'This author knows how to sock it to the reader' *The Times*

'A brilliant writer' *Sunday Express*

'Stephen King without a conscience' Dan Marlowe

'This is an author that does not pull his punches . . . A gripping, and at
times genuinely shocking, read' *SFX Magazine*

'In Laymon's books, blood doesn't so much as drip as explode, splatter
and coagulate' *Independent*

'No one writes like Laymon and you're going to have a good time with
anything he writes' Dean Koontz

'Incapable of writing a disappointing book' *New York Review of Science
Fiction*

'One of the best, and most underrated, writers working in the genre
today' *Cemetery Dance*

Fiends

and

After Midnight

headline

FIENDS first published in Great Britain in 1997
by HEADLINE PUBLISHING GROUP

AFTER MIDNIGHT first published in Great Britain in 1997
by HEADLINE PUBLISHING GROUP

First published in this omnibus edition in 2007
by HEADLINE PUBLISHING GROUP

A HEADLINE paperback

1

ISBN 978 0 7553 3180 2

Typeset in Janson by Avon DataSet Ltd, Bidford on Avon, Warwickshire

Printed and bound in Great Britain by
Mackays of Chatham plc, Chatham, Kent

Headline's policy is to use papers that are natural, renewable and recyclable
products and made from wood grown in sustainable forests. The logging and
manufacturing processes are expected to conform to the environmental
regulations of the country of origin.

HEADLINE PUBLISHING GROUP
A division of Hachette Livre UK Ltd
338 Euston Road
London NW1 3BH

www.headline.co.uk
www.hodderheadline.com

Fiends

This book is dedicated
to the
'Pink Tea'

Warner Law
Clayton Matthews
Arthur Moore
Gary Brandner
Jack Matcha
Charles Fritch
Leo Whitaker
Bob Colby
Marshall Oliphant
Dan Marlow
Francesca Colby
Patricia Matthews
Carol Law
Marilyn Granbeck

And the good old days

'So we'll go no more a-roving
so late into the night'

Contents

Bibliographic Information

Fiends — First appears in this volume.

Kitty Litter — © 1992. First appeared in *Cat Crimes II*, edited by Edward Gorman and Martin Greenberg, published by Donald I. Fine.

The Bleeder — © 1989. First published in *New Blood*, Winter, 1989 issue.

Desert Pickup — © 1970. My first professional sale, published in the 'Department of First Stories', *Ellery Queen's Mystery Magazine*, November, 1970 issue.

The Mask — © 1993. First published in my limited edition short story collection, *A Good, Secret Place*, Deadline Press, 1993.

Eats — © 1985. Originally published in *Mike Shayne's Mystery Magazine*, July, 1985 issue. Reprinted in *The Second Black Lizard Anthology of Crime*, edited by Ed Gorman and Martin Greenberg, 1988. Reprinted as a cartoon in *The Bank Street Book of Mystery*, a Byron Preiss Book published by Pocket Books in 1989.

The Hunt — © 1989. Originally published in *Stalkers*, edited by Ed Gorman and Martin Greenberg, Dark Harvest, 1989.

Slit — © 1993. Originally published in *Predators*, edited by Ed Gorman and Martin Greenberg, ROC, 1993.

Out of the Woods — © 1975. First published in *Ellery Queen's Mystery Magazine*, December, 1975.

Stiff Intruders — © 1980. First published in *Mike Shayne's Mystery Magazine*, March, 1980.

Introduction
The Fox in the Chicken Suit

by Dean Koontz

At the moment Richard Laymon was born, a mysterious rain of one million frogs fell on Cleveland, Ohio, and over seven hundred citizens were severely injured by large plummeting amphibians. In Tibet, at that same hour, the Dalai Lama suddenly levitated twelve feet off his monastery floor and, seized by Tourette's syndrome, began barking like a dog and shouting the word 'gravy' in seventy-nine languages. While the holy man was aloft and shrieking, two archaeologists, at work outside Jerusalem, unearthed the altar of a third-century devil-worshipping cult on which was carved an image of Satan that bore an uncanny resemblance to the Warner Brothers' cartoon character Yosemite Sam. Even as the doctor slapped Richard Laymon's butt and the author's first cry echoed through the hospital delivery room, a group of Carmelite nuns in Boston inexplicably fell into a ferocious hysteria and, racing through the streets of that city, set fire to anyone they encountered who was named 'Herman'. In London, the Queen's favorite feathered hat exploded for no good reason, causing no harm to her august personage but putting her in such a foul mood that, forgetting what century she was in, she ordered the royal hatmaker beheaded. In zoos all around the planet, elephants broke out of their enclosures and squashed anything cute and furry that they could find; for a few minutes, bears addressed startled onlookers in clear, grammatical English, speaking with better diction and projection than the greatest stage actor who ever lived – although according to all reports, none of them had anything interesting to say; and gorillas performed entrechats with a grace that made a ballerina weep. Perhaps the greatest mystery of that fateful day was the bewildering presence of so damn many ballerinas in so many zoos.

Then the world settled into its usual routines. Frogs stopped falling from the sky and were only seen in French restaurants, where they belonged. The Dalai Lama floated back to earth, stopped shrieking about the gravy, and returned to his usual pursuits: prayer, meditation, and betting on the ponies. Wiping the bloodied remains of squashed bunny rabbits off their thunderously huge feet, the elephants ambled back into their enclosures. Their passion for ballet forgotten, the gorillas just ate bananas and stood around scratching their asses. Calm ensued. Peace reigned on God's good earth.

But all the while, Richard Laymon was quietly growing up.

With his sunny face, disarming manner, unfailing cheerfulness, and singularly good humour, he passed through high school and college as smoothly as a fox in an exceedingly convincing chicken suit could pass through a flock of Prozac-numbed hens – that is, of course, if foxes were sufficiently talented tailors to make chicken suits and if hens were able to obtain Prozac prescriptions. If you met Richard Laymon (who, for some reason I don't fully grasp, is known as 'Dick' to his friends) he would strike you as one of the most amiable men you have ever met. He is one of those guys who – were he a movie actor – would most often play the best buddy of the male star: in comedies, he would be lovable and bumbling; in romances, he would be lovable and adroit at bringing the estranged lovers back together after they had quarreled over one stupid misunderstanding or another; in police action pictures, he would be the lovable partner who would be shot stone-cold dead by the villain at the end of act two, sending the star on a flinty-eyed, tight-lipped race for justice and vengeance; in a horror movie, he would be eaten alive. Thus, he was able to appear sufficiently mild-mannered to obtain a job, after college, as a ninth-grade English teacher in a Catholic girl's school. The nuns adored him – and they weren't those crazy damned nuns in Boston who set fire to anyone named 'Herman'; these were *nice* nuns. The students thought Dick was just swell, and their parents thought he was a particularly wholesome young gentleman.

But all the while, Richard Laymon was quietly writing.

Later, he worked in a library at Marymount College, where he probably wore a bow tie, a jacket with leather patches on the elbows, and a look of bookish bemusement. There, I imagine, he kept the card catalogue in impeccable order, dusted the shelves, staffed the lending desk, regretfully sent out overdue notices, murmured of Socrates and Plato to his patrons, and gently reminded boisterous students to whisper at all times. If he were a fox, he would have sewn for himself a chicken suit so thoroughly convincing that any farmer would have reached under him in search of eggs.

He married Ann in 1976, as sweet-tempered and gracious a lady as you would ever hope to meet. In 1979, Ann gave birth to Kelly, a blonde little girl who appeared to have been modeled after the cutest cherubim in certain paintings in the Vatican. No one could look upon this young family without smiling approvingly and feeling that all was right with the world.

In 1980, however, Richard Laymon published his first novel, *The Cellar*. No doubt every nun who had ever known him began to pray for his soul, and every library patron who had ever been alone with him among the stacks at Marymount felt a chill along his or her spine, and all the Catholic school girls to whom he'd taught English said, 'Hey, *cool*!' *The Cellar* was the scariest, fastest-paced, darkest, just-plain-nastiest thriller in years. In that debut, he established a style that has often been imitated but never equaled: plunging, pull-out-all-the-stops, no-limits, in-your-face, shock-packed, take-off-the-top-of-your-head, gonzo suspense and horror that will appall some people and exhilarate others.

Over the years, in nearly thirty novels and numerous short stories, Dick has never compromised his unique vision in order to please the marketplace, yet he has found an audience of devoted readers. Curiously, as I write this, he is better known and more widely admired in England than here in his native country. This situation arose, I believe, because many American editors favored the light diet of 'quiet horror' rather than the meaty stew that Dick cooked up, and along with *good* novels of quiet horror, they shoveled into bookstores uncountable self-conscious pseudo-literary exercises in obscurantism by writers who had yet to learn correct grammar and syntax, books that gave quiet horror – *all* horror – a bad name. Those unreadable tomes, combined with the usual yearly total of 3,568 vampire novels, virtually destroyed the genre on these shores even while Dick was trying to build a career doing something different from the work of others.

He has survived, however, and prospered, because a significant number of readers like a bowl of stew in their literary diet from time to time. By being politically incorrect in his fiction and singularly clear-eyed and cold in his portrayal of evil, he writes stories that read like the work of no one else – which is essential if a writer is to stay afloat in the sea of sameness that is modern publishing. Now that he has written so many books, however, he has revealed himself and can never again quite squeeze all the way back into that chicken suit.

Indeed, when Gerda and I go to the Laymon house for dinner, we sometimes wonder if Ann is really the gentle lady she seems to be or if she is engaged in a masquerade as clever as her husband's. When she's cooking, I pop into the kitchen unannounced – just to be sure that she's adding only herbs and spices to each dish and not anything lethal. When she picks up a carving knife, I ease to the edge of my chair, prepared to leap away from the table and throw myself out of the nearest dining-room window if she should move in my direction instead of toward the turkey or roast. Several times, I've been a bit too edgy, misjudged her intention, and hurled myself through a pane of glass, only to look back into the house from the lawn and see her standing over the roast, looking astonished and bewildered. Too embarrassed to admit my suspicions, I always claim to have been catapulted out of the room by a catastrophic muscle spasm, and I think she buys that story because she keeps giving me the names of medical specialists who might be able to help me – though lately they have all been psychiatrists.

I keep a sly watch on Kelly too. When she was a tiny little girl, she was so cute you could have dangled her from one of the branches of a Christmas tree, and everyone would have been so dazzled by her that they wouldn't have noticed any other decorations – yet she always had an unexpected wit that was more sophisticated and astringent than the average child's sense of humor. One night, when six of us adults sat around the Laymon dinner table, having a grand good time, Gerda realized that Kelly was standing in the doorway, in her pajamas, quietly commenting on our conversation; Gerda nudged me, and when I tuned out the adults and tuned in Kelly, she was funnier than any of us – even though we thought ourselves reasonably amusing. Not long thereafter, during a visit to an amusement park with the Laymons, as we were suddenly swept up in a surging crowd, little Kelly – then no bigger than an elf – reached for my hand, gripping it tightly, and I was touched by her genuine vulnerability and more deeply touched by the fact that she trusted me to keep her safe; yet this *same* little girl eschewed the usual doll house and played, instead, with a miniature haunted castle full of monster figures and beheaded victims. That is a fact, not a comic exaggeration. Now, many years later,

Kelly is a young lady of seventeen, quieter than the sprightly imp of yore, even demure. Nevertheless, she is her father's daughter, with those strange genes, and if at dinner some evening she were to say, 'Let *me* carve the roast, Mom,' I'm certain that I'd have another catastrophic muscle spasm and wind up on the lawn amidst shattered window glass.

I hope that you enjoy this collection of stories as much as I have enjoyed it. I only wish all of you could have the additional pleasure of knowing Dick Laymon and his family as well as I do. In truth, the strangest thing about them is that they tolerate me as a friend.

Fiends

1

Willy had left the window pane for last. Now it was done. He stepped backward, careful to keep his bare feet from landing on pine cones, and looked at it.

Great. Real class. Best damn shack in Wisconsin.

And he didn't look to bad, himself, in the window's reflection. A little bony, but what the hell?

'What a fuckin' stud,' he muttered.

Then he whipped his putty knife at a dead, barkless poplar far across the clearing. It struck blade-first, glanced off, and disappeared into the thick undergrowth near the tree. Turning, he hurled the putty can high toward the lake. It plopped into the lily pads just beyond the shore.

He picked up a red bandanna and wiped the sweat off his face. A mosquito lit on his arm. He watched it for a moment, then rolled it under his fingertip until it disintegrated into a red smear.

'That'll teach you, y'little turd.'

He went into the one-room shack. It still smelled of mildew, but what could you expect from a place that'd been boarded up for three years? Besides, he'd be gone tomorrow.

The mattress in the corner was cluttered. He tossed his handcuffs onto a table in the middle of the room, set his flashlight and pocket knife on the floor, and sprawled backward.

A piece of paper crunched softly as his head pushed it against the mattress. He raised his head and picked up the paper.

It was brown with age. Creases from many foldings obliterated some of the lines.

Holding it above his face, he read the headline:

NORTH GLEN GIRL RAPED, KIDNAPPING FOILED

Foiled, all right. Thanks to that fucking neighbor.

Fix her wagon.

Taking care of that snoopy old bag would be kicks. He looked forward to it.

But not as much as he looked forward to Martha.

Marty.

She'd only been fifteen, way back then. Fifteen and cute and fresh and a virgin.

She had changed a lot since that morning ten years ago when he'd nailed her.

But not her address.

2

After the curtain slid shut and the lights came on in the movie theater, Dan let out a sigh of relief.

'Unimpressed?' Marty asked.

'It was better than a hangover, but just barely.'

'That good?' Grinning, she pulled her hand away from him and stood up. It felt good to get out of the seat. Straining upward on tiptoes, she enjoyed the luxury of stretching her muscles. 'Hope the second show is better.'

'Couldn't be worse. Hungry?'

'For what?'

'How does popcorn sound?'

'Popcorn. Sounds great.' Turning around, she scanned the

people in the rear part of the theater. She had spent most of her twenty-five years in North Glen, and knew most of the faces.

'You want the butter flavoring?' Dan asked.

'But of course.'

'What size Pepsi?'

'Medium.'

'For an extra twenty-five cents, you can get a large.'

She laughed and said, 'Medium will be . . .' Her voice stopped dead as the man near the back of the theater smiled at her and she suddenly recognized him. She sat down fast and scooted low in her seat until the back of her head was against the cushion. She propped her knees against the sticky metal of the seat in front of her. She folded her arms across her belly.

'What's wrong?' Dan asked.

'Nothing.'

'You sure?'

'I'm sure.'

'Okay. I'll be right back.'

She grabbed Dan's arm. 'No. Wait. Don't go.'

He frowned and looked worried. 'What is it?' he asked.

'Do you think we could just leave?'

'You don't want to see the second show?'

'I'm not . . . I feel sort of icky.'

'We can go.'

'You won't mind missing it?' she asked.

'Hell, we can always rent it from Blockbuster if we really want to see the thing. We can leave.'

Dan got to his feet and Marty followed him, sidestepping carefully, trying not to tread on feet, tumble over knees, or bump into heads along the row in front. At the aisle, she took Dan's arm and looked down so she wouldn't have to see that face again.

She kept her eyes fixed on her sandals and the carpet until Dan pushed open the door and they entered the lobby. The lobby lights seemed very bright. Fighting the impulse to look behind her, she hurried with Dan to the exit doors.

'Wait,' she said, and took off her yellow pullover sweater. 'Won't need this outside.'

Dan pushed open the door. The chilly air from the theater followed them outside until the door shut. Then the muggy night settled over them.

Marty took hold of Dan's hand. They walked down the block and round the corner. Dan's old Ford was squeezed into a stretch of the curb between two driveways. He opened the passenger door for Marty.

She climbed in. The air inside was stifling. While Dan walked to the other side, she rolled down the window.

'I'll have the air-conditioning going in a minute,' he said as he dropped into the driver's seat.

'Yeah, right. Mother Nature's air-conditioning.'

'The best kind. Doesn't deplete the stratosphere.'

Marty managed to smile.

When the car was moving, a warm breeze came in through the window. Marty let her arm hang outside and leaned against the door to feel the air's calm touch. 'It's a beautiful night,' she said. 'I love it when it's hot like this. Makes the night seem so . . . friendly. Sort of friendly and quiet.'

'And romantic,' Dan suggested.

'Why don't we go somewhere?'

'Do you feel up to it?'

'I think so,' she said.

'Where to. My place?'

'Nah. This is too beautiful a night to be cooped up.'

'Cooped up?' He put an arm around her shoulders and reached down to her breast. 'I'm not sure I like the sound of that.'

Marty moaned at the gentle pressure of his hand.

'I hate bras,' he said.

'They come off.'

'I wish you wouldn't wear them at all.'

'My parents.'

'I know. Your parents. Christ. You're twenty-five.'

'Am I?'

'You oughta get a place of your own.'

'So I hear.'

'It isn't normal.'

'So you keep telling me. And like I keep telling you, I don't see any reason to move out. I like it there. They like having me. And I don't see any reason to find a place for myself until I'm ready to start a family of my own.'

'Is that a proposal?' Dan asked, not sounding especially amused.

'*This* is my proposal – let's go to the lake.'

'Okay, okay.'

Outside town, the road had no lights but Dan drove fast as if he knew every twist and curve and bump, and he was taking them by instinct.

'The air-conditioning works really good out here,' Marty said.

'Open your vent?' Dan suggested.

Marty opened it. A warm breeze rushed suddenly up her legs and under her skirt. She kicked off her sandals. The floor mat was gritty under her bare feet.

'Can I ask you something?' Dan said.

'Anything you want.'

'What was bothering you at the show?'

The question hit her like a blow to the stomach. She wanted to double over and hold herself.

'You weren't sick, were you?'

'Not really.'

'You were scared. That's why you wanted to get out so fast. Something scared the hell out of you. What was it?'

11

Marty turned her face away and gazed out of the open window. Her arms felt cold. She rubbed them, trying to get rid of the goosebumps.

'Tell me.'

'I saw this guy.'

'Who?'

'Someone I used to know.'

'You saw him during intermission?'

'He was sitting near the back.'

'An old boyfriend?'

She shook her head.

'Was he an old boyfriend?' Dan repeated.

She looked at him. His eyes were on the road and the rearview mirror. He hadn't seen her silent answer. 'No' she said. 'Not a boyfriend. I don't think I want to talk about it, okay?'

'Fine,' he muttered.

'I'll tell you sometime,' she said quietly. 'But not now, okay?'

'Fine. I just wondered if it might be him in the car that's following us.'

Marty groaned. She twisted round and looked out of the rear window. She could see nothing except the curving two-lane road, most of it hidden in shadows cast by the tall forest on both sides. 'Where?' she asked.

'About fifty yards back. No headlights.'

She kept studying the road behind them. And finally she noticed a dark shape against the lighter darkness of the blacktop, moving along like a low, hunching shadow.

3

Near Gribsby, four hundred miles above North Glen, a young man paced the end of a creaking pier.

'About time, huh?' he heard.

He looked toward the shore and saw Tina. She stopped beneath a light, waved, and ran up the pier to meet him. 'Whew!' she said. 'I didn't think I'd ever get away. Relatives can be such a pain in the butt, you know that?'

'I know that,' Brad said. 'The good Lord willing, we'll never be relatives.'

'I didn't mean *that*.'

'I know.' He held out his arms. Tina stepped into them and he kissed the tip of her nose.

'Lousy aim,' she said.

He kissed her mouth. Her lips were warm and open, dry at first, then slippery. He moved his hands on her back, feeling her ribs through the soft thickness of the old sweatshirt that was far too big for her. The sleeves were cut off. He stroked her bare upper arms and slipped his hands into the sleeve holes and rubbed her shoulders. Tina hugged him more tightly.

'I could stay like this forever,' she said.

'We wouldn't get much fishing in.'

'Creep.'

'Ready to go?'

'Nope.'

'Yep.' He kissed her forehead, then pushed her away. 'Climb aboard.' Squatting, he gripped the gunwale and held the boat steady while Tina boarded.

'It's a beautiful night,' she said. 'Get a load of that moon.'

He watched Tina instead. She stood on the deck with her bare feet apart, her hands on her hips, smiling as she looked from the full moon to the bright path it made on the lake.

'Isn't it something?' she said.

'*You're* something.' Brad climbed onto the deck. 'You look like a pirate.'

'Yo ho ho and a bottle of rum.'

'Except for your fanny.' He patted it.

'What about my fanny?'

He stepped back and inspected it, frowning thoughtfully like an artist examining the lines of a statue. 'Nothing is wrong with it . . . exactly.'

'Oh, thank you.'

'But it's not the fanny of a pirate. They've got big, broad butts. Yours is much too graceful and delicate.'

'Sorry.'

'I'll just have to grin and bear it.'

'Bare it?'

The way she smiled made Brad pull her close, holding her lightly, kissing her, finally pushing his hand down the back of her jeans and feeling the cool smooth skin of her buttocks.

Tina squeezed him tightly, and let go.

'Shouldn't we be shoving off?' she asked.

'Should we?' he murmured against the warm curve of her neck.

'The fishies are waiting.'

'Very true. Thanks for reminding me.'

He let her go. Together, they untied the mooring lines. Then Brad turned on the ignition key and pressed the starter button. The twin inboard motors thundered into life. Tina came up beside him. He gave her a swat on the rump.

'If you break it, you buy it.'

'How much?' he asked.

She held onto him as the boat lunged forward. 'You probably can't afford it,' she said.

The bow lifted above the waves.

'You're forgetting, I'm a wealthy man.'

'Right. Your dad owns a bait shop.'

'There are different kinds of wealth,' he said, grinning.

'You're wealthy in worms.'

'How about ten bucks? Is that enough?'

'Plenty.' She smiled up at him. 'You get a discount 'cause I love you so much.'

Brad put a hand on her shoulder. 'Have I wished you happy birthday yet?' he asked.

'No. What're you waiting for?'

'Happy birthday. The big seventeen.'

'Yeah. I'm ancient.'

Brad throttled down. The roar of the motors diminished to a sputtering whisper and the boat slowed, its bow slowly lowering into the waves. 'Time for your party,' he said, and killed the motors. 'We'll let her drift for a while.' He lifted Tina onto the pilot's seat. 'Just sit tight on your priceless fanny.'

'Ten bucks isn't priceless.'

'Right back,' he said, and went below. In the galley, he opened his ice chest. Two glasses were tucked into the crushed ice along with two bottles of champagne. He left one bottle behind and hurried topside.

Tina grinned. 'Hey! Champagne?'

'Happy birthday.'

'Shouldn't you have a towel to wrap round the bottle? They always have towels.'

'A towel, a towel. Good idea. Hold these.' He gave the bottle and glasses to Tina, then rushed below and found a beach towel. It was still damp and smelled of sun tan oil. He tucked it under his arm and picked up a flat, gift-wrapped box. As he reached the top of the steps, he heard a pop. A cork shot past his ear. It thumped the window.

'Almost gotcha!' Tina blurted.

'Good thing you missed.'

'Yeah?'

'How far can you swim?'

'Far. Very far.' She scanned the shores. The nearest was at least a quarter mile away. 'I could make it,' she said.

'This wouldn't.' He tossed the gift sideways. Tina gasped, but he snatched it out of the air with his other hand.

'What if you'd missed?' Tina asked.

'I never miss.'

'But what if?'

'Seriously?'

'Seriously.'

'I would've dived in after it. There's no way I'd let *this* get away. No way in the world.'

'It's something pretty good, huh?'

'It's something *wonderful*.'

'Gonna give it to me?'

'Later. First, we've got to toast the birthday girl.'

4

'Why would he want to follow you?' Dan asked without looking away from the dark, twisting road.

'I don't know,' Marty said.

'You'd better tell me. I've got to figure out how to handle this.'

'Can you lose him?'

'Maybe. For tonight. But he can always go after you tomorrow. He can wait around till he finds you alone. Do you want that?'

'Of course not.'

'Then tell me what he wants.'

'I don't know what he wants. I testified against him once. He went to prison.'

'What did he do?'

'Never mind.'

'Thanks for all the information. At least we know one thing; if it *is* your friend back there, he probably doesn't plan to shake your hand.'

'That's for sure.' She looked out of the rear window and gazed down the road, searching the shadows.

'I'll take you to my place,' Dan said.

'No, not your place.'

'I've got a gun.'

'No!'

'Why the hell not?'

'You want to *shoot* him? That'd be great.'

Dan glanced at her, smiled with one side of his mouth. 'It might not come to shooting.'

'But it might.'

'In that case, may the better aim win.'

A few minutes later, he slowed down in front of his house.

'Keep driving,' Marty said. 'If you get your gun, someone might end up getting killed.'

'Damn right.'

'Keep driving, or you can just let me out and I'll take my chances walking home.'

He made a snorty sound, then muttered, 'I just hope your friend isn't armed.'

Two hundred yards farther, he swung the car sharply onto the narrow road leading to Wilson Lake.

'What are we going to do?'

'I've got a little plan.'

'Dan?'

'Nothing to worry about.' He looked at her and grinned. 'Dan's plans never fail. What does this guy look like?'

'Let's go to the police.'

'I can take care of it.' He slowed down and peered into the rearview mirror until the other car turned. 'He's following us, okay.'

'Dan!'

'Don't worry, everything's fine. How about getting me a flashlight?' He pointed to the glove compartment. Marty opened it, took out the flashlight and snapped the compartment shut.

The flashlight had a ribbed metal casing.

Near the shore, the road widened into a parking lot.

Dan steered onto its hard dirt. As he cruised past several dark cars with couples inside, he kicked off his sneakers, reached down and pulled off his socks.

'Going for a swim?' Marty asked.

'You never know.' He stopped beside a pickup truck and cut the engine. 'Place is sure crowded tonight.' He slipped his bare feet back into his sneakers and stuffed one of his socks into his pants pocket. 'Okay, lets go.'

'Go where?'

'Out there. For a walk. Too many people around here, even if they *are* too busy to see anything. Hand me the light, honey.'

She gave it to him, shouldered open her door, and stepped onto the dirt of the lot. The ground felt nice and cool under her feet. But she put her sandals on, anyway, feeling too vulnerable without them. For a moment, she even considered putting her sweater back on, though the night was balmy and her clothes were sticking to her back and buttocks.

'Shall we take a stroll along the shore?' Dan asked.

'Are you kidding?'

'No.' He looked over his shoulder. Following his glance, Marty saw the dark car turn slowly onto the parking lot. 'Let's go,' Dan whispered, and pulled her hand. 'Don't look back. We don't want your friend to know we're onto him.'

At the edge of the lake, Dan turned on the flashlight.

'What's that for?'

'To see where we're going.'

'There's plenty of moonlight.'

'Your friend has to see where we're going, too.'

'Could you stop calling him that. My friend? He isn't my friend.'

'If you say so.'

She pulled her hand away. It was wet. She wiped it on her skirt.

'What if he's got a knife?' she asked.

'That'll be his tough luck.'

'I like your confidence.'

'No, you don't.' He led her onto a path. To their left, down a steep grassy slope, the water lapped against the shore. The woods pressed close on their side, forcing them to walk single file. They had to duck under low branches.

'Couldn't ask for a better place,' Dan said.

'To hide?'

Dan chuckled, then swung the flashlight so its beam swept across the water. 'Think he saw that?'

'How could he miss it?'

Dan turned off the flashlight and began to unscrew its base.

'What're you doing?'

'Taking it apart.'

'Nice,' she muttered.

'Here, let's get into these bushes.' He dropped two batteries into his palm and pushed Marty. 'You get over there behind that tree.'

'Where'll you be?'

'Right here.'

'Dan . . .'

'I'll just have a chat with this guy. What'd you say his name is?'

'Willy. You aren't going to do something stupid, are you?'

'Me?' He laughed and patted her back. 'Get over there and hide, and don't make a sound. If things get out of hand, try and sneak back to the car. I left the keys under the front seat.'

'Whatever you have in mind . . .'

'Over there. Hurry.'

Marty hesitated. Dan took a quick step toward her, so she turned away. She stepped through the underbrush, feeling its damp leaves cling to her legs, until she came to a birch tree. She crouched behind it to wait, but couldn't see Dan. So she stood up and leaned against the trunk to watch.

Dan was busy doing something with the flashlight and sock. Dropping the batteries into the sock. Knotting it.

Suddenly, he stopped.

Marty heard nothing but the usual summer sounds of crickets and frogs.

Without a sound, Dan stepped into the path. His right hand, down at his side, swung upward. The flashlight glinted moon like the broad blade of a knife as it plunged upward into the man's belly.

5

Something shiny swept up out of the darkness. Willy slashed at it with his knife, but missed. A cold, numbing force crushed his breath. His arms dropped. His knees hit the shoreline path. Dirt and gravel scraped his hands. He tried to gasp, 'Shit!' but couldn't. No air.

No fucking air at all.

6

From behind the tree, Marty saw Dan kick one of the arms. It collapsed, and Willy fell face down.

'Roll over,' Dan said, barely loud enough for Marty to hear. After giving the command, he waited a second. Willy didn't move except to squirm on the ground. 'I said to roll over.'

The gasping shape still didn't do it.

Dan swung the sock with the batteries in its toe. He whipped it against Willy's shoulder. It made a dull thump, and Willy cried out.

'Now, roll over.'

This time, Willy obeyed.

'Why were you following us?'

Willy gasped something that Marty couldn't make out.

'Flattery won't get you anywhere,' Dan said. He walked around to Willy's side and knelt down to look him in the face. 'God, you're an ugly asshole. Why were you following us?'

Willy raised his head, but only for a moment because Dan pushed it back down with the bottom edge of the flashlight. 'Don't move.'

'You're gonna . . .'

'I'm gonna what?'

Marty couldn't quite hear the answer.

'Is that so?' Dan smashed the head of the flashlight against Willy's face.

'I'm gonna cut off your . . .'

Dan stuck the bottom edge of the flashlight under Willy's nose. 'Sharp, isn't it? If I ever run into you again, I'll put your nose where the batteries go.' From the squeal of pain, Marty thought he was already doing it. 'You understand?'

Willy muttered something.

Then shrieked.

Then, sobbing, said, 'I understand.'

'Good. Very good.' Dan stood up, wiping the edge of the flash-light on his pants. 'Just remember, okay?' He whirled the sock until the weighted toe picked up momentum, then crashed it against Willy's head. 'Good night, now,' he said. Willy looked unconscious. 'Come on, Marty. Time to go.'

She stepped out from behind the tree, shaking.

'That should give Willy some second thoughts,' Dan said.

'You bastard,' Marty said. 'You didn't have to . . . torture him!'

'I wanted him to get the message.'

'God, Dan . . .'

'You think I liked doing that?'

She gazed at his face. It was pale in the moonlight. Reaching

21

up, she brushed his messy hair away from his eyes. His forehead was hot and damp under her fingertips. 'Yes,' she whispered. 'I think you liked it. A lot.'

Dan made a sound that was almost like a laugh.

A nasty laugh.

Then he untied the knot from his sock and dumped the batteries into his hand. He slipped them into the metal cylinder and screwed the bottom into place over them. With his thumb, he flicked the switch. Nothing happened. 'Look at that,' he muttered. 'The fucker broke my flashlight.'

Marty walked behind Dan, staring at the ground to keep from stumbling even though her mind paid no attention to the dips and turns and sudden rises of the trail. She didn't hear the water caressing the shore, or the summer night sounds of small animals. She didn't see the lightning bugs that drifted among the bushes, silently glowing and fading. She knew they were there; they always had been. But now she didn't care.

When Dan opened the car door for her, she muttered, 'Thanks,' and climbed in.

'Amazing,' Dan said, sliding into the driver's seat. 'A person could get murdered here and nobody would even notice.'

'They're busy,' Marty muttered.

Dan pushed the key into the ignition, but he didn't turn it. Instead, he stared at the dashboard. Marty wondered what he was waiting for. She said nothing, though. She felt as if he'd turned into a stranger.

Letting go of the key, Dan moved toward the middle of the seat and put his arm across her shoulders. When she faced him to protest, he kissed her.

She pushed him away. 'Cut it out.'

'What the hell's wrong with you?'

'Wrong? You just beat a man senseless.'

'So?'

'And you enjoyed it.'

'Yeah?'

'Yeah!'

'I didn't *exactly* enjoy it. More like, it gave me a nice feeling of accomplishment. You know? Like throwing a touchdown pass.'

'This isn't football.'

'That's right. Maybe I'd better go back and finish him off.'

'Great. Wonderful. Why don't you just do that?'

'He wouldn't ever scare the hell out of you at the movies again.'

'That's a great reason for killing a guy.'

'What did he do to you?'

She said nothing.

'How did he make you so afraid of him?'

'None of your business.'

'I just beat the crap out of the guy for you. Don't I deserve to know why?'

'I didn't ask you to do that. You did it because you wanted to.'

'Crap. That's crap. And don't go around trying to read my mind. This character did something to you. I don't know what he did, but you're my girl and I'm not about to let some asshole go around intimidating you. Clear?'

'Yes,' she said quietly, rubbing her face. 'It's clear. But Dan, don't you see that it's wrong? You can't go around *hurting* people.'

'You can try.'

She turned away from him. 'Take me home. Please.'

7

'This stuff really hits the spot,' Tina said.

'That's what it's for.' Brad refilled both glasses with champagne. He set down the bottle, clamping it between his bare feet to keep it from following the roll of the deck, and put his free arm around Tina.

'You sure know how to throw parties,' she said.

'Better than your parents?'

'Better than the one they threw *me*, that's for sure. Which was no party at all, if you wanta know the truth.'

'I'm sorry.'

'That's okay. I haven't had a party since I was eight. Till now.'

'Ready for your present?' Brad asked.

'Sure.'

He took the package off the seat and handed it to her. 'Happy birthday, Tina.'

She set down her glass and began working on the ribbon. She slipped it off, then unfastened the tape at each end of the package and removed the paper without tearing it.

'Going to save the wrapping?'

'Sure.'

'So you can re-use it sometime?'

'No! I wouldn't re-use it. I'll save it for a keepsake.'

'Oh,' Brad said, and felt a tightness come to his throat.

Tina held the flat, rectangular box by its lid and shook it until the bottom fell onto her lap. Then she folded back the tissue paper inside. 'Brad! Oh, it's beautiful!'

'The saleswoman called it paisley. That's the pattern, I guess. Real colorful and everything, but you can't see it much in this light.'

The dress unfolded as Tina lifted it from the box. She stretched her arms upward, holding it under the moonlight. 'It's just gorgeous! Look how it shines! Oh, thank you. It's wonderful!'

She hugged him tightly, awkwardly, squeezing his neck. But the hug only lasted a moment. Then Tina put the box and wrappings on Brad's lap. 'I'll be back in a jiffy,' she said, and hurried across the deck, the dress in front of her like a wispy dancing partner. Once, she made a dizzy sidestep and almost fell. Brad jumped up to help, but she stayed on her feet and vanished below.

He sat at the stern, waiting.

Finally, the cabin door opened, then latched shut. Brad watched Tina's dark form rise and step into the moonlight.

'What do you think?' she asked.

'Very nice.'

'It's absolutely beautiful in the light. All gold and red and blue. I guess you know that, though.'

'Does it fit all right?'

'Does it?' She posed for him.

'Looks great to me. Is it supposed to cling like that?'

'Sure.' She walked toward him, keeping a hand on the gunwale to steady herself.

The fabric, glossy in the moonlight, sheathed all the rises and hollows of her body until it stopped partway down her thighs.

'It makes me feel naked,' she said. 'Naked and covered with something like baby oil so I'm all slick and shiny.' She rubbed a hand over her ribs. 'Feel,' she said, and stepped into Brad's arms.

Her back was a curving sleekness under the cloth's lubrication.

She moaned. 'It feels so good.' She squeezed him extra hard, grunting with the effort. 'This is just the nicest gift anyone's ever given me.'

'Like it, huh?'

'I love it. Here, you feel.' She tugged Brad's T-shirt off, embraced him and moved lightly against him. The fabric was warm with the heat of Tina's skin, a slippery film between her body and his.

Then Brad noticed that the dress was gathering above his hands. He rubbed upward on her sides, working the dress higher, and slid a hand down until the silken fabric ended and he felt the bare skin of her buttocks.

'Lift your arms,' he whispered.

She raised her arms and he pulled the dress over her head. He draped it across the stern seat. Then he held her hands and looked at her.

He swallowed, trying to get rid of the lump in his throat. 'You're so beautiful,' he said.

'I love you so much,' she said. 'I love you more than anything.'

'I love you, too,' he said.

She moved in against him and unfastened his jeans.

8

When Marty awoke in the morning, the drapes above her bed were bright with sunshine. The drawcord was just out of reach, so she got up quietly and opened the drapes, freeing the sunlight to slant downward onto her bed.

She lay down, closing her eyes against the brightness and enjoying the feel of the heat as she listened to the house. Her mother and father were not yet stirring. She sat up and slipped off her nightgown. As she pulled it over her head, the sunlight touched the skin of her back, warming and soothing, draining away all desire to move. Elbows resting on the knees of her crossed legs, she hung her head and let the sun sink in.

Things should always be this way, she thought.

And her stomach knotted as she half expected to hear the doorbell ring – just as it had rung that other morning, a sunny morning so much like this – when she was fifteen years old.

A warm, summer wind had been blowing through her room that morning, whipping the drapes above her bed and making the light flutter on the pages of *Jane Eyre*. The breeze smelled of flowers and freshly mowed grass, and hinted of a blistering day.

When the doorbell rang downstairs, she didn't want to answer it.

But if she didn't get the door, nobody would, and maybe it was something important.

Rolling reluctantly out of bed, she pressed the open book face down on the sheet to keep her place, then hurried across the carpet to the closet door and pulled her robe off its hook. As she slipped her arms into her robe, the pajama sleeves were shoved up almost to her elbows.

The doorbell rang again.

She fastened the top button of her pajama shirt, hitched up the drooping pants, and tied the robe shut.

The bell rang once more before she got downstairs.

She opened the door. Seeing a total stranger took her by surprise, but there was nothing menacing about his skinny body or his crew cut or his black eyebrows meeting above his nose. His big ears made him look funny.

'Good morning,' he greeted her, bowing his high, narrow head. 'Can I talk to the master of the house?'

'He isn't home right now,' she said.

'When do you expect him back?'

'What's this about?'

'I do odd jobs.'

'Well, I don't know if he'd . . .'

'Can I talk to your mother about it?'

'She isn't . . .'

Marty suddenly realized that she shouldn't be saying such things to a stranger.

'She isn't home,' he said. It wasn't a question. 'I know.' His thin lips curled into a grin. 'They shouldn't have left you alone.'

The door crashed into her. She tumbled backward as the stranger rushed in.

Looking up from the floor, she saw the knife in his hand.

'Stand up,' he said, waving it.

'What do you want?'

'I want you to stand up.'

27

It was hard getting off the floor because her bones felt soft and wobbly. But she did as she was told.

'Your bedroom's upstairs, right?'

She nodded.

'I know. I know all about you, Marty. I've been keeping an eye on you for a long time. Ever since I saw you at the car wash with your old lady. You had on white shorts and a red blouse. I wanted to rip 'em off you and fuck you right there. But I'm not stupid. I waited for just the right time. And guess what? This is it. Let's go upstairs.'

'I don't want to.'

'Start walking.' He waved his knife under her chin.

She began to cry.

He walked behind her, the knife point biting through her robe and pajamas, nipping her back. Up the stairway. Down the hall. Into her sun-bright bedroom.

When he began to strip her, she said, 'Don't. Please.'

He didn't bother to move *Jane Eyre* before shoving her backward onto the bed. By the time he finished, the book's slick dust jacket was ripped off. The covers were broken. The spine was split, and loose pages were scattered over the sheet, spoiled with blood and semen.

Lying back, Marty covered herself with a sheet, curled up on her side, and watched her forefinger draw a line along the edge of the mattress pad.

Why did he have to come back? What does he want?

Me.

He wants me.

Again.

9

The parking space in front of Willy's motel room was empty. He pulled into it.

With a grocery bag in one arm, he opened the door of his room. Air-conditioned. Nice and cool.

He dumped the bag onto his bed. Out fell a plastic bottle of aspirin, his filthy wadded T-shirt, and a coil of clothesline.

He pulled off his boots and jeans, staggered into the bathroom.

In the mirror there, he saw what had been done to him. The crusty gash at the base of his nose. The bruises.

I'll kill his ass, the cocksucker.

Willy took four aspirin tablets, washing them down with handfuls of water. Then he made his way back to the bed. He threw off the blankets and crawled in naked between the sheets.

And moaned.

Slowly, his pain faded.

Everything faded.

In half-sleep, he saw Marty sprawled on a bed, her arms and legs tied to the corners, the sunlight golden on her bare skin.

She looked fifteen for a while.

But then he imagined her changing, growing, getting better, until she became the Marty he'd seen last night.

Before sinking into deep sleep, he made her scream.

10

A young woman named Peggy climbed out of her car. She rubbed her damp hands on her shorts and took a deep breath. Then she walked to the screen door of Mickey's Bait Shop, dust rising behind her white sneakers.

A bell jangled when she opened the door.

'Be right with you,' a voice called from a back room. It wasn't the voice she expected.

Not Mickey's.

But at least it belonged to a man.

She shut the door and hooked it. With a flip of her right hand, she reversed the cardboard sign so it read OPEN on the inside.

The shop was shadowy. It smelled of damp earth, fish, and something else. Machine oil? It smelled good – fresh and masculine.

Boots thumped on the hardwood floor. Cowboy boots, probably. Seemed like half the guys in Wisconsin dressed like cowboys.

'Hi, there,' this one said as he took his place behind the counter.

A good-looking guy, couldn't be older than twenty. His faded blue shirt was open at the throat. From the look on his face, he liked the looks of Peggy.

She took off her sunglasses.

'Can I help you?' he asked.

'I was looking for Mickey.'

'Dad? He was taking a group out on the Eagle Lake.' The son checked his wristwatch. 'He should be back any time, though. You might try the motel.'

'My name's Peggy.'

'Hi. I'm Brad.'

'Nice to meet you, Brad.'

'Is there something *I* can help you with?'

'I could use some bait.' She looked over her shoulder and spotted several tackle boxes on shelves near the door. 'And how about one of those tackle boxes? My old one's all rusted out. Would you show them to me?'

'Happy to.' Brad came around the end of the counter. He wore cowboy boots, all right. And old, faded blue jeans. When

30

she looked at his face, she caught him checking the front of her T-shirt.

'How's life at Camp Wahtooki?' he asked.

'A little lonely.'

'You a counselor there?'

'Yep.'

'Well, what sort of tackle box did you have in mind?'

'Who says I've got a tackle box in mind?'

'You?' he asked, and grinned.

'Me?' Gazing into his blue eyes, she reached forward and gently squeezed his crotch.

His eyes suddenly got very wide. 'Jeez,' he said.

'Let's go behind the counter.'

Brad glanced at the screen door.

'That's taken care of,' Peggy said.

She led him around the counter, knelt in the narrow space behind it, and pulled off her Camp Wahtooki T-shirt. Brad stared. She helped him take off his shirt, then embraced him. When she sucked on his mouth, he finally started to move.

He stroked her breasts.

She lay on the cool floor. It was rough and hard beneath her shoulder blades. Brad unfastened her shorts. Knees up, she raised her buttocks off the floor. Brad pulled the shorts up to her knees, down to her ankles. She kicked them away. Brad opened his jeans and crawled between her legs.

He was big. Even bigger than Mickey. So big it hurt. Stretching her, filling her. She dug her nails into his back, crushed her mouth to his, and met each hard thrust with one of her own. Again and again. Clawing, groaning, together pounding him high and deep.

A face appeared above the counter. A girl's face. She looked sixteen or so. A beautiful face. A horrified face.

It watched.

Somehow, the watching excited Peggy even more.

31

She didn't care where the girl came from. Maybe from a rear entrance. It didn't matter.

Nothing mattered except Brad inside her.

'God, darling!' she gasped, clutching his buttocks.

Nothing but Brad.

His teeth clamped on her shoulder as he plunged.

Nothing.

The girl looking down from above had tears in her eyes. She lifted a hand to wipe them off. Her short sleeve was a shiny swirl of color.

Didn't matter. Nothing mattered.

Nothing, nothing, nothing!

Just THIS!

Peggy's breath caught. She arched against Brad, quaking inside, feeling his wild spurting throbs. 'God!' she cried out. 'Oh God! Yes!'

As she came, she watched the girl's face.

The face suddenly lurched away and was gone.

A while later, Peggy said, 'That was fantastic, Brad.'

'Yeah.'

'Problem?'

'No. It was great. Really.'

'You busy tonight?' Peggy asked.

'Well . . . yeah, I am.'

She ran her hands through his hair. 'Another girl?'

He looked solemn. 'Yeah. My . . . actually, my fiancée. We're . . . we got engaged. Just last night. I don't know . . . I shouldn't have . . . I don't know what the hell I'm doing here with you.'

'Fucking.'

She squeezed his buttocks with both hands. Tightening muscles inside, she squeezed his penis.

It was still big.

It started getting bigger.

'Just once more, darling.'

'No, I don't . . .'

'You want to. I know you do.'

'It . . . isn't right.'

'She'll never know.'

11

Four hundred miles south of Mickey's Bait shop, Willy was driving past the front of Marty's house. A white Pontiac stood in the driveway. The garage door was open. He saw a Volkswagen inside.

Would've been handy if the Pontiac was already gone. But this was fine. This was how he'd figured it. He'd figured on having to wait. In a way, he'd hoped for it.

Gave him time to finish another piece of business.

He turned right, then right again, and came down the back side of the block. The fourth house from the corner was directly behind Marty's place. Only hedges and a drainage ditch stood between their back yards. Both yards had plenty of trees for cover. Willy got out, leaving his rope under the front seat. He walked to the end of the block and turned the corner.

He came to Jefferson, Marty's street, and crossed it.

The house he wanted was the third one up, a small place surrounded by lavish gardens.

That's two things H. Dunning's got, Willy thought. A green thumb and a big nose.

He walked quickly toward the house, keeping his eyes on Marty's place across the street. Bad news if she'd happen to look out and see him.

He hurried up H. Dunning's driveway and took a cobblestone path to the front door.

The doorbell had a weathered note tacked below it. Willy

could hardly read the faded ink, but it seemed to say, 'Bell not working. Please knock.'

He knocked.

'Who's there?' called an old voice from inside.

'Bill Smith. We haven't met, but I live down the block. I was passing by, and happened to notice your beautiful azaleas.'

The door opened.

He knew it would.

'Mr Smith?' The short, smiling woman offered her hand. 'I'm Hedda Dunning.'

Willy took her hand, gripped it tightly, and threw his forearm against her chest. He shoved her backward into the house and followed her, clutching her wrist. He shut the door.

'Young man! What're you . . .?' She squealed when he twisted her arm. It was an old arm, bony and brown. Willy wondered if he was strong enough to break it off.

Probably.

Sobbing, Hedda blurted, 'Leave me alone! Don't hurt me!'

He grinned and took off his sunglasses.

The old woman's weeping eyes narrowed. 'I know you,' she said. 'You're that William Johnson who molested . . .'

'Good memory for an old bag. I've got a good memory, too. Like, I remember your testimony. You fucked me good.'

'Don't you use that language with me, you no-good snake.' She tried to jerk her arm free. She kicked. The toe of her shoe hit Willy's shin.

'Do you think that hurt?' he asked.

She kicked him again.

His fist doubled her. She wheezed and choked as he dragged her into the kitchen. There, he picked her up. Clutching the back of her collar, he opened the refrigerator door. He shoved her head in. He slammed the door on it.

Eggs fell out of the holder in the door. Two of them broke on the back of her head. Willy had to laugh.

Then he stretched her out on the kitchen floor and stripped her naked.

Later, he wanted to see if he really was strong enough to rip off her arm.

He was.

He tore the other arm off, too. But her legs were tougher, and he was a little worn out by the time he got to them, so he gave up after doing no more than breaking the left one out of its hip socket.

He took a Pepsi out of her refrigerator, popped it open, and sat down at the kitchen table.

From there, he had a fine view of Marty's house.

12

Marty's hands were soapy when the telephone rang.

'It's for you, dear,' her mother called from upstairs.

Marty rubbed the sponge once more over the slick surface of the plate, then rinsed off the soap and stood the plate upright in the drain rack. After wiping her hands on a towel, she picked up the phone. 'I've got it,' she called. Then she said, 'Hello,' into the mouthpiece.

'How you been?' Dan asked. There was a flatness in his voice. He sounded weary.

'Not too great. How about you?'

'Well . . .' He was silent for a few moments, then said, 'I'm sorry about last night.'

'Are you?'

'I shouldn't have fought with you like that.'

'Are you sorry for what you did to Willy?'

'He got what he deserved.'

'It wasn't . . .'

'Damn it, Marty!'

'I know you think you did it for me. But you didn't have to brutalize the man.'

'Shit.'

'Dan!'

'When are you gonna grow up? You meet violence with bigger violence. That's how it works.'

'You're wrong. You're so wrong.' Marty's chin started trembling. Her eyes filled with tears. 'I know you did it for me, to protect me. I know that. But it was . . . so horrible! I . . . I just don't know . . .'

There was a long silence on the phone.

'Dan?'

'Yeah?'

'I don't like . . . this other side of you.' Sobbing, she waited for him to speak. But he didn't. 'You tortured him, Dan. You *tortured* him.'

He didn't try to defend himself; he hung up.

Marty put down the phone and stood there, gazing at the wall. Then she ran upstairs to her bedroom, flopped down on her bed and sobbed into her pillow.

Soon, the pillow was warm under her face. Warm and wet. Her body, tired from crying, relaxed. Sleep washed all the pain away as it came down on her, pleasant and heavy, an old friend bringing peace.

When she woke up, she listened to the house. It was silent except for the electric hum of her alarm clock. She glanced at the clock. Almost seven.

Her face felt tight where the tears had dried. Rubbing it with both hands, she thought back to dinner. Her parents had mentioned going over to the Bransons tonight.

Seven-ish.

The house sounded empty. Apparently, they'd already left.

Marty sat up on the side of her bed, wondering what to do.

She couldn't stay alone in the house – not with Willy out there someplace.

If he isn't in a hospital.

Or a morgue.

No, he couldn't be dead. Dan hadn't hurt him enough to kill him.

She kicked off her sandals, unfastened her belt, and slipped off her shorts. Standing, she looked out the window. The neighborhood looked deserted. No kids were playing in the street or yards. Nobody was mowing grass. Even Hedda was missing from the chair on her front porch where she always planted herself after dinner to watch whatever might be going on within eye range.

Marty shut the drapes, then took off her blouse. As she took off her bra and panties, she thought about Dan.

Don't wear any. Give him a big surprise.

Sure thing. No way.

She put on a fresh pair of panties and a new bra. Then she put on a fresh white blouse and a bright yellow skirt that Dan liked.

'Cause it's so short.

He'd have me bare-ass naked if I'd let him.

I must be nuts, she thought as she picked up the phone beside her bed and tapped in Dan's number.

I'm not nuts, she told herself. Everything was fine till last night. Everything was great.

Mostly.

After the fourth ring, his answering machine picked up. The sound of his voice almost made her start crying again.

She waited for the beep, then said, 'Hi. It's me. Are you there? Anyway, I'm sorry about . . . everything. I don't want to lose you over a thing like this. Okay? Anyway, I'm alone and I was thinking maybe you could come over. But I guess you're not home? Anyway . . . give me a call or something. Bye.' She hung up.

Where are you?

She went down the hall to the bathroom. Grimacing at herself in the mirror, she muttered, 'You really blew it, champ. Congratulations.'

She washed her face and brushed her hair, then headed downstairs. On the kitchen table was a note:

Dear,
    We're off for the Bransons. Won't be home till late. If you go off somewhere, be sure and leave a note.
    Love,
    Mom

Marty went to the sink. Empty. The counter, too. Someone had finished the dishes for her and put them away.

She checked the kitchen door to make sure it was locked. Then she made a tour of the house. The front door was locked. She crossed the living room and checked the sliding glass door to the back yard. When she pulled, it rumbled open. No real surprise; the thing was a devil to get locked.

She pushed it with all her strength and pressed the metal switch. Then she tugged again at the handle. The door stayed shut.

After making sure the rest of the house was secure, she returned to the living room. She sat on the sofa, picked up the TV remote, and thumbed the power button.

The television stayed dark.

'Great,' she muttered.

She tried a few other buttons, in case someone had pushed something by mistake. But they didn't help.

Putting down the remote, she got to her feet and stepped over to the television. She braced herself against the walnut top of the console, bent over, and peered down behind it.

The power cord was unplugged.

'Huh?'

How the hell could that happen?

Marty stretched herself across the top of the set and reached down for the cord.

A hand grabbed her between the legs.

13

With his one good eye, Homer Stigg saw a girl up ahead. Seemed funny, a young gal like that walking south this time of the evening. Next town, Mawkeetaw, was a good twenty miles. Not so much as a gas station till then. Nothing but road and forest.

Well, he was heading for Mawkeetaw.

His insides seemed to twist up and quiver.

No, best leave it alone.

Such a pretty young thing. Those legs. That golden hair hanging way down her back. And that dress. That dress wasn't decent. Those colors, though.

Homer had never seen one so shiny and bright. It put him in mind of Joseph's coat of many colors.

Oh, now she was turning around, looking straight at him.

Her face so sweet and lovely. Her dress sticking to her in front. Plain as the nose on your face, she didn't have on a stitch of clothing underneath that dress.

Now her thumb was out and she smiled at him.

Homer's foot lifted off the gas pedal. He felt so tight inside that he thought he might get sick. He hunched over the steering wheel.

Keep on driving, boy. It ain't right to give rides to such sweet young gals.

But what if you leave her there? If you leave her, won't be long before another fella comes along. Maybe a fiend who'll violate the temple of her body.

So he stopped.

Turning his head, Homer watched the girl hurry toward the car. Her dress, all green and red and blue and golden, rippled and shimmered as she came.

Homer leaned across the seat and opened the door for her.

'Thanks,' she said, bending down to look in. 'Where you heading?'

'Down Mawkeetaw. Hop on in, if you wanta go that way.'

She nodded her head and started to climb in. Homer turned away as she reached a leg into the car and her dress started sliding up her thighs.

'That where you live?' he asked. 'Mawkeetaw?'

'No.' The door thumped shut.

'Where you call home?'

'Up north,' she said. Her voice had a hard edge.

Homer pulled onto the road. 'What's your name?' he asked.

'Nothing.'

'Don't you defy your elders, girl.'

After a few moments of silence, she muttered, 'Tina. My name's Tina.'

'Tina what?'

'Never mind.'

'Where's your manners, girl?'

'I'm sorry,' she said, sounding like a little child.

Homer looked at her. Her head was down, her face solemn, her hands folded on her lap. The dress barely covered her lap. Her legs were tawny and smooth.

He wanted to touch them.

Looking away quickly, he leaned forward to ease his tight, sick feeling.

But he was afraid she might get suspicious if he stopped talking. So he said, 'You got family in Mawkeetaw?'

'No.'

'Friends?'

'I've been there a few times for the fair,' she said. Her voice was very quiet.

'You from Gribsby?'

'I never said that.'

'You running away from home?'

'Never mind.'

'I've got me half a mind, girl, to turn this buggy around and take you back. I'll bet Sheriff Diggins, he could find your folks in no time flat.'

'Don't you dare try it,' she said. Her voice was a taut whisper.

Homer looked at her. She met him with steady, narrowed eyes. Her face looked as if it expected a punch, but wouldn't budge an inch. 'I'm not going back,' she said. 'Never. You just try taking me back and see what happens.'

'Keep a civil tongue in your head, girl.'

'I'm not going back.'

'Maybe you are, and maybe you aren't.'

'What do you mean by that?'

His heart was suddenly pumping madly. What *did* he mean by that?

Lord, so confusing.

'I shouldn't have picked you up,' he said. His voice had a dry, raspy sound that frightened him.

'You didn't have to,' Tina said.

'Oh yes, I sure did. I had an obligation. A Christian obligation. It was my duty. I have to save you.'

'Save me?'

'That's right.'

'From what?'

'Fiends. There's all kinds of fiends in this world. Fiends just waiting to get their filthy hands on the sweet, young flesh of girls like you.' He cleared his throat, but the scratchy sound

41

wouldn't go away. 'Just couldn't leave you there on the road. Fiends'd get you for sure.'

She looked at him.

She looked wary.

'Now don't fret, Tina. I won't let them get you. I'll protect you. I sure will.' Reaching out, Homer ran his fingers through her hair.

So soft. Soft and golden, like her skin.

14

When the hand grabbed her, Marty jumped and banged her head on the wall. Then she looked over her shoulder.

Willy grinned.

She kicked and tried to shut her legs, but his hand stayed between them, clutching her, hurting her. An arm wrapped around her hips. It pulled her off the television. When she started to scream, Willy flung her to the floor and dropped on top of her, crushing out the scream.

He rolled Marty onto her back.

She reached for his face, fingers hooked for clawing, but he grabbed her wrists. Pressing them to the carpet, he straddled her hips and sat on her.

Marty bucked and twisted, trying to throw him off. Then she saw his strange grin, so she stopped moving.

'C'mon, horsy! Gideeyap!' He bounced a couple of times.

Marty's knee took him square in the back.

'Naughty horsy!' he bounced harder.

She shot her knee up again. This time, Willy shifted enough to keep it from landing solidly. Then he leaned forward until his face loomed directly over Marty. 'Give Willy a kiss to make up,' he said.

'Go to hell.'

He bent lower and tried to kiss her mouth. She turned away. He pressed his mouth to her cheek and slobbered on her. 'Aren't you glad to see him again?'

'Get off me!' She felt the spittle roll toward her ear. 'What do you want?'

'You'll see.'

'Get off!'

'I plan to.'

'Bastard!'

'I'll let you up. But if you move, I'll kill you.'

He climbed off Marty and stood up.

With his weight gone, her body felt strangely light. She tried to rub the pain out of her wrists, then scratched the backs of her hands. They were itchy and red, the carpet's pattern imprinted in her skin.

As Willy walked toward the hall closet, Marty raised her head. Her blouse had come untucked in the struggle, but its buttons were still fastened. Her skirt was gathered above her waist, exposing her white panties.

She straightened the skirt as Willy came out of the closet.

He had a coil of rope in his hand.

Kneeling beside Marty, he tied a slip knot into one end of the rope.

'Can I sit up now?' she asked.

'Be my guest.'

She sat up and asked, 'What's that for?'

'Hanging you.' He dropped the noose over her head. Reaching behind her, he lifted her hair from under the rope. His hand paused, caressing her neck. Marty felt goosebumps rise under his touch. She heard herself make a tiny, whimpering sound.

'Scared?'

She tried to talk, but couldn't.

Willy laughed. He slid the knot against the front of her

43

throat, then backed away from her and tugged the line. Her head jerked.

'Ow!' she gasped.

'Up.'

Marty slowly got to her feet.

Stall! Do something! Oh, God!

She straightened her blouse and skirt. She scratched her left shoulder as if she had an itch there. Willy watched.

'Another minute,' he said, 'it won't be itchy anymore.'

She shoved her fingers inside the noose and pulled it open.

Willy was too quick.

He tugged his end of the rope and the noose whipped shut, jerking at the back of Marty's neck and flinging her headlong into his arms. He hugged her tightly against his body, gave her rump a painful squeeze with one hand, and said, 'Nice ass.'

'Fuck you.'

'Let's go over to the stairs,' he said. Releasing the grip on her buttock, he stepped backward, paying out rope. Then, using the rope like a dog leash, he led her toward the stairway.

'You won't hang me,' Marty said.

'Don't think so? Maybe you'd better hope I do, honey. 'Cause you know what? I've always known I'd come back and pay you a visit. I've had a lot of years to daydream about it and think about all the things I'll do to you. It's how I used to fall asleep at night in my cell. You were always the last thing on my mind at night. Every night. And I always fell asleep with a boner.'

At the foot of the stairs, he told Marty to stand still. Then he climbed up the stairway backward, paying out rope and keeping the line taut.

'Willy, don't,' she said. 'They'll send you back to prison. You'll spend the rest of your life there. Do you want that? The entire rest of your life?'

'That's if they catch me. But they won't.'

'Yes they will. If you . . . everyone will know you did it. They'll catch you, all right.'

He reached the top of the stairs.

'Willy? Don't do this.' She tried to sound brave, but it didn't work well.

'What'll you give me?' he asked.

A few strides along the upstairs hallway, and he would be standing directly above Marty.

'Anything,' she said. 'Just don't . . . don't hang me. Please. Don't kill me. I'll do anything. Please.'

And then she started to cry.

15

'I want out,' Tina muttered, pressing herself against the passenger door. 'Stop and let me out.'

'As soon as we get to Mawkeetaw,' Homer said. He patted her knee. She pulled it away. 'Scare you? All that talk about fiends?' He forced himself to laugh. His face felt very hot. 'I reckon I oughta apologize, but I won't. Know why? 'Cause I want you scared. Yes, I do. You're a sweet child, and I want you scared. Graveyards, they're full of fearless, sweet young girls.'

'Oh, Christ.'

'Watch your tongue, girl. Take not the name of the Lord thy God in vain.'

Her lower lip started shaking. Then she began to sob.

'Aw, now, don't cry. Nothing to cry about. I'll take good care of you. I sure will. Nothing to fret over, long as you're with Homer.'

He shook his head, upset that he'd let his name slip out.

'Let me go,' Tina said. 'Please?'

'Can't do that. If I let you go, sweetheart, why, a fiend might come by and snatch you up. You don't want that to happen.' He reached a hand toward her. She slapped it away.

'Don't *touch* me!' she blurted.

'Didn't mean nothing by it.' He frowned at her. Tears streaked her face. She sucked in a deep breath and held it, biting her bottom lip. Her arms were crossed in front of her body, hiding her breasts. She was tilted awkwardly to keep her legs out of easy reach. 'Say, you don't think I'm a fiend, do you? I'm not a fiend. Heck no.'

'Then let me go.'

'Can't. Wouldn't be safe. Do you know what they do to pretty girls like you? The fiends?'

So confusing. That awful tightness, his heart thumping, his breath coming so loudly. 'They start with your clothes. Rip them right off you.'

She jerked at the door handle.

Homer jammed his foot down on the brake pedal. The tires screamed as the door flew open and Tina dropped backward through it.

In the rearview mirror, Homer saw her tumbling along the pavement. By the time he had stopped the car to watch, she was no longer rolling. She lay motionless in the grass alongside the road. Her dress of many colors was twisted high. Leaf shadows, stirred by the evening breeze, trembled on the white skin of her buttocks.

Homer pulled her door shut. He pushed the gear shift into reverse.

His hands clenched the steering wheel and he pressed his forehead against it, shaking.

All so confusing.

Never should've stopped.

Never should've picked her up.

Never!

He looked at the rearview mirror.

The girl was on her hands and knees, slowly crawling toward the edge of the forest.

'I'm *not* a fiend!' he cried out. 'I'm *not*!'

He shoved the shift forward, jammed the gas pedal to the floor, and sped away.

16

'Anything?' Willy asked from the top of the stairs.

'Anything!' Marty cried. 'Anything! Just please don't do it! God! Don't! Whatever you want! Anything! Just please please God, don't hang me!'

'Okay. Here's what. Phone that prick boyfriend of yours and tell him to haul ass over here.'

'What?' She sniffed and wiped her runny nose. 'What do you want with him?'

'A little payback.'

'Okay. Okay. I'll do it. I'll call' – she dropped backward – 'him.' Dropped backward grabbing the rope with both her hands.

Willy let go of his end to keep from being tugged off the top of the stairs, and Marty sat down hard. An odd, tickling pain jolted through her.

Before Willy could bring in the slack, she jerked the noose off her head. She got to her feet and ran for the door. Her hand found the knob. She twisted and pulled. The door swung open. Looking over her shoulder, she saw Willy leaping down the stairs three at a time.

She slammed the door and sprinted across the lawn.

At the street, she turned around. The front door opened. Willy stepped halfway out, then took a backward step and shut the door.

He's staying inside!

Afraid to come out and chase her?

She supposed he would probably sneak out the rear of the house.

Unless . . .

He knows I'll have to come back, sooner or later. What if he decides to wait?

No, he'd be crazy to stay inside. He would have to figure she would call the police.

Marty started running toward Hedda's place. She could phone the cops from there.

As she started to cross the street, Dan's car suddenly rounded the corner and pulled to a stop. 'Where you going?' he asked, reaching across the front seat to open the door.

'No place special.'

'Can I give you a lift?'

'Yeah. Okay.' She climbed into his car and pulled the door shut. 'Did you get my message?'

'Message?'

'Guess not. I called you about . . . ten minutes ago?'

'Really? No, I didn't get any message. I thought I'd drop by and . . . you've been crying.'

'Yeah.'

'What's wrong? It's not because of our . . .?'

'Yeah. Of course it is.'

He shook his head. 'I was just coming over to see if we couldn't manage to straighten things out.'

'Nice idea. I had the same thing in mind. That's what I phoned about.'

'You must've just missed me.' He smiled at her. 'Well, where to? Your place?'

'That wouldn't be a good idea. Mom and Dad are there. I want to be alone with you.'

He put his hand against the side of her face.

'How about your place?' she suggested.

'My place it is.'

*

An hour later, Marty was stretched out face down on the bed, naked and sweaty. She felt languid and wonderful. Willy seemed like a problem from long ago and far away.

Dan, sitting on her rump, had been gently rubbing her back for the past few minutes. Now, he swept her hair sideways so it fell over her shoulder.

She was glad to have the hair away from the hot nape of her neck.

She supposed Dan was about to kiss her there.

But he asked, 'What's this?'

'What's what?'

'This mark.'

She suddenly felt sick.

'I don't know,' she said.

'Marty?'

'It's nothing.'

'It looks like a rope burn.' His hands clamped the tops of her shoulders. 'How did it get there?'

'I don't know.'

'Tell me!'

'I don't *know*!'

'It *is* a rope burn, isn't it?'

Marty didn't answer. Dan's fingers tightened on her shoulders. 'That hurts,' she said.

He squeezed harder. 'Who did it to you?'

'Stop that!'

'Who?'

'Who do you think?'

'He put a *rope* around your neck?'

'It doesn't matter. I got away.'

'*When? Tonight?*'

'Yes, tonight. Forget about it, okay? It doesn't matter.'

'When tonight?'

49

'Damn it . . .'

The hands clenching her shoulders suddenly jerked up and down, shaking her.

'Damn it!' she cried out.

'Just before I showed up, wasn't it?'

'Let go of me.'

'The motherfucking bastard. Where was he?'

'I'm not telling you anything. He wants to kill you, you know.'

'He was in your house, wasn't he?'

'No.'

'That's why you were out in the street. That's why you wanted to come over here. Your parents weren't in the house, *he* was.'

'Go to hell,' she said.

Dan climbed off her. 'You stay here,' he said.

Rolling over, she watched him scurry off the bed. He rushed about, snatching his clothes off the floor and putting them on. When he was dressed, he pulled open a drawer of a nightstand beside the bed. He took out a holstered revolver.

'No, don't,' Marty said. 'Put it away. Don't go over there. We can call the cops and have them . . .'

'I'll handle this bum. What the fuck was he going to do, *hang* you?'

'He's probably gone by now.'

Dan took a box of ammunition out of the drawer, opened it, and grabbed a handful of cartridges. He dumped them into a front pocket of his jeans. Then he met her eyes. 'What else did he do?'

'Nothing.'

'Did he rape you?'

'He didn't do *anything*. I got away. Don't go over there, Dan. He wanted me to call you. He *wants* you to come over. I think he wants to kill you.'

'Good. Hope he tries. You stay here till I get back.' Leaning over the bed, he hooked a hand behind her neck and drew her toward him.

She resisted for a moment, then leaned forward and kissed him. 'Be careful. Don't let him hurt you.'

'I'll be fine,' he said, and then he was gone.

Sitting cross-legged on the bed, Marty listened to his footsteps. The front door shut quietly. For a few moments, only the chirping of crickets came to her through the open bedroom window. Then she heard Dan's footsteps by the road. The car door thumped shut. The engine whinnied and started. Gravel crunched under the wheels and the sounds of the car began to fade away.

17

Willy sat in the darkness of Hedda's kitchen, watching. He'd been sitting there for a long time. He didn't mind the wait.

Marty would have to come back. Wherever she'd gone after running off, she couldn't stay away forever. Sooner or later, she'd come home.

Then he would have her.

Nice of her not to call the cops. Stupid, though. Maybe she went off to find that prick boyfriend of hers, get him to handle it.

Willy hoped so.

He got up from the table, stepped over Hedda, and went to the refrigerator. Not much inside. He grabbed a package of cheese, swung the door shut, and returned to the table. There, he unwrapped a thin slice of cheese and began to eat it.

He was working on his fifth slice when a car stopped in front of Marty's house. A Ford. The same Ford that he'd followed to the lake last night.

Willy pulled the plastic wrapping off another slice of cheese as the headlights died and a man climbed out of the car.

The prick.

And he had something in his right hand. A gun?

Figures. Cocksucker likes to play hardball.

Willy folded the slice of cheese in half, then folded it again, making a small, thick square. He stuck it into his mouth.

Across the street, the prick was rushing across Marty's front yard. He disappeared around a corner of the house.

'Gonna sneak up on me?' Willy asked with his mouthful of cheese. 'Real tricky, you dumb-ass shit.'

He got up from the table. His fingers were slippery from the cheese. He wiped them on his jeans and headed for the door. 'So long, sweet stuff,' he said to Hedda.

Outside, the hot night air smelled like moist grass. A welcome change from the bad air of the kitchen.

The prick was nowhere to be seen.

Walking with a casual pace, Willy crossed the street.

He opened the back door of the Ford, climbed in, and shut it quietly.

Kneeling on the floor, he peered out the window at Marty's house.

A light came on in an upstairs window.

Marty's window?

Willy couldn't remember what her bedroom had looked like, that morning ten years ago. He only remembered that it had been very sunny. Very bright and sunny, making Marty's hair shine. Her face had gotten sweaty. There were tiny specks of sweat above her lip. They glistened in the sunlight. She had tears on her cheeks. Her eyelashes stuck together, making little, curly points.

The light in the upstairs window went off.

Willy took the knife from his pocket and opened its blade.

18

'What the hell?' Roger Sanderson knew it was no mirage. It was a real live girl walking slowly through the darkness, her head down. She wore a paisley dress that was torn behind the right shoulder. Roger slowed down and pressed a switch to lower the passenger window.

The girl turned her face toward him and smiled.

'You lost?' he called.

'Me?'

He laughed. 'Climb aboard, mate, and I'll see you to a safe port.'

He watched her get in. Her knees were scraped and filthy. Her dress was very short.

'Nice car,' she said.

'Nice dress.'

She pulled the door shut, and the overhead light went off. 'You like it?' she asked.

Roger switched the light back on. 'Sure looks good on you.'

'Thanks.' She smiled and blushed. Her face was dirty. Tears, dry now, had drawn streaks down her cheeks. 'I'm afraid it got ripped,' she said. 'Back here. See?' She leaned forward and turned her back to Roger. Her skin, where it showed through the rip, was scraped raw.

'How'd that happen?'

'I fell out of a car. Well, actually, I jumped.' Her smile vanished. 'Crazy old guy went weird on me.'

'Had to hit the silk, huh?'

'Oh, it's not silk,' she said, looking down at her dress. 'It's like polyester or something. But it feels like silk, I guess.' She rubbed the glossy fabric and frowned at Roger.

'Hit the silk is a figure of speech,' he said. 'It means to bail out with a parachute.'

'I bailed out, all right. No parachute, though.'

'Did the crazy guy hurt you?'

'Nope. It was the road that banged me up. He just made a few grabs, but you should've heard him talk. Gave me the willies.'

Roger turned off the overhead light, and started driving.

'So, are you a teacher or something?' the girl asked.

'A teacher? What makes you think so?'

'Your lesson about hitting silk. Plus, nobody but teachers talk about stuff like figures of speech.'

'Sorry, Holmes, but I'm a sales rep.'

'I'm not Holmes, I'm Tina.'

'Pleased to meet you, Tina. I'm Roger.'

'I think I like you, Roger.'

'Thank you. I do believe I like you, too.'

19

After Dan left, Marty lay down on his bed and stared at the ceiling. She should've stopped him from going. Somehow, she should've stopped him. It was insane, going after Willy with a gun.

She spent a long time lying there, thinking about it all and worrying.

Finally, she got up, went into the kitchen, opened the refrigerator and took out a can of beer. She carried it into the living room and sank onto the sofa.

And gulped the beer.

Damn him anyway.

Has to prove what a tough guy he is.

It'd serve him right if . . .

No!

God, Dan, you idiot. Who the hell do you think you are, Rambo?

When the can was empty, she flung it across the room. It bounced off the wall and dropped to the carpet.

Then she went into the kitchen and found herself another can of beer. Sipping it, she wandered into the bathroom. She placed the can on the edge of the sink, then sat down on the toilet and urinated. When she stood up and saw herself in the mirror, she shook her head.

Her hair was dark and stringy. Her face was speckled with sweat. She looked down at herself. She was sweaty all over. Her pubic curls were matted down.

She felt pretty sticky down there, too.

So she decided that a shower would be a good way to pass the time while she waited for Dan's return.

If he *does* return, she thought.

Stupid macho jerk.

She picked up her can and took it with her to the bathtub. Squatting beside the tub, she had a couple of swallows, then reached out with one hand and turned on the faucets. While the water rushed out of the spout, she tested its heat with one hand and drank beer with the other.

The can was still pretty full by the time she was ready to step in, so she took it with her.

Holding it above the spray, she raised her other hand to close the shower curtain.

She watched the way her arm angled up to the curtain. It was slender and lightly tanned, and it glistened with wetness. She felt a drop of water slide along its underside, tickling.

The curtain's metal rings clamored along the shower rod as she pulled it shut.

Then she faced the heavy, warm spray.

The water pelted her, flooded her open mouth, spilled down her chin. It drummed her closed eyelids until her eyes ached. Then she bowed her head. It pounded down, matting her hair, streaming down the sides of her face, into her eyes and along her lips and chin. It ran down her shoulders and breasts and belly.

It felt great.

But she wanted to use soap and get herself clean.

Hard to do that with a can of beer in one hand.

So she turned away from the shower. With the spray splattering her back and sliding down her buttocks and legs, she tilted the can to her mouth and drank.

Gulped it down.

All of it.

Then belched.

From the other side of the shower curtain, Willy said, 'Excuse you.'

Marty jumped and her feet slipped out from under her.

20

As she started to fall, she dropped the beer can and made a grab for the curtain rod. It broke loose and she followed it sideways over the edge of the tub. She landed on her back, both legs propped up by the tub.

'Nice fall,' Willy said. 'Nice view.'

She swung her legs down to the floor, clamped a hand between them and crossed her other arm over her breasts. Raising her head, she looked at Willy.

He stared down at her, grinning. 'Pretty as a picture,' he said. 'Wish I had me a camera.'

'Where's Dan?'

'Who?'

'Dan.'

'Oh, the prick?' Willy spread his arms. The front of his T-shirt was soaked with blood. 'I stabbed him with my little knife. Took his billfold. He didn't have much cash to speak of. A shitty thirty bucks and change. You really oughta go out with a better class of guy. Like me.'

'You . . . killed him?'

'Maybe yes, maybe no.'

'God.'

'You really shouldn't have sent him after me, honey.'

'I didn't.'

'Bitch.' Willy took a wallet out of his back pocket and threw it at Marty. It slapped her bare shoulder and bounced off. 'Time to go.' He slipped a faded blue towel off its bar and flung it. It dropped across Marty's knees, but she didn't make a move to take it. 'Now,' he said.

Sitting up quickly, she grabbed the towel.

'Don't just sit there, dry yourself.'

Holding the towel against her body, she carefully got to her knees.

'Now!'

'Turn around,' she said.

'My ass. I'll give you five. One.'

Clasping the towel to her breasts, she reached out sideways with her free arm. She groped blindly, keeping her eyes on Willy.

'Two.'

Her hand found the side of the bathtub. She braced her palm against it and pushed herself up.

'Three.'

She stood up straight.

'Four.'

She glanced from side to side, looking for a weapon. Anything heavy or sharp. Nothing.

'Five.'

She backed away as he came forward.

'You know what happens now?' he asked. 'I'm gonna dry you myself.'

'No.'

'Yep. You had your chance. I counted five. Lucky me.'

'Please.'

Her jerked the towel away from her. 'Nice. Real nice. Last time I saw you stripped, you didn't have hardly any tits at all. Look at 'em now.'

She tried to push past him. He shoved her backward against the wall. With the towel in both hands, he started rubbing her.

'Stop it! Don't!'

'Real nice.'

'You damn bastard!'

'I'm not hurting you.'

'Stop it!'

'How does that feel?'

'You . . .!'

'Honk honk!'

'Bastard!'

He laughed.

Marty drove her knee up, changing his laugh to a squeal of pain. As he started to fold, she shoved him. He fell backward. She leaped over him and ran for the bathroom door.

She rushed through the door and threw it shut. A moment later, a blast slammed the air. A bullet knocked through the door, throwing splinters into her forearm.

As she ran across the front room, she snatched her blouse up off the floor. She thrust her wounded arm through a sleeve. Some splinters caught the cloth. Others flattened down. She hardly noticed the pain as she made for the front door.

She flung it open. As she raced outside, she got her other arm into its sleeve.

A car was parked along the roadside. Willy's Chevy.

The street was deserted. The nearest building, half a block to the south, had no lights in its windows. A couple of hundred yards up the road, the woods began.

The woods and Wilson Lake.

If he catches me there . . .

But it seemed like the only place to go.

The rough asphalt was hot under Marty's feet as she sprinted up the road. She pumped her arms, throwing out her legs as far as they would stretch, her bare feet reaching out but never far enough. Never fast enough.

She kept running, taking gulps of air in quick gasps, her open blouse flapping behind her.

Soon, she felt an unusual warmth inside her legs. In the muscles of her thighs and calves. Though she tried to work them as fast as before, they began to feel tired and heavy. She swung her arms harder to make up for it. The weariness started inside them, too.

But she kept running.

As she took the turn into the woods, she glanced back.

Car headlights came on.

She tried to run faster. With every stride, her arms and legs struggled against the heaviness. Her lungs burned.

But still she kept running.

Finally, she came to the parking lot by the lake.

Last night, it had been crowded with teenaged lovers in cars. Tonight, it was empty.

Nobody to help her.

Marty dashed for the far side of the lot. She heard the racing engine of the car. Blocking her way was a fallen, long-dead tree. She planted a hand on it, kicked her leg into the air, and vaulted it just as the headlights started sweeping the lot.

She squatted with her back against the trunk and shut her eyes. Her hands were slippery against her knees. Sweat streamed down the burning sides of her face. She took deep, painful breaths, hoping to recover quickly enough to do some good.

Then she turned around and looked over the top of the tree trunk.

Willy was out of his car, walking along the other side of the parking lot, peering into the darkness, pausing to listen.

It wouldn't take him long to find her. A few minutes, maybe. *Gotta do something!*

Then she saw the silver path of the full moon shining on the lake.

21

Ahead of him on the dark road, Roger saw a neon sign flashing, WAYSIDE MOTOR INN. The pale blue lights below it read, 'Vacancy.'

'Hey hey!' he said. 'A port in the storm.'

'Hope they've got food,' Tina said. 'I'm starving to death.'

'Mah dear, ports in the storm are renowned for their cuisine.'

He pulled to a stop in front of the motel office. 'You can wait here,' he said. 'I'll be back in a flash.'

Inside the office, he asked for a room with twin beds. The manager, a stooped and bony old crone losing the last of her white hair, squinted out the office window.

'My daughter,' Roger explained. 'The spitting image of her mother, God rest her soul.'

The old woman's watery eyes narrowed at him.

Roger solemnly shook his head. 'Life is so fleeting,' he said. 'Feeble candle flames are we, snuffed, perchance, by a vagrant breeze.'

The old woman seemed to shrink. 'Forty bucks,' she said, and pushed a registration card at him. 'Fill this out.'

As he wrote the requested information on the card, he asked. 'How late does your cafe stay open?'

'Never closes.'

He paid, and she gave him a room key.

Back at the car, he climbed in and said, 'All set. Room sixteen.'

He looked through the cafe windows as he drove by. A lone man sat at the counter. Two couples and a family of six sat at the booths along the wall. 'It doesn't appear crowded. The food's probably greasy enough to lubricate a fleet of Lincolns.'

'I hope it isn't closing.'

'The manager informs me that it stays open continuously.'

'Thank goodness.'

'Thar she blows!' Roger spun the steering wheel. The head-beams lit the side panel of a station wagon, glanced with a blinding flare off the picture window of Room 16, and came to a stop on the brick wall and door. 'We have arrived,' he announced.

'I hope they've got chicken in a basket.'

'Bet they do. I'll just set the luggage in our room, and we'll be off. Unless you want to wash up first.'

'Let's eat now.'

'Do you want to see the room first?'

'I'd sure like to eat.'

'Then eat we shall, without further ado. Or further a-don't.'

'Huh?' Tina asked. Then she grinned and said, 'A joke.'

Roger laughed as he hopped from the car. He hurried around the front and opened the door for Tina. She reached out a hand. Roger helped her out. He held her hand all the way to the cafe, where he let go and said, 'We've got to act properly, now. I'm passing you off as my daughter.'

'Sure thing, Pops.'

He laughed.

Inside, Tina walked briskly to a booth and scooted across it. She patted the cushion beside her and said, 'Sit here, Father.'

'I'll sit over here,' he said. He went to the other side of the table. 'And please take it easy on the father routine.'

'Why don't you sit by me? Do I smell bad?'

'You smell fine.'

'Then why?'

61

'View's better over here.'

She smiled and nodded. 'Do you think I'm pretty?'

'You're a thing of beauty.'

'A *thing*?' She wrinkled her nose.

'That's poetry. John Keats. "A thing of beauty is a joy for ever." '

'Yeah? That's kind of nice.'

She was a joy, all right. Roger watched her pick up the menu and study it, her brow furrowed with concentration. Serious blue eyes, a sweet clear face still lined where tears had washed channels through the dirt, hair the color of gold.

And her body. The way the paisley dress was clinging, he could see that she had a very fine body indeed.

'Look!' She beamed at him. 'Southern fried chicken.'

'This is your lucky day.'

'Sure is.' Her eyes suddenly went sad, and Roger realized that today, perhaps, had not been especially lucky for her.

'Mine, too,' he said.

'Huh?'

'My lucky day. Meeting you. I'm not in the habit of picking up strangers, you know.'

'I didn't know that.'

'Too dangerous.'

'Why'd you pick *me* up?'

'You don't look dangerous,' he said. 'Not dangerous at all, just very lonely and helpless.'

'I'm not all that helpless.'

'Glad to hear it.'

'You might be right about the lonely, though. You're lonely too, aren't you?'

'Sometimes.'

The waitress arrived. He ordered the fried chicken for Tina and a patty melt for himself. Tina asked for a coke, and Roger ordered coffee.

When the waitress was gone, Tina said, 'Do you really think I'm pretty?'

'Very.'

Leaning across the table, she whispered, 'What about my figure?'

'From all appearances, it's in fine shape.'

She nodded in agreement, sat back, and grinned mysteriously. 'Know something?' she whispered.

'What?' His mouth was dry.

'Make a guess.'

'Beauty is truth, truth . . .'

'No. Guess again, silly. Guess what I'm wearing under this flimsy little dress.'

He smiled. 'I don't know. What?'

'Skin. Nothing but skin.'

'Fancy that,' Roger said, and took a drink of water.

22

'Stop!' Willy shouted.

Marty's feet slapped into the water, splashing its coolness high against her body. She waded out until it reached her thighs, then gulped in a deep breath and dived. She stayed below, swimming furiously, until her lungs couldn't hold the air any longer. Then she blew it out in a gush of bubbles and skimmed to the surface. Air! It was fragrant with the night smells of the woods along the shore.

When her breathing became more regular, she trod water and listened. It was difficult to hear much beyond her small area of swirling water and thudding heartbeat and breathing, but she heard enough to know that Willy wasn't swimming after her.

Not on the water's surface.

She squinted at the shore, hoping to see him, but only spotted the top of his car. A chill scurried up her back. Suddenly, she half expected a cold hand to clutch her ankle and drag her down. She thrashed out, flattening into a crawl as her legs rose to the surface. She kept her face down for speed. Her legs kicked, tight and fast. Her arms darted forward, reaching her cupped hands far out and sweeping them down through the water.

She swam hard until she heard Willy's voice from far away.

'Hey out there!' he called.

She said nothing.

'I'd come out and join you, but I haven't got time.'

He doesn't know how to swim?

Either that, or he's just chicken.

'You better come back. Right now.' He said nothing for a while. Then he called, 'Did you hear me? Come outa there!'

She continued to tread water and say nothing.

'Look, you better come out.'

Marty could hardly see him. He probably couldn't see her at all.

If he can't see me, he can't shoot me.

Probably wouldn't be able to hit me, anyway. Not with that pistol.

Marty didn't know a lot about handguns, but she knew they were meant for nearby targets. If you wanted to shoot someone this far away, you should be using a rifle.

And maybe he's scared to fire because of the noise.

'I don't see you coming in,' Willy yelled.

And he wouldn't, either.

I'll just wait him out.

'By the way,' he called, 'I guess I forgot to tell you something about your prick boyfriend. I didn't kill him. All I did was bonk him on the head.'

Marty's mind seemed to freeze.

'He's in the trunk of my car.'

She couldn't think.

'So you better come in now, or I'm gonna open up the trunk and shoot him in the eye.'

Marty buttoned her blouse as she waded out of the lake. When she reached shore, Willy clutched her upper arm and pulled her to his car.

'I want to see Dan,' she said.

'Fuck you.'

He opened the passenger door and shoved her in. The seat felt scratchy against her naked buttocks. Willy shut the door.

She sat up straight and arranged the front of her sopping blouse so it covered her lap.

Willy climbed in and shut the door. 'I like your outfit,' he said.

'Bastard.'

'You wouldn't call me that if you knew the great little place I'm taking you to. Nice little cabin off in the middle of the woods. Stocked up with the best canned food you ever tasted. I fixed the place up real nice for you. It's got real class. Great spot for a honeymoon.'

'*What?*'

'Honeymoon,' he repeated. 'You know. No, I reckon you don't – you still living with your mommy and daddy like a little kid. How come you aren't married, huh? Never found the right man? Guess I set too high of a standard and none of these pricks can live up to me. That right?'

'Go to hell.'

'Anyway, I don't aim to marry you. Thought we'd have us a honeymoon without. We're gonna have a great old time.'

'Eat shit and die.'

'That's no way to talk after all my kindnesses to you and Danny. I could've killed him if I'd wanted. And I could've blown *your* head off.'

'You tried.' She wiped a drop of water off her chin.

'Not hardly. I tried to miss you, that's what I tried to do.'

'Sure.'

'I'm a dead-on shot. You might find that out, sometime, if you give me much more grief.'

A car swung into the parking lot. Marty watched it creep along. It stopped beside them, only a few yards away from her door.

The driver glanced at her, then took off his glasses and turned his back. He scooted toward the girl in the passenger seat.

'Aren't we lucky?' Willy said. 'Hope the girl ain't a pig.' He reached under his seat and picked up Dan's revolver.

'What are you going to do?'

'Just gotta get you something to wear.' He climbed out, shut his door quietly, and walked around the front of his car, the revolver swinging at the end of his lanky arm.

Inside the other car, the couple were embracing, unaware of Willy's approach.

'Watch out!' Marty yelled. 'Get out of here!'

The girl with her back to the passenger door saw Willy approach the driver's window. She stopped moving. For a moment, the boy continued to squirm against her. Then he looked over his shoulder.

'Oh, hello,' he said. He sounded embarrassed and very young.

'Out of the car.'

'Yes, sir.' The boy fumbled along the top of the dashboard and found his glasses, then looked down at his open shirt.

'Get out,' Willy commanded.

'Just a . . .'

The girl said something to him.

The boy reached for the ignition.

Willy stuck the gun muzzle against the boy's ear. 'Out. Now.'

'What do you want?' The kid no longer sounded embarrassed; he sounded terrified.

'You'll see.' Willy opened the door for them, and the interior light came on.

Marty saw how young they were. Sixteen, maybe. The girl might've been even younger – fourteen, fifteen?

The boy climbed out of the car. His fingers moved quickly to button his shirt as if it were very important.

'You, too.'

The girl pressed her back against the passenger door.

'Willy!' Marty said. 'Let her alone.'

'Shut up.'

'Do you want money?' the boy asked.

'Yeah. Good idea.'

The boy reached into his rear pocket. He slid out a wallet. Marty could see his hand shaking.

Willy jerked the wallet away.

'Hey!'

'Shut up, kid.' Willy leafed through some bills, then shut the wallet and stuffed it into his pocket. 'You're filthy rich, you little shit.'

'I'd like to have it back,' the boy said. 'Please? Keep the money, but I'd like to have my billfold back. It was a present.'

'Tough titty,' Willy said.

The boy's eyes narrowed behind his glasses. 'Give it over.'

Willy laughed.

Suddenly, the boy went for him, face turned away, windmilling with aimless fists, crying out, 'Give it you lousy son-of-a-bitch motherfucking bas . . .!'

The gun barrel crashed against his skull.

Marty cringed at the sound of it.

The boy staggered on wobbly legs.

Willy hit him again on the head. Marty turned away.

When she looked back, the boy was lying on the ground and Willy was leaning into the car. 'Your turn, hot stuff,' he said to the girl. 'Come on.' He grabbed one of her hands and dragged her across the front seat.

Her free hand caught hold of the steering wheel. Willy tugged until she let go. Gasping with alarm, she tumbled backward out of the car. She landed on her back, legs in the air.

Making a show of gallantry, Willy helped her stand up. He turned her around and brushed the dust off the back of her knit shorts and jersey.

'Real cute,' he told Marty, looking over his shoulder and beaming her a smile. 'Real class.' He patted the girl's rump. 'You'll look great in this outfit, honey. Think it'll fit? She hasn't got much in the tit department. What do you think?'

'Just leave her alone, Willy.'

'That's twice you've said my name, you dumb fuck.' He faced the girl. 'Take your clothes off.'

The girl stood rigid.

'Come on, hot stuff, strip.'

'The boy's clothes will fit me better,' Marty said.

'Shut up.'

'They will!'

'Strip,' he told the girl.

Marty threw open the door and started to climb out.

Turning, Willy pressed the muzzle between her eyes. It made a subtle ache, way back behind her eyes, like something she felt once while trying on the glasses of a friend. She sat back down in the car, but left the door open and kept her feet on the ground.

Willy jammed the barrel down the back of his jeans. He grabbed the girl's jersey at its waist and tried to lift it. She clamped down both arms, holding it in place.

'Get your arms up.'

She pressed them closer to her sides. Her mouth was a tight line.

'Okay,' Willy said. He let go of her. Taking out the pistol, he knelt by the unconscious boy. His thumb drew back the hammer. 'I'll give you five. Start stripping.'

The girl didn't move.

'One.'

She still didn't move. Marty glanced at the revolver. Its hammer, at full cock, looked like a vicious mouth about to snap shut.

'Two.'

The girl crossed her arms and gripped the bottom of her tight jersey. She peeled it off in a quick, fluid motion.

Marty felt sick for her.

'Three.'

She tucked the jersey under her chin and unbuckled her belt.

'Come on.'

Her fluttering hands opened her waist button, found the zipper tab and pulled.

'Four.'

The jersey fell, but she didn't stop to pick it up.

'Real nice,' Willy said.

Both her hands tugged the tight shorts down her legs.

'Five.'

'There!' she cried out. Naked except for her panties, she hugged her breasts and sobbed loudly. 'There! I'm done! There!'

Willy lowered the hammer with his thumb, then stuck the revolver into his jeans again. He picked up the girl's clothes, shook the dust off them, and tossed them to Marty. 'Get them on,' he told her.

'I'll have to stand up.'

'So stand up.'

He went to the girl and put his hands on her shoulders.

'Keep your mitts off her,' Marty said.

'Shut up and get dressed.'

Holding the clothes, Marty watched him slide his hands down the girl's arms. They moved down her sides. They caressed her hips. They clutched and rubbed her buttocks. Then they tore off her panties.

The girl tried to push him away.

'WILLY!'

He threw her to the ground.

'DON'T!' Marty shouted as he dropped on top of the girl. 'Stop it! Get off her!'

She dropped the clothes, grabbed Willy's arm and tried to pull him away. It was slippery with sweat. He got it free and swung at Marty. The girl under him lashed out with one hand, fingers hooked and spread like claws. Willy pulled up short on his swing at Marty and blocked the girl's attack.

Then he drove a fist down.

Marty heard it connect with the girl's nose. The naked body gave a grotesque lurch and lay still.

Willy got between the girl's legs.

Marty dived, tearing him off her. They rolled on the ground. When they stopped rolling, Willy was on top. He sat on Marty's chest, pinning her arms under her knees. With one hand, he pulled her hair until she gasped with pain. When her mouth opened, he jammed the gun barrel in.

It was thick and cold, and tasted of oil. Its front sight cut the roof of her mouth. It pressed far back toward her throat until she gagged.

23

'Lucky for you a stiff's no fun in the sack.' Willy laughed and pulled the gun out of Marty's mouth. Its front sight chipped a tooth. He climbed off her. 'Get dressed.'

Marty rolled over, choking, spitting gritty bits of tooth into the dirt.

'Now.'

She got to her feet and picked up the girl's shorts.

'Put them on.'

They fitted snugly. After she picked up the jersey, she knelt by the boy. He looked very still. Through the thin fabric of his shirt, she felt his body heat and the rise and fall of his breathing.

'Knock it off,' Willy said.

Ignoring him, Marty went to the girl. In the moonlight, her face looked black with blood. The nose was mashed sideways, its ridge broken.

'Put on her top.'

Marty turned her back to Willy and started to unbutton her blouse.

'Don't be shy,' he said. 'Just think of me as your guy. Which I am. The only guy you're ever gonna have.'

She didn't move.

'Turn around right now or else.'

She turned around. Facing him, she took off her wet blouse. Willy stared at her. Not drying herself, she pushed her hands through the jersey sleeves and pulled it over her head. It stuck to her wet skin.

Willy reached out a hand.

Marty backed away from him. And kept backing away until the side of the car stopped her.

'Sit down,' Willy said. 'Right there. On the ground. Better still, lie down.'

'What for?'

He grabbed the neck of her jersey and pulled. She went to her knees.

'Lie on your stomach.'

She did.

'Now stay that way.'

Kneeling down, Willy went through the boy's pockets. There was only a handkerchief and comb.

'Give him back his wallet,' Marty said.

'Shut the fuck up.'

He climbed into the car, found the girl's leather purse on the floor and dumped it on his lap. Marty, on the ground, couldn't see what fell out. But she saw Willy pick up a billfold and look inside. He grinned. 'Not bad. Kid's got rich folks.'

'Maybe she works.'

'Maybe we'll take her with us.'

'Great idea. Hold her for ransom?'

'Nope,' Willy said. He dropped the purse. 'Ransom, that'd be too much trouble. I'll just take her along for a little variety.'

'Broken nose and all?' Marty asked.

Not answering, he climbed out of the car and went to its front. There, he opened the hood. Her jerked a hose loose and threw it into the lake.

'Finished?' Marty asked.

'Not just yet.' He stepped over the unconscious boy and squatted beside the girl. 'See that? Look at the number I did on her nose.'

'I saw.'

'A real ugly mess, huh? But it's just from the neck up, and that isn't the part that counts. Know what I mean?' He reached down and patted the girl's right breast. 'Guess I'd better not take her with us. Not with her nose like this. People'd wonder.'

'They sure would.' Marty spat out a fleck of tooth. 'They'd ask a lot of questions.'

'Well, since I'm not taking her . . .' He picked up the girl's legs and turned her until the top of her head was toward Marty. Then he dropped her legs and got on his knees between them.

'Willy! No!'

'Yes, yes.' He pulled the pistol out of his belt and aimed it at Marty.

'God, don't.'

He laughed. 'Think I'm gonna pass up a piece like this?' He unzipped his jeans.

'Do me instead.'

'Thanks anyhow.'

'Willy, I'd be better. Hell, she's out cold. She'll just lie there.'

'You're for later. She's for now.'

'Don't do this to her.'

'Jealous?'

'Please.'

Willy, grinning, pulled his penis out of his jeans. It was big and upright.

'I'm not going to let you.'

'Can't stop me.'

'We'll see about . . .'

In the distance, a car engine rumbled and sputtered.

They both looked toward the entrance to the parking area. So far, there was no sign of headlights.

'It'll be here in a minute,' Marty said. 'It'll be the first of a whole bunch. The movie probably just got out. Pretty soon, this place will be crawling with horny teenagers.'

'I'm not quitting now.' Willy started to lower himself onto the girl.

Marty scurried backward, half expecting a bullet to smash through her body. She crawled to Willy's car, stretched across its front seat and reached to the steering wheel.

As she shoved, the blare of Willy's car horn sounded through the night.

24

The driver's door flew open. The revolver came in, swinging. Marty jerked her hand away an instant before the barrel hammered the steering wheel where her fingers had been. The horn went silent.

'I'm gonna fix you for that. Fix you real good. Sit up! We gotta get out of here.'

He jumped into the car and slammed the door.

'Shut your door, damn it! I could've fucked that girl, you stupid bitch. Shut it!' His fist shot sideways, pounding Marty's arm as she leaned away. She pulled the door shut. Willy started the engine and backed up.

The headbeams lit the boy and girl. Their bodies were motionless, but Marty knew they were alive.

Alive and lucky.

Willy's car rolled over the bumpy road, out of the woods, onto the main road.

'Where'd that other car go?' Willy asked.

'I wouldn't know.'

'It was coming.'

'Maybe it turned off.'

'You said a whole bunch were coming.'

'Maybe I was wrong.'

'I oughta kill you.'

She looked out her window. There was nothing to see but dark woods.

She looked at her forearm and saw several places where splinters from the door had torn into her skin. She didn't seem to be bleeding, but the area around the cuts felt tender and sore.

Compared to the rest of her body, her arm was in good shape. Dizzying throbs pounded through her head. The roof of her mouth, cut by the gun sight, felt ragged and painful at the touch of her tongue. The front tooth was crooked and sharp. Her stomach seemed hollow and sour. Underneath the jersey and shorts, her skin itched because she'd still been wet when Willy made her put them on.

You're in great shape, kid.

At least he didn't rape the girl.

Thank God.

Marty slipped a hand down the back of her shorts and scratched her buttocks. They felt clammy.

'Do you mind if I get in the back seat?' she asked. 'I want to lie down.'

'Go on.'

She turned around, crawled awkwardly over the back of the front seat, and dropped onto the rear seat.

'Don't try and pull anything,' Willy warned. 'Remember who's in the trunk.'

'I remember.'

Putting her back to Willy, she curled onto her side and pillowed her head on her arm just above the splinter cuts.

She wanted to take off the damp clothes so that she could get dry.

But she didn't move.

He'll look around and see me.

So what? she thought. This wouldn't be the first time he's seen me naked. Anyhow, he'll only be able to see my back. And what's he going to do about it?

Trembling slightly, Marty struggled out of her jersey. Then she pulled the shorts down to her knees.

The warm night air blowing through the windows rushed against her skin, soothing it, caressing away the itchy dampness.

Willy didn't make a comment, didn't touch her.

He doesn't even know.

The air kept blowing against her, and soon the pains of the body no longer mattered. Only the warm dry smoothness of the moving air mattered. After a while, she fell asleep.

In her dream, Dan was late coming home from work. Apparently, she was married to him. And he was late. And she was worried. But suddenly the front door opened, and Dan came into the bright sunny room. He was naked.

'Where are your clothes?' Marty asked.

'I had to take them off and leave them in the trunk. They're all bloody.'

Now she noticed that Dan was all bloody.

'What happened?' she asked, not terribly concerned. But curious.

'Oh, I had a little run-in with one of your old boyfriends.'

'So, it's *his* blood?

'Mine. But I'm all right.'

He came toward her, arms spread out to hug her. His blood would get all over her. But she didn't mind. She was naked, too. She could simply take a shower. So she opened her arms for him.

Instead of stepping into her arms, he moved a hand up the back of her leg.

Which seemed an odd trick, since he was in front of her.

His fingers delved into the crevice of her rump.

Marty suddenly woke up and felt a hand back there. She flinched rigid. A finger thrust at her anus.

'Bastard!' she yelled.

Willy laughed.

Marty swung an arm down behind her, grabbed Willy by the wrist and jerked his hand away. Still clutching it, she flopped onto her back. Willy was twisted sideways in the driver's seat, watching her over his shoulder.

'Let go,' he said.

Clutching his arm with both hands, she tugged it down and backward.

Willy cried out and seemed to rise higher in his seat.

'Fucking bitch! I'll kill you.' Then he suddenly turned his head forward and yelled, 'SHIT!'

The brakes shrieked.

Marty flew forward and let go of his arm.

The car jerked, throwing her off the seat. She landed on the narrow floor. As she tried to get up, a whining skid sent her sprawling.

Somewhere, a horn blasted. A cry of brakes surged through the night.

But not from Willy's car.

Toward Willy's car.

Marty braced herself for the impact.

It didn't come.

Silence came instead.

The car stopped.

She took deep breaths, trying to calm down.

Nearby, two doors slammed. Then boots scuffled across the asphalt.

Marty thought about getting up from the floor.

But then the footsteps halted near Willy's side of the car and a man said, 'Look what we got here! Got a babe here, butt-naked.' He sounded excited.

'Sure as hell,' said a second voice, also male. It came from the passenger side of the car. 'Hey, honey,' it said. 'Honey, you all right there?'

She didn't move, didn't say a word.

'I think she's out of it, Stu.'

'So's this guy.'

'How come? We didn't hit 'em.'

'Reckon they're stoned.'

'Yeah, bet that's it.'

'Damn near got us killed, fuckin' drug fiends.'

'Let's fix 'em.'

'Fuckers damn near killed us, we oughta fix 'em good.'

The door at Marty's feet opened. Rough hands grabbed her ankles and started dragging her out.

She tried to kick free.

Still dragging her, the man called to his friend, 'Hey, this one's awake!'

'Good deal.'

'Come on over here and gimme a hand.'

He dragged her the rest of the way out of the car. As she fell to the pavement, a blast slammed through the warm night air.

He let go of Marty and called, 'Stu!'

Pushing herself up to her hands and knees, Marty saw her man start backing away fast, holding out his hands. He was a bald, skinny guy, maybe forty years old, and didn't wear a shirt. He made little whimpery sounds as he backed up.

The next shot from Willy's gun punched a hole in the middle of his chest.

25

Roger opened his eyes. Apparently, he'd dozed off. He rolled onto his side. Tina smiled at him. She looked very fresh and young in the mellow lamplight. Her body was a curved mound under the sheet. Her upthrust shoulder was bare. The fine, downy hair on her arms was golden.

'Did you like it?' she asked.

Roger smiled. 'Did I like what?'

'Remember?'

At the touch of her fingers, he squirmed and sighed. 'It's coming back to me,' he said.

'Was I good?' Tina asked.

'Ah, yes. As good as good can be.'

'Be serious.'

'Serious?'

She took away her caressing hand. She snuggled against Roger and pushed her forehead against his chest. 'Be very serious,' she said. She sounded as if she might start crying. Roger held her gently. 'Was I good really?' she asked again.

'You were fine.'

'Only fine?'

'You were fantastic. You *are* fantastic.'

'Really? Don't kid me. Tell me really.'

'Fantastic. Absolutely.'

'How many women have you been with?' she asked, her breath tickling his chest.

'I don't know.'

'Tell me,' she said. Her fingernails lightly scratched his hip.

'Oh, six or seven. Seven, I guess. You're number seven.'

'Now, tell me the truth.' Her fingernails stopped moving. Her hand flattened, warm on his skin. 'How was I? Compared to the others.'

'The best.'

'The very best?'

'Far and away the best. Easily. No comparison.'

'Cross your heart?' Her lips brushed the skin of his chest.

'Cross my heart and hope to die.'

Roger felt her hand move down from his hip. He moaned as her fingers curled around his penis.

'You sure I'm the best?' she asked.

'No doubt about it.'

For a long time, she said nothing. Her fingers continued to hold him. He grew harder and bigger. After a while, she said, 'There's nothing wrong with me?'

'Of course not.'

'Then why?' Her hand went away.

'Why what?'

She didn't answer. She rolled face down and pressed the pillow over her head.

Hearing her muffled sobs, Roger put a hand on her back.

26

Marty didn't know, until she woke up, that she had passed out after the shooting.

Even before opening her eyes, she knew that she was not in Willy's car. This car's engine was quiet. Its air was cool. Too cool. She put a hand on her thigh and felt goosebumps. She moved her feet. The shorts were down around her ankles.

Opening her eyes, she saw the jersey wadded on the seat between her and Willy. She reached for it. Willy's hand came down on hers. He grinned at her. She jerked her hand away, taking the jersey. As fast as she could, she put it on and pulled up the shorts.

Willy laughed.

Marty said nothing. She sat motionless, arms folded across her chest, and wondered if Willy had raped her while she'd been passed out.

No, she didn't think so.

'Real class, huh?' he asked.

'What?'

'The car. Real class. Air-conditioning, the works.'

'How long was I out?'

'Who knows? I didn't time you. Did you see the way I capped those motherfuckers?'

'I saw enough.'

'What a kick.'

She closed her eyes and rubbed her face with both hands.

'Too bad you weren't awake when I moved your Danny boy.'

'Convenient,' she muttered into her hands.

'Huh?'

'I just happened to be unconscious when you changed cars.'

He laughed. 'Not my fault you faint at the sight of a little blood. What, you worried I didn't put Danny boy in our trunk?'

'I don't think he was ever in *any* trunk.'

'Think whatever you want. He's in the trunk.'

'Then stop and show me.'

'Get fucked.'

'You killed him, didn't you?'

'If you say so. See if those bozos got any maps in the glove compartment, huh? I'll show you where we're going.'

'I don't care.'

'Sure you do.' He punched her in the arm. 'Open it.'

She opened the glove compartment.

'What's in there?'

'Some maps, gas receipts, Kleenex.'

And a fifth of Kentucky bourbon that she decided not to mention.

'What about a Wisconsin map?'

She pulled out the stack of maps, found the Wisconsin map and put the others away.

'Open it up.'

She spread the map open.

'Okay. See a town called Marshall up to the left?'

'I can't see anything.'

Willy turned on the ceiling light. It cast a dim yellow glow onto the map.

'Look near the top. A couple of inches from the top. Marshall.'

'I don't see any Marshall. There's a Gribsby here.'

'Down the road from Gribsby.'

'Mawkeetaw?'

'Down a bit more. Marshall. See it?'

'Yeah.'

'Okay. Now, there's a lake over a bit to the right.'

'Cricket?'

'That's her. See a little blue dot beside Cricket?'

'No.'

'A little tiny dot. A speck.'

'I don't see anything there.'

'Well, some maps show it, some don't. Anyhow, that's where we're heading. For the speck.' He turned off the overhead light. 'A real nice little lake. More like a pond. And you know the nice thing about it? Nobody ever goes there. Not a single mother-fucking soul.'

'Why not?' Marty tongued her chipped tooth.

'Fishing stinks. You can't ski 'cause there ain't enough room. And it's harder than hell to find. There's only one way in. You gotta take this shitty little dirt road that's so fucked up you can hardly drive on it. Won't be easy to find at night.'

'Am I supposed to be your navigator?'

'Yep. But we still got a ways to go. You can put it away for a while.'

She folded the map, but did it wrong.

'Nobody ever teach you how to fold a map?' Willy asked.

'My education has been sadly neglected.'

He laughed. 'Bet you learned a thing or two tonight.'

She dropped the map to the floor, and turned her face to the window. In her mind, she saw the shirtless man get knocked off his feet, a hole between his nipples.

'Yeah,' she muttered. 'I learned a thing or two.'

Suddenly, her stomach twisted.

He's a murderer.

It changed things.

Before, she had been a victim for Willy to kidnap and rape and brutalize any way he wanted. Bad enough.

Plenty bad enough.

But now, she was a witness to two murders.

He has to kill me.

I've gotta get out of here!

What about Dan? If he's alive in the trunk . . .

I have to save him.

She took a deep, shaking breath, and said, 'Thirsty?'

'Huh?'

She opened the glove compartment and took out the heavy glass bottle of bourbon.

'Holy shit! Good deal!'

Marty unscrewed the plastic cap, tilted the bottle to her mouth and took two quick swallows.

'Save some for the fishies!'

She handed the bottle to Willy.

He drank. Then he said, 'Good stuff.'

'Sure is,' Marty agreed. She smiled at him. The bourbon seemed to be burning out the bottom of her stomach.

Willy offered the bottle.

'Thanks,' she said, taking it.

'Just don't make a pig outa yourself.'

She tilted the bottle up.

The bourbon splashed against her tight lips. None got into her mouth. She lowered the bottle, wiped her lips dry, and handed it back to Willy.

'Why don't we listen to some music?' she suggested, and reached for the radio.

The bottle knocked her hand away. 'I don't like music.'

'It'd be nice and relaxing.'

'We can relax at the cabin,' he said, and took a swallow. 'Just a couple more hours.'

'Can't we listen to music?'

'Music sucks.'

'Then is it okay if I take a nap?'

'Sure thing. Wanta take off your clothes again?'

'No.'

He laughed.

Marty made a show of stretching and yawning. Then she leaned against the passenger door and lifted her legs onto the seat. She wiggled as if trying to find a more comfortable position, and let her bare feet slip out from under her. They touched Willy's hip.

''Nother drink?' he asked.

'Sure.' She stretched out her arm, pressing her feet harder against him. She pretended to take a swig.

'Have more.'

She pretended to swig again. Then she handed the bottle back to Willy, and sighed loudly.

'Lucky for you my hands are full,' Willy told her.

Grinning, he took a drink.

Marty curled her toes against the side of his leg. She bent toward him. He gave her the bottle. While she lifted it to her mouth, Willy's free hand caressed her legs. She lowered her feet to the floor and scooted a little closer to him. His hand moved up her thigh, but she set down the bottle in its way. Laughing, he took hold of the bottle and picked it up. 'What'll you do when it's empty?' he asked.

'I just don't know,' she said.

'You'll get fucked, that's what.'

'Oh, yeah?' She started to move away from him.

He planted the bottle between his legs and threw an arm across her shoulders, stopping her. She relaxed against him. He lifted his arm off her, retrieved the bottle and drank several large swallows.

He clamped the bottle between his thighs again, and returned his arm to her shoulders.

'Let me.' She reached over and plucked out the bottle. When she raised it to her mouth, Willy's arm pushed downward between her back and the seat. She leaned forward, sipping. His hand went under her jersey.

Marty didn't resist.

She drank, instead.

His hand moved slowly up her side. It was warm and dry. The fingers were long. They caressed her skin as they roamed higher.

Marty took a big swallow of bourbon when the hand found her breast.

It tickled, it massaged, it squeezed.

Lowering the bottle, Marty clutched his hand and pressed it harder against her breast. She moaned. Clamping the bottle between her legs to free her other hand, she grabbed Willy's thigh.

'Go for it, honey,' he said.

Marty squeezed his thigh until it must've hurt. Groaning, Willy dug his teeth into her shoulder. The car swerved. His groaning changed to a gasp of alarm. The hand under Marty's jersey went still as he focused on steering.

When the car straightened out, he laughed and yelled, 'Yeah!' and gave her breast a tweak.

Marty flinched and grabbed his wrist. 'Quit it, now,' she said.

'Yeah?'

'Yeah. I've been through a hell of a lot with you, Willy. I'll probably go through lots more. But not, if I can help it, a windshield.'

'Maybe I'd better pull over, huh?'

'Maybe so,' Marty said.

But he didn't.

27

Roger stroked the length of Tina's back, and kissed her shoulder. Still she continued to cry. He started to ask her what was wrong, but stopped himself. He was tired of asking, and tired of being answered with speechless sobs.

'I wish you'd stop that,' he finally said. 'I hate it when a woman cries. Is it something *I* did?'

A muffled 'No' came from under the pillow.

'Something I *didn't* do or say?'

'It isn't you.'

'Well, that's nice to know. I wish you'd told me that half an hour ago.' He pulled the pillow off her head. She looked up at him. Hair hung in her eyes. She pushed the hair away, and her eyes were red.

'What is it?' Roger asked. 'I mean, you don't have to tell me, but maybe I can help. You never know. I'll help you if I can.'

'Thanks,' Tina said.

'Do you want to talk about it?'

'I don't know.'

'You might feel better if you talk about it. That's what they always say, anyway. I don't know how true it is.'

She sniffed and said nothing.

'Is it a guy?'

She nodded.

'What did he do? Did he hurt you?'

She rolled onto her back and looked at the ceiling. 'I found him with . . . making love with somebody. Right in the store. Right behind the counter. He was going to marry me.' A tear trickled from the corner of her eye, down her temple and into her ear. With a fingertip, she rubbed it out of her ear. She wiped her eyes.

'Who was the girl?'

'I don't know. Someone from Camp Wahtooki. It's a summer camp down the road from town. A *girl's* camp. She was maybe a counselor, or something. She had one of those camp station wagons, so I guess she must be a counselor. The bitch.'

'Do you think the guy is serious about her?'

'It looked serious to me. Brad was screwing her.'

'I mean, have they been seeing each other?'

'I don't know. How should I know? He's with me nearly all the time when he's not working. Maybe she visits him at the bait shop every day. I don't know, I just walked in on him. It was like one of those dumb things that happens on TV. But, hell, you know, I drop in on him all the time and . . . I've never caught him doing *that* before.'

'Did you talk to him about it?'

'Are you kidding?'

'No. Maybe it was completely innocent.'

'How could it be innocent? He was *humping* the bitch.'

'What I mean is, maybe it didn't mean anything.'

'It means plenty when you get down on the floor and stick your weenie in a woman. Doesn't it?'

'Usually,' Roger admitted. 'But the thing is, any normal guy is going to do it to a good-looking gal if the opportunity presents itself. Especially if he's not married. Even if he is, maybe, depending on the guy.'

'God, that's nice.'

'It can be nothing more than a physical thing. There doesn't always have to be a big emotional involvement.'

'*We were going to get married!*'

'So?' Roger said.

She glared at him.

'I'm not claiming it's right. I'm only saying it sometimes will happen, and maybe the guy really does love you and just got . . . involved, carried away. It happens. It almost happened to me. Several times.'

'Almost?'

'I guess the Boy Scout in me won out against the lech. I was married then. Somehow, I always managed to resist the temptations. It wasn't easy. Some of those gals . . . Now I sometimes wish I'd gone ahead. Faithful, boring Roger should've put it to every babe in sight. If I'd known what my dear wife was up to, I would've had myself a field day.'

'She was playing around?'

Roger couldn't answer. He lay on his back and rubbed his face. It made him feel weary and sick to remember. Finally, he said, 'I wanted to kill her when I found out.'

'I wanted to kill myself,' Tina said.

'Instead, we both ran away.'

'Yep.'

'That's because we have high moral character.'

'Is that why?' Tina asked, and smiled.

'But of course. What'd you say the guy's name is? The guy that cheated on you?'

'Brad.'

'Tell you what, why don't you give him a call?'

'I can't do that.'

'Sure you can. I told you that I'd help, didn't I? Well, this is my help. Advice based on years of wisdom. Phone Brad. Give him a chance. Give yourself a chance. Just call and see what happens.'

'I don't know.'

'Go ahead. The phone's right there beside you.'

'I can't just *call* him.'

'Sure you can.'

She shook her head.

'Go on. You want to. I know you want to.'

'I guess so, but . . .'

'Then do it.'

'Well . . .'

'I'll go into the bathroom if you don't want me to listen.'

'No, stay.' She rolled onto her side, facing away from Roger. He put his hand on her bare shoulder.

She swung her feet off the bed and sat up. Leaning forward, she reached to the telephone and lifted its handset.

'Do you know his number?' Roger asked.

She nodded.

'Probably press nine for an outside line, then do the area code and number. That's how these things usually work.'

'Should I reverse the charges?'

'This is on me.' He put his hand on her shoulder again. He could feel her trembling. 'Just go ahead,' he told her.

She tapped in the numbers, and waited.

They both waited.

Then she said, 'Hi, it's me.' Silence. Then, 'I don't know, somewhere down south. Near a place called Wayside, I think . . . I managed . . . Yes, I thumbed . . . I know how dangerous it is. So what? A lot you care . . . You know what I mean. I saw you with her. Behind the counter . . . Yes, that.'

There was a long silence. As she listened to the phone, Tina began to cry softly. Roger kissed the back of her shoulder.

'I don't know,' she said into the phone. 'It hurt, Brad. It really hurt . . . I love you, too . . . Sure, I do . . . You don't have to do that. Just go to bed and I'll see you in the morning . . . The same way I got here . . . No, don't. I'm starting back now, so if you drive down we'll probably miss each other . . . Yes, I'll be careful. Could you give my parents a call and tell them I'm okay? . . . I love you, too.'

She hung up. Then she eased down onto her back, reached up and curled a hand behind Roger's neck. She drew his head down and kissed him on the mouth. 'Thank you,' she said.

'My pleasure.'

Then she got off the bed and picked up her paisley dress.

'What are you doing?' Roger asked.

'I'm going back to Brad.'

'Now?'

'Yup.'

'Why wouldn't you let him pick you up?'

She pulled the shiny dress over her head, saying, 'I can't let him see me like this.'

'Like what?'

'I'm a mess. My dress is torn.'

'How do you plan to get home?'

'Hitch a ride.'

'At this hour?'

'I'll manage.' She buttoned the front of her dress.

'It's too dangerous. Let me drive you.'

'Nah. I'll be fine. It'd be all out of your way, and . . .'

'I don't mind.'

'Thanks, but . . . nah. I'm going back to my *guy*, you know? Wouldn't be right, you taking me. Not after what we did.'

'But it's the middle of the night.'

'I can take care of myself.'

'Why don't you at least stay here till morning? Maybe we can find somebody in the coffee shop. Somebody nice and reliable to give you a lift home. Preferably of the female persuasion.'

'I can't wait that long.' Done with the dress, she stepped over to Roger. 'Thanks so much for everything. You've been great, really great.' She bent over and kissed him.

He didn't let himself enjoy the soft touch of her lips or the warmth of her body. In minutes, she would be gone. He would probably never see her again. It was better, now, to let himself get no closer to her. 'I hope everything works out,' he said.

'Thanks.'

'You really ought to wait for morning.'

'I know, but I can't.'

'It won't be safe out there. Everybody in the world isn't . . . there are lots of nuts out there.'

'Fiends, too,' Tina said. She smiled gently and pushed her fingers through his hair. 'I'll always remember you, Roger.'

'I'll remember you, too. Sure will.'

'You go to sleep, now.'

After watching her leave, he rolled to her side of the bed, reached up and turned off the lamp. Then he lay back. He stared for a long time into the darkness, wondering about what he'd just lost.

28

Willy took a long pull at the bourbon and gave the bottle to Marty.

She pretended to drink while Willy drew his fingernails up the inner side of her thigh. The nails made her squirm with a sickish, hurting tingle. Then his hand pressed between her legs and rubbed her through the soft cloth of the shorts.

The headlights caught a road sign. Willy's hand stopped moving and he read aloud, 'Wayside. Pop, a thousand 'n' twenty-two. Issa biggy.'

There were a few homes scattered along the roadsides, most of them dark at the windows as if abandoned to the night. At the edge of town, the Dairy Queen was open and crowded.

'Lookit all the babes!' Willy slowed down and stared out at them. 'Nice. Really really nice. Hey, lookit the titties on that one!'

'Want her instead of me?' Marty asked, trying to sound annoyed. 'You can take *her* to your cabin.'

'Shit, I'd take ya both. Wouldn' mind that. Wouldn' mind at all. Not a bit. Little variety . . . I'd screw ya one adda time, 'n' both at once. Wouldn' mind that.'

But he kept on driving. Past a closed gas station, into the town's business district. All the stores were closed. Some kept their signs turned on, but most didn't. Every store had a light inside casting a dim, lonely glow onto the deserted sidewalks in front. The marquee of the movie theater near the end of town was dark. Its ticket booth was empty. Through the glass doors of the lobby, Marty could see a man in a purple coat talking with a uniformed girl at the snack counter.

'How come you didn't stop for that queen of tits at the Dairy Queen?' Marty finally asked. 'Thought you wanted . . .'

'You'd of tried to get away.'

'No, I wouldn't. Not anymore. I've been . . . remembering.

How it was the last time.' She rubbed his hand against her groin. 'How good it felt.'

'You were screaming.'

'Just 'cause I was scared. But I loved how you felt. Inside me. I *want* you inside me. Just like before.'

'Liked it, huh?'

'It was the best ever. If we weren't in this damn town, I'd make you pull off the road right now and fuck me.'

'We'll be outa here in a minute.'

'Hurry.' She stood the bottle on his leg. Willy took his hand away from her and lifted the bottle to his mouth. As he drank, Marty squeezed the front of his jeans. His penis was hard. She felt it move under her hand.

The tires bumped over railroad tracks at the end of town.

Pretty soon, Marty thought. Can't let the town get too far behind.

There were houses on both sides of the road. Then an open gas station, a cafe called Bab's Burgers, a motel with its big sign flashing 'Wayside Motor Inn'.

'A motel!' Marty blurted. 'Why don't we go in and get a room?' She gave him another gentle squeeze. 'Think how nice it would be. We'd have a bed.'

They had already left the motel behind, but Marty didn't give up.

'Come on, Willy. It'd be great. You oughta turn around. We'd have a big old bed. And a shower. We could take a shower together. Have you ever done it in the shower? We'd both be all slippery . . .'

'Shit!' Willy blurted. 'Lookit *her*!'

Marty saw her, and groaned.

It was a girl, probably no older than sixteen, slim and blonde and walking backward along the roadside, her arm out, her hand closed, her thumb pointing behind her. She wore a paisley dress skimpy enough to guarantee rides from men.

Willy's foot lifted off the gas pedal.

'Don't stop,' Marty whispered.

The girl took a wide stance, her dress drawing taut across her crotch.

'Shit!' Willy said.

Now the girl was behind them, and Willy's foot was lowering onto the brake pedal.

'Don't stop, honey. You have me.' Marty capped the bourbon bottle and set it on the floor. 'You don't need anyone but me.'

'Need her.'

The car stopped. Marty looked over her shoulder. The girl, bathed in the eerie redness of the rear lights, was starting to jog forward.

So young . . .

Too damn young! Just a kid.

'Drive,' Marty said.

She jerked open Willy's belt, unbuttoned his jeans and pulled the zipper down. He had no underwear on. His penis was a thick, pale column tilting upward, its tip almost touching the steering wheel.

Marty heard footfalls in the gravel. In the side mirror, she saw the girl hurrying toward them.

Closer and closer . . .

Only a few strides away . . .

'Drive!' Marty said and dropped down toward Willy's lap and took him into her mouth and sucked.

Willy stepped on the gas.

'Hey!' the girl yelled.

Willy sped away from her.

Marty slid her mouth, licking and sucking.

'Uhhh, yeah,' Willy gasped. 'Yeah. Oh, babe! Suck me off. Do it, do it! C'mon!'

She had saved the girl.

He might go back to her if I stop.

She kept on.

Gotta get him into the woods. Away from the car and Dan.

If Dan's even still in the trunk.

If Dan's even alive.

If she finished Willy with her mouth, he might not bother taking her into the woods. He might take her straight to the cabin.

Don't wanta go there.

She tried to take her mouth away, but Willy gripped the back of her head and held her down.

Pushed her down, ramming deep.

She gagged and struggled to pull away but Willy only forced her head down harder.

Bite him!

He'd kill me for sure.

But she was choking. It was blocking her throat. She tried to breathe through her nose, but couldn't.

Her hand reached up and found the steering wheel.

She grabbed the wheel and tugged.

Willy's hand leaped away from the back of her head.

Marty, still clutching the wheel, resisting Willy's efforts to turn it, shoved herself up until her mouth was empty.

She was still choking when the car swerved to the side of the road and skidded to a stop.

29

'Coulda got us killed,' Willy said. 'That's twice . . .'

'I'm sorry, sweetheart, but I couldn't breathe. I didn't mean to grab the wheel.' She leaned against him, kissed him, and lowered her hand onto his lap. She lightly wrapped her fingers around him. He was as big as before, wet and slick from her mouth. 'Let's go in the woods now,' she whispered.

'Sure. Why the hell not. Where's the bottle?'

Marty found it under the seat, and sat up with it. Shaking it, she heard sloshing sounds; some bourbon still remained in it.

Willy finished fastening his jeans. Then he shoved the car keys into his right front pocket. He climbed out, the revolver in his hand, and pushed its barrel down the front of his waistband. 'Bring the bottle with ya,' he said.

Marty opened her door. The night air rushed in. It was cooler than before, but felt balmy after the chill of the air-conditioner. She climbed out and shut the door.

Willy came over to her side of the car. 'Let's go this way,' he said. He draped an arm over her shoulders and she led him down a grassy embankment. At the bottom, the ground was springy and wet. Water pressed up between Marty's toes. But the ground was dry on the slope. She climbed higher. Just beyond the top of the ditch, the trees began.

'Don' wanna go far,' Willy said, pulling back at the edge of the forest.

Marty kissed him on the mouth. 'We wanta get away from the road, don't we? 'Case somebody comes by?'

He answered by squeezing her breast. Then he said, 'Gimme the bottle, honey.'

She handed it to him, then led him forward. They walked past tree trunks, clumps of bushes, more trees, deeper and deeper into the woods, farther from the car. Farther from Dan in the trunk.

If he's in the trunk.

Finally, they came to a small, moonlit clearing. 'How about here?' Marty asked.

Willy swung her around. She hugged him. One of his hands slipped under the back of her jersey and roamed her bare skin. The other, holding the bottle outside her jersey, pressed her tightly against him.

The revolver dug into her belly.

Get my hands on it . . .

She lowered a hand, squeezed Willy's thigh, raised her hand to the hard bulge, squeezed and fondled him there as his mouth pressed her lips roughly and his tongue pushed between her teeth. Sneaking her hand sideways, she felt the steel barrel through his jeans.

'Wrong gun,' he gasped into her mouth.

She pulled his zipper down and reached into the open fly.

His hand was no longer under her jersey. It bumped against her hand, and she wondered for a moment what he was up to.

As she slipped him out through his fly, he unfastened the front of her shorts.

That's what.

She raised her hand to his belt buckle.

Her knuckles brushed the wooden grip of the revolver.

Now! Do it now! Grab it!

But her hand wouldn't move. It stayed at the belt buckle, trembling.

Willy started tugging at her shorts. They were tight. He jerked and dragged at them until he got them down around her knees. They were loose there. When he let go of them, they dropped to her ankles.

He pushed his hand between her thighs.

Grab his gun!

A finger slipped into her.

With a gasp, she staggered backward. The shorts caught her ankles. Caught and held and tripped her.

Willy held on.

Held on and went down with her as she fell and smashed her hard against the ground.

The pistol butt rammed into her belly.

The bottle under her back broke.

From the clink it made before bursting, Marty guessed it had struck a rock.

The back of her jersey was suddenly soaked with bourbon. And maybe blood. She felt glass in her skin.

'The bottle broke,' she said.

'Yeah?' Willy pulled his arm out from under her.

'I'm cut,' Marty said. 'It's under my back. It's in pieces. It's cutting me. You've gotta get off.'

'Yeah?'

'Please.' There were pieces buried in her skin. She felt numb in places. Other places were starting to sting, and streams of blood were tickling along the arch of her back. 'Just get off me for a second . . .'

Willy pushed himself up and sat across her hips.

She started to raise her back off the ground, but he clutched her throat and held her down.

'Please, Willy.'

Grinning, he shook his head. Either he was too drunk to understand or care about the glass under Marty, or he liked the idea of grinding her into it.

Pleading, she thought, might only make it worse.

Willy pulled the revolver out of his jeans, tossed it on the wet grass about six feet away, and unbuckled his belt.

'Honey,' Marty said, trying to stay calm. 'Let go of my throat, okay?' She crossed her arms over her belly and started to pull up the jersey. 'I can't get it off without sitting up.'

He leaned back, taking his hand from her neck, and finished opening his jeans. Then he took off his shirt and threw it aside.

As Marty slowly raised her back off the ground, she pulled the jersey up. It was sticky with blood. Shards of glass pulled loose from her back, dropped and tinked against others. When the jersey was off, she flung it away. Sitting upright, she wrapped her arms around Willy and hugged him tightly . . .

And twisted to the left so they tumbled sideways, rolling.

She came down on her side. Though she felt no broken glass, she knew it couldn't be more than a few inches away. So she

97

wrestled Willy onto his back. Stretched out on top of him, she pushed her open mouth against his.

Reaching out with one arm, she patted the dewy grass. Stretched her fingers.

Then had to look.

The revolver lay three or four inches beyond her finger-tips.

Willy squirmed beneath her, trying to force her legs apart.

They suddenly rolled onto their sides. Farther from the gun.

Marty swung a leg over him and forced him onto his back again.

Straddling him, she reached out for the revolver.

He clutched her buttocks and thrust.

Marty grabbed the gun by its barrel.

Willy's penis rammed deep into her, throbbing and squirting.

She swung the pistol and clubbed the side of his head.

Willy yelped. His body jerked rigid, and he suddenly went limp.

Except for the part that was buried in Marty.

Still rigid, it kept jumping and spurting for a few seconds after the rest of Willy seemed to be unconscious.

As fast as she could, Marty climbed off.

On her feet, she took a couple of steps backward, then stopped and reversed the revolver and took aim at Willy.

He wasn't hard any more.

He lay motionless on the ground.

Marty felt blood running down her back, her buttocks, and the backs of her legs. She felt semen dribble out of her and trickle down her left thigh.

Soon, Willy moaned and pressed a hand against his ear. He squirmed a little.

When he opened his eyes, Marty thumbed back the hammer and aimed at his face.

'Don't,' he said. The word came out like a groan of pain and fear. 'Please, don't shoot me.'

'Dirty rotten bastard,' she said.

'Please.'

'Don't move.' Keeping the gun leveled at him, she crouched and picked up his shirt. She wiped herself with it and flung it at him. He cringed as if he expected the shirt to burn him. When it fell onto his legs, he flinched.

'Don't move,' Marty repeated.

Trying to keep the revolver aimed at Willy as much as possible, she put on her shorts. Then she picked up her torn, bloody jersey. She put the gun through its right sleeve and used her left hand to pull the jersey up her arm and over her head. For a few moments, she was blind. But when she could see again, Willy was still on his back.

She changed the gun to her left hand, worked it under the jersey and out through the left sleeve.

'Okay,' she said, the jersey still rucked up above her breasts. 'Pull your pants up.'

As he drew the jeans up his legs, Marty tugged her jersey down. It felt heavy and wet and sticky against her back. It hurt her cuts, but she was glad to be dressed.

She waited for Willy to finish with his jeans. Then she told him to put on his shirt.

When he had it on, she said, 'Stand up.'

'Where we going?' he asked.

'Back to the car. Let's go.'

Trying to get to his feet, he staggered and fell down. But he tried again. This time, he made it.

'Walk ahead of me,' Marty told him.

He turned his back to her and started walking. He walked awkwardly, sometimes stumbling.

Marty followed him, staying a few paces back and out of reach. Soon after they entered the thick trees, she uncocked the gun to prevent it from going off by accident.

It seemed to take a very short time to reach the edge of the woods.

Marty followed Willy down the grassy slope to where the ground was soggy, and up the embankment to the road. Willy stopped beside the car and turned around to face her.

'Open the trunk,' she ordered.

'Okay,' said Willy. But he didn't move.

'Now.'

'Whatcha gonna do if I don't?'

'Shoot you and open it myself.'

'You ain't gonna shoot me.'

'Just open the trunk and . . .'

He lurched toward Marty, reaching for the gun.

She pulled the trigger.

Nothing happened.

Willy grabbed the barrel. As he jerked the gun away from her, he punched her in the face.

Marty dropped to her knees.

'It's single action,' he said. 'You dumb fuck. Gotta *cock* it.'

His fist came in, smashing her face again. And again. And again. She slumped backward.

Willy said something, but she couldn't hear him through the ringing in her ears. She tried to get up. Her legs were bent behind her and her arms wouldn't work right.

Willy walked toward the rear of his car.

Marty struggled to her knees. Her head drooped. It felt as heavy as lead. The side of her face was burning from the punches. She wanted to let her arms fold, to stretch out on the ground and lie there, on and on.

Instead, groaning with pain, she raised her head. She saw Willy open the trunk of the car. She wanted to ask him what he was doing, but she didn't have the strength. Then she saw him raise the revolver, cock it, and aim into the trunk.

'NO!' she screamed.

The gun blasted, leaping in his hand.

Marty struggled to her feet and staggered to the back of the car. Before Willy could grab her, she glimpsed Dan's face in the darkness of the trunk.

The top of his head was partly gone.

'NO!'

She kicked and squirmed in Willy's arms, but couldn't get loose until her teeth found his ear and she bit it hard. His yell of pain stunned her for a second. Then she realized that he had let go of her.

She dashed to the edge of the embankment and jumped as far as she could. She made it almost to the bottom before her heels hit the wet grass. Her legs flew forward and her rump hit the slope. She slid the rest of the way down, then scrambled to her feet and ran, splashing through the soggy grass.

'Stop!' Willy shouted.

Her legs chugged, carrying her up the rise on the other side of the ditch.

From behind her came the sound of a metallic *clank*.

The gun hammer dropping.

But there must've been no live round in the chamber, because there was only the *clank* and no blast.

She reached the top of the slope.

Broke into a sprint for the woods.

A root snagged her foot.

As she lurched forward, falling headlong, a gunshot split the night.

30

Willy grinned when he saw the girl walking backward alongside the road ahead, her thumb out. The same girl he'd tried to stop for, back near that town.

She must've passed his car while he'd been out in the woods with Marty.

She'd gone a pretty good distance, too.

A mighty quick walker.

He stopped his car beside her. 'Want a lift?' he called out the passenger window.

'Man, oh man, *do* I!'

The light inside the car came on when she opened the door, and Willy got a good look at her.

Nice. Real nice.

He always did like the young stuff, and the way this gal's dress was clinging to her skin . . . He watched it slide up her thighs when she climbed into the car.

'Where're you headed?' he asked.

'Gribsby.'

'I'm going as far as Marshall.'

'Oh, that's fine.' Her voice seemed awfully cheerful for so late at night. 'That's great. I'm sure I'll be able to find a ride from Marshall.'

'Probably.'

She sighed loudly with relief or pleasure.

She folded her arms below her breasts, slouched down in the seat, and smiled at him. 'This is great,' she said. 'It sure feels good to be heading home.'

31

Rolling over, Marty crossed an arm over her face to block the bright sunlight. Then she opened her eyes. When the air touched them, they felt raw and burning. She saw that she was stretched out along the edge of a forest.

For a while, she didn't remember. Then it all came back. She moaned as it poured into her like a foul liquid, burning and nauseating.

Suddenly, she sat up. She could see the road.

The road, but no car.

Willy was gone!

The quick movement did it. She twisted sideways and threw up. When the convulsions stopped, she crawled away from the mess.

She heard a car coming. Afraid Willy might be returning, she flattened herself on the ground. After it was gone, she got slowly to her feet. She leaned against the trunk of a birch tree and felt blood begin to trickle down her back.

The forest seemed safer than the road, so she walked into it. Walking hurt badly. Her head was the worst part. It jolted with each step and throbbed madly every time she bent to pass beneath a low limb.

At last, she came to a sunny clearing. Maybe the same clearing as last night. She couldn't be sure. It didn't matter, though. The clearing was bright and well hidden. She only cared about that.

Lying face down on the tall grass, she found it softer than she hoped. It didn't even feel scratchy on her bare arms and legs. It simply matted down under her, soft and dry, as if it had been put there especially to serve as her bed.

She lay with her eyes shut, half awake, half dreaming, and at first she thought that the quietly approaching footsteps were part of her dream. Then she opened her eyes and saw a pair of moccasins.

32

Willy stretched and groaned with lazy pleasure. The sun felt so hot and good. If it weren't for his bastard of a headache, life would be perfect.

The bitch had really given him a wallop with that gun.

He grinned. He'd really given her a wallop, too. With a different kind of gun.

He opened his eyes, lifted his head and looked down his sweaty body at it. Wouldn't do at all if it got sunburned. Especially not now, with so much good stuff ahead.

Speaking of which . . .

He got off the blanket and walked to his shack. 'Here I am, sweetums. William the Conqueror.' He posed in the doorway flexing his muscles.

The girl in the shadows shut her eyes. She lay curled on her side on the mattress, naked, her arms handcuffed behind her back.

Reaching high, Willy plucked a key down from the top of the doorframe. 'Have you been a good girl?' he asked, walking toward her.

'Yes,' she muttered.

'Do you want William to let you go?'

Her eyes opened and she nodded.

Willy leaned over her with the key, opened the left cuff, then the right. His fingers came away bloody. He wiped them on the white skin of the girl's buttocks.

'Now put on your beautiful dress,' he told her.

She sat up and brought her arms slowly in front of her. She frowned at her raw, bloody wrists.

'Oh, did I have the cuffs too tight?' Willy asked.

'Where are we going?' the girl asked.

'It's a surprise.'

She tried to pick up her shining, paisley dress, but her hands wouldn't work. The dress fell. Willy picked it up. She raised her arms, and he put it over them. It drifted down her body.

Willy helped her to stand. Then he fastened every button on the dress.

'Let's go outside,' he said.

As she stepped out the doorway, she raised an arm to shade her face from the noon sun.

'Bright, huh?'

She said nothing.

Willy picked up his handcuffs and rope, then followed her outside. 'Go over to that dead tree,' he told her.

She looked around at him. She glanced at the rope and cuffs in his hand. Then she looked toward the woods that began several yards to the left of the white, barkless poplar.

'Don't try to run,' he said. 'I'll just chase you down, and then I'll *really* have some fun with you.'

She walked to the dead tree.

'That's right. Good girl. Now put out your hands. That's a good girl.'

Her eyes stayed on his eyes, making him a little nervous as he handcuffed her wrists. He knotted the rope to the chain between the bracelets, then flung the coil over a high, thick branch of the poplar. It dropped on the other side. He took the end and began to pull, raising the girl's arms.

'I haven't given you any trouble,' she said quietly. 'I've done everything you asked, no matter how . . . no matter what it was. Why do you have to hurt me?'

''Cause I like it.' He tied the rope to the trunk of the dead tree. 'See how nice I am? I'm leaving you on your feet. Or would you rather sort of *dangle*?'

She shook her head.

'Now guess what I'm going to do,' he said.

Staring into his eyes, she said, 'I don't know.'

'Come on, guess.' His hands roamed the shiny, slick cloth.

ly hot from the sun. He felt her body through it.

rl gritted her teeth.

nna rip the dress off you,' Willy said.

No, don't. Please. It was a present. Don't wreck it.'

He slapped her face.

Then, growling like a dog, sometimes biting the skin underneath, he slowly shredded the dress with his teeth. The girl cried as he ripped. When she finally was naked, he took her from behind with quick hard thrusts that rammed her up off her feet.

Later, he left her hanging in the sun.

He rested in a shaded place near the car and enjoyed the view.

33

When Marty opened her eyes, there was no longer a headache behind them. The curtains rustled with a mild breeze. Light slanted down through the window, laying a slab of gold on the floor. A clock by the bed showed 3:15.

Sitting up, she looked in front of her. A dresser, a closet. Heavy hiking boots stood on the closet floor next to a pair of sneakers. On hangers, she saw a plaid lumberjack coat among many shirts, a dark suit, a colorful sport coat and a white terry-cloth bathrobe.

She got up. The mirror above the dresser threw back her reflection, stunning her. She hardly looked like herself. Her face was swollen and discolored. Her hair was a wild tangle.

Well, her right profile didn't look too bad. Willy had only struck the left side of her face.

Why did he leave me?

She didn't want to think about it.

She opened the bedroom door. The living room was darker

and cooler than the bedroom. 'Jack?' she called softly. No answer came. 'Jack?' Nothing. She walked across the rug, then out the front door. He wasn't on the porch.

He was gone?

Back inside the cabin, she shut the door and locked it . Then she ran to the kitchen and locked the back door. She peaked inside a utility closet. She checked the bathroom. A closet in the living room. Behind all the furniture.

Not looking for Jack anymore.

Searching for Willy.

Shaking and chilled, she shut herself into the bedroom.

'You're a fine specimen,' she told the face in the mirror.

The normal side of her face smiled nervously; the swollen side hardly moved.

Turning around, she stared over her shoulder at the mirror's image of her back. The knit jersey was torn in a few places midway down. It was stiff and brown near the rips.

She took it off.

The large, square bandage – applied by Jack after carrying her to his cabin – was white except for a tiny dot of blood in its center. All around the bandage, her skin was stained. All the way down to her waist. The shorts had soaked up a lot of blood. She took them off.

Dropping the clothes in a heap, she stepped to the closet. She took down the robe. Its hanger fell, making a tinny *ping* when it hit the hardwood floor. She crouched to pick it up, being careful to keep her back straight so the cuts wouldn't pull.

It was then that she saw the dark, glossy stock. She pushed some clothes aside. Propped against a back corner of the closet stood a double-barreled shotgun. Sweeping hangers away, Marty pressed between two clean shirts. They felt cool and fresh on her skin. She hoped that the blood stains on her back were dry.

Her hand closed around the wide, side-by-side barrels. She lifted. The shotgun was heavy. With her arm outstretched, she could barely raise it off the floor. So she dragged it out of the closet.

The shotgun had two triggers. It also had a hammer at the back of each barrel. There was a lever between the hammers. She pressed it sideways with her thumb.

The barrels suddenly dropped, nearly wrenching the weapon from her grip. They hung toward the floor, connected to the stock by a hinge. In each chamber was a round, brass disk with a little nub in the center.

It's loaded.

Marty rested the barrels against the floor, then lifted the stock until the latch snapped. The shotgun was whole again. She returned it to the closet and straightened the hangers in front of it.

Then she put on the robe. It was far too big. She rolled up its sleeves and tied its cloth belt.

Jack was still gone when she went into the bathroom. She took a long shower. Then she dried herself carefully, surprised by the number of cuts and bruises she discovered.

She put on the robe and tied its belt snugly. There was a comb by the sink. She did the best she could with her hair, and opened the bathroom door.

Jack looked up from a magazine. 'How you doing?' he asked.

'A lot better than a few hours ago.'

'Glad to hear it.' He unrolled a leather pouch and started loading tobacco into his pipe.

'Sure is nice of you to help me.' She sat on a rocker across from him. 'Do you mind me borrowing your robe?'

'Not at all.'

'My things are a mess.'

'I noticed.' He struck a match and sucked its flame down to the surface of the tobacco. 'Did you sleep well?'

'Great.'

Jack tamped down the loose ash in his pipe and lit another match. As he drew the flame into the briar bowl, he looked at Marty and raised his eyebrows. He blew a cloud of smoke.

'Smells like a cake baking,' Marty said. 'A chocolate cake.'

Jack shrugged.

'Would it be all right if I use your telephone? I'd like to call my parents and let them know I'm okay.'

'Help yourself.'

'I'll call collect.'

'No need.'

The telephone was on a lamp table at the end of the sofa. Marty stood up and went over to it. She picked up the handset, then tapped in the numbers.

Sitting down on the sofa, she listened to the ringing.

Someone picked up. 'Hello?' asked her father. He sounded tense.

'Hi, Dad.'

'Marty! My God! Are you all right?'

'I'm okay.'

'What in the name of God . . .?'

'I was kidnapped.'

'*Kidnapped?*'

'I just got away a little while ago. I'm all right. You and Mom can stop worrying about me.'

'We've been basket cases.'

'It's all right now. I'm not sure when I'll be home, but . . .'

'Where are you? Where are you calling from?'

'A place in the woods. Anyway, I'm fine. I've got to get going, now.'

'Marty . . .'

'Give my love to Mom.'

'Marty, for . . .'

'Bye for now, Dad,' she said, and hung up.

'Short but sweet,' she said to Jack, and tried to smile. 'I just didn't want to get into it, you know?' She made a small laugh. 'Besides, it was long distance and you were paying.'

'You were actually kidnapped?' Jack asked, and puffed on his pipe.

'Yeah.'

'Guess we'd better make a call to the police.'

'Could it wait? I'm still . . . I don't know. I feel like I need some time, or . . .'

'The sooner you get to the police, the sooner they'll put your kidnappers out of commission.'

'Kidnapper. Only one.'

'Don't you think you should call the police?'

Marty looked into Jack's eyes. They were gentle, confident, comforting. He seemed like a man who *knew* things and could handle tough situations. She would be safe with him. 'How about tomorrow?' she asked.

'Fine with me.'

'Can I stay here till then?'

'You're welcome to stay as long as you want.'

'Really? As long as I want?'

'Sure.' He grinned and puffed his pipe. 'Long as you behave yourself.'

34

Willy took a red bandanna out of his jeans and wiped the sweat off his face. 'Hotter than boiled piss,' he said.

But the shack was just ahead. He would be there in a minute or so. About time! Two hours was too damn long to be tromping through the boonies, especially in this kind of heat.

He was glad he'd done it, though. Now he was sure they were alone. No sign of humanity anywhere nearby. He sure had found himself a great place for a hideout – or Dewey had.

I oughta drop Dewey a card, he thought. 'Hello from your old stomping grounds,' he said aloud.

The girl, apparently hearing him, lifted her head. She was still standing, arms high, under the tree. And still on her feet to keep her weight off the handcuffs.

'Hi, sweet stuff. Miss me?'

She squinted at him and said nothing.

'Looks like you got yourself a little sun,' Willy said, and laughed.

Where she'd had a tan before, her skin now had a deep, rosy glow. Where her skin had been white, she now appeared to be wearing a bright red bikini.

Willy dragged a fingernail down her breast.

She flinched and made a hissing sound between her teeth.

The scratch from his fingernail looked blue-white for a moment, then went red.

'Hurt?' Willy asked.

'Yes.'

'Tough titty.' He laughed.

35

'Are you hungry?' Jack asked. 'I picked up a couple of steaks in town this afternoon.'

'Great. I'm starved.'

'Okay. Why don't you go on and get dressed, and I'll start the barbecue?'

Marty felt her skin heat with embarrassment as she thought about the torn, filthy rags on the bedroom floor. 'Won't this do?' she asked, glancing down at the white robe.

'We don't know each other well enough,' he said.

Marty smiled. 'Oh. I see.'

'Go change,' he said.

She went into the bedroom. On the bed lay two green shopping bags. Inside them she found a white blouse, a pale blue skirt, panties and a bra, and a shoe box containing a pair of white sneakers.

All brand new, the tags still on them.

Blushing, she called out, 'Thank you, Jack! They're great!'

'You're welcome,' he called from somewhere beyond the shut door.

Marty took off the robe. She hung it in the closet, glimpsing the shotgun's stock before she turned away. Then she removed the bandage from her back and made a new one. After that, she removed the tags from the clothes. She started to get dressed.

The bra was slightly too large.

'Wishful thinking,' she muttered. Laughing quietly, she put it on anyway.

Everything else fit well. Looking at herself in the brand new clothes, she felt clean and fresh and very safe.

The night with Willy seemed far away.

Until she saw her face in the mirror.

That brought it all back. Her stomach twisted. She crouched on the floor, shivering, hugging her belly. Then, like an icy wind, it passed. She hurried outside.

The afternoon sun was hot and calming.

She found Jack behind the cabin, standing at a red brick barbecue.

'The clothes are wonderful,' she said.

'You look great.'

'If you're into battered, bruised and ugly.'

He laughed. 'I must admit, I would be interested in seeing what you look like when you haven't just been beaten to a pulp.'

'Consider it done. It's the least I can do for you.'

36

Willy came out of the shack. He was naked. He held his red bandanna in one hand, his leather belt in the other.

The girl raised her head and opened her eyes.

'This is gonna hurt, sweetie. But don't scream too loud, or I'll have to gag you. You wouldn't want that. My hanky's got boogers in it.'

Her dry lips stuck together when she tried to open her mouth. Then they peeled apart. She licked them, and asked in a raspy whisper, 'Why are you doing this to me?'

'Because I can?'

He began to swing his belt.

37

When Jack drove her into the town of Wayside that evening, it looked different from the night before. Golden in the lowering sun. Busy, yet peaceful. And crowded. A dozen people stood in line at the movie theater.

'Would you like to see a show?' Jack asked.

'Would you?'

'Sure.'

Jack parked the car, and they walked to the theater. Inside, they found seats near the front. The lights faded out. And the previews started.

Marty could hardly believe that she was safe and watching a movie.

Only two nights ago, she'd been in a theater with Dan.

She'd spotted Willy . . .

For the next couple of hours, she stared at the enormous screen but noticed little that was on it. She dwelled on the screen in her mind, the one that played a horrible film about Willy.

In that film, she relived it all.

Again and again.

Marty was pulled out of it when the lights came up. She found that she was squeezing Jack's hand.

On the way out of town, Jack asked if she would like some ice cream.

'Sure,' she said.

They stopped at the Wayside Motor Inn, and each had a hot fudge sundae at its all-night burger joint.

Then they were in the car again, rushing along the dark, twisting road.

'Gives me the creeps,' Marty said. She slid across the seat, close to Jack. He put an arm across her shoulders.

'You don't need to be afraid.'

'He's still out there,' she said.

'But he doesn't have you. Not anymore. And tomorrow we'll go to the police.'

'Will you come with me?'

'Of course.'

'What if Willy comes for me tonight?'

'He won't.'

'He might already be at your cabin waiting for us.'

Jack's hand went to the back of her neck. Gently and firmly, he rubbed her there. 'He won't get you. Not tonight. Not while I'm around.'

38

'You look good in stripes. Anyone ever tell you that?' Laughing, Willy scraped the bottom of his chili can. Then he licked the spoon. 'That was funny. Why aren't you laughing?'

The girl, sitting on the mattress with her legs crossed, said nothing. She gazed sullenly down at the can of chili in her hand.

'By the way, sweetie, what's your name?'

She scooped a spoonful of chili into her mouth.

A flashlight lay on the table beside the big, battery powered lantern that lit the center of the room. Willy picked it up, turned it on, and threw its beam in her face.

She shut her puffy eyelids.

'What's your name?' Willy repeated. And then he remembered a game he used to play when he was a kid. He put down the flashlight. He went to the bed and knelt on it, facing the girl. She smelled like sweat and sex. 'Now,' he said, 'what's your name?'

'Tina,' she said.

'You lie!' he blurted, and smacked her hard in the face with his open hand. The blow turned her head sideways. 'What's your name?' he asked again.

She looked at him. She pressed her lips tightly together. They were cracked and bleeding. She said, 'My name's Tina.'

'You lie!' he yelled, and smacked the other side of her face. 'What's your name?'

She glared at him. She said nothing.

'YOU LIE!' He swung. His hand clapped her cheek so hard his fingers tingled and blood flew off her lips.

39

'I'll be just outside the door if you need me,' Jack said from the bedroom doorway.

'I need you,' Marty said.

He grinned. 'Maybe some other time. Goodnight.' He shut the door as he left.

Marty turned off the bedroom light and stood in the darkness. She thought about going out to Jack. But she didn't want to seem pushy.

Some other time.

She took off her clothes and climbed beneath the sheet, wishing he was there beside her, holding her close and warm. His strong arms around her. Caressing her. Not doing anything funny, just being gentle and safe . . .

She woke up with a start.

Her heart was slamming. Her bangs were plastered to her forehead with sweat and the bed was soaked beneath her. She lay there motionless, wondering what had shocked her awake.

The room was pale with a creamy glow of moonlight. The door was still shut. Between the door and the dresser fell a shadow. The shadow was too small to conceal a person. But the open closet made a large darkness.

He's in there.

No, he's not. Don't be ridiculous.

He is!

The sweat seemed to freeze on Marty's skin. She pulled her top sheet up tightly under her chin.

The only sound she could hear was her own loud, thudding heart.

She glanced at the nightstand. There was no lamp on it.

Scissors.

After bandaging her back that morning, Jack had put them in

a drawer of the nightstand. She'd used them, herself, just before supper.

Now, where'd I put them?

On the dresser.

But the dresser stood beside the open closet.

I'll never make it. He'll jump me before . . .

Nobody's in the closet!

Willy is.

Marty inched her leg toward the side of the mattress. After a long time, her right heel dropped over the edge. She kept moving her leg sideways, slowly, slowly, until it was off the mattress all the way to her rump. Her foot on the floor, she started sliding her left leg over.

Eyes on the dark, open closet.

He's watching. If he starts coming, run for it.

At last, both her feet were on the floor.

She raised her back so gradually that the bedsprings hardly made a sound. They were nearly silent, too, when she leaned forward and eased her weight off the bed. She stood up straight, staring at the black closet.

Nothing seemed to move in there.

With six slow, careful steps, she reached the dresser. Her hand patted the top of it.

And found the scissors.

Picked them up. Clenched them tight.

With the tightness of a scream growing in her chest, she sidestepped to the closet. Raising the scissors high, she lurched into the darkness. She drove them down, hard and silent.

Pain seared her thigh.

She tried to stifle her yelp of hurt surprise.

Waving her other hand in the air, she caught the dangling string and pulled. The closet light came on.

Nobody there.

Nobody except Marty.

Marty, naked and sweaty and shaking. Marty, scissors in her hand. Marty with a ragged red gash ripped across the inner side of her right thigh.

She had a sudden urge to sit down on the closet floor and cry. Sit there and cry till dawn.

Instead, she bandaged her leg.

Then she got dressed, putting on the stiff, filthy shorts and jersey that Willy had stolen from the girl by the lake.

Then she took the shotgun out of the closet.

Sneaking through the dark house, she found Jack asleep on the living room sofa. She set down the shotgun. She found his trousers draped over a nearby chair.

His keys were in the right front pocket. His wallet was in the left rear pocket.

She took out a five-dollar bill and slipped the wallet back into his pocket. She kept the keys.

She was tempted to kiss him before leaving.

But she didn't dare.

He might wake up and not let her go.

40

Thrusting and shuddering, Willy erupted inside Tina. Then he relaxed on top of her.

Somewhere along the line, she had fainted.

Just as well. Willy hadn't liked the way she'd just taken it, never saying a word even when the pain made her twitch and weep.

He pulled out and sat back.

A breeze was blowing through the open door and window, giving him goosebumps. He got up and shut them both. The handcuffs lay open on the table. He picked them up. Then he turned off the lantern and made his way through the darkness.

He found the mattress, got to his knees, reached out and touched Tina. Her skin was hot. From its sticky ridges, he knew he was touching her back. He slid his hand down her rump and down the back of her leg to her ankle.

He cuffed her left ankle. After sitting beside her, he attached the other cuff to his own left ankle. The bracelet was almost too small, but he managed to get it on.

Then he unfolded a blanket and lay back, covering himself. He stared at the dark ceiling.

It had been a great day.

Even if the girl wasn't Marty.

At least Marty got what was coming to her.

He'd scared the shit out of her with the noose.

He'd killed her boyfriend. Twice. He grinned. Not every prick gets to die twice.

He'd fucked her. Got her in the mouth, too – almost.

And he'd shot her dead.

That old hollow-point sure made a mess of her back.

He grinned, remembering how she'd been sprawled out in the moonlight, the blood all over her back.

Too bad he'd had to kill her, though.

He'd wanted *Marty* here, not *Tina*.

*Not that there's anything wrong with Tin*a.

Except she ain't Marty.

He sighed. *Oh, the stuff I would've done to her . . .*

41

The attendant at the all-night gas station raised his red, chubby face out of a comic book when Marty stepped up to the window. She smiled at him and slipped a five-dollar bill into the trough under the glass.

'Pump number two,' she said.

He took the bill and nodded.

'Could I ask you something?' she said.

He shrugged.

Before she could start to ask for directions, he frowned and said, 'What happened to your face?'

She shrugged. 'A guy hit me.'

'Slugged you?'

'Yeah. A few times.'

'Sheesh. He really creamed you.'

'I noticed. I felt it.'

'What'd he wanta do that for?'

'He's just a jerk who likes to hurt people.'

'Does it hurt a whole lot? Your face?'

'Some.'

'Guy must be a real creep.'

'He is.'

'Somebody oughta fix his wagon for him.'

'Somebody plans to. Do you know where Cricket Lake is?'

'Sure. You going there?'

'Not exactly. I'm looking for a place close to Cricket, though. It's a small lake. I don't know its name, if it even has one.'

'We got lakes like that all over the place.'

'This one's just west of Cricket.'

'West?'

'Yeah. It has a dirt road leading to it, and one cabin.'

'Oh, I bet you mean the Dewey place.'

'Maybe.'

'The place that Jason Dewey hid out. A little shack by this lake. Jason Dewey, he hid out there . . . guess it must've been three summers back.'

Marty shrugged her shoulders.

'You know about Jason Dewey?'

'No, but . . .'

'He's the guy that chopped up that family down Hingston

way. You must've heard about it. Made all the news. He hacked up the mother and father and all the kids, two or three kids – and the family parrot.'

'A parrot?'

'Yeah.' He grinned. 'He *ate* the parrot. Wild, huh? A real nutcase.'

'He had a hideout somewhere near Cricket Lake?'

'Sure did.'

'How do I find it?'

He gave her directions, but explained that she should wait for morning. 'You ain't gonna find the turn-off in the dark. But if you wanta wait till morning, I'll take you out there myself.'

'I have to go right now.'

He looked disappointed. 'You sure you can't wait?' he asked.

'Sorry. But I've got a wagon to fix. Thanks for the information.'

'Welcome.'

'Pump number two,' she reminded him.

'Five bucks worth.'

42

Two miles west of Cricket Lake, Marty swung the car onto a meager dirt road and stopped. Turning sideways in her seat, she reached up and removed the plastic cover from the dome light. Then she twisted the bulb loose. She put the cover and bulb into Jack's glove compartment, then started driving forward.

The road, little more than a couple of wheel ruts, was hard to drive on. It threw the car around as if trying to rip the steering wheel out of her hands. She held on tightly, fighting to keep control.

A rough bump jolted her teeth together and she bit her tongue. Tears blurred her vision. She didn't dare let go of the wheel, so she tried to blink them away. It didn't work. Tears still blinded her. So she gripped the wheel as hard as possible with her left hand and used her right to rub her eyes clear.

Just then, the road turned.

The car swerved out of the shallow ruts.

She grabbed the wheel and steered along the overgrown center strip, bushes scraping against the right side of the car until she guided the tires again into their twin paths.

She slowed down and took the road more carefully.

Just take it easy. No big hurry. I've got all night.

Just so I get there before morning.

Catch him in his sleep.

If he's there.

God, I hope he's there . . .

43

'Hey,' Willy heard. Something shoved his shoulder. 'Hey, wake up.'

'Huh?' he asked. 'What?'

'I've got to go,' Tina said.

'What?'

'I've gotta go to the bathroom.'

'Shit. You gotta go *now?*'

'I can't help it.'

'Shit,' he said again. Then he said, 'Okay, so I guess we gotta get up. We're cuffed together, case you didn't notice.'

'I noticed.'

Slowly, awkwardly, they both stood up in the darkness. Willy got behind Tina and steered her to the table. There, he turned on the lantern. 'Okay, now we go outside.'

'Together?'

'If you think I'm gonna take off the cuffs at this hour, you're outa your fucking mind. Let's go.'

As they walked in tandem toward the door, Willy saw their reflection in the window. It was the brand new window that he'd installed just before taking off to get Marty. 'Hold it,' he said, and grabbed her shoulders. 'Get a load of the lovebirds. Almost as good as a mirror,' he said.

'Can we go?' Tina asked.

'When I say so.'

In the reflection, he watched his hands vanish behind her shoulders. They reappeared under her arms, then covered her breasts. Her breasts felt hot and slippery. He watched himself squeeze them, watched his fingers pinch her stiff nipples.

She squirmed and made odd little noises in her throat, but didn't protest.

He'd grown hard. He rubbed himself against her back.

In the reflection, he saw one of his hands glide down her belly. It continued downward and went too low to be seen in the window.

He felt her moist curls.

Then his fingertips spread her and slid in.

He saw her smile in the glass.

'Feels good, huh?' he asked.

'This does,' Tina said.

The portrait shattered. Jagged shards exploded into the night outside. Others dropped from above. They plunged down like broken slabs of ice, stabbing and slicing her outstretched arm.

Willy jerked her away from the broken window.

'You bitch!' he yelled as they both stumbled backward, cuffed at the ankles. 'You stupid bitch! You busted my fuckin' window!'

When they fell, Tina landed on top of him. She squirmed and thrashed. Her back and buttocks were hot and slippery. Willy liked how they felt, sliding against his skin.

He didn't know that she was clutching a spike of broken glass until she started to use it on him.

44

After what seemed like more than an hour of slow driving through the woods, Marty rumbled down a slope and spotted a rock, pale in the moonlight, resting in the strip between the ruts.

She jammed on the brakes.

Not quick enough.

The rock scraped and thundered against the car's undercarriage.

When the noise stopped, she wiped the sweat out of her eyes. She eased her foot onto the gas pedal. The car started slowly forward.

Then she saw it.

Ten feet ahead, shining in a stray slant of moonlight, was the rear window of another car.

Willy's car. The one he'd taken after killing the two men on the roadside last night.

Marty hit the brakes and turned off the engine. She opened her door, glad she'd taken care of the ceiling light.

She climbed out and dragged the shotgun after her. Propping its stock on the ground, she crouched behind her open door. She cocked both hammers.

Looking over the top of the door, she could only see the back of Willy's car. She gazed at its trunk. Beneath the dark curving metal, Dan lay dead.

Unless Willy'd moved him.

Dan.

She turned her eyes away from the trunk.

To each side of Willy's car, she could see woods. But not much else, not from her crouched position behind the door. She didn't want to stand up. She liked it fine behind the solid, protective door. But there was no choice.

Slowly, she stood up straight.

She gazed into the darkness, half expecting a gunshot to crack the silence.

No, she thought. He won't shoot me.

He had shot at her before, but only to stop her from escaping. This time, she wasn't trying to escape; she was *coming* to him. He would want her alive.

Hefting the shotgun, she rushed, crouching, to the front of his car. There, she knelt down by the tire. After taking a moment to catch her breath, she raised her head and looked up the road.

The shack, less than fifty yards away, was probably no bigger than her bedroom at home. The walls looked like pale, weathered wood. From where she crouched, she could see a door and a window. The window was lit by a dim, hazy glow. As if a flashlight might be on inside the shack.

She shivered and felt the hairs rise on the back of her neck.

Is he up? she wondered. At this hour?

Up or not, this is it.

'Here I come, Willy,' she whispered. 'Ready or not.'

And she was up and running, shotgun heavy in her hands, pine needles crunching under her shoes, running, fingertip sliding through the trigger guard, running, stopping at the shack's wall, thrusting the barrels in through the broken window . . .

45

Willy, standing naked only a few feet away, grinned at her. He was bloody from head to toe. His arms were high as if he might be hoping to surrender.

Before he had a chance to say anything – before he had a chance to dive for cover – Marty fired.

With a harsh roar, the shotgun spat flame and jumped in her hands and slammed back against her shoulder.

The blast caught Willy in the middle of the chest. It hit him like a hard wind, lifting him off his feet, hurling him backward.

But he didn't go down.

In the light of a battery lantern on the nearby table, Marty saw him, still grinning, start to glide back toward her.

A deathless thing, still up and coming.

She glimpsed shiny, broken rib bones in the pulpy clutter of his chest.

She let out a scream that scorched her throat.

And she thought, *Go for the head!*

She aimed for Willy's face as he came gliding toward her.

It was only then that she noticed the shiny blades of glass jutting out of his eyes. And the wide wedge of glass jammed into his mouth, giving him such a big, strange grin. And the slash across his throat.

She held fire.

A ceiling beam creaked, and Willy began to glide backward again.

Marty suddenly realized that he was suspended by his wrists.

He swung back and forth below the rope like a mutilated Tarzan.

Lowering her gaze, Marty saw that his genitals were gone.

So was his left foot.

When she was done throwing up, Marty entered the shack and looked around. She tried not to look at Willy.

Nobody else seemed to be there.

She found lots of blood, especially on the floor near Willy's dangling body. And on the wall and floor near the broken front window. And on the mattress.

There was a lot of semen on the mattress, too.

He must've brought someone here. Grabbed some other poor girl after I got away . . .

Someone tougher than he counted on.

Tough enough to take him out.

'Hello?' she called.

No answer came.

'Anybody here?'

Still, no answer.

'Whoever you are . . . if you can hear me, thanks. I came here to kill the bastard, but you beat me to it.' Marty suddenly found herself smiling. 'You did a good job on him! You did a *great* job!'

After a few moments, she called, 'Do you need a ride out of here? Or help? Are you hurt? Do you need medical attention? Hello? I'll do anything I can for you!'

Nothing.

She spent a while longer looking around – hoping Willy's tough victim – his killer – might return.

She searched the entire shack.

As she walked out with the shotgun slung over her shoulder, she wondered what had become of the person.

She also wondered what had become of Willy's left foot and his genitals.

She climbed into the car, turned it around, and headed back for Jack's place.

46

The next morning, Tina walked out of the woods and onto the road.

She was barefoot.

She was clean from soaking in the lake last night. The lake water had sure felt good on her sunburn and on a lot of places where Willy had hurt her. She supposed she might've stayed in it all night, but her hands and arms kept on bleeding.

So then she'd waded out and hunted around until she found the remains of her paisley dress under the tree where Willy had torn it off her. Willy had ruined it, shredding it with his teeth like that.

But the shreds had turned out to make very fine bandages. She'd bound the cuts on her arms and hands with bright, shiny rags.

She'd tied a piece around her left ankle, like a broad bandage, to conceal the handcuffs there.

And she'd made herself a bikini top by knotting a few pieces together.

After sunrise, she'd returned to the shack. Willy was anty, and he stank. She'd gotten out as fast as she could.

Outside, she'd used Willy's pocket knife to take the legs off his jeans and make herself a pair of cut-offs to wear. She'd put on the shorts, then dropped the knife into her pocket.

The knife had come in mighty handy in the shack last night. Without it, she'd *still* be cuffed to Willy.

She planned to keep the knife forever.

And keep it always ready, just in case.

Now, walking alongside the road, she heard the sound of an engine. Turning around, she watched a bright blue pickup truck come around a bend.

She put out her arm to hitch a ride.

It was no surprise when the pickup stopped for her. No surprise at all. Not the way she was dressed.

She bent toward the passenger window.

The driver, a nice-looking young man, smiled at her. He wore a T-shirt and tan shorts. His smile looked friendly. 'Can I give you a lift?' he asked, and glanced at her flimsy, makeshift bikini top.

'You aren't some kind of pervert or fiend, are you?'

He suddenly blushed. 'Me? Nope.'

'Better not be,' Tina said. 'I'd hate to have to kill you.'

'You and me both,' he said, and laughed a little.

Smiling, she climbed in.

'Where to?' he asked.

'Home,' she said.

Kitty Litter

'She's here for a kitty!'

My flinch came to an end before the second word was out of her mouth, but my heart still thudded fast and hard. I'd thought I was alone, you see. I was stretched out on my lounger beside my backyard pool, surrounded by redwood fence, enjoying a new *87th Precinct* paperback, savoring the feel of the sunlight and the warm breeze.

The invasion took me by complete surprise.

After the jolt by the imperious voice, I jerked my head sideways and saw the girl.

Already, she was inside the gate and marching boldly toward me.

I knew right away who she was.

Monica from down the block.

Though we'd never actually met, I'd seen Monica around. And *heard* her. She had a loud, nasal voice which she operated primarily to snap back at her poor mother and berate her little friends.

I knew her name because she was often the subject of shouted warnings and threats. I also knew it because she used it herself. She belonged to the odd tribe that refers to itself in the third person.

She was about ten years old, I suppose.

If I had not been so unfortunate as to observe her behavior on previous occasions, I certainly would've been struck by the beauty of the girl striding toward me. She had rich brown hair, gleaming eyes, excellent facial features, a flawless complexion, and a slender body. She didn't look beautiful to me, however.

Nor did she look cute, though she wore a delightful outfit comprised of a pink cap with a jauntily upturned bill, a denim pinafore dress, a white blouse, white knee socks and athletic shoes of pink to match her cap.

She was neither beautiful nor cute because she was Monica.

To my way of thinking, there is no such thing as a beautiful or cute snot.

She halted beyond the foot of my lounger and scowled at me. Her eyes flicked up and down my body.

My swimsuit had never been meant for public inspection. I quickly sheltered myself with the open book. It lay like a pitched roof atop my lap.

'You *are* Mr Bishop?' she demanded.

'That's right.'

'The man with the kitties?'

I nodded.

She nodded back at me. She bobbed on her toes. 'And you're giving them away for free?'

'I'm hoping to find good homes for them, yes.'

'Monica will have one then.'

'And who is Monica?' I asked, though obviously I knew the answer.

She pumped a small thumb against her chest, dead center between the denim straps of her dress.

'You're Monica?' I asked.

'Of course.'

'You want one of my kittens?'

'Where are they?'

In spite of my dislike for this particular child, I was eager to find homes for the kittens. My ad in the newspaper, and the fliers I'd tacked to several neighborhood trees, had not been greatly successful. Of the four kittens born to the litter, I still had three.

They were not getting any younger. Or any smaller.

Soon, they would pass out of the cute, romping, frisky kitten stage altogether. Who would want to adopt any of them, then?

In other words, I had no wish to be choosy. If Monica wanted a kitten, a kitten she would have.

'They're in my house,' I said. 'I'll bring them out for you to . . . inspect.'

As I leaned forward on the lounge and wondered what to do about my immodest swimsuit, Monica scowled across the pool at the sliding glass door of my house.

'It isn't locked, is it?' she asked.

'No, but you stay . . .'

Ignoring me, she skipped off along the edge of the pool.

I took the opportunity to stand, set down my paperback, and snatch my beach towel off the lounge pad. Quickly, I wrapped the towel around my waist.

Corner tucked under to hold the towel, I hurried after Monica. She was already striding briskly past the far end of the pool.

'*I'll* get the kittens,' I called to her. 'You wait outside.'

I did not want her in my house.

I did not want her to ogle my possessions. I did not want her to touch them or break them or steal them. I did not want her to leave the taint of her pushy, pestilent *self* inside the sanctuary of my home.

She reached for the handle of the sliding door. Clutched it.

'Monica! No!'

'Don't have a cow, man,' she said. And then she rumbled open the door and entered.

'Come out of there!' I yelled.

She hadn't gone far. Stepping over the runner, I spotted her standing near the center of my den. Her fists were planted on her hips as she swiveled her head from side to side.

'I asked you to stay outside.'

131

'Where are they?'

I shrugged and sighed. She was in. There was no way to undo it. 'This way,' I said.

She followed me toward the kitchen.

'Why are you wearing that towel?' she asked.

'Because it suits me.'

'Where'd your suit go?'

'It didn't go anywhere.'

'Did you take it off?'

'No!'

'You'd better not've.'

'I didn't. I assure you. I also assure you, young lady, that I'm on the very verge of asking you to leave.'

A small wooden gate was stretched across the kitchen doorway to keep the kittens corralled. I hiked up my towel as if it were a skirt, and stepped over the gate.

I turned around to watch Monica. 'Careful,' I warned.

It would serve her right to fall and mash her impish little nose flat, I thought. But she swung one leg, then the other, over the top of the gate and made it to the other side without misadventure.

She sniffed. Her upper lip reached for the bottom of her nose. 'What's that stink?'

'I don't detect a stink.'

'Monica may barf.'

'You might be smelling the litter box.'

'Yug.'

'There it is, now.' I pointed at the plastic tub. Its desert landscape appeared a trifle bumpy. 'You'll have to get used to some rather unpleasant aromas if you wish to keep a cat in . . .'

'Oh! Kitty!'

She rushed past me, dodged the table, and pranced to the far corner of the kitchen where the cats were at play on their blanket.

By the time I caught up to her, she had already made her pick. She was on her knees, clutching Lazzy to her chest, stroking the little tabby's striped head.

Lazzy had a rather frantic look in her eyes, but she wasn't struggling much.

The kittens rubbed against Monica's knees, purring and meowing.

'She'll take this one,' the girl said.

'I'm afraid she won't.'

Monica slowly twisted herself around. Her eyes said, *How dare you!* Her mouth said, 'Oh, yes, she will.'

'No. I offered you one of the kittens. That isn't one of the kittens.'

'Oh course she is! She's the tiniest, cutest little kitty of the bunch, and she'll go home with Monica.'

'You may have one of the others.'

'Who wants them? They're big! They aren't cute little kitties. *This* is the cute little kitty.'

She nuzzled her cheek against Lazzy's face.

'You don't want that one,' I said.

She started to get up. I grabbed her shoulder and pushed her down until she was on her knees again.

'Now you're in trouble,' she said.

'No doubt.'

'You touched Monica.'

'You're a trespasser in my house. You came in uninvited even after I told you to stay out. You were preparing to leave with property that belongs to me. So I had every right to touch you.'

'Oh, yeah?'

'Yeah.'

'You'd better just let Monica take this cat home, right now, or else.'

In spite of what I'd said about trespassing, etc., her threats could not be ignored. Here I was, a thirty-eight-year-old bachelor wearing next to nothing, alone in my house with a ten-year-old girl.

It wouldn't look good.

The notion of facing accusations sickened me.

'All right. If you want that cat, she's yours. Go on, take her and get out of here.'

With a victorious grin, Monica rose to her feet. 'Thank you,' she said.

'If you want to know the truth, Lazzy always did give me the creeps.'

'The creeps?'

'Never mind.'

Monica narrowed her eyes. 'What's wrong with her?'

'Nothing.'

'Tell. You'd better tell, or else.'

'Well . . .' I dragged a chair away from the kitchen table, swung it around, and sat down on it.

'Is this going to take long?'

Ignoring her question, I said, 'It all started with Lazzy falling in the toilet.'

She gasped as if the cat had suddenly turned white-hot, and tossed her aside.

Lazzy let out a *reeeeooow!* as she twisted and rolled through the air. But she did a quiet, four-point landing. Heading for the blanket, she glanced over her shoulder and gave Monica a look that was clearly miffed.

'You didn't have to throw her like that,' I said.

'She fell in a *toilet*!'

'The toilet had nothing in it except for clean water. Besides, this was some time ago.'

'You mean she isn't dirty any more?'

'She's perfectly clean.'

'Then what's the big deal?'

'She drowned.'

Monica tucked her chin down and gazed at me as if peering over the top of invisible eyeglasses. She folded her arms across her chest. I wondered if she had picked up the stance from an elderly relative. 'Drowned?' she said. 'Puh-leese.'

'I'm serious,' I said.

Monica tilted her head to one side. 'If she drowned, she would be dead.'

I chose not to argue. Instead, I proceeded with the story. 'It began when Mrs Brown gave birth. She was a tabby who belonged to my friend, James, in Long Beach. When he told me about the litter, I expressed an interest in taking one of the kittens off his hands. Of course, I couldn't take one immediately. I needed to wait until they'd been weaned.'

Monica narrowed an eye. 'What does that mean?'

'A kitty can't be taken away from its mother right away. It needs the mother's milk.'

'Oh, that.'

'Yes. At any rate, we set a date for me to visit James and select a kitten. Do you know where Long Beach is?'

She rolled her eyes toward the ceiling. 'Monica has been to the Spruce Goose and the Queen Mary . . . oh, so many times that she is totally *bored* by them both.'

'Then she knows that the drive takes about an hour from here.'

She nodded. She sighed. She looked over her shoulder, apparently checking up on Lazzy.

I went on with my story.

'I drank quite a lot of coffee before setting out in the morning for Long Beach. By the time I reached James's house, I was very uncomfortable.'

This won her attention away from the cat. 'What?'

'I had to pee. Badly.'

'Oh, for heaven's sake.'

'I hurried to the front door and rang the doorbell. I rang it again and again, but James didn't answer. As it turns out, he had forgotten about our date, and gone shopping. I didn't know that at the time, however. I knew only that the door was not being opened, and that my teeth were afloat.'

'You should not be talking to a child about such things.'

'I'm afraid the condition of my bladder is integral to the story. Anyway, I was becoming frantic. I pounded on the door and called out James's name, but to no avail. I considered rushing over to a neighbor's house, but the idea appalled me. How could I ask a stranger for the use of a toilet? Besides, who would allow me inside for such a purpose? There were no gas stations, restaurants, or shopping malls near enough . . .' Monica interrupted me with a sigh. 'Anyway, I had no choice but to let *myself* into James's house. It was either that or . . .'

'You are a very crude person.'

'Not so crude that I wanted to pee outside. And fortunately, matters didn't reach that stage. At the back of the house, I found an open window. The screen was in my way, of course. But I was too desperate to care about niceties. I fairly tore the screen from its moorings, boosted myself through the window, tumbled onto the floor of James's bedroom, and raced for the bathroom.

'As it turned out, the bathroom was where James had been keeping the new litter – with the door shut, you know, so they wouldn't scamper all over the house. And to confine the aroma of the litter box, I'm sure.'

'This is a *very* long story,' Monica complained. 'Long *and* gross.'

'All right. I'll make it quick, then. I burst into the bathroom, pranced about to avoid mashing several kitties underfoot, and prepared to relieve myself. But when I looked down into the toilet bowl . . .'

'Lazzy,' Monica said.

'Lazzy. Yes. Though, of course, that wasn't her name at the time. At any rate, she must've climbed onto the rim of the toilet for a drink, and tumbled in. She was floating on her side, her little face down in the water. I had no idea how long she might've been that way. But she wasn't moving at all. Not of her own accord. She was turning slightly as if being spun by a very slow, lazy whirlpool.

'Well, I fished her right out and laid her out on the floor. She looked horrid. Have you ever seen a dead cat?'

'She was *not* dead. She's right there.' Monica pointed, her arm so straight and stiff that it seemed to be bent just a bit the wrong way at the elbow.

Lazzy lay on her side, head up, licking one of her forelegs.

'She doesn't look dead now,' I agreed, 'but you should've seen her shortly after I pulled her out of the toilet. She had that *awful* look – fur all matted down, ears flattened back. Her eyes were shut, so all you could see were dark slits. And she looked as if she'd died snarling.' I bared my teeth at Monica to give her the idea.

Monica was doing her best to appear bored and annoyed and superior to all this. In spite of her efforts, however, she had a rather slack look to her face.

'The kitten was cold,' I said. 'Sopping. The feel of it sent chills through me. But that didn't stop me from examining the poor thing. It had no heartbeat.'

'I'm sure,' Monica said. But she was definitely looking a trifle distressed.

'The little kitten was dead.'

'No, it wasn't.'

'It had drowned in the toilet. It was as dead as dead can be.'

'Was not!'

'Dead dead dead!'

Monica pounded her fists against her thighs. Red-faced, she snapped, 'You're an *awful* person!'

'No, I'm not. I'm a very nice person, because I brought the dead kitten back to life. I rolled her onto her back and covered her little mouth with my mouth and breathed into her. At the same time, I used my thumb to push at her heart. Have you ever heard of CPR?'

Monica nodded. 'CPR was a robot in *Star Wars*.'

I was glad to find that she was not quite as smart as she thought she was.

'CPR stands for cardiopulmonary resuscitation. It's a technique used to revive people who . . .'

'Oh, *that*!' She suddenly looked very pleased with herself. And very prim and very superior. Her head dipped from one side to the other while her shoulders oscillated. '*So*, the kitty *wasn't* dead. Monica *told* you she wasn't dead.'

'Oh, but she was very dead.'

Monica shook her head. 'Was not.'

'She was dead, and I brought her back to life with the CPR. Right there in the bathroom. Pretty soon, James came home. I told him what had happened, and he let me have the kitten I'd saved. So I named her Lazzy, short for Lazarus. Do you know who Lazarus was?'

'Of course.'

'Who?'

'None of your business.'

'Whatever you say. Anyway, I brought Lazzy home with me. And do you know what?'

Monica sneered at me.

'Lazzy never grew any larger after the day I brought her back from the dead. That was six years ago. She has been the size of a little kitty, ever since. So you see, she's my pet. She's not part of the litter I want to give away. She's the *mother* of the litter.'

'But she's *tinier* than they are!'

'*And* she's been dead.'

Monica stared at Lazzy for a long while. Then she turned to me, no longer looking the least bit shaken. 'She isn't *either* the mother. You made the whole thing up just so you could keep the cute one.'

She rushed over to the blanket, snatched up Lazzy and hugged her and kissed the dark brown M on her honey-colored brow.

'Put her down,' I said.

'No.'

'Don't make me take her from you.'

'You'd better not.' She glanced at the kitchen doorway behind me. 'You'd better get out of my way, or you'll be in very very bad trouble.'

'Put down Lazzy. You may still take one of the other kittens, but . . .'

'Get out of the way,' she said, and walked straight toward me.

'As soon as you've . . .'

'Mr Bishop said, "Come into my house. I have a little kitty for you." ' She halted and leered at me. 'But when Monica went into his house, he told her a urine story and he took off the towel he was wearing and he said, "This is the little kitty I have for you. His name is Peter." '

I could only gasp, 'You!'

'And he told me to pet Peter and kiss Peter. I didn't *want* to do it, but he grabbed me and . . .'

'Stop it!' I blurted, and stumbled sideways out of her way. 'Take the cat! Take her and get out of here!'

As she strutted by, taking away my Lazzy, she winked at me. 'Thank you so much for the kitten, Mr Bishop.'

I watched her leave.

Just stood and stared as she sashayed through the den and stepped over the threshold of the open sliding door. Immediately after setting foot on the concrete, she burst into a run.

Apparently afraid I might find a smidgen of nerve and attempt to retrieve my cat.

But I didn't move a muscle.

An accusation such as she had threatened to make . . . How does one disprove such a thing? One doesn't. Such an accusation, once made, would cling to me like leprous skin for all the days of my life.

I would forever be known as a pervert, a child-molester.

So I let her *steal* my dear Lazzy.

I stood frozen with terror and *let* her.

And from outside came a familiar *reeeeoooow!* followed by a quick harsh yelp – the sort of yelp a girl might make if the cat in her arms decided to claw its way to freedom – followed by a thudding splash.

I still stood motionless.

No longer terrified.

Amused, actually.

The poor dear. Fell and got herself all wet.

Lazzy leaped over the threshold and came scampering through the den, fur abristle over the ridge of her spine, her tiny ears swept back, tail curled up in a small, bushy question mark.

She slowed down, then rubbed her side against my bare ankle.

I picked up my tiny little cat. I held her in front of my face with both hands.

From outside came more splashing sounds.

Cries of 'Help!' and 'Help!'

Was it possible that Monica's bag of tricks did not include swimming?

I dared not get my hopes up.

There were no more cries for help. I did hear some choky gasps and quite a good deal of splashing, however, before silence replaced the disturbance.

I carried Lazzy out to the poolside.

Monica was at the deep end. Face down, arms and legs spread out, hair drifting above her head, blouse and jumper shimmering slightly.

She rather looked like a skydiver enjoying a freefall, waiting for the very last moment to pull her ringcord.

'I suppose I ought to pull her out,' I told Lazzy. 'Give her some CPR.'

Then I shook my head.

'No. Not a good idea – a man my age putting his hands on a ten-year-old girl? What would people say?'

I headed for the sliding glass door.

'Why don't we go pay a visit to James? Who knows? Maybe someone will be lucky enough to find Monica while we're away.'

Lazzy purred, her little body vibrating like a warm engine.

The Bleeder

The spot of wetness on the sidewalk at Byron's feet looked purple in the mercury glow of the streetlight. It looked like a drop of blood.

He squatted down and peered at it. Then he pulled a flashlight out of the side pocket of his sport jacket. He thumbed the switch. In the bright, somewhat yellowish shine of its beam, the spot appeared crimson.

Might be paint, he thought.

But who would be wandering around at night dripping red paint?

He reached down and touched it. Bringing his fingertip close to the flashlight glass, he inspected the red smear. He rubbed it with his thumb. The stuff was kind of watery. Not gooey enough for paint. More like blood that had been spilled very recently.

He sniffed it.

He could only smell mustard from the hot dog he'd eaten during the last show, a smell strong enough to overpower blood's subtle aroma. But it wouldn't have masked the pungent odor of paint.

Byron wiped his finger and thumb on his sock. Still squatting, he let the beam of his flashlight drift over the concrete ahead. He saw a dirty pink disk of flattened bubble gum, a gob of spit, a mashed cigarette butt, and a second drop of blood.

The second drop was three strides away. He stopped above it. Like the first, it was about the size of a nickel. Sweeping his light forward, he found a third.

Maybe someone with a nosebleed, he thought.

Or a switchblade in the guts.

No, a *real* wound and there'd be blood everywhere. Byron remembered the mess in the Elsinore's restroom last month. During intermission, a couple of teenagers had gone at each other with knives. He and Digby, one of the other ushers, had broken it up. Though the kids only had minor wounds, the john had looked like a slaughterhouse.

Compared to that, this was nothing. Just a drip once in a while. Even a nosebleed, he thought, would throw out more gore.

On the other hand, the person's clothing, or a handkerchief, might have soaked up most of it – so that only a fraction of the spillage actually hit the sidewalk.

Just a little drip now and then.

Just enough to make Byron very curious.

The trail of blood was going in his direction, anyway, so he kept his flashlight on and kept a lookout.

'What, the streetlights aren't bright enough for you?'

He turned around.

Digby Hymus, known to the gals who worked the refreshment stand as the Jolly Green Dork, came striding down the sidewalk. The thirty-year-old retired boxer had removed his green usher's jacket. Its sleeves were tied around his neck so he looked as if he were giving a piggy-back ride to someone who'd been mashed by a steam roller. His arms were so thick with muscle that they couldn't swing close to his sides when he walked.

'Hate to tell you this, By, but you look like a goddamn retard with that flashlight on.'

'Appearances are often deceiving,' he said. 'Take a gander.' He aimed his flashlight at the nearest spot of blood.

'Yeah? So what?'

'Blood.'

'Yeah? So what?'

'Don't you find it intriguing?'

'Probably some babe sprung a leak in her . . .'

'Don't be disgusting.'

'Hey, you're the guy so interested in blood. You've got a real ghoulish streak, you know that?'

'If you can't say something nice, don't say it.'

'Screw you,' he said, and walked across the road to his parked car.

Byron waited until the car sped off, then continued to follow the trail of blood. He stopped at the corner of 11th Street. His apartment was five blocks straight ahead. But the drops of blood went to the right.

He paused for a moment, considering what to do. He knew that he ought to go on home. But if he did that, he would always wonder.

Maybe the bleeder needs help, he told himself. Even a slow leak could be fatal if it went on long enough. Maybe I'm this person's only chance.

Maybe I'll be a hero, my story will be on the news.

Then guys like Digby – gals like Mary and Agnes of the snack counter – wouldn't be so quick to poke fun at him.

His mind made up, he turned the corner and began to follow the blood up 11th Street.

The television. He could see it now. Karen Ling on the five o'clock news. 'Byron Lewis, twenty-eight-year-old poet and part-time usher at the Elsinore theater, last night came to the aid of a mugging victim in an alley off 11th Street. The victim, twenty-two-year-old fashion model Jessica Connors, had been assaulted earlier that evening in front of the theater where Byron worked. Bleeding and disoriented, she had staggered several blocks before falling unconscious where she was later discovered by the young poet. Byron made the grisly discovery after following Jessica's trail of blood. According to paramedics, Jessica was only minutes away from death at the time she was found. Her survival is being attributed to Byron's quick actions

145

in applying first aid and summoning paramedics. She is currently recovering, and extremely grateful, at Queen of Angels Hospital.'

Byron smiled.

Just a fantasy, he told himself. But what's wrong with that?

The bleeder will probably turn out to be an old wino who cut his lip on a bottle of rotgut.

Or worse.

You'll probably wish you'd gone straight home.

But at least you'll *know*.

Stopping at Harker Avenue, he found a spot of blood on the curb. No traffic was nearby. But Byron believed in playing by the rules. So he thumbed the button to activate the WALK sign, waited for the signal to change, then started across.

If the bleeder had left any drops on the road pavement, passing cars must have obliterated them.

He found more when he reached the other side.

The bleeder was still heading north on 11th Street.

And Byron realized, with some dismay, that he had crossed an invisible border into Skid Row.

In the area ahead, many of the streetlights were out. They left broad pools of darkness on the sidewalk and road. Every shop in Byron's sight was closed for the night. Metal gates had been stretched across their display windows and doors. He glanced through the checkered grating in front of a clothes store, saw a face at the window, and managed to stifle a gasp of alarm.

Just a mannequin, he told himself, hurrying away.

He made a point to avoid looking into any more windows.

Better just to watch the sidewalk, he thought. Watch the trail of blood.

The next time he looked up, he saw a pair of legs sticking out of a tenement's recessed entryway.

The bleeder!

I did it!

Byron rushed to the fallen man. It *was* a man, unfortunately. A man with holes in the bottom of his shoes, whose grimy ankles were blotched with scabs, whose trousers were stained and crusty with filth, who wore a ragged sweatshirt that had one empty sleeve pinned up.

No left arm.

His right arm was folded under his head like a pillow.

'Excuse me,' Byron said.

The man kept snoring.

Byron nudged him with a foot. The body twitched. The snoring stopped with a startled gasp. 'Huh? Whuh?'

'Are you all right?' Byron asked. 'Are you bleeding?'

'BLEEDING?' The man squealed and bolted upright. His head swiveled as he looked down at himself. Byron helped by shining the light on him. 'I don' see no blood. Where? Where?'

Byron didn't see blood on the man, either. But he saw other things that made him turn away and try not to gag.

'Oh God, I'm bleedin'!' the man whined. 'They musta bit me. Oh, they's always bitin' me. Why they wanna bite on ol' Dandy! Where'd they get me? They after ol' Dandy's stump again? Jeezum!'

Byron risked a look at Dandy, and saw that the old man was struggling with his single arm to pull his sweatshirt off.

'Maybe I've got the wrong person.'

'Oh, they's after me.' The shirt started to rise. Byron glimpsed the gray, blotchy skin of Dandy's belly.

'Gimme yer light, duke! C'mon, gimme!'

'I've gotta go,' Byron blurted.

He staggered away from the frantic derelict – and saw a spot of blood farther up the sidewalk.

Dandy wasn't the bleeder, after all.

'I'm sorry,' Byron called back. 'Go back to sleep.'

He heard a low groan. A voice sunken in fear and disgust said, 'Aw, looky what they's done to me.'

If only I'd left the guy alone, he thought.

Real neat play. I should've gone on home.

But he'd come this far. Besides, he couldn't turn back without passing Dandy. He might cross to the other side of the street, but that would be cowardly. And he was no less curious than before.

The drops of blood led him to the end of the block. He waited for the traffic signal to change, then hurried into the street. This time, the trail continued over the pavement. A good sign, he thought. Maybe the bleeder had crossed so recently that no cars had yet come by to wipe out the spots.

I'm gaining on him. Or her.

Oh, he did hope it was a woman.

A slender blonde. Slumped against an alley wall, a hand clamped to her chest just below the swell of her left breast. 'I'm here to help you,' he would say. With a brave, pained smile, she would say, 'It's nothing. Really. Just a flesh wound.' Then she would unbutton her blouse and peel the bloody side away from her skin. She wore a black lace bra. Byron could see right through it.

He imagined himself taking out his clean, folded handkerchief, patting blood away from the cut, and trying not to stare at her breast. His knuckles brushed against it, though, as he dabbed at the wound. 'Excuse me,' he told her. 'That's okay,' she said. 'Come with me,' he suggested. 'I'll take you to my apartment. I have bandages there.' She agreed, but she was too weak to walk without assistance, so she leaned against him. Soon, he had to carry her in his arms. He wasn't huge and powerful like Digby, but the slim girl weighed very little, and . . .

'Hey you.'

Startled, Byron looked up from the sidewalk. His heart gave a quick thump.

She was leaning against the post of a streetlamp, not against a wall. She was a brunette, not a blonde. She wasn't holding her chest.

Her hands, instead, were roaming slowly up and down the front of her skirt. The skirt was black leather. It was very short.

Byron walked toward her. He saw no blood on her shiny white blouse. But he saw that most of the buttons were undone. She didn't wear a black lace bra like the bleeder of his fantasy. She didn't wear one at all, and the blouse was open wide enough to show the sides of her breasts.

'Looking for someone, honey?' she asked. Running the tip of her tongue across her lower lip, she squirmed against the light post. As her hands slid upward, the skirt rose with them. It lifted above the tops of her black fishnet stockings. The straps of a garter belt were dark against her pale thighs.

Feeling a little breathless, Byron looked her in the eyes. 'You aren't bleeding, are you?' he asked.

'What do you think?' She eased the skirt higher, but he didn't allow his eyes to wander down.

'I don't think you understand,' he said. 'I'm trying to find someone who's bleeding.'

'Kinky,' she said. 'What's your name, sweet thing?'

'Byron.'

'I'm Ryder. Wanta find out how I got my name?'

'Have you been standing here long?'

'Long enough to get lonely. And hot.' One of her hands glided up. It slipped inside her blouse. Byron saw the shapes of her fingers through the thin fabric as they fondled her breast.

He swallowed. 'What I mean is, did you just get here?'

'Few minutes ago. You like?' She eased the blouse aside, showing him the breast, stroking its erect nipple with the edge of her thumb.

He nodded. 'Very nice. But the thing is . . . did you see anyone go by?'

'Just you, Byron. How about it?' She stared at the front of his slacks. 'You look mighty sweet to me. I bet you taste real fine. I know *I* do. You wanta find out just how fine, too, I'll bet.'

'Well . . . see, I'm looking for someone who's bleeding.'

Her eyes narrowed. 'That'll cost you extra.'

'No, really . . .'

'Yes, really.' She curled her lower lip in, and nipped it. Then she pushed the lip outward as if offering it to Byron. A trickle of blood rolled down. When it reached her chin, she caught it on the tip of her index finger. She painted her nipple with it. 'Taste,' she whispered.

Byron shook his head.

Ryder smiled. More blood was dribbling toward her chin. 'Oh? Do you want it someplace else?'

'No. I'm sorry. Huh-uh.' He backed away from her.

'Hey now, buster . . .'

He whirled around and ran.

Ryder yelled. He understood why she might be upset, but that was no reason to call him such names. They made him blush, even though nobody seemed to be around to hear.

I'm hearing, he thought as he dashed up the sidewalk. And I'm not half those things she's calling me. She knows it, too. She saw.

Crazy whore.

By the time he reached the other side of the next street, she had stopped shouting. Byron looked back. She was gone.

While he gasped for air, he swept the beam of his flashlight over the sidewalk. He saw no blood spots.

I lost the trail!

His throat tightened.

It's all her fault.

He stomped his foot on the sidewalk.

Calm down, he told himself. It's not over yet. You still had the trail when you ran into her.

The DON'T WALK sign was flashing red, but Byron didn't care. After all, he hadn't even *looked* at the signal the first time across. Now, it just didn't matter.

Old Dandy'd been bad enough. But Ryder!

Running into people like that made traffic signals seem pretty trivial.

No cars were coming, so he hurried back across the street.

Nothing to it.

He smiled.

When he found a spot of blood on the sidewalk, a thrill rippled through him.

'Ah ha!' he pronounced. 'The game's afoot!'

Now I'm talking to myself? Why not? I'm holding up fairly well, all things considered.

Spying a second drop of blood, he understood how he had lost the trail. The bleeder hadn't crossed the road, but had headed to the right along Kelsey Avenue.

Byron quickened his pace.

'Gaining on you,' he said.

As he hurried along, he realized that the spots on the sidewalk were farther apart than they used to be. The distance between them had been irregular from the start – but anywhere from three to five feet, usually. Now, it seemed more like eight to ten feet from one drop to the next.

Is the wound coagulating? he wondered. Or is the bleeder running dry?

What if the blood stops entirely?

If that happens, I'll never find her.

Or find her too late – dead in a heap.

Neither outcome suited Byron.

He broke into a run.

A few strides after passing the entrance of an alley, he lost the trail again and staggered to a halt. Turning around, he returned to the alley. His flashlight reached into it, and a spot of red gleamed on the pavement two yards ahead.

Odd, he thought. In his fantasies, he'd imagined finding the bleeder in an alley. What if it *all* would happen just the way he'd pictured it?

Too much to hope for, he told himself.

But he felt a tremor of excitement as he entered the alley.

He shined his light from side to side, half expecting to find a beautiful woman slumped against one of the brick walls. He saw a couple of garbage bins, but nothing else.

She might be huddled down, concealed by one of the bins.

Byron stepped past them. Nobody there.

He considered lifting the lids, but decided against it. The things would stink. There might even be rats inside. If the bleeder was in one of them, he didn't want to know.

Better not to find her at all.

This was supposed to be an adventure with a glorious and romantic outcome. It would just be too horrible if it ended with finding a body in the garbage.

He kept going.

Ten strides deeper into the alley, his pale beam fell upon another drop of blood.

'Thank God,' he muttered.

Of course, there were several more bins some distance ahead – dark boxes silhouetted by faint light where the alley ended at the next road.

I'll find her before then, Byron told himself.

Any minute, now.

A black cat sauntered across the alley. It glanced at him, eyes glowing like clear golden marbles.

Good thing I'm not superstitious, he thought, the back of his neck tingling.

'If only you could talk,' he said.

The cat wandered over to the right side of the alley. Back hunched, tail twitching, it rubbed its side against a door.

A door!

Byron tipped back his head and inspected the building. He thought that it might be an apartment house. Its brick wall was three stories high, with fire escapes at the windows of the upper floors. All the windows were dark.

He stepped toward the door. The cat leaped and darted past him.

He almost grabbed the knob before noticing that it was wet with blood.

A chill crept through him.

Maybe this isn't such a great idea, he thought.

But he was so *close*.

Still, to enter a building where he didn't belong . . .

This might very well be where the bleeder lived. Why had she entered from the alley, though, instead of using the front? Did she feel that she had to sneak in?

'Strange,' Byron muttered.

Maybe she simply wandered down the alley, lost and dazed, and entered this door in the hope of finding someone who would help her. Even now, she might be staggering down a hallway, too weak to call out.

Byron plucked a neatly folded handkerchief from his pocket, shook it open, and spread it over his left hand. He turned the knob.

With a quiet snick, the latch tongue retracted.

He eased the door open.

The beam of his flashlight probed the darkness of a narrow corridor. On the hardwood floor gleamed a dot of blood.

He stepped inside. The hot air smelled stale and musty. Pulling the door shut, he listened. Except for the pounding of his own heartbeat, he heard nothing.

His own apartment building, even at this hour, was nearly

always filled with sounds: people arguing or laughing, doors slamming, voices from radios and televisions.

His building had lighted hallways.

Hallways that always smelled of food, often of liquor. Now and again, they were sweet with the lingering aromas of cheap perfume.

Nobody lives here, he suddenly thought.

He didn't like that. Not at all.

He realized that he was holding his breath as he started forward. He walked slowly, setting each heel down and rolling the shoe forward to its toe. Sometimes, a board creaked under him.

He stopped at a corner where this bit of hallway met a long stretch of corridor. Leaning forward, he aimed his beam to the left. He saw no blood on the floor. His light reached only far enough down the narrow passage to reveal one door. That door stood open.

He knew that he should take a peek inside.

He didn't want to.

Byron looked to the right. Not far away, a staircase rose toward the upper stories. Beyond that was a foyer and the front entrance.

He saw no blood on the floor in that direction.

I'll check that way, first, he decided. He knew it would make more sense to go left, but heading toward the front seemed safer.

He turned the corner. After a few strides, he twisted around and checked behind him with the light. That long hallway made him very nervous. Especially the open door, though he couldn't see it from here. Instead of turning his back on it, he began sidestepping.

He shined his light up and down the stairway. The balustrade flung crooked, shifting bars of shadow against the wall.

What if the blood goes up there?

He didn't want to think about that.

He checked the floor ahead of him. Still, no blood. Coming to the foot of the stairs, he checked the newel cap and ran his light up the banister. No blood. Nor did he find any on the lower stairs. He could only see the tops of five, though. After that, they were above his eye level.

I don't want to go up there, he thought.

He wanted to go up there even less than he wanted to search the far end of the hallway.

Sidestepping through the foyer, he made his way to the front door. He tried its handle. The door seemed frozen in place.

He noticed that his light was shining on a panel of mailboxes. His own building had a similar arrangement. But in his building, each box was labelled with a room number and name. No such labels here.

This came as no surprise to Byron. But his dread deepened.

I've come this far, he told himself. I'm not going to back out now.

Trembling, he stepped toward the stairway. He climbed one stair, then another. The muscles of his legs felt like warm jelly. He stopped. He swept his light across two higher treads that he hadn't been able to see from the bottom. Still, no blood.

She didn't go this way, he told himself.

If she did, she's on her own.

I didn't count on having to search an abandoned apartment house. That'd be stupid. God only knows who might be lurking in the empty rooms.

Byron backed down the stairs and hurried away, eager to reach the passage that would lead to the alley door.

He felt ashamed of himself for giving up.

Nobody will ever know.

But he hesitated when he came to the connecting hallway. He shone his light at the alley door. Twenty feet away. No more than that. He could be outside in seconds.

But what about the bleeder?

You'll never know, he thought.

You'll always wonder.

Suppose it *is* a beautiful young woman, wandering around in shock, slowly bleeding to death? Suppose you're her only chance?

I don't care. I'm not going upstairs.

But what about that open door?

He could take a look in there, couldn't he?

He swung his light toward it.

And heard the soft murmur of a sigh.

Oh, my God!

He gazed at the doorway. The sigh had come from there, he was sure of it.

'Hello?' he called.

Someone moaned.

Byron glanced again at the alley door, shook his head, and hurried down the corridor.

So much for chickening out, he thought, feeling somewhat pleased with himself in spite of his misgivings.

I'll be a hero, after all.

'I'm here,' he said as he neared the open door. 'I'll help you.'

He rushed into the room.

He jumped the beam of his flashlight here and there. Shot its bright tunnel into corners of the room. Across bare floorboards. Past windows and a radiator.

At his back, the door slammed shut.

He gasped and whirled around.

And stared, not quite sure what he was seeing.

Then a small whimper slipped from his throat and he stumbled backward, urine running hot down his leg.

The man standing beside the door grinned with wet, red lips. He was hairless. He didn't even have eyebrows. Nor did he appear to have a neck. His head looked as if it had been jammed down between his massive shoulders.

His bloody lips grinned at Byron around a clear plastic tube. A straw of sorts. Flecked inside with red.

The tube curled down from his mouth to a body cradled in his thick arms.

The limp body of a young man whose head was tipped back as if he found something fascinating about the far wall. He wore jeans and a plaid shirt. The shirt hung open. From the center of his chest protruded something that resembled a metal spike – obviously hollow inside – which was joined with the plastic tubing. A single thin streamer of blood stretched from the hole, across his chest, and down the side of his ribcage.

It was the streamer, Byron knew, that had left the trail of drops which led him there.

He pictured the monstrous, bloated man carrying the body block after block down city streets, drinking its blood as he lumbered along.

Now, the awful man shook the body. His cheeks sank in as he sucked. Some red flew up through the tubing. Byron heard a slurpy hollow sound – the sound that comes from a straw when you reach the bottom of a chocolate shake.

Then came another soft sigh.

'All gone,' the man muttered.

His lips peeled back, baring red teeth that pinched the tube.

He dropped the body.

The spike popped out of its chest and swayed at the end of the tubing.

'Glad you're here,' he said. 'Got me an awful thirst.'

Wrapping his thick fingers around the spike, he stepped over the body.

Byron spun around, ran, and leaped. He wrapped his arms around his head an instant before hitting the window. It exploded around him and he fell until he crashed against the pavement of a sidewalk.

He scurried up and ran.

He ran for a long time.

Finally, exhausted, he leaned against a store front. Panting for air, he looked where he had been.

Now *that's* a trail of blood, he thought.

Too weak to go on, he let his knees unlock. He slumped down on the sidewalk and stretched out his legs.

His clothes, he saw, were shredded from the window glass.

So am I, he thought.

But that thing didn't get me.

Smiling, he shut his eyes.

When he opened them again, he saw a woman crouching beside him. A young, slim blonde. Really cute. She looked a lot like the one he'd hoped to find at the end of the trail. 'You'll be all right,' she said. 'My partner's calling for an ambulance.'

She nodded toward the patrol car idling by the curb.

Desert Pickup

'All *right*!' He felt lucky about his one. Walking backward along the roadside, he stared at the oncoming car and offered his thumb. Sunlight glared on the windshield. Only at the last moment did he manage to get a look at the driver. A woman. That was that. So much for feeling lucky.

When he saw the brake lights flash on, he figured the woman was slowing down to be safe. When he saw the car stop, he figured this would be the 'big tease.' He was used to it. The car stops, you run to it, then off it shoots, throwing dust in your face. He wouldn't fall for it this time. He'd walk casually toward the car.

When he saw the backup lights come on, he couldn't believe his luck.

The car rolled backward to him. The woman inside leaned across the front seat and opened the door.

'Can I give you a ride?'

'Sure can.' He jumped in and threw his seabag onto the rear seat. When he closed the door, cold air struck him. It seemed to freeze the sweat on his T-shirt. It felt fine. 'I'm mighty glad to see you,' he said. 'You're a real lifesaver.'

'How on earth did you get way out here?' she asked, starting again up the road.

'You wouldn't believe it.'

'Go ahead and try me.'

He enjoyed her cheerfulness and felt guilty about the slight nervous tremor he heard in her voice. 'Well, this fella gives me a lift. Just this side of Blythe. And he's driving along through this . . . this *desert* . . . when suddenly he stops and tells me to get out and take a look at one of the tires. I get out – and off he goes! Tosses my seabag out a ways up the road. Don't know why a fella wants to do something like that. You understand what I mean?'

'I certainly do. These days you don't know who to trust.'

'If that ain't the truth.'

He looked at her. She wore boots and jeans and a faded blue shirt, but she had class. It was written all over her. The way she talked, the way her skin was tanned just so, the way she wore her hair. Even her figure showed class. Nothing overdone.

'What I don't get,' he went on, 'is why the fella picked me up in the first place.'

'He might have been lonely.'

'Then why'd he dump me?'

'Maybe he decided not to trust you. Or maybe he just wanted to be alone again.'

'Any way you slice it, it was a rotten thing to do. You understand what I mean?'

'I think so. Where are you headed?'

'Tucson.'

'Fine. I'm going in that direction.'

'How come you're not on the main highway? What are you doing out here?'

'Well . . .' She laughed nervously. 'What I'm intending to do is not . . . well, not exactly legal.'

'Yeah?'

'I'm going to steal cacti.'

'What!' He laughed. 'Wow! You mean you're out to lift some cactuses?'

'That's what I mean.'

'Well, I sure hope you don't get caught!'

The woman forced a smile. 'There *is* a fine.'

'Gol-ly.'

'A sizable fine.'

'Well, I'd be glad to give you a hand.'

'I've only got one shovel.'

'Yeah. I saw it when I stowed my bag. I was wondering what you had a shovel for.' He looked at her, laughing, and felt good that this woman with all her class was going to steal a few plants from the desert. 'I've seen a lot of things, you understand. But never a cactus-napper.' He laughed at his joke.

She didn't. 'You've seen one now,' she said.

They remained silent for a while. The young man thought about this classy woman driving down a lonely road in the desert just to swipe cactus, and every now and then he chuckled about it. He wondered why anybody would want such a thing in the first place. Why take the desert home with you? He wanted nothing more than to get away from this desolate place, and for the life of him he couldn't understand a person wanting to take part of it home. He concluded that the woman must be crazy.

'Would you care for some lunch?' the crazy woman asked. She still sounded nervous.

'Sure, I guess so.'

'There should be a paper bag on the floor behind you. It has a couple of sandwiches in it, and some beer. Do you like beer?'

'Are you kidding?' He reached over the back of the seat and picked up the bag. The sandwiches smelled good. 'Why don't you pull off the road up there?' he suggested. 'We can go over by those rocks and have a picnic.'

'That sounds like a fine idea.' She stopped on a wide shoulder.

'Better take us a bit farther back. We don't wanta park this close to the road. Not if you want me to help you heist some cactus when we get done with lunch.'

She glanced at him uneasily, then smiled. 'Okay, fine. We'll do just that.'

The car bumped forward, weaving around large balls of

cactus, crashing through undergrowth. It finally stopped behind a cluster of rocks.

'Do you think they can still see us from the road?' the woman asked. Her voice was shaking.

'I don't think so.'

When they opened the doors, heat blasted in on them. They got out, the young man carrying the bag of sandwiches and beer. He sat down on a large rock. The woman sat beside him.

'I hope you like the sandwiches. They're corned beef with Swiss cheese.'

'Sounds good.' He handed one of them to her and opened the beer. The cans were only cool, but he decided that cool beer was better than no beer at all. As he picked at the cellophane covering his sandwich, he asked, 'Where's your husband?'

'What do you mean?'

He smiled. It had really put her on the spot. 'Well, I just happened to see that you aren't wearing a ring, you understand what I mean?'

She looked down at the band of pale skin on her third finger. 'We're separated.'

'Oh? How come?'

'I found out that he'd been cheating on me.'

'On *you*? No kidding! He must have been crazy.'

'Not crazy. He just enjoyed hurting people. But I'll tell you something. Cheating on me was the worst mistake he ever made.'

They ate in silence for a while, the young man occasionally shaking his head with disbelief. Finally, his head stopped shaking. He decided that maybe he'd cheat too on a grown woman who gets her kicks stealing cactus. Good looks aren't everything. Who wants to live with a crazy woman? He drank off his beer. The last of it was warm and made him shiver.

He went to the car and took the shovel from the floor in the back. 'You want to come along? Pick out the ones you want and I'll dig them up for you.'

He watched her wad up the cellophane and stuff it, along with the empty beer cans, into the paper bag. She put the bag in the car, smiling at him and saying, 'Every litter bit hurts.'

They left the car behind. They walked side by side, the woman glancing about, sometimes crouching to inspect a likely cactus.

'You must think I'm rather strange,' she confided, 'picking up a hitchhiker like I did. I hope you don't think . . . well, it was criminal of that man to leave you out in the middle of nowhere. But I'm glad I picked you up. For some reason, I feel I can talk to you.'

'That's nice. I like to listen. What about this one?' he asked, pointing at a huge prickly cactus.

'Too big. What I want is something smaller.'

'This one ought to fit in the trunk.'

'I'd rather have a few smaller ones,' she insisted. 'Besides, there's a kind in the Saguaro National Monument that I want to get. It'll probably be pretty big. I want to save the trunk for that one.'

'Anything you say.'

They walked farther. Soon, the car was out of sight. The sun felt like a hot, heavy band pressing down on the young man's head and back.

'How about this one?' he asked, pointing. 'It's pretty little.'

'Yes. This one is just about perfect.'

The woman knelt beside it. Her shirt was dark blue against her perspiring back, and a slight breeze rustled her hair.

This will be a good way to remember her, the young man thought as he crashed the shovel down on her head.

He buried her beside the cactus.

As he drove down the road, he thought about her. She had been a nice woman with obvious class. Crazy, but nice. Her husband must've been a nut to cheat on a good-looking woman like her, unless of course it was because of her craziness.

He thought it nice that she had told him so much about herself. It felt good to be trusted with secrets.

He wondered how far she would have driven him. Not far enough. It was much better having the car to himself. That way he didn't have to worry. And the $36 he found in her purse was a welcome bonus. He'd been afraid, for a moment, that he might find nothing but credit cards. All around, she had been a good find. He felt very lucky.

At least until the car began to move sluggishly. He pulled off the road and got out. 'Oh, no,' he muttered, seeing the flat rear tire. He leaned back against the side of the car and groaned. The sun beat on his face. He closed his eyes and shook his head, disgusted by the situation and thinking how awful it would be, working on the tire for fifteen minutes under that hot sun.

Then he heard, in the distance, the faint sound of a motor. Opening his eyes, he squinted down the road. A car was approaching. For a moment, he considered thumbing a ride. But that, he decided, would be stupid now that he had a car of his own. He closed his eyes again to wait for the car to pass.

But it didn't pass. It stopped.

He opened his eyes and gasped.

'Afternoon,' the stranger called out.

'Howdy, Officer,' he said, his heart thudding.

'You got a spare?'

'I think so.'

'What do you mean, you think so? You either have a spare or you don't.'

'What I meant was, I'm not sure if it's any good. It's been a while since I've had any use for it, you understand?'

'Of course I understand. Guess I'll stick around till we find out. This is rough country. A person can die out here. If the spare's no good, I'll radio for a tow.'

'Okay, thanks.' He opened the door and took the keys from the ignition.

Everything's okay, he told himself. No reason in the world for this cop to suspect anything.

'Did you go off the road back a ways?'

'No, why?' Even as he asked, he fumbled the keys. They fell to the ground. The other man picked them up.

'Flats around here, they're usually caused by cactus spines. They're murder.'

He followed the officer to the rear of the car.

The octagonal key didn't fit the trunk.

'Don't know why those dopes in Detroit don't just make one key that'll fit the door and trunk both.'

'I don't know,' the young man said, matching the other's tone of disgust and feeling even more confident.

The round key fit. The trunk popped open.

The officer threw a tarp onto the ground and then leveled his pistol at the young man, who was staring at the body of a middle-aged man who obviously had class.

The Mask

The Palace Theater screened a different horror classic every Saturday at midnight. Allan Hunter hadn't missed one in over a year. Tonight, he'd watched the original *Nosferatu* with Max Schreck.

Though he owned a car, he'd always made the two-mile journey from his apartment to the Palace afoot. The trip *to* the theater was enjoyable, but it was the return trip that he craved. He knew there were dangers. A more sensible man would drive to and from the movies rather than risk a mugging, or worse. But if he drove, safe and insulated inside his car, he knew he would miss the thrill.

For Allan relished the mysteries of the night.

Apartment windows enticed him. If dark, who slept within? Or who didn't sleep, but lay awake or made love or stood at the black windows, peering out, perhaps watching him wander by? If still aglow in the deep hours of the night, who was about inside, doing what?

The shops and stores along the way, locked and deserted, intrigued him. If their fronts were barricaded by iron gates, all the better. The accordion gates tantalized Allan. They whispered of the owner's fear. He often stopped and peered through them, wondering what needed such protection through the night.

Each time a car swept past Allan on the quiet streets, he tried to glimpse who was in it, and he wondered, going where? People heading home after work, after a late film or party? A lover on his way to a rendezvous? A wife fleeing her brutal husband? A maniac on the prowl for his next victim? Often when a car went by, he imagined that its brake lights might suddenly flash on, that it might swing to the curb in front of him, that its door might fly open and someone call to him – or leap out and rush him. Just *thinking* about that gave Allan goosebumps.

And so did thinking about what might lurk in the dark spaces along his route: recessed entryways and those narrow gaps he encountered where two buildings didn't quite join – and alleys. Such places gave him a delicious tingle. He always quickened his pace to get past them. Often he couldn't force himself to glance in, appalled by the possibilities of what he might find. Derelicts, or worse.

There *were* derelicts abroad. Some slept in entryways, or on bus-stop benches. Some, curled in shadows, glared at him as he hurried by. Others shambled along the sidewalks or down the streets, clutching secret prizes. Or trudged behind rattling supermarket carts piled high with bizarre shapes. Allan found no magic, no excitement, in contemplating such wrecks. They scared him, disgusted him. They hardly seemed human at all.

They were the worst thing about walking home after the midnight movies.

Whenever possible, he crossed the street or even backtracked to avoid confronting one. But sometimes he was caught by surprise and had no choice but to endure the stench, the maniacal jibbering, the whiny plea for money.

With such mad, vile creatures lurking in the night, it was little wonder that Allan rarely encountered normal people during his treks home from the movies.

Most of those he saw were in the midst of rushing to or from their parked cars. Occasionally, he spotted someone walking a dog. Once in a great while, a pair of joggers. Never a jogger out by himself, always with a companion. Sometimes a lone man hurrying along. Almost never a woman.

No woman in her right mind, he thought, would wander about the city alone at this hour.

When the woman came into sight as he walked home after *Nosferatu*, he thought she must be mad – or wildly reckless. Even though she was a block away, he could see she was no derelict. Her stride was too steady as she approached the corner. Her hair, silvery in the streetlight, looked trim and well groomed. She wore a pale blouse, shorts that reached almost to her knees, white socks and dark shoes.

Certainly not a derelict.

A prostitute? Allan had never encountered any prostitutes in this neighborhood. And wouldn't a streetwalker be dressed in something exotic or scanty?

This woman looked more like a co-ed who'd wandered too far from campus. Or like one of the young teachers at the high school where he taught – Shelly Gates or Maureen O'Toole, for instance. Or like some of the women he liked to watch when he made his weekly trips to the supermarket. Casually dressed, trim and neat and clean.

Allan realized that he had stopped walking.

How strange to see someone like her roaming about at this hour!

She had come to a halt at the street corner, her head turned away. She seemed to be checking for traffic, preparing to cross the intersection.

But then she turned around.

She had no face. Allan's heart slammed.

What's wrong with her!

She walked briskly toward him.

No face!

He glanced at the street, tempted to race across and escape. But when he looked at the stranger again, she was closer. Close enough for him to see the shimmer of fabric that draped her face. Silver, glossy. It hung from her forehead, slotted with holes for her eyes and mouth, and fluttered below her chin.

A mask!

Allan heard himself moan. Chills chased up his back. His scalp prickled.

He leaped off the sidewalk and sprinted for the other side of the street.

What if she comes after me?

He sprang over the curb, dodged a parking meter, and looked back.

She had stopped. Her head was turned his way.

She's watching me. Oh God, she's watching me. But at least she's staying put.

Allan swung his eyes to the sidewalk and hurried for the corner. He didn't want to see her again, but in his mind she was crossing the street, pursuing him. He had to look again.

Checking over his shoulder, he saw her still standing motionless, still watching him.

At the corner, he rushed to the left. A few strides, and the wall of a Wells Fargo bank sheltered him from the stranger's view. He slowed and caught his breath.

Safe.

'Christ,' he muttered.

He'd walked the night streets countless times, seen his share of weird derelicts, watched hundreds of horror films, read scores of fright books.

But he'd never been spooked like this.

Spooked? Scared nearly witless.

By a piece of silver cloth no bigger than a hanky.

As he walked along, he began to feel ashamed of himself. What a coward, running like that. The woman had looked perfectly normal except for the mask. And the mask itself had been nothing hideous. A simple square of fabric. Possibly silk. Nothing to inspire panic.

She's *gotta* be a nut case, going around like that.

Nothing wrong with running away from a lunatic.

But what if she's sane? What if she only wears the mask

because her face is disfigured? She walks at night when there's almost nobody around to see her, and wears her mask just in case. In case someone like me comes along. So her face won't gross me out.

And I ran away as if she were a monster.

What an awful life she must live. And I came along and made it worse.

Good going.

Allan considered turning around, going back and searching for her. But he didn't have the nerve.

He couldn't get the woman out of his mind. He thought about her constantly: that night as he lay in bed; Sunday as he corrected papers, labored on his vampire novel, read and watched television; all week long. At school, every slender, blonde student in his classes reminded him of her. So did two of the teachers, Shelly and Maureen, even though Maureen was a redhead. They all forced him to remember the woman in the mask, and his shame.

The more he thought of her, the more certain he grew that she wasn't crazy. She was a sensitive young woman cursed with a hideous face. She led a solitary, lonely life, willing to venture from her home only in the dead of night, and then with her face concealed.

He could imagine the anguish she must've felt when he fled from her.

If only he had held his ground. Smiled as she approached. Said, 'Good evening.' It was too late for that, however. The most he would ever be able to do was apologize for adding to her misery.

To do that, he would need to find her again.

But he'd spotted her some time after 1 a.m. That's when he would need to go looking. If he tried it on a school night, he'd be wasted the next day. He had to wait for the weekend.

At last, Friday arrived. Allan awoke feeling nervous and excited. Tonight, he would go out searching for her.

What would he say if he found her? How would she react? She might hate him for running away. *How could you do that, you bastard! I'm a human being, not a freak!*

Or she might indeed, after all, turn out to be utterly mad.

'Is something bothering you?' Shelly asked him during lunch.

'Me? No.'

'Are you sure? You've been acting strange all week.'

'I have?'

Shelly glanced at Maureen. 'You've noticed it, haven't you?'

Maureen, who rarely spoke, studied her sandwich and shook her head. 'He seems fine to me.'

'It might help to talk about it,' Shelly told him. 'You aren't sick, are you?'

'I feel fine.'

'If it's too personal . . .'

'Leave him alone,' Maureen said. 'He doesn't want to talk about it.'

'You *have* noticed!'

Maureen shrugged. Her eyes met Allan's. 'You don't have to say anything. It's none of our business.'

'Of course it's our business. We're his buddies. Right, Allan?'

He smiled. 'My buds. Right. I do appreciate your concern, really. Thanks. But it's nothing. I'm just a little bit nervous about this gal I'll be seeing tonight.'

'Ah-ha!' Shelly's eyes gleamed. 'A gal! Go for it, Romeo!'

'That's wonderful,' Maureen said.

'Anybody we know?' Shelly asked.

'*I* don't even know her. Not exactly. She's just somebody I met last weekend. At the movies. She sat across the aisle from me. We didn't even talk. But if she's there tonight . . .'

'Whoa!' Shelly held up her hand. 'Hold on. One second. She was at that midnight creepshow thing you go to on Saturday nights? And you don't know her? So where do you think you'll find her tonight?'

Allan felt heat wash over his face. This is what comes of lying, he thought. He shook his head and forced himself to laugh. 'Geez, I don't know. Guess I *won't* be seeing her tonight. You're right.'

'Boy, you must have it bad. You don't even know what day it is.' She nudged Maureen with her elbow. 'Looks like we've got a case of love at first sight.'

'I don't even know her,' Allan protested.

'She must be quite a fox.'

'Quit teasing him,' Maureen said. 'Let him eat his lunch.'

Shelly laughed. 'So what's she got that we ain't got?'

No face, Allan thought.

But he only shrugged. Then Jake Hanson came to their table and the conversation turned to obnoxious students, as it often did. When the bell rang and Allan got up from the table, Shelly said, 'Hey, good luck with the fox. Don't do anything I wouldn't do.'

Allan headed for his fifth-period class, wishing he'd kept his mouth shut.

Finally, the school day ended. On the way home, he stopped off at Blockbuster Video and picked up six tapes. Horror movies. Two of which he hadn't already seen. They would help pass the time.

He ran one during supper, but his mind was on the masked woman. He hardly noticed the movie. Then he tried to work on his vampire novel, but gave up after an hour. As he sat in his recliner to watch the next movie, he thought, What's the use? I might as well stare at the wall.

And then he had a very welcome thought.

It came in the form of Shelly's voice saying, 'So where do you think you'll find her tonight?'

Shelly was right.

Why get all worked up when I probably won't find her tonight, anyway? We ran into each other on *Saturday* night. Why not wait for then?

Yes!

I'll stay home tonight, enjoy my movies, go to bed at a reasonable hour . . .

The feeling of relief was immense.

Then Saturday arrived. The hours crept by. He told himself that he didn't *have* to approach the masked woman. He could take a different route home from the theater, and avoid her. For that matter, he could stay home.

And miss the midnight showing of *The Cabinet of Dr Caligari*? He'd already seen the film six or seven times. A shame not to watch it again, though. He could always drive his car.

No. I'll walk. I'll take my usual route. If I see her, I'll apologize. And that will be the end of it.

After supper that night, he sat in his recliner and watched *The Texas Chainsaw Massacre*, then *I Spit on Your Grave*. For minutes at a time, he was able to forget about the masked woman. When the movies were over, he took a shower. He shaved. He combed his hair and splashed some Chaps on his cheeks. Instead of wearing his favorite outfit for the midnight show – old blue jeans and his Bates Motel T-shirt – he put on a good pair of Dockers and a plaid sports shirt.

In the bedroom mirror, he shook his head at himself.

What the hell am I doing? You'd think I really *did* have a date.

Hey, maybe she won't recognize me dressed up like this. She couldn't have gotten a very good look at my face.

At a quarter past eleven, he left his apartment. He gave his parked car a long look as he walked by it.

So much easier if I just drive.

He couldn't.

He had to make an attempt to find her.

Tense and shaky, he walked to the Palace. He usually bought nachos and a Pepsi at the refreshment counter. But tonight he had no appetite. He took his seat. He glanced about at the familiar crowd, fearing that *she* might've come to watch the movie. Then the lights dimmed. He rubbed his sweaty hands on the legs of his trousers, and faced the screen.

The Cabinet of Dr Caligari began.

He stared at it. But in his mind, he saw the masked woman. Saw himself approaching her. What if she's bonkers? What if she's dangerous? What if she lifts the mask to show me her face and it's horrible? Worse than anything ever created by Tom Savini or Stan Winston? Worse than the ugliest fantasies of Clive Barker?

He tried to calm himself.

Maybe she won't show up.

He had never run into her before. Last Saturday night could have been a fluke. She might've been out on a special errand, or something.

Maybe I'll never see her again.

As much as he dreaded the encounter, however, he found himself troubled by the idea of never seeing her again. It was more than a need to set matters right. He'd known that all along, he supposed.

She frightened him, but he longed to learn her secrets.

All the mysteries of the night, so eerie and tantalizing, seemed banal compared to the woman in the mask. She was the ultimate mystery.

Mad or sane? What lurks beneath the mask? What possesses her to walk the empty streets? Does she have a tortured soul? What stories might she tell of children shrieking at the sight of her, of heartless abuse, of solitary years locked away from daylight? How does it feel to be shunned?

He could learn the answers.

Tonight.

The lights came up.

Allan walked into the night. By the time he'd walked a block, he was alone.

His mouth was dry. His heart thudded. His legs trembled.

He gave no thought to the windows above the street, barely glanced through the accordion gates of the closed shops, paid no attention to passing cars, looked into dark entryways and the gaps between buildings and the alleys for no reason other than to search for her. As he hurried along, he noticed a few derelicts. He saw them, felt neither fear nor disgust, and turned his eyes away to look for the masked woman.

Finally, he came to the block where he'd encountered her. The sidewalk stretched ahead of him, deserted. He slowed his pace. He gazed at the corner.

Where are you?

Maybe I'm early. No. If anything, *Cabinet* was five or six minutes longer than *Nosferatu*. Maybe I'm too late, then.

But if she'd come this way, we should've run into each other already.

Maybe she stayed home tonight. Or chose a different route.

He stopped. It was just about here that he'd been halted by the sight of her. She'd appeared from the right, walked to the corner and turned her back to him as if intending to cross the street. It was here that he'd been standing when she turned around.

He waited.

Dribbles of sweat slid down his sides.

I ought to just keep walking. If she doesn't show, she doesn't show.

He checked his wristwatch. One twenty-eight.

Give her five minutes.

When he looked up from his watch, she was already past the corner and striding toward him.

He gasped and staggered backward.

Cool it! he told himself. This is it. You wanted to see her, here she is.

The silver fabric shrouding her face shimmered and swayed as she walked. Her hair gleamed in the streetlights. Instead of shorts and a blouse like last week, she wore a dress. It looked purple and shiny. It hung from her shoulders by narrow straps, draped the swells of her breasts, tapered down to a sash at her waist, flared out at her hips and drifted against her striding thighs. It was very short. Her legs looked long and sleek. She wore sandals, not shoes and socks.

Allan's heart thundered.

She's gorgeous! Except for that damn mask. What horrors did *it* conceal?

She must be mad. No sane woman would walk these streets at such an hour – and *not* in a dress like that!

Don't just stand here, gaping at her.

He started walking toward her.

Her sandals made soft clapping sounds on the concrete. Her skirt briefly took on the shape of each thigh that swept against it. The ends of the sash swung by her side. The silken fabric clinging to her breasts trembled and jiggled.

Maybe she is a whore, after all.

If so, she might wear the mask merely to conceal her identity. Or to make her look enigmatic. Her face might not be ghastly, after all.

Now, only a few strides separated Allan from the woman.

In the darkness behind the mask's eye slots, he could see nothing except mere specks of reflected light. A vague hint of lips showed through the slot at her mouth.

I've got to say something. Apologize. At least.

He was walking straight toward her, so he angled to his right.

Her head turned.

He managed a smile.

They passed each other.

He breathed in her perfume. A scent so strange and delicious it forced him to sigh, to look back at her.

She halted as if she felt his gaze.

'Excuse me?' he said. Damn, but he sounded like a scared kid!

She turned around.

'Do you remember me?' he asked.

'Oh, yes.' Her voice was low, breathy. In spite of the narrow gap at her mouth, it stirred the mask like a soft breeze.

'I . . . I guess I kind of . . . lost my cool last week. I'm really glad you came along.' He shrugged. 'I wanted to apologize.'

'Apologize? For running from me?' she asked.

'I'm really sorry.'

'What's your name?'

He hesitated. 'Allan.'

'Allan what?'

She wants my *last* name? Good God, she'd be able to look me up, find me. 'Hawthorne,' he lied. 'Allan Hawthorne.'

She stepped toward him, mask and dress glimmering, and reached out her hand. Allan shook it. But when he tried to let go, her fingers tightened. She held him in a firm, warm grip. 'I'm Ligeia,' she said.

The name surprised him. 'Really? Ligeia? There's a story by Poe . . .'

'I know,' she said in her strange, hushed voice.

'I really like Poe.'

'We have that in common, then. Come with me.' She pulled him by the hand. And kept his hand in hers as she led him slowly down the sidewalk.

'Uh . . . Where are we going?'

'Does it matter?'

'I don't know.'

'You're free to leave, if that's your wish.'

'No. No, that's okay.'

She nodded slightly, then turned her head forward.

Allan hoped to see under her mask, but it curved around the

side of her face, hiding her almost to the ear. It hung from a headband, a folded scarf that was tied at the back. The way the silver cloth was tucked in over the top of the scarf, it flowed down smoothly except for a slight bump made by the tip of her nose. Her chin didn't seem to touch the draping fabric at all.

They walked in silence for a while.

He wished she would say something.

Finally, he broke the silence himself. 'I really felt awful about running away.'

She stopped and turned toward him. 'It was this,' she said. Her other hand came up. Her fingertips glided down the glossy mask, easing it inward. Ever so briefly as the fingers slid down, the mask took on the contours of her face. Though her eyes remained hidden, Allan glimpsed a veiled suggestion of slender nose and cheeks. Her lips appeared for an instant, bare in the opening. Her fingers drifted the fabric against a small bulge of chin. Then she breathed. The hints of her face dissolved behind a silver tremor.

Allan tried to swallow. He wished his heart would slow down.

'I frighten you, don't I?'

'A little,' he whispered. 'I guess.'

'We fear the unknown,' she said. 'But we're enthralled by it.'

'Yes.'

'Do I enthrall you, Allan?'

He let out a small, nervous laugh. 'I don't know. You sure . . . make me curious.'

'You wonder what the mask hides.'

'Yes. And . . . and why you walk around at an hour like this.'

'So I won't be seen.'

'But why?'

'My face, of course. Come along.' She turned away, pulling at his hand, and they resumed walking. 'I like the night,' she said. 'It holds such secrets.'

'But its dangerous.'

'Not for me. The mask protects me. People keep their distance. They take me for a madwoman.'

'I guess . . . I was afraid of that, myself.'

'I know.'

'You're not, though.'

'You don't think so?'

'Hope not.'

Laughing softly, she squeezed his hand. 'I think I like you, Allan.'

'I think I like you, too.'

'Shall we be friends?'

'Sure,' he said.

She looked at him. '*Are* you sure?'

'Yeah. I mean, why not?'

'You're still frightened of me, aren't you?'

'A little, maybe.'

'I won't hurt you.'

'It's just . . . you know, the mask. If I could see your face . . . Is it . . . is something wrong with it?'

'My face is my own.'

'How can we be friends if you're hiding behind a mask, if you won't let me see what you look like?'

She gave no answer, but led him into an alley. His mouth went dry. His heart slammed. As they left the lights of the street behind, he peered into the darkness. High walls on both sides. Dumpsters ahead. But no lurking derelicts that he could see. Though the alley appeared deserted, he trembled with dread and excitement.

Ligeia halted. She put her hands on his shoulders.

'Is my face *so* important?' she asked.

Oh, God! She's going to take off the mask. Now. Right here in the alley. In the dark.

'Is it?' she asked again.

'Uh. I guess not. Not really.'

'You said we can't be friends unless you know what I look like.'

'That isn't quite what . . .'

'Suppose I'm not pretty? Would you run from me again?'

'No.'

'Suppose I'm horribly ugly?'

'Is that why you wear the mask?'

'Perhaps.' Gently, she rubbed his shoulders. 'How important is my face to you, Allan? Does it need to be beautiful? Or can you accept me without . . . passing judgement on it?'

He managed to whisper, 'Yes.'

'Yes what?'

'I don't need to see.'

She glided forward, wrapped her arms around Allan and drew him close against her. He felt the heat of her body, the push of her breasts, the cool smoothness of the mask against his face. Her lips met his mouth.

Her lips felt wonderful. Warm and moist.

So long since the last time he'd held and kissed a woman. The feel of her shocked him with desire.

But she *must* be hideous, or why . . .?

He didn't care. She smelled of strange, jungle blossoms. Her sweet breath filled him. He slid his tongue into her mouth and she sucked it in deep and writhed against him, rubbing him with her sleek body as her hands clutched his back.

His own hands roamed Ligeia's back, caressing the skin above the top of her dress, roaming lower, sliding the fabric against her, following her curves down past the sash. He filled his hands with the soft, firm mounds of her buttocks. And knew they were bare beneath the fragile veil of the skirt. Moaning into her mouth, he pulled the skirt up.

Ligeia grabbed his wrists. She forced his hands down to his sides and leaned away, shaking her head. She breathed hard. The mask clung around her mouth, wet.

'What's wrong?' Allan whispered.

'Nothing. You're . . . I've got to leave now.'

He took a step toward her. She stopped him, hands against his chest.

'I'm sorry,' she said. 'Perhaps we'll see each other again.' She backed away from him.

'Don't go.'

Without another word, she whirled and fled.

The moment she vanished from sight, Allan ran to the mouth of the alley. He spotted her to the right, dashing up the sidewalk, her shimmering dress afly, her arms pumping, her long bare legs striding out, her sandals clapping the concrete.

'Ligeia!' he cried out.

She didn't look back.

What if I never see her again?

Maybe that'd be for the best, he told himself. What sort of relationship could we have, anyway? She has to wear that mask. Too grotesque to go anywhere without it.

I'd be better off . . .

She darted around the corner.

'No!' he yelled into the night, and sprinted after her.

The hell with the mask, he thought as he raced up the sidewalk. Who gives a shit! Who gives a shit *what* she looks like!

He ran harder than he'd ever run before.

Pounded around the corner.

Skidded to a halt when he saw her no more than fifty feet away.

Obviously, she hadn't thought he would pursue her. She was walking slowly, head down, arms swaying limp at her sides, sandals scuffing along. She seemed lost in her thoughts, crushed by a burden of dejection.

Ligeia, Allan thought. What have I done to you?

He ached to rush forward and take her into his arms and make everything all right.

That might only make matters worse.

Is she upset because I got carried away in the alley? *She's* the one who started it. And that dress! Nothing on under it. What did she expect?

Maybe that isn't it. Suppose she's falling in love with me and knows it can't work. Maybe that's why she fled.

Whatever the reason, she was probably in no mood for Allan to put in an appearance.

He couldn't just walk away, though.

So he decided to follow her. He crept closer to the building fronts, ready to duck out of sight if she should start to turn around, and made his way forward, matching her pace.

Find out where she lives, he thought. She's bound to head for home, sooner or later.

He felt guilty, sneaking after her. Spying on her. It seemed like a betrayal. But he kept at it, knowing that if he quit he might lose her forever.

It went well for two blocks.

Then she stopped at a street corner. Though there seemed to be no traffic, she stood and waited for the light to change. As Allan watched, she began to turn around. He rushed forward, dodged into an entry way and stepped on the ankle of a derelict huddled in the darkness. The filthy old man flinched, moaned. With a gasp, Allan lurched away from him and staggered into the middle of the sidewalk.

He jerked his head forward, spotted Ligeia at the corner.

Facing him.

'Ligeia!' he called. 'Please!'

She flung herself around and leapt into the street. Without checking for traffic.

'Look out!' Allan cried.

The teenager bearing down on her yelped. Ligeia tried to lean out of his way. The teenager swerved, but not in time.

The bicycle slammed into her, tumbled her to the pavement,

twisted away and hit the curb, its abrupt stop hurling the kid against the handlebars.

Ligeia, sprawled in the street, started to push herself up.

As Allan ran to help, the kid jumped from his bicycle, let it fall, and hurried toward Ligeia. She was crouched, trying to stand, her back to him. 'Geez, lady. You okay?'

She looked over her shoulder at him. Her mask gleamed in the streetlights.

'Yeeeah!' he gasped, and bolted for his bike.

Even before he got to it, Ligeia was up and running. The kid started to pick up his bike, but dropped it and scampered out of the way when he saw Allan bearing down on him.

Allan hurdled the rear wheel.

Ligeia had already made the other side of the street.

'Wait!' he called.

She didn't look back, didn't slow down.

She was fast. Not as fast as Allan, but almost. It took all his speed to gain on her.

'Please! Stop!'

She *had* to be hurting. A patch of skin over her right shoulder blade was scraped raw. Her skirt was torn, and drooped away from the scuffed cheek of her buttock. Her pumping arms showed Allan abraded elbows. Her whole body must be afire with pain.

'Why are you *doing* this?' he gasped.

'Leave me alone!' she cried out.

'No! You need me! I need you!'

'You . . . don't *know* me!'

'I know you're lonely. I know I *care* about you. We can't lose each other. Please.'

'You'll hate me!'

'Bullshit!'

'I'm . . .'

'I don't give a flying fuck if you look like Godzilla!'

Reaching out, he grabbed her left arm. She tried to twist free

184

of his grip. 'Stop that!' he snapped. And tugged her to a halt. Turned her roughly toward him.

Clutching both her upper arms, he pushed her backward and pinned her against the accordion gate of a pharmacy. It rattled as she hit it.

'Settle down.'

She quit struggling. She gasped for air. Her breath gusted out the front of her mask.

'Are you okay?' he asked.

She shook her head.

'You shouldn't have run.'

'Obviously.'

The remark made his throat tighten. He drew Ligeia gently against him. And her arms wrapped around him. He pressed his face against the mask, felt her cheek through its slick fabric. They held each other for a long time.

Then Ligeia whispered, 'I don't want to lose you so soon. Before we've even . . .'

'You won't.'

'You haven't seen my face.'

'It doesn't matter.'

'Think so, huh?' She squeezed Allan hard against her, then eased him away. 'I . . . I've got to show you.'

He nodded. He felt as if his heart might crash out through his ribcage. 'You don't have to.'

'I do. Better that you see it now, than . . .' Ligeia quit without finishing. She raised her hand to the headband across her brow. Hooked it with her fingertips. Peeled it back. The mask slid up her face.

More than her mask was coming off.

Her hair, too.

Oh God!

Her arm dropped to her side, mask and wig clutched in her fist.

Allan gaped at her.

She stared at him. She caught her lower lip between her teeth. After a few moments, she said, 'At least I'm not Godzilla.'

She let the mask and wig fall. Reaching up with both hands, she unpinned her hair. She shook her head, ran her fingers through the flowing red tresses. Her green eyes shimmered with tears.

'Maureen?'

'Don't hate me,' she said in the voice he knew so well, a voice so different from the breathy tones of Ligeia. 'Please.'

'How could I hate you? But I don't . . . Why? Why the mask? What's going on?'

'I just got tired of the buddy treatment, Allan.' A tear fell from the corner of each eye. They made silver trails down her cheeks. 'Day in, day out. You never . . . I'm not your buddy. I never wanted to *be* your buddy. So maybe it made me a little crazy and . . .'

'A lot crazy. Something might've happened to you, wandering around at night like this.'

She sniffed and rubbed away the tears. 'I just wanted you to notice me.'

'God, Maureen.'

'I wanted to show you that I'm a woman.'

His throat tightened. 'I always knew you were a woman. But it never entered my mind that you might want to . . . get involved with me. You never said anything. You never gave me any reason to suspect it.'

'I know. I know. I wanted to. I just couldn't. But then . . . I guess it was seeing *Phantom of the Opera* a few weeks ago that gave me the idea. I thought, what if he doesn't realize it's me? What if I'm a stranger he meets in the night? A mysterious, seductive masked woman. The way you're into spooky stuff, I figured it might work.'

'It sure worked, all right.'

'Too well, I guess. Back in the alley, I just couldn't . . . let it go any further. It wouldn't have been right. It wasn't me you wanted. It was Ligeia. Not plain old ordinary me.'

'She was . . . the most exciting woman I ever . . . She was fantastic.'

'I guess you must be awfully disappointed.'

'I don't know. I suppose so. It was the mystery, you know? It was the unknown and being afraid of who she was, what she might look like under the mask. Now that it's you . . .'

'It was always me.'

'Yeah, but . . .'

'It was. It *is*. I *am* Ligeia.' Crouching, she picked up the mask and wig. She put them on and took hold of Allan's hand.

'I don't think that'll work.'

'Won't it?' she asked, her voice low and breathy.

'I know it's you.'

'Do you?'

'Of course.'

'You know nothing.'

Allan felt a chill crawl up his spine.

She led him along the sidewalk. 'Maureen is a spineless, pitiful creature of the light. I despise her.'

'Hey, come on. You don't have to do this.'

'I belong to the night.'

'Cut it out, okay? I'm *glad* you're Maureen.'

'I'm *not* Maureen. Call me again by that vile name at your peril.'

'Oh, for godsake.'

She pulled him into the darkness of an alley. She pushed him against a brick wall.

'This is ridiculous,' he muttered, his voice trembling. 'Let's get out of here.'

She lifted his hands to her breasts. He felt them, warm and firm through the slick fabric. She rubbed his palms against her stiff nipples.

'You're making me nervous. I wish you'd stop this. We're gonna have to look each other in the face, Monday morning.'

'You won't be looking *me* in the face. I'm Ligeia.'

'Come on, we both know you're not.'

She released his wrists. 'Lift my mask,' she whispered.

His heart kicked. 'What for?'

'You'll see.'

'I don't need to see. I know who you are.'

'Then why are you afraid to lift the mask?'

'You already took it off.'

'That was in the light. I am a woman of the darkness.'

He tried to laugh. 'You're pretty good at this. But I think we oughta get going.'

'I showed you Maureen. I didn't allow you to see Ligeia. The true face of Ligeia shuns the light. But you may look upon it now, if you have the courage.'

'I'm not afraid.'

'Then lift the mask.'

He stared at the fabric draping her face, tried to see her eyes and mouth behind the black slots. 'I know it's you,' he murmured. But he thought, *What if it's not?*

Ridiculous. Crazy.

But he couldn't force himself to lift the mask.

'Who am I?' she asked, her breath stirring the cloth.

'Ligeia.'

'Yessss.' She pulled him forward against her.

They embraced, they kissed, they squirmed breathless as they caressed and explored each other. She winced once when Allan touched the scrape behind her shoulder. He whispered, 'I'm sorry' into the warm pit of her mouth. Then he was on his back on the alley pavement. Maureen straddling him, bare to the waist. As he squeezed her breasts, she sank down and impaled herself.

Afterward, she lay on top of him and kissed him through the mouth slot of her mask.

He sighed. He'd known Maureen for three years. Three years wasted, he thought. So much missed.

'I must leave you now,' she whispered.

'No. I'll walk you home. Or we could go to my apartment.'

'Not tonight, my darling.' She pushed herself up, and Allan sighed with a feeling of loss as he slid out of her. Standing, she raised the top of her dress and arranged the shoulder straps. 'Farewell.' She turned away.

'Hey! Don't leave!'

She ran from the alley.

Allan knocked on the door of Maureen's classroom ten minutes before the start of first period Monday morning.

'Come in.'

He entered. She pushed back her chair and stood up, smiling. She wore a sleeveless, yellow sundress. She looked radiant. The sight of her made Allan's heart race. How could he have known her so long and never realized how beautiful she was?

Her bright green eyes watched him as he approached her desk.

'Good morning, Ligeia,' he said.

'Huh? Ligeia?'

He grinned. 'Still up to your tricks.'

She frowned with confusion. 'What?'

'Saturday night was great. The greatest.'

'Oh? You got together with your mystery woman?'

'Sure did.'

'Must've gone pretty well.'

'You oughta know.'

Her frown deepened. 'How would I know?'

'How about having dinner with me tonight?'

The frown vanished. A corner of her mouth curled up. 'Are you kidding?'

'Not a chance.'

'What about this other gal of yours? Ligeia? You just met her, and now you want me to go out with you?'

'She won't mind.'

'She must be very understanding.'

'What she doesn't know won't hurt her. I don't think we'll be seeing each other again. Not till next Saturday night, anyway.'

'You some kind of a two-timer?'

'Yep.'

The door opened. A couple of students came in.

'Look,' Maureen said, 'we can talk about this later. I've gotta get the spelling list onto the board.'

'Fine.'

He turned away, nodded a greeting to the kids, and paused at the door.

He looked back.

Maureen, facing the chalkboard behind her desk, wrote 'fantasy' with her right hand. Her left arm hung at her side.

Allan stared at her elbow.

She looked back at him. She raised her eyebrows. 'Is something wrong?'

'Your elbow,' he murmured.

She smiled. 'Just had a little mishap over the weekend.' She rubbed the dark crust of scab, then turned again to the chalkboard.

Eats

I'm a trained investigator, so I knew right away that the dame who walked into my office had class. How did I know? She had blue hair on her head and a poodle tucked under one arm. I took my feet off my desk.

'My name is Mabel Wingate,' she said.

'Want me to stand up and cheer?' I asked through my mouthful of sandwich.

She tittered. 'Isn't he delightful!' She put the question to the pooch, chucking it under the chin. 'Do you think he might be good enough to share his sandwich?'

It was salami and Swiss on an onion roll with lettuce and onions and plenty of mayo. I'd just bought it at Lou's Deli down the block. I'd taken only one bite. I didn't want to part with it.

'This is my lunch, lady,' I said.

'You don't mind, do you?' she asked.

'Are you planning to hire me?'

'We shall see.'

I'm not an idiot. If I didn't fork over some of my sandwich to Snuggles or Snookums or whatever its name was, the old gal would find herself a different gumshoe. (I needed the work. Things had been slow lately, ever since I got on TV for plugging one of my clients. What can I say? Mistakes happen.)

'You don't watch much television, huh?' I asked.

'Please,' she said. 'The sandwich.'

'Oh, sure.' I set it down on my desk. She reached for it. 'Ah ah!' I snapped. 'Not the whole thing.'

'No, of course not. Excuse me.'

She waited, hovering over my desk and watching while I scooted back, slid up my trouser leg, and pulled the shiv out of my boot. I pressed its button. The blade flew and snapped into place.

'Dear me,' Mabel said. She was impressed. Her mouth looked like a doughnut.

'My toadsticker,' I told her.

'I do hope you've washed it.'

I've seen what dogs eat. Washed or not, pooch wouldn't care. I pinned the sandwich to my desk top and tried to keep its insides from slopping out as I cut. It made a real mess. 'There you go,' I said.

Mabel snatched up the biteless half. 'You're a dear,' she told me. She smiled at the dog. 'Isn't he a dear, Muffin?'

Muffin licked its chops.

But Mabel was the one who ate the sandwich.

She wolfed it down, then eyed the remains of my half. I stuffed the last of it into my mouth before she could make a grab for it.

'That certainly was tasty,' she said. 'I haven't eaten properly in ages.'

I had already noticed she was skinny, but I hadn't given it much thought. After all, it's chic to look like a cadaver.

'Have a seat,' I told her.

She sat down. Muffin licked some mayo off her chin.

'Someone,' she said, 'wants to poison me.'

'I see.'

'It's frightful. I hardly dare touch a bite. I'm withering away to nothing. You must help me.'

'I charge three hundred beans a day,' I said.

'Three hundred what?'

'Dollars.' It was double my usual rate, but I figured she could handle it. She wore diamond earrings, a pearl necklace, and eight rings. I knew that none of the jewelry was fake because of her blue hair and poodle.

'That sounds a trifle steep,' she said.

'You get what you pay for,' I explained. 'I'm the best.'

She rolled her eyes toward the ceiling as if she doubted my word.

'You don't want to pinch pennies,' I said, 'when your life's on the line.'

'I suppose you're right.'

'Of course I'm right.'

She set Muffin on the floor. It skittered under the desk and started chewing on one of my boots. I used my other boot to fend it off while Mabel took a checkbook out of her purse. Usually, I insist on cash. A lot of my clients (back when I had clients) were deadbeats. But I figured I could trust Mabel.

She made out the check to Duke Scanlon, Private Investigator. Then she filled in the amount. I licked my lips and stopped kicking Muffin. She signed the check and slid it across the desk. It got mayo on it. 'Will that be enough,' she asked, 'to retain your services for a week?'

'Consider me retained. For starters, what makes you think someone wants to poison you?'

'I don't *think* someone wants to poison me, I *know*.'

'Has there been an attempt on your life?' I asked.

She rolled her eyes again. She was good at it. 'My dear young man – may I call you Duke?'

'Duke it is, Mabel.'

'Duke, now see here, had I been poisoned already I would hardly need your services. I would be pushing up daisies like my dear husband, Oscar.'

'What happened to Oscar?' I asked.

'Why, he died, of course. That's what happens when one is poisoned.'

'Ah-ha,' I said.

'Ah-ha, indeed. It was dreadful. He barely had a chance to swallow. One moment he was complaining that the hollandaise had curdled, and the next moment he was in it.'

'Eggs Benedict?' I asked.

'Precisely.'

'When did this happen?'

'April fifteenth,' Mabel said. 'That's over a month ago, and I haven't eaten properly since then. Whoever murdered Oscar, you see, intends to do the same to me.'

Muffin tried to climb my leg. Smiling at Mabel, who couldn't see what was going on, I bent over and patted the little cutie on the head and gave its ear a twist. It bit my wrist, then scampered away and hopped onto Mabel's lap looking pleased with itself.

'What did the police find?' I asked.

'The police? Ha! I told them and *told them* that Oscar had been poisoned, but would they listen? No. As far as they were concerned, poor Oscar simply dropped dead from a bum heart.'

'Did Oscar *have* a bum heart?'

'He most certainly did by the time *they* saw it.'

'Was an autopsy performed?'

'Of course,' she said.

'No traces of poison were found?'

'No, but I've discussed the matter with my physician and he assures me that there are several varieties of poison which might go undetected.'

'He's right,' I told her.

'Of course. He's a doctor.'

'Do you have any idea who might have . . .'

'You wouldn't have another one of those delicious sandwiches, would you?' she interrupted.

'Not on me,' I said.

'Then let's discuss the rest of the details over lunch. I'm famished.'

I was all for it. Not only was I starving, but this called for a celebration. I was two thousand one hundred dollars richer than I'd been ten minutes ago, and the case would be a cinch. All I had to do was go through the motions.

Because Mabel Wingate was in no danger of being poisoned. Her late husband, Oscar, had been dropped by a faulty ticker, not Eggs Benedict. It was good enough for the cops; it was good enough for me.

Shrinks probably have a name for Mabel's condition – the way her mind turned things around to help her cope with the sudden shock of her Oscar's death. I have a name for it, too – bananas.

Mabel was bananas and rich.

I stood to make out like a bandit.

'Not a peep about this to the chauffeur,' she warned as we left the building.

'Yamamoto's,' Mabel told him.

He started driving. 'I'm not big on Japanese food,' I said.

'None the less, I am.'

So Yamamoto's it was. Mabel left Muffin in the limousine with Herbert the chauffeur, and we went in. 'I just adore sushi,' she said as we sat at a corner table.

'Sushi? She the waitress?'

'You have a lot to learn, Duke.'

She ordered the same meal for both of us. When the waitress left, she started right in on the case. 'One of my relatives,' she said, 'is obviously the villain. With Oscar out of the way, you see, the entire family fortune fell into my hands. Once I'm out of the way, they'll inherit oodles.'

'Who, exactly, will get the oodles?' I asked.

'According to the terms of our will, the wealth would be divided equally among our three children. We also provided handsome amounts for each of our servants.'

'So you figure one of the kids poisoned Oscar?'

'Or one of their spouses,' Mabel said. 'Or one of the servants. Or a combination.'

'In other words, you suspect everyone.'

She nodded.

'So they all have a motive. But who had the opportunity? Who was present at the time of Oscar's death?'

'They all were. Wingate Manor is a rather large estate. All of our children live there with their spouses. The servants were also in the house that morning: Herbert the chauffeur, George the butler, Wanda the maid, Kirk the stable boy and, of course, Elsie the cook.'

I counted on my fingers. 'That makes eleven suspects,' I said. 'Any grandchildren?'

'Not one.'

'Well, it makes a big bunch. Maybe we can narrow it down a little.'

Before we could start narrowing it down, the food arrived. I stared at it. I wished I was back at Lou's Deli. 'What *is* this stuff?' I asked.

'Sushi, my dear.'

'It looks like dead fish.'

Mabel tittered.

I put my nose close to the plate, and sniffed. The last time I'd smelled something like it, I was a kid in a rowboat trying to grab bait out of a minnow bucket. It was a hot day, and most of the minnows were belly up. 'I'm not going to eat this,' I said.

'Oh, but you must. Until you catch the killer, you'll need to act as my food taster.'

'What are you getting at?' I asked.

'Eat,' Mabel said.

For three hundred dollars a day, I'll eat anything. So I forked a critter, held my breath so I couldn't smell it, and put it into my mouth. It tasted the way I was afraid it might taste.

Mabel watched me chew. She hadn't touched her food yet. I

swallowed, and tried to wash the taste out of my mouth with water.

Mabel kept watching.

I got the picture. She was waiting to see if I'd keel over.

'Oscar didn't die in a restaurant,' I said.

'No,' said Mabel. 'But one can't be too careful.'

'Nobody's going to sneak into the kitchen of a restaurant to poison you,' I said.

'One never knows.' She pointed her fork at something on my plate that looked like an octopus tentacle.

I ate one, and gagged.

'Now that.'

That looked harmless. It looked like a cake of crisp rice – sort of. But it tasted like something that had been left overnight in the cloudy old water from a goldfish bowl.

Mabel watched me eagerly. I didn't keel over, but I wanted to.

'Fine,' she said. 'Now we trade plates.'

We traded, and she dug in. It made me feel sick, watching her stuff such junk into her mouth. I flagged down the waitress and ordered a double Scotch on the rocks.

The Scotch helped. I drank, and tried not to look at Mabel.

This job, I decided, was not turning out to be such a picnic.

That's how it started. After leaving Yamamoto's Sushi Bar and Bait Shop, we took the limo to Wingate Manor. It was quite a snazzy joint.

Mabel introduced me around as the son of an old school chum who was down on his luck and would be living in for the next week. The living in part came as a surprise, but I didn't complain. After all, the place was like a luxury resort complete with pool, sauna, a tennis court, stables, and a television in every bedroom. No wonder the two daughters, the son and their assorted mates weren't eager to move out.

None of them struck me as killers. That came as no big

surprise, since I'd already decided Mabel's deck was short a few cards.

At cocktail hour, we all sat around the pool. George the butler passed out drinks. I wanted Scotch, but I got a vodka gimlet – the same drink as Mabel. After I took a sip, she managed to switch glasses with me. She was quite artful about switching. I don't think anyone caught on.

George passed around a tray of snacks. Canapes, Mabel called them. Since I was the guest, she said, I should be first to help myself. I ate one. It was a miniature sandwich with liver inside. I'm not big on liver, but it sure beat sushi. I didn't keel over. Mabel took one.

Later, the rest of the clan headed into the dining room. I could smell a roast. My stomach grumbled. I had one foot in the dining room when Mabel grabbed my arm and stopped me.

'Duke and I will be dining later,' she told the others. 'We have some matters to discuss.'

She led me into the study. 'I can't let them see that I've hired a taster,' she explained.

'No,' I muttered. 'I guess not.'

'They'd know I'm onto their game.'

'Right,' I said.

Bananas.

I could have used a few bananas, just then.

Finally, the dining room was cleared. Our turn. The roast was cold, but it tasted great. Mabel watched and waited. I poured gravy over my mashed potatoes. I took a big bite. She raised her eyebrows. I sipped the red wine. I ate a yucky chunk of broccoli.

We stared at each other.

'How are you feeling?' she asked.

'Starved.'

'You're doing splendidly,' she said. We traded plates and glasses.

This went on for the next five days. Breakfast, lunch, cocktails and dinner, whether we were taking our meal at the estate or at a restaurant, I tested all the food and drinks first. Then we switched, and Mabel ate her fill. Except for one return trip to Yamamoto's, it wasn't half bad.

I spent my days swimming, riding horses, and sometimes playing tennis with members of the clan. A certain son-in-law named Aaron showed a nasty streak on the courts. He liked to slam balls at my face. He was a doctor when he wasn't hanging around the estate. If I had to pick a poisoner, it would have been him.

But I didn't have to pick.

Nobody had any intention of poisoning Mabel. She didn't need a private eye or a food taster. She needed a shrink.

I knew that all along.

On Friday afternoon, four hours after our second trip to Yamamoto's, my stomach couldn't hold out for the cocktail hour. I snuck into the kitchen. Elsie the cook wasn't around. The snacks were ready. I took a loaded tray of canapes out of the refrigerator, set it on the counter, and picked up one of the tiny sandwiches. Muffin, who had grown very fond of my boots during the past few days, was busy gnawing at my ankle. I peeled open one of the snacks and sniffed it. Liver, yuck. I tossed it across the kitchen, and Muffin went scampering after it.

The dog gobbled it down.

Adios, Muffin.

Muffin may or may not have been poisoned by the canape. Its ticker might've just chosen that moment to go on the fritz.

Sure.

I'm a trained investigator. I don't believe in coincidences.

Mabel wasn't bananas, after all.

In a way, that made me feel good. I'd grown fond of the old dame. I was glad to find out she wasn't a loony.

I returned the tray of poisoned snacks to the refrigerator. Then I stashed the mortal remains of Muffin in the pantry and went up to my room to fetch Slugger.

Slugger is my .38 caliber snub-nosed revolver. I don't have a permit to carry a concealed weapon (it got lifted after I dropped that client mentioned earlier), but I didn't plan to go up against a killer without my equalizer, so I tucked Slugger under my belt. I pulled out my shirt-tail to keep him out of sight, and went outside to the pool.

By five o'clock, the whole gang was there.

'Has anyone seen Muffin?' Mabel asked.

Nobody had seen Muffin. That included me.

George came out with a tray of cocktails. We took our glasses. I sipped. Mabel tried to sneak her usual switch, but I shook my head. 'Not necessary,' I whispered. She raised her eyebrows, then smiled.

She looked around to make sure nobody was within earshot, then whispered, 'Have you unearthed the killer?'

George returned with the tray of poisoned appetizers.

'Put them on the table,' I ordered.

'I'm to pass them, sir,' he said.

'Do as Duke says,' Mabel told him.

With a nod, George set the tray on the poolside table. 'Now,' I said, 'go and bring out the other servants. Everyone.' He left.

Sally, the wife of Aaron the doctor, saw George depart without passing snacks. 'What gives?' she asked.

'This gives,' I answered, and pulled out Slugger.

Everyone except Mabel started yelling at me. 'See here!' I heard. And, 'Put that away!' And, 'He's berserk!' One of Mabel's daughters covered her ears and shouted, 'Oh oh oh, he's going to murder us all!'

'Quiet!' Mabel called out. 'Duke is a private detective whom I hired to protect me.'

That shut them up. Some looked surprised, others confused, a few miffed. Aaron looked more miffed than anyone. I was glad he didn't have a tennis racquet handy.

'Line up,' I commanded.

They formed a line with their backs to the pool.

'What is the meaning of this?' Sally asked.

'You'll soon find out,' I said.

When the servants showed up, I made them stand in line with the rest of the gang.

'Mabel,' I said. 'The tray.'

She went to the table and hefted the tray.

'One canape apiece,' I told her.

She walked slowly down the line of eleven suspects, making sure that each of them took one of the little sandwiches.

'Okay,' I said. 'When I count to three, I want every one of you to eat your snack.'

'This is ridiculous!' snapped Sally.

'Just a little test,' I explained. I didn't bother playing games with the count. I rattled off, 'One two three.'

They all ate.

Except Aaron. He threw his canape at me.

'You're the poisoner!' I shouted. I aimed Slugger at his snarling face. 'Freeze!'

Aaron froze.

The other ten didn't. They dropped. Some pitched onto the concrete. Some flopped into the pool.

Mabel looked at me. 'You idiot!' she yelled.

'Oh, boy,' I muttered.

In this game, some cases are tough. Some are a lead-pipe cinch. You win a few and you lose a few. You hope it all evens out in the end, but if it doesn't . . . well, that's the way the cookie crumbles.

I wouldn't have it any other way. I'm a sleuth, a snoop, a gumshoe. I'm the guy you call when the chips are down and your back's to the wall. I'm Duke Scanlon, Private Eye.

The Hunt

Still there. Still staring at her.

Kim, seated on a plastic chair with her back to the wall, felt squirmy. Except for the door frame, the entire front of the laundromat was glass. The florescent lights overhead glared.

To the man in the car outside, it must be like watching her on a drive-in movie screen.

She wished she'd worn more clothes. But it was a hot night and very late, and she'd postponed doing her laundry until nearly every stitch in her apartment needed a wash. So she'd come here in sneakers, her old gym shorts from high school, and a T-shirt.

Probably why the bastard's staring at me, she thought. Enjoying the free show.

No better than a Peeping Tom, the way he just sits there, gazing in.

When Kim had first noticed him, she'd thought he was the husband of one of the other women. Waiting and bored, choosing to spend his time in the comfort of his car, maybe so he could listen to the radio – and ogle her from a discreet distance.

Soon, however, two of the women left. The only one remaining was a husky middle-aged gal who kept complaining and giving orders to a fellow named Bill. The way Bill listened and obeyed, he had to be her husband.

Kim didn't think that the stranger in the car was waiting for them.

They finished. They carried their baskets of clean clothes out to a station wagon, and drove off.

Kim was the only woman left.

The stranger stayed.

Every time she glanced his way, she saw him staring back. She couldn't actually see his eyes. They were masked in shadow. But she felt their steady gaze, felt them studying her.

Though she was unable to see his eyes, enough light reached him from the laundromat to show his thick neck, his shaved head. His head looked like a block of granite. He had a heavy brow, knobby cheekbones, a broad nose, full lips that never moved, a massive jaw.

Wouldn't be so bad, Kim had thought, if he looked like some kind of wimp. I could handle that. But this guy looked as if he ate bayonets for breakfast.

She'd wanted to move away from her chair near the front. Wait at the rear of the room. Hell, duck down out of sight behind the middle row of machines.

But if she did that, he might come in.

I'm all right as long as he stays in the car.

I'm probably all right as long as Jock's here.

She didn't know Jock's name, but he *was* one. The big guy might even be a match for the stranger. He appeared to be a couple of years younger than Kim – maybe nineteen or twenty. He had so much muscle that he couldn't touch his knees together if his life depended on it. Nor would his elbows ever rub against his sides. His sleeveless gray sweatshirt was cut off just below his chest. His red shorts were very much like Kim's, but a lot larger. He wore them over sweatpants.

She watched him, now, as he hopped down from one of the washers and strutted to a nearby machine. He thumbed a button. The door of the front-loading drier swung open. A white sock and a jockstrap fell to the floor.

Kim's stomach fluttered.

He's done.

She forced herself not to glance out the window. She forced

herself not to hurry. She tried to look casual as she rose from her chair and strolled toward the crouching athlete.

'Hi,' she said, stopping beside him.

He looked up at her and smiled. 'Hello.'

'I'm sorry to bother you, but I was wondering if you could do me a favor.'

'Yeah?' His gaze slipped down Kim's body. When it returned to her face, she knew he would be willing to help. 'What sort of favor?' he asked.

'It's nothing much, really. I just don't want to be left alone in here. I was wondering if you could stick around for a few minutes and keep me company until my clothes are finished. They're in the driers, now. It'll just be about ten more minutes.'

He raised his eyebrows. 'That's it?'

'Well, if you could walk me out to my car when I'm done.'

'No problem.'

'Thanks. I really appreciate it.'

He stuffed the rest of his laundry into a canvas bag and tied the cord at the top. Standing up, he smiled again. 'My name's Bradley.'

'I'm Kim.' She offered a hand, and he shook it. 'I sure appreciate this.'

'Like I told you, no problem.'

Kim stepped to a washer across the aisle from him. He watched as she braced her hands on its edge and boosted herself up. Watched her breasts.

Maybe it wasn't such a hot idea asking him for help.

Don't worry, she told herself. He's just a normal guy.

She slumped forward slightly and cupped her knees to loosen the pull of the fabric across her chest.

'You live near here?' Bradley said.

'Yeah, a few blocks. Are you a student?'

'A sophomore. I live off-campus, though. I've got my own apartment. Do you come here often?'

'As un-often as possible.'

He laughed softly. 'Know what you mean. Chores. I hate them.'

'Same here. Especially laundry. It gets kind of spooky here.' Her head turned. She wanted to stop it, couldn't, kept turning until she saw the parked car and the grim face behind its windshield. She quickly looked back at Bradley.

'If you get spooked, why do you come here so late?' he asked.

'No waiting for machines.' Then she added, 'Famous last words.'

Bradley frowned. 'What is it?' He glanced toward the front, then scowled at her. 'What's the matter?'

Kim felt her mouth stretch into a grimace. She shook her head. 'Nothing.'

'Is it that guy out there?'

'No, it's . . . He's been watching me. Ever since I got here. He just sits there, staring at me.'

'Oh yeah?' Bradley glared in the man's direction.

'Don't! Jesus! Just pretend he's not there.'

'Maybe I ought to go out and . . .'

'No!'

He turned to Kim. 'You don't know who the guy is?'

'I've never seen him before.'

'No wonder you're worried.'

'I'm sure it's nothing,' she said, beginning to tremble again. 'He probably just likes to look at women.'

'*I* like to look at women. That doesn't mean I hang around laundromats like a goddamn pervert.'

'He's probably harmless.'

'Doesn't look harmless to me. Who's to say he isn't some kind of freak like the Mount Bolton Butcher?'

'Hey, come on . . .'

Bradley's face went pale. His eyes widened. They roamed

down Kim, and returned to her face. 'Christ,' he muttered. 'I hate to tell you this, but . . .' He hesitated.

The change in him frightened Kim. '*What?*'

'You . . . you're a dead match for his victim profile.'

'What are you talking about?'

'The Mount Bolton Butcher. He's had eight victims, and they all . . . they were all eighteen to twenty-five years old, maybe not as pretty as you, but almost. And slim, and they all had long blonde hair parted in the middle just like yours. You look so much like the others that you could all be sisters.'

'Oh shit,' Kim muttered.

'I was going with a girl who kind of fit the profile. Not as much as you do, but it had me worried. I was afraid, you know, she might end up raped and dismembered like . . . Is there a back way out of here?'

'Hey, come on. You're really . . .'

'I'm not kidding.'

'I know, but . . . It probably isn't him, right? I mean, he hasn't . . .'

'He hasn't nailed anyone in two months, and the cops think he might've left the area, or died, or been jailed for something else. But they don't *know*. They're just trying to calm people down, saying stuff like that. Have you ever been up around Mount Bolton?'

Kim shook her head. It felt a little numb inside.

'I tell you, it's one big mean wilderness. A guy could hide out for years if he knew what he was doing. So maybe he laid low for a while, and maybe now the urge has gotten the best of him, and . . . Not much of anyone goes camping up there anymore. If he wanted a new victim, he might have to come down into town for one.'

'This is really starting to give me the creeps.'

'Just sit there a minute. I'll check the back.'

Bradley walked up the aisle between the rows of silent washers and driers. He stepped past the coin-operated vending machines where patrons could purchase drinks, snacks, detergent or bleach. He tapped out a rhythm as he walked by a long, wooden table where people earlier had separated and folded their laundry. Then he disappeared into a recessed area at the rear of the room. He was out of sight for just a second.

When he stepped into the open again, he met Kim's eyes and shook his head.

Not once did he glance toward the man in the car as he came back to her. 'Nothing but a utility room,' he said. 'The only way out is the front.'

Kim nodded and tried to smile. She felt a corner of her mouth twitch.

'You think your stuff is about ready?'

'Close enough.' She hopped off the washer. Bradley picked up his laundry bag and stayed at her side as she headed for the pair of driers near the front.

'Your car's in the lot?' he asked.

'Yeah.'

'I'll get in with you. If he thinks we're really together, maybe he won't try anything.'

'Okay,' Kim said. Both driers were still running. She could see them vibrating, hear their motors and the thumps of the tennis shoes she'd tossed into the nearer of the two.

She swung her laundry basket off the top of that machine, set it at her feet, crouched and opened the front panel. The motor went silent. Reaching inside, she lifted out a handful of warm clothes. They still felt a little damp, but she didn't care.

'If he follows us when we leave,' Bradley said, 'maybe we can lose him. But at least you won't be alone. As long as I'm with you, he'll think twice before he tries anything.'

She dropped more clothes into the basket, and looked up at Bradley. 'I really appreciate this.'

'I'm just glad that I'm here to help.'

'Do you really think he might be the Butcher?'

'I hope we don't find out.'

What if you're *the Butcher?*

The thought came suddenly, and seemed to turn her stomach cold inside.

No. That's ridiculous.

Looking away from him, she continued to unload the machine.

What's so ridiculous about it? Bradley seems to know a lot about the Butcher. And he wants me to take him in my car. Once we're alone . . .

For all I know, he's been lying from the start.

Maybe he's *with* the other guy. They might be working together.

Don't let him in the car, she told herself. Walk out with him, but . . .

'Oh, shit,' Bradley muttered.

Her head snapped toward him. He was standing rigid, eyes wide as he gazed toward the front.

Kim sprang up and whirled around.

The stranger filled the doorway. Then he was inside, striding toward them.

He wore a dark stocking cap. His face was streaked with black makeup. His black T-shirt looked swollen with mounds and slabs of muscle. The sling of a rifle crossed his chest. So did the straps of a harness that held a sheathed knife, handle down, against the left side of his rib cage. Circling his waist was a web belt loaded down with canvas cases, a canteen and a holster. He wore baggy camouflage pants. Their cuffs were tucked into high-topped boots.

Bradley, fists up, stepped in front of Kim. His voice boomed out, 'Stop right there, mister.'

A blow to the midsection dropped Bradley to his knees. A knee to the forehead hurled him backward. He hit the floor sliding and lay limp at Kim's feet.

She whirled away and tried to run. A hand snagged the shoulder of her T-shirt. The fabric tugged at her, stretched and ripped as she was twisted sideways. Her feet tangled. She crashed against the floor.

The man grabbed her ankles, tugged her flat. His weight came down on her back. An arm darted across her throat and squeezed.

Kim woke up in total darkness. She lay curled on her side. Her head ached. At first, she thought she was home in bed. But this didn't feel like a bed. She felt a blanket under her. The surface beneath the blanket was hard. It vibrated. Sometimes, it pounded against her.

She remembered the man.

Then, she knew where she was.

To confirm her fears, she tried to straighten her legs. Something stopped her feet. She reached out. Her fingers met hard, grooved rubber.

The spare tire.

The car stopped. Kim had no idea how long she had been trapped inside its trunk. Probably for an hour. That's about how long it should take, she knew, to drive from town to the wilderness surrounding Mount Bolton.

Ever since regaining consciousness and realizing she was in the trunk of the man's car, she had known where he was taking her. After a period of gasping panic, after prayers for God to save her, a numbness had settled into Kim. She knew she was going to die, and there was nothing she could do about it. She told herself that everyone dies. And this way, she would be spared such agonies as facing her parents' deaths, the deaths of other loved ones and friends, her own old age and maybe a lingering demise in the grip of cancer or some other horrible disease. Has its advantages.

God, I'm going to die!

And she knew what the Butcher did to his victims: how he raped them, sodomized them, tortured them with knives and sticks and fire.

The panic came back. She was whimpering and trembling again by the time the car stopped.

She heard the engine quit. A door thudded shut. Seconds later, a muffled jangle of keys came from behind her. She heard the quiet clicks of a key sliding into the trunk lock. The clack of a latch. Then, the trunk lid swung up, squeaking on its hinges.

A hand pushed under her armpit. Another thrust between her legs and grabbed her thigh. She was lifted out of the trunk, swung clear of the car, and thrown to the ground. The forest floor was damp, springy with fallen pine needles. Sticks and cones dug against her as she rolled onto her back. She stared up at the dark shape of the man. He was a blur through her tears.

'Get up,' he said.

Kim struggled to her feet. She sniffed and wiped her eyes. She lifted the front of her torn T-shirt, covering her right breast and holding the fabric to her shoulder.

'What's your name?' the man asked.

Kim straightened her back. 'Fuck you,' she said.

A corner of his mouth curled up. 'Look around.'

She turned slowly and found that she stood in a clearing surrounded by heavy timber. There was no sign of a road, though she suspected they couldn't be far from one. The car couldn't have traveled any great distance through the underbrush and trees. She faced the Butcher. 'Yeah?'

'Do you know where you are?'

'Got a pretty good guess.'

'You're a tough little thing, aren't you?'

'What've I got to lose?'

'Not a thing, bitch. Look to your right. There's a trail sign.'

She looked. She spotted a small wooden sign on a post at the edge of the clearing.

'Stick to the trail,' he said. 'You'll make better time.'

'What are you talking about?'

'You've got a five-minute headstart.' He raised an arm close to his face. With the other hand, he pushed a button to light the numbers on his wrist watch. 'Go.'

'What is this?'

'The hunt. And your time is running.'

Kim swung around and dashed away from the man. She didn't head toward the trail sign. Instead, she ran for the end of the clearing. This was the way the car had come. She might reach a road.

He's not going to let me get away, she thought. This is just part of it. A goddamn game. I'm not going to get out of here alive.

That's what he thinks.

I haven't got a chance.

Oh yes I do, oh yes I do.

She dodged a bush, raced through the gap between two trees, and shortened her strides when she met a downslope.

Car couldn't have come this way, she realized. The bastard must've turned it around before he stopped. Knew I'd try this.

I'm running *away* from the road.

She wondered how much time had passed. Her five minutes couldn't be up yet.

He won't give me five, she thought. He's probably already after me.

But she couldn't hear anything back there. She heard only her huffing breath, her heartbeat, her shoes crunching pine needles and mashing cones and snapping twigs.

I'm making too much noise.

Then a foot slipped out from under her. She saw her leg fly up. Saw the treetops. Slammed the ground and slid on her back, forest debris raking her shirt up, scraping her skin. When the skid stopped, she lay sprawled and didn't move except to suck air into her lungs.

I can't run from him, Kim told herself. He'll catch me easy. Gotta sneak. Gotta hide.

Sitting up, she peered down the slope. It wasn't heavily wooded. The dense trees were off to the sides. She stood. She glanced toward the top. No sign of him yet. But time had to be running out.

In a low crouch, she traversed the slope. Soon, she left the moonlight behind. The dark of the forest felt wonderful – a sheltering blanket of night. She walked slowly, trying not to make a sound as she stepped around the trunks of spruce and fir trees, ducked under drooping branches.

The place smelled like Christmas.

Play it right, she told herself, and maybe you'll see another Christmas.

How good is this guy? she wondered. Is he good enough to track me through all this in the dark?

He wouldn't have let me go if he wasn't sure he'd find me.

There must be a way. I just have to be smarter than him.

He's after me by now, she thought. Even if he did wait the whole five minutes.

Kim stepped behind a tree, turned around, and scanned the woods. Except for a few milky flecks of moonlight, the area was black and shades of gray. She saw the faint shapes of nearby trees and saplings. Nothing seemed to move.

You won't spot him till he's right on top of you, she realized, recalling his dark clothes and makeup.

She looked down at herself. Her legs were dim smears, her shorts dark, but her T-shirt almost seemed to glow. Muttering a curse, she pulled it off. She tucked it into the front of her shorts, so it hung from her waist. That was better. She was tanned except for her breasts, and they weren't nearly as white as the shirt.

Turning around, Kim made her way toward a deadfall. The roots of the old tree formed a clump nearly as high as her head. Bushes and vines had grown around the trunk. She considered climbing over the dead tree, but decided to bypass it, instead.

As she neared the mound of dirt-clogged roots, she noticed a space between the trunk and the ground. Kneeling, she peered into the opening. It was exposed, but she would be out of sight if she squirmed to where a thick nest of bushes grew in front of the trunk.

The idea of being trapped beneath the dead tree didn't appeal to her. Probably a host of nasty creatures under there – ants, spiders, termites, slugs. They would crawl on her.

Besides, she told herself, if it looks like a good hiding place to me, it'll look like one to him. If he comes this way, he'll check it out. And he'll have me.

Forget it.

She hurried around the root cluster and headed to the right of the deadfall. With the barrier at her back, she broke into a run and didn't bother moving from tree to tree for concealment. She dashed as fast as she could, staying clear of trees, dodging occasional clusters of rock, circling patches of underbrush. At last, winded and aching, she ducked behind a trunk. She bent over and held her sweaty knees and gasped for air.

That little burst of speed, she thought, ought to put some ground between us. He can't run all-out, not if he's tracking me.

How can he track someone in the dark? she wondered. It wouldn't be easy, even in daylight, to follow her signs. What does he look for, anyway? Broken twigs?

Kim pulled the T-shirt from her waist band and mopped her wet face, her dripping sides, her neck and chest and belly. As she tucked the shirt into her shorts again, she wondered if the Butcher might have a night-vision device. Maybe an infra-red scope, or something.

That would explain a lot.

He seemed so sure he'd find me.

Maybe took it out of his car while he was giving me the headstart.

How can I hide from something like that?

They pick up body heat? she wondered.

What if I bury myself?

That idea seemed just as bad as hiding under the deadfall.

Sighing, Kim leaned back against the tree. Its bark felt stiff and scratchy. A quiet scurrying sound made her flinch. But it came from above. Probably a squirrel up there, she thought.

What about climbing a tree?

Even if the Butcher figured out that she had gone up a tree to hide, there were thousands. She could climb high enough to be invisible from the ground. The limbs and foliage might even offer some protection from a night scope, if he had such a thing.

If he does find me, Kim thought, he'll have a damn tough time getting to me.

He could probably shoot me out of it. That won't be easy if I'm high enough. And he might be afraid of the noise. The sound of gunfire would carry a long distance. Somebody might hear it.

Besides, I'd rather be shot than taken alive. Quick and clean.

If he doesn't shoot me down, his only other choice is to go up after me. That'll make *him* vulnerable.

'All *right*!' Kim whispered. 'Let's make it even tougher.'

She stepped out from under the tree. Crouching, she studied the ground. Here and there, the faint gray shapes of rocks jutted through the mat of pine needles. She gathered several, choosing those that were large enough to fill her hand – large enough to do some real damage. When she had six, she spread her shirt on the ground. She piled them onto the shirt, brought up its corners, and knotted it to form a makeshift sack.

Swinging the load at her side, Kim wandered through the trees until she found a stand of five that were grouped very closely together. Their branches met and intertwined, forming a dark mass.

Perfect.

She hurried to the center tree, saw that it had no handholds within easy reach, and went to the tree beside it. The lowest limb of this one was level with Kim's face. After the first limb, it looked as if the going would be easy.

The shirt full of rocks presented a problem. Kim thought about it for a while. Then, she opened the knot and retied it so that the untorn sleeve was free. She pushed her left hand through the neck hole and out the short sleeve, then slid the bundle up her arm. With the weight of the rocks tugging at her shoulder, she swung the load out of the way against the side of her back.

She shinnied up the trunk, struggled onto the limb, stood, and began climbing carefully from branch to branch. It wasn't as easy as she had supposed. Soon, her heart was slamming and she had to fight for air. Stopping to rest, she leaned away from the trunk and peered down. She couldn't see the ground – just a tangle of lower branches.

I'm pretty high, she thought.

Damn high. Jesus.

Her throat tightened. Her stomach fluttered. Her legs began to tremble. She turned suddenly and hugged the tree. I'm safe up here, she told herself. I'm not going to fall. She reminded herself of her days on the high school gymnastics team. That wasn't so long ago, she thought. This is no tougher than the uneven parallels. I've stayed in pretty good shape.

She still had to cling to the tree for a while before she found the nerve to relax her hold.

Just a little bit higher. Don't look down, and you'll be okay.

She got her knee onto the next branch, crawled up, stood on it, swung her foot around the trunk to another, pushed herself higher, and soon the process of climbing occupied all her thoughts, leaving no room for fears of falling.

When her movements began to sway the upper reaches of the tree, Kim knew she was high enough. She straddled a branch, scooted forward until she was tight against the trunk, and wrapped her legs around it.

For a long time, she stayed that way. Then, the rocks began to bother her. The sleeve of the T-shirt felt like a hand on her shoulder, trying to drag her backward. Rough edges of rock pushed against her skin through the fabric.

Easing away from the trunk but still keeping it scissored between her legs, she swung the bag onto her lap. She draped it like saddlebags over a branch just overhead and to the right.

Relieved of the burden, she inched forward again and embraced the tree.

Kim dreamed that she was falling, flinched awake, found herself slumping sideways, and clutched the trunk. Cheek pressed to the bark, she saw that morning had come. Dust motes floated in golden rays slanting down through the foliage. Out beyond the branches, she saw the bright green of nearby trees. Tilting her head back, she saw patches of blue, cloudless sky. She heard birds singing, a soft breeze whispering through the pine needles.

My Christ, she thought, I made it through the night.

She'd even, somehow, drifted off to sleep some time before dawn.

She felt numb from the waist down. Hanging onto an upper branch, she stood and held herself steady. Sensation returned to her legs and groin and rump, making them prickle with pins and needles. When they felt normal again, she removed her shorts, climbed to a lower branch and urinated. Returning to her perch, she put her shorts back on. She sat down, one arm around the trunk, and let her legs dangle.

Now what? she wondered.

Obviously, she had eluded the Butcher. She wondered if

he'd passed this way in the night and kept on going. Maybe he'd never even come close.

Maybe he'd given up, finally, and gone away.

That's wishful thinking, Kim warned herself. He won't give up. Not this easily. A, he wants me. B, I can identify him. He isn't going to let me waltz out of here.

On the other hand, he would've found me by now if he'd actually been able to follow my signs.

Maybe he *did*, she thought. Maybe right now he's taking a snooze under the tree.

No. If he knew I was up here, he would've tried to take me. *I lost the bastard.*

The trick, now, is to find my way back to civilization without running into him.

Trying it in daylight seemed foolhardy.

Waiting for nightfall was torture. There was no comfortable way to sit. Kim changed positions frequently, mostly sitting, sometimes standing, occasionally hanging by her hands from higher branches to stretch and take the weight off her legs.

Hunger gnawed at her, but thirst was far worse. She ached for a drink of water.

In spite of the shade provided by the upper areas of the tree, the heat of the day was brutal. Sweat dribbled down her face, stinging her eyes. It streamed down her body, tickling and making her squirm. Her skin felt slick and greasy. Her shorts felt as if they were pasted on.

For all the wetness on her skin, her mouth had none. As the day dragged on, her lips became rough and cracked. Her teeth felt like blocks of gritty stone. Her tongue seemed to be swelling, her throat closing so she had difficulty when she tried to swallow.

At times, she wondered if she could risk waiting for dark. Her strength seemed to be seeping away with the sweat pouring out of her skin. Spells of dizziness came and went. If I don't climb down pretty soon, she thought, I'm going to fall. But she held on.

Just a while longer, she told herself. Again and again.

Finally, dusk came. A refreshing breeze blew through the tree, swaying it gently, drying her sweat.

Then, darkness closed over the forest.

Kim began to climb down. She was ten or twelve feet below her perch when she remembered her T-shirt. She'd left it resting on a branch up there.

It seemed like miles away.

But she couldn't return to civilization wearing nothing but her shorts.

She began to cry. She wanted to get down. She wanted to find water. It just wasn't fair, having to climb back up there again.

Weeping, she struggled upward. Finally, she tugged the loaded shirt off the branch. Hadn't needed the damn rocks anyway. She plucked open the knot and shook the shirt. The rocks fell, thumping against branches, swishing through pine needles. She stuffed the empty rag into the front of her shorts so she wouldn't lose it, then started her long climb down to the forest floor.

When Kim dropped from the final limb, she had no clear memory of the descent.

She found herself walking through the woods. Her hands felt heavy. She looked at them, and saw that each held a rock. She didn't remember picking them up. But she kept them.

Until she heard the soft, windy sound of rushing water. Then she tossed them down and ran.

Soon she was kneeling in a stream, cupping cold water to her mouth, splashing her face with it, sprawling out so she was submerged, the icy current sliding over her body. She came up for air. She cupped more water to her mouth, swallowed, sighed.

Kim didn't think she had ever felt so wonderful in her life.

Until she was suddenly grabbed by her hair and jerked to her knees.

No! Not after all this!

His hands clutched her breasts, tugging her up and backward against him. She squirmed and kicked as he hauled her to the bank. There, he threw himself down, slamming her against the ground. He writhed on top of her. His hands squeezed and twisted her breasts. He grunted as he sucked the side of her neck.

Reaching up behind herself, she caught hold of his ear. She yanked it. Heard tearing cartilage, felt a blast of breath against her neck as he cried out. His hands flew out from under her. He pounded the sides of her head.

Stunned by the blows, Kim was only vaguely aware of his weight leaving her body. She thought she should try to scurry up and run, but couldn't move. As if the punches had knocked the power out of her.

She felt her shorts being tugged down. She wanted to stop *that*, but still couldn't make her arms work. The shorts pulled at her ankles, lifted her feet and released them. Her feet dropped and struck the ground.

Rough hands rubbed the backs of her legs, her rump. She felt the press of a whiskered face. Lips. A tongue. The man grunted like a beast.

Then he grabbed her ankles, pulled and crossed her legs, flipping her over.

Kim stared up at the man.

He pulled a knife from his belt. Its blade gleamed in the moonlight. He clamped the knife between his teeth and started to unbutton his shirt.

She stared at him.

She tried to comprehend.

He was skinny, wearing jeans and a plaid shirt. His hair was a wild bush.

He's not the Butcher!

He pulled his shirt open.

A roar pounded Kim's ears. The man's head jerked as if he'd been kicked in the temple. A dark spray erupted from the other side. He stood above her for a second, still holding his shirt open, the knife still gripped in his teeth. Then he fell straight backward.

Kim's ears rang from the sound of the shot. She didn't hear anyone approach.

But then a man in baggy pants and black T-shirt was standing near her feet. He pointed a rifle down at the other man, and put three more rounds into him.

He slung the rifle onto his back. He crouched, picked up the body, and draped it over his shoulder. Turning to Kim, he said, 'Get dressed. I'll give you a lift back to town.'

'No way,' she muttered.

'It's up to you.'

He strode into the trees, carrying the body.

'Wait,' Kim called, struggling to sit up.

He halted. He turned around.

'*He's* the Butcher?' she asked.

'That's right.'

'Who are you?'

'A hired hand.'

'Why did you *do* this to me?' she blurted.

'Needed bait,' he said. 'You were it, bitch. I figured he'd sniff you out, sooner or later. He did, and I took him down. Simple as that.'

'How did you find me?' Kim asked.

'Find you? I never lost you. Climbing the tree was a pretty good gimmick, I'll give you credit for that. Glad you dumped the rocks, though. Great timing. That's what brought him out of cover.'

'Why didn't you shoot him right then?'

'Didn't feel like it. Coming?'

'Fuck you.'

He left.

Kim followed the stream. Early the next morning, she came upon a two-lane road. She walked alongside it. Finally, she heard the approach of a car. Just before it came into view around a bend, she lifted the torn front of her T-shirt to cover herself.

The car, a green Jeep, stopped beside her. A park ranger leaped out and hurried over to her. 'My God, what happened to you?'

She shook her head. 'Can you take me to the police?'

'Certainly.' His eyes traveled down Kim in a way that reminded her of Bradley in the laundromat. She wondered how Bradley was doing. She wondered if she wanted to see him again. 'You look like you've had a rough time of it,' the ranger said.

'Yeah.' Swaying forward, she took a quick lurching step to keep herself from falling. The ranger gripped her arm and held her steady.

'Are you all right?' he asked.

'I'll live,' Kim said. Her lips twitched into something that felt almost like a smile. She said it again. 'I'll live.' It sounded very good.

Slit

The library would be closing in five minutes. Charles knew that the last of the students had already left. He was alone with Lynn.

He saw no point in heading off into the stacks to shelve books, so he lingered beside the circulation desk, arranging volumes in the cart and sneaking glances at her.

She sat on a high stool behind the desk. Her empty loafers were on the floor. Her feet, in white socks, curled over a wooden rung of the stool. Charles could see one smooth calf, the crease behind her knee, and a few inches of bare thigh. Her legs were parted as far as the straight, denim skirt would allow. The skirt's hem looked so tight against the side of her thigh that Charles wondered if it might leave a red mark on her skin.

She was leaning forward, elbows resting on the desktop, hands on cheeks, head down as she looked through *Kirkus*. Her white blouse, tucked into the skirt, was taut against her back. Charles could see the bumps of her spine, the soft curves of her ribs, the pink hue of her skin through the fabric, the slim bands of her bra.

He squatted down and placed some books on the lower shelf of the cart. This angle allowed him to see Lynn's right breast. It was there beyond the underside of her arm, a sweet mound cupped by the tight blouse, its front hovering just above the edge of the desk.

It would look so much better without the bra. The seams, the pattern, the stiffness. All in the way.

Charles pictured himself slicing through its straps.

223

Lynn reached out, turned a page, flinched and blurted, 'Ow! Damn!' She jerked her hand up. She held it rigid in front of her face, fingers spread and hooked. A gleaming dot of blood bloomed on the pad of her index finger.

Charles felt his mouth go dry. His heart thudded. Heat rushed through his groin. He moaned.

She glanced over at him. Her face was red, her teeth bared. Her eyes returned to her hand. She looked as if she didn't know what to do with it. She shook it a couple of times like a cat with a wet paw, then pressed the bleeding fingertip between her lips.

'A paper cut?' he asked.

She nodded.

'I hate those things,' he said.

A cut. A slit.

He stayed crouched, hard and aching.

Lynn took the finger away from her mouth. It left some blood on her lips. She scowled at the wound, then gave Charles a tight, twisted smile. 'It's not that they hurt so much, you know? They're just so . . .' She shuddered. 'They're like fingernails skreeking on a blackboard.' She licked the blood from her lips, then returned the finger to her mouth.

'Would you like a bandage?' Charles asked.

'Do you have one?'

'Oh, sure. I'm always prepared.'

'Like a Boy Scout, huh?'

'Yeah.' Rising from his crouch, he hoped that the books on the cart's top shelf were high enough. They were. Their tops reached up past his stomach.

He turned away from Lynn and hurried into the office behind the circulation desk. There, he took a bandage from the tin inside his briefcase. He adjusted the front of his pants to make the bulge less apparent. But it still showed. He took his corduroy jacket off the back of a nearby chair, put it on, and fastened the middle button. He looked down. The front of the jacket nicely concealed his secret.

When he came out, he found that Lynn had turned around on her stool to face him. 'It's stopped bleeding,' she said.

'Yeah, but paper cuts. You rub them the wrong way and flip back the skin and . . .'

'Yuck. I guess I will take a bandage. Would you like to do the honors?' She held her hand toward Charles.

'Sure,' he said. Trembling, he stripped the wrapper off the adhesive strip. He moved closer to Lynn, halting when the wet end of her finger was inches from his chest. He stared down at the slit – a crescent across the finger's pad, rather like the gills of a tiny fish, pink under a thin white flap. The edge of the flap was away from him.

'Do you think I'll live?'

'Sure.' His voice came out husky. He felt terribly tight and hard.

'Are you okay?' she asked.

'Yeah. Cuts make me nervous.'

'You aren't gonna faint or anything, are you?'

'Hope not.' He fumbled with the bandage, peeling the shiny papers away from its sides. He let them fall. They drifted down like petals plucked from a flower, and settled on her shirt.

Pinching the sticky ends of the bandage, he lowered the gauze center toward Lynn's cut.

He wanted to hurt her.

No! Don't!

He wanted to grab her finger and rub his thumb back, flipping up the little edge of skin, making her jerk and cry out.

Not Lynn! Don't!

As fast as he could, he pressed the bandage to her cut and flipped the adhesive ends around her finger. He whirled away and rushed for the office.

'Charles?' she called. 'Charles, are you all right?'

He didn't answer. He dropped onto his swivel chair, hunched over and grabbed his knees.

It's over, he told himself. You didn't do it. Lynn can't even suspect . . .

He heard her quiet footsteps behind him. She put a hand on his shoulder. 'What's wrong?' she asked.

'Just . . . cuts. They upset me.'

Her hand squeezed him through the corduroy. 'If I'd known . . . What is it, a phobia or something?'

'I guess so. Maybe.'

In a lighter tone, she said, 'That probably explains why you carry bandages around, huh?'

'Yeah.'

She patted his shoulder. 'Maybe you'll feel better if you get some fresh air,' she said. 'Why don't you go ahead and take off? I'll close up the library.'

'Okay. Thanks.'

He waited until she was gone, then carried his briefcase outside. The night was dank and misty.

Feverish with memories of Lynn's cut, he lingered near the library entrance. Soon, the upper windows went dark. He pictured her up there, alone in the stacks, lowering her bandaged finger from the switch panel, starting down the stairwell.

His Swiss Army knife was a heavy lump against his thigh. He slipped his hand down into his pants pocket. He caressed the smooth plastic handle.

And savored thoughts of slitting her.

Just wait for her to come out . . .

No!

He turned from the library and walked quickly away.

In his apartment three blocks from campus, Charles went to bed. But he didn't sleep. His mind swirled with images of Lynn.

Don't think about her, he told himself.

You can't do her.

But it would be *so* nice.

But you can't.

Lynn was a graduate student. Like Charles, she earned a small stipend by working part-time at the Whitmore Library. Everyone knew they worked the same hours. Too much suspicion would be focused on him.

Besides, he really liked her.

But damn it . . .!

Forget about her.

He tried to forget about her. He tried to think only about the others. How they yelped or screamed. How their faces looked. How their skin split apart. How blood spilled out like scarlet creeks overflowing banks of ripped flesh, spreading and running, forming new streams that slid along velvety fields, that settled to create shimmering pools in the hollows of the body, that flowed down slopes.

So many faces. So many bodies flinching with surprise or thrashing in agony. So many flooding slits.

All belonged to strangers.

Except for the face and body and cut of his mother. Struggling to stop the confusing flood of images, fighting to keep his mind off Lynn, he concentrated on his mother. Her voice through the door. *Honey, would you be a dear and get me a Band Aid?* He saw himself enter the steamy bathroom, reach high into the medicine cabinet for the tin of bandages, take out one and step to the tub where she reclined. The water was murky. Patches of white suds floated on its surface. From her chest rose shiny wet islands, wonderfully round and smooth, each topped by a ruddier kind of skin that jutted up in the center. Looking at the islands made Charles feel strange and squirmy.

His mother held a razor in one hand. Her left leg was out of the water, its foot propped on the rim of the tub under one of the faucet handles. The cut was midway between her knee and the place where the water rippled around the wider part of her leg. *I'm afraid I nicked myself shaving*, she said.

Charles nodded. He gazed at the wound. He watched the strands of red slide down her gleaming skin. They made the bath water pink between her legs. She had a hairy place down there. He couldn't see her dingus. He stared, trying to find it even though he knew he shouldn't be looking at that place. But he couldn't help himself. He felt sick and tight.

You didn't cut if off, did you?

Cut off what, honey?

You know, your dingus.

She laughed softly. *Oh, darling, mommys don't have dinguses. Here.* And then she took gentle hold of his hand and guided it down into the pink, hot water. She slid it against her body. Against a cut – no, not just a cut – a huge, open gash with slippery edges. He tried to jerk his hand away, but she tightened her grip and kept it there. *Go on, feel it*, she said.

But doesn't it hurt? he asked.

Not at all.

It was almost as long as his hand. Warm and slick inside. And very deep. She squirmed a little as his fingers explored.

Her voice had a funny sound to it when she said, *I'm made this way. All mommys are.* She released his hand, but he kept it there. *That's enough, now, honey. You'd better put that Band Aid on my leg before I bleed to death.*

Then Charles had the bandage ready. As he lowered it toward the small bleeding cut on her leg, she said, *You aren't gonna faint or anything, are you?* But it wasn't his mother's voice. He turned his head. The woman sprawled in the tub was Lynn.

At dawn, groggy and restless, Charles climbed out of bed. He didn't know whether he had slept at all. Maybe a little. If so, his sleep had been a turmoil of dreams so vivid that they might have been memories or hallucinations.

He felt better after a long shower. Returning to his bedroom, he sat down and stared at the alarm clock. A quarter till six. That gave him just more than ten hours before returning to work at the library. And seeing Lynn again.

He saw her naked beneath him, writhing as he slit into her creamy skin.

'No!' he blurted, and stomped his foot on the floor.

There were ways to prevent it. Tricks. He'd worked out *lots* of tricks over the years to feed his urges – to ease the needs, to keep some control.

Weller Hall seemed huge and empty. Charles knew that it wasn't empty. But he saw no one as he eased the door shut and made his way to the staircase. Those few students and professors unlucky enough to be burdened with 'eight-o'clocks' were already snug in the classrooms, probably yawning and rubbing their eyes and wishing they were still in bed.

He climbed four creaky stairs, then stopped. He listened. Beyond the sounds of his own rough breathing and heartbeat, he heard a distant voice. Probably Dr Chitwood. Dr Shithead to the students who had to suffer through his mandatory (this being a university of Methodist origin) History of Christianity class. Known as Heist of Christ. Not only mandatory, but boring, and forever scheduled for 8 a.m.

It was one of only three classes taking place in Weller Hall on Monday, Wednesday and Friday at such an ungodly hour. Chitwoods's room was right at the top of the stairs.

Grinning, Charles pulled out his knife. He pried it open and dug into the smooth, worn wood of the banister. He carved a neat, two-inch slot down the rail's top. He scraped it clean of splinters. Crouching, he ran his thumb over a grimy stair. He rubbed his thumb against the pale cut on the handrail, darkening it with dirt, camouflaging it.

Using needle-nosed pliers, he snugged an injector blade into the slot.

He straightened up and admired his work.

The edge of the blade protruded just a little bit above the surface of the rail. It was hardly visible at all.

Shivering with excitement, Charles hurried outside. He waited on a bench and watched the entrance to Weller Hall.

This'll be great, he thought. It was always great.

But he'd never done it on campus before. He began to worry about that. He even considered returning to the stairway and pulling out the blade. He could walk into town and set up the trap somewhere else, somewhere safer.

He didn't want to do that, though. Too often, the trick ended up wasted on somebody old and ugly. He couldn't take a chance on that happening. He needed to slit a co-ed, a fresh young woman. One like Lynn.

The minutes dragged by. When people began wandering into the building, Charles feared that he might miss the event. He waited a while longer, fidgeting. Then he rose from the bench, trotted up the concrete steps, and rushed inside.

A few students were wandering the corridor, lingering near doorways, entering classrooms. Nobody on the stairs. He strolled to the far side of the hall. He removed a paperback copy of *Finnegan's Wake* from his briefcase, opened the book, leaned back against the wall, and pretended to read.

From here, he had a good view of the stairway.

The book trembled in his hands.

He held his breath when a couple of girls walked past him and turned toward the stairway. They looked like freshmen. They acted like freshmen, the way they talked so loudly and laughed and gestured.

The girl on the razor's side of the stairs held books to her chest with her left arm. Her right arm swung free. At the first

230

stair, she rested her hand on the banister. It slid up the rail as she began to climb.

Her shiny blonde hair swayed against her back. She wore a sleeveless sweatshirt. Her arms were slender and dusky. Her white shorts were very tight. Charles could see the outline of her panties. Skimpy things.

His heart slammed.

As she stepped from the third stair to the fourth, she jerked her hand off the railing.

Got her!

But she didn't flinch or cry out. She simply chopped her hand through the air. Some kind of damn gesture to accompany whatever inane point she was making to her friend.

She was almost to the landing before her hand returned to the banister.

Charles sighed. He felt robbed.

It's not over yet, he told himself.

She'd been so perfect, though. Pretty and blonde and slender like Lynn. A few years younger, but otherwise just right.

I couldn't have seen the look on her face, anyway, he consoled himself.

From above came a thunder of footfalls.

Charles perked up. Heist of Christ was out, the students stampeding to escape. In seconds, the first of them rounded the landing and rushed down the lower flight. Trembling with excitement, Charles watched those near the banister. A boy in the lead. Luckily, his arm was busy clamping books to his hips. Behind him came a lithe brunette, breasts jiggling the front of her T-shirt. But she carried a book bag by its straps and didn't bother with the rail.

Coming down behind her was a fat guy in a sweatsuit. But behind him was a real beauty with flowing golden hair, her shoulders bare, her torso hugged by a bright yellow tube top. Her hand was on the banister!

Yes!

'Ow! Shit!'

The fat guy.

No!

He jerked his hand off the railing and halted so abruptly that the blonde nearly crashed into him. He lifted his hand to his crimson, stunned face. Blood dripped off, streaking the front of his sweatshirt. 'Fuckin' A! Looka this! Jeeeeez!'

Kids started to crowd around him.

Before long, someone would find the razor.

Releasing a long sigh, Charles closed his book. He tucked it under one arm, picked up his briefcase and strolled up the corridor.

Later that morning, after his seminar in Twentieth Century Irish Literature, Charles sat on a park bench along one of the campus walkways. The bench was fairly well hidden by hedges at both ends and an oak to the rear.

He took two X-Acto blades from his briefcase. Each was about an inch in length, V-shaped, with fine sharp edges. At the blunt end of each blade was a tab that could be slid into one of the several handles which were part of the kit. Charles hadn't brought the handles with him.

With the blades cupped in one hand, he pretended to read Joyce. He watched the walkway. People kept coming by.

Patience, he told himself.

Before he could find time to plant the blades, a couple roosted on the bench across from him. They had bags from the Burger King a block from campus. Charles waited while they ate and gabbed. He waited while they snuggled and kissed. Finally, they wandered away, the guy with his hand down a back pocket of the girl's short denim skirt.

He checked the walkway. Clear at last!

Working quickly, he planted one blade upright in a green

painted slat beside his right thigh. He scooted away from it, then dug a place for the other blade on a slat of the backrest. After checking again for witnesses, he inserted the blade.

Then he roamed across the walkway and settled down on the bench where the sweethearts had wasted so much of his time. They'd left a fry behind. He brushed it to the ground. He opened *Finnegan's Wake*, and waited.

People came by. A lot of people. Alone, in pairs, in small groups. Students, instructors, professors, administrators, ground keepers. Male and female. Slender, lovely girls. Plain girls. Slobs.

Into the afternoon, Charles waited.

Nobody sat on the bench.

Nobody.

Still, Charles waited. Over and over again in his mind, beautiful young women sat down on the bench. Their faces twisted and went scarlet. They leaped up, shrieking. They hurried away, blood from gashed buttocks spreading across the seats of shorts and skirts and jeans, blood from ripped backs staining blouses, T-shirts, flowing down the bare skin of those who wore tube tops or other varieties of low-backed garments.

In his best fantasy, it was Lynn who sat on the bench. Wearing a white bikini.

He often returned to that one while he waited.

Lynn stopped in front of him.

He gazed up at her, puzzled. She wasn't wearing a bikini. She wore a white cotton polo shirt, pink shorts that reached almost to her knees, and white socks and sneakers. Her huge leather shoulder bag hung against her hip.

'Hi, Charles,' she said. 'How's it going?'

He shrugged. He tried to smile. He was reasonably certain this was Lynn, not a figment of his imagination.

'Ready to head on over to the salt mines?' she asked.

He glanced at his wristwatch. Ten till four. Impossible! He couldn't have been sitting here *that* long.

'I guess it's time,' he muttered.

Lynn tilted her head to one side. 'Are you all right?'

'I didn't get much sleep last night.'

'I had kind of a restless night, myself. So, are you coming?'

'Sure. Yeah. I guess so.' He put his book away, lifted his briefcase and rose from the bench. With a last glimpse at the other bench, he started walking with Lynn.

It's Fate, he thought. He'd *tried* to direct his need away from Lynn, but his efforts had failed. They were meant to fail. He was being guided by forces beyond his control, forces that had ordained Lynn to bleed for him.

'Check out my finger,' she said as they walked along. She raised it in front of his face.

The bandage was gone. Charles saw a tiny curve of white fringe on the pad of her finger. His heart thudded. 'It looks good,' he said.

'Almost as good as new.' She smiled as her upper arm brushed against him. She lowered the hand to her side. 'If it wasn't for your first-aid, no telling what might've happened. Who knows? I might've bled to death.'

Charles knew she was joking. But his heart pounded even harder. Heat spread through his groin. 'From a paper cut?'

'Of course. Happens all the time. It's the leading cause of death among librarians and editors. Honest to God.' She looked at him. 'You *do* know how to smile, don't you?'

'Sure,' he muttered.

'Let's see one.'

He tried.

'Miserable,' she said. 'You know, you'd be a pretty handsome fellow if you'd smile once in a while.'

He gazed at her. He pictured how her face would look with bright red blood streaming down it. He imagined himself licking the blood from her cheeks and lips.

'That's more of a leer than a smile, actually,' Lynn said. 'But it'll do. You just need more practice.'

Even after all the books were shelved, Charles stayed in the second-floor stacks.

If he went downstairs, he would see Lynn. She would be sitting on her stool behind the circulation desk, checking books in and out, or maybe wandering the floor, cheerfully offering suggestions to students in need of assistance.

As long as I don't see her, he told himself, nothing will happen.

A few students came up. Some searched for books, while others slipped into carrels along the far wall and studied. There were girls, but he paid them no attention. It would be Lynn, or no one.

He ducked into a carrel himself. For some unknown reason, it had been placed in a corner away from the lights. That suited him well. He felt snug and hidden.

He folded his arms on the desk top and put his head down.

Maybe I'll sleep, he thought.

He closed his eyes. He pictured Lynn suspended from a ceiling beam, wrists tied, arms stretched high, feet off the floor. He had no rope, though. Too bad. Go back to his apartment and get some? The emergency exits had alarms. He couldn't leave the library without passing Lynn's desk.

Maybe use my belt, instead?

That had worked before. He'd put a loop around the girl's hands and nailed the other end high on a wall.

No hammer. No nails.

A rope would be better, anyway. Even though he didn't have one, he liked the image of Lynn hanging helpless. He knew she was wearing a polo shirt. In his mind, however, she wore a regular blouse. With buttons. And he saw himself slicing off the buttons, one by one.

*

Charles flinched awake when someone stroked the back of his head. He jerked upright in his chair. Lynn was standing close beside him, frowning down with concern on her shadowy face.

'You really zonked out,' she said. Her voice was little more than a whisper in the silence.

'I'm sorry. I didn't . . .'

'That's okay.' Her hand stayed on the back of his head, caressing his hair. 'I was a little worried about you, though. You just disappeared.'

'I was shelving books up here. I felt so tired . . .'

'No problem.' A smile tilted the corners of her mouth. 'I thought maybe you were trying to avoid me. You've been acting so strange ever since last night.'

'I've been *feeling* pretty strange.'

'Are you still upset because I cut myself?'

'In a way, I guess.' He stood up. The chair made a loud squawk as it was scooted away by the backs of his knees. The noise made him cringe.

'I haven't been quite myself, either,' Lynn said.

He turned to face her. 'Really?'

'Really.' Gazing into his eyes, she took hold of his hands. 'The way you acted last night . . . You were so sweet, getting me the bandage and everything, putting it on my finger even though you have that phobia about cuts. I just suddenly realized . . . how really special you are, Charles.'

'Me?'

'Yeah, you.' She lifted her hands to his face. Gently caressing his cheeks, she eased against him. She tilted back her head. She pressed her mouth against his lips. After a slow, soft kiss, she looked up into his eyes. 'We're all alone,' she whispered. 'I've already locked up for the night.'

All he could say was, 'Oh.' He was trembling. His heart was punching his breath ragged. His groin was tight and the way

Lynn pressed against him, he knew she must be able to feel his erection.

She stepped back to make a space between their bodies. Her hands roamed over his chest. 'I was awake all night,' she said. 'Thinking about you.'

'I was awake thinking about you, too.'

'You were?' He heard a tremor in her voice.

'Yes.'

'Oh, man.' She made a soft, nervous laugh. 'I should've cut myself a long time ago.'

Her trembling fingers unbuttoned his shirt. She spread it open. She kissed his chest.

With one hand, Charles stroked her back. With the other, he dug into the pocket of his pants. He squeezed the plastic handle of his knife.

Staring into his eyes, Lynn plucked at the bottom of her polo shirt. She pulled it free of her shorts, drew it over her head and dropped it to the floor.

Charles felt as if his breath had been sucked from his lungs. He struggled for air.

Lynn fumbled at the waist of her shorts. The garment slipped down her legs. She stepped out of it, nudged it away with her sneaker.

The plastic knife handle felt greasy with sweat.

'Do you like how I look?' Lynn whispered.

Charles nodded. 'You look . . . beautiful.'

So beautiful. Slender and smooth, naked except for her skimpy white bra and panties, her white socks and sneakers.

She had a calm, dreamy look on her face. A hint of a smile. Arching her back, she reached both arms up behind her.

'Don't,' Charles murmured.

Her eyebrows lifted. 'I was just going to unhook . . .'

'I know. Let me?'

Her smile brightened. 'Sure.'

Charles pulled out his knife. As he opened the blade, he watched Lynn – ready to grab her if she should try to flee.

Her smile went crooked. She stood motionless, eyes on the knife. 'You're kidding, right?'

'I have to.'

She lifted her gaze to his face. She seemed to be studying him. Then she shrugged one shoulder. 'Go ahead, Charles.'

'Huh?'

'If you have to, you have to. I'll buy a new one.'

'Oh.'

She put her hands on his hips. He felt them shaking slightly. They squeezed him when he cut through each of the shoulder straps. Then he slid his blade under the narrow band between the cups of her bra. She closed her eyes. Her mouth hung open. He heard her raspy breathing. He tugged, severing the band.

The bra fell away.

Lynn opened her eyes. A smile fluttered on her face. 'This is pretty kinky,' she said, her voice husky.

She shivered when he rubbed the blade's blunt edge down the top of her left breast. In the glow of the nearest florescent light, he saw the smooth skin go pebbly with goosebumps. Her nipple grew. He pressed it down with the flat of the blade, and watched it spring up again. Lynn groaned.

She tugged open his belt. She unfastened the button at the waist of his jeans, jerked his zipper down, feverishly yanked his jeans and underwear down his thighs.

Can't be happening this way, Charles thought. Never had anything like this happen. He wondered if he might be asleep, dreaming.

But he knew that he was very much awake.

Lynn's fingers curled around him.

'Do my panties,' she whispered. 'With the knife.'

He cut them at the sides. The flimsy fabric drooped, but the panties didn't fall. They clung between her legs until she reached down. A small pull, and they drifted toward the floor.

'This is so weird,' she gasped. 'I've never . . . nothing like this.'

Her soft, encircling fingers slid on him. Up, and down.

The knife shook as Charles moved it toward her chest. Just above her left breast, he pressed the point against her skin. Gently.

'Careful there,' she whispered. 'You don't want to cut me.'

'I do, actually.'

Her hand slipped away. She stood up very straight, searching his eyes. 'You're kidding, aren't you?'

'No.'

'But you *hate* cuts.'

'I'm sorry. As a matter of fact, I love them. They . . . they do something to me.'

'You mean like they turn you on?'

'Yes.'

'But that's crazy!'

'I guess so. I'm awfully sorry, Lynn.'

'Hold on, now.'

'I *have* to do it. I have to cut you up.'

'Oh my God.'

He shook his head. 'You're so beautiful, and . . . I guess I love you.'

'Charles. No.'

He stared at the knife point denting her skin. A slit all the way down to the tip of her breast . . .

Lynn grabbed his hand, twisted it. As Charles yelped, the elbow of her other arm crashed against his cheek. Stumbling backward, he heard his knife clatter to the floor. His pants tripped him. He slammed the side of the study carrel and fell.

Lynn scurried, crouched, and came up holding the knife.

Charles got to his knees. He gazed up at her. So beautiful. Scowling at him, naked except for her white socks and sneakers. The blade of the knife in her hand gleamed.

'Oh, Charles,' she murmured.

Tears stung his eyes. He hunched over, clasped his face with both hands, and wept.

'Charles?'

'I'm sorry,' he blurted. 'God, I'm so sorry! I don't know why I . . . I'm sorry!'

'Charles.' Her voice held a note of command.

He rubbed tears from his eyes and lifted his head.

Lynn stared down at him. She nodded slightly. A corner of her mouth was trembling.

She flicked her wrist. She flinched and grimaced as the blade cut a tiny slit. She closed the knife and lowered it to her side.

Charles watched the thin ribbon of blood. It started just below her collar bone and trickled down. It ran along the top of her breast, split in two, and one strand began a new course down the pale round side while another made its slow way closer to her nipple.

'Come here,' Lynn whispered.

Charles was embarrassed horribly the next day in the pharmacy.

Lynn was giggling.

She plopped three boxes of condoms down on the counter. The clerk, a young man, glanced from her to Charles. He looked amused.

'You got something against safe sex?' Lynn asked.

The clerk blushed. 'No. Huh-uh.'

Charles wanted to curl up and die.

'Ring these up, too, while you're at it.' Onto the counter, Lynn tossed three tins of adhesive bandages.

Out of the Woods

A sound like footsteps outside the tent shocked me out of half-sleep. Another camper? Not likely. We were far from the main trails and hadn't seen a backpacker in three days.

Maybe it was no one at all. Maybe a twig or pine cone had dropped from a nearby tree. Or maybe the smell of food had drawn an animal to our camp. A big animal.

I heard it again – a dry crushing sound.

I was afraid to move, but forced myself to roll over and see if Sadie was awake.

She was gone.

I looked down the length of my mummy bag. The unzipped screen was swaying inward. A cool damp-smelling breeze touched my face, and I remembered Sadie leaving the tent. How long ago? No way to tell. Maybe I had dozed for an hour, maybe for a minute. At any rate, it was high time for her to come in so we could close the flaps.

'Hey, Sadie, why don't you get in here?'

I heard only the stream several yards from our campsite. It made a racket like a gale blowing through a forest.

'Sadie?' I called.

Nothing.

'Saay-deee!'

She must have wandered out of earshot. Okay. It was a fine night, cold but clear, with a moon so round and white you could sit up for hours enjoying it. That's what we'd done, in fact, before turning in. I couldn't blame her for taking her time out there.

'Enjoy yourself,' I muttered, and shut my eyes. My feet were a bit cold. I rubbed them together through my sweatsocks, curled up, and adjusted the roll of jeans beneath my head. I was just beginning to get comfortable when somebody close to the tent coughed.

It wasn't Sadie.

My heart froze.

'Who's out there?' I called.

'Only me,' said a man's low voice, and the tent began to shake violently. 'Come outa there!'

'What do you want?'

'Make it quick.'

'Stop jerking the tent.' I took my knife from its sheath on the belt of my jeans.

The tent went motionless. 'I've got a shotgun,' the man said. 'Come outa there before I count five or I'll blast apart the tent with you in it. One.'

I scurried out of my sleeping bag.

'Two.'

'Hey, can't you wait till I get dressed?'

'Three. Come out with your hands empty, four.'

I stuck the knife down the side of my sweatsock, handle first to keep it from falling out, and crawled through the flaps.

'Five, you just made it.'

I stood up, feeling twigs and pine cones under my feet, and looked into the grinning, bearded face of a man who bore a disturbing resemblance to Rasputin. He had no shotgun. Only my hand-ax. I scanned the near bank of the stream behind him. No sign of Sadie.

'Where's the shotgun?' I asked. Then I clamped my mouth shut to keep my teeth quiet.

The man gave a dry, vicious laugh. 'Take that knife outa your sock.'

I looked down. I was wearing only shorts and socks, and the

moonlight made the knife blade shine silvery against my calf.

'Take it out slowly,' he warned.

'No.'

'Want to see your wife again? If I give the signal, my buddy will kill her. Slit her open like a wet sack.'

'You've got Sadie?'

'Back in the trees. Now, the knife.'

'Not a chance.' I pressed my knees together to keep them from banging against each other. 'You'll kill us both anyway.'

'Naw. All we want's your food and gear. See, we gotta do some camping. You understand, pal.' He grinned as if a glimpse of his big crooked teeth would help me understand better. It did.

'What did you do?' I asked, trying to stall for time. 'Rob a bank?'

'That, too. Now are you gonna get rid of that knife or do I signal Jake to start cutting?'

'Better signal Jake,' I said, and grabbed my knife.

'You sure?'

'I'm sure. Just one favor, though. Do you mind if I tell my wife goodbye?'

He grinned again. 'Go on.'

'Thanks,' I said. Then I yelled, 'Goodbye, Sadie! Sadie! Goodbye, Sadie!'

'Enough.' He came forward, holding the ax high, shaking it gently as if testing the weight of its head. All the time, he grinned.

My knife flew end over end, glinting moonlight, and struck him square in the chest. Hilt first.

He kept coming. Finally, I backed into a tree. Its bark felt damp and cold and rough against my skin.

'There's no Jake,' I said to distract him.

'So what?' he answered.

I raised my hands to block the ax and wondered if it would hurt for long.

Then a chilling, deep-throated howl shook the night. A mastiff splashed through the stream. Huge, brutish, black as death. The man had no time to turn. He only had time to scream before Sadie, snarling, took him down and began to rip his throat.

Stiff Intruders

'What are you doing here?' Charlie demanded of the dead woman.

She didn't answer. She was leaning back in Charlie's lawn chair, the very chair he wanted for himself, the chair he sat in every morning to drink his first two mugs of coffee. This was his favorite part of the day: so quiet, the air still cool and fresh from the night, the sun gently warming. But now, this!

'Hey!' he shouted.

She didn't stir. She simply sat there, hands folded on her lap, ankles crossed casually. Charlie sipped his coffee and walked around her. She wore a sleek, blue evening gown. Inappropriate wear, Charlie thought. A sun dress or swimsuit would be just the thing, but a formal, off-the-shoulder gown was unsuitable, even pretentious. Not that she could be held accountable.

Charlie went into the kitchen for a refill of coffee. As he pushed through the door to the backyard and saw her still sitting there, the injustice of it overwhelmed him. He decided to nudge her off the chair and let her fend for herself.

That's exactly what he did. The woman flopped and sprawled, and Charlie took his seat.

After a few moments, he moaned in despair. He simply couldn't enjoy his coffee in front of her.

Emptying his cup on the grass, he got to his feet and rushed into the house. He wanted to pound roughly on Lou's bedroom door. That might rub Lou the wrong way, however, so he rapped lightly.

'Knock off the racket!' Lou yelled.

'May I come in?'

'Suit yourself.'

Charlie opened the door and stepped into a room stinking of stale cigar smoke. Lou was in bed, covers pulled high so that only his face showed. The chubby face, flat nose and bulging eyes always reminded Charlie of a pug named Snappy he'd once owned. Snappy, who nipped anything in sight, generally had a sweeter disposition than Lou. Especially in the morning.

'Get up, Lou. I want to show you something.'

'What?'

'Get up, get up!'

Lou moaned and sat up. 'This better be good,' he said.

'Oh, it's not good, but you'd better see it.'

Muttering, Lou climbed from bed. He put on his slippers and robe, and followed Charlie to the backyard.

'See,' Charlie said.

'Who is she?' asked Lou.

'How should I know?'

'You found her.'

'Just because she was sitting in my chair doesn't mean I know the lady.'

'What was she doing in your chair?'

'Not much.'

'How come she's on the grass?'

'She was in my seat, Lou.'

'You shoved her off?'

'Certainly.'

'That was rude, Charlie.' Lou knelt down beside her. 'Nicely dressed, isn't she?'

'Certainly better dressed than you left yours,' Charlie said.

'I won't quibble with that.' He tipped her head back and touched her bruised throat. 'A nylon stocking,' he said. 'Maybe a scarf. Not my style at all.'

'I haven't accused you of anything,' Charlie protested.

'No, that's right. Thanks. You've gotta be wondering, though.'
Charlie shrugged.

'You read my book, right?'

'Certainly.'

In fact, Charlie had not read it. He hadn't read any book since *Silas Marner* in high school. But Lou was proud of *Choke 'Em Till They Croak: the True Story of the Riverside Strangler in His Own Words*. He had every right to be proud. The book, written during his last two years in prison, had been a hardbound bestseller. The paperback rights went for $800,000, and Ed Lentz was signed to play Lou in the Universal film.

'First,' Lou said, 'if she wasn't a blonde, I left her alone. Second, I took the clothes home to dress up my mannequins. Third, I didn't use no scarf, I used my thumbs. That's how come they called me Thumbs.'

'Certainly, I know all that.'

'Fourth, I didn't dump 'em in other people's backyards. That's rude. I left 'em on the freeway exits.' He poked her with his foot. 'Not my style at all.'

'But the police?'

'Exactly. We've gotta get rid of her.'

'What'll we do with her?' Charlie asked.

Lou pulled a cigar out of his robe pocket. He peeled off the wrapper and tossed it into the grass. He poked the cigar into his mouth and lit it. 'What we'll do,' he said, 'we'll deposit her at the bank.'

They stored her in the trunk of Charlie's Dodge until after dark that night. Then they went for a drive. Charlie, a former wheel man who drove getaway cars during numerous successful robberies and one failure, stole a Ford Mustang from the parking lot of an apartment building in Studio City. Lou followed him in the Dodge. On a dark, curving road in the Hollywood Hills, Lou picked the lock of the Mustang's trunk. They transferred her into the trunk, and left the

Mustang behind the Santa Monica branch office of Home Savings and Loan.

'That was certainly a chore,' Charlie complained afterward.

'I got a kick out of it,' Lou said.

Two days later, while reading the morning paper, Lou announced, 'They found our body.'

'Oh?'

' "Dancer found slain," it says. "The body of twenty-nine-year-old ballet dancer Marianne Tumly was found late Sunday night, the apparent victim of strangulation. Miss Tumly, understudy of Los Angeles ballerina Meg Fontana, disappeared Friday night after the company's performance of *Swan Lake*. Her body was discovered in the trunk of a car abandoned in Santa Monica, according to police officials." ' Lou began to mumble, apparently finding no more worth sharing.

'You don't suppose they'll connect us, do you?' Charlie asked.

'Not a chance.'

For several days, Charlie drank his morning coffee in the backyard, enjoying the fresh air, the sunlight, the silence and peaceful solitude. On Saturday, however, he found the body of a lean brunette occupying his chair.

He stared at her. She stared back.

'This is ridiculous,' he said. 'Well, you're not going to ruin my day *this* time!'

But she did.

Though Charlie sat in Lou's wicker chair, back turned so she was out of sight, he could almost feel her studying the back of his head. Irritated, he went inside to refill his mug. As he poured steaming coffee from the percolator, he got an idea. He went to the linen closet. Before resuming his seat, he covered the woman's head with a striped pillow case.

That almost worked. Unfortunately, Charlie half expected her to peek out from under the pillow case. Every few seconds, he looked over his shoulder to check. It finally became too much for him. He rushed into the house and barged into Lou's bedroom. 'Lou!' he cried. 'There's another one!'

Lou's scowl turned to a grin. 'A busy man, our strangler.'

Late that night, they put her in the trunk of a stolen Firebird. They left the Firebird in a parking lot at Los Angeles International Airport.

Though the newspaper ran stories for several days about the disappearance of a dancer – another member of the troupe performing *Swan Lake* – her body wasn't found until Thursday night. It made the Friday morning paper.

After reading the article aloud, Lou lit a cigar. 'We did real good on that one, Charlie. If we'd wrapped her up better to hold in the aroma, she might've gone another week. Know what I'd like to do, I'd like to put the next one . . .'

'*What* next one?' Charlie demanded.

'We've had these gals two Saturday mornings in a row. Number three's gonna pop up tomorrow, you can bet on it.'

'Lou!'

'Huh?'

'Let's lay for the strangler. If he comes along tonight with another corpse, we'll nab him!'

'What then?'

'We'll make him take it away.'

Lou watched his smoke float toward the ceiling. Then he said, 'Good idea. Excellent idea. I'd like to meet the guy.'

Charlie, sitting on a stool near the backyard fence at midnight, heard a car in the alley. It stopped just on the other side of the fence. He heard the engine die, then the quiet bump of a closing door.

So this is how he does it, Charlie thought. Just drives up the alley and brings her in. But the rear gate? It's always locked. How . . .?

Behind Charlie, something thudded against the redwood fence. He turned and looked up. A blonde woman grinned at him over the top. He heard a grunt. The woman seemed to leap. She towered over him for a moment, then folded at the waist. Charlie jumped out of the way. He gaped at her. She hung there, swaying slightly, like the body of a gunslinger draped over a saddle. Another grunt came from behind the fence. Her legs flipped high, slender and pale in the moonlight. Then she dived to the grass. She performed a somersault, and lay still.

Charlie glanced toward the garage. Its side door stood open. In the darkness of its gap was the red glow of Lou's cigar.

He motioned frantically for Lou to join him.

Quickly, he crouched at the corner of the fence. The wood jolted against his back, and he saw an arm hook over the top rail. After a gasp and a scuffling sound, a leg appeared. Then, in one quick motion, the man swung over and dropped to the grass. He landed silently on his feet, less than a yard from Charlie.

Crouching, he lifted the body. He flung it over his shoulder.

'Now,' said Charlie, 'you may kindly toss her back over the fence and take her away. Clutter someone else's yard.'

Still holding the body, the strangler turned to Charlie and said, 'Huh?'

'I said take her away!'

'How come?' he asked. He was younger than Charlie had imagined. His shaved head was shiny in the moonlight. In his tight T-shirt and jeans, his stocky body looked dangerous.

'Because,' Charlie answered in a subdued voice, 'you've been putting them in *my* lawn chair.'

'I thought you liked it.'

'*Liked* it?'

'Sure.'

Charlie was relieved to see Lou ambling toward them, puffing vigorously on his cigar.

'You took good care of 'em,' the younger man continued. 'You know?'

'Why'd you bring them here?' Lou asked.

The man spun around. Charlie dodged the woman's left heel.

'Did you know about me?' Lou asked. 'Is that it?'

'Know what?'

'I'm Thumbs O'Brien. The Riverside Strangler.'

'No fooling?'

'Did you read my book, kid?' Lou's voice was eager.

'What book?'

'Never mind.' Lou sounded disappointed. 'So how come you're leaving stiffs in our backyard?'

'Like I was telling this guy, you took good care of 'em. I mean, the first, I was bringing her up through the alley here. It's dark, you know. So I just heaved her over the fence.'

'How did she get in my chair,' Charlie asked.

'I got to thinking, you know? How comfortable can it be on the grass? So I hustled her over to the chair.'

'Decent of you,' Lou said.

'You guys took care of her real good.'

'Thank you,' Lou said.

'That's why I came back. I figured I'll let you take care of the others, too.'

'Tell me this,' Lou said. 'Why'd you do it?'

'I just told you, you took real good . . .'

'He means,' Charlie explained, 'why did you kill them?'

'Oh.' He grinned. 'She told me to.'

'Who did?'

'Isadora.'

'Who?' asked Lou.

'Isadora Duncan. You know, Isadora! She wants 'em for her dance troupe.'

Lou tapped a column of ash from the tip of his cigar. 'They won't do her much good dead.'

Charlie groaned at Lou's display of ignorance. '*She's* dead,' he explained. 'Isadora is. Her scarf caught in the wheel of her car. A long time ago. In the twenties, I believe.'

'No kidding?' Lou nodded at the young strangler. 'So you're fixing her up with a bunch of dancers. I get it.'

'May I ask,' Charlie inquired, 'how large a group she requires?'

'Oh, big. Real big.'

'How big?'

'Fifty-two.'

Charlie imagined fifty-two more bodies in the backyard on his lawn chair. 'I won't have it!' he blurted. 'Lou!'

''Fraid that's too much, kid.'

'Too much?'

'Yeah. Sorry.'

Charlie watched the woman fall. He watched the brief struggle. It was no contest, really. The kid didn't have a scarf handy, but Lou had his thumbs.

On a sunny, cool morning toward the end of the week, Charlie carried his coffee mug outside and stopped in surprise.

'What are you doing here?' he asked.

Lou, in sunglasses and a Dodger ballcap, was sitting on his own lawn chair. A cigar tilted upward from his mouth. Propped against his upraised right knee, he held a spiral notebook. 'How's this sound?' he asked. '*Save Your Last Dance for Me: the True Story of the Swan Lake Strangler in His Own Words.*'

'It sounds like a lie,' Charlie said.

'You gotta take liberties,' said Lou, 'when you're a ghostwriter.'

Special

1

The outlaw women, wailing and shrieking, fled from the encampment. All but one, who stayed to fight.

She stood by the campfire, a sleek arm reaching up to pull an arrow from the quiver on her back. She stood alone as the men began to fall beneath the quick fangs of the dozen raiding vampires.

'She's mine!' Jim shouted.

None of his fellow Guardians gave him argument. Maybe they wanted no part of her. They raced into the darkness of the woods to chase down the others.

Jim rushed the woman.

You get her and you get her.

She looked innocent, fierce, glorious. Calmly nocking the arrow. Her thick hair was golden in the firelight. Her legs gleamed beneath the short leather skirt that hung low on her hips. Her vest spread open as she drew back her bowstring, sliding away from the tawny mound of her right breast.

Jim had never seen such a woman.

Get her!

She glanced at him. Without an instant of hesitation, she pivoted away and loosed her arrow.

Jim snapped his head sideways. The shaft flew at Strang's back. Hit with a thunk. The vampire hurled the flapping body of an outlaw from his arms and whirled around, his black eyes fixing on the woman, blood spewing from his wide mouth as he bellowed, 'Mine!'

Jim lurched to a halt.

Eyes narrow, lips a tight line, the woman reached up for another arrow as Strang staggered toward her. Jim was near enough to hear breath hissing through her nostrils. He gazed at her, fascinated, as she fitted the arrow onto the bowstring. Her eyes were on Strang. She pulled the string back to her jaw. Her naked breast rose and fell as she panted for air.

She didn't let the arrow fly.

Strang took one more stumbling stride, foamy blood gushing from his mouth, arms outstretched as if to reach beyond the campfire and grab her head. Then he pitched forward. His face crushed the flaming heap of wood, sending up a flurry of sparks. His hair began to blaze.

The woman met Jim's eyes.

Get her and you get her.

He'd never wanted any woman so much.

'Run!' he whispered. 'Save yourself.'

'Eat shit and die,' she muttered, and released her arrow. It whizzed past his arm.

Going for her, Jim couldn't believe that she had missed. But he heard the arrow punch into someone, heard the roar of a mortally wounded vampire, and knew that she'd found her target. For the second time, she had chosen to take down a vampire rather than protect herself from Jim. And she hadn't run when he'd given her the chance. What kind of woman *is* this?

With his left hand, he knocked the bow aside. With his right, he swung at her face. His fist clubbed her cheek. Her head snapped sideways, mouth dropping open, spit spraying out. The punch spun her. The bow flew from her hand. Her legs tangled and she went down. She pushed at the ground, got to her hands and knees, and scurried away from Jim.

Let her go?

He hurried after her, staring at the backs of her legs. Shadows and firelight fluttered on them. Sweat glistened. The skirt was so short it barely covered her rump and groin.

You get her and you get her.

She thrust herself up.

I'm gonna let her go, Jim thought. They'll kill me, and they'll probably get her anyway, but . . .

Instead of making a break for the woods, she whirled around, jerked a knife from the sheath at her hip, and threw herself at Jim. The blade ripped the front of his shirt. Before she could bring it back across, he caught her wrist. He yanked her arm up high and drove a fist into her belly. Her breath exploded out. The blow picked her up. The power of it would've hurled her backward and slammed her to the ground, but Jim kept his grip on her wrist. She dangled in front of him, writhing and wheezing. Her sweaty face was twisted with agony.

One side of her vest hung open.

She might've had a chance.

I got her, I get her.

Jim cupped her warm, moist breast, felt its nipple pushing against his palm.

Her fist crashed into his nose. He saw it coming, couldn't believe it, had no time to block it. Pain exploded behind his eyes. But he kept his grip, stretched her high by the trapped arm, and punched her belly until he could no longer hold her up.

Blinking tears from his eyes, sniffing up blood, he let go. Her legs folded. She dropped to her knees in front of him and slumped forward, her face hitting the ground between his feet. Crouching, he pulled a pair of handcuffs out of his belt. Blood splashed the back of her vest as he picked up her limp arms, pulled them behind her, and snapped the cuffs around her wrists.

2

'That one put up a hell of a scrap,' Roger said.

Jim, sitting on the ground beside the crumpled body of the woman, looked up at the grinning vampire. 'She was pretty tough,' he said. He sniffed and swallowed some more blood. 'Sorry I couldn't stop her quicker.'

Roger patted him on the head. 'Think nothing of it. Strang was always a pain in the ass, anyway, and Winthrop was such an atrocious brown-noser. I'm better off without them. I'd say, taken all round, that we've had a banner night.'

Roger crouched in front of the woman, clutched the hair on top of her head, and lifted her to her knees. Her eyes were shut. By the limp way she hung there, Jim guessed she must still be unconscious.

'A looker,' Roger said. 'Well worth a broken nose, if you ask me.' He chuckled. 'Of course, it's not *my* nose. But if I were you, I'd be a pretty damn happy fellow about now.' He eased her down gently and walked off to join the other vampires.

While they waited for all the Guardians to return with the female prisoners, they searched the bodies of the outlaws, took whatever possessions they found interesting, and stripped the corpses. They tossed the clothing into the campfire, not one of them bothering to remove Strang from the flames.

Joking and laughing quite a bit, they hacked the bodies to pieces. The banter died away as they began to suck the remaining blood from severed heads, stumps of necks and arms and legs, from various limbs and organs. Jim turned his eyes away. He looked at the woman. She was lucky to be out cold. She couldn't see the horrible carnage. She couldn't hear the grunts and sighs of pleasure, the sloppy wet sounds, the occasional belch from the vampires relishing their feast. Nor could she hear the women who'd been captured and brought in by the other Guardians. They were weeping, pleading, screaming, vomiting.

When he finally looked away from her, he saw that all the Guardians had returned. Each had a prisoner. Bart and Harry both had two. Most of the women looked as if they'd been beaten. Most had been stripped of their clothes.

They looked to Jim like a sorry bunch.

Not one stood proud and defiant.

I got the best of the lot, he thought.

Roger rose to his feet, tossed a head into the fire, and rubbed the back of his hand across his mouth. 'Well, folks,' he said, 'how's about heading on back to the old homestead?'

Jim picked up the woman. Carrying her on his shoulder, he joined the procession on its journey through the woods. Other Guardians complimented him on his catch. Some made lewd suggestions about her. A few peeked under her skirt. Several offered to trade, and grumbled when Jim refused.

At last, they found their way to the road. They hiked up its moonlit center until they came to the bus. Biff and Steve, Guardians who'd stayed behind to protect it from outlaws and vampire gangs, waved greetings from its roof.

On the side of the black bus, in huge gold letters that glimmered with moonlight, was painted, ROGER'S ROWDY RAIDERS.

The vampires, Guardians and prisoners climbed aboard.

Roger drove.

An hour later, they passed through the gates of his fortified estate.

3

The next day, Jim slept late. When he woke up, he lay in bed for a long time, thinking about the woman. Remembering her courage and beauty, the way her breast had felt in his hand, her weight and warmth and smoothness while she hung over his shoulder on the way to the bus.

He hoped she was all right. She'd seemed to be unconscious during the entire trip. Of course, she might've been pretending. Jim, sitting beside her, had savored the way she looked in the darkness and felt quick rushes of excitement each time a break in the trees permitted moonlight to wash across her.

The other Guardians were all busy raping their prisoners during the bus ride. Some had poked fun at him, asked if he'd gone queer like Biff and Steve, offered to pay him for a chance to screw Sleeping Beauty.

He wasn't sure why he had left her alone during the trip. In the past, he'd never hesitated to enjoy his prisoners.

But this woman was different. Special. Proud and strong. She deserved better than to be molested while out cold and in the presence of others.

Jim would have her soon. In privacy. She would be alert, brave and fierce.

Soon.

But not today.

For today, the new arrivals would be in the care of Doc and his crew. They would be deloused and showered, then examined. Those judged incapable of bearing children would go to the Donor Ward. Each Donor had a two-fold job: to give a pint of blood daily for the estate's stockroom, and to provide sexual services not only for the Guardian who captured her but also for any others, so inclined, once he'd finished.

The other prisoners would find themselves in the Specialty Suite.

It wasn't a suite, just a barracks-like room similar to the Donor Ward. But those assigned to it did receive special treatment. They weren't milked for blood. They were provided good food, not the slop doled out to the Donors.

And each Special could only be used by the Guardian who had captured her.

Mine will be a Special, Jim thought. She's gotta be. She *will* be. She's young and strong.

She'll be mine. All mine.

At least till Delivery Day.

He felt a cold, spreading heaviness.

That's a long time from now, he told himself. Don't think about it.

Moaning, he climbed out of bed.

4

He was standing guard in the north tower at ten the next morning when the two-way radio squawked and Doc's voice came through the speaker. 'Harmon, you're up. Specialty Suite, Honors Room Three. Bennington's on his way to relieve you.'

Jim thumbed the speak button on his mike. 'Roger,' he said.

Heart pounding, he waited for Bennington. He'd found out last night that his prisoner, named Diane, had been designated a Special. He'd hoped this would be the day, but he hadn't counted on it; Doc only gave the okay if the timing was right. In Doc's opinion, it was only right during about two weeks of each woman's monthly cycle.

Jim couldn't believe his luck.

Finally, Bennington arrived. Jim climbed down from the tower and made his way across the courtyard toward the Specialty Suite. He had a hard time breathing. His legs felt weak and shaky.

He'd been in Honors Rooms before. With many different outlaw women. But he'd never felt like this: excited, horribly excited, but also nervous. Petrified.

5

Honors Room Three had a single large bed with red satin sheets. The plush carpet was red. So were the curtains that draped the barred windows, and the shades of the twin lamps on either side of the bed.

Jim sat down on a soft, upholstered armchair. And waited. Trembling.

Calm down, he told himself. This is crazy. She's just a woman.

Yeah, sure.

Hearing footfalls from the corridor, he leaped to his feet. He turned to the door. Watched it open.

Diane stumbled in, shoved from behind by Morgan and Donner, Doc's burly assistants. She glared at Jim.

'Key,' Jim said.

Morgan shook his head. 'I wouldn't, if I were you.'

'I brought her in, didn't I?'

'She'll bust more than your nose, you give her half a chance.'

Jim held out his hand. Morgan, shrugging, tossed him the key to the shackles. Then the two men left the room. The door bumped shut, locking automatically.

And he was alone with Diane.

From the looks of her, she'd struggled on the way to the Honors Room. Her thick hair was mussed, golden wisps hanging down her face. Her blue satin robe had fallen off one shoulder. Its cloth belt was loose, allowing a narrow gap from her waist to the hem at her knees. She was naked beneath the robe.

Jim slipped a finger under the belt. He pulled until its half-knot came apart. Then he spread the robe and slipped it down her arms until it was stopped by the wrist shackles.

Guilt subdued his excitement when he saw the livid smudges on her belly. 'I'm sorry about that,' he murmured.

'Do what you're going to do,' she said. Though she was

trying to sound tough, he heard a slight tremor in her voice.

'I'll take these shackles off,' he said. 'But if you fight me, I'll be forced to hurt you again. I don't want to do that.'

'Then don't take them off.'

'It'll be easier on you without them.'

'Easier *for* you.'

'Do you know why you're here?'

'It seems pretty obvious.'

'It's not that obvious,' Jim said, warning himself to speak with care. The room was bugged. A Guardian in the Security Center would be eavesdropping, and Roger himself was fond of listening to the Honors Room tapes. 'This isn't . . . just so I can have fun and games with you. The thing is . . . I've got to make you pregnant.'

Her eyes narrowed. She caught her lower lip between her teeth. She said nothing.

'What that means,' Jim went on, 'is that we'll be seeing each other every day. At least during your fertile times. Every day until you conceive. Do you understand?'

'Why do they want me pregnant?' she asked.

'They need more humans. For guards and staff and things. As it is, there aren't enough of us.'

She gazed into his eyes. He couldn't tell whether or not she believed the lie.

'If you don't become pregnant, they'll put you in with the Donors. It's much better for you here. The Donors . . . all the Guardians can have them whenever they want.'

'So, it's either you or the whole gang, huh?'

'That's right.'

'Okay.'

'Okay?'

She nodded.

Jim began taking off his clothes, excited but uncomfortably aware of the scorn in her eyes.

'You must be a terrible coward,' she said.

He felt heat spread over his skin.

'You don't seem evil. So you must be a coward. To serve such beasts.'

'Roger treats us very well,' he said.

'If you were a man, you'd kill him and all his kind. Or die trying.'

'I have a good life here.'

'The life of a dog.'

Naked, he crouched in front of Diane. His face was inches from her tuft of golden down. Aching with a hot confusion of lust and shame, he lowered his eyes to the short length of chain stretched taut between her feet. 'I'm no coward,' he said, and removed the steel cuffs.

As the shackles fell to the carpet, she pumped a knee into his forehead. Not a powerful blow, but enough to knock him off balance. His rump hit the floor. He caught himself with both hands while Diane dropped backward, curling, jamming her thighs tight against her chest. Feet in the air, she slipped the hand shackles and trapped robe under her buttocks and up the backs of her legs. They cleared her feet. Her hands were suddenly in front of her, cuffs and chain hidden under the draping robe.

As her heels thudded the floor, Jim rushed her. She spread her legs wide, raised her knees, and stretched her arms out straight overhead. The robe was a glossy curtain molded to her face and breasts.

Jim dived, slamming down on her. She grunted. Clamped her legs around him. He reached for her arms. They were too quick for him. The covered chain swept past his eyes. Went tight around his throat. Squeezed.

Choking, he found her wrists. They were crossed behind his head. He tugged at them. Parted them. Felt the chain loosen. Forced them down until the chain pressed into Diane's throat.

Her face had come uncovered. Her eyes bulged. Her lips peeled back. She twisted and bucked and squirmed.

When he entered her, tears shimmered in her eyes.

6

The next day, Jim let Morgan and Donner chain her to the bedframe before leaving.

She didn't say a word. She didn't struggle. She lay motionless and glared at Jim as he took her.

When he was done but still buried in her tight heat, he whispered, 'I'm sorry.' He hoped the microphone didn't pick it up.

For an instant, the look of hatred in her eyes changed to something else. Curiosity? Hope?

7

'What are you sorry about, Jim?'

'Sorry?'

'You apologized. What did you apologize for?'

'To who?'

'You've gone soft on her,' Roger said. 'Can't say I blame you. She's quite a looker. Feisty, too. But she's obviously messing you up. I'm afraid someone else'll have to take over doing the Honors. We'll work a trade with Phil. You can do his gal, and he'll do yours. It'll be better for everyone.'

'Yes, sir.'

8

Phil's gal was named Betsy. She was a brunette. She was pretty. She was stacked. She was not just compliant, but enthusiastic. She said that she'd hated being an outlaw, living in the wilds, often hungry and always afraid. This, she said, was like paradise.

Jim had her once a day.

Each time, he closed his eyes and made believe she was Diane.

9

He longed for her. He dreamed about her. But she was confined to the Specialty Suite, available only to Phil, so he would probably never have a chance to see her again. It ate at him. He began to hope she would fail to conceive. In that case, she would eventually be sent to the Donor Ward.

A terrible fate for someone with her spirit.

But at least Jim would be able to see her, go to her, touch her, have her.

And she would be spared the final horror which awaited the Specials.

Doc had judged her to be fertile, however, so Jim knew there was little chance of ever seeing her again.

He was in the Mess Hall a week after being reassigned to Betsy, trying to eat lunch though he had no appetite, when the alarm suddenly blared. The PA boomed, 'Guardian down, Honors Room One! Make it snappy, men!'

Jim and six others ran from the Mess Hall. Sprinting across the courtyard, he took over the lead. He found Donner waiting in the corridor. The man, gray and shaky, pointed at the closed door of Honors Room One.

Jim threw the door open.

Instead of a bed, this room was equipped with a network of

steel bars from which the Special could be suspended, stretched and spread in a variety of positions.

Diane hung by her wrists from a high bar. There were no restraints on her feet. She was swinging and twisting at the ends of her chains as she kicked at Morgan. Her face wore a fierce grimace. Her hair clung to her face. Her skin, apparently oiled by Phil, gleamed and poured sweat. The shackles had cut into her wrists, and blood streamed down her arms and sides.

Phil lay motionless on the floor beneath her wild, kicking body. His head was turned. Too much.

She'd broken his neck?

How could she?

Even as Jim wondered, he saw Morgan lurch forward and grab one of her darting ankles. Diane shot her other leg high. With a cry of pain, she twisted her body and hooked her foot behind Morgan's head. The big man stumbled toward her, gasping with alarm. He lost his hold on her ankle. That leg flew up. In an instant, he was on his knees, his head trapped between her thighs.

Morgan's dilemma seemed to snap the audience of Guardians out of their stunned fascination.

Jim joined the others in their rush to the rescue.

He grabbed one leg. Bart grabbed the other. They forced her thighs apart, freeing Morgan. The man slumped on top of Phil's body, made a quick little whimpery sound, and scurried backward.

'Take Phil out of here,' said Rooney, the head Guardian.

The body was dragged from under Diane and taken from the room.

'What'll we do with her?' Jim asked.

'Let her hang,' Rooney said. 'We'll wait for tonight and let Roger take care of her.'

They released her legs and backed up quickly.

She dangled, swaying back and forth, her eyes fixed on Jim.

He paused in the doorway. He knew he would never see her again.

10

He was wrong.

He saw her a month later when he relieved Biff and began his new duty of monitoring video screens in the Security Center. Diane was on one of the dozen small screens. Alone. In the Punishment Room.

Jim couldn't believe his eyes. He'd been certain that Roger had killed her – probably torturing her, allowing the other vampires small samples of her blood before draining her himself. Jim had seen that done, once, to a Donor who tried to escape. Diane's crime had been much worse. She'd murdered a Guardian.

Instead of taking her life, however, Roger had merely sent her to the Punishment Room. Which amounted to little more than solitary confinement.

Incredible. Wonderful.

11

Night after night, alone in the Security Center, Jim watched her.

He watched her sleep on the concrete floor, a sheet wrapped around her naked body. He watched her sit motionless, cross-legged, gazing at the walls. He watched her squat on a metal bucket to relieve herself. Sometimes, she gave herself sponge baths.

Frequently, she exercised. For hours at a time, she would

stretch, run in place, kick and leap, do sit-up and push-up and handstands. Jim loved to watch her quick, graceful motions, the flow of her sleek muscles, the way her hair danced and how her breasts jiggled and swayed. He loved the sheen of sweat that made her body glisten.

He could never see enough of her.

Every day, he waited eagerly for the hour when he could relieve Biff and be alone with Diane.

When he had to go on night raids, he was miserable. But he did his duty. He rounded up outlaw women. Some became Specials, and he visited them in Honors Rooms, but when he was with them he always tried to pretend they were Diane.

Then one night, watching her exercise, he noticed that her belly didn't look quite flat.

'No,' he murmured.

12

Throughout the winter, he watched her grow. Every night, she seemed larger. Her breasts swelled and her belly became a bulging mound.

He often wondered whose child she was bearing. It might be his. It might be Phil's.

He worried, always, about Delivery Day.

13

During his free time, he began making solitary treks into the wood surrounding the estate.

He took his sub-machine-gun and machete.

He often came back with game, which he delivered afterwards to Jones in the kitchen. The grinning chef was always delighted to receive the fresh meat. He was glad to have Jim's company while he prepared it for the Guardians' evening meal.

14

Spring came. One morning at six, just as Bart entered the Security Center to relieve Jim of his watch, Diane flinched awake, grimacing. She drew her knees up. She clutched her huge belly through the sheet.

'What gives?' Bart asked.

Jim shook his head.

Bart studied the monitor. 'She's starting contractions. I'd better ring up Doc.'

Bart made the call. Then he took over Jim's seat in front of the video screens.

'I think I'll stick around,' Jim said.

Bart chuckled. 'Help yourself.'

He stayed. He watched the monitor. Soon, Doc and Morgan and Donner entered the cell. They slung the sheet aside. Morgan and Donner forced Diane's legs apart. Doc inspected her. Then they lifted her onto a gurney and strapped her down. They rolled the gurney out of the cell.

'I'll pick 'em up in the Prep Room,' Bart muttered. 'That's what you want to see, right?' He leered over his shoulder.

Jim forced a smile. 'You got it.'

Bart fingered some buttons. The deserted Punishment Room vanished from the screen, and the Prep Room appeared.

Doc and his assistants rolled the gurney in.

He soaked a pad with chloroform, and pressed it against Diane's nose and mouth until she passed out. Then the straps were unfastened. After being sprayed with water, she was rubbed with white foam. All three men went at her with razors.

'Wouldn't mind that job,' Bart said.

Jim watched the razors sweep paths through the foam, cutting away not only Diane's thick golden hair, but also the fine down. The passage of the blades left her skin shiny and pink. After a while, she was turned over so the rest of her body could be lathered and shaved.

Then the men rinsed her and dried her with towels.

They carried her from the gurney to the wheeled, oak serving-table. The table, a rectangle large enough to seat only six, was bordered by brass gutters for catching the run-off. At the corners of one end – Roger's end – were brass stirrups.

Feeling sick, Jim watched the men lift Diane's limp body onto the table. They bent her legs. They strapped her feet into the stirrups. They slid her forward to put her within easy reach of Roger. Then they cinched a belt across her chest, just beneath her breasts. They stretched her arms overhead and strapped her wrists to the table.

'That's about it for now,' Bart said. 'If you drop by around seven tonight, that's when they'll be basting her. She'll be awake then, too. That's when the panic really hits them. It's usually quite a sight to behold.'

'I've seen,' Jim muttered, and left the room.

15

He returned to the barracks and tried to sleep. It was no use. Finally, he got up and armed himself. Steve let him out the front gate. He wandered the woods for hours. With his sub-machine-gun, he bagged three squirrels.

In the late afternoon, he ducked into the hiding place he'd found in a clump of bushes. He lashed together the twenty wooden spears which he'd fashioned during the past weeks. He pocketed the small pouch containing the nightcap mushrooms which he had gathered and ground to fine powder.

He carried the spears to the edge of the forest. Leaving them propped against a tree, he stepped into the open. He smiled and waved his squirrels at the north tower. The gate opened, and he entered the estate.

He took the squirrels to Jones in the kitchen. And helped the cheerful chef prepare stew for the Guardians' supper.

16

Just after sunset, Jim went to the Security Center and knocked.

'Yo.' Biff's voice.

'It's Jim. I want to see the basting.'

'You're a little early,' Biff said. Moments later, he opened the door. His mouth made a tight little O and he folded as Jim rammed a knife into his stomach.

17

Diane was awake, sweaty and grunting, struggling against the restraints, gritting her teeth and flinching rigid each time a contraction hit her.

Jim stared at the screen. Without hair and eyebrows, she looked so *odd*. Freakish. Even her figure, misshapen by the distended belly and swollen breasts, seemed alien. But her eyes were pure Diane. In spite of her pain and terror, they were proud, unyielding.

Doc entered the Prep Room, examined her for a few moments, then went away.

Jim checked the other screens.

In the Donor Ward, the women had been locked down for the Guardians' evening mealtime. Some slept. Others chatted with friends in neighboring beds. Jim made a quick count.

In the Specialty Suite, Morgan and Donner were just returning a woman from an Honors Room. They led her to one of the ten empty beds, shoved her down on it, and shackled her feet to the metal frame. Jim counted heads.

Thirty-two Donors. Only sixteen Specials. Generally, however, the Donors were older women who'd been weakened by the daily loss of blood and by regular mistreatment at the hands of the Guardians. The Specials were fewer in number, but younger and stronger. Though some appeared to be in late stages of their pregnancies, most were not very far along, and many of the newer ones had probably not even conceived yet.

It'll be the Specials, Jim decided.

He watched Morgan and Donner leave the Suite.

In the Mess Hall, Guardians began to eat their stew.

In the floodlit courtyard, Steve and Bennington climbed stairs to the north and west towers, carrying pots of dinner to the men on watch duty. When they finished there, they should be heading for the other two towers.

Morgan and Donner entered the Mess Hall. They sat down, and Jones brought them pots of stew.

Doc entered the Prep Room. He set a bowl of shimmering red fluid onto the table beside Diane's hip. He dipped in a brush. He began to paint her body. The blood coated her like paint.

In the Mess Hall, Baxter groaned and staggered away from the table, clutching his belly.

In the Banquet Room, there was no camera. But Jim knew that Roger and his pals would be there, waiting and eager. The absence of the usual table would've already tipped them off that tonight would be Special. Even now, Roger was probably picking five to sit with him at the serving table. The unfortunate four would only get to watch and dine on their usual fare of Donor blood.

In the Mess Hall, Guardians were stumbling about, falling down, rolling on the floor.

In the Prep Room, Doc set aside the brush and bowl. He rolled the serving table toward the door. Diane shook her crimson, hairless head from side to side and writhed against the restraints.

Jim rushed out of the Security Center.

18

'All hell's broken loose!' he shouted as he raced up the stairs to the north tower. 'Don't touch your food! Jones poisoned it!'

'Oh shit!' Harris blurted, and spat out a mouthful.

'Did you swallow any?' Jim asked, rushing toward him.

'Not much, but . . .'

Jim jerked the knife from the back of his belt and slashed Harris's throat. He punched a button on the control panel.

By the time he reached the front gate, it was open. He ran out, dashed across the clear area beyond the wall, and grabbed the bundle of spears.

The gate remained open for him. Apparently, the poison had taken care of the Guardian on the west tower.

Rushing across the courtyard, he saw two Guardians squirming on the ground.

At the outer door of the Specialty Suite, he snatched the master key off its nail. He threw the door open and rushed in.

'All right, ladies! Listen up! We're gonna kill some vampires!'

19

Blasts pounding his ears, Jim blew apart the lock. He threw his gun aside, kicked the door, and charged into the Banquet Room.

Followed by sixteen naked Specials yelling and brandishing spears.

For just an instant, the vampires around the serving table continued to go about their business – greedily lapping the brown, dry blood from Diane's face and breasts and legs as Roger groped between her thighs. The four who watched, goblets in hand, were the first to respond.

Then, roaring, they all abandoned the table and attacked.

All except Roger.

Roger stood where he was. He met Jim's eyes. '*You dumb fuck!*' he shouted. 'Take care of him, guys!'

The vampires tried. They all rushed Jim.

But were met, first, by Specials. Some went down with spears in their chests while others tossed the women away or slammed them to the floor or snapped their spines or ripped out their throats.

Jim rushed through the melee. He halted at the near end of the table as Roger cried out, 'Is *this* why you're here?' His hands delved. Came up a moment later with a tiny, gleaming infant. 'Not enough to share, I'm afraid.' Grinning, he raised the child to his mouth. With a quick nip, he severed its umbilical cord.

One hand clutching the baby's feet, he raised it high and tilted back his head. His mouth opened wide. His other hand grasped the top of its head.

Ready to twist it off. Ready to enjoy his special, rare treat.

'No!' Diane shrieked.

Jim hurled his spear. Roger's hand darted down. He caught the shaft, stopping its flight even as the wooden point touched his chest. 'Dickhead,' he said. 'You didn't really think . . .'

Jim launched himself at Diane. He flew over her body, smashed down on her, slid through the wide V of her spread legs and reached high and grabbed the spear and rammed it deep into Roger's chest.

The vampire bellowed. He staggered backward. Coughed. Blood exploded from his mouth, spraying Jim's face and arms. He dropped to his knees and looked up at the infant that he still held high. He lowered its head toward his wide, gushing mouth.

Jim flung himself off the end of the table, but he knew he would be too late.

He landed on the spear. As its shaft snapped under his weight, bloody vomit cascaded over his head. Pushing himself up, he saw the baby dangling over Roger's mouth. The vampire tried to snap at its head, but the tide of rushing gore pushed it away.

Jim scurried forward. He held the child in both hands until Roger let go and slumped against the floor.

20

Afterwards, the Donors were released.

They helped with the burials.

Eleven dead Specials were buried in the courtyard, their graves marked by crosses fashioned of spears.

Morgan, Donner and the Guardians, who'd all succumbed to the poison, were buried beyond the south wall of the estate.

The corpses of Roger and his fellow vampires were taken into the woods to a clearing where two trails crossed. The heads were severed. The torsos were buried with the spears still in place. The heads were carried a mile away to another crossing in the trail. There, they were burned. The charred skulls were crushed, then buried.

After a vote by the women, Doc and three Guardians who'd missed the poisoned squirrels were put to death. Jones had also missed the meal. But the women seemed to like him. He was appointed chef. Jim was appointed leader.

He chose Diane to be his assistant.

The child was a girl. They named her Glory. She had Diane's eyes, and ears that stuck out in very much the same way as Jim's.

The small army lived in Roger's estate, and seemed happy.

Frequently, when the weather was good, a squad of well-armed volunteers would board the bus. Jim driving, they would follow roads deep into the woods. They would park the bus and wander about, searching. Sometimes, they found vampires and took them down with a shower of arrows. Sometimes, they found bands of outlaws and welcomed these strangers into their ranks.

21

One morning, when a commotion in the courtyard drew Jim's attention, he looked down from the north tower and saw Diane gathered around the bus with half-a-dozen other women. Instead of their usual leather skirts and vests, they were dressed in rags.

Diane saw him watching, and waved. Her hair had grown, but it was still quite short. It shone like gold in the sunlight.

She looked innocent, glorious.

She and her friends commenced to paint the bus pink.

Joyce

Barbara bolted out of the bedroom and straight into Darren's arms. He caught her, held her.

'What's wrong?' he asked. 'What is it?'

'Suh . . . somebody under the bed!'

'Oh. I'm sorry. Did she frighten you? It's only Joyce.'

'*Joyce?*' Barbara struggled out of Darren's embrace and gaped at him. 'But you told me . . . you said she was dead!'

'Well, of course she is. Do you think I would've married you if I still had a wife? It's just like I said, the brain aneurysm three years ago . . .'

'But you've got her under the bed!'

'Sure. Come on, I'll introduce you.'

Darren took Barbara by the hand and led her into the bedroom. She staggered along beside him. On the floor by the bed was her suitcase, the one she'd taken with her on the honeymoon, unpacked that evening, and after her shower with Darren had decided to tuck out of sight.

'Luggage doesn't go under the bed,' he explained. 'I keep it out in the garage.'

Barbara stood there, trembling and gasping inside her new silk kimono, trying to stay on her feet as Darren carried the suitcase over to the door. Then he knelt and slid Joyce out from under the bed.

'Darling, meet Joyce.'

Joyce lay stiff on the carpet, her wide blue eyes gazing toward the ceiling, her lips curled in a smile that showed the edges of her straight, white teeth. Wisps of brown hair swept across her forehead. Thick tresses flowed from beneath her head – a rich, silken banner that extended past her right shoulder. Her arms, close to her sides, were reaching upward from the elbows, hands open. Her legs were straight, parted slightly. Her feet were bare.

She wore a white negligee, a skimpy number with spaghetti straps and a plunging neckline. It was every bit as short as the nightie that Barbara had delighted Darren by wearing on their wedding night, and every bit as transparent. The way he'd dragged Joyce from beneath the bed had twisted it askew, pulling its deep V sideways so her right breast rose bare through the gap.

Smiling over his shoulder at Barbara, Darren said, 'Isn't she lovely?'

Barbara dropped.

When she came to, she found herself lying in bed. Darren was sitting on its edge, a worried look on his face, a hand inside her kimono gently caressing her thigh. 'Are you all right?' he asked.

She turned her head.

Joyce stood beside the bed, six feet away, still smiling. The nightie blew softly, stirred by the breeze from the window. Though it concealed nothing with its sheer fabric, at least it had been straightened so her breast no longer stuck out.

She has a better figure than me, Barbara thought.

She's more *beautiful* than . . .

Barbara looked away, frowned at Darren. Though she wanted to sound calm, her voice came out high and childlike when she asked, 'What's going on?'

Darren shrugged. He stroked her thigh. 'It's nothing to be upset about. Really.'

'Nothing to be upset about? You've got your dead wife *stuffed* in your bedroom . . . and wearing *that*!'

He smiled gently. 'Oh, she isn't stuffed. She's freeze-dried. I found a place that does people's deceased pets. She looks wonderful, doesn't she?'

'Oh, God.' Barbara murmured.

'And that's her favorite nightgown. I don't see why she should be deprived of it, but if you'd rather she wear something a bit more modest . . .'

'Darren. She's dead.'

'Well, of course.'

'You bury dead people. Or cremate them. You don't . . . keep them.'

'Why not?'

'It just isn't done!'

'Oh, if I couldn't have had her preserved so nicely, I suppose there'd be some reason to dispose of her. But look at her.'

Barbara chose not to.

'She's as fresh as the day she died. She doesn't smell. What's the problem?'

'The problem? The problem?'

'I don't see any problem.'

'You've had her here . . . in your house . . . all along?'

'Sure.'

'Under the bed?'

'Well, only when I expected you to come over. I was afraid you might not take it well, so I felt it best to keep her out of sight.'

'Under the *bed*? When I was here? All those nights I spent here, she was . . . Oh, God. You had this . . . this *stiff* under the bed while we . . .'

'Not just any stiff. My wife.'

'Oh, that's supposed to make it okay?'

'She *was* my wife, darling. What was I supposed to do, throw her out like an old shoe? I loved her. She loved me. Why should we part, just because she stopped being alive? I would've been . . . so lonely without her. And look at it from her point of view. Do you think she would've *enjoyed* being put in a hole, all by herself? Or burnt to ashes? Good Lord, who would want a fate like that? Instead, she's here in her own house where she belongs, with her husband. Isn't that the way *you* would want it? Really? It's what I'd want for myself. It's what I'd want for you if, God forbid, you should stop living before I do. So we would always be together.'

'I suppose,' she muttered, 'it would be better than . . . those other things.'

'No doubt about it.'

'You should've told me, though.'

'I was waiting for the right time. I'm just sorry you had to find out about her . . . the hard way. She must've given you quite a shock.'

'Yeah, I'll say.'

'You've taken it really well, though. You're a champ.' With that, he spread open her kimono.

'Darren!' She swept it shut. Fast. And looked at Joyce. Who didn't seem to be watching. The former wife's gaze was directed, not at Barbara, but toward the open window beyond the bed, which she seemed to find pleasing, possibly a little amusing.

'Now, now,' Darren said. 'Relax.'

'But Joyce.'

'She can't see what we're doing. For heaven's sake, she's dead.'

'I don't care. Not in front of her. No way.'

'Now you're being silly.'

'Silly! Goddamn it!'

'Shhh, shhh. Calm down. It's all right. I'll take care of her.'

Darren bent low, parted just enough of Barbara's kimono to expose her groin, kissed her softly there, then climbed off the bed. Stepping in front of Joyce, he took off his velours bathrobe. 'Forgive me?' he asked. Then he draped the robe over her head. It hung down nearly to her waist.

He stepped away from her. He faced Barbara. He smiled. 'Better?'

'Can't you just put her out in the hallway or something?'

Darren looked disappointed. 'That wouldn't be nice. This is her bedroom, too, you know. I can't just put her out.'

Barbara sighed. This would be their first night together in the house as man and wife. She didn't want to make a stink. Besides, it wasn't really so bad now that Joyce's face was out of sight. 'All right,' she said.

'I could put her back under the bed, if you'd . . .'

'No, she's fine there.' Under the bed, she would be so much closer. Directly beneath them as they made love. Awful.

Darren stepped over to the light switch.

'No, leave the lights on.'

'Are you sure?'

'I don't . . . want to be in the dark with her.'

'Whatever you say, darling.'

As he returned to the bed, Barbara sat up and took off her kimono. She glanced at Joyce, then lay down and shut her eyes.

Darren sank down on top of her. He kissed her mouth. 'I'm so proud of you,' he whispered.

'I know. I'm a champ.'

'You are. You truly are.'

Barbara couldn't help it: every now and then as Darren kissed her and fondled her and plunged inside her, she looked over at Joyce. His other wife. His dead wife. Standing there shrouded by a bathrobe. Which wasn't pulled low enough in front to hide how the diaphanous nightie, drifting in the breeze, brushed against the dark tuft of hair between her legs.

He used to make love to her, Barbara thought.

Here, on this same bed.

Does she know? Does she know he's doing it to me, now, right in front of her? Is she jealous?

Don't be ridiculous.

Barbara tried to shake off the notion. But couldn't.

At the proper moment, she faked an orgasm.

It took a while for Darren to recover. Soon after he was breathing normally again, he whispered, 'See, it was just fine.'

'Yeah.'

'She didn't bother you at all, did she? Joyce, I mean.'

'Not really.' A lic. Why not?

'I bet she made it better for you. She did for me.'

What Barbara thought was, *Oh, my God.* What she said was, 'I don't know. Maybe.'

A while later, Darren said, 'Maybe I should turn the lights off now.'

'No. Leave them on.'

'You aren't still spooked, are you?'

'Just a little.'

'Well, that's all right. I'm sure she'll take a little getting used to.'

I'll never get used to her, Barbara told herself. Never.

Soon, Darren fell asleep. Barbara tried to sleep, but her mind was in a turmoil. She'd just married a man who kept his dead wife in the bedroom. Liked her there. As much as admitted that it turned him on to have her standing nearby while he made love.

Weird. Disgusting.

But it calmed Barbara whenever she thought about how things would be once she'd gotten rid of Joyce. Calmed her enough so that she was almost able to fall asleep.

Each time she started to drift, however, she lurched awake with a sickening dread and had to look. To make sure Joyce hadn't moved, hadn't pulled the robe off her head, hadn't crept closer to the bed.

The bitch seemed to be staying put.

Of course.

All that ever seemed to move was the nightie, blown by the breeze so it floated against her belly and pubic curls and the tops of her legs.

*

When Barbara woke up, the bedroom was bright with sunlight. She'd fallen asleep after all. Somehow. In spite of Joyce.

Joyce.

She didn't want to see her, fought the urge to turn her head, instead gazed at the ceiling and tried to appreciate the feel of the warm breeze caressing her body.

I can't spend another night in the same room with her, she thought. Just can't. I've gotta make Darren listen to reason.

She turned her head toward the other side of the bed.

Darren was gone.

No! What if he took his robe with him? What if *she's* uncovered?

Barbara snapped her head the other way.

Joyce was gone.

Gone where?

Barbara bolted upright. Heart thudding, she scanned the room. No sign of the corpse. She blew out a shaky breath and filled her lungs with the sweet morning air.

Not here. Maybe Darren came to his senses and . . .

She went cold inside and her skin crawled with goosebumps. *He put her under the bed!*

Moaning, she flung herself off the mattress. She rushed to the middle of the room and there, a safe distance away, dropped to her hands and knees and peered into the space beneath the bed.

No Joyce.

Thank God.

But where *is* she? What's Darren done with her?

At least she's not here. That's the main thing.

Calming down slightly, Barbara got to her feet. She brushed some carpet lint off her hands and knees. She was still trembling, still shivery with gooseflesh.

I can't live like this, she thought as she returned to the bed.

She put on her silk kimono, wrapped it snugly around herself and tied the sash. Then she turned toward the closet. She wanted her house slippers.

What if Joyce is in there?

She stared at the shut door. And decided it could stay shut. She could do without her slippers.

Heading for the bedroom door, she noticed that her suitcase was missing. Darren must've taken it out to the garage.

Maybe he'd also taken *Joyce* out to the garage.

If only.

Fat chance.

She halted at the doorway, leaned forward and swiveled her head from side to side. The corridor looked clear. She rushed for the bathroom. Its door was open. No sign of Joyce. She entered and locked the door. Then had a few bad moments as she approached the tub. But the tub was empty. Barbara sighed, relaxed a little.

She used the toilet, washed her face, brushed her teeth, sat on the edge of the tub and tried to work up her courage for venturing out of the sanctuary of the bathroom.

This is crazy, she told herself. Why should I be scared of Joyce? She can't hurt me. Can't do anything but freak me out. And make me wonder if I'm married to a crazy man.

He's not crazy. He cares about her, that's all. Can't bear to part with her.

Jesus H. Christ on a crutch.

He damn well *will* part with her. It's her or me.

Right. What'll I do? Where'll I go? I gave up my apartment. I already quit my job, for godsake. Guess I can always find . . .

Why should *I* be the one to leave? *She's* the dead one.

Just gotta talk to Darren. If he'll only listen to reason and put her away someplace, everything will be okay.

Barbara forced herself to leave the bathroom. As she walked

down the corridor, someone stepped out of the bedroom. She flinched before realizing it was Darren.

He'd already gotten dressed. He wore one of the bright red aloha shirts they'd bought on Maui. It hung loose down past the front of his Bermuda shorts. His legs looked darkly tanned above the tops of his white socks. He had his Reeboks on.

'Morning!' he said, smiling as he hurried toward her. 'You sure slept in, didn't you?'

Then she was in his arms. She hugged him, kissed him. My Darren, she thought.

He felt solid and warm and comfortable.

When they released each other, he said, 'I have a surprise for you.'

'You've put Joyce in storage?'

His smile faltered. 'Don't be silly. I made a trip to the doughnut shop. Maple bars!'

He knew how she loved maple bars. But she couldn't work up much enthusiasm as she said, 'Oh, that's sweet.'

Taking her hand, he led her into the kitchen. On the counter, the pot of coffee was ready. On the table, a heaping platter of doughnuts, including four maple bars, waited. In the corner, smiling, staring at Barbara as she entered, stood Joyce.

Her hair was done up in a ponytail. She wore a fresh white blouse. The bra beneath it, faintly visible through the thin fabric, was black. Her blouse was tucked neatly into the elastic waistband of her glossy blue shorts. She wore white socks and blue L.A. Gear athletic shoes.

'You dressed her,' Barbara muttered.

Darren grinned. 'She didn't dress herself.'

'Why?'

'Isn't that obvious?' He laughed softly and picked up the coffee pot.

'I mean, why did you dress her?'

'Oh. Well, it wouldn't be right for her to go around all day in

285

her nightgown.' He filled the mugs with coffee and set them on the table. He pulled out a chair for Barbara.

'I'll sit over here,' she said. And took the chair on the opposite side of the table. So she wouldn't have her back to Joyce. So she could keep an eye on her.

Darren sat down in the chair he'd intended for Barbara. He took a sip of coffee. 'Actually, I did keep Joyce in her bathrobe for a while, at first. I thought to myself, why bother putting clothes on her? It got depressing, though. There she was, day and night, standing around in her robe. It made her seem . . . oh, I don't know, like an invalid.'

Tempted to make a remark, Barbara bit into a maple bar instead.

'So then I decided to start dressing her up. Off with that tired old bathrobe, on with . . . well, whatever the occasion demanded. Nightwear at night, casual things for daytime wear, one of her nifty little bikinis for poolside . . . she always liked to join me out by the pool, though she wasn't much for swimming. For more formal occasions – a birthday, Thanksgiving, that sort of thing – a lovely evening gown. Whatever seemed right.' Smiling, he bit into a jelly doughnut.

'Like having a life-size Barbie doll.'

'You're my Barbie doll,' he said, his voice muffled by dough-nut, white powder and red jelly on his lips. 'She's my Joycie doll.'

Joyce smiled at the top of Barbara's head.

'Isn't it . . . difficult to dress her? I mean, she's stiff, isn't she?'

'Oh, we manage. Some outfits are trickier to get on her than others, but we make do the best we can.'

Barbara started to take another bite of maple bar. But it would be a muddy lump in her mouth like the first one, and tough to swallow. She set down the bar and drank some coffee.

'Is something wrong with your maple bar?'

'It's fine,' she muttered.

Frowning with concern, he leaned forward slightly. 'Is it Joyce?'

'Of course it's Joyce. What do you think?'

'We went through all this last night, darling. I thought you understood.'

'My God, you dress her up like she's *real*.'

'She *is* real.'

'But she's *dead*! You cart her around from room to room. You *dress her up*! You put a *bra* on her. Probably panties too, for all I know.'

'Would you prefer her *without* panties?' he asked. Raising his eyebrows, smiling slightly, he bit again into his doughnut.

'I'd prefer her *gone*!'

Nodding, he chewed for a while. He swallowed. He sipped his coffee. 'You'll get used to her. Once you've gotten to know her better, I'm sure you'll . . .'

'I want her out of here.'

'Out of the kitchen?'

'Out of the *house*. Preferably in a fucking *graveyard*!'

'Oh, dear. You *are* upset.' The look of sorrow on Darren's face made her heart ache for him.

'I'm sorry,' she murmured. 'I am. I love you so much. But Joyce . . .'

'She frightens you, doesn't she?'

Barbara nodded.

'She doesn't bite, you know.'

'I know.'

'She doesn't *do* anything.'

'She looks at me.'

'They're only glass eyes,' Darren explained gently.

'They're not hers?'

'Hers didn't fare well in the . . . process. But if they bother you . . . Back in a sec.' He pushed himself away from the table and hurried from the kitchen.

While he was gone, Barbara studied Joyce's face. Glass eyes. They sure looked real. Too real, too bright and aware. Did it make things any better, knowing they were fake? For a few moments, she thought so.

They're not Joyce.

They're not her dead eyes. Nothing much more than a couple of shiny marbles poked into her sockets.

Sockets.

The *real* Joyce hasn't got eyes. Were they gouged out? Popped? Dragged out with forceps? Did they just shrivel away in the 'process' and fall out?

Those beautiful, lively eyes gazing at the top of Barbara's head were pieces of glass stuck into pits.

Do *they* ever fall out?

Does Darren take them out lovingly, from time to time, and polish them up?

Barbara stared at Joyce. No eyes. God! Those aren't her eyes. They're covers. Hatches put there to conceal a pair of hideous cavities.

Cringing, she looked away. Thanks for telling me, Darren. Thanks a lot.

'Here we go,' he said, bustling into the kitchen. 'This'll be just what the doctor ordered.' He kissed the top of Barbara's head, then hurried around the table.

She looked up in time to watch him slide sunglasses onto Joyce's face. They were much like those worn by the Highway Patrolman who'd stopped Barbara last month for making an unsafe lane change on the Santa Monica Freeway. Wire rims, teardrop shaped lenses with silver reflective surfaces.

'How's that?' Darren asked. Stepping away, he admired the effect. 'Make her look rather dashing, don't you think?'

Now I can't tell where she's looking, Barbara thought. But she didn't want to hurt Darren's feelings. He was *trying* to help. 'That's a lot better.'

Maybe it is better, she told herself. Now, at least, her eyes are out of sight. Maybe I can forget about them. Forget they aren't eyes, just socket hiders.

Darren sat at the table, looking pleased with himself. 'For every problem, there's a solution.'

'Guess so,' Barbara said. She picked up her maple bar and forced herself to eat it.

When Darren asked how she would like to spend the day, she suggested going to the beach. 'Fabulous idea,' he blurted. 'It'll be like we're still on our honeymoon.'

'Just the two of us, right?'

'Of course.'

'You don't want to take *her* along?'

'Joyce'll be fine right here.' He winked. 'She's really pretty much a home body.'

In the bedroom, Barbara tied her string bikini into place, then covered up with a blouse and shorts, and slipped into sandals. Darren came in while she was making the bed. 'I'll get the towels and things while you're changing,' she told him.

'I'll be done in a jiff,' he said, and winked.

Before they left, Darren carried Joyce into the living room. He set her down on the sofa, tucked a pillow under he head and pulled off her shoes. 'All comfy?' he asked. He patted her leg, then took the beach bag from Barbara's hand and led the way to the door.

It was wonderful to get out of the house. Away from Joyce. At the beach, they roamed along the shoreline, holding hands. They spread towels on the sand, massaged each other with sun block, stretched out side by side, lay motionless under the heavy sun and soothing breezes.

Exhausted after a night of so little sleep, Barbara slumbered peacefully.

Later, they explored the pier. They wandered the souvenir

shops. They rode the bumper cars. Darren sank a basketball three times in a row and won her a furry, pink teddy bear. They ate fried clams and homemade potato chips on a bench high above the ocean.

Then they returned to the sand. They spread their towels again, lay down, and again Barbara fell asleep.

She awoke when Darren kissed her shoulder. 'We'd best be on our way.'

Her stomach twisted, knotted itself into an icy clump.

'Not yet.'

'We don't want to burn.'

'We won't. The sun block . . .'

'Nevertheless. We should be getting back.'

'It's still early.'

He glanced at his wristwatch. 'It's after three.'

She nodded. She forced herself to smile.

Her smile became genuine as she pulled the shorts up her legs. 'I know, let's go to a movie!'

'A movie?'

'Sure. A matinee. It'll be great!'

'Well . . .'

'Please? This is out last day together before . . . it'll be off to work for you in the morning. We won't have another chance to *do* anything till next weekend. Please?'

'Sure. Why not?'

They returned to the car, drove to a parking structure near the Third Street Mall, then went to a cineplex. Of the six movies playing there, one was scheduled to begin in fifteen minutes. Darren bought tickets, and in they went.

Soon, the theater darkened. Too soon, the movie ended.

'It sure will be great to get home and take a nice shower,' Darren said as they walked through the lobby. He patted her rump. 'Together.'

'Why don't we stay for another?'

'Really, darling. I think one's enough.'

'Please? You know how I love movies.'

He smiled. 'How's this? We'll drop by the video store on the way home and rent a couple for tonight.'

She sighed. She didn't want to *start* anything. 'All right. If you'd rather do that.'

So they drove to a video store.

Barbara studied the shelves of tapes, shaking her head, unwilling to make a choice. Over and over again, she found reasons not to accept videos Darren selected. She'd already seen this one, that one didn't sound very good. 'Don't worry,' she said several times. 'We'll find something. There must be *something* decent around here.' And they kept on looking.

She managed to stretch out their search for more than an hour.

Finally, Darren said, 'Let's just grab a couple. I'm starving.'

Barbara grabbed two that she'd noticed when they first came in.

Back in the car, she said, 'Why don't we have a bite to eat before we go home?'

'Take-out?'

'I'd rather eat *in* a restaurant. It's so much more fun.'

'Look how we're dressed.'

'We don't have to go any place fancy. Jack-in-the-Box or Burger King. Whatever.'

Darren drove to Burger King. They ate at a table. While Barbara slowly consumed her meal, she tried to think of another way to delay their return home.

Give it up, she finally thought. I've stalled him as long as I can without making a fuss. We can't stay away forever. Might as well get it over with.

So, when the meal was done, they climbed into the car and drove through the dusk, heading for home.

Where Joyce would be waiting.

Maybe we'll be in luck, Barbara thought, and the house burnt down while we were out.

Fat chance.

They rounded a corner, and there it was. Still standing.

'Did you have a good time?' Darren asked as he swung into the driveway.

'Wonderful. I really hate for it to end.'

'Nothing's ended, darling.' He stopped the car, leaned toward Barbara and stroked the back of her head. 'Our life together has only begun. We'll have so many fine times.'

'I suppose so.'

'No supposing about it.'

She followed him into the house. Darren carried the sack of video tapes into the living room and set it down at Joyce's feet.

'She won't have to watch the movies with us, will she?' Barbara asked. 'Couldn't you . . . maybe put her in another room?'

'I could. But the sooner you get used to her the better. Don't you think?'

'I don't think I'll ever get used to her.'

'Oh, you will, you will. Give it time. Now, you go along and start your shower. I'll be along in a minute.' He winked. Then he crouched, slipped his arms under Joyce, and lifted her off the sofa.

Barbara's heart slammed. 'Where are you taking her?'

'The guest room.' He grinned. 'Time to get her out of the daytime attire.'

She hurried ahead of them and shut herself into the bathroom. Trembling, she took off her clothes.

The daytime attire, she thought.

He's stripping her. Then he'll be waltzing in here and putting his hands on *me*.

That's what *he* thinks.

She thumbed down the lock button, then went to the tub and turned on the shower.

He'll just have to choose, she thought as she adjusted the faucets. Joyce or me. He can't have it both ways.

What if he chooses her?

I can't lose him. Not over a damned stiff!

Sighing, Barbara stepped to the door and unlocked it.

She climbed into the tub and slid the glass door shut. The hot spray felt wonderful splashing against head and face, sliding down her body.

His hands will be clean, she told herself. They'll be all soapy when he rubs me. They won't have Joyce on them.

But she'll be waiting when we come out.

Dressed in her little see-through nightie.

God!

Standing around in her nightie and shades while we watch the movies. Then standing by the bed while we make love.

I can't take much more of this.

Maybe I shouldn't let him have me again till she's out of the house.

No, he'd end up resenting me. I can't do anything to *make* him get rid of her. He'd hold it against me forever. It has to be his decision.

If only she hadn't been preserved so well. If she was rotten or stinky, he sure wouldn't have kept her around.

What if I go to the market tomorrow while he's at work, pick up some really stinky cheese, poke some into her mouth? Poke some into her *everywhere*?

Yuck! I'd have to touch her.

There are always gloves for that.

Darren will think she's going bad.

And get rid of her?

What if he probes around and finds the cheese?

Would it be worth the risk?

Barbara flinched, startled, as the shower door rumbled open. She turned. Joyce stared in at her, smiling. No silver shades, no nightie.

'No!' She staggered backward as Joyce rose, lifted high by Darren behind her. 'Get her *out* of here!' She slipped. Her rump smacked the bottom of the tub. 'Ow!'

'Darling! Are you all right?'

'No! Get her out of here! What's the matter with you?'

'This'll be a great way for you to get better acquainted. Really. Did you hurt yourself?'

'I'll live.' Barbara scooted backward and drew her legs up to her chest as Darren stepped into the tub with Joyce. Holding the body against him with one arm across her belly, he slid the shower door shut.

The spray splattered off Joyce's shoulders. Water spread down her body in shiny streamers.

'Please!' Barbara begged. 'I don't *want* to get better acquainted. Take her away!'

'You'll be fine once you've gotten to know her.'

'The water'll ruin her! You'd better . . .'

'Oh, no, she's quite durable. Stand up, now, darling.'

'Darren!'

'Is it really asking so much? Just stand up. Please.'

Trembling, breathless, Barbara struggled to her feet.

Darren smiled at her from behind Joyce's shoulder. 'Now, come a little closer. Be careful you don't fall.'

She took a few small steps forward, and stopped.

'Closer.'

She moved closer.

'Closer.'

'No. Come on.' One more step, and she would *meet* Joyce.

'Okay,' Darren said. He blinked water out of his eyes. 'You're doing fine. Really. You're making great progress. Now, I want you to touch her face.'

'Don't make me.' Her voice came out whiny.

'I won't make you do anything. Do it for me. Do it for us. Please. You must get over this phobia about Joyce.'

'It's not a *phobia*.'

'Then we'll be able to get on with our lives. I'm sure you'll even come to *like* her. She'll make a fine companion for you while I'm away at work every day. Now, please. Touch her face.'

Barbara raised a wet hand toward Joyce's cheek. And hesitated, fingers shaking.

Joyce gazed at her with merry, shining eyes.

Glass stuffed in pits.

'You're so close now,' Darren urged her. 'Don't stop now.'

Holding her breath, Barbara placed her fingertips against Joyce's cheek. She prodded it gently. She stroked it. The skin felt smooth and stiff. Like a fine leather shoe.

From behind Joyce's shoulder, Darren beamed at her. 'I'm so proud of you!'

Barbara lowered her arm. 'I did what you asked. Now will you take . . .'

She gasped as the body lurched forward. Its hands brushed her sides. Before she could leap away, *other* hands clutched her. Darren's hands. They grabbed her sides, jerked her forward. Tight against Joyce.

She turned her head just in time to avoid a collision with Joyce's face. Their cheeks rubbed.

Darren kissed her, pressed his lips against hers above Joyce's shoulder. Pushed his tongue into her mouth.

He can't be doing this!

Not with Joyce in the middle!

But he *was* doing this, Joyce in the middle, her hard breasts shoving into Barbara's breasts, her belly and groin and thighs tight and stiff against Barbara. And *moving*. Rubbing against her as Darren writhed and moaned and thrust with his tongue.

Barbara chomped.

Darren cried out. His hands leaped off her.

She drove her hands against Joyce's hips and rammed her away, slamming Darren against the tile wall beneath the shower nozzle. He grunted as his head thumped. Blood exploded from his mouth.

Barbara staggered backward to get away from the four feet sliding her way.

She spit out a chuck of Darren's tongue.

She hadn't meant to bite it *off*, but . . .

Horrified, she watched the bloody slab flop onto Joyce's belly button.

I've ruined him!

'Look what you made me do!' she yelled.

Darren didn't answer. Nor did he move. During the fall, he'd slipped lower so his head was under Joyce. His arms lay limp against the bottom of the tub. His legs were stretched out to either side of Joyce's legs. His genitals showed through the crevice between her thighs.

The water cascading down on Joyce sent Darren's tongue sledding down her belly.

Barbara took another step backward. Her foot landed with a splash.

The tub was filling!

He's gonna drown!

Dropping to a crouch, she grabbed Joyce's ankles. She pulled. The body slid toward her. She worked her hands up the legs, scooting Joyce along beneath her toward the rear of the tub.

Darren's face came into view.

The water was up past his ears. His eyes were shut, his mouth hanging open. His mouth brimmed with blood.

'You'll be okay!' she cried. 'I'll save you!'

His eyes opened.

Thank God!

Red spray exploded like a geyser as he shrieked, 'BITCH!'

He sat up fast. His chest met the top of Joyce's head and raised her body. She came up rigid like a plank lifted at one end.

Barbara, lurching to get away from Darren, slipped.

And fell forward, her knees driving down into Joyce's belly.

Krrrrrrk!

Joyce's head jumped forward, chin poking into her throat, face rolling against her chest. Between her breasts, her head was upside down, ponytail toward Barbara, the stump of her snapped neck straight up, catching spray.

Darren roared with rage.

Barbara snatched up the head by its ponytail.

As Darren leaned forward and reached for her, she whipped Joyce's head against the side of his face. It caved in his cheekbone and bounced off, its glass eyes flying out and shattering against the front of the tub. Darren's eyes rolled upward. He slumped. She swung the head around and around by its ponytail, and struck him again. This time, Darren's left eye popped from its socket and dangled by a cord. The third blow mashed it. The fourth sent teeth flying from his mouth.

'Joyce is durable, all right, you bastard!'

She kept on bashing his head until Joyce's broken skull parted company with her scalp. This happened while Barbara was winding up for another strike. Her weapon suddenly went nearly weightless. She cringed as airborne head bones crashed against the shower door. Some bounced off and rained down on her shoulder and back.

She threw down the sodden mop of hair.

Then she tore off Joyce's right arm and used it on Darren until it broke apart. She had to pause and catch her breath before ripping the left arm from its socket.

She smashed it down on the collapsed rag of Darren's face.

The arm didn't last long.

It wasn't easy breaking off Joyce's legs. But she managed. They proved to be well worth the effort.

A Good, Secret Place

The new kid came up the street from the house where Eddie and Sharon used to live. We'd seen him once before, the day he moved in. Even from a distance, we'd wanted nothing much to do with him. For starters, he couldn't have been older than about twelve. For finishers, you could tell he was a dork.

So there we were, Jim and I, playing catch in my front yard on one of those really fine summer nights just at dusk. The neighborhood was so quiet about the only sound was the hardball smacking into our mitts. And this new kid came strolling up the street.

It was pretty obvious what he had in mind. He was wearing a mitt.

Not just any mitt – a first baseman's glove. Have you ever noticed that the real dopey kids of this world *always* use a first baseman's glove? I think it's because they're scared of the ball. A big leather scoop like that let's them go for it without getting too close.

Anyway, he didn't come onto the lawn. He stayed at the edge of the street, off past Jim's side, and watched us. We pretended he wasn't there. Easy enough for Jim, since he didn't have to look at the kid. He kept his face toward me as we fired the ball back and forth. Once in a while, he rolled his eyes toward the sky.

Other than being too young for us and wearing that stupid first baseman's glove, the kid was dumpy. He looked like he hadn't washed his hair for a month, and greasy strands hung down his forehead. He had a face like a pig. Fat, with little pink eyes. And a red nose that was runny, so he kept sniffing and every so often he'd stick his tongue up to lick the snot off his lip. He wore a red shirt with yellow flowers on it. It hung unbuttoned at the bottom. His belly bulged out through the gap like gray pudding. Lower down, you could see his boxers. Like he'd hitched them up, but forgotten to hitch up his pants. They were white with blue stripes. His pants, which looked about ready to drop, were plaid Bermuda shorts. They had huge, swollen pockets, and reached down to his knees. Below his fat calves, he wore black socks. He wore sandals on his feet.

I'm not joking. That's actually what the kid looked like.

He was a real prize.

I tried to keep my eyes off him, but it wasn't easy, the way he just stood there off to the side of Jim, watching us throw. I wished he would go away. And I felt like a jerk for ignoring him. He didn't say anything. He just stood there, sniffing and licking his snot, and sort of smiling.

Pretty soon, he started to sock his fist into his mitt.

I really couldn't take that. It's no fun at all, being left out of stuff.

So I called, 'Heads up, kid,' and threw him the ball. I didn't burn it in, nothing like that. I tossed it high and easy and right to him. He lit up for a second, then looked alarmed as the ball got closer. Ducking and turning his face away, he reached up with his huge scoop of a glove and didn't even come close. The ball flew past him and went sailing off down the street. About the time it bounced on the pavement, he checked his mitt. He frowned, like he was really surprised to find it empty. Then he said, 'Sorry.'

That was the first word I ever heard him say. Sorry.

Then he went chasing after the ball.

'Good going, Ricky babes,' Jim said.

'What do you want? What was I supposed to do, ignore him?'

'Now we'll probably be stuck with the little creep.'

'It's getting dark, anyway. Maybe we'd better call it a night pretty soon.'

'Yeah, I'm all for that.'

But we had to wait for the ball. The kid took a while trying to find it. Finally, he dug it out of the flower bed in front of the Watson house and came loping up the street. Still a ways off, he gave it a throw.

'God!' Jim muttered. 'What is he, a girl?'

It was my ball, my fault, so I had to chase it down. I wasn't eager to pick it up, considering it had been in the kid's hand and was probably sticky. So I snatched it off the grass with my mitt. By the time I got back with it, the kid was stepping over the curb, walking toward Jim.

'Getting pretty dark,' I said. 'I guess we'd better call it quits for now.'

'Do we *have* to?' the kid asked.

I didn't like the sound of that 'we.'

'Yeah, we'd lose the ball.'

'Well, all right.' He sniffed and backhanded some goo off his upper lip. 'I'm George Johnson. We just moved in.' He swung a pudgy arm out behind him. 'Over there.'

'I'm Rick. This is Jim.'

Luckily, he didn't try to shake hands with us.

'You guys sure are good.'

'It just takes practice,' I said, figuring he meant we were good with the ball.

'You want a Twinkie?' He shoved a hand down into a bulging front pocket of his shorts and pulled out a cellophane pack. The twin, cream-filled yellow cakes inside looked pretty smashed.

'Thanks anyhow,' I said. 'I just had dinner.'

'Please,' George said. 'They're good.'

'What the hell,' Jim said. He stuck his mitt under his arm, took the package from George, said 'Thanks,' and ripped it open. He scooted one of the mooshed Twinkies off the cardboard backing and held it toward me.

'There's only two of 'em,' I said. 'You eat it, George.'

'Oh, I got plenty. I want it to be yours.'

Well, it *had* been wrapped up. So I went ahead and took it.

Jim and I both had our mouths full when George said, 'Will you be my friends?'

How can you say no to a kid who has just given you a Twinkie?

'Yeah, well . . .' I said.

'What the hell,' Jim said.

The next day, we made the mistake of riding our bikes past George's house. We were heading for the Fashion Mall, a good place to hang out and watch the babes – especially Cyndi Taylor. She was a varsity cheerleader and didn't know we existed, but she had a summer job working at Music World. We could pretend to brouse through the CDs and tapes for about an hour, and spend the whole time scoping her out. I know, that might sound kind of dumb. You wouldn't think so, though, if you'd ever seen Cyndi.

The only thing was, George must've been keeping a lookout. We hadn't even gotten past his house when the screen door banged and he ran out, yelling, 'Hey, guys! Wait up!'

Jim gave me a disgusted look, but George was still in his pajamas so I figured we were safe. We swung our bikes to the curb.

'Hiya, George,' Jim said.

George stopped beside us, huffing and grinning. 'Hey, where we going?'

'Nowhere,' I said. 'Just tooling around.'

'Great! I'll be right out!'

'That's all right,' Jim said. 'Don't you have something else you've gotta do?'

'Nope!' And off he ran, his big butt bouncing the seat of his pajamas.

The screen door whammed shut.

'Terrific,' I muttered.

'Let's beat it,' Jim said.

So that's what we did.

We sprinted our bikes for the corner, sped around it, then cut down the first alley. All the way to the mall, we kept glancing back, afraid George might be on our tails. But he wasn't.

He didn't show up at the mall, either.

He ruined everything, anyway. I couldn't quit thinking about him. He'd been so damn excited about coming with us. He'd probably rushed to get dressed, and yelled something to his mom like, 'Hey, I'm going off with my pals!' He'd probably been hurrying out to the garage for his bike when he saw we were gone. I wondered if he'd cried. I wondered how he explained to his mom that his friends had left him behind. I felt like a jerk.

I couldn't even work up much excitement watching Cyndi Taylor glide around the music store. I'd look at her, but mostly I'd see George. I've been ditched a few times. I know how it feels.

And it doesn't always feel much better when you're the one who did the ditching.

To get home that afternoon, we took a back route so we wouldn't have to ride past George's house.

Every night since school let out, we'd been playing catch in my front lawn after dinner. But not that night. I cut across backyards to reach Jim's place. He had a pool, so he also had a fence. I scrambled over the fence. Jim was waiting. We shot the ball back and forth across the length of the pool. Later on, Jim stood on the diving board. I threw just out of his reach, trying to get him to fall in. After a couple of close calls with him teetering and flapping his arms, he said, 'I go in and wreck my mitt, it's your ass!'

'Language!' his mom called from inside the house.

When it was almost too dark to see the ball, someone turned on the lights. Then his sister, Joan, came out with a friend. They were both seniors and wearing bikinis. They didn't talk to us or anything, but it was great while it lasted. They splashed around, all shiny in the water, while we fired the ball from one end of the pool to the other. I think they liked having us there. They floated around on their backs quite a lot.

But then I guess Jim's mom noticed what was going on and got scared we might bean someone, so she told us to quit.

We went up into the living room and played some Super Mario Brothers till it was time for me to go home.

I took the front way. Off in the distance, I could see George's house. I realized that, somewhere along the way, I'd stopped feeling rotten about ditching him.

When it was time to set out for the mall the next day, I sped over to Jim's place. He was waiting on his driveway.

'Wanta drop by George's house and see if he wants to come along?' Jim asked, grinning.

'In your dreams.'

'The little shit.'

'You said it.'

Not only had I quit feeling sorry for the twerp, but I'd found myself really resenting the way he'd messed with our lives. Hell, we couldn't play catch in my frontyard, we couldn't ride our bikes past his house. We were like fugitives on our own block, hiding from him. And *then* we felt guilty about it. I did, anyway. And I didn't like it. He had no right. So the hell with him.

We coasted down Jim's driveway. At the street, Jim swung to the right.

'This way,' I said, and swung my bike to the left.

'Are you kidding?'

'Screw him.'

We picked up a lot of speed by the time we reached George's house. Neither of us looked at it. I didn't hear the screen door slap shut, so I figured we must've shot past too fast for the little scuzz.

Then I looked back.

George, hunched over the handlebars of his ten-speed, swooped down his driveway and swerved into the street. He pumped his pedals like a madman trying to catch up.

'Oh, no,' I muttered.

Jim glanced back. 'Terrific. You and your great ideas.'

'Hey, wait up!' George yelled.

'Wanta ditch him?' Jim asked.

'God *damn* it! The hell with ditching him.' I slowed down. So did Jim.

George closed the gap. Riding between us, he matched our speed. 'What's up?' he asked.

'Not much,' I said.

'Where'd you guys go yesterday?'

'Nowhere,' I said. This hot feeling went through me. It was shame, whether I wanted it or not.

'I got a sudden case of the trots and had to go home,' Jim explained. 'Sorry we couldn't wait for you. But it would've got pretty messy on the street, you know?'

'Gosh, I'm sorry.'

'Shit waits for no man,' Jim added.

George laughed. 'So, you okay?'

'Fine,' Jim muttered, and gave me the eye.

'So, where we going?'

Jim had saved us with the trots story. Now it was my turn. 'The pool. Over at the Jefferson Recreational Center.'

George's smile faded. 'The pool?'

'That's right,' I said.

He looked confused. Frowning at Jim, he said, 'Don't you *have* a pool?'

Jim didn't miss a beat. 'Sure, but all the babes are at the public pool.'

'You got your trunks with you, George?' I asked.

He gave our bikes a once-over. 'Where's yours?'

'Wearing 'em,' I said, and patted the seat of my jeans. 'Underneath.'

'Oh.'

'You'd better go get your trunks,' Jim said, 'and we'll meet you at the pool.'

'I don't know where it is.'

Jim gave him directions. George listened, frowning and nodding, then made sort of a nervous smile and said, 'Okay. Guess I can find it.'

'Great,' Jim said.

'See you there,' I said.

George swung his bike around and pedaled for home.

Jim and I gave each other grins. We headed for the mall.

At Music World, we roamed up and down the aisles pretending to look at stuff while we watched Cyndi. I felt a little guilty about the dirty trick we'd played on George, but forgot about it when Cyndi came over to us. It was almost too much for me, being this close to her. The way she looked and smelled made me ache.

'Can I help you find something?' she asked.

I didn't trust myself to speak. All I could do was shake my head.

'We're just browsing around,' Jim said, the way he always did when she or one of the others came over like this.

'Fine. If you need any help, be sure to let me know.'

'We will,' Jim told her.

She smiled and walked away.

'Oh, man,' Jim whispered. 'What I'd give . . .'

'Yeah.'

After she'd left, we had to settle for watching her from a distance. She spent a while helping other customers, and then Bobbi Andrews came into the store. She was the head cheerleader, but nothing at all like Cyndi. While Cyndi was slender and graceful and beautiful, Bobbi was squat and had a face like a rabbit. She was really popular, anyway. There were three reasons for that: her pep and two humongous knockers. I couldn't care less about any of that. Personally, I thought she was a waste.

But she was Cyndi's best friend.

They got together near the back of the store and started talking.

We figured that Cyndi was too busy with her to notice us, so we wandered down the aisle for a better view. We were pretty careful about it. We pretended to be greatly interested in various CDs and albums in the trough along the way, and got to the end of the aisle.

Cyndi was close enough to touch if I leaned forward far enough. She stood in the next aisle, leaning back slightly. The edge of the trough just behind her pressed a dent into her pleated skirt – into her rump, too. I could see the straps of her bra through her white blouse. The way her head was turned, I could see the fine, downy fuzz on her smooth cheek.

'. . . by ten, I think,' Bobbi was saying when I started to listen. 'No later than eleven.'

'No problem,' Cyndi told her. 'Don't worry about it. We'll just be pigging out and watching movies.' Grinning, she nudged Bobbi with her elbow. 'At least till my parents hit the sack. You won't miss much. Just don't forget to bring that extra sleeping bag.'

'Hope Doris doesn't fart in it.'

Cyndi elbowed her again, and laughed.

Then Jim elbowed me, and we got away before they could notice we'd been near enough to hear them.

Outside the store, Jim grabbed my arm. 'Did you *hear* that?'

He was flushed and breathless. 'She's having a *slumber* party. Are you thinking what I'm thinking?'

I was.

'You think it's tonight?' he asked.

I knew she didn't work at Music World on weekends. This was Friday. 'It's gotta be either tonight or tomorrow night.'

'Yeah!'

We took the back route to my house so we wouldn't have to pass George's place. When we were safely out of sight in the garage, Jim said, 'Wonder if he's still at the pool.'

'You'd think he might get the message,' I said.

'Kids like that *never* get the message.'

In the house, I asked if Jim could stay the night. Mom saw no problem with that. She suggested he stay for supper, too. Then we made a trip by the backyards to Jim's place. He got his mom's permission. After he put together his sleeping bag and overnight stuff, we returned to my house.

It didn't take long to set up the tent, toss in a couple of pads from the patio lounges, and arrange our sleeping bags.

But the waiting took a *long* time.

Nothing in the world takes longer than waiting for something really great to happen.

Finally, Dad got home from work. Finally, we ate supper. Finally, darkness came and we went out to the tent.

We had to wear our pajamas and leave our clothes behind. That was how we'd always done it in the past, and we didn't want to make my parents suspicious by doing anything differently. It wouldn't be a problem. They expected us to make a few trips back and forth to brush our teeth, use the john, that sort of thing. Once they were off to bed, it would be a cinch to sneak our clothes out.

We took two flashlights into the tent with us. And a couple of cans of Pepsi and a bag of onion-flavored potato chips. We zippered the fly screen, but left the flaps open to get some air. Inside, we sat cross-legged on our sleeping bags and started snacking.

'This is so neat,' Jim said.

'The chips?'

'You know.'

'God, I can't believe we're gonna do it.'

'I just hope we can see something.'

'It's a one-storey house,' I said, 'so they sure won't be upstairs.'

'As long as they don't shut all the curtains.'

'They won't. They can't. It'd be too cruel.'

Jim laughed softly. 'When do you think we oughta get going?'

'We'd better wait till after eleven.'

'Man, I hope we don't miss everything.'

'Bobbi won't even be getting there till then. Anyway, they'll probably be messing around all night.'

'We wanta be there in time to see 'em change.'

'Change into what?'

I wasn't the one who asked that.

George was the one who asked that.

We both flinched and jerked our heads toward the front of the tent. And saw George crouched on the other side of the fly screen, his piggish face gray in the darkness. We shined our flashlights on him. He squinted and said, 'Hiya, guys.'

'What're you doing here?' I snapped.

'You having an over-nighter?' he asked, just as calm as if he hadn't heard me.

'This is private property,' Jim told him.

'Can I have some potato chips?'

'You can't come in here,' I said. 'There isn't enough room.'

'I gave you guys my Twinkies.'

'Okay, okay,' I said. I didn't want to argue with him, just get rid of him. So I unzipped the screen and handed out the bag. 'Help yourself. You can have them all.'

'Gee, thanks.'

'Why don't you take them home,' I said, 'and share with your parents.'

'Oh, they're out.' He stuffed a handful of chips into his mouth.

'Give some to your sitter,' Jim said.

'Sitter?'

'They didn't leave you alone, did they?' I asked.

'Sure. Always do.'

'Great,' Jim muttered.

'So, where we gonna go?'

'Nowhere,' I said.

'We gonna go look in windows?'

How long had he been listening to us?

'We aren't going anywhere,' Jim said.

'I'll go with you. I like to look in windows. You get to see all kinds of neat stuff.'

'What are you,' Jim asked, 'a little pervert?'

George laughed, spraying out some potato chip crumbs.

'You'd better never be looking in *my* windows,' I told him.

'Or mine,' Jim added.

'Nah. I only like to see girls.'

'You been spying on my sister?' Jim asked.

George shook his head and jammed his mouth full of potato chips.

'He knew about your pool,' I reminded Jim.

'Yeah. You been snooping around my house?'

'Huh-uh. Honest.'

'You better never, man.'

'I'll give you some good stuff if you let me come with.'

'You're not coming "with",' I said.

'Please?'

'Good stuff like what?' Jim asked.

'Twinkies.'

'That's no big deal. What else?'

'Cut it out,' I told Jim. 'He's got nothing we want.'

'I'll getcha some booze,' George said.

'Really?' Jim sounded interested.

'Forget it,' I said.

'What kind?'

'Anything. Pop's got a whole big bar in the den. And he's got a wine cellar.'

'You can get us a bottle of wine?'

'Sure.'

'Your old man'll kill you,' I said.

George shrugged. 'He won't know any better. 'Sides, who cares if he finds out? I'll swipe us a bottle, okay?'

'Cool,' Jim said.

'Are you nuts?' I asked.

'Are you? Come on. We can tie one on on the way over to Cyndi's.'

'Good going,' I muttered. I couldn't believe he'd spoken her name in front of a sleeze like George.

'Who's Cyndi?' George asked.

'Nobody,' I said.

'Is she the girl we're gonna spy on?'

'Go on home and get the wine,' Jim said. 'But don't come back till eleven. We aren't leaving till then.'

'Promise you won't go without me?'

'Cross my heart and hope to die,' Jim said. 'Now get going.'

George shoved the potato chip bag through the fly screen, then sprang up, and ran off through the dark.

'You asshole!' I yelled.

'I know what I'm doing.'

'You *ass*hole! You told him Cyndi's *name*! You told him where we're *going*! Well, *I'm* not going. Not if that sleazy little shit's coming with us. No way. I'm not gonna have him spying on Cyndi.'

'Like he's been spying on my sister?'

That slowed me down. 'You think he's been doing that?'

'You think he *hasn't*? Like you said, how does he know about the pool?'

'He might've heard splashing, or . . .'

'From the street? Huh-uh. He's been snooping around. I bet he's even climbed over the fence. Joan's window is right there, man.'

'That doesn't mean he's ever looked in.'

'Hey, he confessed. He *said* he looks in girls' windows.'

'Not Joan's, though.'

'Like I'm sure he'd admit it. Get real. And what do you suppose he was doing in *your* backyard tonight?'

'Trying to find us, probably.'

'Yeah, maybe. Or maybe he came along to check out your parents' bedroom. Maybe he comes along *every* night to look in their window. Maybe he gets a charge out of watching your mom undress.'

'She shuts the curtains,' I said, feeling kind of hot and awful inside.

'Yeah, but does she shut them all the way? If there's even the tiniest open space between . . .'

'That dirty bastard better *not* be watching Mom.'

'I bet he does. Maybe my mom, too. Maybe Joan *and* Mom. And your mom. Maybe every gal in the whole neighborhood. You heard him. He *likes* to look in windows.'

'If he ever spied on my mom . . .'

'We gotta teach him a lesson. That's how come I said he can come along. You think I want his wine and Twinkies? We'll take him with us, all right. And then we'll nail his rotten Peeping Tom ass.'

We lay down on top of our sleeping bags, heads toward the front of the tent so we could keep a lookout for George, and hatched our plans.

At about ten-thirty, the light came on in my parents' bedroom. Mom stepped up to the window and pulled the curtains shut. After a while, the light went off. But a faint, trembly glow showed through the curtains. It came from their TV, which they liked to watch in bed till after the eleven o'clock news. They weren't likely to get up again except maybe to use the john.

'Ready to go?' Jim asked.

'Pretty soon.'

We waited a while longer. I was feeling awfully nervous. Not so much about sneaking into the house for our stuff. About the rest of it.

Finally, I said, 'Okay.'

We crawled out of the tent and crossed the patio to the back door. We didn't try to be quiet shutting the door and heading for the bathroom. Jim went in. I waited in the hall. When he flushed the toilet, I used the noise as a cover to rush into my bedroom. I flicked on the light, found a coil of rope in my closet and gathered up our clothes. Quick as I could, I turned the light off. Then I waited in the darkness at the doorway until Jim flushed the toilet again. While it made its gushy running sounds, I hurried to the back door. I opened it, stepped outside, checked my parents' window to make sure nobody was looking, and ran to the tent.

I kept watch through the fly screen.

Before long, Jim came out.

He crawled into the tent.

'Any problem?' I whispered.

'No sweat.'

We turned on our flashlights just long enough to sort out our clothes. Then, in the darkness, we stripped. It felt weird, being naked, feeling the warm air on my body, the sleeping bag under my rump. It might've been kind of exciting if there'd been nothing on my mind except going to Cyndi's house. But George had ruined things.

313

Once all my clothes were on except my shirt, I wrapped the rope around my waist. It had to go around several times. I did it carefully so the coils weren't all bunched on top of each other, but arranged flat against my skin. I tucked the ends underneath.

I'd just put on my shirt when Jim whispered, 'Here he comes.' Quickly, I fastened the buttons.

We picked up our flashlights and crawled outside.

Jim pressed a finger to his lips. George nodded, and raised the grocery sack he was carrying.

I led the way. We stopped at the side of the garage.

'You got the stuff?' Jim asked.

'Sure.' George opened the sack. He lifted out a wine bottle. 'I got the Twinkies, too.'

'Great. Put it away.'

'Don't you want some now?'

'Later.'

'We know a good, secret place along the way,' I whispered. 'We'll stop there and have a little party.'

'Neat!' George said.

The hike to our 'good, secret place' took about twenty minutes.

It was a railroad underpass beneath Jefferson Avenue.

If George hadn't been with us, Jim and I would've walked over it just as fast as possible and been mighty glad to leave it behind us.

Even in daylight, the place gave us both the creeps.

We'd never gone down there at night.

I felt jittery the whole time as we walked toward it.

Partly, I was worried that we might be spotted by cops or by someone we knew in the cars that went by. I turned my face away every time a car approached us from the front.

Mostly, though, I was scared about going down into the underpass.

We'd explored it quite a few times. From what we'd found,

we knew that other people used the place. There was writing on the concrete walls, some of it pretty weird and sick. And there was always a lot of junk scattered around: empty booze bottles, smashed beer cans and cigarette packs, a ratty blanket or two, even an old, stained mattress. Clothes, too. Like a flat, dirty sneaker, a sock, somebody's old underwear, a pair of pants.

Once, we got pretty excited when we spotted a bra. Jim had picked it up. It was caked with dry mud, and one of the shoulder straps was torn loose.

Our best discovery was a copy of *Penthouse* magazine. It must've gotten soaked a while before we found it, because its pages were all stiff and swollen, and a lot of them were stuck together. We peeled them apart and got to see quite a few pictures. We took that magazine with us, and Jim kept it hidden in his room.

Our most revolting discovery was a used condom. We didn't touch that.

The creepiest thing we ever found down there, I guess, was the remains of a campfire – a circle of scorched rocks around a heap of ashes. In with the ashes were a couple of charred cans and a whole bunch of small bones. We figured they were probably turkey bones, or something. Until I found the skull. I picked it up and blew off the ashes. It had a short snout and pointed teeth. Jim said, 'God, that's a cat!' I yelled and dropped it. The skull hit a rock and shattered.

After that, we'd stayed clear of the underpass.

I sure didn't look forward to going back tonight.

I would've chickened out except for one thing: it was the perfect place for making George wish he'd never messed with us.

Too soon, we got there.

Jim halted just short of where the bridge's guard rail started. We stood there, silent, and waited for a car to pass. When it was out of sight, another set of headlights showed in the distance.

Jim must've figured the driver couldn't see us yet. He whispered, 'This way, quick,' and stepped off the sidewalk.

'Where we going?' George asked.

'It's a great place,' I told him. 'Nice and private.'

Before the car got much closer, we followed Jim into the trees. We were hidden by the time it whooshed by. We crept past a few trees, then began climbing down a steep, bushy slope toward the tracks. To the right, the tracks stretched off across an empty field, shiny in the moonlight. To the left, they vanished in the black mouth of the underpass.

A couple more cars sped by, but they didn't worry me. We were low enough for the guard rail to prevent anyone from seeing us.

The weeds were dewy. They made my jeans wet to the knees. I slipped once or twice. George landed on his butt once. But finally we made it down the slope and climbed a small embankment to the tracks.

'That's our place,' I told George.

'Under there?' He didn't sound thrilled.

Jefferson Avenue was four lanes wide, so the dark area beneath it looked like a tunnel. We could see the gray of moonlight at the other end, but it was too dim to show us much of anything in the underpass.

'Hope nobody's there,' I muttered.

'Keep your eyes peeled,' Jim said. 'And get ready to run like hell.'

'Can't we just stay here?' George asked.

Jim shook his head. 'Somebody might see us from the road. Let's go.'

'I don't know,' George said.

'You wanted to come along,' I reminded him.

'Yeah, but . . .'

'Hey,' Jim said. 'If you want to run around with the big guys, you've gotta do what we do.'

'Or you can go on home,' I said. 'It's up to you, but *we're* going in there.'

He hung back while Jim and I stepped over a rail and started walking down the middle of the tracks toward the underpass. I really hoped George would chicken out. I didn't want to go under there, didn't want to nail him, wanted only to have him out of our lives so we could hurry on to Cyndi's house.

But he shrugged and came after us.

There were two sets of tracks. They ran side by side, several yards apart. Ahead of us, broad concrete supports stood between them.

We waited until we were just under the edge of the bridge, then switched on our flashlights. George dug into the paper sack and came up with a big, six-volt lantern.

'All *right*,' Jim whispered.

We shined our beams into the darkness. George's was really huge and bright. We swept our lights all over the place before going any further.

'Looks okay,' Jim murmured.

It didn't look okay. Not at all. But at least we didn't spot anyone.

Jim aimed his beam at the nearest support. The concrete was scrawled with names and dirty words and dates and drawings. The drawings were pretty crude. The biggest was an old one that I'd seen plenty of times before. It showed a cartoonish gal with huge tits and her legs spread apart. Jim and I used to call her 'The Beave'. Since the last time we'd been here, somebody'd added a mammoth erection just underneath her. It was aimed between her legs, and squirting like a geyser.

Normally, we would've had a good time studying the artwork and making remarks. But George was with us. And we were in a hurry to get to Cyndi's. And this was night.

Neither of us got cute.

'Check the other side, George,' Jim said.

317

'Me?'

'You got the good light. Make sure nobody's hiding behind those things.'

'Aw, geez.'

'Just do it,' I told him. 'We don't want some damn wino jumping us.'

George moaned, but did as he was told. He crept past the support, shined his lantern behind it, raised the light to check the backsides of the other three supports, and swung it every which way. 'Okay over there,' he said, his voice shaking. He hurried back to our side of the tunnel. 'Want me to open the wine?'

'Might as well,' Jim said.

George squatted, set down his sack, and lifted out the bottle. He stood up with it. Jim held his light on its neck while George picked at the foil with a dirty fingernail.

I took the opportunity to look around. I stayed put, but swept my light here and there. It gleamed off the glass of an empty bottle a few feet away. Over near the wall was a rag, maybe a shirt. It was surrounded by broken glass, cans, mashed cigarette packs. Halfway up the wall was an enormous black Swastika. I'd seen it before, but the drawing beside it was new to me – a rump with a hard-on shoved into its hole.

I decided to quit looking around.

George had the wine bottle clamped between his legs, a Swiss Army knife in his hands. He pried out the knife's corkscrew, then bent over and started twisting it into the top of the bottle.

Once it was in deep, he started pulling and grunting.

'Awful tight,' he muttered.

'Why don't you give it a try,' Jim said to me.

George handed over the bottle. I set my flashlight on the ground, pinned the bottle between my legs the same way he'd done, and tugged on the knife.

At first, the cork wouldn't give.

'Hurry it up,' Jim said. 'We don't wanta be late to Cyndi's.'

It moved just a little.

Then it slid out fast. As it popped free, Jim shot an arm across George's chest, whipped a leg behind him, and flung him backwards. George yelped with surprise. Grunted when he slammed the ground.

I knew this was what we'd planned, but Jim's sudden attack probably surprised me as much as George.

I put the knife and bottle down fast.

George, wheezing for air, didn't struggle as Jim rolled him over and dropped onto his rump.

I pulled up my shirt. I unwrapped the rope. By the time I was on my knees beside them, Jim had both George's arms bent up behind him.

'Guys!' George gasped. 'What're you . . .?'

'Shut up,' Jim snapped. 'We aren't gonna hurt you.'

I started tying George's hands together.

'Hey!' he said. 'Don't! Don't!'

'Calm down,' Jim told him.

'Is . . . is this . . . some kinda 'nitiation?'

'Sure,' Jim said.

'Is not!' I said. 'Why'd you wanta say that? He'll think he's . . . It's no initiation, George. You're not joining something. We just wanted to be left alone, damn it, but you wouldn't get the message. You're *not* our friend. You're a fat, grubby little pain in the ass!'

George started blubbering.

'*And* a Peeping Tom!'

'Yeah!' Jim joined in. 'You been spying on my sister, you dirty pervert!'

'Who else you been spying on?'

'Nuh . . . nobody!'

'I bet,' Jim said.

'Yeah,' I said. 'And you think you're gonna go with us to Cyndi's, you got another thing coming!'

Jim climbed off him, grabbed him by the feet and shoved his legs up till his calves were mashed against the backs of his thighs. Done with the hands, I looped the rope around his ankles, pulled it taut, and tied his feet together.

By the time I finished, George was bawling.

'You'd better cut that out,' Jim warned him. 'Somebody might hear you.'

'They might *come* for you,' I added.

'Puh . . . Please!'

'I'd be *very* quiet, if I were you,' Jim said.

'From now on,' I said, 'you just stay away from us.'

We stepped back. Jim turned off George's lantern and picked up the wine bottle. He took two packs of Twinkies out of the sack. I twisted the cork off George's knife and put the knife on the ground a couple of yards away from him. Then I picked up my flashlight and stuffed it into my pocket.

'If you're still here when we get back,' I told him, 'we'll untie you.'

'*If* we come back,' Jim added.

As we hurried out into the moonlight, George blurted things like 'Please!' and 'Don't leave me here!' and 'Come back!' But he cut it out when we were about halfway up the slope.

'Here,' Jim said, and offered me a pack of Twinkies as we walked across the bridge.

I shook my head. 'I don't want to eat his stuff. I mean, we double-crossed him.'

Jim grinned. 'Got him good, huh?'

'Maybe we oughta go back down and let him go.'

'Are you nuts? We've already wasted enough time. Besides, the little dork would probably *still* wanta come with us. He'll think we were joking or something, and we'll be right back where we started.'

'Yeah, I guess so.'

'Anyhow, he'll probably get loose and be outa there in five minutes.'

'I don't know. I tied him pretty good.'

'So maybe it'll take him ten. Don't go feeling sorry for him. He asked for it, he got it.'

'Yeah. Maybe he'll stay out of our face after this.'

'And stay away from our windows. I ever catch him spying on Joan or Mom, he'll think he got off easy tonight. I'll cut off his dick and make him eat it.'

'Oh, gross.'

'Give him a Hostess weenie.'

I elbowed Jim, and laughed.

He made me hold the wine bottle while he unwrapped his Twinkies. 'You don't know what you're missing,' he said through a mooshy mouthful.

Watching him, I could almost taste the things. Pretty soon, I said, 'He owes us, you know.'

'Huh?'

'For all the crap he put us through.'

'Damn right.'

'Besides, he ate our potato chips.'

'Sure did.'

I took the other package from Jim, gave him the bottle back, tore off the cellophane and started eating. I was about halfway through my first Twinkie when Jim took a drink of the wine.

He sighed. 'Good stuff.'

He passed the bottle to me. I had a couple of swallows. It made my mouth pucker. When it hit my stomach, it seemed to turn into fire. 'Thlightly impertinent,' I said.

That got a big laugh out of Jim.

We walked along, taking slugs of wine and bites of Twinkie,

swinging the bottle out of sight every time a car approached from either the front or the rear. Once we got away from Jefferson, there were a lot fewer cars. By then, the Twinkies were gone and the bottle was almost half empty. I was feeling pretty great.

'Let's save the rest,' Jim said.

'What for?'

'For us, stupid.'

We yucked it up.

After calming down, Jim said, 'Hey, we don't wanta get polluted.'

'Speak for yourself.'

'Where's the cork?' I gave it to him, and he squeezed it into the bottle's neck. 'We'll save it for the return trip.'

That sounded like a fine idea.

He carried it the rest of the way to Cyndi's house.

Except for a lamp at the end of the driveway, Cyndi's house was dark. Not even the porch light was on.

'What gives?' Jim asked.

'I don't know.'

'This is her house, isn't it?'

'Sure.'

We'd both been there before. Three times, we'd followed her home after school, first to find out where she lived, then later just because we liked to watch her walk, books clutched to her chest, hair golden in the sunlight, skirt swinging.

'Sure looks like her house,' Jim muttered.

'That's because it is.'

'Maybe they're around back.'

So we hurried across the frontyard and made our way alongside the house. The windows there were dark. So were those in the rear, and those along the other side. I was shaking pretty badly the whole time, scared of getting caught, thrilled by our search for the girls. I could see why a guy like George might get a kick out of sneaking around like that. It was a real charge. But the charge died when we got to the street.

'Well, shit,' Jim said.

'We must've gotten here too late.'

'Thanks to George, the little shit.'

'Damn it!'

'This *is* the right house, right?' Jim asked.

'Of course it's . . . hey! Maybe we've got the wrong night! Maybe it's *tomorrow* night. All we did was guess, remember?'

'Yeah! Bet it is tomorrow night.'

'All right! So no big deal. We'll come back.'

We turned away from Cyndi's house, and started walking.

'Tomorrow,' Jim said, 'we won't have to waste time fooling around with George. He won't come anywhere near us from now on.'

'Right. And we'll get away earlier. Mom and Dad are going out. They won't be getting home till really late.'

'Man!'

'We can leave at like ten or something!'

'Fantastic! This calls for a drink!'

We passed the bottle back and forth a couple of times. We probably would've polished it off and gotten ourselves really smashed, except the bottle got smashed first. Jim stumbled on a raised section of sidewalk. He went lurching forward and the bottle flew. It exploded on the sidewalk in front of us.

Scared that somebody might've heard the noise, we ran two blocks and didn't stop till we reached Jefferson.

When the guard rails of the bridge came into sight, my stomach went kind of cold. The last thing I wanted to do was go down to the underpass.

'Wonder how Georgie-porgie's doing,' Jim said.

'I guess we'll have to find out.'

'I bet he's already home.'

'Yeah,' I said. 'I hope so.'

'I just hope he's learned his lesson. It'd sure be a pain if we had to go through this again tomorrow night.'

'When he sees us coming from now on,' I said, 'he's gonna run the other way.'

''Less he liked it down there.'

'Nobody could like it down there.'

'I don't know. He's a pretty weird kid.'

'No kid's that weird. It's too damn creepy.'

Jim laughed. 'Hope he crapped his pants, the little shit.'

At the other side of the bridge, we ducked into the trees and started down the slope. I only looked once at the underpass. The idea of George being tied up in that dark, awful place made me feel kind of sick.

Jim and I both fell on our cans a few times before we got to the bottom of the slope. The wine might've had something to do with that.

Finally, we got to the tracks.

We walked between the rails, our flashlights off. With every step, I felt shakier. I told myself that George probably *had* gotten loose and run home. We wouldn't need to go under there, at all, just shine our lights in, make sure he was gone, and leave.

He'd probably left my rope behind. It could stay right where it was. I sure didn't need the rope badly enough to go in after it.

Just where the tracks disappeared into the darkness, we stopped and turned on our flashlights. The shiny rails gleamed. About twenty feet ahead, the rail on the left was draped with rope.

My rope. It had to be.

George *had* worked himself loose.

Now, we could go home.

Jim's flashlight swung away from the rail, away from the rope, off to the side where we'd left George.

324

Just as I'd expected, George wasn't there.

But he wasn't gone.

Jim's light found him a couple of yards closer to the wall.

We both gasped. I felt like I'd been kicked in the belly.

We ran toward George, our beams jerking all around as we tried to spot who'd done it to him. We saw no one.

We stopped by his body but didn't look down at him. Darted our lights everywhere else. We were both panting, even though we hadn't run very far. Jim made these weird whiny sounds every time he sucked in a breath.

'See anyone?' I asked.

'Huh-uh.'

'Maybe . . . they're gone.'

I swept my light across the center supports. Four broad, concrete walls. A crazy or two or three might've been lurking behind every one of them. I knew one of us should go to the other side for a look. I didn't have the guts to do it, though.

'Let's . . . get,' Jim whimpered.

'Can't leave him.'

We shined our flashlights down at George. He lay sprawled on his back, his shirt wide open, his boxer shorts and Bermudas hanging off one foot. He was bloody all the way down to his knees.

'What'd they . . . *do* to him?'

I shook my head.

George's eyes were shut. One was swollen so it looked like a hardboiled egg with a slit across it. I'd seen a boxer on TV one time who had an eye like that after going eleven rounds with the heavyweight champ.

George's neck was shiny red, but I didn't see any wounds on it.

He was so fat and dumpy that he actually had tits. I thought about how the other guys probably gave him grief about them when he had to dress for gym class. Then I thought how there wouldn't be any more gym classes for him. Because of us.

I moved my light down his fat belly.

He looked so lonely and pitiful.

'Where'd all the *blood* come from?' Jim whispered. Stepping behind my back, he moved sideways past George's hips. Then he froze. The pale beam of his light slanted down between George's legs. He let out a terrible groan, staggered out of my way, whirled around and started to puke.

I pointed my flashlight at George's groin.

And knew where all the blood had come from.

Blood *still* trickled out of the raw open slot where his dick should've been.

I went numb and started to sway. I thought I might pass out, and hoped I wouldn't fall on *him*. Then my arm got grabbed. I yelped. But it was only Jim.

I started to cry. 'Look . . . look what we did.'

'We didn't.'

'They cut off his dick,' I sobbed.

'No.'

'They *did*! Look! Didn't you see?' I pointed my light at the bloody opening.

'They didn't cut off his dick, you dope. He never had one. George is a girl. They didn't cut off nothing. They banged her.'

'What?'

'She's a *girl*. Georgina or something.'

'Oh, my God.'

'Don't know why she'd sneak around spying on Joan, but . . .'

'Didn't.'

I flinched so hard it made every bone in my body hurt. Jim actually jumped and cried out. Then we shined our lights on George's face. Her eyes were open. One eye was, anyway – the one that wasn't swollen shut.

She pushed herself up with her elbows. 'Spying on you guys,' she said. 'You're who I looked at. You two, not girls.'

'You're . . . alive!'

'Yeah.'

'Why'd you make us think you were dead?' Jim demanded.

'Just wanted to hear whatcha had to say.'

'Shit!'

'I'm just glad you're alive,' I said. I wiped my eyes with my shirttail, but couldn't stop crying. I dropped to my knees beside her and put a hand on her shoulder.

'It's okay,' she said.

'No it's not! God, I'm so sorry! If we'd known . . .'

'How bad are you hurt?' Jim asked. He crouched down next to me.

'My face don't feel too good.'

'Is that all?'

''Cept for my twat.'

'They raped you?' Jim asked.

'Yeah. *He* did. Just one. He really stank. You shoulda smelled him.'

'We never should've left you here,' Jim said. 'We never would've, if we'd only known you were a girl.'

'If we'd gone to the pool today like we told her . . .'

'Aw, I didn't show up anyhow,' she said. 'You woulda found me out.'

I sniffed, and wiped my face again.

'I only just wanted to be your friend,' she said, her voice going higher.

'You can be our friend,' I said.

'Sure,' Jim said.

'Honest?'

'Yeah, honest,' I told her. 'This *was* an initiation. I was just lying about all that stuff I told you.'

'Really?'

'Yeah.'

'From now on,' Jim said, 'we'll never ditch you again.'

'You guys sure had me going. I was starting to figure you hated me.'

'Naw. We were just kidding.'

Her bloody face smiled. She sat up.

'You'd better not move,' I said. 'We'll have to get you an ambulance or something.'

'I'm okay.'

'You can't be okay,' Jim said. 'All that blood.'

'Oh, I was a virgin. But not anymore.' She looked at each of us. 'You guys wanta bang me? You can if you want, now we're pals.'

I went kind of speechless.

'Not tonight,' Jim said. 'Thanks anyway.'

I nodded.

'You sure? I'm kinda sore, but if you want . . .'

'Some other time,' Jim told her.

'Well, okay.' She sighed as if she were a little disappointed, then got to her feet. She shook her foot clear of the tangled boxers and Bermuda shorts. 'Wanta see something cool?' she asked.

'We oughta just get out of here,' I said.

'You guys gotta see this.' She stepped over to her lantern, bent over as if she didn't mind us looking at her butt, picked up the lantern and turned it on. 'Come on,' she said.

We followed her across the tracks.

Joined her on the other side of the nearest concrete support.

Where she shined her light on a bum.

He was slumped against the support, shirt open, pants down around his ankles. His head was down. Cradled in his arms was a pile of loose guts.

George grinned at us. 'Knew he didn't get far.'

'Holy shit,' Jim muttered.

Crouching, George plunged her hands into the guts. They squirmed around like a bunch of wet snakes. Pretty soon, she came out with her knife. 'Didn't wanta lose this,' she said. She stood up and cleaned the knife on the front of her shirt. 'Betcha didn't figure he'd get into my initiation, did you?'

We shook our heads.

We walked back to the other side of the tracks. There, George stepped into her boxers and Bermudas. As she pulled them up, she said, 'So, what're we gonna do tomorrow?'

After Midnight

This book is dedicated to
Tom Corey
Friend, Photographer, Musician,
Construction Guru
and the Builder of Alice's Garage
&
To Donna, René and Amina
his special gals

Introduction

Hello.

I'm Alice.

I've never written a book before, but figured I might as well start by saying who I am.

Alice.

That's not my real name. I'd have to be an idiot to tell you my real name, wouldn't I? Identify myself, then go on to write a book that tells more than anyone should ever know about my private life and adventures and passions and crimes.

Just call me Alice.

Sounds like 'alias', doesn't it?

I'm somebody, alias Alice.

Anyway, names are the only things I'll lie about. I'll make up names for *all* my characters, because they're real people – or were – and I don't want any trouble. If I start giving true names, no telling where it might lead.

Obviously, that'll have to go for *place* names, too. Not just people. I don't want to give away *where* stuff happened, or someone might start putting two and two together.

Except for the names of people and places, everything else will be completely true. I promise. I mean, why bother to write my story if I'm not going to tell the truth? What would be the point?

For that matter, what *is* the point?

Why am I sitting down to write this book?

I'm not doing it for the money. I *would* do it for the money, but how can you get paid for a book without letting someone know who you really are? How do they make out the checks? I haven't figured that out yet, but I'm working on it.

I'm not doing it for fame, either. How can I make myself famous if nobody knows who I am?

But I want to write it anyway.

My story only happened about six months ago, but I already feel it starting to slip into the past. If I don't hurry and get it down the way it was, I'm afraid I'll lose it.

I'll never forget the main stuff, but little pieces are sure to fall away and others will change on me.

I want a record of how it *really* was. Every detail. So when I read it, later on, I'll have a way to live it all over again.

Also, it might come in handy if they ever try to prosecute me. It'll give the complete truth about my side of things, and might help me off the hook.

Or maybe it won't.

I might be better off burning it.

Anyway, here we go.

Chapter One

It Starts

I've already explained my name is Alice (but not really). I was twenty-six years old when all this took place last summer, and living in a comfortable little room over the garage of my best friend's house.

That was Serena.

She had it all. Not only the huge old house at the edge of the woods, but a husband named Charlie and two kids – a four-year-old named Debbie who was every bit as beautiful as her mother, and a baby named Jeff.

Some people have all the luck, don't they?

I mean Serena, not me.

What it mostly boils down to is genes. Serena was hugely, incredibly lucky in the genes department. Which is to say, she was born beautiful and smart. When you've got that going for you, everything else is a whizz. It was only natural for Serena to marry a handsome, wealthy fellow, move into a great house, and have a couple of terrific kids.

I didn't make out quite so well in the genes department.

My parents were a couple of duds. Good, hard-working people, but duds. Not that I hold it against them. It wasn't their fault; they came from duds, themselves, and couldn't help it. Just as I can't help who *I* am.

And I don't resent who I am.

You can't do anything about your genes, so you have to do the best you can with what you've got.

I did all right.

This isn't meant to be an autobiography, so I won't bore you with the details of my youth. This is supposed to be about what happened because of the stranger who showed up on that night last summer, so I'll skip to there.

As already stated, I was living in the room over Serena's garage. I paid a monthly rent. She had tried to talk me out of paying (she really had no use for the money, anyway), but I insisted. Even though I was between jobs, I had some savings. I was glad to part with it, so as not to be considered a freeloader.

Even if a person doesn't look like a beauty queen, she can still keep her dignity.

Am I giving you the impression that I'm an ugly, pathetic cow?

Writing is harder than it looks, I guess. Especially if you want to tell something the way it really is and not mislead people.

The fact is, I'm not and never was ugly. My face doesn't stop clocks. But then, it doesn't stop traffic, either. People have said I have a 'sweet' face, and I've been called 'cute'. Not many people have ever used the term 'beautiful' in connection with me. Those who did – like my parents – were either blinded by prejudice in my favor, lying outright to spare my feelings, or hoping to lay me.

George Gunderson used to call me 'beautiful' and 'gorgeous', but you should've seen George. I was probably the only gal in the history of his life who didn't run away screaming. Besides, he was just flattering me to get in my pants. Guys are that way, in case you never noticed.

Anyway, I'm not exactly beautiful or gorgeous. I just have an ordinary, fairly pleasant-looking face. My natural hair color is brown, but I tint it a nice, light shade of blonde. My eyes are brown. So are my teeth.

Just kidding about the teeth.

Maybe I shouldn't joke around like that. After all, this is

supposed to be a serious book. People do tell me, though, that I've got an interesting sense of humor.

My two greatest attributes, if you listen to what other people say, are my sense of humor and my smile. They also say I'm a 'nice' person, and that I'm 'caring.' But what do they know?

Though I'm nothing special in the face department, I do have a damn good body on me. I'm large for a woman (five-foot ten), and used to be on the husky side. Hell, I was fat and dumpy. But my first year at college, I pulled myself together and got into shape. Ever since then, I've stayed fit. I look great in a swimsuit – and even better out of one.

But mostly, I keep my main assets well hidden. I don't like for guys to see what I've got.

Back when I was dumpy, they never wanted to look at me or be seen with me. After I got into shape, though, I had to fight them off. Just about all of them were total jerks. They didn't want to know me or have fun. All they cared about was the fact that I was 'built'.

According to several charmers, I was 'built like a brick shithouse'.

I don't even know what a brick shithouse *looks* like.

What the hell *is* a brick shithouse? Why would anyone want to compare *me* to one? It's not only crass, but it doesn't even make sense.

When you come right down to it, most guys stink. By the time I was twenty-six and living above Serena's garage, I'd pretty much given up on them.

But then came the night the stranger showed up.

It was a hot night in July. Serena and Charlie were off on a vacation with the kids, and wouldn't be coming back for a week. In the meantime, I had the entire house to myself. They always encouraged me to stay in the real house whenever they went away. They said it made the house look 'lived in', so it wouldn't be a target for burglars. Maybe they believed what they were saying. Personally, though, I think they were just being nice to me. They figured I would much rather spend the week in their house than in my room above the garage.

They were partly right. They had a wonderful kitchen, a master bathroom with a sunken tub that was absolutely heavenly, and a den with a thirty-five-inch television. Whenever I had the run of the house, I prepared great meals for myself, lounged in the bathtub, and spent hours watching the big-screen TV.

In the master bedroom was a king-sized bed about three times the size of my bed in the garage. The walls and closet doors on both sides of it were lined with mirrors, and another huge mirror was fixed to the ceiling directly above the mattress. Serena told me they were Charlie's idea. They probably were. Serena must've like them, too, though. The mirrors wouldn't have gone up if she hadn't approved. She and Charlie were both a couple of gorgeous specimens, so it's hardly any wonder that they liked to watch each other – and themselves.

The first time I ever stayed overnight in the house, I tried out their bed. I looked pretty good in the mirrors, myself, but I also looked very *alone* sprawled out in the center of that enormous mattress. And then I got to thinking about Serena and Charlie, and how this was *their* bed. Time after time, they'd probably made love right in the very place where I was lying. Right on the very sheet. But now it was me on the sheet, not Serena, not Charlie. To make a long story short, my imagination ran wild and nothing could stop it. Even after I finally fell asleep, my mind wouldn't settle down. All night long, I thrashed about and sweated, plagued by feverish dreams – or hallucinations – so vivid they seemed real.

When I woke up the next morning, I was so worn out and ashamed of myself that I vowed never to spend another night in Serena and Charlie's bed. From then on, I always returned to the garage for bedtime.

It suited me.

As much as I liked their kitchen and bathroom and television, I often got the willies at night. The place was too big – more rooms than you could use, a hallway that ran from one end of the house to the other, windows all over the place and too many doors. You always had to worry that someone might be peering at you through a window – or already inside, hiding and ready to jump you.

Not at all like my small, cozy place above the garage.

My place was about twenty-five feet square, a single room with a kitchenette and 'half a bath' – meaning I had a fully equipped bathroom, minus a tub. From the middle of the room, with the bathroom door open, I could see every door and window. I could also hear the slightest sound.

After entering my quarters, I never failed to look around to make sure nobody had crept in during my absence. And I listened. An intruder might hide motionless and holding his breath, but I figured I would be able to hear his heartbeat.

I always felt very safe, back in my own room.

But *getting* to it could be hard on the nerves.

On that hot July night when the stranger came, I'd stayed in the house until after midnight. Normally, I would've left earlier. But this was the first day of Serena and Charlie's vacation, and I hadn't had the house to myself since their spring trip to San Francisco. As a result, I'd forgotten the wisdom of early departures. So I stayed too long in their house that night.

Overdid it.

Serena and Charlie have a lovely swimming pool in the back yard. With no other houses nearby and a wild forest behind their property, the pool is like a private, woodland pond.

A pond that I avoided like a swamp.

Except when I was house-sitting, nobody around to look at me or interfere.

The day everything started, Serena and Charlie didn't get away until early afternoon. In the driveway, I gave everyone goodbye kisses, wished them a great time, then waved as Charlie backed his car toward the road.

As soon as they were out of sight, I celebrated my new freedom by running up to my room, throwing off my clothes and jumping into my new, two-piece swimsuit. I'd already packed a small bag with things I might need during the day. I grabbed it and hurried down to their house.

First, I made myself a Bloody Mary. Then I went out to the pool.

Slick with oil and gleaming with sunlight, I spent all afternoon relaxing on the lounger, drinking this and that drink, reading a paperback mystery, daydreaming and napping. Now and then, when I grew terribly hot and drippy, I went into the water for a chilly, refreshing swim.

It was a luscious afternoon.

I drank too much and slept too much and got too much sun and loved it.

Later, I barbecued a steak on the outdoor grill. I ate it by the pool. After supper, I figured I'd had enough outdoor living for one day, and moved inside. I took a long, hot shower, soaping myself all over to get the oil off. When I rinsed, my skin gleamed. It had a warm coppery glow from the sun.

My tan was great, but it made me look a little silly in the bedroom mirrors. That's because of the places where I *wasn't* tanned. I looked as if I were wearing a swimsuit made from the skin of someone else, a stranger who'd never been out in the sunlight.

I used some of Serena's skin lotion to keep myself nice and moist. Then I slipped into Charlie's blue silk robe, went into the den, and watched television. I just loved their big-screen TV. It made everything look huge.

Their house was too far out of town for cable, so they had a satellite dish. The little TV in my own room was hooked up to the same system, so I knew how to work it.

You could get a zillion shows.

I found a movie that started at eight. While I was watching it, night came so I had to get off the couch and shut the den curtains. I don't like curtains being open at night. Somebody might be out in the dark, looking in. You can't see him, but he can see you. It really gives me the creeps.

That particular night, I felt more edgy than usual. It was probably a case of first-night jitters. Or else a premonition.

I turned on a couple of lamps to make the den bright.

I'd planned to take a long bath by candlelight after the movie. When the time came, though, I changed my mind. I much preferred to stay in the bright den with the television on, its volume good and loud. I'd lost every desire to go wandering through the dark house or to sit all alone in the hot water, surrounded by silence and flickering candle flames and shadows.

With the change of plans, I wanted popcorn – at least until I thought about the long journey to the kitchen. There were windows all along the way – enormous windows and sliding glass doors and walls of glass – every one of them facing the pool area, the back lawn and the woods. If only I'd remembered to shut those curtains before dark!

With the curtains wide open, it would almost be the same as if the house didn't have any rear wall, at all.

I had walked that particular gauntlet before.

That's true. I'd often walked it at night when the curtains were wide open and I was all alone in the house. Sometimes, I hadn't even gotten a case of the jitters. Usually, though, I found myself hurrying along, goosebumps from head to toe, afraid to even *glance* toward the windows, absolutely certain that someone horrible must be gazing in at me.

Tonight, I was already feeling too damn jumpy.

The popcorn wasn't worth a trip that might scare me half out of my wits, so I went ahead and watched the next movie without any.

It ended a little after midnight.

Which was late. Normally, eleven o'clock would've been about the right time for letting myself out of the house and hurrying to my room above the garage.

As late as it already was, I didn't feel the least bit sleepy. Maybe because I'd taken all those naps beside the pool.

So why not stay and watch one more movie?

Why not? Because if I watched another, I would have to make my trip to the garage at 1:30 or 2:00.

Way too late.

My swimsuit was still in the master bathroom. I decided to leave it there. Since I had nothing else to put on, I stayed in Charlie's robe. I liked wearing it, anyway. It was very lightweight, and felt slippery and cool against my skin. Also, it made me feel funny, sometimes, knowing it was his. Funny in a good, familiar sort of way.

My purse was with me on the sofa, so I didn't need to go searching for it. I didn't have to wander around the rest of the house to make sure all the doors were locked, either. I'd taken care of that before the sun went down. I'd also made sure that every light was off except for those that were supposed to stay on all night: the one in the foyer and a couple out in front of the house.

Serena and Charlie never lit up the rear of the house – the deck or pool or yard – except when they were out there. (And sometimes not even then.) I never asked them why. If it was me, though, I would've kept them off because of the woods.

Who knows what they might attract? There were things in the woods that might see the lights and come over to investigate. Nasty, wild things that belonged in the deep woods, not in your back yard. Not in your house.

Chapter Two

The Stranger

Midnight.

I wished I was already back inside my safe little place above the garage.

Before I could *be* there, though, I had to *get* there.

Getting there was the bad thing about staying in Serena and Charlie's house. It was the price that had to be paid. Not a terrible price, really. I'd always been willing to pay it for the luxury of using their house.

I mean, it was my choice to stay after dark, to stay until midnight. I *could've* returned to my place before sundown, or even kept out of their house entirely and avoided the whole problem.

Or, having stayed late, I could've avoided the return trip by *remaining* in the house.

But here's the deal.

It only takes me two or three minutes to step outside, hurry over to the garage, climb the flight of stairs to my door, unlock it and get inside. If I'm *really* scared, I can probably do it in less than a minute.

The trip always frightens me, but it doesn't last long. If I avoid it by spending all night in the house, however, I end up being tormented for hours and hours, not a few minutes.

It makes sense to me.

I do things my own way, that's the thing. If enjoying the luxuries of the house means I have to make a scary rush back to my own place in the middle of the night, so be it. I'll pay the price.

Anyway, it was time to go. Past time.

So I shut off the television, then turned off all the lamps in the den. After that, there was only darkness except for a dim, gray glow of moonlight that seeped in through the curtains. I opened the curtains. The glow brightened a lot. I stepped up close to the glass door and looked out.

With the den dark behind me and the area behind the house spread with moonlight, I felt invisible.

I took my time, gazing out. I wanted to be completely sure it was safe before unlocking the door and stepping into the night.

Impossible, of course.

You can *never* be sure it's safe.

The full moon, that night, was very bright. It laid a dazzling silver path across the surface of the swimming pool. The concrete around the pool looked gray like dirty snow. The lawn beyond the concrete was as dark as the water. Like the water, it had a path of moonlight. The path on the grass was as dim as old iron, but led straight to the brilliant path that came over the pool toward me.

At the far end of the lawn, the forest started. The tops of the trees looked as if they'd been misted with silver spray-paint. Below their tops, the trees were completely dark. So dark they looked *gone*. They cast a black shadow over part of the lawn.

I saw nobody.

But there was so much blackness.

Someone might be lurking at the border of the woods, or even closer than that.

In the pool, for instance.

The water level is a foot or more below the rim, so the far wall casts a shadow along its entire length. A dozen faces – *two* dozen – might be hidden in that strip of blackness ... all of them watching me. The near side of the pool could provide another hiding place, not because of any shadow but because the concrete edge, itself, blocked my view of whatever might be waiting beneath it.

If he preferred to stay dry, an assailant might simply wait for me, nearby but out of sight, with his back pressed to the very wall of the house. I wouldn't be able to spot him there until I'd opened the door and leaned out. And that might be the end of me.

Or he might position himself around the corner to jump me in the space between the house and the garage.

Do you see what I mean about safety?

I stared out the door for a very long time. Even though I saw nobody, I couldn't quite force myself to move. I kept thinking about all the places where someone *might* be.

My breath kept fogging up the glass. I guess that's because the air-conditioner was on in the house. Every now and then, a milky white cloud would ruin my view. I had to sway to one side or another, or crouch, in order to find some clear glass. Sometimes, I wiped away the fog with my hand or forearm or the front of my robe.

The way I'm telling it, you must think I was standing there forever and that I'm a hopeless coward.

It sort of *felt* like forever, but it probably wasn't more than fifteen or twenty minutes.

And even though I'm not the bravest person in the world, it's a fact that I'd made the trip from the house to the garage many times in the past, often at very late hours of the night. Serena and Charlie did a lot of traveling. I'd lived above their garage for three years, and I *always* came over when they were away.

Sometimes, I hardly gave a glance out the door before sliding it open and walking out. That was rare, but it happened. More often, I spent five or ten minutes. A couple of times, I'd been so spooked that it had taken me more than an hour to work up my courage to leave.

But I'd *always* gone, sooner or later.

So I wouldn't call myself a hopeless coward.

I'm a *hopeful* one.

Finally, you decide it's time. You *hope* nobody's out there waiting to jump you, because you can't be sure. Then you take a deep breath, flip open the lock, roll open the door, and go for it.

That night, the time finally came.

I was trembling quite a lot by then. Also, my robe was hanging open because I'd been using it to wipe the glass. I pulled it shut, tightened the silk belt, took a deep breath that trembled on its way in, and unfastened the lock.

I pulled, and the door rolled away to my right.

Things looked so much clearer, suddenly.

Just at that moment, before I'd even had a chance to step outside, someone crept out of the blackness at the edge of the woods.

I almost made a sudden break for the garage. But I held back.

If I darted out and ran, he would see me for sure.

And do what? Chase me down?

Holding my breath, staying absolutely motionless except for my right arm, I slowly reached sideways and found the door handle. I pulled gently, easing the door along its tracks. It made a soft rumbling sound, which the stranger didn't seem to hear.

As I slid the door shut in front of me, I kept my eyes on him.

If he noticed me, he gave no sign of it. His head didn't seem to be fixed in my direction. It turned this way and that. A few times, he even glanced over one shoulder or the other.

The full moon lit his hair and shoulders, but not his face. Most of his front was vague with shadow. I could make out his silhouette clearly, though. He was wearing shorts, but no shirt. When I caught a side view, he didn't seem to have breasts.

That was my big clue as to his gender.

The stranger still might've been a girl – maybe a thin and shapeless tomboy – but I doubted it.

346

This was a guy.

A guy who'd come sneaking out of the woods and was making his way closer and closer to the house.

Soon, the door bumped softly shut in front of me. I fastened its lock, then took one step backward and stopped.

I knew *exactly* what to do.

Hurry over to the telephone and call the police.

It's what I *intended* to do.

But the telephone was out of reach. To put my hands on it, I would need to abandon the glass door and make my way through the darkness to the other end of the couch.

That couldn't be done without losing sight of the intruder.

So I stood where I was, and watched him.

He still seemed unaware of my presence. Maybe that was an act, but I doubted it. Though he was stealthy about the way he approached the house, he didn't seem to be in any hurry.

Maybe he cut the phone line and knows I can't call for help.

Don't be ridiculous, I told myself. That's movie stuff, cutting phone lines. Nobody does it in real life.

Do they?

More than likely, he didn't even know I was in the house: I'd turned off the lights fifteen or twenty minutes before he put in his appearance. For all he knew, nobody was home.

But how long had he been watching?

What if he'd started watching *before* the lights went out?

Suppose he's been watching me all day?

When that thought shoved its way into my mind, I suddenly felt sick with fear.

What does he want?

Maybe nothing. Maybe he's just a guy who happens to enjoy wandering around in the middle of the night. Maybe just someone who got lost in the woods and only now has managed to find his way out.

Or a harmless nut of some kind.

Or . . .

A burglar. A rapist. A killer.

Trembling, I watched him step onto the concrete directly across the pool from where I stood.

He had no weapons or tools that I could see.

But his shorts had pockets.

Near the edge of the pool, he stopped. He seemed to stare straight at me.

He can't see me, I told myself. The room's completely dark. The moon is probably glaring on the door glass.

His head swiveled slowly from side to side. He turned around in a complete circle as if to make sure he wasn't being observed. Then he took off his shorts.

They appeared to be cut-off jeans. First he had to unbuckle his belt. After the belt was open, he unfastened a button or snap at his waist and lowered the zipper. Bending over, he drew the shorts down his legs. Then he stepped out of them and stood up straight.

The moon, high in the sky behind him, rimmed his body with white so I could see right away that he didn't have on a stitch of clothing.

Though his front was poorly lighted, I could see the general gray of his bare skin all the way from his face down to his feet. His eyes and mouth looked like dim smudges. His nipples were like an extra set of eyes spaced wide apart on his chest. His navel was just a small, dark dot. Down from there was more skin, then a nest of hair and his penis.

He stood there for a while as if he wanted me to take a good, long look at him – even though I *know* he couldn't see me standing on the other side of the glass door.

Then he looked around, turning his head and body. When he turned, I got a side view.

It made me feel a little sick.

And very frightened.

He wants to shove that into me.

No, he doesn't, I told myself. He doesn't even know I'm here.

He'd better not. If he knows, he won't quit till he nails me with that thing.

The prowler sat down on the concrete, swung his legs over the edge of the pool, scooted forward and slid down into the water.

Chapter Three

In the Water

You suddenly couldn't see him at all. He'd vanished. I stared at where he'd been, but he was gone as if he'd turned invisible.

Not invisible, but black.

The pool looked empty. I knew it wasn't, though.

I pictured him swimming underwater for a few more seconds, then bursting out, hurling himself onto the pool's edge and dashing at my door.

The door might slow him down, but it wouldn't stop him.

I mean, it was *glass.*

I tried to prepare myself for the shock of a sudden assault.

Don't scream, just turn around and run like hell.

Go for the kitchen.

Grab one of the butcher knives.

I saw him.

Out near the middle of the pool, the back of his head and then his buttocks slid across the moonlight's silver path. He seemed to be on his way to the shallow end, doing a leisurely breast stroke.

Not coming for me, after all.

Not yet.

But the pool had tile stairs underwater at a corner of the shallow end. When he came to them, he might climb out.

I stepped a little closer to the glass door.

He didn't swim toward the stairs. Instead, he kept to the center. At the end of the pool, he stood up. His wet skin gleamed in the moonlight, but only down to his waist. There, the black water cut him off. He looked as if he'd lost his lower body – legs, ass, and the all the rest – as if whacked apart by a terrible sword.

The saber.

I suddenly remembered Charlie's saber. It hung on hooks above the fireplace in the living room, along with a framed citation that had something to do with the Civil War service of his great-great-grandfather.

The saber was an actual relic of the war.

It hadn't belonged to Charlie's ancestor, though; Serena had bought it for him as a Christmas present.

We'd all fooled around with it, now and then.

It was about four feet long, and sharp.

Out in the pool, the stranger turned around. He eased down into the water, his body disappearing until nothing was left except his face. Then he started swimming again, apparently on his way to the deep end.

I stepped backward, turned away from the glass door and went to get the saber.

I'd forgotten that the foyer light was on. It was halfway down the long corridor, too far away for its brightness to reach the doorway of the den. But I saw it the moment I stepped out. Seeing the foyer light, I also remembered that the living room curtains were wide open.

The wall out there was mostly glass from one end to the other, from floor to ceiling. Like the wall of an aquarium.

From anywhere near the deep end of the pool, the stranger would have a fine view in.

I muttered a curse.

To be honest about it, I said 'Shit.'

I hated my stupidity for not remembering to shut the curtains before dark. Bad enough that I'd missed out on popcorn because they were open, but now I couldn't even go for the saber.

Obviously, I *could* go for it if I wanted to.

But I'm not that stupid.

Suppose, so far, the guy had no idea that anyone was in the house? He sees me sneaking through the living room, trying to get the saber, and he'll know I'm here.

He'll assume I'm alone.

Maybe he'll like the looks of me. Even though I'm no glamour queen, I've got a great figure and I *am* wearing a clingy, revealing robe.

And he is already naked and aroused.

Maybe, so far, he'd only been interested in a little midnight skinny-dipping. But seeing me . . .

No way.

I wasn't going to risk it.

I'll wait till he tries to break in.

And maybe he won't, I thought. Maybe he really did come here only to use the swimming pool. He might do a few laps, then walk back into the woods and that'll be the end of it.

He might be breaking in right now.

I stepped back into the den. This time, I shut the door behind me to make sure no light could possibly sneak in from the foyer.

It had already dimmed my night vision. Except for the outside glow coming through the glass door, everything in the den looked much darker than before.

From where I stood, I could only see a small section of the pool. The stranger wasn't in sight, and that worried me. So I hurried.

My bare left foot kicked a leg of the coffee table. From the sound, you'd think I'd struck the table with a hammer. My toes crumpled. Pain rushed up my leg. Tears flooded my eyes. My mouth flew open to let out a cry of agony, but I kept quiet and hobbled sideways and fell backward onto the couch. The couch scooted and bumped the wall. Flinging my leg up, I clutched my ruined foot.

From the feel of things, I figured two or three toes might be broken.

But the pain subsided after a couple of minutes.

Wet-faced and breathless, I fingered my toes. I wiggled them. They felt sore and kind of tired, but they seemed okay otherwise.

I wondered what the stranger was up to.

But I no longer wanted to look. I wanted to remain right where I was. The couch felt good under my back, even though my rear end was hanging off the cushion and I had to keep at least one foot planted on the floor to stop myself from sliding off.

Maybe I should swing my legs up, make myself comfortable, and stay put.

I wasn't *required* to stand at the door and watch the stranger swim his laps.

He would go away, sooner or later.

Go away, or break in.

If he tries to break in, I'll go for the saber. If he doesn't, I'll just . . . What if I don't hear him?

Such a huge house, he could make almost any kind of noise at the other end and I'd be none the wiser. Especially now that I'd shut the den door.

Also, there was the air conditioner.

The house had central air.

I couldn't hear its machinery. The compressor, or whatever, was outside and pretty far away. But the den had a couple of vents and an air intake. They didn't make enough noise to notice, usually. Just soft, breezy, breathy sounds. But now they seemed as loud as a gale.

The stranger could hurl a brick through the living-room window and I probably wouldn't hear it.

Turn off the air.

The control box was mounted on the hallway wall, not far from the den. Only minutes ago, I'd been standing within reach of it. Too bad I hadn't thought to reach out and flick it off. But my mind had been on the saber, not on the quiet noise of the air conditioner.

So, do it now.

I pushed myself off the couch and stood up. My toes ached, but not badly. I hardly limped at all on my way to the door. I wrapped my hand around its knob.

And suddenly wished, badly, that I hadn't shut it.

What if I open it and he's standing right there?

I pictured him on the other side of the door, naked and hard, dripping water onto the hallway carpet, grinning at me. He'd grabbed Charlie's saber on his way through the house, and held it overhead with both hands like a Samurai all eager to split me down the middle.

My imagination likes to torture me with stuff like that.

I figured he probably wasn't really there, or even in the house at all.

But my hand and arm felt frozen. I couldn't force myself to open the door.

Then all of a sudden I got to thinking the knob might start to turn in my hand and *he* might throw the door open, crashing it into me and rushing in.

This was just my imagination at work, and I knew it.

But it scared me.

I let go of the knob and backed away from the door, pretty much expecting it to fly open. But it stayed shut. So then I turned around and faced the sliding glass door.

From where I stood, I could see the pool. Not much of it, though.

And not the stranger.

Where is he?

This time, I was extra careful crossing the room. My feet hit nothing. As I neared the door, I put a hand forward. Soon, my fingers touched the cool glass.

I eased closer, peering out.

Still no sign of him.

When my breasts met the glass, I stopped. This was about as close to the door as I could get without bumping my nose or forehead.

I stared out.

Where'd he go?

He didn't seem to be in the pool, and he obviously wasn't standing nearby on the concrete or lawn.

Maybe he'd gone away.

Maybe he's already in the house.

The chill from the glass, seeping through my robe, was making my nipples ache. I eased back a little to get away from it.

The glass in front of my face had fogged up, so I wiped it with my hand.

And that's when I saw him.

He was in the pool, after all.

Maybe he'd been below the surface for a while. Or maybe he'd been floating somewhere that I couldn't see him.

Anyway, there he was.

He drifted on his back near the middle of the pool, his arms spread out, his legs apart. He didn't move a muscle. The water, calm and almost motionless itself, rippled around him, turned him slowly, eased him along as if it had a vague destination for him but wasn't in any hurry.

His wet skin shone like silver in the moonlight.

He looked asleep.

He was probably awake, though, feeling the lift of the water beneath him, enjoying its cool lick, relishing the warm breezes drifting over the regions of his skin that weren't below the surface.

He looked as if he might be waiting for a lover to come, drawn to him by his open naked body, lured by the invitation of the pillar of flesh that stood tall and ready, shiny in the moonlight.

What if it's me?

What if he's waiting for me?

He wants me, knows I'm watching, thinks he can lure me out of the house.

You've got another think coming, buster. You can wave that thing in the air till hell freezes over, or IT does. I'm not stepping one foot outside.

Just because he looked beautiful in the moonlight didn't mean he wasn't a rapist, a killer, a madman.

There *had* to be something wrong with him. A normal person doesn't sneak out of the woods in the middle of the night, strip naked and go for a dip in the swimming pool of a total stranger.

Maybe he knows Charlie or Serena and they told him it's okay.

That hadn't occurred to me before.

But it seemed highly unlikely. Virtually impossible. For one thing, they wouldn't give someone permission to use the pool in their absence without telling me about it. After all, I'd *be* here and take him for an intruder.

For another thing, I knew all their friends. The man in the pool wasn't one of them.

I didn't think so, anyway.

It was hard to tell exactly what his face looked like, but I was pretty sure that a body as fine as his didn't belong to anyone I'd ever seen around the house or pool.

Serena and Charlie were sociable people. They *did* like to invite friends over for pool parties. But I was the only one with permission to use it when they were away. That's another reason I knew this guy didn't belong here.

Nobody but me was allowed in the pool when they weren't home.

As far as I knew, anyway.

And I knew plenty. I'd been living over the garage for three years, and I could see the pool from my windows.

People just didn't show up and start using it. Whenever I'd seen anyone at the pool, Serena or Charlie or both of them had been there, too.

Of course, I hadn't spent all my time watching for pool activity. Things might've gone on, now and then, that I didn't know about.

But not much.

I've seen squirrels, raccoons, deer and other animals come out of the woods to drink at the pool. I've watched Charlie swim his laps at dawn when he probably assumed I was asleep. I've even observed the times, fairly often in the summer, when Serena and Charlie went skinny-dipping late at night. They kept the pool lights off, of course, and spoke in whispers or not at all. Whenever they used the pool that way, they always ended up making love. They did it right out in the open, so they must've figured I was asleep or blind. Whereas, actually, I happened to be looking out my window.

I was looking out my window more than anyone would've guessed, but I'd never found a *stranger* in the pool.

Not until tonight.

He'd hardly moved at all in the past few minutes. Just drifted this way and that on his back. I began to wonder if maybe he'd fallen asleep. If asleep, he must've been having a doozy of a dream.

The telephone rang.

After midnight, and it suddenly let out a loud jangle in the silence and darkness of the den.

I jumped and yelped.

Out on the pool, the stranger's head jerked sideways in the water. I couldn't see his eyes, but I knew he was staring straight at me.

Chapter Four

The Phone Call

Not that he could see me.

If you're in real darkness and someone else is out in the moonlight, he doesn't stand a chance of spotting you.

But I felt his eyes on me.

I flinched as the phone rang again.

A phone isn't meant to ring that late at night. It scares you. Even if you're *not* alone in the house and spying on a prowler, the ringing rips through your nerves.

Friends don't call after nine. Not unless there's an emergency.

It rang again, and I flinched again.

Out in the pool, the man rolled over, turned and started gliding toward me with his head up.

The phone rang again as I took slow backward steps away from the glass door.

Why did it have to be so loud?

I knew he could hear it. Maybe not this particular phone, but a general clamor. I'd been swimming in the pool myself, sometimes, when people called. Even with the doors and windows shut, you could hear rings and chirps and warbles and tweets from all over the house. I don't even know how many phones Serena had, but at least five – maybe seven or eight. It was a big house, and there were phones in nearly every room.

The only answering machine was in the den.

With me.

After the fourth ring came clicks that meant the machine was responding.

I kept creeping backward.

Outside, the stranger arrived at the side of the pool. He stood up, put his hands on the concrete edge, and seemed to stare straight at me.

I'm not big on distances. My guess, though – he was only twelve or fifteen feet away from the glass door. And I was on the other side of it, five or six feet back.

More clicks from the machine.

A man's voice said, 'Ah, you finally got yourself an answering machine. Hope it's not because of me. But it probably is, huh? Who's the guy you got to record the greeting for you?' A pause. 'Never mind. It's none of my business, I guess. Anyway, are you there? Judy? If you're there, would you pick up? Please? I know you probably don't want to talk to me, but . . . I don't want to lose you. I love you. Are you there? Please, talk to me.'

He went silent.

The man in the pool jumped, planted a foot on the edge, and climbed out.

'The thing is, I'm not going to call again. I'm not going to beg you to change your mind. I'm not going to plead with you. I've got to hang onto a little of my dignity, you know?'

The man started walking slowly toward the glass door.

'So this'll be it. The ball's in your court. If you really want it to be over, fine. I'll accept that. I'll never bug you again. It'll be adios, Tony. Forever. I don't want that to happen, but hell . . . Are you there, Judy? It feels weird, talking to you this way. Would you please pick up, if you're there?'

The stranger arrived at the door and peered in.

Could he see me?

Could he hear the quick loud thudding of my heart?

I stood motionless, staring at him. He had his arms raised like a guy who's been ordered to 'stick 'em up'. His open hands were pressed against the glass. So was his forehead. But his nose didn't touch the glass. Neither did his chest or belly or legs. Nothing else touched except for the tip of his penis, which looked like a smooth and strange little face pushing against the glass to help him search for me.

'Okay,' Tony said to the answering machine. 'If that's how you want it. Anyway, I've moved to a new place. I couldn't stand being in the old apartment anymore, not after everything that'd happened there.' He sounded as if he were trying not to cry. 'I'll give you my number, and you can call me if you want to. If you don't call, I'll understand.'

As Tony gave his new telephone number, the man outside took a step away from the door, reached down and grabbed the handle and jerked it.

Snatching up the phone with one hand, I blurted, 'Tony!'

With my other hand, I slapped up the light switch.

A lamp came on by the couch.

The sudden brightness hurt my eyes, made me squint, obliterated my moonlit view of the stranger. The sliding door was now a mirror. It showed me a hollow, transparent version of the coffee table, the lamp, and me.

I saw myself with the phone against my left ear. I stood crooked, still bent sideways to the right as if frozen in my reach for the light switch. My belt had come loose. The open robe seemed to split me down the middle. It still covered my left side from shoulder to thigh, but my entire right side was bare to the gaze of the stranger.

If he was still there.

He must've leaped back when the light first came on.

Now he returned, looming out of the darkness just beyond the door and pressing his body against the glass.

Tony was talking into my ear. I didn't pay much attention, but he seemed to believe I was Judy.

The stranger gaped in at me. With his body pressed to the door, the lamplight reached him. He looked awful – grotesquely flattened and spread out – like an alien creature trying to ooze through the glass.

'HELLO!' I shouted into the phone. 'POLICE! I WANT TO REPORT A PROWLER!'

'Huh?' Tony asked. 'A prowler?'

The stranger writhed against the glass, licked it, rubbed it with his body and open hands as if making believe it was me.

From where I stood, it *looked* like me.

My reflection was superimposed over him.

He couldn't see that, though. And didn't need to, because he had a great view of the *real* me.

'YES! HE'S IN THE YARD! HE'S TRYING TO FORCE HIS WAY IN. THIS IS 3838 WOODSIDE LANE. YOU'VE GOT TO GET OVER HERE RIGHT AWAY!'

'Who is this? This isn't Judy?'

'HE'S A WHITE MALE, ABOUT TWENTY YEARS OLD, SIX FEET TALL, A HUNDRED AND EIGHTY POUNDS, WITH SHORT BLOND HAIR.'

'Is this for real? Do you really have a prowler?'

'YES! AND HE'S NAKED, AND HE'S TRYING TO GET IN! YOU'VE GOT TO SEND A SQUAD CAR RIGHT AWAY!'

'Holy shit,' Tony said.

'PLEASE HURRY!'

'Do you want me to hang up and call the police?'

Taking the phone away from my mouth, I yelled at the man, 'THE COPS ARE ON THE WAY, YOU SICK BASTARD! THEY'LL BE HERE IN TWO MINUTES!'

I know he heard me, but he seemed to be lost in his own world of skin and glass and me.

Watching him, I saw myself. I looked like a ghost being molested by a mad, drooling mime. He writhed against me, caressed me, kissed me, then suddenly went rigid and started to jerk, shaking the door in its frame. For a moment, I thought he was having a seizure.

In a way, he was.

When I realized what was going on, I gasped and turned my head away.

My eyes met the light switch.

I shot my hand out and flipped it down. Darkness clamped down on the room.

The door stopped shaking.

I looked.

The stranger took a few steps backward, then whirled around. He ran to the edge of the pool, dived in, and swam for the other side.

While I watched him, I heard Tony's tiny, faint voice coming from the phone's earpiece down by my side.

The stranger boosted himself out of the pool, scurried over the concrete, swooped down and snatched up his shorts. He didn't put them on. Clutching them in one hand, he dashed onto the lawn and ran toward the woods.

I lifted the phone.

Tony sounded frantic. '. . . okay? Hello? What's happening?'

'I'm here,' I said.

'What happened? What's going on?'

'I think it's all right now. He just ran away.'

'You'd better call the cops.'

'He thinks I just did. That's what scared him off.'

'Maybe you'd better call them for real.'

'I don't know. He's gone now.'

'How do you know he won't come back?'

'Thanks a lot, Tony.'

'Sorry. Are you okay?'

'Just a little shook up. I'm all by myself, and he came sneaking out of the woods behind the house.'

'You said he was naked?'

'Yeah. Well, he took off his shorts and started swimming in the pool.'

'Weird. You don't have any idea who he was?'

'Not a clue. Just some guy who came out of the woods.'

'Miller's Woods?'

'Yeah.'

'That's bad. A lot of real oddballs hang around in there.'

'This is the first time anyone ever come sneaking out to use the pool. That I know about, anyway.'

'You're lucky that's all he did.'

'Yeah,' I said. I thought about what he'd done on the door, but kept my mouth shut about it.

'You really should call the cops,' Tony told me.

'I know. You're probably right.'

'They keep finding bodies in those woods.'

He wasn't telling me anything new. 'Now and then,' I said. 'But most of them weren't *killed* there. They were just dropped off, you know? It's not like there's necessarily a homicidal maniac hanging around in the woods.'

'*I* sure wouldn't want to live near them.'

'Well, I don't mind. I like it, normally. It's nice and peaceful.'

'You live there *alone*?'

'I'm alone tonight.'

'Maybe you shouldn't be. I know you don't want to hear this, but you really *can't* be sure he won't come back.'

'I wish you'd stop saying that.'

'You sound like a nice person.'

'Thanks.'

'I'd hate to think you might end up . . . you know.'

'I won't,' I told him.

'Do you have a name?' he asked.

'No, actually I'm one of those people who isn't that lucky.'

He laughed a little, and I smiled.

'My name's Alice,' I said. (That isn't really what I told him. I told him my true name, which is a secret as far as this book is concerned . . . unless you're smart enough to find my hidden message.)

'Hello, Alice,' He said.

'Hello, Tony.' (Tony isn't his real name, either, by the way – in case you were daydreaming when you read the introduction. Tony, Serena, Charlie, Judy etc. – all made up. The same goes for Miller's Woods, and so on. Just thought I'd remind you.)

'I guess I dialed a wrong number,' Tony said.

'I guess you did.'

'I was trying to call this gal . . .'

'I know. Judy. She must've dumped you, huh?'

'Something like that.'

'You probably called her once too many times after midnight.'

'Think so?'

'It scares people. You shouldn't do it.'

'Maybe not.'

'Besides which, it makes you sound desperate. If you want to get back on Judy's good side, you don't want her to think you're desperate about it.'

'You're probably right.'

'You bet I'm right.'

'Good thing I dialed the wrong number,' he said.

'I'm glad you did. My creepy visitor would probably *still* be here.'

'So, what are you going to do?'

'Nothing. Go to bed, I guess.'

'You shouldn't stay there. Not by yourself.'

'I'll be fine.'

'Is there a neighbor you could stay with for the rest of the night?'

'Not exactly. Nobody nearby.'

'What about . . .?'

'Anyway, I'll be fine. I really don't think he'll be coming back tonight. As far as he knows, the cops are on the way over.'

'I hope you're right,' Tony said.

'So do I.'

'I'd hate to read about you in the paper.'

'Me, too.'

He laughed quietly. Then he said, 'I'm serious about this, though. Is there a friend you can call? Someone who might be willing to come over? Maybe a relative?'

'None.'

'What about heading over to a motel?'

'At this hour?'

'Most of them over by the highway are open all night. You might have to ring a bell, or something, but . . .'

'I'm not going to any motel. Are you kidding? I'm probably ten times safer staying right here than if I try to drive over to one of those places at this hour. Anyway, haven't you ever heard of Norman Bates?'

'You'll be fine if you don't take a shower.'

'I'll just stay home and take one.'

Tony was silent for a few moments. It made me wonder what he was thinking about. Then he said, 'Look. Why don't I come over there? Just so you won't be alone in case this guy decides to try something.'

His suggestion didn't come as a huge surprise. Still, it made me feel uneasy.

'I don't think so, Tony. Thanks for asking.'

'I realize we don't know each other very well.'

'We don't know each other period,' I pointed out. 'You called the wrong number and we've been talking for about five minutes. Now you want to come over?'

'I'm worried about you.'

'Maybe you are and maybe you aren't. Maybe this whole thing's a set-up. It's pretty convenient, you just happening to call here when you did.'

'I dialed the wrong number.'

'Maybe you did and maybe you didn't.'

'Jeez,' he said.

For a few moments, he was silent.

Then he said, 'Anyway, it's getting pretty late. I'd better hit the sack. Good luck with your intruder, Alice. It was nice talking to you. Pretty much. Bye.'

He hung up.

Chapter Five

Exit

After that, I put down the phone and crept through the darkness to the sliding door.

The other side of the glass was smeared where the stranger had licked it, where he'd rubbed it with his wet face. It looked like a dirty car windshield after you've run wipers across it.

I found a clean place next to the mess his face had made, and peered out as if gazing over his shoulder.

The warnings from Tony made me nervous. Maybe the stranger *would* sneak back.

Maybe, next time, he wouldn't let a door stop him.

Not that it had actually *stopped* him, this time.

I could still picture him writhing against it.

Trying my best to ignore the image, I must've spent about ten minutes pressed to the glass. I had to make sure the coast was clear. But I couldn't get the awful picture out of my mind.

If he'd still been there – the glass gone – my right breast might've been pushing against his bare chest. He could've been squirming against me, rubbing me, spurting on me.

I finally stumbled backward to get away from the door.

The moonlight showed what he'd left on the glass.

It made me feel sick. Trembling, I turned away. I shut the curtains, then found my purse on the couch and made my way to the other door. I opened it and stepped into the hallway. This time, I was glad to see the foyer light.

This time, too, I wasn't afraid of being seen.

That's not quite true. The idea of being seen frightened me; it just didn't stop me. I walked swiftly down the hall and into the living room. Almost nothing showed on the other side of the glass wall. Just darkness. But the glass gave back an image of me.

Me, striding across the carpet, my purse swinging by my hip, the robe flowing around me, my legs flashing out long and bare as if the robe were an exotic gown with a slit up its front.

I looked like the heroine of a gothic romance.

Or a madwoman from a horror movie.

Especially when I reached up with both hands and lifted the saber off its hooks above the fireplace.

The saber felt good and heavy.

I stepped away from the fireplace, turned toward my dark image in the glass, and watched myself slash the air a few times.

Was *he* watching?

With the wall of glass in front of me and the foyer light behind my back, I could probably be seen clearly all the way from the edge of the woods.

I raised the saber high.

'You want me, pal?' I asked. 'Come and get me.'

I swung the blade a few more times.

I felt powerful and excited. I looked pretty cool, too.

But then I started to feel stupid and silly and even a little scared, so I turned away from the glass and hurried toward the foyer.

Normally, I would've left the house through the sliding door in the den. That was just my habit. It probably started because the den was where I spent most of my time, after dark. I'd be in it for hours watching the big-screen television, so I generally felt comfortable there and didn't want to wander through the huge, empty house on my to get out. So simple just to use the door that was there, slip outside, slide it shut and hurry over to the garage.

Not tonight.

I just couldn't. Not after what the stranger had done on the other side of it.

Somebody will have to clean that up, I thought.

Not me. Not tonight, anyhow.

Standing in the foyer, I wondered if there was anything I needed. I had my keys inside my purse. Since I planned to come back first thing in the morning, there was no reason to take my swimsuit, towel, oil, paperback, etc.

The doors were locked. I'd turned off all the lights except for those that were supposed to remain on all night.

I suddenly remembered the air conditioning.

Serena and Charlie usually turned it off before retiring – except when the weather was terribly hot.

When I was in command, I often forgot about the thing and left it going all night.

Since I'd just now thought of it, I rested the saber against my shoulder and marched up the hallway. At the thermostat, I flicked the switch to the Off position.

'What a good girl am I,' I whispered.

Then I wondered which door to use.

Not the den door, that was for sure.

Serena and Charlie's bedroom had a sliding door. So did the living room, and the dining room beyond that. But all those doors could be seen from the back yard, the pool and the woods. If the stranger was watching, he might see me leave the house. He might even see me go to the garage.

And know where to find me.

I decided to leave by the front door.

First, though, I had to pee. The guest bathroom was just off the hall on my way back to the foyer, so I went in. I'd given little Debbie a Winnie the Pooh nightlight for her second birthday, and there it was, spreading a soft glow through the dark.

I didn't touch the switch for the overhead lights.

Late at night, it's always best to avoid turning on lights. At least if you're in a room with windows. The sudden brightness, where a moment earlier the windows had been patches of empty black, announces you to the world, gives away your exact location.

The bathroom had a pair of high, frosted windows that were clearly visible from nearly anywhere outside the front of the house.

So I settled for the light from Pooh bear.

With the door open and the lights off, I placed the saber and my purse on the rug just in front of the toilet. Then I took off the robe, draped it over a towel bar, and sat down.

Too bad I'd already shut off the air conditioning. Not because I suddenly felt hot, but because I was so noisy. Without the air going, the only sound in the house seemed to be me.

Talk about giving away your location!

Leaning forward, elbows on my knees, I could see out the open bathroom door. I kept watching. I half expected someone to drift by in the hallway, or come in.

The thoughts gave me gooseflesh. Prickly bumps sprouted all over me, the way they do sometimes when I try to squash a really awful spider in the corner of a ceiling and it gets away and falls on my bare arm.

I felt crawly all up and down my body.

Nobody showed up in the doorway, though.

Finally, I got finished. I was reluctant to flush, but did it anyway. In the silence, the noise of the flush was like a sudden roar.

So loud that *anything* might've happened somewhere else in the house: phones might've rung; somebody could have shouted out my name; the stranger might've smashed the glass of a window or door.

At last, the noise subsided.

I put the robe on, belted it shut, then crouched and picked up my purse and the saber. In the doorway, I stopped. I leaned forward, easing my head into the hall, and looked both ways.

Nobody.

Of course.

I stepped out and walked quickly to the front door.

Getting it unlocked and open would've been tricky with my left hand, since I'm a righty. So I switched the sword to my left hand. With the blade resting against my shoulder, I used my right hand to unfasten the deadbolt, turn the knob, and pull the door open.

It swept toward me.

For some reason, the porch light was off.

It shouldn't have been off.

And nobody should've been standing on the front stoop, but someone was.

A tall, dark figure reaching for me.

I shrieked.

Through the noise of my outcry, he said something. I couldn't hear it, though. Still shrieking, I swung the saber at him.

A left-handed, feeble try.

He staggered backward to avoid the blade.

It missed him, but he stumbled off the edge of the stoop and fell backward. He landed on the grass. A *whoomp!* exploded out of him; the impact with the lawn must've knocked his wind out.

I leaped over the threshold, ran across the stoop and hopped down. Stradling his hips, I raised the saber high with both hands and swept it down as hard as I could.

It chopped his head down the middle, cleaving his face in half. It split his head open most of the way to his neck, but his jaw stopped the blade.

He thrashed and gurgled between my feet.

My saber was stuck, either between a couple of his lower front teeth or in the bone of his jaw. I shook it and tugged it. Instead of coming loose, it jerked his head this way and that.

At last, it came out.

I was all set to give him another chop, but he'd quit moving. He looked pretty dead.

Pretty isn't a great choice of words, under the circumstances.

Anyway, there was no good reason to give him another whack.

I felt too shocked and worn out to do much of anything, so I just kept standing over him, his hips between my ankles. I had the sword clutched in my right hand, but held it off to the side so blood wouldn't rub off or drip on me.

I stood there for a long time.

Staring down at the body.

It was lit by the dim glow from a lamp near the driveway.

It wore a short-sleeved plaid shirt, blue jeans and loafers. No socks.

It sure wasn't my prowler.

I figured it was probably Tony.

Chapter Six

Discoveries

My guess was right.

When I finally recovered enough to move, I stepped away from him, put my saber down on the grass, then crouched beside him and searched the pockets of his jeans.

He had a comb and handkerchief in his left front pocket. A wallet in the left back pocket. In the right front, a leather key case and some coins. In the right back, a pistol.

A pistol!

Had he come here planning to stand guard and protect me? Or to use the gun against me?

I put his things into the pockets of my robe, but the gun was too heavy. It felt like a hand tugging down on my pocket. Afraid it might ruin the robe, I took it out and carried it.

Back inside the house, I shut the door. I sat down on the cool marble floor of the foyer and inspected my findings.

The white handkerchief looked clean. I didn't study the comb very closely; combs can be gross. He had eighty-five cents in change. Six keys in his leather case. Thirty-eight dollars in the bill compartment of his wallet.

The wallet was *full* of stuff, but I won't bore you with a list. I'll cut to the chase, as they say. It contained two foil-wrapped condoms – meant for me? – and a driver's license that identified him as Anthony Joseph Romano.

His date of birth was two years earlier than mine, which made him twenty-eight. The photo must've been taken a few years ago, because he hardly looked old enough to be out of high school. He had short blond hair, freckles across his nose, and a friendly smile.

371

It made me feel bad, looking at him.

Knowing I'd killed him.

He'd probably driven over here to protect me. Nothing more sinister than that.

He thought he was being a good guy.

Like they say, 'No good deed goes unpunished.'

I felt rotten about killing him, but not particularly guilty. It wasn't *my* fault he paid me a surprise visit and got his head chopped open for the trouble. I hadn't *invited* him over.

He should've minded his own business.

Not only had he gotten himself killed, but he'd put *me* into a horrible situation.

What was I supposed to do now?

I stopped looking at his photo, and checked the address on his driver's license. 4468 Washington Avenue, Apt. 212. (Sounds like a real address, doesn't it? I made it up.) I knew the general area. It wasn't far from here. Less than ten minutes. After hanging up the phone, he must've grabbed his pistol and hurried right out to his car . . .

No.

He probably hadn't come here from the Washington Avenue address. He'd moved to a new place because of all the memories. That's one of the reasons he'd tried to phone Judy – to let her know his new phone number.

Unless he'd made the move a couple of months ago, the address on his driver's license almost had to be wrong.

I gave the wallet another search. Sure enough, tucked into the bill compartment was a folded slip of paper with an address scribbled on it in pencil: 645 Little Oak Lane, Apt. 12. (But not really.) This was probably his new address.

I put the paper back where I'd found it, set the wallet aside, and picked up the pistol.

It was a small, stainless steel .22 automatic with a black plastic handle. The fine print in the steel told me that it was a Smith & Wesson.

The safety wasn't on.

I dropped the loaded magazine into my hand, then pulled back the slide. Tony didn't have a bullet in the chamber. I shoved the magazine back up the handle until it clicked into place, then worked the slide, watching through the port to make sure it fed in a round. Then I thumbed the safety on.

After that, I just kept sitting there.

I didn't have the energy to get up.

Besides, get up and do *what*?

Deal is, I didn't know what to do next. So I just sat there, staring.

I've *gotta* do something, I kept telling myself.

What's the best course of action if you've just butchered an innocent man?

The answer probably seems obvious to you: call the cops and tell them the whole truth about everything.

Or fudge a little, maybe. Claim that he was holding the pistol when I opened the door. To make that version work, I would only have to take the gun outside and put it into his hand.

Which hand? That always trips up the criminals on TV. They stick the gun into the right hand of a lefty.

I'm a tad smarter than that.

Tony'd been carrying the weapon in his right rear pocket. Also, he'd reached for me with his right hand.

Reached for *me*? Maybe he'd been reaching for the doorbell button.

In either case, the evidence seemed to prove him a righty.

Not that it mattered. I had no intention of planting the pistol on him.

I had no intention of calling the cops, either.

Right now, you're probably thinking, *Oh, you stupid idiot! A guy you've never seen before in your life showed up in the middle of the night with a gun! It's a clear case of self-defense! Call the cops right now! Fess up! They probably won't even charge you with anything!*

Wrong.

Calling the police might be smart for *you* to do, but you're probably one of those people who's never gotten in trouble. A good, upstanding citizen.

If I were you, I probably *would* call the cops and admit everything. And I'm sure it'd turn out hunky-dory.

But I'm not you.

I'm me, alias Alice.

I could've gotten away with calling about the prowler. I might have actually done it, too, if the phone had been handy. It would've been safe. My troubles were several years earlier and in a different state. Cops coming over to save me from a prowler wouldn't even know about me or what I'd done.

But if they came to investigate Tony's death, they'd investigate me.

They'd run my prints.

Find out who I am.

After that, I wouldn't stand a chance.

So Tony had to go.

Tony *and* his car, if he'd driven one here.

Obviously, I had a long night ahead of me. But I stayed sitting on the marble floor for a while longer, wondering what to do first, where to start.

Finally, I decided to start by changing my clothes.

No matter what I might end up doing, I didn't want to do it wearing Charlie's robe. I liked the robe too much. It was bound to get bloody if I kept it on.

Whatever got bloody would have to be destroyed.

For that reason, I couldn't wear clothes belonging to Serena or Charlie. I wasn't eager to sacrifice any of my own clothes, either, but figured it had to be done.

Which meant a trip to my place above the garage.

Now that my mind was made up, I stuffed Tony's hanky and comb and everything else into the pockets of my robe. Everything except the pistol. I held on to that.

Then I went out the front door again.

I didn't plan to go back inside the house until everything was taken care of, so I locked the door and shut it after me.

Just for the hell of it, I went over to the porch light, reached up and gave the bulb a twist.

It turned easily.

The light came on, almost blinded me.

'Very interesting,' I muttered.

Had Tony loosened it? Had someone else? Or had the bulb simply worked its way loose all on its own, with nobody's help? (Light bulbs do that, you know. Almost as if they're living creatures unscrewing themselves for sport or for reasons we'll never guess.)

I left it screwed in.

All the better to see by.

Here's the deal: I wasn't worried about anyone noticing Tony's body on the lawn. That could only happen if a person came down the driveway.

Not likely to happen at this hour of the night – or morning.

His body couldn't be seen from the street because a thick, tall hedge stood in the way. Hedges also ran along both sides of the lawn.

In addition to that, we had no neighbors.

None close enough to worry about, anyway.

There were vacant lots to the right and left, and a string of vacant lots across the road. The nearest house, a couple of lots to the left, was empty and up for sale. The nearest occupied house stood about a quarter of a mile to the right, and on the other side of the road.

We were pretty much alone out here.

It couldn't hurt to leave the light on. But then I thought, why take the risk? I wouldn't have any use for the porch light until I came back from the garage.

As I reached up for the bulb, though, my eyes strayed over to Tony.

I hadn't really seen him before. Not in halfway good light, anyway.

From the chin up, he was a horrible wreck.

You wouldn't recognize him as the guy in his driver's license photo.

He looked like a nightmare.

Considering the gory ruin of his head, I was surprised to notice how clean his clothes seemed to be.

With the light still on, I went over to him and checked more carefully. His shirt had a few spots of blood on it, but nothing obvious. His jeans seemed fine.

Why not?

First, I took the purse off my shoulder and removed my robe. I left them on the dry concrete of the front stoop. Then I crouched over Tony and stripped him. It wasn't easy, especially because the night was so hot. Even though I'm in pretty good shape, I ended up out of breath and sweaty.

When I was done, I slipped into his loafers. They were a little too big for me, but I could walk in them okay. I carried his jeans and shirt over to the stoop and dropped them.

Then I stretched out naked on my back for a rest.

The concrete felt cool and nice.

Too nice. I could hardly force myself to get moving again.

Finally, though, I stood up to put his clothes on. I started with the shirt. It was very large, and hung halfway down my thighs. But it would do just fine. Next, I slipped his shoes off and climbed into the blue jeans.

They were way too big. When I had them all the way up around my waist, my feet were still inside the denim legs. Also, I had a huge amount of spare room inside the waistband.

Looking down the gap, I could see all the way to my knees. I fastened the belt, anyway. It had enough holes to let me cinch it tight and keep the jeans from falling. With that taken care of, I bent over and rolled up the legs. The cuffs reached almost to my knees. I looked like I was wearing waders.

The jeans felt too hot and too heavy.

I needed them, though. I wanted the pockets; otherwise, I could've gotten rid of the jeans and just worn the shirt like a dress.

What I finally did was use the saber to cut the legs off. I took the legs off very high, then slit the sides almost up to the belt.

After that, the jeans felt light and airy.

What was left of them.

I returned all of Tony's belongings to the pockets where I'd found them. I also slipped my own key case into a pocket.

Then I unlocked the front door and went back inside the house, but only long enough to put my purse and Charlie's robe in the living room.

I left again.

Reaching up, I unscrewed the porch bulb. It was pretty hot by then, and made my fingertips smart.

Chapter Seven

Clean Up

Ever try to carry around a dead guy?

Let me tell you, it isn't easy.

So I left Tony sprawled on the lawn, right where he'd fallen, and went hiking up the driveway without him.

On the road, just to the right of the driveway entrance, a car was parked at the curb. It was the only car in sight.

The driver's door was locked, but one of Tony's keys did the trick. I climbed in and tried a key in the ignition. The engine started. Keeping the headlights off, I swung away from the curb, did a U-turn, and drove into the driveway.

When the trunk seemed to be even with Tony, I stopped the car. I got out and opened the trunk. It looked pretty empty except for the spare tire. Leaving it open, I went over to Tony.

I picked up his legs by the ankles, turned him, and started dragging him toward the driveway. The grass was still wet from the sprinklers. The wetness helped his body slide, but also made my footing tricky. A couple of times, my feet flew out from under me and I landed on my butt, which didn't feel too swift.

By the time we reached the edge of the driveway, I knew we had a problem. Not to be too graphic about it, his split head had left a trail across the grass. The stuff on the grass wasn't what worried me, though. Most of it would go away after the automatic sprinkling system had gone through a few cycles. Birds, ants, and so forth would take care of the rest. The problem, for me, was whatever might get on the driveway. I didn't want to wake up in the morning and find bloodstains on the concrete. They'd be hard to get rid of.

At first, the only possible solution seemed to be a plastic bag over Tony's head to catch whatever might want to slop out.

But I was in no mood to run around hunting for a bag.

Finally, I came up with a simple answer to the problem. All I had to do was turn the car sideways so its rear jutted out over the grass.

So that's what I did. The driveway was wide enough to make it fairly simple.

I lined the car up with Tony, backed up until the rear tires almost went off the edge of the driveway, then climbed out and looked at him.

Loading his body into the trunk was going to be a bear.

And messy, too.

But it couldn't be avoided.

Before getting started, I took off the shirt and cut-off jeans and tossed them onto the driver's seat. For one thing, I didn't want them to get gory. For another, the night was too hot for clothes, especially if you're doing hard work.

I stepped out of the shoes and left them on the driveway.

Then I walked onto the slippery wet grass, straddled Tony's hips, bent down, clutched his wrists and straightened up, pulling him. His back came off the ground. But then, instead of continuing to rise, he slid on his butt and went scooting between my legs. I scurried backward, trying to stay with him, and bumped into the rear of the car.

'Shit!'

He was up to his waist beneath the car like a grease monkey going under to make repairs.

Hanging on to his wrists, I waddled forward to drag him out. He just lay beneath me, staring at the show while I hobbled over him, my breasts lurching from side to side between my down-stretched arms.

By the time I'd left his head behind me, I was doubled over like a contortionist, my arms straining backward between my legs. At last, he started to slide.

I shuffled onward, pulling him.

He finally cleared the car. By then, I was huffing and sweaty again.

I sat down on the rear bumper.

'Should've minded your own business,' I muttered. 'You wouldn't be dead, for one thing. For another, you wouldn't be putting *me* through all this shit.'

He didn't answer.

He probably figured, though, that I didn't have much room for complaining. I was still alive, after all, whereas he wasn't.

I was inconvenienced, but he was toes up.

'This is more than a little inconvenience, buddy,' I told him. 'This is a major pain in the ass.'

The night was way too hot for such work. Sweat was pouring down my body. It made my eyes sting. It tickled my sides and back.

How nice it would've been, just then, to go around back and jump in the pool.

Thinking about the pool, I remembered the prowler. A funny thing, though. The thought of him didn't frighten me, disgust me, thrill me – nothing. He'd lost all his powers to intimidate or fascinate me. Probably the moment I put the saber through Tony's head.

His fault.

All his fault.

True enough, I thought. That bastard got Tony killed as sure as if he'd been the one swinging the sword.

I oughta kill his ass for doing this to Tony and me.

If I went swimming, he might show up and give me the chance. I should take the pistol or saber with me, just in case.

But which?

I couldn't exactly *swim* with either weapon.

Forget it. Forget which weapon to take, forget having a swim. Time's a-wasting.

Tony had to be dealt with.

I tried again.

This time, I straddled his head instead of his hips. Bending down, I jammed my open hands underneath his shoulders and grabbed his armpits. When I lifted him, he started to slide away. Instead of letting him go, I hauled back on him, pulled him against me and hoisted him up.

His full weight shoved against my chest.

Instead of rushing forward and throwing him headlong into the trunk, the way I'd figured, I found myself suddenly staggering backward. I fell, and he came down on top of me. His split-open head mashed against my face.

I wanted to scream.

But you can't scream with your mouth shut. God knows, I kept it shut. If I hadn't, it might've ended up full of Tony's brains or whatever.

So the scream only happened in my mind.

Twisting and bucking, I threw him off me.

I crawled away from him. Still on my hands and knees, I lost my steak supper on the grass. The steak, and then some. I couldn't stop vomiting. After a while, nothing came out except slobber.

Finally, I did stop. I crawled away from the glop, stayed on all fours while I tried to catch my breath, then struggled to my feet. Bending over, I put my hands on my knees. I stayed that way for a few minutes.

I felt stuff sticking to my face.

When I had the strength to move again, I wiped my face with both hands, then squatted and rubbed my hands against the damp grass.

I wanted to take a shower.

I wanted to *scrub* Tony off me.

His blood and goo.

But that would have to wait. First I needed to deal with his body.

I wandered over to it, being careful where I stepped with my bare feet.

'What the hell am I gonna do with you?' I asked.

'That's *your* problem,' he seemed to tell me. 'You should've thought of that before you split my head open, you dumb bitch.'

He was sprawled face down, the way he'd landed after I threw him off me.

I grabbed the elastic waistband of his skivvies, hoisted him to his knees and started dragging him backward. We made it about halfway to the trunk of the car before the elastic gave out. The shorts tore away, and he flopped.

I tossed the useless rag into the trunk, straddled his butt, grabbed him by the knobs of his hip bones and hauled him up.

It seemed to be working.

I reared back, bringing him higher and higher.

Then my hands slipped off his hips. I wasn't ready for that. Not at all. I flew backward, slammed the rear of the car and tumbled into the trunk with my feet kicking at the sky.

It hurt so much that my eyes filled with tears.

He was *dead*, but beating up on me.

And *defeating* me.

'Bastard!' I shouted at him.

I could almost hear him laughing at me.

Crying, I twisted my body around and crawled out of the trunk.

Tony was sprawled on the grass.

'Think you can beat me?' I asked him.

'Think it?' I could hear him taunt me. 'I *know* it! You're too weak to get me in the trunk. I'm too big, and you're too weak. I'll still be lying here tomorrow when the sun comes up. I'll still be lying here *next week* when Serena and Charlie come home.'

'Oh, no you won't,' I said.

But he was right in a way.

Not about me being too weak. I was in great shape, and I probably *could've* lifted him if everything hadn't been so wet and slippery.

He was right about his size.

He was too *big*.

I took care of that with the saber.

He lost ten or eleven inches very quickly.

I figured his head wouldn't make that much difference, though. It probably didn't weigh more than ten or fifteen pounds. So after tossing it into the trunk, I removed both his arms. They didn't come off as easily as his head. I couldn't just whack them off with a couple of good blows, but had to really work at it. And the arms were easy compared to his legs.

This was very rough work for a hot night.

When I had Tony down to his torso, I stuck the sword in the ground, got down on my knees, wrapped my arm around his chest, and picked him up.

At that point, he was still pretty heavy.

But manageable.

His torso shook the car when I dumped it into the trunk on top of his other parts.

I slammed the trunk shut.

By then, I was *really* tuckered out.

Not to mention filthy.

So exhausted I could hardly walk, I stumbled away from the driveway, found a clean place on the lawn, and flopped. The cool, wet grass felt wonderful. I lay on my back, panting for air, sweat pouring off my body.

In my mind, I was floating on the cool water of the pool.

That's how I'll spend tomorrow, I told myself. This whole mess will be over by then, and I'll do nothing all day except float around in the pool and drink ice-cold cocktails and sunbathe.

Something in the grass under my back started to bother me. A stone or a twig, probably. It had been pushing against me from the start, but I'd been too worn out to care.

Now, I rolled over to get away from it.

Flat on my stomach, I crossed my arms under my face. They were sticky, though, and didn't smell very good, so I got them away from my face and spread them out. With nothing for a pillow, I lowered my head onto the lawn.

But I didn't like having my face in the grass.

The grass tickled. Especially where it brushed against my eyelid and lips. Also, I wondered what sort of bugs might be under me. I didn't want ants or spiders crawling on my face, getting into my nostrils, my mouth, my eyes.

For that matter, I didn't like the idea of bugs crawling on me *anywhere*.

I wondered what might be drawn to me by the smell of Tony's blood.

Before you know it, I felt tiny creatures scurrying all over my bare skin. Most of them were probably just in my mind, but they seemed real enough.

That ended my rest period.

I got to my feet and staggered across the lawn. At the front of the house, in the space between a couple of bushes, was a coiled garden hose. Charlie used it, every so often, to wash the car in the driveway.

I used it to wash me.

The first water to blast out of the nozzle was warm from cooking inside the hose all day. I aimed the hard stream at my hands and forearms. It hit me with such force that it hurt, but it sure knocked the blood and filth off me.

Even before I finished hosing off my arms, cold water was shooting out. I adjusted the nozzle. The rough, narrow rod of shooting water spread out and became a spray. I could've made it a gentle, light shower, but I kept it powerful enough to do the job.

Raising the nozzle, I aimed down at the top of my head. The water drummed my skull, froze my scalp, matted my hair, rushed all the way down my body. I flinched under the frigid attack. I cringed and shuddered. After the first shock, though, it didn't feel so horrible. The spray was no less cold, but I must've been getting used to it. Pretty soon, it seemed pleasantly cool.

I moved the nozzle around, spraying myself straight in the face, under my arms and down my sides, and so on. When the water hit certain areas – where I was still especially hot – it again felt ice cold.

Soon, I was as clean as I could get without soap and hot water.

I felt human again.

But thirsty. Afraid of choking if I shot the water straight into my mouth, I aimed the nozzle sideways in front of my lips, darted my head forward and took bites out of the spray. It worked pretty well. But sometimes I didn't get away quickly enough. Then, the water pelted the inside of my cheek, making quick hollow tapping sounds, and flooded my mouth. I ended up choking a couple of times, but nothing serious.

After taking care of my thirst, I went on spraying myself.

Why stop?

For one thing, it made me feel so much better after all that hot, dirty work.

For another, I deserved a treat. I'd gotten Tony safely stowed inside the trunk of his car, so the worst part of the job was over. Now, it was just a matter of driving him away.

But to where?

Until I could figure out a good place to leave his car, there was no reason to quit enjoying the hose.

Just take it somewhere far away, I thought. The farther away, the better.

Oh, really? How do you think you'll get home?

How far away is *his* place? I wondered. Not the old place, but the new one. Which street was it on?

I tried to picture the writing on the slip of paper in his wallet.

Little Oak Lane!

Not far away, at all.

Well, four or five miles, but I could walk a distance like that in about an hour.

What if I drop the car off – with him in it – right where he lives? Perfect!

They might not find his body for days.

And when they do, they won't have a clue as to where he went to get himself killed.

That matter solved, I dragged the hose across the lawn, being careful not to step in anything nasty. Along the way, I stopped and gave the saber a long, hard squirt. It was planted half a foot deep in the earth, and vibrated as the water struck it.

When I got in range of Tony's car, I twisted the nozzle. The spray tightened into a stiff tube of water that reached all the way. My aim was too high, at first. The water slammed against the rear window and seemed to explode off the glass, sending a shower skyward while most of the water sluiced down the top of the trunk. I lowered the nozzle slightly and hit the edge of the trunk lid dead on, nailed it where I'd touched it the most and where it was most bloody. The water blasted it, rumbling and bursting away.

Then I did the rear bumper, then the back tires.

Done with the car, I adjusted the nozzle to make a soft spray. For a while, I watered the lawn. Along with the lawn, I watered whatever of Tony was spread around. Even in the lousy yellow light from the porch and nearby lamps, I could see rusty stains on the grass, and small bits of him. My vomit, too.

Soon, the grass looked green again.

I carried the hose back to its place near the front of the house, arranged it in a proper coil, gave my hands a final rinse, then reached in between the bushes and shut the water off.

Not much remained to be done.

I gathered the two denim legs that I'd cut from Tony's jeans. With one of them, I wiped the saber.

I thought about taking the saber into the house, but I was naked and dripping and didn't want to bother. I certainly couldn't take it with me. So I slid it inside the severed legs of the jeans and hid it in the bushes.

That was pretty much the end of the clean up.

Chapter Eight

Tony Goes Home

I was still wet when I put on Tony's jeans and shirt. They stuck to me. I slipped my feet into his loafers, then climbed into the driver's seat.

The car started fine. With a couple of easy maneuvers, I straightened it out. It ended up with its front toward the road.

Before taking off, I gave the lawn a final glance.

Everything looked okay.

Daylight might be another story, but I intended to take a good, long look at the whole area after the sun came up and make sure nothing showed that shouldn't.

Feeling weary but good, the job nearly done – and the worst of it definitely over – I gave the car some gas and headed for the road.

At the top of the driveway, I turned left. There was no traffic in sight, so I kept the headlights off and drove along the two-lane country road by moonlight. With the windows wide open, the night air rushed in. It felt wonderful, blowing against me. And it smelled so fine, too. Sweet and moist and woodsy.

I almost turned on the radio. It would've been great to be tooling along through the darkness with a summertime song in my ears. But I was on a stealth mission. I kept the radio off, so the only sounds came from the car's engine and the hiss of its tires on the pavement and the wind rushing by.

It was lovely, even without a song.

It made me want to go out every night – but not with a dismembered body in the trunk.

Just drive and drive along the empty country roads in the

moonlight, smelling the smells of the night, feeling the soft rush of the wind. Just roam with nowhere to go. And with nothing to give me that tingly little scared feeling deep down inside.

Of course, maybe the scared feeling gave the trip a little extra flavor.

It's hard to tell the difference, sometimes, between fear and excitement.

Anyway, the good part of the trip only lasted a few minutes. Coming to the town limits, I had to slow down and put the headlights on. Then I headed for Little Oak Lane, which I figured was in the newer residential area on the other side of town.

If I hadn't been in Tony's car (with him in the trunk), I probably would've made a straight shot through the middle of downtown on Central Street. I like to call it 'the scenic tour', because there's nothing worth seeing in downtown Chester. (Not the town's real name. I've dubbed it Chester in honor of Chester from *Gunsmoke* – because it's a really lame town that just limps along.)

Downtown Chester fills both sides of Central Street for five blocks. And that's about it. The street gets pretty crowded during the day, though I can't imagine why. Maybe it's people looking to buy discount lamps or old-lady shoes. For any serious shopping, you go elsewhere. Like to the Ralph's supermarket or the mall or the Wal-Mart or Home Depot – none of which is anywhere near Chester's business district.

When I came to Central, I slowed down and looked. The street was well lighted, and almost empty. But not empty enough. A couple of drinking establishments must've still been open. I spotted about a dozen parked cars, two or three people roaming around, and even one car heading toward me.

So I got away from Central and drove an extra block before turning.

On this road, nothing was open. I saw nobody milling about.

No cars were coming, either. I glimpsed some activity when I looked down sidestreets, but nothing to worry me.

I only had two real concerns about the drive. First, that somebody would recognize Tony's car and remember that it was on the move that night. Second, that *I* might be seen behind the wheel.

Neither problem was likely to arise unless somebody got pretty close to us.

Which never happened, as far as I could tell.

I did take detours, a couple of times, to avoid approaching vehicles. Once, I even pulled to the curb, shut off the engine and headlights, and ducked until a car'd gone by. Later, driving past a jogger, I turned my head aside so he wouldn't be able to see my face.

I also had to wait at an intersection for an old bum lady to push her shopping cart across the street in front of me. Normally, a person like that would've given me the creeps.

But she didn't spook me at all.

I just worried that she might get a good look at me. Hunched over her shopping cart, though, she never glanced in my direction.

Soon after she'd gone by, I came to Little Oak Lane. Stopping under a street light, I pulled the slip of paper out of Tony's wallet and checked the address.

645 Little Oak Lane, Apt. 12.

It was only a block away.

A two-story, stucco apartment house with a subterranean parking lot.

Near the entrance, a driveway swooped into the lot.

Rolling slowly past it, I glanced down the concrete ramp.

Awfully well-lighted down there.

The little tremor in my belly grew large.

I drove around the block to give myself time to think. On the one hand, the building's lot seemed like the perfect place to drop off Tony's car. He probably had an assigned parking space in there.

Where better to leave his car than precisely where it *should* be?

Seeing it there in the morning, who would ever guess he'd gone somewhere in the middle of the night and gotten himself killed?

And his body might not be discovered for days.

On the other hand, someone might enter the parking lot and see me.

Which would screw up everything.

What are the chances?

Slim, I told myself. Very slim. The danger would only last for a minute or two – long enough to drive in, locate Tony's space, park his car, jump out and run back up the ramp to get outside.

Worth the risk.

I came to that conclusion just in time to make the turn.

Oh, God, here we go!

I swung to the right and drove slowly down the ramp into the lot. Nobody seemed to be coming or going. The place looked deserted except for the parked cars. Lots of them. I began to worry about finding a space for Tony's car.

That turned out not to be the problem.

Among the twenty or so parked cars, I found three empty spaces. But they were labelled with letters, not numbers.

L, R and W.

That was the problem.

One of them had to be reserved for Tony's car.

But which one? He rented apartment 12, not apartment L, R or W.

After making one full loop through the lot, I stopped and tried to think.

I sure didn't want to leave Tony's car in the wrong slot. That would make it *really* conspicuous. Better to abandon it on a street than to leave it in someone else's space.

A one-in-three chance of getting it right made for lousy odds.

I needed a clue, and fast. At any moment, one of the two missing cars might return and I'd be seen.

Think!

If Tony had been worried about forgetting the letter of his parking space, wouldn't he have written it on the same paper as his address?

I hauled out the paper again and double-checked it.

645 Little Oak Lane, Apt. 12.

No L, no R, no W. Nothing except the address.

Forget it! Park and get out of here!

No, wait!

Could there be a correlation between Tony's apartment number and any of the letters?

With the help of my fingers, I counted to the twelfth letter of the alphabet.

12 was L!

Fabulous!

It didn't make anything certain, but at least it was a clue.

I swung his car into space L, shut off the headlights, killed the engine, put the keys in my pocket, and pulled out Tony's handkerchief. With that, I wiped the steering wheel, shift lever, interior door handle, and every other surface that I might've touched. Then I climbed out, locked the door, and shut it so gently that it hardly made a noise.

For the next minute or so, I used the hanky to wipe the outside. The rear of the car was still wet from getting hosed. That didn't worry me much. It was just water. It would dry soon enough.

I saw no traces of blood.

Tucking the hanky into my pocket, I headed for the driveway ramp. It seemed like an endless distance away. I listened for sounds of approaching cars. And for footfalls. The only sounds came from Tony's loafers on my feet, clumping along the concrete. They sounded loud and hollow.

Finally, I reached the ramp.

My legs felt shaky as I hurried to the top.

Suddenly, I was out!

In and out, slick as a whistle, unseen!

I almost clapped my hands, but didn't. Someone might glance out a window to see who'd made the noise.

Feeling light and free, I quickened my pace.

I'd be home in an hour.

Five, six miles.

Maybe a little longer than an hour. At a good pace, I can make four miles in an hour. But it might take an hour and a half for six miles.

Then I got to thinking.

Suddenly, I wasn't certain of the mileage.

The drive had *felt* like a lot more than six miles. I must've been in the car for half an hour.

Half an hour, averaging about thirty miles per hour . . .

Fifteen miles!

But I did make those detours, pull over once, drive around the block while I was trying to make up my mind, and sit in parking lot for a few minutes trying to figure out which slot to use.

So maybe the distance was more like ten or twelve miles.

It can't possibly be that far!

But I had no way of knowing for sure.

During the drive over, I hadn't paid any attention to the clock *or* to the odometer.

If only I'd checked the odometer before starting out from home . . .

Or set the tripometer.

Oh, my God!

I stopped walking.

Was Tony's car *equipped* with a tripometer?

I tried to call up an image of the dashboard. I pictured a dashboard, okay, and it had a tripometer, but I didn't know whether my picture was accurate. Maybe I was just imagining the device.

But if Tony *did* have one, and if he'd set it to zero before coming to my rescue . . .

I had to go back.

Chapter Nine

The Lost Detail

So many little details to think about.

And if you don't think about them, too bad, tough toenails, you're done for.

Just don't kill anyone. That's my big advice to you, if you're reading this. I've heard that books are supposed to be meaningful and help a person gain insights into themselves, or life, or something. So maybe that's what you should get from my book – don't kill anyone or you'll be sorry.

Of course, I guess any person with half an ounce of sense knows that already.

The bad part is, even if you know better, you might end up doing it anyway.

Like me.

I sure never *set out* to split open Tony's head. It could have happened to anyone. It's all a matter of circumstances.

Just like we're all at the mercy of our genes – which pretty much decide everything about how we look and act and even what diseases we'll probably get – we're also at the mercy of circumstances.

All of a sudden, WHAM! and we've killed someone.

You might be pretty smug and sure you'll never do it, but just try popping out of your house in the middle of the night and finding a stranger on your doorstep about to grab you. See what happens then.

See what *you'd* do.

It's you or him, and you figure he's there to rape or kill you.

If you don't get him fast, he'll get you.

I bet you'd whack him if you could.

And then what would you do, after he's splayed out on your lawn as dead as a carp?

I know, you'd call the cops.

And ruin your life.

The thing is – do you want the straight scoop?

Even if you're a goody-two-shoes who has never been in trouble in your life, you'll be walking into a nightmare if you bring the cops into the picture. For one thing, maybe the courts won't see the killing as self-defense. You might get convicted of murder or manslaughter and end up in jail. But suppose you make out fine with the legal system? They either don't hit you with criminal charges at all, or you get acquitted. Great. Congratulations. But what about the friends and relatives of the guy you killed?

Ever hear of a wrongful death lawsuit?

Ever hear of revenge?

I think about stuff like this.

I bet you'd think about it, too, if you ever killed somebody.

Even by accident.

You'd sure *better* think about it. Do you *really* want to call the cops? Especially considering this: if you don't call them – and you're smart and lucky and have the guts to do whatever it takes – the whole situation might *go away*.

Just like it never happened.

Me, that's what I wanted.

I wanted it to go away.

I would've done *anything* to make it go away, and that included making a return trip to Tony's car in the parking lot.

I hated to go back, but I *had* to.

With a simple push of a button, the tripometer's wheels would spin to 000 and the cops would lose their best clue about where Tony got killed.

I was sure glad I'd thought of it.

On my way to the parking lot, I tried to think of any other details that needed my attention.

I came up with nothing else in connection with Tony's car or apartment. Just set back the tripometer, and leave.

But several details would need to be taken care of, back home.

I made a mental list of them:

1. Immediately retrieve the saber from where I hid it in the bushes.

2. First thing in the morning, check the lawn carefully and clean up any remaining blood or debris. Whatever little pieces of Tony I might find in the grass (and there shouldn't be much) could go down the garbage disposal in Serena's kitchen.

3. Make sure to clean off the glass door where the stranger made his mess. (This had nothing to do with covering up Tony's death, but was for my own peace of mind.)

4. Clean the saber and return it to its proper place on the living room wall.

5. Get rid of Tony's stuff. If suspicion somehow ended up falling on me, I'd better not get caught with his jeans, shirt, wallet, shoes, etc.

That was all I could think of.

But I felt as if I must be forgetting something.

I kept going over the list in my mind, wondering what I'd missed.

And came up with:

6. Check the street in front of the house, just in case. He'd parked there. Maybe he'd dropped something.

7. Check the driveway.

Hell, check everywhere. And double-check. Make sure there's absolutely nothing that might lead anyone to think Tony was there, or that anybody'd gotten killed.

That should cover it.

But I *still* had an uneasy sensation that I'd forgotten a very important piece of evidence.

What could it be?

Maybe nothing. Have you ever started off on a trip feeling *absolutely certain* you'd forgotten something? Maybe you'd neglected to turn off the coffee pot, or you'd left behind your swimsuit or toothbrush? But you can't think of *what* it is, so you don't go back? Then it turns out that you hadn't forgotten anything at all?

I've had that happen to me.

Just as often, though, it turns out that the feeling was right and you *did* forget something.

Anyway, I still hadn't thought of it by the time I arrived back at Tony's building.

Then I had bigger things to worry about, such as being seen in the parking lot. I'd been lucky, last time. Going back down would be pressing my luck. Tempting fate. I didn't like it.

But I did it.

Dripping sweat, breathing hard and trembling, I walked to the bottom of the driveway. Nobody seemed to be around, so I ran all the way to Tony's car. I stopped beside it, huffing, and dug the keys out of my pocket. Then I unlocked the door, opened it, leaned in and stared at the dashboard.

A tripometer!

He *did* have one, and it showed 14.2 miles.

Divide it in half, you get 7.1 miles.

Almost certainly, that was the distance to Serena and Charlie's house.

Tony *had* set his tripometer.

My God! I thought. What if I hadn't thought of it?

Reaching into the car, I stabbed the reset button with my forefinger. The numbers spun back to form a row of zeros.

The evidence was erased.

With the hanky, I wiped the front of the button.

Erased?

Something about that word.

I locked and shut the car door and wiped its handle.

Erased.

Backing away from the car, I looked around. So far, so good. I headed for the driveway ramp, walking fast.

Erased?

Why did that word stick in my head? Should I erase something? Was there an incriminating note that needed to be . . . ?

The tape!

I chugged my way up the driveway.

That's it! The audio tape on Serena and Charlie's answering machine!

How could I possibly have forgotten about *that*? It had Tony's message on it, all that stuff he was trying to tell Judy.

The dead man's voice on a tape in Serena's home.

My God, how could a detail like that slip my mind?

At the top of the driveway, I hurried over to the sidewalk. Once more, I'd made it away from the parking lot undetected. Plus, I'd erased the mileage from the tripometer *and* I'd remembered the lost detail – the message tape.

Simple enough to get rid of that.

I added it to my mental list of things to do at home.

Erase it right away, tonight, as soon as you get back. Bring in the saber, then erase the tape. Maybe destroy it entirely, just to be sure. Burn it.

Leaving Tony's apartment building behind me, I walked to the corner of the block. There was no traffic in sight. I jogged across the street, then slowed to a long, easy stride.

Pace yourself, I thought. It's more than seven miles. That's a pretty good hike.

Should take less than two hours, though.

What if Tony taped the call?

I felt a flutter deep inside.

If he did . . .

He didn't, I told myself. Nobody does that.

Most people don't, anyway. It would be a very strange, abnormal thing to do. Illegal, too, unless you tell the other person about it.

But if he did record it, he's got my address on tape. My voice and my name, too. The minute the cops search his room, they'll find out everything.

BUT PEOPLE DON'T TAPE THEIR CALLS!

Of course they don't. And only a fool would return to Tony's in order to destroy a tape that doesn't even exist.

But might.

I'd have to actually go inside the building, break into his room . . .

I've got his keys.

But the risk! For nothing! For a tape that doesn't exist.

I continued walking, determined not to go back for the non-existent tape.

And I wouldn't have gone back, either.

I would've kept on walking home, but all of a sudden, from thinking about tapes and answering machines and telephones, something popped into my mind that made my insides go cold and squirmy.

Redial.

Chapter Ten

The Third Key

SHIT!

I had to go back again.

Almost nobody tapes their own telephone conversations, but damn near *everyone* has a redial button.

After our talk, Tony'd had no time to make another call. He'd probably dropped everything, grabbed his gun, rushed out to his car and sped over to guard me.

So a touch of the redial button on his phone would place a call to Serena's phone.

Unless the cops were very stupid or careless, they'd pay me a visit within hours of finding Tony's body.

I had to take care of the redial.

I turned around and headed back.

This is crazy!

But what choice did I have?

When you kill someone, you've *got* to clean up afterward. Not just the body and gore, but the rest of the pieces, too. Tripometers, telephone messages, redials, the whole nine yards.

It sucks big.

If you don't take care of every detail, you go down.

Not me.

When I was about to cross the last intersection before Tony's building, a car turned onto the road a block to my right. I lurched backward fast, heart slamming. Before the car even got close, I found a good place to hide behind a clump of bushes. I crouched there, gasping for breath, sweat pouring down my face and trickling down the nape of my neck. Tony's shirt clung to my back and sides. The seat of his jeans felt damp against my butt.

Waiting for the car to pass, I picked up the front of the shirt and wiped my face.

And wished I were back home so I could jump into the swimming pool.

That suddenly made me picture the prowler in it, drifting on his back, and how the moonlight glinted on his body.

His gorgeous body.

Stop that! I told myself. He's a disgusting pervert! And this is all his fault. If he hadn't come along, Tony would still be alive. I wouldn't be here in the bushes, hot and miserable and hiding like a criminal. And I wouldn't need to break into Tony's apartment in the middle of the night.

The car passed me and kept on going.

I stayed hidden for a while.

Cars have rearview mirrors.

When it was out of sight, I stood up, plucked the clinging clothes away from my skin, and returned to the street corner.

I stared at Tony's building.

Talk about pressing your luck.

I felt like running away.

But the details had to be taken care of, or I'd be sunk.

I started to cross the street.

What'll I do when I'm inside?

1. Find Tony's telephones. (Remember, he might have more than one.)

2. Make a few random calls on any phones I find to make absolutely sure redial won't give away Serena's number. (Also, if the cops manage to check Tony's phone records, there'll be calls originating from his place *after* the one to Serena. That should help.)

3. Check around to make sure there's no tape recording of his call. If there is, take it. But there won't be.

4. How about leaving his wallet and keys in his room? That way . . .

No, I'd better keep them. No telling where my fingerprints might be. And what if I should need his keys again, later on? Keep that stuff and get rid of it later.

Anything else while I'm in his room?

Just be careful about fingerprints and stuff.

And don't get caught.

What if he has a roommate?

That idea gave me a scare, but only for a few seconds. Tony was twenty-eight years old. Apparently, he'd just moved into the new place because of Judy. He'd loved her so badly. They'd spent so much time together at his old place that he just couldn't stand to be there without her.

A guy like that doesn't have a roommate.

Probably.

The danger would be from tenants of other apartments who might notice me in the building's entryway and corridors.

Nobody'll see me. Not at this hour of the night.

What about security cameras?

As I approached the front stairs, I spread the collar of my shirt and lifted it, pulling the shirt up to hide most of my face.

You didn't do this in the parking lot, stupid.

Fear slammed through me again.

Had there *been* security cameras in the parking lot?

I didn't know.

I hadn't noticed any, but I hadn't been looking, either.

Instead of climbing the stairs to the front doors, I made a third trip to the parking lot. This time, I searched high and low for video cameras.

I was awfully damn shaken up.

What the hell would I do if I *found* cameras?

I didn't have the slightest idea, but I'd probably be sunk. There I'd be on video tape somewhere, delivering Tony's car in the middle of the night – even wiping it for prints!

I felt sick inside just thinking about it.

Thank God, there didn't seem to be any video equipment down there.

As you might've already noticed, the parking lot didn't have a gated entrance, either. *Anyone* could've driven or walked in, as I proved. Frankly, the lot had no security whatsoever.

Nor did the rest of the building, as I soon found out.

This might surprise some of you. You might even think I'm lying. Because if you live in a place like Los Angeles or New York City, you probably think *every* apartment house in the world has security measures like a Wells Fargo bank.

But you're wrong.

In Chester, we did have plenty of buildings designed to foil criminals. But we also had some that were wide open – ungated, unguarded, uncameraed, and virtually unlocked. They were usually older places that didn't charge you a fortune in rent.

They aren't only in Chester, either.

I'd lived in a few of them, myself, before coming to town and moving in over Serena and Charlie's garage. They weren't so bad. You had to worry about prowlers, but at least you had your freedom. You weren't locked in a cage, and your every move wasn't caught on video tape. There's a lot to be said for that.

Even if you *aren't* doing something bad.

If you *are* up to no good, a lack of security is splendid.

After finishing my search for video cameras, I didn't even bother going back outside. I just trotted up a stairway near the front of the parking lot, came to an unlocked door, opened it and found myself inside the foyer.

The foyer and corridor were dimly lighted.

I saw no one.

Nor did I hear any sounds from the rooms as I sneaked down the corridor looking for apartment 12.

Everyone's asleep, I thought.

God, I hope so.

I felt like a wreck. My mouth was dry, my heart slamming, my whole body dripping with sweat. I was panting for air like a worn-out dog. And shaking like crazy.

The nasty green carpet silenced my footfalls.

But every so often, a board creaked.

What if somebody hears me?

What if a door suddenly opens?

A door wouldn't even have to open – each had a peephole. Someone might look out at me and I'd never even know.

I felt sick with fear.

If anybody sees me, it blows the whole deal.

What'll I do?

Pray it doesn't happen.

At last, I came to number 12. As quietly as possible, I reached into the right front pocket of my cut-offs and pulled out Tony's key case. I unsnapped it.

Of the six keys, two belonged to Tony's car.

Four to pick from, but one of them didn't really look like a room key. It might go to a padlock, or something.

So I selected a key from the remaining three.

You can't fool around with a bunch of keys and not make *some* noise. They clinked and jingled, sounding awfully loud in the silence.

When I finally had the key pinched between my thumb and forefinger, I couldn't hold it still. My hand shook so badly that the tip kept scraping around on the face of the lock, and wouldn't go in the hole.

At last, it went in.

But just the point of it. I tried to force it in the rest of the way, but it wouldn't go.

When that sort of thing happens, sometimes you've got the key upside down. So I turned it over and tried again.

No luck.

Wrong key.

With more clinking and jingling, I fumbled about for key number two.

By the time I had it ready, my hand was shaking worse than ever. The key bumped and scratched against the lock, and kept missing the hole. I used my left hand to hold my right hand steady. That didn't help a lot, but it helped some. Enough.

I made it to the hole.

This time, the key slid in all the way.

Yes!

But I couldn't turn it.

Shit!

No matter how hard I twisted the key, all it did was rattle deep inside the lock somewhere. It wouldn't turn. The damn thing seemed to be frozen in an upright position.

Letting the bunch of keys dangle, I looked at my hand. I had a red imprint on my thumb and forefinger.

I wiped my hand dry on the front of my shirt, then tried again. This time, I twisted the key so hard that I started to worry about breaking it.

So I quit and let go again.

What the hell is wrong? I wondered. The key fit. It had gone in all the way. Why wouldn't it turn?

Maybe it's the wrong damn key.

But it *fit*!

Sure. Okay. It's the right size to go in the hole, but not completely right.

Obviously not right enough to unlock the door.

I jerked it out, turned it over, then tried to stick it back in.

This time, it would only go halfway in.

I muttered, 'Shit,' yanked it out, then fumbled for the third key. And dropped the whole case. It landed on the carpet in front of the door with a quiet thump and a loud jangle.

I crouched and grabbed it.

Then stood again, holding my breath and glancing up and down the corridor.

Nothing happened.

I took a deep breath, sighed with relief, and got back to work.

Having dropped the case, I'd lost track of the third key.

All three 'door' keys – including the two failures – looked pretty much alike.

So I picked one at random.

As I aimed it for the lock hole, the door swung open in front of my face.

Chapter Eleven

Apartment Twelve

A young woman inside the room frowned out at me. Maybe 'frown' isn't the right word, since she didn't seem angry. She looked concerned or confused.

God only knows how I must've looked.

I felt as if the floor had dropped out from under me.

What's she doing here?

Nobody's supposed to be here!

'Are you all right?' she asked.

'I . . . I must have the wrong apartment, or . . .'

'This is twelve,' she said, then glanced at the number on the door as if to make sure of it.

She must've just gotten out of bed. She had a crease on her cheek, her short blonde hair was mussed, and she wore wrinkled pajamas.

She was probably two or three years younger than me.

And beautiful.

Not exotic, glamorous beautiful.

Wholesome, girl-next-door beautiful, like an Iowa cheerleader.

I would've given my left arm to look half as good as this gal.

'Where are you trying to go?' she asked.

'Maybe I'm in the wrong building.'

She shrugged.

'Is this 645 Little Oak Lane?'

Why hadn't I said 465? She would've told me, 'Oh, no, this is 645. I'm afraid you *do* have the wrong building.' And that would've been the end of the situation.

But I was curious, for one thing. I wanted to find out what was going on.

For another thing, the damage was already done. She'd seen me.

And I didn't know what to do about it.

After hearing the address, she nodded and looked more confused than before. 'You seem to be in the right place, but . . .'

'Doesn't Tony live here?' I asked.

'Tony?'

'Yeah, Tony.' I tried to remember his last name. 'Romano.'

'What?' Now, she seemed confused *and* surprised. 'Tony Romano?'

'Is this his apartment?'

'No. This is *my* apartment.'

'But you know him, don't you?' I asked.

'Sure. Do you?'

'He gave me this address.'

'What for?'

'He said he lived here. And that . . . I should come over tonight. He gave me his keys. See?' I held up the key case in front of her. 'I was supposed to let myself in. And wait for him.'

'Huh?'

406

I shrugged.

'But he doesn't live here,' she said.

'What do you mean?'

'This isn't his *place*. It's mine. He lives over on Washington Avenue.'

'Are you sure?'

'I'm sure, all right. I used to spend half my life over there. Why on earth did he give you *my* address?'

'I don't know.'

But I suddenly had a pretty good idea how I'd gotten the wrong address – and who *she* was.

'Are you Judy?' I asked.

'Yeah?' She said it softly, like a question.

I put on a big smile. 'You're Tony's girlfriend!'

'Not anymore. But yeah. We were . . .' She shrugged.

'It's nice to meet you. My name's Alice.' I held out my hand, and she shook it.

'Hi, Alice,' she said.

'So, why did he give me *your* address?' I asked.

'I have no idea. It's weird. But Tony can *be* weird, sometimes. Why don't you come on in? Maybe you should call him, or something.' She opened the door wider and I stepped into her apartment.

Only a single lamp was on. It didn't do a very good job. It cast a yellowish light that left corners of the living room in shadows.

I looked around and didn't see anybody.

From the looks of the furniture, Judy wasn't exactly rich. She had an old armchair, a sofa with threadbare cushions, a few lamps and small tables, and bookshelves against most of the walls. The shelves were crammed with books, mostly paperbacks.

After shutting the door, she said, 'Tony does oddball stuff, sometimes.'

'Yeah, I've noticed.'

'Isn't that one of his shirts you're wearing?'

I forced a smile.

Wearing his jeans and shoes, too.

She wasn't likely to recognize them, though. Most blue jeans and brown loafers look pretty much alike. Besides, I'd customized Tony's jeans.

'I'm just borrowing his shirt for the night,' I told her. 'Mine got spilled on.'

'So you saw him tonight?' She didn't sound suspicious, just curious.

'Yeah, we had dinner together.'

'How's he doing?'

'He really misses you.'

She winced slightly. 'I miss him, too. Sometimes. Not that I'll ever go back to him. Would you like something to drink? A Pepsi or a beer or something?'

'Okay, sure.'

'How about a beer?'

'Great!'

Being careful not to touch anything, I followed her into the kitchen.

She turned on a light and went to the refrigerator. The top of her kitchen table was hidden under a computer and piles of books and papers.

'So, how do you know Tony?' she asked.

Without even pausing to think, I said, 'We met at a bar. The Cactus Bar and Grill.'

'Really?' She set a couple of beer bottles on the counter, then reached up and opened a cupboard. 'I ate there with him once. I'm surprised he went back. He thought they had lousy margaritas.'

'He sure put down a lot of them the night we met.'

'No kidding.' Shaking her head, she filled a pair of glass mugs with beer. Then she turned around and handed one to me.

'All he could talk about was you,' I said. 'And how much he loves you.'

'Really?' Her smile seemed a little sad.

'Yeah. He's miserable.'

We went into the living room. Judy sat in the armchair, and I took the sofa.

I still had no idea what I was doing.

That's not quite true.

I was stalling.

Playing things by ear.

Because I had no idea what to do.

Shoot her?

I was sitting on Tony's pistol. It made my butt hurt on the right side, and I would've been glad to take it out of my pocket.

But *shoot her?*

Gunshots in a place like this, at an hour like this, would probably wake up half the people in the building.

I'd be shafted.

'So you don't think you'll get back together with Tony?' I asked, then tried the beer. It was very cold and bitter and I liked it a lot.

'Not a chance,' Judy said. 'Did he tell you why we broke up?'

For a while, I couldn't answer because I was busy swallowing that wonderful beer. Then I said, 'I think it was too painful for him to talk about.'

'He was probably too embarrassed.'

'Really?'

'Yeah. It's not the sort of thing you want to tell people about. Especially not a woman.'

'Oh, well, you don't have to . . .'

'*I'll* tell you. Hey, I've *got* to tell you, if you're going with him now. He beat me up.'

'He *beat you up?*'

'Yeah.'

'My God! Why'd he do that?'

Judy's face suddenly changed from nicely tanned to bright red. 'Well, he was drunk. It was a sex thing. He wanted to do something, and I wouldn't let him.'

'So he *pounded* you?'

She nodded. Her face was scarlet.

'What did he want to do?' I asked.

'It doesn't matter.'

An idea struck me. Frowning, I leaned forward and said, 'Do you want to know why I'm *really* wearing Tony's shirt? Because he ripped mine off me. Tore it right off.'

She looked shocked. 'Tonight?'

'Yeah.'

'Jeez. Was he drunk?'

'As a skunk,' I said.

''Cause, I mean, he's not usually like that. How long have you known him?'

'Just a few days.'

'He must be in really bad shape. I mean, we went together for months, and he never pulled anything like that. He drank too much a few times, but he never *attacked* me. He was always so sweet. You wouldn't have thought he had a mean bone in his body. Till that night he went berserk on me.'

I nodded eagerly.

We've both been there, girl!

'Tonight,' I said, 'was the first time he ever got ugly with me. I couldn't believe it. He'd seemed so gentle, before. Like a really sensitive, sincere guy.'

'Exactly,' Judy said.

'But, boy . . .' I shook my head. 'Not tonight. He scared me half to death.'

'What did he do?'

I drank some more beer, sighed, then set the mug down on the table in front of the sofa and said, 'Well, he came over to my place for dinner. After that we went and saw *Independence Day*. Everything was fine till after the movie. We went back to my place and had a few drinks. We were planning to fool around, but my roommate came home. She always shows up at exactly the worst possible time.'

Judy smiled slightly. 'That's what roommates are for.'

'Do you have one?' I asked, suddenly worried.

'Not since college.'

'They can be a real pain in the butt,' I said.

'No kidding.'

'Anyway, the three of us sat around and had a few drinks. And I could tell that Tony was starting to lose his patience. He wanted to . . . you know, mess around. But we couldn't do it in front of Jane. Finally, he said it was time for him to go home. And he asked me if I wanted to come with him. So I said, "Sure," and we left.'

'Was he okay to drive?' Judy asked.

'No. Hardly. But neither was I. I mean, we were both pretty looped. We shouldn't have driven at all. But I wanted to get out of there, too, before something happened between him and Jane. She was starting to look at him a certain way, you know? Besides, I was interested in seeing where he lived. He'd been kind of funny about the place, like he didn't want me there for some reason.'

'Strange. He had *me* there all the time.'

'Well . . .' I shrugged. 'Who knows? Maybe that had something to do with it. You know? The way he feels about you, maybe he thought I might – taint the place, or something.'

'That'd be really strange.'

'Anyway, he didn't take me there, after all. He drove us into the woods, instead.'

Chapter Twelve

Tony Tales

'Drove into *what* woods?' Judy asked.

'Miller's Woods.'

'You're kidding. At night?'

'Yeah. Tonight.'

'You *let* him?'

'Like I said, we were both a little smashed.'

'My God.'

'We went to that picnic area. With the fireplaces and tables?'

Judy nodded. 'I've been there a few times. Never at night, though.'

'Well, that's where we went.'

'Was anybody around?'

'Just me and Tony. Which is what he wanted, I guess . . . to have me out there alone. Anyway, we went over and sat on one of those tables.'

'You got out of the car? Weren't you frightened?'

'Yeah, sort of. As a matter of fact, that was the whole problem. It was so dark and spooky. I had this awful feeling like we were being watched. I wanted to get the hell out of there. But Tony kept saying there was nothing to worry about. And he laughed at me for being scared.'

'That wasn't very nice,' Judy said.

'I didn't think so, either. I thought it was rotten. So I *really* wasn't in any mood to fool around with him. Anyway, we were sitting on top of a picnic table with our feet on the bench. Tony had a bottle of tequila. He drank from it with one hand and rubbed my back with the other. Before you know it, he snuck that hand under my blouse. Then he started trying to unhook the back of my bra, so I told him to stop it.'

'Naturally, he didn't.'

'Of course not. He went ahead and unhooked my bra, so I stood up on the bench and said, "I mean it, Tony. Not here. This place gives me the creeps."

'He said that's what he likes about it. So I said, "Let's just go over to your apartment, okay?" Then I jumped off the bench and started walking away, but he suddenly leaps up and grabs me by the collar and jerks me off my feet. But he catches me, you know? So then I'm leaning against him and he reaches around in front and rips my blouse open. I mean, he was just vicious about it. It was a pullover, and he tore it apart right down the front and ruined it. Which is the *real* reason I'm wearing his shirt right now.'

Judy nodded, a solemn look on her face. 'Not because yours got spilled on.'

'That was a little fib. I'm sorry. I never thought I'd end up telling you this stuff.' I tried to smile, making it look like a strain. 'You're really a good listener, Judy.'

'Thanks. I've been through a few of these things, myself.'

'Guys are such awful pigs.'

'They can be.'

'He completely ruined my blouse.'

'He's ruined a couple of mine, too,' Judy said. 'And a good dress.'

'Tore them?'

'Different things.'

I could tell she didn't want to go into details, so I went on with my story. 'The whole thing just scared the hell out of me,' I said. 'Him flipping out like that. And also, you know, being in those woods. I really panicked. I just wanted to get away. But he wouldn't let me. He jerked my shorts down and threw me onto the picnic table. I tried to get up, but he slugged me in the stomach.'

Judy winced as if she could feel the blow, herself.

'That knocked my wind out. All I could do was squirm on the table. It felt like I was drowning. Then the next thing I know, he's on top of me. We're both naked and he's . . .' I made a face. 'You know.'

'Screwing you?'

'Yeah.'

Her face suddenly went crimson again, and she said, 'In the right place?'

'Huh?'

'Never mind.' She was really flustered. 'It's none of my business. Forget I asked, okay?'

'You mean, did he do it to me in the vagina?'

'Well. Yeah.'

'Yeah, that's where.'

Grimacing, she said, 'And not with anything funny?'

'What do you mean, funny?'

'He obviously didn't, or you wouldn't have to ask.'

'What'd he do to *you*?'

'Nothing. I wouldn't let him. That's why he beat up.' She smiled a little sadly. 'You should've seen me afterward. I was a wreck. You look like you lucked out.'

'This was my lucky night, okay.'

'You got off without too much damage. That's all I meant.'

'I guess that's true.'

'How did it turn out?' she asked.

'Where were we?'

'On the picnic table.'

'Oh, that's right. He was screwing me. In the vagina. With his penis. Without a condom.'

'Well, at least you don't have to worry about AIDS or anything. I happen to know that he's perfectly healthy.'

I laughed.

Couldn't help it.

Luckily, I didn't have a mouthful of beer. It would've spewed.

Judy raised her eyebrows as if she hoped I might let her in on the joke.

'As a matter of fact,' I said, 'he isn't.'

'Isn't?'

'Perfectly healthy.'

'What do you mean?'

'He probably has a major headache, right now. If he's awake yet.'

'Awake?'

'I knocked him out cold with his tequila bottle. He'd left it on the table where I could reach it. So while he was busy humping me, I grabbed it and gave him a good one. Busted it against his head.'

Judy's mouth dropped open. She gaped at me, an odd look in her eyes as if she might be tempted to laugh, herself.

'Knocked him out cold,' I said. 'But he was still on top of me, so I rolled over. He fell off me *and* the table, and whacked the bench, then rolled off *it* and landed on the ground. Took a pretty good fall.'

'Was he all right?'

'Not really. He was out like a light and his head was bleeding. He wasn't dead, though.'

'Where is he now?'

'I don't know. And I don't care. He's probably on a back road, somewhere, walking home. But he won't have an easy time of it. I was still really angry at him, you know? A bit *more* than angry. I was furious. I mean, he'd raped me. Wouldn't you call that a rape?'

'I'd call it a rape,' Judy said.

'So would I.'

'Are you going to press charges against him?'

'I don't think so. I think I've punished him pretty good *without* the cops. You know what I did? I left him there in the woods completely naked. Out cold, and naked as the day he was born. I kept his shirt, since he'd wrecked mine. All the rest of his clothes, I burned in one of the fireplaces. His underwear and everything. Except his shoes. I threw those into the woods. He'll never find them. Then I hopped into his car and drove off.'

'You really left him there?'

I grinned. 'Seemed like a good idea. Part of my revenge. But it didn't seem like *enough* revenge. So I thought I'd drive over to his apartment and trash the place. Just to teach him a lesson, you know? Teach him that he can't do that sort of thing to a girl.'

'So why did you come *here*?'

'I thought *this* was his place. I'll show you.' I drank the last of the beer, set the mug on the table again, then pulled Tony's wallet out of my rear pocket. Taking out the slip of paper, I walked over to Judy's chair. 'See this?' I handed it to her.

She scowled at it. 'That's *my* address. It's also my handwriting. I gave this to Tony . . . months ago. When we first met.'

I sighed and shook my head.

She held the paper toward me.

'You might as well keep it,' I told her. On my way back to the sofa, I stuffed Tony's wallet into my pocket.

'What made you think this was *his* address?'

'I found it in his wallet. I just assumed it was where he lived. Pretty stupid, huh?'

From the look in Judy's eyes, she seemed to agree. But she didn't make any sort of crack about it. All she said was, 'You should've checked his driver's license.'

'He didn't have it with him.'

'He *didn't*?'

'He'd gotten it revoked.'

416

She gasped. 'You're *kidding*!'

'No. They took it away from him about a week ago. For drunk driving and leaving the scene of an accident.'

'My God! An accident?'

'It wasn't anything serious. Nobody got hurt. But Tony sped off, afterward. He got caught about a mile away. He was lucky he didn't end up in jail.'

'Poor Tony,' Judy said.

'Yeah. He's been having a hard time of it, lately. He just can't get over losing you.'

'Jeez.'

'Anyway, that's why he didn't have a license. When I found the address in his wallet, I just automatically figured it must be where he lived. So here I am. Guess I would've figured out something was wrong when none of his keys fit the door.'

'I heard you trying them,' Judy explained.

Trying to look embarrassed, I asked, 'Did I wake you up?'

'No. I wasn't asleep. I'd *been* asleep, but then I had this horrible nightmare that woke me up. Really freaked me out.'

'I hate nightmares.'

'Me, too. I think they're scarier than real life.'

'Think so?'

'Sure,' she said. 'Nightmares just give you raw fear. If the same stuff happened in real life, you'd still be scared, but you'd also be thinking rationally and trying to figure things out. How to get away, that sort of stuff. In nightmares, all you have is the fear. Just fear, and nothing else. That's what makes them so terrible.'

'But you wake up from nightmares,' I pointed out.

'I sure woke up from this one tonight. And then I wasn't very eager to fall asleep again. If you go back to sleep too soon, you know, you can wind up back inside the same nightmare. So I got up and went to the bathroom.'

'*That* gives me the creeps,' I told her. 'Going to the john in

417

the middle of the night. I always think I hear things.'

'I heard *you* trying to unlock the door.'

'Oh, wow. That must've freaked you out.'

'I didn't think it was *my* door. I thought it might be the one across the hall. But the sounds went on a lot longer than they should've, so I looked out the peephole.'

'And there I was.'

'There you were.'

'You sure scared the hell out of me, opening the door like that.'

'I didn't mean to scare you,' Judy said. 'I just thought you looked like you needed help.'

'You were right about that.'

She didn't say anything for a few seconds, just looked at me like maybe she was worried about hurting my feelings or making me mad. Then she said, 'Now it's Tony who needs the help.'

'What?'

'I don't blame you for what you did to him,' she said. 'I'm sure he deserved it. Maybe even worse. But . . . I owe him. If I hadn't dumped him, none of this bad stuff would've happened tonight.'

Funny, but she was absolutely right about that.

Then she said, 'It sounds as if he's . . . come apart at the seams.'

'He really has,' I said.

Chapter Thirteen

Ringing Up the Dead Guy

'I just can't leave him out there,' Judy told me.

'He's probably on his way home, by now.'

'But he was still unconscious when you drove off and left him, wasn't he?'

'Dead to the world.'

'So for all we know, he might *still* be out cold.'

'I guess it's possible,' I admitted. 'Look, I have an idea. Why don't you give him a call?'

It seemed like a fine idea. Judy didn't know that he'd moved to a new apartment. She would obviously dial his old number and get a recorded message explaining that Tony's phone was out of service.

'Maybe he's already home by now,' I added.

'It's worth a try.'

Judy leaned forward in the big, old chair and stood up. Her phone was on the lamp table near the end of the sofa. As she walked over and picked it up, she said, 'I can't imagine he's home, though. Not if he had to walk.' She picked up the handset and started to tap in a number. 'It's an awfully long way from Miller's Woods to his place.'

'Especially if you're bare-ass naked,' I said.

Which made her laugh. 'You're terrible,' she said.

'Yep.'

Listening at the earpiece, she suddenly frowned. 'His number's been changed,' she muttered. 'They're going to . . .' She stopped to listen.

They're giving her the new number!

419

I couldn't even *begin* to figure out the ramifications of that.

While I sat there, stunned, she tapped in a series of numbers.

A moment later, she met my eyes and said, 'It's his machine.'

'Maybe you'd better hang up.'

'He might be monitoring.'

Should I stop her?

Maybe not. This could be a good deal.

Or a disaster.

'Hi, Tony,' she said. 'It's me, Judy. Are you there?' She stopped talking. She waited.

Leave it at that! Don't say another word!

'I guess you're not home. Okay. Well, I just called to see how you're doing. Give me a call back if you want to. I'm still at the same number. So long.'

She hung up.

'We'll probably get to him before he even hears it,' she said.

'I imagine so,' I said.

'It's funny that he changed his number. Do you know why he did that?'

I couldn't come up with a good lie right off the bat, so I just said, 'No idea.'

'Maybe it has to do with his accident.'

'Could be.'

'At any rate, he hasn't gotten home yet. I'm sure he would've picked up.'

'You can bet on that. He's been dying to get a call from you. But you never know, maybe he's taking a shower or something. We probably ought to wait a few minutes and try him again.'

Judy shook her head. 'No. I don't want to wait any longer. I need to go out and find him.'

'Want me to come with you?'

'You don't have to,' she said, and turned away.

'Sure I do,' I said. From my seat on the sofa, I watched her stride into a nearby room and switch on a light. At the other end of the room was a rumpled bed.

Judy stepped out of sight.

Raising my voice, I said, 'I can't have you going out there all by yourself. Something might happen to you.'

'I'll be all right,' she called.

'Maybe. But what if you're not? I'm the one who left Tony stranded. I'd feel awful.'

'You hardly even know me.'

'I'd feel awful, anyway. You're a nice person.'

A quiet laugh came from the bedroom. Then Judy said, 'Well, I'm not sure how nice I am, but thanks.'

'You *are* nice. And trusting. I mean, I'm a complete stranger, but you let me in here in the middle of the night. You even gave me a beer.'

'Well, we've got a mutual friend, I guess. Or enemy.'

'I want to help you look for him. Really.'

'Fine with me. I might be a nice person with a lot of sterling qualities, but I am a chicken. It'll be great to have you along.'

'You and me, Judy.'

She came out of the bedroom. Her pajamas were gone, and she was no longer barefoot. She wore white socks and blue sneakers, a pale blue skirt, and a short-sleeved white blouse that looked crisp and cool. Most of the blouse's buttons weren't fastened yet. It wasn't tucked in, either, and hung down like a miniskirt. Only a few inches of her real skirt showed in front of her thighs.

'You're wearing a skirt?' I asked.

'It's a hot night.'

'Tony'll like that.'

'I guess so,' she said.

'And no bra.'

She laughed. 'Hot night. Besides, look who's talking.'

'I have an excuse. Tony wrecked mine.'

'I don't *need* an excuse. You're not my mother.' Grinning, she looked down and worked on fastening the rest of her buttons. 'It's not like I'm trying to do Tony any favors,' she said. 'I just want to be comfortable.'

'That's fine,' I said. 'Hell, you look great.'

'Thanks. I feel great. This is kind of fun, in a way. It's like going out for an adventure.'

I found myself grinning. 'Yeah,' I said. 'It is.'

Finished with her buttons, she hurried into the kitchen. She came back with her purse and slipped its strap onto her shoulder. 'All set,' she said. 'You ready to go? Do you want to hit the bathroom first?'

'Ah. Maybe so. Good idea.'

She pointed the way.

I went in, turned on the light and shut the door. The bathroom was small, but very clean. A wonderful, flowery aroma filled the air. It seemed to come from a bar of soap on the sink.

Not wasting any time, I took the .22 out of my back pocket, pulled my cut-offs down and sat on the toilet.

While I peed, I wondered what the hell I'd gotten myself into.

A complete disaster, that's what.

I'd actually brought Tony's car – and corpse – to Judy's building, not his.

Even if I could somehow learn the location of his new apartment – which seemed impossible – the plan was blown anyway because I'd come face to face with Judy.

Killing her wouldn't fix everything, but it had to be done.

The worst part of it was, I liked her.

Too bad I hadn't shot her right away. It would've been easier. Now that I knew her, it was going to be tough.

I kept staring at the pistol in my hand.

Maybe I should just do it. Go out there and shoot her right now.

With my thumb, I switched off the safety. It had been hiding a small red dot.

Wait till she turns around. Get up real close behind her, then put a couple in the back of her head.

Don't let her know what's coming. That way, she won't be scared.

And won't scream, either.

Maybe she'll scream because it hurts.

I imagined it all happening, and it made me feel sick.

Let it wait, I told myself. There's no big hurry. We'll be leaving in a few minutes. Wait till we're someplace where nobody will be likely to hear the gunshots.

Right away, I felt better.

I still had to kill her, but not until later.

I thumbed the safety back on, then reached over and set the pistol on the edge of the sink.

When I was done at the toilet, I pulled up my cut-offs and fastened the belt tight enough to keep them from falling down. Instead of putting the pistol into my back pocket, I slipped it into the right front pocket. That way, it would be easier to take out.

Then I washed my hands.

There was a mirror above the sink.

I hardly recognized myself. My hair looked strange – damp, ropey and coiled. My face was shiny with oils and sweat. The afternoon in the sun had turned it a dark, coppery color. My eyes looked all wrong – the whites too white, the gaze too intense.

I looked a little mad, a little wild.

Like someone well suited for bloody work.

I washed my hands with hot water, using the nice soap. When I finished, my hands smelled like spring flowers. I rinsed my face with cold water. I cupped some water to my mouth, and had a few swallows.

After drying, I used the towel to wipe the faucet and toilet handles and the light switch. I put the towel back on its bar, then shut off the light with the edge of my hand. Standing in the dark, I slipped my hand under the front of my shirt and grabbed the doorknob to let myself out.

'Ready?' Judy asked.

'All set,' I told her.

Our beer mugs were gone.

Along with my fingerprints!

Smiling, I said, 'You cleaned up already?'

'Yeah. I hate coming back to a mess. Did you want your mug?'

'I just thought I might have a drink of water.'

'It's already washed, but I'll get you a clean one.'

Already washed!

'Never mind,' I said, pleasantly relieved. 'We'd better go.'

'Are you sure? It wouldn't be any trouble.'

'Yeah. Hey, I'd just end up having to pee again.'

'Okay.'

'Let's go.'

Judy walked in front of me. I followed her toward the door, the pistol swinging in my pocket, rubbing against my thigh. She opened the door, then stepped aside.

I went out into the hallway. Nobody was there.

Judy came after me, using the outside knob to pull the door shut. Then she gave it a couple of twists and shoves to make sure the door was locked.

Which took care of any prints I might've left on the knob. Side by side, not saying a word, we walked down the silent hall to the foyer. There, she whispered, 'Where'd you park Tony's car?'

'In the lot.'

'*This* lot?'

'Yeah.'

'You found an empty space for it?'

'I put it in L. Is that okay?'

'Fine. That's right next to mine.'

As we hurried down the stairway, she said, 'I've got an idea. Why don't we leave it there and take my car?'

'Are you sure you want to?' I asked.

What does this do to my plan?

Not that I actually *had* a plan anymore.

'This whole business is pretty hairy,' she said. 'Going to the woods at this time of night. I'd just rather be doing it in my own car. At least I can be pretty sure it won't break down on us.'

'Fine by me,' I said. 'You drive.'

'You point the way.'

We came out of the stairwell into the parking lot.

Nobody else seemed to be around.

My loafers clopped loudly on the concrete floor. Judy's sneakers were nearly silent.

'If we find Tony,' she said, 'we'll bring him back here so he can drive himself home. Unless he needs emergency treatment.'

'There's his car,' I said, pointing at it.

'Yeah.'

It looked just fine sitting there. A few shiny drops of water sparkled on the trunk and rear bumper, but I saw nothing to worry about.

'That's a good place for it,' Judy said. 'Nobody ever parks there but guests. It can stay right where it is for a few days, if he needs to be hospitalized or something.'

'I don't really think he'll need to be hospitalized,' I told her.

Chapter Fourteen

Night Riders

'Exciting, isn't it?' Judy said as we reached the top of the driveway ramp.

'What is?' I asked.

'This. Going out like this.' She swung her car onto the road and picked up speed. 'I never go anywhere this late at night. I'm almost always asleep by now.'

'Me, too,' I said, but I wasn't really paying attention.

I was preoccupied, just then, with my feelings of relief. Now that we'd left the apartment building behind us, I was finally free of Tony.

I mean *free*!

He and his car were *gone*!

Adios, toot-toot, bye-bye!

I would never go near them again, and nobody would ever find out what I'd done.

Not even Judy.

I looked over at her. She kept turning her head, glancing around like an eager tourist. There wasn't much to see, though, unless you're fascinated by empty streets, porch lights and darkness.

'It *is* exciting to be out like this,' I told her.

'Sort of spooky, too,' she said.

'If you think it's spooky now, wait till we get to the woods.'

'I can hardly wait.'

'Do you know how to get there?' I asked.

'I can find Miller's Woods all right, but I'm not sure about the turn-off to the picnic area. How about you?'

'I'm pretty sure where it is.'

We were nearing the business district, so I said, 'You'd better not take Central. When I came through, there were some unsavory characters hanging around.'

'We can do without unsavory characters,' she said.

A block short of Central, she turned onto the same street I'd used earlier. It looked deserted.

'The fewer people see us,' I said, 'the better.'

'You're probably right.'

'Two gals by themselves.'

'Are you trying to scare me?'

'We just have to be careful, that's all. You never know who might be out there.'

'Most people are all right,' Judy said.

'Not the sort who are cruising the roads at this hour.'

'We are.'

'We're the exception. Anyway, it only takes one lunatic to spoil the night.'

'You're a regular cockeyed optimist,' she said.

'That's me.'

'Maybe instead of a lunatic, we'll run into a wonderful, charming stranger.'

'Run over one?'

'*Into*.' She turned her head and smiled at me. 'You're a trouble maker.'

'Yep.'

'I know 'em when I see 'em. I'm one, too.'

'You? A trouble maker? You seem like such a *nice* girl.'

'I'm that, too.'

'How can you be nice *and* a trouble maker?'

'I make benign mischief.'

Normally, I might've laughed at that. It was a pretty cute thing to say, *benign mischief*. But it almost made me cry.

Here Judy was, out in the middle of the night on a mission of mercy. Having herself an *adventure*. She's nervous but excited and having fun, saying cute stuff, and she doesn't have the slightest inkling that I'm going to leave her dead in the woods.

It was awfully sad if you think about it.

And I couldn't *help* but think about it, riding along in the car with her.

On her last ride.

Too bad she wasn't an ugly, snotty, miserable bitch. Then I wouldn't have felt so bad.

'Are you okay?' she asked after a while.

'I guess so.'

'You're kind of quiet. Worrying about lunatics?'

'Sure am.'

'Well, I think we'll be perfectly safe as long as we stay in the car. We really shouldn't need to get out, I don't think.'

'Maybe not,' I agreed. 'Depending on Tony.'

'With any luck, we'll find him walking along the roadside before we even have to go into the woods.'

'I sure hope so,' I said.

But I didn't really think it stood much chance of happening.

We were nearly to the town limits when Judy said, 'Uh-oh.'

'What?'

'Here comes your lunatic, now.'

'Very funny.' Twisting sideways, I looked out the rear window and saw a pair of headlights in the distance.

'Man,' Judy said, 'he's really barreling down on us.'

'Just drive normal,' I told her. 'Don't speed up or anything. It might be a cop.'

'That'd be fine by me.'

The car bore down on us, full speed.

'What the hell is he *doing*?' Judy blurted.

The headbeams surged in through the windows and glared off our rearview mirror.

'God!' Judy cried out. 'He's going to ram us!'

But he didn't.

At the last instant, the car swerved to our left.

It started to roar past us, then slowed enough to match our speed.

It wasn't a cop car.

Cops don't drive Cadillacs. Not in Chester, they don't. Not in any town I've ever heard of. This thing looked like a giant old gas-gulping monster that belonged in a junk yard, not on the road. A real old clunker, but its engine sounded *hot*.

As it tooled along beside us, the guys checked us out.

Two of them.

Judy gave them a glance, then turned her face straight forward.

I was leaning toward the dashboard so I could look past her. I had a lousy view of the driver, but the one in the passenger seat looked like a tough guy. He stared back at us. He looked all of about eighteen years old and had a crew cut. A cig dangled off his lips. He wasn't wearing a shirt.

'Real charming,' Judy said quietly, as if addressing the windshield.

'Don't do anything. Don't even look at them.' As I gave that advice, I settled back into my seat and stopped looking at them myself.

A few seconds later, the car sped past us and swerved into our lane, barely missing our front bumper. Judy hit the brakes. As I was thrown forward, she flung an arm across my chest. Her arm didn't stop me, but my hands did. I slammed them against the dashboard.

The Cadillac pulled away from us.

'You okay?' Judy asked.

'Yeah. Thanks.'

'Bastards,' she muttered.

We were moving along at a crawl.

The Cadillac kept going, gaining speed, and soon vanished around a bend in the road.

Judy gave us a little gas. As we picked up speed, she took a deep breath. Then she said, 'Maybe you'd better put on your seatbelt.'

'Not me.'

'Huh?'

'I don't use them. I'll take my chances with the windshield.'

'Yeah?' She gave me a look, but there wasn't enough light in the car to see whether she was smiling, smirking, frowning, or something else. 'I'll keep mine on,' she said. 'Safety first.'

'No faith in your own driving?' I asked.

She laughed.

We glided around the bend. Ahead of us, the road was dark except for the moonlight. No sign of the Cadillac.

'You think they're gone?' Judy asked.

'Looks that way,' I said. 'But things aren't always how they look.'

'I guess they were just fooling around.'

'Looks that way.'

'Could've gotten ugly. Maybe this wasn't such a hot idea, after all.'

'What?' I asked.

'Coming out to look for Tony. I mean, what if those two guys had gotten *serious*?'

'Do you want to call it off and go back?'

She didn't answer for a few seconds. Then she said, 'I guess if they'd meant to nail us, they would've done it.'

'Probably.'

'Probably just wanted to give us a thrill.'

'As long as they don't show up again,' I said, 'we might as well keep going. We're more than halfway there.'

'Gone past the point of no return?'

'Yep.'

'Gotta keep going, then.'

'You and me, babe.'

She turned her head toward me. Again, I couldn't see her expression. She said, 'Can you imagine what a couple of guys like that might do if they got their hands on Tony?'

'On *Tony*?'

'Yeah.'

'Wouldn't be pretty.'

'I'd like to be there to see it,' Judy said.

'Whoa! What kind of talk is that? We're on a mission to rescue the guy!'

'That doesn't mean I wish him a full and rewarding life of health and happiness. Not after what he did to me. And to *you*, for that matter. It'd be sort of neat to see him really get creamed by a couple of punks.'

'I did a pretty good job on him,' I said.

'But just think what a couple of punks like that might do.'

'You shock me, Judy. I am truly shocked.'

'Sure you are.'

'Now, give me a clue. Why exactly *are* we driving out here to rescue him?'

'Good question.'

'Maybe we *should* turn back.'

'Nah,' she said. 'Can't.'

'Why not?'

'It's my fault he's out here tonight. I'm the one who made him nuts. He wasn't a bad guy before I made him crazy. It's my fault he beat *me* up, and it's my fault he attacked *you*.'

'That's ridiculous.'

'No, it's true. I got him into this mess, so I've now gotta help him get out.'

'Whether you want to or not.'

'Yeah, sort of. No, I want to. I mean, we had a lot of great times together. Before he went off the deep end.'

'You just feel sorry for him.'

'Maybe. I don't know. I was in love with him. That sort of

thing . . . I can't just pretend it never happened. He was the most important thing in my life for a while. The things we did . . . they're all part of me, and always will be . . . in spite of everything else.'

'You're nuts,' I said.

She laughed softly. 'Think so?'

'Yeah. You sound like you're *still* in love with him.'

'Maybe with the way he used to be.'

'Well, that guy's gone forever.'

'I know. It can never be the same. But still, I owe him. For the good times, and because this crazy stuff happened because of me.'

'You gonna kiss and make up with him?'

She let out a sharp laugh. 'No way!'

'Yep. And you'll take him back to your place . . . supposedly so he can pick up his car. But before you know it, you'll be asking him in for a beer. Maybe a coffee. Then wham! You're all over each other.'

'Not a chance.'

'Next thing you know, it's Humpty-Dumpty time.'

'No!' she blurted, laughing, and slapped my leg. 'That's not going to happen. No way! Not in a zillion years.'

I happened to know she was right.

'It's what *he'd* like to have happen,' I said. 'He wants you back.'

'Well, I don't want *him* back.'

'He kept pretending *I* was you.'

'He what?'

'Yeah. He'd shut his eyes whenever we were making love, and call me Judy.'

'Oh, my God.' She sounded appalled. 'Really?'

'Yeah. He even did it tonight when he had me on the picnic table.'

'While he was *raping* you?'

432

'Yeah. He kept saying stuff like, "How do you like it, Judy? Huh? Big enough for you, Judy? Oh, Judy, you're so tight and wet. I love your tight, wet pussy." '

'*Tony* said that?'

'Not exactly. I cleaned it up a little. He didn't say pussy.'

'Oh.' She stared straight out the windshield. Her face looked gray in the moonlight, but I bet its true color was bright red.

'That's when I hit him with the bottle,' I explained.

'Good going.'

'Like I told you, guys are pigs.'

'I'm willing to concede that *he* is.'

'Trust me, they all are.'

'I wouldn't go along with that,' she said. 'Not a hundred percent.'

'Ninety percent?' I asked.

She said, 'Ninety-nine.'

So then I *had* to laugh.

'I tell you what,' she said. 'When we *do* find Tony, I'll run him over.'

'All *right*!'

Chapter Fifteen

Into the Woods

But she was joking, of course. About running him over. She wanted to rescue Tony, not kill him.

More's the pity.

If she'd been sincere in her desire to murder the guy, I might've changed my mind about killing her.

433

No, not really.

Here's the deal. No matter how much I might like Judy (and I liked her plenty), no matter how much she might despise Tony (though I frankly believe she still loved him in spite of everything), no matter *ANYTHING* – she had to die.

Didn't she?

Because if she lived, she could tell on me. I'm not saying she *would*. But she might. And then where would I be?

Up the infamous Creek of Shit without a paddle, that's where.

Kill her, and I'm home free.

Well, not completely. There was still the little problem of the redial button on Tony's phone. If he even *had* a redial button. Wherever his phone might be. In his mystery apartment, wherever that might be.

I wished I could get to it, but I didn't know how.

What could it show the cops, anyway? Only that Tony's last call had been to Serena and Charlie's phone.

It didn't prove that anyone had answered it.

Serena and Charlie were away on a trip. I, of course, never heard the phone ring because I never left my room over the garage.

There was only one problem with that.

Phone records would show that the call had lasted a while. Four or five minutes? Which would lead the cops to figure he either talked to someone, or left a message on the answering machine.

My insides shriveled.

They'll want to hear Tony's message.

But I couldn't *let* them hear it.

One little button on a telephone was going to destroy me if I couldn't come up with a way to find Tony's new apartment.

'We're almost there, aren't we?' Judy asked.

For a second or two, I didn't know what she was talking about. Then I saw the woods on both sides of the road. 'It'll be pretty soon,' I said. 'The turnoff. It'll be on the right. Shady Creek Picnic Area.'

'I hope he's okay.'

'But not *too* okay?'

'Medium okay, medium hurt. Maybe in great pain, but with no permanent damage.'

'You're so caring, Judy.'

'I just hope he's there. I thought we'd find him before now. You know, on his way home.'

'Don't forget, he's naked. He probably hides when a car comes along.'

'Yeah. We might've gone right by him.'

'Or he could've taken a different route.'

'What other route? There's *only* one way to get back to town from out here.'

'If you stick to the roads,' I said. 'But maybe he took a shortcut through the woods.' I spotted the sign up ahead and said, 'Here it comes.'

Judy slowed down.

'I bet we'll find him here,' I said as she made the turn.

'You hit him that hard?' she asked.

'No. He's probably conscious by now. But if *I* were in his shoes . . . or shoeless and bare-ass naked, as the case may be . . .'

Judy laughed softly.

'I might just decide to stay put. At least I'd be in the middle of nowhere and surrounded by trees, so I wouldn't need to worry about everyone *seeing* me.'

'You'd have to go home eventually.'

When she said that, I immediately thought of my prowler. Maybe he was a guy who *hadn't* gone home eventually.

'I might just decide to stay in the woods,' I said, 'and live like Tarzan.'

'Yeah. I can just see Tony swinging through the trees.'

'*I said grab the VINE!*'

Judy laughed, shaking her head. Then she said, 'Ouch.'

'How would you know?' I asked.

'It's *gotta* hurt.'

'I guess so.'

I *knew* so. I bit one, once. Chomped it right off, in fact. You should've seen the guy! It hurt, all right.

Don't go feeling sorry for him, though. And don't think I'm some kind of evil person or nut. He shouldn't have gone and stuck it someplace where it didn't belong. Especially not after I'd begged him not to.

He got no worse than he deserved.

But you should've heard him scream! It hurt, all right! And then he went crazy trying to get it out of my mouth. He yelled, 'Give it back! Give it back, you fucking bitch!' I guess he figured they could sew it back on for him at a hospital. But I wouldn't let him have it. He kept yelling and hitting me, but I went ahead and chewed it up. After I swallowed it, he *really* went berserk and almost killed me.

Anyway, enough about that. Like I said near the front, this book isn't an autobiography. I just had to tell you about that incident because of how it fit in with what Judy and I were saying on the road to the Shady Creek Picnic Area.

I didn't tell Judy about it, though.

I never told *anyone* about it, until now. Not even my mom or the people in the hospital where they took care of me afterwards. I made up a story about getting beaten up by a mugger, and the guy never told.

I don't know what ever happened to him.

Well, I can vouch for two or three inches. Not the rest, though. When I got better and went back to school, we had a new principal. He got hired because the one before him had suddenly and mysteriously left town.

Anyway, that's *really* more than I intended to tell. I guess I'll leave it in, though. Why not? It's the truth. And it also goes to show you what pigs men are – even school principals.

I only have one regret about what I did to him.

No mustard!

That's a little joke.

Anyway, I've strayed away from the real story.

When I left off, I'd just told Judy the old Tarzan joke about grabbing the vine, and we were having some laughs about that. She was driving us along the road to the picnic area. She thought we might find Tony there. I was sitting in the passenger seat, and had Tony's pistol in the front pocket of my cut-offs. I'd be using it on her pretty soon.

The next thing you know, we came to the end of the road. The pavement spread out into a clearing with logs laid out to show you where to park. There were places for six or eight cars, but no other cars were there. Judy drove up to one of the logs and stopped.

The beams of our headlights reached out into the picnic area, lighting a couple of the green wooden tables.

'I don't see him,' Judy said. 'Do you?'

'No. But we weren't up here. We were down by the creek. If you want, I'll run down and see if he's there.'

'No, don't do that. We'd better stay in the car.'

'What if he's still unconscious?' I asked.

'I don't know.'

'I'll just run down and take a quick look.'

'No, don't.'

'It'll only take a minute.'

'I'll go with you,' Judy said, and shut off the headlights.

The night dropped down on us.

'My God,' she said. 'It's dark out here.'

'Do you have a flashlight?'

'Sure. Back in my bedroom. Maybe I should go get it.' But she was kidding. Instead of turning the car around, she shut off its engine and unfastened her seatbelt.

'Ready?' I asked.

'Not hardly. I don't want to go out there.'

'Then stay here. That's fine. I'll just go . . .'

'No way. If you're going, I'm coming with you.'

'Then we might as well get it over with,' I said, and opened the passenger door. The car's overhead light came on.

'Much better,' Judy said.

I climbed out. My legs were trembling. I was shaking all over, and sweating. My heart was pounding like mad. I was a genuine wreck.

For one thing, the place gave me the creeps. As a general rule, I don't like to be in forests at night. Plus, a lot of bad stuff had gone on in Miller's Woods, and I was a little nervous about the prowler. He might be nearby. After his visit to Serena and Charlie's house, he'd gone back into the woods only about a mile from here.

My other reason for being a wreck is that I had to kill Judy. It stank, but there was no way out of it. And this was the perfect place for it.

Dark as death, secluded, and within reasonable walking distance of home if I took the shortcut through the woods.

When we shut our doors, the light in the car went out.

We met in front, but didn't say anything. As if we were afraid to speak. Afraid of who might hear us.

Side by side, we walked up the gentle slope toward the place where we'd seen the picnic tables. We could still see them, but now they looked so dark and vague that they hardly seemed real.

Here and there, tiny dabs of moonlight made it down through the trees. A soft, warm breeze was blowing. It might've felt good, if things had been different. Just then, there *was* no such thing as good. Good, for a while, seemed to be gone from the face of the earth.

We walked past the picnic tables, and went on to the crest of the hill. There, we stopped and gazed down toward the creek. I saw a few places that looked like moonlight glinting off water. And I saw a flat shape that might've been a picnic table. But nothing looked very clear or very real. Mostly, there was only darkness.

'I've got a bad feeling about this,' Judy whispered.

What are you, psychic?

'What kind of bad feeling?' I asked. I didn't really want to know, but I had to ask.

'Like we're really going to regret going down there.'

'You don't have to go down.'

'Yeah. I do.'

Brave, innocent, stupid Judy.

Chapter Sixteen

Killing Judy

As we made our way down the slope, I reached into the front pocket of my cut-offs and took hold of the pistol. With my thumb, I flicked its safety off.

'Tony?' Judy called softly. 'Are you there?'

I slipped the .22 out of my pocket, but kept it by my side, out of sight.

'Tony?' she called again. 'It's Judy. Are you down there?'

I didn't want her to know what was coming, so I slowed down a little. She was about one stride downhill from me and two feet to my left when I brought the pistol up and fired point blank at the side of her head.

That should've done it.

But on the way up, the muzzle of the pistol snagged her ear.

I must've been standing too close. Probably because of the darkness.

She yelped, 'Ow!'

The pistol spat out a bright, quick flash. In that instant, I saw the tilt of Judy's head and the angle of my pistol.

And I couldn't tell if I'd gotten her.

But she cried out, grabbed her head above the ear and fell, tumbling crookedly.

On her way down, I took aim but decided not to fire again.

For one thing, I didn't want the noise. If you haven't been around a .22, you might think it just makes a tiny bang like a cap gun, or something. But it's more like a strong firecracker. *BAM!* My ears were ringing from the shot, and the sound of the blast must've carried for a mile.

I probably could've heard it from my room above the garage, if I'd been there.

My prowler *must've* heard it, unless he'd left the woods entirely.

He's the other reason I didn't put a few more rounds into Judy. The fewer I used on her, the more I'd still have in the pistol in case I met *him* on my way back home through the woods.

Him, or some other creep.

(What about the guys in the Cadillac? Were they gone for good?)

So instead of using Judy for target practice as she tumbled down the slope, I thumbed the safety on and hurried after her. She rolled all the way to the bottom, her arms and legs flopping around. When the ground leveled out, she rolled over a couple more times and stopped.

She came to rest in a patch of moonlight.

Her white blouse had come unbuttoned. It was wide open, leaving her bare to the waistband of her skirt. The skirt had gotten pushed up around her hips.

Except for the patch of white fabric between her legs, she looked like somebody who'd just gotten herself raped and murdered.

Raped and murdered.

An idea suddenly leaped into my head.

A brilliant idea.

I slipped the pistol into my pocket, then picked Judy up by the ankles and dragged her toward the picnic table. Along the way, she groaned a couple of times.

Still alive.

But she didn't struggle at all, just remained limp.

I stopped dragging her when the backs of my knees met the edge of the picnic table's wooden bench. I lowered her feet to the grass.

With such deep darkness, I couldn't see any blood on her. But her head *had* to be bloody. So I took off my shirt – Tony's shirt – and put it near the end of the bench, out of harm's way.

After that, I straddled Judy, squatted down, grabbed her sides just below her armpits, and pulled her up to a sitting position. Then I hugged her against me and stood up.

A good thing I'd taken off the shirt. Her face was so slippery against my shoulder and breast, it must've been covered with blood.

Though Judy felt awfully heavy, she didn't weigh nearly as much as Tony. I managed to seat her on the bench and lean her backward against the edge of the table. Then, keeping a hand on her shoulder so she wouldn't tip over, I climbed on top of the table. I crouched down, grabbed her, and hauled her up.

Then I stretched her out so she was lying lengthwise on her back.

By that time, I was sweating like a hog. I wanted to get it done, though, so I didn't waste any time resting.

First, I pulled the blouse off her shoulders and about halfway down her arms. Which made her bare all the way down to the

441

top of her skirt. It also pinned her arms against her sides, in case she might wake up and try to struggle.

Second, I rucked her skirt up around her waist. I was tempted to take it off her entirely. Some guys do that, preferring their victim naked. But most of them, when it gets to a certain stage, are in an awfully big hurry to *get in*. They'll just shove the skirt up and go for it. Some guys even *like* you to be wearing clothes when they screw you. It turns them on.

I know all about this sort of stuff.

When you're built 'like a brick shithouse', you learn plenty.

I'm what you might call an expert.

Anyway, never mind.

After I'd shoved up Judy's skirt, I spread open her legs about as wide as they would go, so her feet hung over the sides of the table.

Next, I had to rip her panties off. A guy who wants to rape you will hardly ever just pull them down. He has to do it with violence. If he has a knife, he'll cut them off you and maybe cut you a little bit in the process. Some guys will tear them off with their teeth. That can hurt, too. Accidently on purpose, they'll bite more than your panties. Usually, though, they rip them off you with their hands. That's how I decided to do it.

On my knees between Judy's legs, I slipped a hand inside the crotch of her panties. The flimsy fabric was moist. I jerked it sideways hard and fast. Half the crotch panel ripped away from her waistband. One more tug, and it tore completely off. I let go, and the tattered flap fell against the table top. She still wore the narrow strip of elastic low across her belly, but there was nothing in the way.

Then I went to work on her.

Coming to my senses afterward, I found myself sprawled on top of her. I was completely naked. She was slippery underneath me, and still alive. I felt the slight rise and fall of her chest, the thump of her heartbeat.

Suddenly, a hot sickness rushed through me.

What have I done?

Blown everything.

All I'd wanted to do from the start was clean up after myself, make it impossible for anyone to suspect me of killing Tony – destroy every link to me, wipe out every trace.

What'll I do?

For starters, I pushed myself up. Our bodies came apart with quiet, wet sounds. I climbed off her, got down from the top of the table, and sat on the bench. Leaning forward, I put my elbows on my knees and tried to figure a solution.

I must've looked like that statue, The Thinker.

The famous one by the sculptor, Godzilla.

Just kidding. Rodin, right?

The Thinker, but a female version and built like a brick shithouse.

Thinking, *How the hell do I get out of this?*

What a mess.

If only I'd kept things simple! But no! I had to get clever and tricky. Make them think she was murdered by a rapist. Brilliant idea!

In the process, I'd turned her into a petri dish of Alice samples.

So clean her up!

Sure thing, I thought. What about the *marks* I'd put on her body?

The Thinker returned to thought.

Suddenly, I sat up straight and blurted, 'Yes!'

First, I had to find my clothes. I slipped into my shoes – Tony's loafers. Then I hunted for my cut-offs. I found them on the ground where I'd thrown them during the frenzy with Judy. I put them on the bench so they wouldn't get lost again.

Carrying Tony's shirt, I went to the creek. Though I could hear the quiet gurgle and see bits of moonlight glinting on the water, the embankment took me by surprise. It was like stepping off a stair in the darkness. I gasped and fell and hoped like hell I wouldn't go down on a sharp rock.

Luckily, I hit nothing but water. It was about a foot deep. It splashed up cool against my face and underside as my hands and knees punched through the surface. The rocky bottom hurt my knees a little, but not much. The shirt protected my hands.

I eased myself all the way down into the water so it covered me and glided gently over me. It felt wonderful. It probably wasn't very clean, though. Not like the swimming pool.

Thinking of the pool, I couldn't help but remember the prowler. I pictured him floating on his back, and how he'd gleamed with moonlight. So beautiful and dangerous. Then he was out of the pool and squirming against the glass door, throbbing and spurting.

If they find some of that stuff on Judy . . .

That'll cinch it for sure.

My brilliant idea was suddenly more brilliant than ever.

But it would require a trip to Serena and Charlie's house.

It'll be worth it.

Not wasting another moment, I pushed myself out of the water. With the sodden shirt in my hands, I climbed the bank and hurried to the table.

Judy was sprawled on top, the same way I'd left her.

Sitting on the bench, I dumped the water out of my shoes. Then I put them on again, climbed the bench and bent over her. Starting at her face, I washed her with the shirt. Water spilled off her, running onto the table, dribbling through the cracks between its boards and hitting the ground under the table with quiet splattery sounds.

I thought the water might wake her up, but it didn't. She stayed limp.

I mopped her neck, her shoulders and breasts, then decided I needed more water. So I hurried back to the creek. This time, I didn't fall in. With the shirt sopping again, I returned to Judy and worked my way lower down her body.

I made two more trips to the creek for water.

By the time I was done cleaning Judy, I'd drenched her from head to ankles and scrubbed every inch of her with the shirt.

Every inch of her front, anyway.

I didn't turn her over, or see any reason to.

She gave me no trouble at all, just stayed limp except for a few times when she squirmed. Now and then, she made soft moaning sounds.

I washed the shirt out a final time and put it on the bench with my cut-offs.

It took a while, in the darkness, to find a good stick. There were plenty to choose from, though. I finally came up with a piece of branch about four feet long. At one end, it was just about the right thickness to wrap my fingers around. From there, it tapered down to about half that size. It had a few small limbs along the way, but I snapped them off.

Then I knelt on the table and went back to work on Judy.

Right away, she flinched and cried out and tried to sit up.

I clubbed her down with the heavy end of the stick. Four or five blows to the head and face, and she was limp again. After that, I focused on the places where I might've left bruises with my teeth and hands.

Really laid into her.

The heavy end made thunking sounds when it struck her. The other end whistled each time I swung it down, and whapped her skin like a switch.

She never flinched or cried out. Those early blows to the head had done her in.

At least for now.

Exhausted and drenched with sweat, I went down to the creek. I rolled in the cool water, then lay on my back for a while with only my face in the air. It felt great. But work still needed to be done.

Not quite ready to get going, I stayed in the water and made a list in my head:

1. Make sure Judy is dead.
2. Wipe my fingerprints off her car.
3. Run back to Serena and Charlie's house.
4. Collect the sample off the glass door.
5. Run back here.
6. Add the sample to Judy's body.
7. Go home.

It all had to be finished before sunrise. How much time did that give me? Two or three hours, probably.

Plenty of time.

But not if I spent the rest of the night relaxing in the creek.

So I climbed out and returned to the table. Kneeling on the bench, I put my ear close to Judy's mouth. She didn't seem to be breathing. Nor could I find a pulse at her neck or wrist.

She seemed to be dead.

But I'm no expert on that sort of thing.

I had to be completely sure.

The best way, I decided, was to cave in her head with a rock. Why use a rock? Because I didn't want to fire my pistol again, I had no knife or saber, strangling or suffocating her seemed iffy, and drowning her in the creek would've been too much work. With a good, heavy rock, I could crack open her skull and spill her brains out and *know* she was dead.

To get one, I returned to the creek.

Standing in the water, I reached down between my feet and plucked out a rough-edged rock the size of a baseball.

It should do the job fine.

With the rock clutched in my right hand, I climbed onto the bank and took a couple of strides toward the picnic table.

And stopped.

The top of the table was speckled with moonlight.

A flat, empty surface.

Judy was gone.

Chapter Seventeen

Gone

NO!

She wasn't on the table, but she couldn't be *gone*. Maybe she'd rolled off and fallen.

I ran to the table.

Without enough light to see if she was on the ground, I searched for her with my feet. I circled the entire table, sweeping my feet this way and that, hoping to kick her.

No Judy.

I tossed the rock away, dropped to my hands and knees, and crawled under the table. The ground was soggy.

No Judy.

I crawled backward. Clear of the table, I scrambled on my knees to the bench where I'd left my clothes. My shirt and cut-offs were still there.

So was the pistol.

My panic faded a little.

I stood up, quickly put on the shorts, and pulled the pistol out of my pocket. Turning slowly, I scanned the area. Judy couldn't have gone far. In her shape, she was lucky she'd been able to move at all, much less get down from the table and sneak into the trees.

Unless she had help.

The prowler, for instance.

The idea sickened me with dread, but only for a moment.

Nobody had come to Judy's rescue. I was almost certain of that. I can't explain exactly why, but I'd sensed from the start that we were alone in our clearing by the creek. I'd felt the solitude, the privacy. I'd never doubted it.

'Judy?' I asked. I didn't call it out, but spoke in a normal voice. And knew she was near enough to hear me.

Probably hiding in the bushes of trees just beyond the table, not daring to move because she knows I'll hear her.

'Where are you, Judy? It's me. Alice. Are you all right? I'm sorry I ran off and left you, but . . . I thought you were dead. Somebody ambushed us. Do you remember that?' (I figured her memory might be fuzzy about a lot of stuff, because of being shot in the head etc.) 'You got shot and went down, and I ran for my life.'

I saw no movement in the darkness of the woods. I didn't hear anyone, either.

'Then I came sneaking back and saw this awful woman. She had you on top of the table. She was beating you with something. I wanted to help you, but . . . I wouldn't have stood a chance, you know? I mean, she had a gun. She would've shot me, just like she shot you.'

I stopped telling the story, and listened.

Nothing.

'She finally quit beating you and went away,' I said. 'She ran into the woods. I followed her for a couple of minutes to make sure she was really leaving, then I came back to help you, but . . . Where are you?'

No answer.

I wondered whether she was already out of earshot, or unconscious again – or just didn't believe me.

'It's safe for now,' I told her. 'But that woman might come back pretty soon. You'd better come out. I know you must be scared and confused – and in terrible pain – but if she comes back . . . Please, Judy! I'm scared. Let's get out of here! I'll drive you to the emergency room.'

Drive?

What if Judy *wasn't* cowering in the darkness beyond the table or unconscious or sneaking deeper into the woods?

What if she was circling around me?

Going for her car!

I snatched my shirt off the bench, then whirled around and raced to the slope. I chugged my way up it, pumping hard with my arms, the pistol in one hand, the shirt in the other. The wet shirt slapped my side. My breasts leaped about wildly. Halfway up the slope, one of my loafers flew off. I didn't dare stop for it.

At any moment, Judy might reach her car, climb in and drive away.

I knew it would happen.

It WON'T happen! Look what I did to her! How can she make it to the car? She can't.

But she will.

I was doomed. I'd been doomed from the start of all this, and I'd known it, but I'd resisted.

In my mind, I heard the engine start. I heard it kick over again and again, roaring defeat at me.

But I didn't hear it for real.

Not yet.

Dashing over the crest of the hill, I saw the vague shape of the car in the darkness ahead.

No sign of Judy.

Of course not. She was already behind the wheel, concealed in darkness behind the windshield, reaching for the ignition.

I dodged a picnic table and sprinted toward the car.

With every stride, I expected the headbeams to shoot out and blind me.

But they didn't.

The engine didn't turn over.

The headlights stayed dark.

Nothing happened.

Staggering to a halt, I ducked down a little and peered through the open window of the driver's door.

Nobody there.

Nobody in the back seat, either.

With the last of my energy, I jogged in a circle around the car to make sure it was safe. Then I slipped the .22 into my pocket and pulled open the driver's door. The car filled with light. Squinting, I dropped into the seat. The key was in the ignition. Judy must've left it there when we set out to search for Tony. I jerked the door shut and the light went out.

For a while, I just sat there streaming sweat and gasping for breath.

I could barely put my thoughts together, I was so pooped.

But I knew I'd lucked out. I'd gotten to the car first. Judy had lost her chance to drive away.

My skin itched from the heat and sweat. When I couldn't stand it any longer, I rubbed myself with the shirt. It was still wet. It felt cool and wonderful.

I started feeling better about things.

Nobody ever said it would be easy, I told myself. It's a tricky business, trying to get away with this sort of thing. There are bound to be setbacks.

By and large, I'd handled matters fairly well so far. I would've met with complete success if I hadn't gone to Judy's apartment by mistake.

Pretty big damn mistake.

Bigger for her than me. She'd be dying because of it.

I rubbed my face and chest again, then leaned sideways and

used the shirt to wipe off the interior handle of the passenger door. I also did the window still and dashboard. Then I sat up straight and wiped the steering wheel.

As I did that, I realized that one of my shoes was gone.

Gotta go find it.

Time's a-wasting.

I pulled out the ignition key. With the key case in one hand and my shirt in the other, I climbed out of the car. Again, the light came on. In its glow, I saw the strap of Judy's purse on the floor. She'd apparently shoved her purse underneath the driver's seat.

I started to reach for the strap, then stopped myself.

What do I need her purse for? Just have to get rid of it later, like Tony's wallet.

I would've been better off if I'd never touched Tony's wallet. That's what got me into this.

Finding that paper with the wrong address.

So I decided to leave Judy's purse untouched.

Standing in the V of the open door, I did some more mop-up with my shirt. Then I shut the door and wiped its outside handle.

I dropped Judy's keys into a pocket of my cut-offs, then went around the car to take care of fingerprints I might've left on the outside of the passenger door.

The surface of the parking area was pavement littered by old leaves and twigs. I doubted that my bare foot was leaving any tracks. To make sure, though, I opened the passenger door. The interior light came back on, and spilled a yellow glow onto the pavement. I did a couple of tests with my bare foot. Nothing showed, so I shut the door and wiped it again and took off.

I headed back to the scene of Judy's escape.

She'll be down there, somewhere. Maybe trying to crawl away, or hiding in the bushes.

Maybe watching me.

About halfway down the slope, I found my shoe. I slid my

foot into it. Then I put the shirt on. It stuck to my skin. I left it unbuttoned so air could get in.

About the next step I took, my shoe slipped on the wet grass. I started to drop backward, but caught my balance in time and stayed on my feet.

Close call, I thought. What if I'd fallen and really hurt myself? Bumped my head on a rock, or something, and got knocked out cold? Then *I'd* be the one in big trouble. Judy could come up here and finish me off. Or take her car keys and escape. Lucky thing . . .

Would she?

What if she saw me fall, tumble down the slope, and not get up? Would she come out of hiding?

She might.

Or she might figure it's a trick.

I took a few more strides, then pretended to trip over a rock or something. Yelling, 'AHHH!' as loud as I could, I windmilled my arms, stumbled a couple of times as if trying to regain my footing, then plunged headlong.

I wanted it to look real.

It suddenly was real.

I slammed against the ground. It knocked my wind out and seemed to kick me into the air. I flipped over. The ground kept battering me, shoving me along. I twisted and rolled and flopped, arms and legs flying, all the way to the bottom.

Like Judy after her fall down the same slope, I came to rest on my back.

History repeats itself.

At least I hadn't been shot in the head.

I felt plenty bruised and scratched and battered, though. And I'd lost *both* shoes.

Plus the pistol.

I should've been able to feel its weight against my right thigh, but the pocket had an awful lightness.

So much, I thought, for another brilliant idea.

Now what?

I had two choices. Either forget the trick and go looking for the pistol, or stay on my back and pretend to be unconscious.

I felt vulnerable without the gun. But I could get along without it for a while. I didn't need artillery for handling Judy.

Just stick with the plan for ten or fifteen minutes, I told myself. See what happens.

It might be a waste of time.

On the other hand, searching for her in the dark woods would probably be a waste of time, too. If she'd found herself a good hiding place, and didn't make any noise, I'd hardly stand a chance of finding her. Unless I tripped over her, or something.

This way, at least, was restful.

Just don't fall asleep, I warned myself.

There probably wasn't much danger of that. Though I was worn out, I didn't feel sleepy. I was too tense for that. And too uncomfortable. The tumble down the slope had bruised and scratched me. I felt small pains in a dozen places, and I itched in about a dozen more.

I ached to rub my injuries, scratch my itches.

But I couldn't do it.

Judy might be watching.

Or so I thought, anyway, until she shrieked, '*No!*' into the night somewhere far away.

Chapter Eighteen

Cries in the Night

Either Judy, or someone else.

It had to be Judy, though. A woman's voice, and coming from the right direction. Who else *could* it be?

If it was Judy, she'd missed my tumble down the slope and she wasn't watching me now. My fall had roughed me up, but accomplished nothing. I got to my feet, wincing a couple of times.

Standing there, I searched my pockets. Tony's wallet was still in my back pocket. I still had all the keys, too. Apparently, nothing had fallen out except the gun.

I wiped the sweat off my face and rubbed my hurts and itches and stared into the woods.

Nothing to see.

I heard the trees whispering quietly with the breeze. Birds and crickets and other forest sounds. But not another outcry.

Okay, I thought. What's going on?

She'd shrieked like someone scared witless, or hurt, or both. So, was it real or fake?'

If fake, she must be trying to lure me into a trap. A gutsy move. A crazy move. Hell, I was bigger and tougher than Judy. I'd already beaten the snot out of her. And I had a gun. Her only real chance of survival was to *avoid* me.

But you never know with people. They do weird, stupid stuff sometimes. Especially when they're scared. Maybe Judy thought she could out-smart me.

Maybe she'd figured out a great, flawless trap.

On the other hand, she might be in real trouble.

Either way, I didn't have a choice. I had to go looking for her. And finish her off, unless somebody's already saved me the trouble.

I wasn't going anywhere, though, without the pistol.

I wanted to find my shoes, too, but they didn't matter much. The. 22 mattered plenty.

Turning away from the woods, I searched the grassy area around my feet, looking for the gun. I'd been aware of losing my shoes early in the fall, but didn't have a clue as to when the gun had slipped out of my pocket.

It didn't seem to be nearby, so I began to study the route of my fall. For the most part, the slope was clear of trees. A lot of moonlight got through. Before even starting to climb, I picked out half a dozen chunks of darkness. A couple of them would probably turn out to be my shoes. I saw nothing that might be the pistol, though.

I started trudging up the slope, taking it slowly, hunched over, my knees bent and my arms swaying. I must've looked like a kid playing elephant. It was a nice, relaxing posture. But I was too tired and hot to be comfortable. My shirt stuck to my back with sweat. My eyes stung. My face and chest itched with trickles of sweat.

I started out thinking the pistol would be the real problem. Because it was flat and so much smaller than the shoes, it might disappear in the grass. I even worried that I might not be able to find it at all.

But I found it first, only about fifteen feet up the slope. The way I was bent over with my arms swaying, I almost brushed it with my fingertips before seeing it. The pistol lay nestled in the thick grass. In the moonlight, its stainless steel finish looked gray like dirty snow.

I snatched it up.

Then I rubbed it against the front of my cut-offs to wipe off the dew from the grass.

Afraid of losing it again, I kept it in my hand.

A few minutes later, I came across one of the loafers. I slipped my foot into it and went looking for the other.

One shoe off and one shoe on . . .

'Help!'

This time, I recognized Judy's voice. Or thought so, anyway. It's how she might've sounded, squealing out a plea to be saved.

She's gotta be in deep shit.

Or else a great actress.

But my guts told me this wasn't faked.

So did my skin. Though burning hot and slick with sweat, I felt goosebumps spreading up my thighs and belly and breasts. The hairs on my arms stiffened. Prickles scurried up my back and the nape of my neck. My nipples tingled and got hard. Goosebumps crawled over my cheeks, my forehead. My scalp crawled.

It's pretty much what happens every time I get a strong case of the creeps, the willies, the heebie-jeebies.

And I had them now.

Something about the sound of Judy's cry for help, maybe. Or what it triggered in my imagination.

Something awful had happened to her.

Or someONE.

Something or someone worse than me.

Turning around slowly, being careful not to slip on the wet slope, I stared at the woods. There was nothing to see.

Judy's cries had come from deeper in. The first had sounded nearer than the second. Was she running away from a pursuer? Or was she already caught, and being carried?

If he kills her, I'm in business.

But killing her was *my* job. It gave me a queer feeling to think of it being done by someone else.

Who? My prowler?

I hurried to find the other shoe. No more cries came from the woods while I hunted for it.

Is she already dead?

Did she get away?

This might sound odd, but I didn't want either to be true.

Finally, I found the loafer. I slid my foot into it, then turned around and started making my way down the slope again – carefully. I'd found out the hard way that the slope was tricky and not as gentle as it seemed.

Safe at the bottom, I broke into a run. And ran like crazy until I came to the picnic table. There, I stopped and listened. Mostly, all I heard were my heartbeats and my hard breathing.

What's he doing to her?

The sick bastard.

I thought about what he'd done to the glass door.

Might not even be him.

I stepped past the end of the table, took my usual route to the creek, and knelt in the water. Then I twisted around and sat down on the bottom. A tricky thing to pull off, one-handed. But I managed to do it and keep the pistol high and dry.

No, not because I was afraid of getting my ammo wet.

As a fan of mysteries and thrillers, I've read enough to figure out that most people who write them don't know squat about firearms. (That goes double for the people who make movies and television shows.) One thing I know, and some of them don't, is that ammo won't get hurt by a little dip in the creek.

The reason I kept the pistol high was in case I needed it fast. I didn't want to shoot it and find out, too late, that I had a barrel full of water. I wasn't sure about a .22, but some guns can blow up if you pull a stunt like that.

(Anyway, I just wanted to make that clear. I don't want you to read my book and think I'm one of those idiots who worries about a little water wrecking my ammunition.)

Okay.

So there I was, sitting in the creek and holding my pistol overhead while I rested and cooled off. The water sure felt good. Cool and smooth. With my left hand, I cupped some of it into my mouth.

And there I sat.

Not really wanting to move.

The water felt great, rushing against me. And it tasted great, too. Fresh and woodsy.

But I was wasting time.

Scared to move.

On my right, the woods loomed high, hiding the moonlight. A kingdom of darkness. It was where I needed to go. Judy was over in that direction.

But so was whatever horrible creature or person had made her shriek.

I didn't want to go there.

I felt safe in the creek. And the area to my left seemed even safer. That's where the picnic table was. The one I'd had Judy on. I could see a bit of it through the trees. In that same direction was the slope to the parking lot. And Judy's parked car. And the roads out of the woods.

In that direction, nothing bad would happen to me.

I could even drive away in Judy's car, leave it somewhere in town, and walk home.

I *wanted* to do it.

To put an end to all this. To stop being scared and tired and hurt. To go home and lock myself in my good, safe room above the garage and maybe never come out again.

I *longed* to do that, and forget all about Judy.

And save myself.

Whatever got her might get me.

Leaning forward, I lowered my shoulders and head into the creek.

I would've looked very odd to anyone watching me.

All they'd see was my arm sticking up, holding the pistol high. Like the Lady of the Lake with better weaponry.

I've got a gun, gang. What the hell am I scared of?

I stayed under for a while longer. Then my lungs started to ache, so I came up for air. And struggled to my feet. And trudged through the knee-deep water, my shirt clinging like someone else's sodden skin, my shorts so wet and heavy that they hung low on my hips, ready to fall.

I climbed the bank on the side of the creek where the forest began. With the pistol clamped under my left armpit, I tugged my cut-offs up and tightened the belt. Then I took off my loafers, emptied them, and put them on again.

I was shivering slightly. No matter how hot the air is, it always feels chilly when you first come out of water. Also, I hadn't gotten over being scared.

The pistol gave me enough courage to go on, but it didn't make me fearless.

I was still vulnerable.

After all, a .22 doesn't pack much punch.

And I'd never counted the rounds in the magazine, so I didn't know how many cartridges were left. They were singlestacked, I knew that. Fully loaded, a magazine that size might hold about eight or ten.

I'd already fired one.

And maybe it hadn't been fully loaded to start with.

I could find out how many rounds were in the gun. But not without unloading it. Which didn't seem like a great thing to try. In the dark, I might drop a couple of cartridges and lose them on the ground. Or what if somebody came along while I stood there with a handful of loose ammo?

Doesn't matter, anyway. When I run out, I run out.

Let it be a surprise.

I started walking into the dark woods, keeping the pistol down close to my side, raising my left arm in front of me for protection against crashing into tree trunks or low branches. I walked slowly, unsure of where my feet might land. Very soon, the chill from the water went away. The air again felt hot and heavy. Here, surrounded by trees, I felt no breeze at all.

I walked without knowing where to find Judy.

Just that her cries had come from deeper in the woods, somewhere east of the creek.

I walked slowly in that direction and tried not to make much noise.

Chapter Nineteen

The Search

Soon, I began to think it was a waste of time. I might search till dawn and never find Judy.

How *could* I find her? Miller's Woods went on for miles, and she might be almost anywhere. Maybe I'd already missed her. I might've walked on past her and left her behind. With any step I took, she could've been a hundred yards away to the north or south. Or sprawled unseen in the darkness five feet away.

It would take a huge stroke of luck for me to find her.

And maybe that wouldn't be so lucky.

Maybe I'd be luckier *not* finding her.

If she'd faked the outcries, a trap was waiting for me. If she *hadn't* faked them, I might have to face whatever had torn those shrieks out of her.

Even if I couldn't find Judy, *it* might find me.

It or he.

Probably a he.

Most monsters are.

At any moment, he might jump me from behind. Take me

down and drag me away. Do things to me so I would cry out in terror and pain just like Judy.

The pistol might not do much good if he caught me by surprise. Or if there turned out to be more than one guy.

I knew what it was like. All of it. To be jumped from behind. To be outnumbered. To be beaten and tortured. To be raped, gang-banged, sodomized and all the rest.

No, not *all* the rest.

I hadn't been killed.

Not yet.

I'd been *left* for dead, but not killed.

I'll tell you about it. I hadn't planned on getting into stuff like this, but what the hell. Why should I keep it a secret?

It happened when I was eighteen, and got a flat tire on a highway outside Tucson. I was alone. Alone, I tried to change the flat. But three guys in a pickup truck stopped to 'help'. They helped me, all right. Drove me off into the desert and spent all night 'doing' me, doing everything that popped into their sick ugly heads. By the time they were done with the fun, I apparently seemed to be dead. So they dug a grave for me, rolled me into it and covered me up. Then they drove off and left me. I would've ended up dead for real, but I'd landed at the bottom of the grave with an air pocket under my face. I also would've ended up dead if they hadn't been such lazy bastards. They'd dug the grave too shallow, hadn't bothered to pile some heavy rocks on top, and so I managed to crawl out. Then I was picked up by a family of off-roaders who happened to come along in a Jeep.

You might think nothing would scare me, after being through a deal like that.

But guess what.

It's the opposite. *Everything* scares me.

You've probably heard the saying, 'What doesn't kill me makes me stronger'. It might be true, as far as it goes. I have gotten stronger and stronger from all the bad stuff. But I've also gotten more and more afraid.

So even as I crept through the dark woods hoping to find Judy, I shivered with fear and felt ready to scream and wanted to run for home.

If the fear wasn't bad enough – and it was plenty – I also had accidents. I was trudging through rough wilderness, not hiking on a path through a park. All I could see were a few bits and pieces of moonlight, dim gray blurs that might be anything, and blackness that might be *nothing*.

I hated walking into the black places. I might drop into a pit or step on a body or get leaped on by a madman. And the gray places weren't much better.

Three or four times, I tripped and fell down.

Twice, I scraped the top of my head against low limbs.

Countless times, I was whipped across the face by unseen branches or bushes.

Only once did I get the *real* shaft. Striding through a black place, I walked straight into the end of a large, broken limb. I never saw it coming and didn't even slow down. Just plowed into it. It slammed into me above my belly button. It probably would've plunged all the way through and killed me if it hadn't been so thick. Instead of skewering me, though, the branch gouged me, caved me in, punched my breath out and knocked me backward. I fell sprawling.

For a while, I twisted and squirmed and couldn't breathe.

When I was able to catch a breath, I curled onto my side and clutched my belly. The wound felt raw and seering hot. Not very deep, but awfully painful. I held it with both hands and cried.

Finally, I was ready to get up. I found the pistol on the ground beside me, then struggled to my feet.

Judy no longer mattered much.

I really had no hope of finding her, anyway.

And so what? With or without me, she probably wouldn't leave the woods alive. Not unless she'd faked those cries, which I doubted.

Even if she gets away, I told myself, she doesn't know who I am or where I live.

She knows me face.

So what? Unless she bumps into me at the supermarket . . .

What if she describes me to a police artist?

That could be bad. Sometimes, those drawings turn out to to look exactly like the suspect. I might be watching the TV news in a few days and end up staring at my own face. Most of the people in Chester would see it, too. Even though I pretty much kept to myself, I wasn't a total recluse. I'd be recognized, for sure.

On the other hand, maybe Judy wouldn't be able to describe me. Though we'd spent time together in her well-lighted apartment, she hadn't gotten a good look at me *after* I shot her in the head and pounded the daylights out of her with a stick. It's very common for head injuries to screw up your short-term memory.

That's what I've read, anyway.

In my own experience, I've always been able to remember every detail no matter *where* I got injured, in the head or otherwise.

I wouldn't have minded a little memory loss, here and there. Especially if I got to pick which memories to dump.

Memories can be a real pain.

While I was thinking about all this, I kept on sneaking through the woods. I'm not sure, though, whether I was looking for Judy or for a way out. I just kept moving along, trying not to get hurt again. I still couldn't stand up straight or take a deep breath because of ramming into the branch.

Every now and then, I imagined how it would feel to catch a branch that way in the middle of my face. That was almost enough to make me sit down and wait for dawn. But I kept moving, anyway.

I needed to finish with Judy and get back to Serena and Charlie's house before daylight.

The lawn might have some Tony on it. The saber was still hidden in the bushes. I needed to do a whole slew of other chores, too, like make sure nobody would ever hear Tony's voice on the answering machine, and burn his wallet and . . .

Firelight!

In the distance ahead of me and off to my left, I saw bushes and low-hanging tree branches that trembled with yellow-orange light.

This is it! Has to be!

I made my way slowly toward the glow, trying to be quiet.

Let this be it! Let it be Judy!

I walked as close as I dared to the firelit clearing, then crawled even closer and peered through a gap in the bushes.

And found her.

Found a tent, a campfire, and Judy.

The green tent was pitched a few yards to the right of the fire. The fire, burning brightly, cast its glow far enough to shine on Judy.

Nobody else seemed to be there.

But *someone* belonged to the campsite. Someone had pitched the tent, built the fire, and captured Judy. Someone had *put* her this way.

She stood under a tree limb, her arms high, her wrists tied together. The rope went over the top of the limb. I couldn't see where it came down, but the other end must've been tied to a tree somewhere behind her. She wasn't dangling, or standing on tiptoes, but she didn't have enough rope to let her slouch. She looked as if she were *stretching* for the ground. Her back was arched. Her skin was pulled so taut that all her ribs showed. Her breasts were drawn high. Her belly looked flat and long. She stood with her legs pressed tightly together. Her feet, flat against the ground, weren't tied.

When I'd left her on the picnic table, she'd been wearing her shoes and socks, her skirt, and her blouse. The skirt had been rucked up around her belly and her blouse had been pulled half off, but she'd still had them on. Now, they were gone.

All she wore now was a hat and a gag.

An old, felt hat covered her head all the way down to the eyebrows. Her upraised arms pinned the brim up against its sides. The strange hat must've belonged to her attacker. Maybe he'd jammed it on her head to hold a bandage against her gunshot wound. Or maybe he liked how she looked in it.

The hat made her look like some sort of beautiful hillbilly girl. Maybe the Feds had stripped and tortured her, trying to make her give up the location of her moonshine still.

Of course, she couldn't tell any secrets with the gag in her mouth. It looked like a red bandana. The sort of thing you might see tied around the forehead of Willy Nelson or around the neck of a too-cute-for-words dog. In this case, it was stuck in Judy's mouth and tied somewhere behind her neck.

A gag like that could suffocate someone. But Judy seemed to be okay. From where I watched, I could see her ribcage expanding and contracting. She was able to breathe, if only through her nose.

Her eyes were shut. She couldn't be unconscious, though, and still stand that straight and rigid and hold her head up.

Probably just resting.

She'd had a hard night.

Mostly because of me. Well, *all* because of me, in the sense that I'd dragged her into the whole mess.

Just goes to show what a wrong address can do.

But I'd also been the one who shot her and beat her with a stick. From my hiding place behind the bush, I could see plenty of bruises and scratches and swollen places on her body. Most of them had been put there by me.

Maybe all of them.

Some bastard had grabbed her, brought her here, stripped her, tied her under the tree, shoved that silly hat onto her head and gagged her mouth, but I wasn't sure he'd hurt her.

Don't forget the shrieks.

He'd probably raped her. He *must've* raped her. You don't grab a gal and strip her naked and hang her by a rope, that way, and *not* rape her. Logic tells you that.

I couldn't tell by looking, though.

This may sound funny, but I *hoped* he hadn't done it.

Judy didn't deserve that kind of treatment. She was a beautiful, fine, sweet girl, and I liked her. I never saw her as my enemy. Only as my problem.

She could 'finger' me.

So she had to go.

But not like this?

I hated it to be like this.

But in part of my mind, I knew it was perfect! This was like a best-case scenerio. *I* wouldn't be murdering her at all. And therefore, nobody could ever pin it on me. They'd nail *this* bastard for it, or nobody. And they'd likely figure he's the one who chopped Tony into little pieces, too.

Because of this guy, whoever he might be, suspicion would never fall on me. I ought to be cheering him on.

But I couldn't.

I didn't *want* him to rape her, kill her, touch her.

Weird, huh?

I'm not sure how to explain it. Maybe I'm not even sure *why* I felt that way. It wasn't that I wanted to save her, or spare her the pain, or anything like that.

I mean, I did and I didn't.

I would've *loved* to spare her, but she had to go.

The thing is, I had to be the one to do it.
Not this guy, whoever he might be.
Not this stranger, this interloper, this *thief*.
She was mine, not his.

Chapter Twenty

Choices

Opening her eyes, Judy stared straight at me. I caught my breath. My heart pounded faster.

Can she see me?

I didn't think so. I was well hidden in the bushes.

If I can see her, she can see me.

Maybe so, I thought. But I still doubted that she'd spotted me. She didn't react, just stood there the same as before, stretched tall, her skin agleam in the firelight.

I raised the pistol and took aim.

Judy still didn't react, so she was obviously unaware of me and the gun.

I aimed for her heart.

She was about twenty-five or thirty feet away. That's farther than it sounds, when it comes to hitting a target with such a small handgun.

I could certainly hit her. But *where* wasn't certain at all.

Shooting for her heart, I might just as easily hit her in the neck or shoulder or breast or stomach. I might only nick her in one side or the other.

The chances of killing her with the first shot were slim.

It might take three or four rounds to do the job.

Then what would I have left for the guy who'd brought her here?

And where the hell was he, anyway?

Asleep in the tent? Maybe. Or maybe wandering the woods to gather firewood.

Or sneaking up on me.

When that little idea popped into my head, I got goosebumps again. They went scurrying everywhere. I brought the gun back close to my body and dropped onto one knee. Twisting from side to side, I checked behind me.

Nothing but darkness.

And I couldn't even see the darkness very well. The campfire had ruined my night vision.

My hearing was okay, though. I heard nobody trying to sneak up on me.

Doesn't mean he isn't.

I turned forward again and studied the campsite. Judy's head was now bowed and her eyes seemed to be shut. Maybe she'd fallen asleep or passed out.

Other than that, everything looked the same.

I stared at the tent. It was about as high as my chest (if I'd been standing up) and maybe seven or eight feet long. Big enough for one or two guys sleeping lengthwise. No light seemed to be on inside it. With that kind of material – nylon, I guess – the light would've seeped right through. From where I stood, I couldn't see whether or not the front was open.

The longer I watched the tent, the more certain I felt that Judy's attacker must be inside. Cozy in his sleeping bag, and fast asleep. After all, he'd had a long and busy night. And that's what guys do after they've screwed you – they sleep.

If he *was* asleep in the tent, I could do whatever I pleased.

But what *should* I do?

1. Kill them both?
2. Kill him and rescue Judy?
3. Avoid him and rescue Judy?
4. Avoid him and kill Judy?
5. Avoid them both, go home, and hope for the best?

Other possibilities entered my mind. Most of them involved trying to capture the guy, and what I might do with him afterward. Or what Judy and I might do to him. Or what the three of us might do together.

That stuff didn't seem practical, though.

Too risky.

Basically, I had only the five realistic choices. I gave them a lot of thought. Each had merits and disadvantages. After a while, though, I managed to rule out the plans that involved killing the man.

You don't want to kill your fall guy.

That whittled the choices down to three. Should I kill Judy, rescue her, or go home?

If I went home, the guy would still have her as a prisoner to torture, rape and murder as he wished. From a purely logical standpoint, I couldn't ask for anything better. But I hated the idea. He had no right to her. She was mine, not his.

Which didn't seem like a very good argument.

I mean, this was supposed to be about my survival. If the guy kills her, I'm home free. I'd be a fool to interfere just because of some bizarre emotional thing about Judy.

The logic nearly convinced me to leave her.

But then I found a fairly good argument against it.

What if he doesn't kill her?

It seemed ridiculous, at first. A guy in his position *had* to finish Judy off. You can't let a girl live after this sort of thing. She'll tell on you.

But something might go wrong.

Maybe he doesn't have what it takes to finish her off. Or what if she escapes? Or maybe somebody comes along and scares him away or arrests him or . . . who knows? I could think up plenty of scenarios.

Hell, I'd gotten away a few times myself. I'd gotten out of tougher jams than this one Judy was in.

If I could do it, she could, too. She might not be as tough as me, but she was likely smarter.

Anyway, I just couldn't count on the guy killing her. And that gave me the excuse I'd been looking for. The option of walking away was no good.

That left me with two choices. Do I kill her or rescue her?

Judy obviously needed to be killed. And I should do it quietly, with a rock. But should I do it here, or 'rescue' her and take her somewhere else to do it?

If I did it here, the guy would still have her body. I didn't like certain aspects of that, but I *really* liked the aspect that he might get caught with it.

On the other hand, if I 'rescued' her, we could go somewhere else and have plenty of privacy. I liked the idea of that. I liked it a lot. But disliked the possibility that she might escape from *me*.

Whereas she wouldn't stand a chance of escape if I walked over and bashed her head in while she dangled there.

It was a hard decision.

I kept going back and forth.

I couldn't make up my mind.

So finally I decided not to decide. I would play it by ear.

In the clearing, Judy still hung with her head down and her eyes shut. But the campfire had dwindled. Her skin no longer shimmered so brightly with the golden light. She looked darker now, and less distinct.

If I waited a while longer, the fire might dwindle down to nothing and I would have darkness on my side.

Then again, I might be running out of night.

I'd lost track of time, but figured it had to be after three o'clock in the morning. Maybe even after four. Waiting any longer would be foolish.

Carefully, I stood up. My body felt stiff and sore, but I managed to rise without groaning or making any other sound. With the pistol in my right hand, I crept away from the clearing. Then I slowly circled around to the other side, staying in the darkness. Finally, I approached the campsite from behind Judy.

The fire had dwindled even lower. Judy was little more than a dark shape hanging below the limb, a silhouette against the fire's dim glow.

There was still no sign of the man who had put her there.

From my new position, I could see the front of the tent. Its flaps were shut. I figured he must be inside.

Fast asleep.

Standing motionless for a while, I watched and listened. Then I moved in with slow, gentle steps. Though I tried to be silent, a little noise couldn't be helped. The ground was covered with old leaves and twigs. The leaves sounded like wads of paper crinkling and crunching under my shoes. Some twigs broke like toothpicks. Others snapped like pencils.

I kept my eyes on Judy. She never flinched or raised her head, never reacted in any way to the sounds of my approach.

When I was only a few strides away from her, I realized that I didn't have a rock yet.

Stopping, I squatted and studied the ground. There were old, dead branches scattered around, but no rocks. None nearby, anyway.

Too bad I didn't have the one from the creek.

It's not that there were no rocks in sight. I saw a whole bunch of them. But they were out in the middle of the campsite. Three or four boulders, large enough to sit on, were arranged near the fire. I couldn't really use one of those. But dozens of smaller rocks, stacked about a foot high, formed a low wall around the fire.

Most of them looked to be the right size for pounding out Judy's brains.

Most of them would probably be hot, too. But there had to be some that wouldn't burn my fingers, and I only needed one.

To get it, of course, I would need to abandon the darkness and enter the clearing. Stride out past Judy. Search for my rock out in the open, directly in front of the tent.

Why not?

Judy's head was down and the tent flaps were shut.

Besides, her mouth was gagged. Even if she saw me, she couldn't cry out.

Also, I had the pistol. If things went sour, I could start shooting people.

Before going anywhere, I made sure the safety was off.

The gun shook like crazy in my hand. I was plenty scared. But this wasn't the creepy sort of fear that gives you goosebumps. This was the kind that makes your heart pound like a club, makes you shake like a lunatic and sweat like a glass full of ice in a heat wave. It makes your legs feel so weak you think they've decided, on their own, to keep you from walking into trouble.

But I *made* mine walk.

There's this thing about me. Maybe you've already noticed it. I'm the sort of gal who gets things done. I'll do almost anything, no matter how dangerous or messy or awful it might be, if I figure it's a thing that needs doing.

I wanted a rock, so I made myself go for it.

Staying about five feet away from Judy's left side, I walked softly past her. She just stood there, arms high, head down. Except for her breathing, she didn't seem to move at all.

When I was in front of her, I looked back. I'd expected a better view, but the flames had sunk very low. She was bathed in a murky glow that trembled with shadows as if I were looking at her under water.

I couldn't even tell whether her eyes were shut.

But she didn't act as if she saw me.

I kept walking.

I glanced at the tent, scanned the clearning ahead of me, checked over each shoulder, eyed the tent again, and several times twisted around for a brief look at Judy.

And wished I could see her better.

Darkness was good for sneaking around, and I should've been grateful for it. But I'd expected more firelight. I wanted to be able to see what I was doing – and see Judy.

So when I reached the fire, I crept around to the other side, crouched down by a small pile of wood, and started adding sticks to the shaky remains of the flames.

Chapter Twenty-one

A Hell of a Gal

Within a few seconds, the fire grew brighter. I added more sticks, and larger ones. They crackled and snapped, crawling with flames.

As I built up the fire, I kept watch on the front of the tent. It stayed shut. No light or sounds came from inside.

I added larger sticks and chunks of branches.

It seemed crazy, even to me. Had I lost my mind? Did I want to get caught?

Who knows?

I kept telling myself that nobody wakes up just because a fire outside the tent is getting larger.

But it was getting louder, too. A lot more snapping and crackling. And every so often, a burning stick would go off with a *bam*!

I refused to stop adding wood, though, until the fire was large and bright.

Bright enough for its light to spread over Judy.

When her skin gleamed like molten gold, I stood up. I started to step around the fire, then realized I'd forgotten to grab a rock.

Bending over, I patted a few of the rocks along the top of the fire circle. They all felt hot enough to scorch my fingers.

Neat play.

If I'd been taking care of business, I would've found one *before* building up the fire.

Too late, now.

But the far side of the wall wasn't being lapped by flames, so I hurried over there. Sure enough, several of the rocks were only mildly warm.

After switching the pistol to my left hand, I used my right to pick up one I liked. It was shaped like a large wedge of pie, and must've weighed three or four pounds. Perfect.

On my way over to Judy, I turned around completely a couple of times. The clearing, now alive with firelight, looked deserted. Nobody seemed to be peering out at us from the woods. The tent was dark, its flaps still shut.

Judy's head still hung down. She didn't seem to know I was there.

I slipped the pistol into my pocket, held the rock behind my rump so she wouldn't be able to see it, and walked up to her.

Where my shadow fell on Judy, her shine vanished. I stepped sideways enough to let the firelight reach her.

Her skin was so sweaty she looked as if she'd been rubbed with oil.

'Judy?' I whispered.

She didn't stir.

I slid my left hand gently up her side. She was slick and smooth and hot.

'Judy?' I asked, a little louder.

She still didn't respond. My hand was just below her armpit, so that's where I patted her a few times.

'Judy. Wake up. It's me.'

Nothing. So I gave her a good, solid smack in the same place. Her breasts lurched. With a gasp, she jerked her head up. She looked into my eyes.

'It's okay,' I said. 'I'm here to save you.'

Her eyes flicked from side to side, studying me. She moaned into her gag.

I glanced over my shoulder to make sure nobody was coming. Then I faced Judy again and went into my routine. 'I thought you were dead,' I told her. 'Somebody ambushed us and you went down. Do you remember?'

She shook her head slightly from side to side.

'I ran away. But you were gone when I came back. So I've been looking for you. I've been searching all over. I had no idea . . . Then I saw the firelight. Just hang on, I'll get you out of here.'

She nodded, moaning again.

'I'll take the gag off, but you've gotta be quiet.'

Keeping the rock out of sight, I reached up with my left hand and tried to work the bandana loose. It was too tight. So I stepped around behind her, set the rock down on the ground, and used both hands to work on the knot.

Why was I even bothering?

Why not just bash her head open and be done with it?

Maybe for the same reason I'd wasted time building up the fire. Whatever reason that might've been.

Just to delay things? To put off the moment when I would have to kill her?

Maybe.

How should I know? I'm not a shrink.

All I know is that I needed to take her gag off. After a minute or two, the knot came loose. I untied it and slipped the bandana out of her mouth. I stuffed it into my pocket, then picked up the rock and stepped around to her front.

She was taking deep breaths through her open mouth like someone who'd been held underwater way too long.

'Are you okay?' I whispered.

She nodded, and kept on taking huge breaths.

'Who did this to you?' I asked.

'Don't . . . know.'

'You don't *know*?'

'It's all . . . dark. Blank.'

'Do you remember how you got here?'

Her head shook slightly.

'Or who beat you up?'

'No.'

'Or tied you like this?'

'Just . . . we were walking. You and me. Looking for Tony. And then . . . I don't know. Somebody must've . . . brought me here.'

'But you don't have any idea who?'

'Did Tony?' she asked.

'I don't know,' I told her. 'I never saw who did it, either. But somebody shot you and then must've carried you here. Maybe it *was* Tony. Do you think he would shoot you?'

'I don't know. Yeah. Maybe. He was awfully . . . crazy about me.'

'Does he own a gun?'

'Yeah.

'Maybe it *was* Tony,' I said. 'Do you think he's in the tent over there?'

'Don't know.'

'He might be,' I told her. 'I'm pretty sure *someone's* in it.'

476

'Oh, God.'

She sounded frightened.

'Don't worry. I'll get you out of here.'

'Hurry, okay? Please?'

'Tell me if he comes out.'

She nodded.

'Tell me if *anyone* comes out. We don't know for sure it's Tony.'

'Okay.'

'I'll have to untie you.'

'Okay.'

Not wanting to set the rock down again, I slipped it underneath my shirttail and shoved a corner of it down inside the right rear pocket of my shorts.

Then I reached high with both arms. As I stepped in against Judy, the front brim of her hat shoved me in the face. 'Let's get rid of this,' I whispered, and gently lifted the hat off her head.

She winced.

'Sorry.'

'It's okay.'

Her hair looked wet. Shiny golden curls were matted flat against her scalp. If there was blood, I couldn't see any. But another red bandana, folded into a pad, was clinging to the side of her head above her ear. Her ear had a crusty nick on top. The pistol sight must've done that.

Turning away, I gave the hat a fling. It sailed across the firelit darkness and landed in some nearby bushes.

Just as I faced Judy again, the makeshift bandage lost its grip and fell. It dropped softly onto her shoulder. I stuffed it into a pocket, then looked closely at her gunshot wound.

The bullet had taken an upward course, gouging a path through her hair and scalp. The furrow looked shallow and about half an inch high. The hair around it was stained a rusty color, but the wound didn't seem to be bleeding anymore.

'You were really lucky,' I whispered.

'I don't feel so lucky.'

'It just nicked you.'

'It hurts like crazy.'

'I feel like I've got the worst hangover in history.'

'Must've been the beer.'

'Sure,' she said. And a corner of her mouth tilted upward, trembling. I guess it was supposed to be a smile. The other corner of her mouth, red and swollen from when I'd worked her over with the stick, didn't move at all.

'We'll get you some aspirin,' I told her. 'But first we have to get you out of here.' Reaching for the rope around her wrists, I leaned forward. Our bodies met. I couldn't help that. It was necessary if I wanted to work on the rope. My shirt was open. We were bare against each other except for my shorts.

'Sorry about this,' I whispered.

'It's fine.' When she said that, I felt her breath against my lips. I was slightly taller than Judy, but her head was tipped back. Every time she exhaled or spoke, soft air brushed my lips and entered my mouth.

Our difference in size made her breasts level with mine. Our nipples met. Hers were hard, too.

'Scared?' I asked.

'Yeah.'

'Same here. But don't worry. I'll get you out of this.'

'Hurry, okay?'

'I'm trying. Where are your clothes?'

'I don't know.'

'Maybe they're in the tent.'

'Yeah.'

'Unless he burnt them. Or maybe he left them in the woods somewhere.'

'I . . . they're just gone. I don't know where. I was like this when I came to.'

'This is a tough knot,' I told her. Which was sort of a lie. I was only fiddling with the thing, not really trying to undo it.

'You can get it, can't you?' Judy asked. She sounded worried.

'I'll get it.'

'What if he comes out?'

'Just give me a warning. I'll take care of him.'

'But he has a gun.'

'He does?' I asked, forgetting.

Judy hesitated a moment. Then she said, 'He *must* have one. He shot me, didn't he?'

'Yeah. I forgot about that for a second. My God, if he comes out with a gun, we've had it.'

'Maybe you oughta run and try to get help.'

'And leave you here? No way. We're in this together. You and me, honey.'

Murmuring, 'Thanks,' she eased her head forward. Her cheek brushed against my jaw. Then she rested her face against the side of my neck. 'You're risking your life for me,' she whispered.

'I'm a hell of a gal,' I told her.

'Yeah,' she said. 'You are.'

A few moments later, I told her, 'This knot's *really* giving me trouble. I can hardly hold my arms up.' With that, I lowered them and put them around her. 'Don't worry, I'm not quitting. I just need to rest for a minute.' I gave her a gentle hug. She winced and stiffened. 'Sorry. Did that hurt?'

'Yeah, a little.'

'He must've really done a number on you.'

'I guess so. I don't even know what he did. But I'm . . . awfully sore. All over. Inside, too.'

'The dirty bastard.'

'He'd better not've made me pregnant.'

'Don't worry about it. If we don't get you out of here, it won't matter.'

'Trying to cheer me up?'

'How am I doing?' I asked.

'A lousy job.'

I gave her rump a pat, then said, 'I'd better get back to work.' Reaching high again, I started to fool with the knot.

'If you get me out of this,' she whispered, 'I'll owe you my life.'

'Forget about it,' I said.

'I'll do *anything* for you.'

'Anything?'

'Anything.'

Chapter Twenty-two

Here Comes Trouble

'Okay,' I said. But was she serious? She sure sounded serious, all right. Not only about doing 'anything' for me, but about her memories of what had happened to her.

Her *lack* of memories.

But what if she was lying?

What if she remembered *everything*?

'What's wrong?' Judy whispered.

'Huh?'

'You're suddenly . . . all tense. I can feel it.'

'It's the knot,' I said. 'It's too tight.' Shaking my head, I let go of the rope. I put my arms around her.

'Are you quitting?' she asked. She sounded scared like a little kid in the dark.

'No. No way. I'll never quit on you. I just have to figure out another way.'

'What about the other end of the rope?' she asked. 'He tied it to a tree behind me.' She went rigid. I suddenly knew exactly what she'd meant about *me* going all tense. She felt as if a live current had zipped through her body. But hardly missing a beat, she said, 'Maybe it'll be easier. Why don't you go over and give it a try?'

'You *did* see him,' I said, letting go of her and taking a step backward.

She shook her head. 'I didn't see *anyone*. All I know is that it's tied to a tree back there. I didn't see who did it, or when, or *anything*. I turned around and saw it there, that's all.'

'What are you so nervous about?'

'What do you think? Jeez, Alice. If we don't get out of here, that guy's gonna come out of his tent and kill *both* of us.'

'Is he?'

'*Yes! What do you think is going on?*'

I put my hands on her sides and said, 'Why don't you tell me?'

She stared into my eyes. She was breathing hard again, her ribs rising and falling under my open hands. I could feel tremors running through her.

'Do you think I did this to *myself*?' she whispered.

'No, of course not. But I think you know more than you're telling me.'

'Look, just get me down. Please. I don't care about anything else. I don't care what you did. I just want down from here before he . . .'

'Tell me the truth,' I said. 'The truth shall set thee free.'

'You shot me. Okay? Then you put me up on the picnic table and . . . I don't know what. You were *doing* stuff to me. And then you went at me with a stick or something. I think you knocked me out with it. When I woke up, you were gone. So I climbed off the table and hid in the bushes. And then later I ran for my life. I kept running till *he* caught me. *Now* will you get me down from here? Please? I don't know why you did any of that stuff, and I don't care. I'll never tell anyone. I promise. It's just between you and me, okay? Just get me out of here.'

'You lied about everything,' I muttered. My fingers ached from digging into her ribcage, but I didn't let go.

'I meant it about owing you,' she said. 'I meant that. Get me out of here and I'll do *anything* for you. I'll give you all my money, everything I own. I'll go with you. I'll live with you. I'll be your slave. I'll be your lover. Whatever you want. *Anything*. Just get me out of here.'

'What makes you think I want any of that?' I asked.

'Don't you?' It sounded more like a challenge than a question.

'I'd like to have the truth,' I said. 'How's that? How about the truth right now?'

'Like what?'

'What about this guy?' I asked. 'Who is he?'

'I don't know. I don't *want* to know. He's *horrible*.'

'More horrible than me?'

'You're not so bad. When you're not trying to kill me.'

'Haven't lost your sense of humor.'

'Just get me away from him. Please. I'll never tell on you. I promise. Cross my heart and hope to die.'

'Nobody keeps their word anymore.'

'I do.'

'That's a good one, coming from a liar.'

'I'm telling the truth now,' she said. 'If you get me away from this guy, you'll never regret it. I'll never do anything to hurt you. Never. I'll never say a word against you. I'll *lie* for you. I'll take blame. I'll do whatever it takes. I swear to God.'

'What's he *do* to you?'

'We don't have time. Come on, Alice. If he wakes up . . .'

'*Does* he have a gun?'

'I don't know.'

'How did he get you?'

'He jumped me from behind. I'll tell you everything later, okay? We haven't got time for this. You've gotta untie me. Please!'

'Shhh. Raise your voice, and you'll wake him up.'

'Maybe I *should*,' she blurted. 'Maybe I *will*! Stop screwing around and get me down from here!'

'Shut up!'

'Get me *down*!'

I clamped her left nipple between my thumb and forefinger and twisted it. She flinched and writhed. Breath hissed out around her teeth. 'Just shut up,' I told her.

She jerked her head up and down.

'Now, tell me about our friend in the tent. I take it he's not Tony.'

'No,' she said, and panted for air.

'Who is he?'

'I don't know.'

'What does he look like?'

'Big.'

'Big? What's big?'

'*He* is.'

'How big?'

'I don't know. Don't just keep . . . Do you *want* him to catch us?'

'He doesn't scare me,' I said.

'Then you're dumber than you look.'

I gave her a very hard pinch and twist. She cried out and squirmed. Then, gasping for air, she blurted, 'You stupid bitch, now you've done it. He's gonna come out!'

'I'm trembling.'

'You oughta be! We'll be next.'

'Huh?'

'He's got a body in the tent with him. Some dead woman. He *eats* her.'

'*What?*'

'*He eats a dead woman in his tent!*'

I didn't like the sound of that.

But I didn't have time to give it much thought, because I heard the tent flaps whap open behind me.

Letting go of Judy, I spun around. The weight of the pistol slapped my left thigh. A good thing, since it reminded me that I had it in the wrong pocket.

I went for it left-handed as this *guy* crawled out of the tent.

In spite of Judy's description, I still expected him to be my prowler.

But he wasn't.

My prowler was sleek and handsome.

Not a fat, bald, drooling slob.

He really *was* drooling, too. Slobbering all over the place as he struggled to his feet.

Grunting.

Naked.

Filthy with old blood that looked brown and crusty.

Coated with curly, filthy hair all the way down from his shoulders to his feet.

Only one part wasn't hairy. It jutted out in front of him, so big he was getting drool on it.

He lumbered toward me, hunched over, his arms outspread as if he wanted to give me a bear hug. But he had a knife in one hand, a hatchet in the other.

No kidding.

They didn't look any too clean, either.

He grunted and laughed as he picked up some speed and charged at me.

You've gotta be kidding!

I had this urge to laugh. But what came out was a scream. Behind me, Judy screamed, too.

This might've been hilarious in a movie.

I mean, the guy was such a monstrosity! It crossed my mind that all this was some sort of a gag. But I figured it must be real.

I forced my eyes away from him just long enough to glimpse a shadowy body inside his tent. I couldn't be sure, but it looked like a woman. And it looked dead, to me.

I started firing.

Better late than never. The deal is, I'd had a little trouble with the pistol. I began to go for it when the guy first came crawling out of the tent. But it was down at the bottom of my pocket, and I had to drag it out with my left hand. I'm a righty. So after I got the pistol out, I spent a few moments switching it to my right hand. Only after that did I start pumping bullets into him.

I pulled the trigger fast.

BAM-BAM-BAM-BAM-BAM!

But he didn't go down.

He was backlit by the fire, so I couldn't see where I was hitting him. I *had* to be hitting him, though. I'm an okay shot and this was close range and he was a large target charging straight at me. How could I miss a thing like that?

I couldn't, that's how.

I was hitting him, all right. But the little .22s weren't doing the job.

In another second, he'd be on me. I had Judy at my back, so I dodged sideways, holding fire. He tried to follow me, but he was too big and clumsy. He couldn't change course in time.

Judy kicked out at him. She was probably trying for his nuts. I heard the *smack* sound of her bare foot meeting his skin, but he didn't cry out or drop.

He plowed into her.

His body slammed against Judy and crashed through her, knocking a grunt out of her as he sent her flying backward and upward, twisting at the end of her rope. Stumbling past where she'd been, he managed to turn around and start coming after me again.

Judy came swinging toward his back like Tarzan on the attack. But I don't think she meant to do it. She was at the mercy of the rope and the whims of motion.

She meant what came next, though.

As the guy staggered toward me, Judy raised a slim bare leg and kicked him in the back of his head. She rebounded away from him, spinning wildly.

He grunted, stumbled forward and fell to his knees.

I ran up to him, fired a shot into the top of his shiny head, then pranced backward out of reach, not sure what to expect.

What I *hoped* was that he'd drop like a sledge-hammered bull.

But instead, he squealed and started crawling forward, trying to get up.

I glanced at the pistol. If I'd been out of ammo, the slide would've been locked back. It was forward. Which meant I had at least one more round.

There might be a couple, but I could only count on one.

So I wasn't eager to use it.

As he stumbled to his feet, I hurried around behind the campfire. He lurched toward me, hunched over, arms out like before as if he wanted to give me a big, friendly hug. He still had the knife in one hand and the hatchet in the other.

By now, he had a face of blood from my shot to his head. The rest of his body was a mess, too. A worse mess than before. Now, it wasn't just the woman's old, dry blood. It was *his* blood, too, and plenty of it. It was pouring out of four or five holes in his chest and belly.

Have you ever seen those cartoons where a character gets all shot up, then drinks a glass of water and suddenly he's squirting out of every hole?

It was like that.

Except these holes weren't really squirting. They were flowing like garden hoses when the water is just barely turned on.

A guy shot up like that shouldn't have still been coming at me. And he certainly shouldn't still have a hard-on. What kind of a freak *was* he?

'You're dead!' I shouted as he lumbered closer. 'Fall down, you motherfucking idiot! Don't you know when you're dead?'

He raised his head slowly and grinned at me.

What a nice thing. What lovely teeth. Brown and crooked. Maybe it was just my mind playing tricks, but I thought I could see shreds of flesh caught between some of them.

I gagged.

He stopped just on the other side of the fire. Still grinning, he drew back his right arm. He was getting ready to throw the hatchet at me.

I stuck my own right arm straight out over the fire, shouted, 'Eat this!' and fired.

Instead of going into his open mouth the way I wanted, my bullet slashed his right cheek open and punched a hole through his earlobe.

My slide locked back.

I gasped, 'Shit!'

He hurled the hatchet. It flew at me over the fire, tumbling, coming straight for my face.

I dodged it. The damn thing came so close that I felt a gust of air against my left cheek. And I'd lurched sideways too fast. I stumbled, trying to stay on my feet. Then I fell.

The bastard cried out, 'Ah-*ha*!'

He thought he had me.

As he staggered his way around the fire, I rolled over, got to my hands and knees, and tried to scurry up. My feet slipped on the dewy grass. I fell and banged my knees, and he gained on me.

'Get *away* from me!' I yelled.

He grunted and kept coming.

He was almost on me by the time I made it up and launched myself out of reach.

'Thata girl!' Judy cried out.

Cheering me on from the sidelines.

'Get his ax!' she yelled.

I'd already thought of that.

I'd already spotted it, too. The hatchet lay flat on the ground about fifteen feet beyond where I'd been standing before my fall.

I could get to it, but I needed a lead. I'd have to swoop down and snatch it up. Without a good lead, he might end up on my back.

'Die, you bastard!' I yelled as I ran.

He giggled. *Giggled!* Do you believe it?

Maybe he had a right to giggle. He'd taken all the bullets I could throw at him. Now, he was only a few strides behind me. He'd be on top of me if I slowed down to pick up the hatchet. And he'd probably plunge his knife into my back.

So I didn't slow down, I dived. Slamming the dewy grass, I slid on my chest and belly, my arms reaching out ahead of me. In mid-slide, I grabbed the hatchet with my right hand. As I skidded to a stop, I flipped onto my back.

Grinning, the big boy sank to his knees in the grass just beyond my feet.

He clamped the knife between his teeth, then leaned forward and clutched my ankles. Grunting, he jerked them apart. He started pulling me toward him.

I don't know what the hell he thought he was doing.

Well, maybe he wanted to pull me closer in order to work some sort of mischief on me. If you can call rape and murder mischief, which I'm not sure would be proper.

Anyway, he obviously wasn't thinking straight.

How *could* he, with all those bullets in him?

I slid toward him on the seat of my cut-offs. He kept forcing my legs farther apart as if he wanted to dive between them. Judy dangled in silence from her limb.

When he dragged me close enough, I raised the hatchet high and swung it down with all my might. It got him in the back of the head.

WHUNK!

Chopped him deep, the hatchet busting through his skull and into the mush underneath. Blood and stuff flew up, glistening in the firelight.

He grunted.

He farted.

Then he plunged forward.

Like he had it all planned to land on top of me and pin me down, crush me, suffocate me, kill me with his corpse.

I jerked the hatchet, trying to turn him away. With a slurp, it jumped out of his head and I was left holding it. Before I could scoot out of the way, he bumped me in the stomach. Then his head slid lower as if he wanted to shove it down the front of my cut-offs. It was too big to fit in, though. So it stayed outside. The next thing I knew, it was shoving at my crotch. As he kept on falling, his head acted like a plow and pushed me ahead of him.

By the time he'd finished, I was in the clear.

Chapter Twenty-three

Survivor

Utterly worn out, I lay on my back and figured I might stay that way for an hour or two. But the top of the guy's head was jammed between my legs, big and leaking blood through my cut-offs and making me all sticky down there.

So I squirmed to get away from it.

When nothing of me was touching him anymore, I sprawled and shut my eyes and took deep breaths.

Vaguely, I knew that I had to get up. A lot needed to be done. But I had no interest in moving.

'Alice!' Judy called.

'Yeah?' I answered, not even bothering to lift my head.

'Are you okay?'

'I guess.'

'Is he dead?'

'Pretty sure.'

'That's great. You really did great. You saved our lives.'

'Yeah.'

'Can you come over here and cut me down?'

I didn't answer, just sighed and stayed on my back.

After a minute or two, Judy said, 'Please?'

'What's your hurry?' I called to her.

'This isn't very comfortable.'

No kidding, I thought.

Even though the ground felt good under my back, I wasn't very comfortable, either. I ached just about everywhere. I was sweaty and itchy. And I didn't like how my cut-offs were soaked with the dead guy's blood. I needed a bath and a bed.

'Alice?'

'Yeah?'

'Come on, okay? Please?'

'Yeah, yeah. I'm coming.' I picked up the hatchet, got to my feet, and stood over the body. It wasn't a pretty sight, I can tell you that. You should've seen the butt on this guy. It would've ruined your appetite for a week.

Anyway, I thought about going for his knife. It had fallen out of his mouth when I chopped him. It was probably on the ground underneath him, somewhere in the region of his waist.

Only one problem about getting it.

I didn't want to touch him.

'What're you doing?' Judy asked.

'Nothing.'

I'd managed to keep Tony's loafers on, so I sat down on the grass near the side of Fatso the Friendly Corpse. Drawing in my legs, I swiveled around so my feet were aimed his way. Then I leaned back, braced myself up with my arms, placed the bottoms of my shoes against his hip and buttock, and *punched out*.

His body lurched and shook, but didn't go much of anyplace. So I kept ramming it with both feet, shoving it and kicking it until finally he rolled onto his side as if he wanted to take a look at this gal who was making his life so difficult.

The knife was a little lower than where I'd expected to find it. Good thing I hadn't tried to grab it by reaching under him. I might've gotten a handful of something that wasn't a knife.

Anyway, I picked it up.

The fire had dwindled quite a bit, by then. On my way over to it, I found the .22 on the ground. I couldn't remember dropping it, but there it was. When I put the pistol into the right rear pocket of my cut-offs, I noticed that I'd lost the rock I'd tucked back there.

I kept losing stuff.

It was turning into a trend.

Near the campfire, I set down the hatchet and knife on one of the larger rocks. Then I went to the small pile of firewood and started adding pieces to the flames. Soon, a pretty good blaze was going.

I emptied my pockets to find out what I still had.

The pistol. Two red bandanas and one white handkerchief. Judy's keys, Tony's keys, my keys. And Tony's wallet.

Inspiration striking me, I dropped Tony's wallet and keys into the fire.

'What're you doing?' Judy asked.

'A little house-cleaning.'

I put everything else back into my pockets. Down in the fire, flames wrapped the black leather wallet and key case.

So much for my fingerprints.

I realized, of course, that the keys wouldn't burn. I'm not stupid. Maybe some of the things in Tony's wallet would survive the fire, too. But that was fine. His stuff, being found here in the campsite with everything else, would probably make the cops think Tony was just another victim of Fatso.

I stood there, added more wood, and even turned the wallet over with a stick to make sure it was burning okay.

Then I retrieved the knife and hatchet. I dropped the hatchet into the fire, but kept the knife. After watching for a while to make sure the handle was catching fire, I started toward the tent.

But changed my mind. For one thing, I'd seen more than enough nasty stuff for one night. The remains of Fatso's last victim, last lover, last meal – whatever – were in there. I didn't need to see her close up and personal.

For another thing, why risk leaving evidence of myself inside or near the tent? I happen to know that people *always* leave stuff behind at crime scenes: a telltale hair or fingerprint; samples of their own blood, saliva, semen, etc.; maybe a hat, maybe a glove. This one serial killer in L.A. actually got caught because he lost his *wallet* at the scene of a crime and it had his driver's license in it. Talk about morons!

But here's the deal. I couldn't possibly leave any evidence of myself in or around the tent if I stayed a safe distance away from it.

So I avoided the tent and headed for Judy.

She was all golden and gleaming in the firelight, standing there straight and rigid with her arms high, like before. The gag was gone, but she was breathing hard, anyway.

Gasping for air and staring at me.

'You saved my life,' she said. Her voice sounded rough and shaky.

'I know.'

'I'm not your enemy.'

'Who said you are?'

'Nobody. But look . . . I know you think I'll tell on you, but I won't.'

'Tell about what?'

Looking me straight in the eyes, she said, 'You killed Tony.'

'Really?'

She nodded. 'That was his wallet you threw in the fire, wasn't it? His wallet and keys.'

'Who's to say?'

'Me. You killed Tony. Then you were trying to cover it up, but you came over to my place by mistake. So then you figured you had to kill me, too. Because I'd be able to recognize you. And you *still* want to kill me, don't you?'

'That's right, Sherlock.'

'Well, don't. Okay? You don't have to.'

'Afraid I do.'

'No, look. Like I said, you saved my life. I'm not going to do anything that'll hurt you or get you thrown in jail or anything.'

'It doesn't bother you that I killed your old lover-boy?'

She didn't answer right away.

493

'Come up with a good one,' I suggested.

'It bothers me,' she said. 'Sure it does. We *were* in love. But maybe he deserved what he got.'

'And maybe he didn't,' I said.

'Either way, he became my enemy when he attacked me. And you *became* my friend when you killed Milo.'

'Fatso? You know his name?'

She nodded. 'Milo. That's all I know. And I know that you saved me from him. I would've ended up in the tent.' She shuddered, and I actually saw her chin tremble. She said, '*You're* my friend now. And forever. I won't betray you.'

'There's only one way I can be sure of that,' I told her.

She glanced at the knife in my hand. Then, very quickly, she said, 'No, look, I've got a plan.'

'Let me guess,' I said. 'The plan is for me *not* to kill you.'

'Will you *listen*?'

'I've got places to go . . .'

'I'm Milo's *victim*!' Judy blurted. 'I've got his sperm in me to prove it!'

'You do?'

'What do you think? The first thing he did was rape me. He got me about ten minutes after I ran away from you.'

The idea of it sickened me. That filthy, bloody slob, grunting and drooling on top of Judy while he shoved his vile cock into her.

'I'll tell the cops *I* killed him,' she said.

'Sure.'

'No, listen. I'll say that Tony and I came over to park and mess around. We were going at it on the picnic table when all of a sudden this *stranger* jumps us and kills Tony. See? That gets you off the hook for Tony.'

'I'll be off the hook for Tony the second I kill you.'

'I wouldn't know about that. Maybe, maybe not. But I don't think you really *want* to kill me. You don't, do you?'

'Just go on with your story.'

'Okay. So Milo kills Tony, and I make a break for it. But he catches up to me. I can show the cops right where it happened. My clothes'll be there. Most of them, anyway.'

'Yeah. Your panties are over by the picnic table somewhere. In pieces.'

'I'll say Tony did that. He *has* done it.'

'Yeah.'

'But they'll find everything else in the place where Milo got me. They'll find other stuff there, too, if they really look for it.'

'Like what?'

'You know.'

'Your blood and his semen?'

Nodding slightly, she said, 'And I guess our footprints. Anyway, it'll all back up my story. And then I'll explain about him bringing me to the camp, here, and hanging me up like this.'

'Which he did,' I threw in.

'Right! And the cops'll find that poor woman in the tent, and they'll know I would've been next. They'll figure Milo was some kind of Dahmer. I'll be a hero for killing him. And you'll never enter the picture.'

'How do you plan to explain killing him?'

'Easy. While Milo was asleep in the tent, I got my hands loose and found his gun.'

I switched the knife to my other hand, then reached into my pocket and pulled out the pistol. I raised it in front of her. 'This one, right?'

'Right.'

'It's Tony's gun,' I explained. 'How do *you* get hold of it?'

'Easy.' A smile twitched at the unhurt corner of Judy's mouth. 'Tony took it with him when we were making out on the picnic table. He would've *done* that, too. We came here sometimes, did I tell you that? We hardly ever stepped a foot out of the car, but

Tony knew this was sort of a dangerous area, so he always brought his .22 along, just in case.'

'Why didn't he use it when Milo attacked?'

'It was in the pocket of his jeans, and his jeans were down around his ankles. He couldn't reach it in time. Then, after he was dead, Milo took the pistol. And kept it.'

'Where?'

'In a pocket.'

'A pocket of what?' I asked.

'He was wearing overalls most of the time. You know, *bib* overalls?'

'Cute. The pig dressed up like a farmer.'

'Yeah. And he kept the gun in his pocket. So when I finally got my hands free, I snuck into his tent and found it. But he woke up and came after me. That's when I start shooting him. Just like you did. From there on, my whole story can be almost exactly the same as how it really happened, but it'll be me instead of you.'

'I could leave you the loafers to wear,' I suggested. 'That way, you'd match the footprints.'

'Good idea.'

I nodded, frowning, wondering. 'It's not a bad plan,' I admitted. 'Almost sounds like something *I* might've come up with.'

'It'll work.'

'That's what *you* think.'

'What's wrong with it?'

'Lots of stuff.'

Chapter Twenty-four

Friendly Persuasion

'Like what?' Judy asked. 'What's wrong with my plan? Tell me. Maybe we can work it out.'

'I'm running out of time, here.'

'Alice, look. I'm giving you a chance to walk away from everything. If we can work this out, the cops will think nobody was involved but me, Tony and Milo.'

'Here's one little problem,' I told her. 'Tony's body is in the trunk of his car. Which is parked in the garage of *your* apartment building.'

She gaped at me. For a few seconds, she looked stunned and lost. But she recovered fast. 'Easy,' she said. 'Take my car. Drive to my place, put my car back where we got it, and come back here in Tony's car. Park it where mine is, now. Then just leave his body in the trunk and be on your way. I'll say Milo put him in the trunk. Hey, that'll be perfect! He knocked me out and left me on the picnic table. That way, I'm out cold while he hauls Tony's body over to the car. But before he can make it back, I come to and run into the woods. Then he hunts me down and, you know . . . the rest.'

'That sounds okay. But where are you while I'm driving the cars back and forth?'

'I'll stay right here in camp.'

'Like a good little girl,' I muttered.

'Okay. Well, leave me tied up. But if you do, you'll have to come back and cut me loose after you've dropped off Tony's car. I mean, I can't exactly be found like this or it'll blow the whole story.'

'It'll blow the story if I help you. They'll wanta know who cut the rope.'

'Then just untie the knot.'

I shook my head.

She stared into my eyes and said nothing for a few moments. Then, in a softer voice, she said, 'You don't have to do it now. It can wait till you come back.'

'When I come back?'

'From switching the cars.'

'Oh. Right.' I pulled one of the bandanas out of my pocket, wiped the knife clean, and tossed the knife to the ground. Then I stepped behind Judy.

'What're you doing?' she asked.

'I don't want you yelling for help.'

'I won't. I promise. Don't put that on me. Please.'

'There are other ways to shut you up,' I said.

She didn't argue after that, but just stood motionless while I put the gag into her mouth and tied it behind her neck.

Then I stepped around to the front.

She stared into my eyes. She was breathing hard again, air hissing through her nostrils.

'I'm not switching the cars,' I explained. 'It's a stupid idea. Somebody'd probably see me. Anyway, I'm too tired to play any more games. What I'm going to do, Judy, is leave you here just as you are.'

She nodded slightly.

'I'm not going to kill you. Okay?'

Her nod grew a little more enthusiastic.

'I mean, you helped me out with Fatso. If you hadn't kicked him in the head . . . I don't know, maybe he would've gotten me. So I owe you for that. Besides, none of this is your fault. I just bumped into you by mistake. Wrong address. I was afraid Tony might have a redial button . . . *Whoa!*'

Judy's eyebrows lifted.

We needed to talk.

Instead of bothering to untie the gag, I hooked a forefinger underneath it at each corner of her mouth, pulled roughly, and dragged it down over her chin. The bandana hung around her neck like a dog scarf.

And like a dog, she panted for air.

'What about redial?' I asked. 'Did Tony have it?'

'Just . . . wait.'

'Come on. Did he? I know he moved to a new apartment and you've never been there, but what sort of phone did he have at his old place? He might've taken it with him. Did it have redial?'

'If I tell . . .'

'You'd *better* tell, unless you wanta die right now!'

'No gag, okay? Please?'

I punched her in the belly. A good hard one. Her breath gushed against my face. She couldn't fold over because of the way she was hanging; instead, the blow made her knees jump up and sent her swinging backward.

When she swung forward, I caught her by the sides. I stopped her, held her steady for a moment, then took a couple of steps backward so I could see her better.

Mouth agape, she wheezed for breath. Her eyes were shut tightly. She kept her knees high, so all that held her up was the rope around her wrists.

She *really* looked as if she were being stretched. Her arms and torso actually seemed longer and skinnier than before. Her belly was sunken in. Her ribcage was high and bulging. Her breasts were pulled almost flat against her chest.

'It's okay,' I said. 'Put your feet down.'

She just kept hanging there, gasping.

'Put them down and stand up.'

She didn't.

Instead, she blurted, 'I just . . . I just . . . You didn't have to . . .'

'Shut up and tell me about his redial!'

'Okay. Okay.'

'Stand up!'

She lowered her legs until her feet met the ground. Though she still had to stand tall, she no longer looked as if she were being pulled apart on the rack.

'Now,' I said, 'what about it?'

'He doesn't. Have it.'

'Have you been to his new place?

She shook her head.

'Then how do you know what kind of phone he has?'

'I . . . gave it to him.'

'*What?*'

'His phone. I gave it to him. When we were . . . going together. He . . . I don't think he'd . . . get rid of it.'

'I'm sure he wouldn't,' I said. 'Not if it came from you. And it didn't have redial?'

'No. Huh-uh.'

'Are you sure?'

'I'm sure.'

'You've told me a lot of lies tonight,' I pointed out. 'How do I know this isn't another one?'

'I swear. Honest to God.'

'Why'd you buy him a phone that didn't have redial?'

Her face contorted with confusion or pain or disgust – hard to tell which, since it was sort of battered. She said, 'Huh?'

'If you're buying your boyfriend a new telephone, why do you get him one that doesn't have a redial button?'

'I don't know. It didn't . . . I didn't *buy* it for him. It was my *old* phone. I got a new one . . . I was going to throw it away, but . . . he asked me for it. So I gave it to him.'

'Why do you want to lie about a thing like this?' I asked her.

'I'm not lying.'

'Did you forget about Tony's *answering machine?*'

'No. That's what it was . . . an answering machine. The one I gave him.'

'I don't think so. Tony told me that you never *had* an answering machine.'

'But . . . That's not so.'

'Oh, yes it is. Why did you lie about it?'

'I didn't. Honest.'

'You lie like a rug, Judy.'

'So do you.'

'But I'm *running* this show,' I said, and started to unbuckle my belt.

'What're you doing?'

I pulled the belt out of its loops, and my cut-offs fell down. I stepped out of them.

'Hey,' Judy said. She sounded like a kid again. 'Come on, Alice. Don't.'

'Admit you lied.'

'Haven't you hurt me enough?'

'I saved your life. Remember? You said I can do anything I want.'

'Why do you want to *hurt* me?'

'Because you lied. Admit you lied.'

'Okay. I lied. Okay?'

'You didn't give him his phone?'

'No.'

'You wanted me to leave here thinking he *didn't* have redial. Why?'

'I don't know.'

I swung the belt. My sidestroke, at a slightly downward angle, caught her just above the hip then curled around and lashed her across the buttocks. She jerked and gasped.

'Why?' I asked again.

'I don't *know* what he's got!' she blurted.

'Then why did you lie?'

'You won't . . .'

'Won't what?'

'Believe me.'

'Try me.'

'It was just . . . just because . . . I didn't want you to worry.'

'*What?*'

'Your . . . You must figure . . . redial's got your number. If he *has* it. You're scared.'

'*Does* he have it? Do you know?'

'He's got it.'

'Shit!'

'It's . . . I know his answering machine. It's got . . . everything.'

'*Fuck!*'

So then I sort of lost it.

I whipped the hell out of her with Tony's belt, lashing her with all my strength, circling her as I swung.

Finally, my arm fell to my side, spent. The belt swaying by my leg, I stumbled around to Judy's front.

She was limp, her feet on the ground but her knees bent, all her weight on the rope again.

The fire had burnt down low, so I couldn't see her very well.

I staggered over to it, squatted, and added some twigs and branches. I could hardly catch my breath. Sweat poured off me. The shirt was clinging to my back and my loafers felt slimy inside. I didn't like being this close to the fire. It was too damn hot. But I wanted the fire bright, so I kept adding fuel for a while.

Finally, the light reached Judy and turned her to polished gold. Along with her other injuries, she now had stripes. In some places, the stripes bled. All down her body, her skin was shiny with blood and sweat.

I rose from my squat and hobbled over to her.

She was panting for breath and crying. It made her shake a lot.

I picked up my cut-offs, then stood to the side and watched her.

She was *really* shaking. It made me wonder if she had a fever.

'Sorry you made me do that to you,' I said.

She raised her head and looked at me.

'Now, I suppose you'll tell on me.'

Her head moved slowly from side to side.

'No?' I asked.

When she spoke, her lips made some small bubbles. Red bubbles of spit and blood.

She said, 'You . . . saved . . . me.'

'You're not gonna tell?'

'Milo . . . did . . . it.'

As I worked Tony's belt into the loops of my cut-offs, I said to Judy, 'How do I know you're not lying again?'

She didn't answer.

I fastened the belt, then looked down at the knife on the ground.

I knew that I ought to finish her off.

I'd told her that I wouldn't, though. And besides, you should've seen her. She looked so vulnerable and hurt, hanging there in the firelight. And so beautiful. And she had that bandana hanging around her neck.

I bet you couldn't have killed her, either.

'You'd better not tell on me,' I said to her. 'If the cops ever come looking for me, I'll hunt you down. And what I'll do to you . . . you'll wish I'd left you for Milo.'

She moved her head slowly up and down.

'Hang in there, honey,' I said. And then I left.

Chapter Twenty-five

On the Way Out

Dumb, I know.

Just call me Miss Sentimental. I knew better than to walk off and leave her alive, but that's exactly what I did. My heart got in the way of my brain.

I'd gotten to like her. That was the problem. It isn't easy to kill someone you like. Let that be a warning to you.

Of course, as I wrote early on, it's better not to kill anyone at all. Hell, look what happened to me all because I got carried away and whacked Tony with my saber. An *accident*, and look at all the shit that's already flown because of it. And we've still got plenty of book to go, so you don't even know the half of it yet.

You give some poor jerk a chop in the head and you're in for a world of troubles. So try not to do it.

Anyway, I left Judy behind, hanging by the rope and pretty beaten up – but alive – and hurried out of the clearing.

After so much time with the firelight, the woods seemed blacker than a pit. I walked slowly, feeling my way with both hands, trying not to crash into anything or fall down again. Before long, I'd lost all sense of direction and didn't know *where* I was.

Somewhere in Miller's Woods, that's all I knew for sure.

But I still had high hopes of finding my way home before dawn.

As I trudged through the woods, my night vision returned. No longer completely blind, I could make out the shapes in the darkness.

I kept thinking about how stupid I'd been about Judy. If only

I'd finished her off, I would now be completely in the clear. The cops would never in a million years connect me with anything.

Now, I was in Judy's hands.

She probably *would* finger me. Why not?

Because I'd saved her from the clutches of Milo?

I'd also spared her from myself.

I mean, I'd hurt her, but I hadn't killed her. So, really, I'd saved her life *twice*.

She *owed* me, and she knew it, but she would probably spill everything to the cops anyway. As you may have noticed, she's a goody-two-shoes. A regular Girl Scout. A gal like her might be grateful to me and she might lie sometimes – for instance, if she's trying to pull a trick on someone planning to kill her – but she'll have this compulsion to be truthful to the cops.

She'll rat me out.

Which wasn't exactly a sudden revelation. I'd known it all along. Sort of. Even while she'd been telling me about her big plan to leave me out of the picture, I'd never quite believed she would carry out her end of it.

Maybe she'd *thought* she would.

Or maybe the whole business had been a lie to save her ass.

Well, *something* had saved her ass. I'm not sure what. Maybe a combination of things.

Such as a ton of luck. Plus the facts that she was beautiful and friendly and all that. And I knew it was only by a mistake of mine that she got dragged into this whole mess in the first place. Then I had to feel sorry for her because she'd gotten herself raped by Milo. Then I had to feel grateful because she kicked him in the head. Then she confused me with promises about never telling on me.

Those are probably some of the things that saved her, but maybe not all of them.

Who knows why stuff happens?

Not me, that's for sure.

I'm *interested*, and I like to look for answers, but the answers don't seem to be very simple and I've got a feeling that there're secret forces at work. Genes, for instance. Or Fate. Or God. Or gremlins. Or certain stuff you don't want to admit, not even to yourself. I mean, who the hell knows? Maybe we aren't even *supposed* to know the real answers.

Maybe 'the truth *is* out there,' like they say on the TV show, but that doesn't mean we can ever find it out.

All I knew for sure was that I *didn't* kill Judy, so now my life was in her hands.

It made me feel like a patsy. A softie. A dope.

But it made me feel good, too, somehow. I liked knowing that she was still alive back there at the camp. And that she was only alive because of me.

In a few hours, she would probably be back in her apartment.

Even if she couldn't get out of the rope, somebody would be sure to find her soon.

Maybe not.

Though I knew Miller's Woods pretty well (at least in daylight), I wasn't exactly sure where the campsite was located. It might've been in a remote part of the woods, not close to any trails. I mean, if you're going to do what Milo'd been doing to people, you'd make sure to set up camp where a bunch of nature lovers won't stumble into it.

He must've had plenty of confidence in its remoteness, or he wouldn't have built a fire. He'd not only built the fire, but he'd left it burning – and Judy dangling – while he went to bed in his tent.

That's confidence.

Or stupidity.

He must've been awfully sure, too, that he'd tied Judy so well she didn't stand a chance of getting loose.

What if she can't get loose and she doesn't get found?

She could die at the end of that rope.

That'd be fine, I told myself. If she dies that way, it won't be my fault. Milo put her there, not me. But she'll be just as dead, so she won't be able to tell on me.

I wondered how long it would take her to die that way.

A few days?

Hell, somebody would probably find her before that. Or she'd work her way out of the rope.

I could go back and save her.

Yeah, right. In my condition, I'd be lucky to make it home. I sure couldn't turn back, now, and go hunting for the camp.

Maybe tomorrow. Get some rest, and go looking in daylight.

1. Why would I want to?
2. I probably couldn't find the campsite again, even if I tried.
3. If I *did* find it, the cops might be there waiting for me.

Maybe I'm a sentimental fool, but I'm not crazy.

Eventually, after trekking through the woods for at least an hour, I made my way into familiar territory. I'd really hoped that I might come out in Serena and Charlie's back yard, but it didn't work out that way. The familiar territory was only the creek.

But I sure was glad to find it.

I worked my way out to the middle of the creek (without falling!), sat down, leaned back, and let the wonderful, chilly water rush all over me. It felt so good it hurt.

I was in awful shape. I'd never been so worn out in my life, and I still had a long hike home. At least a mile through the woods. It made me almost cry, just thinking about it.

The night was still dark, though. I still had time. So I lay in the water with just my face out, and rested for a while. Soon, the water didn't feel so cold. It seemed cozy and almost warm.

A nice bath. Gotta have a nice, long bath when I get home.

Then I thought about how to get there. I'd made the hike between home and the picnic area many times during my three years living above Serena and Charlie's garage. Never in the dark, though. I'd always been afraid of the woods at night.

They even frightened me a little in daylight. Though I loved the solitude and quiet, I'd always been aware that someone might be lurking nearby, watching me, stalking me. Not that I'd ever discovered anyone doing that sort of thing. But I'd felt the potential. I'd even felt the urge, myself, to sneak around and spy on other people I found in the woods.

A few times, I'd surrendered to the urge.

But that's another story.

The deal is, I knew how to get home from the picnic area by hiking through the woods. But I wasn't too sure about doing it at night. The trails got tricky in places. I might miss a turn-off and end up lost. There were slopes and ditches to contend with. I might take a bad fall. Or walk into a broken limb and skewer myself.

What about taking Judy's car?

At first, the idea seemed incredibly idiotic. For one thing, somebody might see me driving it. For another, what would I *do* with her car afterward? Where would I leave it?

I'd be asking for trouble.

On the other hand, I had Judy's keys in my pocket. Her car was waiting for me just up the slope from the creek and it could get me home in less than ten minutes.

Fantastic!

I'd park it in the garage, directly under my room, where it would be safely hidden. I could dispose of it later – tomorrow night, for instance.

I was awfully tempted.

It'd be so easy!

But it'd be so *incriminating*, too. What if I got caught with Judy's car?

Then came a thought that changed everything.

If I leave it here, somebody might get suspicious and go looking for her.

That settled the matter.

With her car gone, no park personnel or random visitor or cop would start wondering who it belonged to. And if a friend or relative should report Judy missing tomorrow or the next day, her car wouldn't be found in Miller's Woods to give searchers a starting place.

I *had* to take it home.

Feeling fairly rested and revived and eager to get started, I stood up in the creek and waded ashore. Then I crouched in the bushes for a couple of minutes to make sure the coast was clear. I didn't see or hear anyone. So I walked over to the picnic table, my shoes squelching with every step. At the table, I sat on the bench, took off my loafers, and dumped the water out of them.

I put one of them back on, then changed my mind.

They were Tony's shoes. Evidence. I really didn't need them anymore, since I planned to be driving home instead of walking. Also, disposing of them here and now would save me from having to deal with them later.

I still had one bandana, and used it to wipe the shoes clean. Then I threw them into the bushes behind the picnic table.

For a while, I thought about getting rid of the rest of Tony's stuff. But that would mean driving home naked. I might get away with it, but the risk was too big. If I happened to drive past a cop . . .

Besides, everything except the belt would be easy enough to burn.

And *none* of it could be traced back to Tony, I was pretty sure of that.

Barefoot, dressed in nothing but the cut-offs and shirt, I walked away from the picnic table and headed for the slope below the parking area. I couldn't see Judy's car. It had to be up there, though.

It better be!

I trudged slowly up the slope. The dew made the grass slippery.

I remembered the big, fake tumble I'd taken on this very hillside in hopes of tricking Judy. And how the pistol had fallen out of my pocket.

Suddenly alarmed, I slapped my pockets.

No pistol!

For a moment, I thought I'd lost it again. Panic hit me. But then I remembered that I wasn't *supposed* to have it. I'd gotten rid of Tony's pistol on purpose, back at the camp.

What a relief!

But then, still in a fret, I checked the soggy pockets of my cut-offs to make sure I hadn't lost the keys.

I felt only two sets.

Which scared me all over again until I recalled that I'd thrown Tony's keys into the fire and I only *wanted* to have two sets: mine and Judy's.

What if I tossed in the wrong keys?

With a groan, I stopped climbing the slope and pulled both key cases out of my sodden pocket and studied them. I recognized my tan leather case right away. But I wasn't too sure about Judy's.

Find out soon enough.

I hurried the rest of the way up the slope, trying to ignore the nasty cold feeling in my stomach. At the top, I spotted Judy's car.

It was still the only car there.

Breathless from the climb, I walked slowly over to it.

After checking inside and underneath the car to make sure I was alone, I opened the door. The overhead light came on inside. I climbed in and shut the door.

And hoped I hadn't thrown the wrong keys into the fire.

It wouldn't have surprised me much, the way things had been going so far.

The first key I tried didn't fit.

But the second did. I twisted it, and the engine started.

'All *right!*' I blurted.

Keeping the headlights off, I backed up and turned around. I drove out of the parking area. Enough dim light came down through the trees to let me see the pavement of the road out. I didn't put the headlights on until I came to the main road north of the woods.

Chapter Twenty-six

Home at Last

You might find this hard to believe, but I made it back to Serena and Charlie's house without any trouble at all. I saw nobody. Every road I traveled was empty. I could hardly believe my luck, especially figuring how lousy most things had gone that night.

The night was still dark, but starting to get pale in the east by the time I swung into the driveway.

I checked the front lawn on the way by, but couldn't see much. So I drove ahead, stopped in front of the garage, and climbed out of the car. Standing there, I scanned the rear of the house, the pool area and lawn, and the dark border of the woods.

Everything looked fine.

No sign of my prowler.

The truth is, he didn't worry me.

For one thing, I figured he was probably long gone by then.

I'd made him think I was on the phone with the cops, so this was probably the last place where he wanted to be.

For another thing, I was too worn out to care.

Also, I'd killed Milo the Monster, so what did I have to fear from a nice, clean-cut pervert like my prowler?

Just *let* him come, I thought.

Over by the side of the garage door, I tapped the code number into the key pad of the remote control box. The motor hummed and the door started its noisy rise.

I returned to Judy's car. When the garage door was all the way up, I drove inside and parked in the empty space beside my own car.

The space was where Serena and Charlie sometimes parked their Land Rover. Not often, though. They rarely bothered to put it in the garage. Usually, they parked on the driveway so they'd be close to the house.

But they were gone for a week, and so was their Land Rover.

Nobody would have any reason to open the garage door and find a stranger's car inside.

I killed the headlights and engine, removed the key from the ignition and shoved the key case into my pocket. Leaving the windows down and the doors unlocked, I climbed out. I glimpsed Judy's purse on the floor, but didn't touch it.

The garage door was still open. Nervous about that, I hurried over and thumbed the button to start it shutting. As it rumbled down, I returned to Judy's car and closed the driver's door. Then I went to the side door of the garage and let myself out.

With that door locked behind me, I gazed up the stairway to my room.

And wanted to climb it.

Go in and clean myself up and fall in bed and not get up for hours and hours.

But I had a few matters to take care of, first.

Such as the saber.

I found it in front of the house, hidden in the bushes. Leaving it encased in the denim legs of Tony's jeans, I carried it to the front door. The door was locked, of course. In my key case, though, I kept a full set of house keys. It took me a minute to find the right one, but then I unlocked the door, let myself in, and set the sword down on the foyer floor.

Then I went out again to look around. The sky was slightly lighter than before. It looked like dusk – the way things are in the evening a while after sundown and just before night takes over. Not the greatest for trying to see. I would need to inspect the area again in daylight. But I had to do it right away, even in such mediocre light, just in case there might be something nasty in plain sight.

A finger, for instance.

An ear.

Whatever.

First, I inspected the driveway between the house and the road. Then I walked back and forth a couple of times on the road in front of the house.

Everything looked fine.

So I returned to the front lawn and started traipsing over it, head down, studying the grass. This search paid off. I found a few small pieces of Tony. Some skin and muscle, I guess. Nothing anyone would be likely to recognize as human, but I picked them up, anyway. You can't be too careful about such things.

The left front pocket of my cut-offs had nothing important in it – just a bandana and hanky, so I stuffed the pieces in. Better than carrying them around in my hand, I figured. But they didn't feel very pleasant. There was nothing between them and me except a thin, wet layer of cloth. They sort of rested against my thigh, soft and gooshy. I tried to tell myself this was no worse than wandering around with some raw chicken in my pocket. It didn't help much, though. For one thing, I've never roamed around with raw chicken in my pocket. I mean, who does? I really couldn't trick myself into thinking it wasn't Tony.

I felt pretty disgusted and crummy.

This was the sort of thing you'd find *Milo* doing.

With the stuff in my pocket, I couldn't concentrate too well on my search anymore. So I decided to quit and try again later.

Before going back into the house, I sat on the stoop and checked the bottoms of my bare feet. They were wet. Bits of grass and leaves clung to them. I didn't see any blood, though.

I took off my shirt and used it to clean my feet. Then I went inside, carrying it.

In the kitchen, I turned on the light and made sure the curtains were all shut. Then I draped the shirt over the back of a chair. Stepping up to the sink, I dug into my pocket and pulled out the Tony parts. They were slimy. They also had some ants crawling on them, which didn't make me feel too great about hauling them around in my pocket. I stuffed them down the garbage disposal. With water running, I switched on the disposal to grind them up.

Then I washed my hands very quickly, snatched my shirt off the chair and rushed over to the laundry room, which was just off the kitchen.

I tossed the shirt into the washing machine, then whipped off my belt. My cut-offs dropped to the floor. I stepped out of them. Standing there bare naked, I checked myself for ants. I was feeling itchy, but couldn't find any critters. So I picked up the cut-offs and emptied the pockets. The shorts, hanky and bandana went in with the shirt.

I set the keys aside, added detergent to the wash, and started the machine. While it was filling, I hurried to the foyer and slipped the saber out of the denim legs. Sword in one hand, legs swinging in the other, I returned to the laundry room. I tossed the legs into the machine with the other stuff.

Back in the kitchen, I stood at the sink and washed the saber. It *looked* clean even before I started. I must've done a pretty good job on it with the hose. But I scoured the thing with a rag and liquid soap, being especially careful to get at the crevices where the blade joined the handle.

You can never get rid of *all* the blood. That's what I'd read, anyway. Police investigators would take the sword apart and find traces, no matter what I might do.

I wasn't doing this for the police.

I was cleaning it so Charlie or little Debbie wouldn't notice blood on the saber next time they took it down to play 'charge' or 'Peter Pan' or something.

With a dish towel, I wiped every bit of water off the sword. Then I dried my own bare front, which had gotten splashed.

On my way into the living room, I changed my mind about hanging up the weapon right away. What if some water or blood was trapped inside the handle, and leaked on the wall?

Besides, I sort of liked having it handy.

So I took it with me.

In the den, I set it down and turned on a lamp. Right away, I looked toward the sliding glass door where my prowler had been. I couldn't see it, though. The curtains were shut.

Thank God.

What I *didn't* need to see, on top of everything else, was the mess my prowler had left behind.

With a feeling of relief – and a touch of nausea just from thinking about what he'd done – I turned my attention to the answering machine. It blinked a tiny red light to let me know we had a message.

I poked the 'new message' button.

The quiet hiss of rewinding tape seemed to last a long time. When it stopped, Tony said, 'Ah, you finally got yourself an answering machine. Hope it's not because of me. But it probably is, huh?'

Listening to him, I felt strange.

515

So much had happened in the hours since he'd made that call. Especially to him.

But my own life would never be the same, either. Nor would Judy's.

Or Milo's, for that matter.

All because Tony had dialed a wrong number.

He'd probably only been one digit off, or reversed something. And *WHAM!*

Just goes to show what can happen because of a little mistake.

'The thing is,' he was saying, 'I'm not going to call again.'

How right you are, I thought.

But I didn't laugh, I wrinkled my nose.

And kept listening.

He sounded like a pretty nice guy.

When he started in about moving to a new place, I pulled open a drawer of the telephone stand and hunted for something to write with. There were plenty of ballpoints and pads of paper. And some miniature tape cassettes. I snatched up a pen and note pad just as he started to give his new phone number.

While I was busy writing, his call ended.

That's because I had picked up and blurted, 'Tony!'

My voice wasn't there. Nothing else was there. The tape stopped, and the machine made a few beeps to let me know there were no more messages.

I frowned at Tony's phone number for a few moments, not sure why I'd bothered to copy it down.

Maybe it would come in handy for something.

But probably not.

It was only on paper, though. I could burn it easily enough, later on – along with the rest of the note pad, so nobody would ever be able to discover the *imprint* of Tony's number.

For now, though, I had another matter to deal with.

I opened the answering machine, pulled out the tape, and replaced it with a spare cassette from the drawer.

Then I stood there, staring at the machine and wondering what to do next.

Get everything together.

Seemed like a good idea. With the note pad and cassette in one hand, I picked up the saber. Then I headed for the laundry room. Along the way, I noticed my favorite blue silk robe draped over a chair in the living room, where I'd put it such a long time ago. It had pockets and I needed pockets. But I was awfully hot and sweaty and dirty, so I decided to save the robe for later.

I walked on through the kitchen and entered the laundry room. The washing machine was still going, of course. My belt lay on the floor, and the two sets of keys were on a shelf beside the washer.

Except for Judy's car and the odds and ends in the washer, that was everything.

I wanted to keep it all with me.

But I left it in the laundry room for a couple of minutes while I rushed into the kitchen. Serena keeps a drawer full of small bags. I grabbed one, returned with it, and loaded it up with the two sets of keys, the tape cassette and note pad. I wound up the belt and stuffed it inside, too.

Leaving the washer to finish its business, I carried the saber and bag into the living room. There, I grabbed Charlie's robe.

In the hallway, I stopped just long enough to flick the air conditioner on. Then I went to the end of the hall and entered Serena and Charlie's bedroom. It was dark with the curtains shut. I didn't turn any lights on, though. I just walked straight through to the master bathroom.

I swung the door shut with my elbow, bumped it with my rump to make it latch, then elbowed the light switch. I needed a hand, though, to lock the door. So I held the sword between my legs and thumbed down the lock button.

After that, I hung the robe on a hook. I set my bag on a

counter near the sink and took the saber with me to the sunken bath tub.

I set it down on the tile floor beside the tub.

Not that I'm paranoid, or anything. I just wanted to be safe. And what good is a weapon if it's out of reach when you need it?

While the tub was filling, I used the toilet. Then I stood in front of a full-length mirror and looked at myself.

What a wreck.

My hair, dark and clinging to my scalp, looked as if I hadn't shampooed it in a month. Everywhere, my skin looked greasy. I must've had about two dozen scratches on my front and back. Several of them had bled. I didn't have much blood on me, probably thanks to spending time in the creek. But some of the scratches looked like bright red threads across my skin. I had plenty of welts and bruises, too.

The grand-daddy of all my injuries was my stomach, where I'd walked into that broken branch. It had rammed me and gouged me raw. Skin was ruffled up around the edges of the wound, and I had a bruise the size of a grapefruit.

Nothing looked bad enough to require medical attention, though.

I'd gotten off lucky.

At least compared to a few other people I could think of, such as Tony, Milo, the gal in Milo's tent, and even Judy.

Three out of four needed a coroner, not a doctor.

I wondered how Judy was doing.

Probably still hanging there. Her wrists had been tied together *very* well. She might not be able to get loose at all. Not without help, anyway.

Watching myself in the mirror, I raised my arms high and crossed my wrists. I stood as Judy had been standing, probably *still was*. It made my breasts lift and my belly sink in. I've got a terrific build, but I looked even better that way.

Anybody would, I guess.

Maybe that's why guys like to string up their victims by the wrists.

No. It might be one of the reasons, but not the main one. I'd spent enough time with Judy to know the truth about that. I sure did like how she looked so stretched and taut, but more important was that her whole body was right there dangling in the open. Nothing was hidden.

You had total access.

You could swing her. You could spin her. You could wander around her, look at any part of her. You could pick up her legs and spread them apart. Touch any part of her. Hurt any part of her.

I turned around slowly, staring at my reflection in the mirror.

And wished I could see Judy again.

Chapter Twenty-seven

Splish-splash

Over at the tub, I shut off the faucets and eased myself down into the deep, hot water. It made my scratches sting a little, and felt like burning oil on the raw gouge from the branch. None of the really bad pain lasted more than a few seconds, though.

I leaned backward, easing myself down. Soon, my whole body was submerged except my face. The back of my head lightly rested against the rear of the tub. My buttocks lightly rested on the slippery tiles of the bottom. Nothing else of me touched the tub. I felt cool air on my face. Everywhere else was water. Its liquid heat surrounded me, wrapping me, caressing me softly all over, whispering in my ears, licking me between the toes and sliding into every crease and crevice.

It was luscious.

Heavenly.

After so many rough hours of fear and pain and strenuous labor, I'd come to a place of peace. My arms drifted beneath the surface, weightless and limp by my sides. My legs, open and bent at the knees, lingered at mid-depth as if held off the bottom by ribbons of silk. I heard little more than the quiet lapping of water. My muffled heartbeat sounded calm. Breathing slowly, I felt hot currents rub against my chest and breasts.

I supposed it would be a good idea to sit up, soap myself and shampoo my hair. But I couldn't force myself to abandon the luxury of lounging motionless.

Suspended in the lazy heat.

After a while, my mind seemed to slide off into the air and drift out over the woods. I wasn't searching for anything, just drifting. But when I saw the glow of a campfire, I went down for a closer look.

I found Judy suspended from the limb like before, shiny as oil and glowing with firelight. She still wore the red bandana loose around her neck.

But all her injuries were gone.

She looked beautiful.

As I walked up to her, she said, 'I knew you'd come back, Alice.'

'Then you knew more than me.'

'I've *always* known more than you,' she said, and gave me a sly grin.

'I didn't even know how to find this place,' I told her.

'How *did* you find it?'

'Just luck. It's been my lucky night.'

'Mine, too,' Judy said.

'How do you figure that?'

'You came back for me, didn't you?'

'Yeah. I did. I couldn't just leave you here.'

'You're such a softie.'

'That's me,' I said, and smiled.

'Give me a kiss, you softie.'

Her words shocked me, thrilled me. I laughed and shook my head. 'No, I don't think so. Thanks anyway, but . . .'

'You don't have to be afraid of me,' she said.

'I'm not afraid of you.'

'You love me, don't you?'

'No!'

'You came back because you love me.'

'That isn't why.'

'Then why?'

'Only because it was wrong to leave you here. And because I don't want you to die like this. I wouldn't be able to stand it if you died like this. You never did anything to hurt me. And you helped me with Milo.'

'You love me, don't you?'

'Stop saying that.'

'Kiss me, and I'll stop saying it.'

'I don't want to kiss you.'

'Yes, you do.' She slid her tongue slowly across her lips, moistening them so they glistened. 'Don't worry. It won't hurt a bit.'

'I know it won't hurt,' I said. 'That's not why.'

'Then why?'

'Just because.'

'I'll never tell,' she said. 'I promise. Nobody will ever find out about this. It'll be our secret, just between you and me.'

'I don't know.'

'Yes, you do. You've wanted to kiss me from the start.'

'No.'

'Everywhere. You've wanted to kiss me everywhere. My mouth, my breasts . . .'

'Shut up.'

'Everywhere.'

'No.'

'Do it, Alice. Now. I want you. And I want you more than anything.'

I nodded, trembling. Then, I leaned in until our bodies met, and kissed Judy lightly on her open lips.

Her arms and legs clamped around me.

'Now I've got ya, bitch!'

But it wasn't Judy saying that.

It was a man, his voice low and scratchy and *gleeful*.

This wasn't Judy at all, not anymore. It was Milo, face bloody and eyes bulging, squeezing me so hard with his arms and legs that I was sinking deep into the soft bulges of his body, being enveloped by him. As I tried to scream, his mouth covered mine. His writhing lips felt slimy. He stuck his tongue into my mouth. Only it wasn't his tongue. It was hard and thick, and he shoved it in deep. Thrust it down my throat.

I'll bite it off, you . . .!

I suddenly came wide awake and found myself staring up through the water.

Shit!

I rammed my elbows against the bottom of the tub and burst through the surface fast, choking. I sat there, wracked with coughs. Some water had found its way into the wrong place, that was for sure. Probably not much, but enough to keep me coughing for a while.

After I finished, my chest ached every time I took a deep breath.

I was okay, but didn't feel much like trying to relax in the water again. For one thing, I might catch another snootful. For another, I didn't want any more dreams.

Dreams are so damn weird. If you ask me, the point of every single dream and nightmare is just to torment you. That's all any of them ever do. They scare the crap out of you or they humiliate you. Or else they tantalize you with a situation that is really fabulous, wonderful beyond belief – only to jerk it away from you.

They twist things.

They really suck.

And they seem to be ten times worse – more real and more twisted – when you're really tired.

I was hugely tired, so I didn't dare relax again. I opened the bathtub drain and got to my feet. The water almost came up to my knees. The tub was so large, though, that I didn't need to worry about it overflowing. As the water gurgled out, I slid the plastic curtain shut, turned the faucets on, and lifted the gizmo to start the shower.

The hot, stiff spray hissed down, pelting my scalp and face and shoulders. It felt great.

But two things were wrong.

First, the water made too much noise coming out, splashing my skin, pattering against the plastic curtain, raining against the water pooled in the tub. It made me worry about all the things I *couldn't* hear. In other rooms, phones might be ringing. A window might be breaking. Someone could even kick open a door and I wouldn't be able to hear it.

Second, the frosted white shower curtain hung between me and my saber.

What if I *needed* it?

After worrying for a while, I slid open the shower curtain, bent over and picked up the saber. I brought it in with me. Then I shut the curtain again and set the sword on the bottom of the tub.

I couldn't hear any better, of course, but now I had a weapon. That made things all right.

I went ahead with my shower, sudsing myself all over with a bar of soap, then shampooing my hair, always being careful where I put my feet.

Naturally, nobody came along and tried to attack me.

They never attack you when you're ready for them.

How about if old Mother Bates had swept open the shower curtain and found Janet Leigh facing her with a *cavalry saber*! Would've changed the course of movie history.

Anyway, *I* was ready. But nobody came.

Just as well. I'd had a long night.

When I was done with the shower, I turned off the water and opened the curtain. Squatting down, I picked up the sword. Then I climbed out of the tub, set the sword aside and stepped over to the towel rod.

Two matching bath towels hung there. They both looked clean, but I could tell that they weren't fresh from the laundry. I didn't know which had been used by Serena, which by Charlie, so I just grabbed one and started drying myself with it. The towel was enormous, thick and soft. As I buried my face in it, I wondered who it had rubbed, and where. Not that it mattered much. I was just curious, that's all. Either of them using it on any parts of themselves was fine with me, and nice to think about.

After drying myself, I dried the sword. I was very careful doing that, because I didn't want to cut the towel.

Then I applied some of Serena's roll-on deodorant to my underarms. I knew this was hers, not Charlie's, because I recognized the scent.

I used Serena's hair brush. The mirror was fogged up, except near the bottom, so I had to squat very low in order to see my head in it. I gave my hair a quick brushing, then stood up again.

Finally, I put on Charlie's silk robe and left the bathroom. Of course, I took along my sword and bag of goodies.

While I'd been in the tub, the sun had come up. Even with most of the curtains shut, the house was filled with grayish light.

In the laundry room, I took all my things out of the washing machine. I loaded them into the drier and started it. Then I went to the front door.

I opened it and walked to the edge of the stoop.

Morning was here, all right. The sun was still very low in the east. It spread brilliant, golden light across the lawn, making the dew sparkle. There didn't seem to be any breeze at all. The warm, moist air smelled of flowers and grass. Birds twittered in the distance. I heard a woodpecker somewhere. Insects were humming and buzzing. It was as quiet and peaceful all around me as a forest glen.

It was lovely.

When I stepped down, the grass felt warm and wet under my bare feet. I wandered slowly, looking for bloodstains and pieces of Tony. I saw a few butterflies. And some bees. But nothing bad.

The lawn seemed fine.

I was about to take a closer look at the driveway, but heard the far off sound of a car engine. It sent a tremor through my stomach. I figured the car must be coming here. Quickly, I turned around and walked toward the front door.

The car sound grew louder.

Cops?

No way, I told myself. They couldn't be after me. Not yet, anyway, and probably never.

What if it's Serena and Charlie?

Maybe something had gone wrong with their trip. It hardly seemed likely. Anything was possible, though. People *do* return home unexpectedly.

I felt cold and sick inside with the idea that it might be them. I could probably hang up the sword and clear out the clothes drier in time, but what about Judy's car in the garage?

I leaped onto the stoop, planting wet footprints on the concrete, and rushed to the front door.

The car sounded as if it had almost reached the driveway.

Brakes squeaked a bit.

I shoved open the door and ducked inside.

Before I had a chance to shut the door, though, I heard a familiar sound.

THWAP!

I'd rarely been outside at this time of the morning, but I'd sometimes heard such a sound coming through my windows above the garage.

It was the *Chester Tribune* smacking the pavement near the end of the driveway.

Standing in the doorway, I shook my head and smiled. I felt like a dope for being so scared.

After the sound of the car engine faded, I went to get the paper. On my way up the driveway, I looked again for evidence of Tony.

There was nothing.

The paper had landed on the pavement a few yards down from the top, so I didn't need to go all the way to the road. I went the rest of the way to the top, anyhow, just to take a look around.

Everything seemed fine.

I walked back and forth on the road in front of the house, searching.

Satisfied that there was nothing to find, I returned to the driveway. On the way down, I picked up the newspaper. I peeled off its rubber band and unrolled it.

The headline read:

ALICE SOUGHT IN MURDER SPREE!

Just kidding.

I half *expected* it to say that, but it didn't.

I don't remember what the hell the headline was. It had nothing to do with me.

As I carried the *Tribune* down toward the house, though, it gave me an idea.

Chapter Twenty-eight

Yvonne

Until I've had a cup of hot, black coffee, I'm useless in the morning. And this qualified as morning, even though I'd never gone to bed.

Back inside the house, I tossed the *Tribune* onto the kitchen table and set to work making a pot of coffee. I knew right where to find everything. Before long, the cozy aroma of coffee filled the kitchen.

I had to wait for the pot to fill, though, so I sat at the table and looked through the newspaper. It didn't contain a single story about anything I'd been involved with last night.

Nothing in the Obituary section, either.

None of which came as much of a surprise.

When the coffee was ready, I poured myself a mugful. I almost took it outside to drink it by the pool. That would've been nice on such an early, lovely morning. On my way to one of the back doors, though, I remembered what the prowler'd done. That changed my mind. So I returned to the kitchen table and looked at the newspaper again while I enjoyed my first mug of coffee.

I went straight to the movie ads. I like movies. Chester had a cineplex with six theaters. Not bad for such a worthless little town. Some good stuff was playing. I checked the times on a couple of them, and wondered about going to a movie today.

Why not? I deserved a treat, the way I'd toughted it out and taken care of so many problems.

One problem still needed to be dealt with, though.

Tony's redial.

I now had a plan.

If it works, I thought, I'll take in a movie afterward to celebrate.

When I went for a refill on my coffee, I checked the clock on the kitchen wall.

6:20.

I should probably wait until after 8:00 to try out my idea.

To help pass the time, I decided to make myself a huge breakfast. Normally, I don't have any breakfast at all – just coffee. But I'd had a long, hard night. I'd gotten enough exercise to kill off a high-school football team, picked up scads of minor injuries (food heals), and must've burnt off one or two zillion calories. I deserved a *feast*.

While a skillet full of bacon was sizzling on a burner, I made myself a Bloody Mary. I prepared it my special way – half tomato juice and half vodka, double the usual amount of Worcestershire Sauce and Tabasco to give it a real bite. After stirring it around with ice cubes, I squeezed a slice of lime into it. Then I sprinkled ground pepper over the top.

It tasted so fine.

I sipped it while I finished tending to the bacon, made some toast and fried a couple of eggs. After buttering the toast, I topped each slice with an egg. Then I sat at the table and devoured it all.

One of the best things you can put in your mouth is a piece of buttered toast that's dripping with egg yellow. Try it by itself, or with a chunk of egg white and a bite of bacon. Wash it down with coffee or a Bloody Mary. Mmmmm.

I hated to see the last of it go.

After breakfast, I did the dishes and skillet by hand and put everything away. I was tempted to have another Bloody Mary, but resisted the urge. One had been enough to make me feel pleasant. A second might knock me off my feet.

I needed to have my wits about me – and my feet under me – for taking care of the redial problem.

Before leaving the house, I hung the saber on the wall where it belonged. I also hung Charlie's robe in the bedroom closet and put on my swimsuit from yesterday. The swimsuit was all I had to wear, because I didn't want to use Tony's clothes again now that they'd been washed. In the laundry room, I emptied the drier and stuffed everything into a grocery bag.

Carrying my bags, my purse, and the *Chester Tribune*, I left the house and went up to my room over the garage.

It was nice to be in my own place again. It felt so safe and cozy. I wished I could stay – climb into bed and bury myself under the covers and sleep for ages.

Maybe later.

A lot later.

First, I needed to hide Tony's things. I hung up his shirt in my closet, just as if it were my own. I folded the cut-offs and slipped them into a dresser drawer where I kept other pairs of shorts. The handkerchief and bandana also went into drawers. I put the note pad and both sets of keys in my purse. I hid the cassette tape in a chest pocket of an old flannel shirt near the back of my closet.

That left nothing except the severed denim legs of Tony's jeans. They certainly weren't incriminating, so there was no reason to hide or destroy them. I decided to take them out to the car with me. They might make good rags. So I folded them and set them near my purse.

Next, I took off my swimsuit. I put on thong panties and a bra, then stood like a dope and wondered what else to wear.

Making the decision wasn't easy. Mostly because I didn't really know what I'd be doing. Also, maybe, because I needed sleep. And the Bloody Mary might've had a little to do with it.

Finally, I made up my mind and got dressed.

With my purse, the morning newspaper and the denim legs, I hurried downstairs and let myself into the lower part of the garage.

I took Judy's car.

I didn't like the idea of driving it around. I wanted to dump it somewhere and be done with it, but using my own car for a mission like this would've been idiotic.

Judy's car, at least, couldn't be traced to me.

And I doubted that anyone would recognize me. Not in my sunglasses and red wig.

Yeah, I had a wig on.

I kept a small collection of them, just in case. A gal never knows when she might want to alter her appearance a bit. Or a lot.

The curly red hair looked pretty damn gawdy, but that was the idea. Gawdy all the way. My lipstick was too bright, too red. My gold hoop earrings were the size of bracelets. If people saw me, *that's* what they would see. They'd never stand a chance of recognizing – or identifying – me, Alice.

I drove to the busy area near the highway. Some of the locals call it 'motel row.' But it had a lot more than just motels. Along both sides of the highway were tons of restaurants and gas stations, and even some fruit stands and gift shops.

There were also scads of public telephones.

You hardly ever find phones in enclosed booths, anymore. I didn't want to deal with highway noise, so I parked the car and went into a restaurant called Pokey's. The hostess was busy seating a family, so I went straight for the restrooms. Near the end of the corridor, I found two public phones between the doors marked Guys and Dolls.

Nobody was using them.

I took the note pad and a pen out of my purse. After checking the newspaper, I jotted down a number I'd found on the masthead.

Then I dropped a quarter into the phone and made the call.

'*Tribune* circulation,' a woman's voice told me. 'This is Yvonne. May I help you, please?'

'I hope so,' I said. 'This is Mrs Tony Romano. I'm afraid we didn't receive our newspaper this morning.'

'May I have your phone number, please?'

I read her Tony's number off the pad, and figured she was probably tapping it into a computer.

'Yes. You *should've* gotten it by now, Mrs Romano. I'll . . .'

'The thing is,' I said quickly, 'we haven't been getting it since our move. We just recently moved to a new place. I was wondering if there might be a mix-up and maybe it's still being delivered to our old address on Washington.'

'Hmm. No. We have it here as being delivered to 8448 Adams.'

I wrote the address on my note pad.

'Is that your correct address for delivery?' Yvonne asked.

'Yeah, it is.' Laughing softly, I said, 'So much for my theory.'

'Well, I'll make sure we get this straightened out for you, Mrs Romano. We'll have this morning's paper to you within the hour.'

'Thank you very much.'

'Thank *you* for being a subscriber, and we do apologize for your inconvenience.'

'No problem. Thanks again. Bye-bye.'

I hung up and grinned.

After glancing around to make sure nobody had an eye on me, I wiped the handset and number pad with a tissue. Then I walked out of Pokey's and climbed into Judy's car.

Next stop, Tony's place!

I felt brilliant.

Of course, the trick would've fallen flat if Tony hadn't been a *Tribune* subscriber. Lucky me, he was. And lucky me, he'd been prompt about giving the paper his change of address.

If my luck held, I would walk up to Tony's front door and find it unlocked.

Which was *sure* to happen.

Sure.

In my dreams.

Too bad I'd gotten rid of Tony's keys. I could've stepped right up to his door, unlocked it and walked in easy as pie. But last night, I'd been sure there was no possibility of learning his new address. I'd been *positive*. There just wasn't any way to do it, not without drastic steps such as questioning people in his old building.

Besides, I'd already thrown his keys in the fire before Judy told me that she knew for a fact he had redial.

If only I'd kept them!

Thought I was so smart, throwing all that stuff in the fire.

Yeah, yeah, burn the evidence! Great idea!

Shit!

Of course, the keys would probably still work fine. All I had to do was drive over to Miller's Woods, hunt around until I find the campsite, dig the keys out of the cold campfire, hike back to the car and drive all the way over to Tony's . . .

That's all.

And in the meantime, maybe the cops might find Tony's body.

If they haven't already.

And they get to his place ahead of me.

What if they're already there?

Tony's address on Adams was only a few blocks away from Judy's apartment building. Just for the sake of caution, I made a slight detour and drove to her place, first. The neighborhood probably would've been crawling with cops and curious neighbors if Tony's body had been discovered. But it was quiet, so I drove on.

As I drove, I wondered how to get inside his apartment.

I had no idea.

I planned to play it by ear.

Now, you might be asking yourself, *All this over a redial button? Is she nuts?*

Maybe.

I wondered about that myself.

But I kept picturing a cop in Tony's apartment. He notices the redial feature and thinks, *This'll have the last number Tony ever called! It might even belong to the murderer! Check it out!* So he gives it a try. Next thing you know, Charlie's voice is in his ear, saying, 'Thank you for calling. Nobody is available to answer the phone, right now, but if you'd like to leave a message . . .'

This'll *really* get the cop going. Especially if he ever lays his hands on the phone company records and finds out what *time* Tony made the call – and how long it lasted.

He'll be very eager to pay Charlie a visit.

But Charlie and Serena are out of town for the week.

And the only person with access to the house and phone is me.

Not a pretty picture.

But I now had a chance to make it go away.

All I had to do was get inside Tony's apartment and make one telephone call.

Worth a little risk, don't you think?

I thought so.

But then, I'd been through a lot, so maybe I wasn't thinking very straight at the time.

Chapter Twenty-nine

Murphy

Leaving Judy's car parked around the corner, I walked back to 8448 Adams.

It was an old, single-level building with eight small units and an open, grassy courtyard in the middle. I didn't know Tony's apartment number. So instead of entering, I just looked the place over and kept walking.

Each front door had a mailbox nearby. Too bad. If you're in a complex with a bank of mailboxes, the post office requires names on all the boxes. But when you've got your own box, like at this place, you don't need to put your name on it. And nobody does.

Three of the units had newspapers in front of them.

One of those was probably Tony's.

But which?

Had the *Tribune* delivery person shown up yet with the replacement? If not, I could simply wait for him and see what he does.

But there was a slim chance that he'd already been here and gone. (He certainly wouldn't have left a *second* paper on the doorstep.) If he'd already shown up, I would have an awfully long wait.

There was just no way to know for sure.

Anyway, I didn't have time to waste. I had to get this done and get going.

Maybe the car ports or garages would give me a clue as to Tony's apartment number. So I headed for the end of the block to look for an alley entrance.

And heard a distant siren.

Oh, my God!

The sound froze me.

My mind went nuts. The cops had found Tony's body, knew I'd killed him, knew where to find me, and were swooping in for the arrest. In a matter of seconds, squad cars would roar around the corners and shriek to a halt. Cops would leap out and come at me with their guns drawn.

I had an urge to break into a run.

The siren's cry grew louder.

They can't know it's me! How can they know it's me?

Just play innocent, I warned myself. Admit nothing. Stay calm.

What can they really prove?

As the siren noise bore down on me from behind, I turned my head and looked over my shoulder.

Siren blaring, lights aflash, an ambulance sped by me and kept going.

I laughed at myself. But my heart was thumping like mad, and I was suddenly out of breath.

Even after the ambulance was out of sight, I stood there gasping, trying to calm down.

Not enough sleep, that was the problem.

That, and a little too much stress.

Maybe I should've had that extra Bloody Mary with breakfast, after all.

I've gotta get out of here!

But I couldn't just give up on Tony's place without at least trying to get in. It was almost a miracle that I'd been able to find out his address. I was *meant* to come here, get inside somehow, and take us off his redial.

Just go for it!

I turned around and walked back to his building. I wasn't sure what to do. Go door to door, maybe, saying my car broke down and I need to use a phone . . .

MANAGER

It was a sign near the door of apartment one.

The building manager would *have* to know Tony's apartment number. And he or she would have keys for it.

I hurried over and rang the doorbell.

I did it with a knuckle.

Knuckles don't leave fingerprints.

Nothing happened, so I rang it again. This time, a man's voice called, 'Hang on, there! I'm on my way!'

A few seconds later, the front door swung open. The screen door still stood in the way. Through the gray mesh, I could barely make out the man on the other side.

'Well, hello there,' he said.

'Good morning,' I said.

'Take a step backward, and I'll open the screen. Don't wanta knock you on your keester, do I?'

I took a step backward, and he swung the screen door open. He held it wide with an outstretched arm. He was maybe about thirty years old. He had messy brown hair and wore glasses. He also wore a Bear Whizz Beer T-shirt that showed a grizzly bear peeing in a woodland stream. His shorts appeared to be swimming trunks, even though the apartment building didn't seem to have a swimming pool. He was barefoot.

Not much to look at, but he had a nice smile and I sort of liked the glint in his eyes.

'My name's Fran Johnson,' I told him, and held out my hand.

'Murphy Scott.' He gave my hand a hearty shake as if we were old pals. 'Pleased to make your acquaintance, Fran. And what brings you here, this fine morning?'

'I'm looking for my boyfriend, Tony. Tony Romano.'

'Ah, Tony!'

'He lives here, doesn't he?'

'He does indeed. I helped him move in last Saturday. Apartment six, directly across the way.'

Nodding, I muttered, 'Six, I know,' and glanced over my shoulder at the unit on the other side of the lawn. It was one of the three with a *Tribune* on the stoop.

I faced Murphy again and said, 'The thing is, he isn't . . . I'm afraid something might be wrong. We were supposed to meet for breakfast this morning, but he didn't show up. I waited over an hour for him.'

Frowning, Murphy shook his head.

'Have you seen him at all this morning?' I asked.

'Nope. I just got up.'

'I phoned him a few minutes ago, but all I got was his answering machine.'

'Maybe he screens his calls.'

'But I told him it was me, and he still didn't pick up.'

'He might've been indisposed at the time. That sort of thing happens. He could've been taking a shower, for instance.'

'Maybe, but . . .'

'A lot of possibilities.' With a sheepish look on his face, Murphy said, 'Sometimes, guy's just . . .' He shrugged. 'Were you getting along all right?'

'Sure. I mean, as far as I know. Nothing *seemed* to be wrong. And we had this date for breakfast.'

Frowning past my shoulder, Murphy said, 'He hasn't picked up his paper yet. Maybe he just overslept or something.'

'But he didn't answer his phone.'

'Why don't you go over and give his doorbell a ring or two?' Murphy suggested.

'I already tried, but . . . okay.'

While Murphy watched, I walked across the grass to unit six and pushed the doorbell with my knuckle. The sound of the ringing gave me flutters in the stomach.

What if he comes to the door?

Yeah, right. In his condition?

But somebody else might open it.

A cop. A friend. A twin.

Be ready for anything. Stay cool.

The door stayed shut.

I rang the bell a few more times, then turned around and headed back for Murphy. As I walked toward him, he checked me out.

Normally, I don't like it when guys do that.

Most guys are pigs.

Anyway, I didn't mind Murphy looking me over. I'd only just met him, but I already knew he wasn't some kind of asshole. Also, I could tell that he liked what he was seeing, and I can't say I blamed him.

Along with my red wig, bright lipstick and enormous earrings, I wore a yellow blouse the color of a lemon. I would've preferred a halter top, but had to keep my midriff covered because of the injury. To make things interesting, I'd left a few of my upper buttons undone. Plenty of cleavage showed.

My legs were scratched and bruised, too, so I couldn't wear my really short, snug shorts. I'd chosen a skirt, instead. A light, full skirt of forest green. It drifted against my legs and had a slit up one side. In a certain light, you could see through it.

The whole outfit was intended to draw men's eyes. To attract them and *dis*tract them. They would see the flamboyant redhead, the stacked and leggy broad – not me.

My shoes, actually, weren't part of the outfit. The costume screamed out for something like gold lamé slippers or snake-skin boots. But I wore white sneakers for comfort and speed.

Murphy, watching me, shook his head and smiled.

'What?' I asked.

'Tony's gotta be either nuts or dead to miss a breakfast with *you.*'

I must've blushed. I sure felt very hot all of a sudden.

'The thing is,' I said, 'he's diabetic. Did he tell you about that?'

Murphy lost his smile. 'Oh, man,' he said. 'No, he didn't say anything about that. Diabetic? Maybe we'd better have a look. I'll go get the keys.'

He vanished inside, but his screen door barely had time to swing shut before he pushed it opena dn came out. As I followed him across the courtyard, I scanned the rest of the apartments. I saw nobody.

He pulled open Tony's screen door and knocked a couple of times on the wooden door. But he didn't wait for a response. He stuck a key into the lock, turned it, and pushed the door open. Then he called out, 'Tony?'

We both listened, but heard nothing.

'Tony? It's Murphy, the manager. Are you here?'

Still no answer, so Murphy stepped inside. I crouched, picked up the *Tribune* by the rubber band around its middle, and entered behind him. We were in a small, tidy living room.

I saw Tony's answering machine on a lamp table beside his couch. 'Maybe I'd better wait here,' I whispered. 'In case he's . . . indecent or something.'

'No problem,' Murphy said, and hurried away to search the apartment.

The moment he stepped into the bedroom, I rushed forward, tossed the newspaper onto Tony's couch, swung my purse behind my back to get it out of the way, and picked up the telephone.

At the sound of a dial tone, I started to tap numbers into the keyboard.

The three-digit local prefix.

Then four random numbers.

In the earpiece, I heard quiet, ringing sounds.

YES!!!

Murphy, coming out of the bedroom, looked at me and shook his head.

I gave him a smile, then spoke into the mouthpiece. 'Barb? It's me, Fran.'

Murphy hurried on, apparently to check the kitchen.

'I got the manager to let me into his apartment, but he doesn't seem to be here.' Then I called out, 'Murphy, any sign of him?'

'Nope.'

To the ringing phone, I said, 'I guess it's good news. I was really afraid he might've had another seizure.'

Murphy came back into the living room, his eyebrows raised, his head shaking.

'Any sign of him?' I asked.

'Nothing. He's not here.'

I gave Murphy a grateful smile, then told the phone, 'He's definitely not here . . . No, I don't know if his car's here.'

'I'll go look,' Murphy said.

A moment later, he was gone. The screen door clapped shut behind him.

I hung up.

Then I flipped up the plastic cover of the answering machine, took out Tony's tape cassette, shut the cover and gave it a quick wipe with my skirt. I tucked the tiny cassette down the front of my panties.

After that, I picked up the phone and tapped in another set of random numbers.

This time, somebody picked up after the first ring. A man's voice said, 'Hello?'

I didn't say a thing.

'Hello? Who is this?'

'This is Margaret,' I said, 'from Westside Marketing Research . . .'

'Not interested,' he said and hung up.

I still had the apartment to myself. As I tried a new number, I noticed a calendar beside the answering machine. It was the kind that has a small, separate page for each day of the year. The number showing on the right was yesterday's date.

The thick stack of pages on the left side of the center rings told me that Tony was in the habit of turning them over, not ripping them out.

From the other end of the line came a busy signal.

With the edge of a fingertip, I flipped the calendar page over so today's date showed.

Then, hearing a quick approach of footsteps on the outside walkway, I said into the phone, 'Maybe so. I sure hope so, anyway.'

As the screen door opened, I turned around and smiled at Murphy.

He came in, shaking his head. 'Car's gone,' he whispered.

'Thanks, Murphy.' Into the phone, I said, 'Tony's car is gone . . . I have no idea . . . Well, I'd much rather be stood up for a breakfast date than have Tony in a coma, or something. I'm *glad* we didn't find him, you know? . . . Right, I'll let you know if I find out anything. Bye-bye.'

I hung up, then said to Murphy, 'That was Tony's sister. She's even more worried than I am. I made the mistake of calling her from the restaurant . . . They're really close. I thought she might know where he was. But I only ended up scaring her half to death.'

'He's probably fine,' Murphy said.

'I sure hope so.'

'Ready to go?'

No! My fingerprints were all over the phone.

'Yeah,' I murmured. 'I guess.'

He frowned slightly, but turned around and started toward the door.

'I don't . . .'

He looked back. 'What?'

'. . . feel so good.'

Chapter Thirty

MDS

I let out a moan and tried to look nauseated. Bending over, I put my hands on my knees.

'Are you sick?' Murphy asked.

'No, no. I'll . . . be fine. Just . . . I'm a little dizzy, that's all. I'd better just . . . I'll be fine in a minute. I'm sorry.'

'Hey, no problem.'

'I'd better sit down,' I said, and sank to the floor.

Murphy squatted in front of me, looking appalled. 'What's the matter? Do you need an ambulance, or . . .?'

'No. No. I'm . . . I get this way. It's my . . . condition kicking up.'

'Condition?'

'MDS.'

'I don't know what that is.'

As far as I knew, neither did anyone else. I'd just then made it up. 'Morning Dehydration Syndrome,' I explained.

'Huh?'

'It's because I missed breakfast, and . . .' I trailed off and hung my head.

'Dehydration?' he asked.

'Water. I need . . . water.'

'Okay. Hang on.' Murphy sprang up, dodged past me, and went rushing for the kitchen.

The answering machine was next to my shoulder and slightly behind me. I stood up quickly and turned around. As I listened to cupboards squeak and water run, I picked up the telephone's handset, wiped it all over with my skirt and returned it to its cradle. Then I gave the phone's keypad a quick rub. When the kitchen faucet shut off, I sank to one knee. I was struggling to rise as Murphy trotted in with a glass of water.

'Be careful,' he said.

Wobbling, I made it to my feet. But as I reached for the glass, I lost my balance accidentally on purpose and fell toward Murphy, bumping the glass. The whole load of water caught me in the chest. It drenched the top of my blouse, doused my exposed cleavage, soaked through my bra, and poured down between my breasts.

As I sagged and grabbed Murphy by the shoulders, some of the water underneath my blouse even raced down my belly and soaked the top of my skirt.

He wrapped his arms around me and pulled me against him.

'My God,' he gasped. 'Are you okay?'

'I . . . yeah. Just . . . a little dizzy. Just . . . I'll be . . . fine . . . In a minute.'

'Are you sure?'

'You won't let me fall, will you?'

'I don't think so,' he said, and I felt his arms tighten against my back. He still seemed to be clutching the glass in one hand. His other hand was open and pressing firmly against me.

'I'm not too heavy, am I?' I asked.

'No. No, not at all.'

'I'm starting to feel better.'

He didn't say anything, but his open hand began to move up and down a little, caressing my back.

'Good thing you're so strong,' I told him. 'I would've fallen flat on my face.'

'Sure glad that didn't happen.'

'I'm really sorry about all this.'

'No need to be sorry about anything.'

'It's so embarrassing.'

'Nothing to be embarrassed about.'

'Stumbling around like a drunk.'

'These things happen. But we'd better get some water into you.'

'Instead of "onto" me?'

He laughed quietly, his chest shaking against my breasts.

'What I really need is a towel,' I said.

He laughed again. Then he said, 'I think you *are* feeling better.'

'You don't feel so bad yourself.'

He didn't laugh at that one. He just made a sound like, 'Mm?' and seemed to tighten up slightly. 'I'd better get you that water,' he said. 'If I let go of you . . .?'

'I'll be okay.'

He loosened his hold. Easing backward, he stared at my face. He looked worried. 'Okay?'

'So far, so good.'

He backed away from me. The front of his pale blue T-shirt looked wet from where he'd been pressed against me. 'You steady?' he asked, looking from my face to my blouse and up to my face again.

'Fine,' I said.

'I'll just be gone a second.'

'Why don't you see if Tony has some beer?'

'*Beer?*'

'Yeah. A good, cold beer. That'd be a lot better than water.'

He grinned. He glanced at my blouse again, and said, 'Beer's *always* better than water.'

'Especially on a hot day like this.'

'I don't know about borrowing Tony's beer, though – if he has any. I hardly know him, and . . .'

'Yeah, you're right. And maybe he wouldn't want *me* drinking it. Maybe he wouldn't even want me to *be* here.' I shrugged. 'I mean, the way he stood me up this morning, no telling what's going on. Maybe he's decided to hate me, or something.'

'I can't imagine that.'

'*I* can. Guys are such . . . Maybe we'd better get out of here before he shows up and starts trouble.'

Murphy frowned and nodded, then said, 'If you'd like a beer, I've got plenty of cold ones over at my place.'

BINGO! His place. Exactly where I wanted to go. I planned to seduce him, then act as if I hadn't really wanted him to do *that*. Afraid I might charge him with sexual assault, he would make damn sure he never told the cops about me. Brilliant, huh?

'Are you sure?' I asked. 'I don't want to . . . you know, make a nuisance out of myself.'

'Be glad to have you.'

'That'd be great.'

'Let me put this away,' he said, and headed for the kitchen with the glass.

When Murphy was out of sight, I looked down to check my blouse. The water had drenched me in the middle, but more on the left side than the right. The pink of my skin showed through the yellow fabric. On the left, I could also see the outline and pattern and red color of my bra. And my nipple. Not the *color* of my nipple, but the way it was sticking out as if it wanted to poke a hole through the thin, wet layers of my bra and blouse.

No wonder Murphy's had such trouble keeping his eyes away.

As water started running in the kitchen, I bent over and looked at Tony's floor. There were just a few damp places on the carpet. Most of the water had ended up on me.

Soon after the kitchen faucet shut off, a cupboard squeaked open and I heard the quiet thump of the glass being set on a shelf. Then the cupboard bumped shut.

I took another look at my left breast. My blouse still clung to it, and my nipple still jutted out. My right one was erect, too. I could feel it that way, but it didn't show so much because that side was fairly dry.

'Still on your feet,' Murphy said. He looked both happy and nervous as he came toward me.

'I'll be fine now.'

'You still want the beer, don't you?'

'You bet.'

I walked out ahead of him, going slowly and trying to look a little shaky on my feet. Then I waited in the sunlight while he locked Tony's main door and eased the screen door shut. Coming over to where I stood, he took hold of my arm and led me carefully across the courtyard.

'My place is sort of a mess,' he warned.

'Is your wife out of town, or something?'

'Who's married?'

'You're not?' I tried to sound surprised, but I wasn't. After all, he didn't wear a wedding ring.

'Not me,' he said.

'That's a surprise. I thought all the good guys were taken.'

He shook his head and laughed softly. 'I'm not taken. And what makes you think I'm a "good guy"?'

'I can tell.'

He held the screen door open for me. His main door wasn't completely shut, so I pushed it out of my way and stepped into his apartment.

As Murphy came in, he asked, 'Want the air conditioning on?'

'It's up to you.'

'I usually like to leave it off in the mornings. You know, keep the place wide open so the air can get in.'

'That's fine.'

'But if you're hot . . .'

'This is nice.'

'Okay.' Leaving the main door wide open, he stepped around me and spread his arms. 'Home, sweet home. Make yourself comfortable and I'll get us a couple of cold ones.'

'Great.'

Over his shoulder, he said, 'I don't usually drink in the morning.'

'What do you usually do?'

'Read and write.'

'Ah,' I said.

Murphy disappeared into the kitchen.

Unlike Tony's living room, this one had bookshelves standing against every available wall. They were loaded with hardbounds and paperbacks in a fabulous disarray.

The whole room was in disarray.

Cluttered with books, mostly.

But a lot of other stuff, too.

You couldn't even see the top of the coffee table. Along with all sorts of mail and magazines and a few pens and pencils, it was cluttered with three Pepsi cans, a couple of wadded napkins, and a paper plate littered with an empty brie wrapper, a used knife smeared with white cheese, and cracker crumbs.

I moved a couple of pillows aside. As I sat down, I slipped the strap of my purse off my shoulder. I put the purse down between my hip and the end of the couch, where it wouldn't be in the way.

'What do you write?' I called.

'Crap that nobody wants to publish.'

'That sounds lucrative.'

I heard him laugh.

Then he came walking in with two beer bottles in one hand, two large glass mugs in the other, and a plastic bag of pretzels hanging from his teeth.

He set it all down on the coffee table without moving anything out of the way.

'There we go,' he said. After tossing the pillows aside, he sat on the couch.

Not far away from me, but not very close, either.

He poured beer into the mugs, and handed one of them to me. Then he opened the pretzels and placed the bag on the couch between us.

Turning toward me, he hoisted his mug and said, 'Down the hatch.'

We bumped our mugs together.

I took a drink. The beer tasted great.

Murphy drank, too. When he came up for air, he said, 'There goes my writing for the day.'

'Not much of a loss, if it's crap.'

He laughed. 'You're right.'

'*Have* you had stuff published?'

'Oh, sure. I do all right. Not as well as I'd like, but not too badly.'

'What do you write?'

'Crime novels.'

'*Murder* mysteries?'

'Sort of.'

'Cool.'

'*TRIBUNE!*'

The sudden shout made me jump. Beer slopped out of my mug and splashed the middle of my chest – like the water, but not as much. And colder!

A moment later, I heard the slap of a newspaper smacking concrete outside.

Turning my head, I looked out the screen door and across the courtyard. A rolled *Tribune* lay on the stoop in front of Tony's door.

Murphy, frowning, leaned forward to see past me. 'Well,' he said. 'That's odd.'

Chapter Thirty-one

The Offer

'Kind of,' I said, and shrugged and changed the subject. 'I'm sure klutzy this morning.' I reached out and took a wadded napkin off the coffee table.

Murphy watched me blot the beer off my chest, but he said, 'Tony already *had* a paper. Why would they bring him another one?'

'Some sort of mix-up?' I suggested, and slid the damp ball of paper down between my breasts. 'They usually just do that if you call.'

'But he *got* his. And he's not even *home*.'

I grinned and pulled out the napkin. 'It's a *mystery*, isn't it? You're a mystery writer. What do *you* think?'

He made a face, narrowing one eye and turning down a corner of his mouth. 'Well, let me think. Obviously, someone called the *Tribune* and asked for a new paper to be delivered. Since Tony is gone, it'd be stretching things to assume that *he* made the call.'

'Wouldn't make any sense at all,' I agreed.

'So somebody *else* must've asked for the paper.'

'But why would anyone want another paper delivered to Tony's place?' I asked.

'Elementary, my dear Fran.'

'Oh?'

'Sure. It was some sort of a mix-up.'

I laughed and drank some more beer.

'It was delivered to Tony's *by mistake*!' he pronounced.

'Sent to the wrong address?'

'Exactly!'

'You're a genius!'

'You bet,' he said, and laughed. 'Somewhere along the way, somebody misunderstood the address, or wrote it down wrong, or hit a wrong computer key . . . something like that.'

'You're a regular Travis McGee,' I told him.

He beamed. 'You know McGee?'

'Sure.'

'Well, now. I'd give you a beer, but you've already got one.'

'Well, I'll take another when this one's done. Maybe I've read some of *your* stuff. What name do you write under?'

'My own.'

'Murphy Scott?'

Looking pleased that I'd remembered, he said, 'That's it.'

'What are some of your books?'

'There've only been two so far. That have gotten published, anyway. *Deep Dead Eyes* and *The Dark Pit*.'

'Neat titles,' I said.

'Thanks.'

'How are the books?'

'Brilliant.'

'I thought you said they're crap.'

'That was before I found out you're a reader.'

'That makes a difference?'

'Sure. To someone who isn't a reader, I might as *well* be writing crap.'

I laughed. 'You're weird, you know that?'

'Maybe a little. How about you?' he asked. 'Are *you* weird?'

'What do you think?' Reaching out, I grabbed a few pretzels out of the bag between us. 'You're the mystery writer. What do *you* make of me?' I chomped a pretzel and grinned at him.

Taking a long drink, he gazed at me over the upper rim of his mug. Then he set down the mug, turned sideways on the couch so he faced me, and said, 'I'll say this about you. You're not what you seem.'

It made me feel a little sick to hear him say that.

And it probably showed on my face.

Suddenly, the pretzel in my mouth went so dry I had a hard time swallowing it. I had to wash it down with some beer. Then I asked, 'What do you mean?'

'Well,' he said, 'you're not really a redhead. That's either a dye job or a very good wig, I'm not sure which.'

'What makes you think it isn't natural?'

'A couple of things. Redheads usually have light skin and freckles, whereas you've got a nice dark tan. Also, you have brown eyes and eyebrows.'

'Ah. Okay. You're right. It's a wig. Anything else?'

'I guess that's about it,' he said.

Alarms went off inside me.

I could tell by the look in his eyes that there was something else.

Something a lot bigger than my hair color.

'What is it?' I asked.

He shrugged. 'This and that. Why don't you tell me?'

'Tell you what?'

'Who you really are.'

'I'm just me.'

'And what's really going on.'

'Nothing's going on.'

'Hang on,' he said. 'I want to show you something.'

'Okay.'

I sat there with my beer while he got up and walked over to a corner of the living room. There, he crouched over a cardboard box and opened its lid.

I thought about bolting.

I also thought about attacking him.

But I had no idea what he knew – or what he thought he knew.

Besides, I sort of liked him.

He took a book out of the box, then came back to the couch and handed it to me. A hardbound copy of *Deep Dead Eyes* by Murphy Scott.

The front picture showed a dead woman under water. You seemed to be looking down at her from the surface of a lake or river as if you were in a rowboat or something. She was a few feet below the surface, and sort of blurry. She seemed to be naked, but you couldn't make out the details very well. What you could *really* make out was the way her eyes were gazing up at you.

'That's for you,' Murphy said.

'Really? Thanks. Will you autograph it for me?'

'Sure thing. But first, take a look at the back cover.'

I flipped the book over. On the back of the dust jacket was a black-and-white photograph of Murphy standing in front of a tree. In jeans and a plaid shirt, he looked like a hunter or fisherman. The picture, taken at an odd upward angle, looked as if the photographer had been more interested in the tree than in Murphy. The tree sure looked a lot more menacing than the author.

'Do you recognize me?' he asked.

'Sure. Nice picture.'

'Thanks. And it shows that I *am* who I say I am, right?'

'A writer, you mean?'

'Yeah.'

'That's either you, or you've got a twin.'

'It's me,' he said.

'I believe you.'

'Want the autograph now?'

'Sure.' I handed the book to him.

Holding it, he bent over and searched the cluttered table

until he found a pen. Then he stepped around the table, sat on the couch and opened the book on his lap. He turned to the title page. At the top right corner, he scribbled the date. Then he smiled at me and asked, 'Do you want it personally inscribed?'

'Sure.'

'To . . .?'

'Me.'

'Fran?'

'Sure.'

'*Are* you sure? Is Fran the name you want on here? Is Fran your *real* name?'

'Why shouldn't it be?'

He made a little shrug, then lowered his head and wrote a brief message in the book. Below the message, he scratched his autograph. Then he passed the book to me.

The inscription said:

To Fran,
My mysterious and beautiful guest –
Tell me your story.
Who knows? Maybe my next book will be about you.
Warmest Regards,
Murphy Scott

I lifted my eyes to his. 'Thanks,' I said, and shut the book.

'How about it?'

'Tell you my story? What makes you think I *have* a story?'

'Your red hair.'

'And what else?'

'Your telephone call to Tony's sister.'

'What about it?'

'It was a fake. You were still on the phone with her when I came back from checking for Tony's car. Remember?'

'Yeah.'

'And you told her that Tony's car was gone?'

I nodded.

'Well, I could hear the busy signal.'

'No, you couldn't.'

'Yes, I could. I was standing right next to you. I heard it coming out of the earpiece. It was very quiet, but . . .'

'There *wasn't* any busy signal. I was talking to Tony's sister.'

'The question is, why?'

'She was worried about him.'

'You weren't talking to her. You were talking to a busy signal. But that's all right. Okay? I just want to know what's going on. I'm curious. Maybe it *is* something I can write about. And maybe I can help you.'

'Who says I need any help?'

'You've gotta be awfully desperate to put on a disguise and come over here the way you did – make up a story about being stood up for *breakfast.*'

I shook my head and tried to look stupid.

'And *Morning Dehydration Syndrome*? You've got to be kidding.'

'Just because *you've* never heard of it . . .'

He smiled and shook his head. 'And the second *Tribune*? You must've called in the request for it. My guess is, you needed to get into Tony's apartment for some reason, but you didn't know which one it was. So you called for a replacement paper. You wanted to see where it got delivered.'

'You *oughta* be a writer,' I told him, smiling and shaking my head. 'With an imagination like that . . .'

'Am I wrong?'

'Dead wrong.'

'Oooh. Don't say things like that, okay? To a writer, that sounds like some sort of ironic foreshadowing. I'm not at all interested in getting myself killed. I'm fascinated by your situation, that's all.'

'You don't even know my situation.'

'Tell me about it.'

'What do you *think* is going on?' I asked him.

'Tony had something in his apartment, and you wanted it. You *had* to get it. Maybe you figured you just couldn't wait for the *Tribune* guy, so you thought up the breakfast story and came to my door, hoping you could trick me into letting you into his place. While I was searching for him, you tried to take care of your problem, whatever it was. And you made the fake call to his sister to add a touch of verisimilitude to your story.'

Laughing, I said, 'What a crock.'

'Was he blackmailing you? What?'

'He stood me up for breakfast.'

Murphy raised his right hand and said, 'No matter what, I'll never tell a soul.'

'Nothing to tell.'

'I'll give you a thousand dollars for your story.'

'Haw!'

'And if it's something usable, we can work out a deal so you get a percentage of everything.'

'You really *are* curious.'

'Nothing like this has ever happened to me before,' he said.

'Nothing like what?'

'I'm minding my own business when a gorgeous mystery woman comes to my door and drags me into her intrigue.'

Gorgeous?

'It's a first,' he said. 'This sort of thing just doesn't happen in real life. Not to me, anyway. At least it never did until this morning.'

'Maybe I'd better leave.'

'No, don't. Please. You've got no idea how great this is. For me. Do you want another beer? Something else? Just name it. I *have* to know what's going on. Was Tony blackmailing you? Did he have pictures of you, or . . .?'

I shook my head.

'What'll it take for you to tell?' he asked.

'I guess I'll take another beer,' I told him.

Nodding, he stood up. 'You won't run off, will you?'

'Not a chance.'

He raised his eyebrows as if he wanted to know why.

'I *can't* run off,' I explained. 'I might have to kill you.'

Which was a joke. I didn't intend to kill him. There'd be no need for it. Like I already mentioned, I planned to ensure his silence by getting him to screw me.

Chapter Thirty-two

Leverage

Entering from the kitchen with two fresh bottles of beer, Murphy looked eager and excited and not at all worried. He sat down on the couch and filled our mugs with beer.

I took a drink, then said, 'Before you get too comfortable, you'd better shut the front door. And get your checkbook.'

'Sure. Okay.'

He got up again, closed the main door, disappeared into another room, and came back with it.

I held out my hand.

'You want to *see* it?'

'You're curious about *my* story, I'm curious about yours.'

'Well . . .' He shrugged, then handed the checkbook to me.

I flipped through his check stubs. He hadn't been very diligent about keeping track of his balance, but I performed some simple math along the way. By the time I came to the final stub, he seemed to have about twelve thousand dollars, give or take a few hundred. I looked up at him and said, 'Not bad.'

'Well, I just got an advance.'

I felt a little giddy. When you don't have a job and your bank balance is less than two hundred bucks, twelve thousand looks like a fortune.

I gave Murphy a frown. 'You could've offered me a little more than a thousand.'

'Well . . . How much *do* you want?'

'How about ten?'

'*Ten* thousand? I wouldn't have anything left to live on. Whatever I've got now, it'll have to last me for *months*.'

'How many months?'

'I don't know. It all depends. Six or eight, maybe. And I have an estimated income tax payment coming up in September. That'll clean me out if I don't get something else by then. And I probably won't. The taxes always clean me out.'

'Suppose you give me five thousand?' I suggested.

He grimaced.

'Five thousand in cash, up front, and you can have my story. I'll sign a paper, giving you all the rights to it. You won't have to cut me in for a percentage or anything, even if it's a bestseller or blockbuster movie. How does that sound?'

'I don't know,' he said.

'If you get low, just don't pay your estimated tax on time.'

'Easy for you to say.'

'My story could make you a lot of money.'

'I don't even know if I can *use* your story. I don't know what it is.'

'And you never will unless you cough up the five grand.'

He scowled at me, but with a glint in his eye. He almost seemed to be smiling as he sat down on the couch and reached for his beer. He drank some. Then he said, 'Just give me a hint.'

'A hint?'

'Something to whet my appetite. Enough to make me take the risk. I mean, five thousand dollars ... That's a load of money.'

'Suppose I tell you that I killed two people last night – in self-defense – and one of them was probably a serial killer?'

He gaped at me.

'What do you say to that?' I asked.

'If it's true ...'

'It's true.'

'Do the police know about it?'

'I don't think so. *I* sure didn't tell them. But they'll find out eventually. Today, probably. But maybe not till tomorrow or the next day. It all depends on when certain things turn up.'

'Bodies?'

'Basically.'

'*You* should tell the cops. Especially if ... you said you killed them in self-defense, right?'

'That's what I said.'

'Is it true?'

'Pretty much.'

'*Pretty much*? You mean it *wasn't* self-defense?'

'No, it was. Yeah. It's just ... all sort of complicated.'

'You've *gotta* tell the cops.'

'Bullshit. Don't give me that.'

'Is Tony one of the people you killed?'

'I'm not saying. I'm not telling you anything else. Not till I've got the money.'

Scowling, he took off his glasses. He rubbed his eyes as if he were suddenly feeling very tired. Then he muttered, 'Man, oh man.'

'How about it?'

He shook his head. 'This is a real mess. I had no idea you'd *killed* anyone.'

'Wouldn't be much of a story for you if I hadn't.'

'But how can I write it?'

'You're a *fiction* writer. Turn it into fiction. Change all the names – not that you know *my* real name, anyway.'

'I guess I could do that. But if anyone finds out . . .'

'*I'll* never tell, you can bet on that.'

'What if they catch you?'

'They won't. I've covered my tracks. There's absolutely no evidence connecting me to anything.'

'There's me,' he said.

'I know.'

He gave me a weary smile.

'Don't worry,' I said. 'You don't know enough to do me any harm. What could you tell the cops?'

He shrugged slightly. 'Not much.'

'At this point, you don't know who I killed, or how, or where. For all you know, I've been lying about everything. Also, you don't know who I am. You don't even really know what I look like.'

With a smile, he said, 'So, you don't think you'll have to kill me?'

I smiled back. 'Only if you don't pay up.'

'I don't suppose you'll take a check?'

'Cash only.'

'I'll have to pay a visit to the bank.'

'I'll have to go with you.'

'Sounds good to me,' he said. 'But you might want to think twice about going in. They have those security cameras.'

I grimaced. He was right about the cameras. Even with the wig on, I didn't like the idea of being caught on video tape. But if I didn't go inside with him . . .

'How do I know you won't snitch on me?' I asked.

'I won't. But I don't expect you to believe it.' He shook his head. He drank some beer. 'There must be a way.'

I drank some beer and frowned and tried to think of something, too.

After a while, he said, 'I don't know.'

'Come on. You're the writer. Think of something.'

'Well, I've got no intention of turning you in. You might just try a flying leap of faith.'

'Yeah, right. You seem like a good guy, Murphy, but I'm not ready to trust you with my life.'

'Suppose you *had* something on me? If I turn you in, you turn me in.'

That seemed like a pretty good idea. I should've thought of it myself. But I saw a big problem with it. 'What are you going to do,' I asked. '*Kill* somebody?'

'Maybe nothing quite that drastic.'

'It'd have to be drastic. Something you'd at least go to prison for. And something that nobody could know about except me, so you'd be completely in my hands.'

He shrugged.

I felt a sudden rush of heat that must've turned my face bright red.

Murphy saw.

'What?' he asked.

Feeling all squirmy inside, I said, 'Nothing.'

'Come on. Have you got an idea?'

'Well . . . yeah, but it's pretty far out.'

'That's not always a bad thing. Sometimes, far out's the only way to go. Let's hear your idea.'

'How would you like to rape me?'

It was his turn to get red. His mouth drooped open. He said, 'Uh. What?'

'Told you it was far out.'

'Rape you?'

'Right. Well, more like *pretend* to rape me.' I tried to smile, but didn't do a very good job of it. I felt awfully embarrassed and excited. I was trembling like mad. Streams of sweat were dribbling down my sides.

'Geez,' Murphy said. 'I don't know.'

'You'd have to really go through with it, though. We can't just *say* you did it. I'd need the physical evidence to prove my case against you.'

Looking flushed and disoriented and a little amused, he said, 'And this would be so you'd have leverage to keep me from tipping off the bank teller, or someone, that I've got a killer in my car?'

'Basically.'

'Which I have no intention of doing, anyway.'

'So you say.'

'It's the truth.'

'This'll be my insurance. I won't even go with you to the bank. I'll stay here and wait. If the cops come to arrest me, they'll find a rape victim in your bed.'

'You're nuts,' he said, looking terribly nervous but amused.

'Think so?'

'Definitely.'

'How about it?'

'It's not rape if you consent, so it wouldn't really be a crime.'

'Nobody'll ever know I consented. And we'll make sure it looks like a rape. I'm already pretty banged up from last night, so . . .'

'I suppose you'd need to bang *me* up, just to make it look good.'

'Some. Yeah. Good idea.'

'You're very big on tricky stuff,' he said.

'It seems like a great solution to me. I mean . . . *I'm* willing to go through with it if you are. What about you?'

'I've got a suggestion.'

'Yeah?'

'Why don't we hold off on the so-called "rape" till after I get back from the bank? You'll already have your money, then. There won't be anything hanging over our heads, so we'll be able to relax and take our time and . . .'

'And *I* won't have anything to hang over *your* head when you go into the bank.'

'You've gotta have that leverage, huh?'

'Yep.'

'But if we wait till afterwards . . .'

'I'm starting to think maybe you don't want to do it at all.'

When I said that, he smirked and set down his beer mug and moved the bag of pretzels out of the way. I put down my mug, too.

He reached over and clutched the front of my blouse with both hands.

'Do you want me to rip it off you?' he asked.

'Gotta make it look good.'

'What'll you wear later?'

'We'll think of something.'

'Do you want me to do it right here?'

'We were sitting here having a couple of beers. You invited me in after we came back from Tony's apartment.'

'And what were we doing there?' Murphy asked, still clutching my blouse.

'He'd stood me up for breakfast.'

'You're going to stick with that story?'

'Sure. After we'd looked for Tony, I wanted to wait for him in his apartment. But you wouldn't let me.'

'But you'd killed him.'

'Who, me? For all you know, he isn't even dead. Anyway, you wouldn't let me stay in Tony's place, but you said I could come over here to wait for him. You said we could have a couple of beers and wait for him together.'

'Very good. Maybe *you* should be the writer.'

'Maybe so,' I said. 'Anyway, so I just innocently sat here and had a couple of beers with you while I was waiting for my boyfriend to get home, and all of a sudden you grabbed the front of my blouse and *ripped* it open.'

As I said, '*ripped*', he did it.

Chapter Thirty-three

Getting Down to Business

Tore my blouse wide open.

My buttons went *pup-pup-pup*. The tail came jerking up out of my skirt's waistband.

Murphy shoved the blouse off my shoulders, then stopped and held it there. 'How's that so far?' he asked. His voice sounded pretty shaky.

'Not bad at all,' I said.

'Thanks.'

'Now, hit me in the face.'

'I can't hit you.'

'Go ahead.'

'No way.'

So I slapped him, knocking his head sideways and putting a handprint on his face. He looked startled. 'Like that,' I told him.

'Maybe this isn't such a good idea,' he said.

'You don't think so?'

'Why don't I just go to the bank and . . .'

Hooking a finger under the right cup of my bra, I stretched aside the flimsy red fabric, freeing my breast.

Murphy stared at my naked breast and moaned.

'Go ahead and feel,' I said.

'I don't think . . .'

'Don't think, just do,' I said. With that, I took hold of his wrist, pulled his hand away from my blouse and pressed it against my breast.

His hand felt smooth and cool.

He had a look on his face like a teenage kid who'd never done anything like this before. Embarrassed, confused, astonished, thrilled, grateful.

I was giving the guy a real treat.

Maybe giving myself a treat, too.

'Now what're you gonna do?' I asked. I had a little tremble in my voice that wasn't supposed to be there.

Staring into my eyes, he squeezed my breast gently and then let go and put his arms around me. He pulled me toward him and touched his lips softly against mine. With one hand, he took off his glasses. He set them on the back of the couch, then kissed me again, this time pushing firmly against my open lips, his mouth open slightly, his breath going into me.

I started feeling soft and lazy inside. As if the kiss was sapping my strength away. And my worries. And my plans. I felt all vague and peaceful. I almost could've drifted down into sleep, but I felt a curious eagerness about what Murphy was doing to me and what he might do next.

His phone rang.

We both flinched.

It rang again.

He took his mouth away from me and whispered, 'I'd better get it.'

I nodded.

Murphy grabbed his glasses, then got up from the couch.

I untwisted myself and leaned back against the cushion. I felt as if I'd been dragged roughly from a wonderful place and abandoned.

I felt a little better, though, when he sidestepped past my knees and I saw the front of his shorts.

Arriving at the lamp table, he picked up his phone just after the fourth ring.

'Hello? . . . Oh, hi, Harold . . . No, it's fine. What's up?'

He turned toward me, made a face that made me smile, and ogled my exposed breast. Then his eyes lowered to my belly as if drawn by my injury down there. I knew how awful it looked, but I didn't try to cover it. He frowned at the bruised and gouged skin, then met my eyes with a look of concern.

I wiggled my eyebrows at him.

Brightening up slightly, he said into the phone, 'Yeah. Sure I've heard of him . . . Yeah, I saw those movies . . . He does? . . .' Looking me in the eyes, he suddenly grinned. 'The most exciting book he's read all year? Cool . . . Uh-huh . . . Sure . . . Yeah, maybe we'll at least get an option out of it . . . Right, can't hurt . . . *Five* copies? Geez. I guess they think I get 'em free . . . Yeah, I know . . . Today? They *can't* get them today. Don't they know I'm out here in the boonies? Where are they, in L.A.? . . . Oh. Same difference. Anyway, I don't care who they are, I'm not driving to Culver City. Not today. It's about a six-hour drive, and I've already got plans.'

He gave me a smile.

I flexed a muscle to make my breast hop, and his eyes got very wide.

'I don't care,' he said into the phone. 'The best I can do is send them overnight express, and I'm not too sure about that . . . Well, they're always like that. They want everything yesterday, and then you drop everything to get the books off and you end up never hearing from them again anyway . . . I know . . . Well, let me have the address. I'll get the books to them as soon as I can.'

He couldn't seem to find a pen or paper on the lamp table.

Leaning forward, I snatched a ballpoint and the *TV Guide* off the cluttered table in front of me. Then I twisted around and reached them over to him.

'Thanks,' he whispered.

He dropped the *TV Guide* onto the lamp table and started to write on its back cover.

'Got it,' he said, and read the address back to Harold. Then he listened and nodded and said, 'Okay. No problem. And thanks. You never know, maybe this'll turn into something . . . Right. Take it easy. Bye.'

He hung up the phone and said, 'My agent.'

'Sounds like he had some good news for you.'

He shrugged. 'Yeah. Well, sort of. Some bigwig movie producer's all hot for *The Dark Pit*. I'm supposed to drop everything and . . .'

'I heard.'

'It's no big deal.'

'They want to make a *movie* out of your book? Sounds like a big deal to me.'

'These things usually don't go much of anywhere. These movie people . . . They'll tell you it's the greatest book in the history of the world, then they'll offer you about three hundred dollars for an option.'

'Three *hundred*? You're kidding.'

'That'd just be for rights to fool around with the book for six months or something. And then you'd get maybe a hundred thousand if it goes into production.'

'*That's* a lot.'

'But you never get it, because nothing ever gets that far.'

'Some stuff must.'

'Yeah. But not much. It's mostly a big waste of time. I don't jump through hoops for those guys anymore.'

'*I* would, if I were you.'

He smiled and said, 'You being *you*, you might.'

'What's that supposed to mean?'

'You're not *me* standing here looking at *you* right now.'

'I'll keep,' I told him, and drew my blouse shut to hide my breast. 'You shouldn't pass up a fabulous opportunity like this.'

'I know,' he said, and leered.

'I don't mean *me*.'

'I do,' he said.

He held out a hand. I took it, and he pulled me to my feet. I stepped around the end of the coffee table. When I was standing in front of him, he let go of my hand. With both his hands, he slipped my blouse off my shoulders and down my arms. It drifted to the floor behind me.

'What'll you do about the books?' I asked.

He shrugged. 'Maybe call Federal Express.'

'You don't want to deliver them today?'

'I've got better things to do,' he said, and slid his gaze down my body.

Blushing, I said, 'I could go with you.'

'It's an awfully long drive.'

'I don't mind. I could tell you my story on the way.'

'We'll see.'

'If I can stay awake.'

'Maybe you can take a nap while I go to the bank. You do still want your money, don't you?'

'Darn right,' I said.

'And I can't go get that till after I've raped you?'

'Darn right again. So you'd better get to it.'

'Are you sure you feel up to it?'

'You bet.'

'You're awfully banged up. What happened to you? All these bruises and everything?'

'Rough night.'

'Were you in *fights*?'

'Sure. Fights, falls, collisions. You name it, it happened. But don't worry. I'm fine.' Bending down, I raised a foot and started to pull off my shoe.

Murphy put a hand on my shoulder to hold me steady.

'Thanks,' I said. I tossed the shoe toward the couch. It landed on the floor with a thump. 'They've gotta be artfully arranged,' I explained.

He shook his head. 'Of course.'

I shifted to my other leg, pulled off my other shoe, and tossed it across the room. Then I stood up straight and smiled at him.

'Anything else?' he asked.

'Just be a little careful around my stomach.'

'What happened there?'

'Nailed by a tree branch. Walked right into it in the dark. But maybe I'll tell you all about it in the car. If we ever get there.'

'I guess you want me to get on with it.'

'Good guess, Sherlock.'

'Where do you want me to start?'

'Surprise me.'

With a silly smile on his face, he put his arms around me and drew me forward. His mouth came at mine. I slapped him. The blow sent his glasses flying off his face. He looked startled and hurt.

'None of that kissy stuff,' I said. 'Get rough. This has to look good.'

'Why does it have to *look* good? Nobody'll ever know it happened.'

'They will if you double-cross me.'

'I'd never . . .'

'You're a guy. Guys do stuff like that.'

'Not me.'

'Guys'll stab you in the back, lie . . .'

'Not me.'

'But I don't know that for sure, do I?'

'Guess not,' he admitted. Then he started to unhook the back of my bra.

And I suddenly realized that I still had the miniature cassette tape from Tony's answering machine hidden inside my panties. If this went much further . . .

'Rough!' I snapped and shoved him away.

As he came back at me, I tore the bra off, myself, and threw it to the floor. 'Take me to your bedroom,' I gasped.

He grabbed my arm, but I pulled free.

He looked confused.

'My God, do I have to draw you a picture?'

'I don't want to hurt you,' he said.

'Pretend it's a game.'

'But . . .'

I whirled around and ran from him.

Instead of coming after me, he went hunting for his glasses. So I stopped. With my back to him, I quickly slipped a hand down my skirt and plucked the cassette out of my panties. It was wet and slippery.

What'll I do with it?

My purse was on the couch, all the way across the room. No way of getting there without Murphy seeing me and wondering what I was up to.

I had no idea where to hide the cassette, so I kept it in my hand. I wiped it against the back of my skirt as I turned to face Murphy again.

He didn't seem to know where his glasses had landed after I'd knocked them off his face.

'There on the table,' I said, pointing.

'Ah.' He found them, picked them up, checked them out, and put them on his face. 'Thanks,' he said.

'Now come and get it,' I blurted, and ran.

This time, he chased me.

All right!

He probably could've caught me if he'd tried, but he stayed a stride or two back. I made straight for the doorway of his bedroom and lunged through it.

Murphy close on my heels, I raced across the floor and leaped onto his bed.

Luckily, his curtains were shut.

I stopped in the middle of his springy mattress. Bouncing, I turned around to face him.

He stopped at the foot of the bed and gaped up at me, his face strange with perplexity and delight.

'What're you staring at, big guy?'

He didn't answer, just watched.

Even though I wasn't bouncing very hard, my breasts were flying around like crazy. And he was gazing at them as if mezmerized by how they jumped and lurched.

'What're you gonna do now, hotshot?' I asked. 'Just gonna stand there gawping at my boobs?'

Bending over, he reached out and grabbed my ankles and pulled.

I let out a squeal and landed on my back.

He jerked my ankles wide apart. My left leg came out of the slit in my skirt, and was bare all the way up to my hip. 'How's that?' he gasped.

'Shut up and fuck me,' I said.

Chapter Thirty-four

The Art of Seduction

Off came his Bear Whizz Beer T-shirt. He pulled it up his torso and over his head. While his eyes were behind the T-shirt, I stuffed the cassette tape underneath the pillow.

As he tossed the shirt aside, I braced myself up on my elbows so I could see him better.

He was slim and nicely built, and had a good tan.

Still in his shorts, he planted a knee on the mattress and got ready to climb up.

'Why don't you get rid of the shorts?' I said.

'Huh?' he asked.

'And how come you're wearing *swimming trunks*? You don't even have a pool.'

'They're comfortable.'

'Well, take them off.'

More flustered than usual, he said, 'I don't . . . I'm not wearing any . . . you know, underwear.'

'Good. Take off the trunks and get up here.'

'You gonna look?'

'Of course I'm gonna look.'

'Do you *have* to?' he asked.

'You're some rapist.'

'I'm not a rapist.'

'Are you a virgin?'

'No,' he said. 'It's just that . . . we hardly even know each other.'

'You've already seen plenty of me,' I informed him. 'And you're about to see the rest. So let's have a look at you.'

'Well . . .'

'When do you plan to stop blushing?'

'Sometime next year, I should imagine.' Bending over, he pulled down his trunks. When he stood up straight, they were out of sight. 'There,' he said.

'Wow,' I said.

He gave me a twitchy, embarrassed smile.

'Get up here,' I said.

'Just a second, I'd better grab a condom.'

'No, don't. You're raping me. I need your semen for evidence. You can't use a rubber.'

'I don't know if that's such a good idea.'

'It's the whole point.'

He looked hurt.

So I said, 'Well, it *was* the whole point, anyway. Before you got me all worked up like this.' Squirming a little and staring him in the eyes, I undid both the buttons that held my skirt together at the hip. I spread the skirt open. I still had my panties on, but nothing else. There was about as much to my panties as a pirate's eyepatch. The band and patch were red like my bra. 'I've still gotta have the *evidence*,' I explained.

He gaped at me for a while, his mouth hanging open. Then he said, 'We really need to use protection.'

'I won't get pregnant. You don't have to worry about that. I just finished my period.' A fib, but so what?

You should've seen him go red. Guys really hate to hear about your period. Normal guys, anyway. Perverts are a different story. I knew this pervert named Jack, and he used to keep track of my time of the month so he could . . . Never mind. I can't tell every story I know, or you'd never find out what happened between me and Murphy. Anyway, believe me, you don't *want* to know about Jack. He was mental.

Murphy, still on the subject of condoms, said, 'It's not just about you getting pregnant.'

'I know. You're worried about diseases.'

'Yeah.'

'Do you have any?' I asked.

'No.'

'Neither do I.'

'I still think we'd better . . .'

'Don't you believe me?' I asked. 'You think I'm *lying*?'

'You might be. Hell, *you're* afraid I'll turn you in the minute I get alone. Why can't *I* be afraid you'll give me AIDS and kill me?'

'I haven't been with a guy in about five years,' I told him. 'I don't shoot up drugs. I haven't had any blood transfusions. And I've had annual check-ups. I'm not gonna give you any disease.'

'Five years?' he asked.

'I've been saving myself for you.'

He smiled and said, 'Right.'

'By the look of things, it was well worth the wait.'

'Thanks, but I still want to use a condom.' He turned away and walked toward his dresser.

'Come on, no. I want to feel *you* in me.'

As he pulled open a drawer, he looked over his shoulder at me.

'You wear one of those,' I said, 'it's like getting fucked by a balloon.'

He laughed softly and shook his head. 'It's not much better from this end, believe me.' Then he started searching through the drawer. 'Maybe after we've known each other longer . . .'

'Next time, I'll bring a note from my doctor. If there is a next time.'

'I hope there will be,' Murphy said.

I said, 'Me, too.'

Then I pulled the skirt out from under me and pushed it aside until it fell to the floor. On my back, I brought my knees up to my chest and peeled my panties off.

Murphy found what he was looking for, turned around and came back toward the bed with a foil packet pinched between his thumb and forefinger.

'Would you like me to do the honors?' I asked.

'Like what?'

'If you *have* to wear it, I might as well get the fun of putting it on you.'

'Okay. If you want to.'

Sitting up, I swung myself around. I sat on the edge of the

bed, my feet on the floor. 'Right here.' I spread my knees and patted the side of the mattress.

Murphy stepped in between my legs.

'Man, look at that thing.'

He glanced at it and shrugged.

'Looks like a cannon.'

Blushing deep red, he muttered, 'No it doesn't.'

'Hope it doesn't go off by accident.'

'Hey.'

'Might blow out my eye.'

'Jeez.'

I grinned up at him. 'What?'

'Do you have to talk about it?'

'Just admiring the equipment.'

'Do you *have* to?'

'I don't *have* to.'

'It's just . . . sort of embarrassing.'

'Okay. I'll stop talking about it.'

'Thanks,' he said.

'Me and my big mouth,' I said.

'That's all right.'

'But are you *sure* you want to cover this baby up with a nasty old rubber?'

'That's the only way I'll . . . yeah. I'm afraid so. Sorry.'

'Okay. It's a shame, but if you insist . . .'

'I do.'

'Okay. Well, give me that thing.'

He handed the packet to me. I tore it open and pulled out the condom. It felt warm and slimy. 'Yuck,' I said. 'I *really* want this in me. What is it, *used*?'

'Just pre-lubricated.'

'I know, I know. I was kidding. But yuck. I mean, really.'

'We don't have to do this,' he said, and placed his hands gently on my shoulders.

'Don't have to use the rubber?'

'Not if we call the whole thing off.'

I looked up at him. 'Do you *want* to call it off?' I asked.

'Do I look like it?'

'Hardly.'

He started to rub my shoulders. And kept rubbing them as I leaned forward.

But it wasn't the condom I put on him.

It was my mouth.

He gasped and arched his back and squeezed my shoulders. But he didn't complain or try to pull back.

Dropping the condom, I clutched his buttocks. I dug my fingernails in, drew him closer to me and slid my lips down his thick shaft, taking him into my mouth until no more could fit in.

He stood rigid and moaned.

I pulled slowly back, sucking as I went.

He shuddered.

I squeezed his buttocks and went down again, my lips a tight, sliding ring.

'Don't. Uh. Y'better stop.'

Up again, pulling at him, sucking.

'Ahhh!'

Down, taking him in deeper and deeper.

'No, y'gotta . . . I'm gonna . . .!'

I jerked my head up suddenly and he popped out of my mouth with a wet slurp. I tugged his ass. As he stumbled toward me, I shoved at the floor with my feet, springing up from the mattress and wrapping my arms around his back.

He fell forward, trapped between my thighs. I fell backward, pulling him down on top of me.

On the way down, he prodded my right thigh so I shifted a bit to take care of the aim.

My back hit the mattress.

And in he went.

He was awfully big, but I was juicy.

Pre-lubricated.

He went sliding in all the way. It felt huge, but I liked how it filled me and stretched me. I hugged him tightly and clamped my legs around him.

Grunting, he tried to push himself off me.

For about two seconds.

Then, with a moan, he kissed me and shoved his tongue into my mouth and jammed a hand in between us and grabbed one of my breasts and thrust at me with his hips and throbbed deep inside me, spurting.

'So much for condoms,' I whispered.

I held him hard against me.

The moment he finished pumping, though, he started to struggle so I let him go. He didn't have any mattress under his knees. As he squirmed backward, he no sooner got out of me than he slid off the edge of the bed.

Raising my head, I found Murphy on his knees. He was red and gasping, and had a dazed look in his eyes.

He still had his glasses on and they'd gotten knocked crooked.

I gave him a cheerful smile.

'That was a . . . lousy trick,' he said.

'I thought it was a *good* trick. Hell, so did you. You loved it. You went nuts.'

He shook his head, glanced between my legs, then turned his head away and straightened his glasses.

'There's nothing to worry about,' I told him. 'I didn't *give* you anything – expect maybe the quickest, hottest fuck of your life.'

'I wanted to use a condom.'

'I didn't. And you didn't *need* one.'

'I sure hope not,' he said, and stood up.

He was sticking straight out as if pointing at something across the room.

'Wanta do it again?' I asked.

'No.'

'Are you sure?'

He glanced at me, looked away, then turned to me again and stared at my sprawled, naked body.

'How about it, big fella?'

Though he frowned as if angry at me, he was rising. 'You're a real piece of work,' he said.

'Yep.' Writhing, I rubbed my breasts and licked my lips. 'How about another piece?'

His smile broke out. 'Don't you think I'd better get to the bank?'

'Don't you want to rape me again?'

'Who raped who?'

I laughed. 'You loved it. And you'd love to do it again, wouldn't you?'

'Don't you want me to get the money?'

'Yeah. Sure. I want the money, but . . .'

'Then I'd better go.'

'Okay. But first you have to tie me up.'

'*Tie you up?*'

'Of course. I'm your prisoner.'

'That's crazy.'

'If you call the cops on me, I want them to find me naked and tied to your bed.'

'*I'm not going to call the cops.*'

'This'll be my insurance. Now, go find some ropes or something, okay?'

Chapter Thirty-five

Tied

'How's that?' he asked.

Stretched out spread-eagled on his bed, I strained at the ropes. They creaked a little, but held. 'Excellent,' I said.

He stood near the end of the bed and stared down at me. He was a little out of breath. And hard. 'Anything else I can do for you?' he asked.

'Climb on.'

'Don't you want the money?'

'Yeah, I want it.'

'Then you'd better let me leave, don't you think?'

'You'd better put some clothes on first.'

'Thanks for the reminder.'

I watched him go to the closet and take out a pair of jeans and a short-sleeved shirt. When he had them on, he sat at the end of the bed to put on his socks and shoes. 'Any last minute instructions?' he asked.

'Small bills.'

'How small?'

'I don't know,' I said. 'But that's what the gangsters always want. Small bills.'

He looked over his shoulder at me and smiled. 'My gal, the crime wave.'

My gal?

He'd said it in a kidding way, but I liked it.

'Anyhow,' I said, 'big stuff is hard to spend.'

'Let's at least get most of it in hundreds and fifties,' he suggested. 'Otherwise, you'll have an awful lot of cash to lug around.'

'I guess that'll be okay.'

He turned away and finished putting on his shoes. Then he stood up and faced me. He looked good. 'Any other orders, Vito?' he asked.

'One more. You'd better gag me so I can't cry out for help.'

'Why on earth would you want to cry out for help?'

'Because you're holding me prisoner.'

'But I'm *not* holding you prisoner.'

'I know that, you know that, but the cops won't know that, will they?'

'The cops again.'

'Just find a handkerchief or something and tie it around my mouth.'

'You might suffocate.'

'Tie it loose.'

He smirked and shook his head, then turned away and went to his dresser. I heard a drawer open. A minute later, he said, 'I don't think my handkerchiefs are big enough.'

'Well, find something.'

He left the room. I heard his quick footsteps, a drawer sliding open and shut, then more footsteps. He came back with a white dish rag.

'How's this?' he asked.

'Perfect.'

Kneeling beside me on the mattress, he wound the towel into a thick strip. I lifted my head off the pillow and opened my mouth. He stuffed the towel in. Then he knotted it behind my neck.

'Okay?' he asked.

I said, 'Uhhh,' into the rag.

Grinning, Murphy said, 'I should've done this to you a long time ago.'

I said, 'Haw haw.'

'Will you be okay like this?' he asked.

If I don't get a stuffed-up nose.

I nodded.

'I'll get back as fast as I can,' he said. Bending down, he kissed me on the forehead.

Then he hurried away. I heard his footsteps as he wandered around the apartment. I didn't know what he was doing, but figured he was probably getting his keys, wallet, checkbook, that sort of thing. Then he took a leak. He flushed the toilet. He washed his hands. Finally, the front door thudded shut.

I was alone.

Tied up and gagged.

And I liked it.

The mattress felt good underneath me.

I could breathe okay through the dish towel.

The room was hot, and everything had a yellow hue because of the sunlight seeping through the curtains. A breeze was gently lifting the curtains. It smelled of flowers and mowed grass. Every so often, I felt the air sneak softly over my body.

It may sound strange, but I actually liked the feel of being pulled by the ropes. My whole body felt lean and taut.

I thought of Judy hanging by her wrists in the firelight, and how fine she'd looked.

Is she still there? I wondered.

Maybe she'd already managed to work her way loose. Or maybe someone had found her and set her free.

Maybe she's still there, just the way I left her.

She's there and I'm here. We're both naked. We're both tied and helpless. We have our wounds, but we're beautiful – stretched taut and lean.

While thinking about her, I must've slipped off into sleep.

Soon, she came walking over to the foot of the bed. The red bandana hung loose around her neck, and that's all she wore. She held a knife in her right hand. 'Well, well, well,' she said. 'Look at you.'

'I'm sure glad to see you,' I said, and wondered vaguely how I was able to talk through my gag. Then I realized that the gag was gone. 'I've really missed you, Judy,' I said. 'I've missed you so much.'

'I've missed you, too,' she said.

'How did you manage to get free?'

She raised her left arm and showed me the rough, bloody stump at her wrist. 'Had to gnaw my hand off,' she said.

'My God.'

She smiled sweetly and shrugged. 'Ah, it wasn't so bad. You do what you've gotta do. Looks like you're in a predicament, yourself.'

'Not really.'

'You don't think so?'

'No. This is just to look good in case Murphy gets the cops on me.'

'He won't do that.'

'You never know,' I said. 'Guys'll stab you in the back.'

'Not this one. He loves you.'

'He *loves* me? Do you think so?'

'Sure. He's head over heels.'

'I don't know.'

'Trust me,' Judy said.

'I sure hope you're right.'

I hoped so badly that she might be right. It made me feel excited and sad and warm to think that Murphy might actually love me.

It made me feel a little like crying.

'I *know* he loves you,' Judy assured me. 'But that doesn't mean he'll come back and untie you.'

'Oh, he will.'

'Maybe he will and maybe he won't. Do you want me to cut you loose, just in case?'

It didn't seem necessary. After all, I was sure that Murphy

would soon be back. But I liked having Judy in the room with me, and wanted her to come closer.

So I said, 'Yeah, maybe you'd better.'

Smiling, she strolled over to the bed. She climbed onto the mattress, swung a leg over me, and sat on my belly. Then she leaned forward. Her left breast looming over my face, she started to saw at the rope around my right wrist. Her breast shook with the quick movements of her arm.

Then it stopped.

She'd quit trying to cut through the rope.

I pulled, but my arm was still tied down.

'Why are you stopping?' I asked.

'I changed my mind. I don't think I'll cut you loose, after all.'

'Why not?'

'Just remembered something.'

'What?' I asked, with a bad feeling starting to chill my stomach.

'*You* didn't cut *me* down.'

'I know, but . . .'

'Why should I cut you down, when you left me hanging in the woods?'

'I had to,' I said.

'And I had to chew my hand off, or I'd still *be* there. You know what? It hurt.'

'I'm sorry.'

'You oughta be.'

'I am.'

'Prove it,' Judy said.

'How?'

'Kiss me.'

Her breast hovered low over my face, swaying slightly, looking golden in the soft sunlight coming in through the curtains. Her nipple was just above my mouth.

Opening my mouth, I raised my head off the pillow.

I flicked her nipple with my tongue.

'Not there,' she said, and thrust the gory stump of her wrist into my mouth.

'*Eat it!*' she yelled.

Shocked awake, I cried out – into my dish rag – and tried to sit up.

The ropes held me down.

I struggled to fill my lungs, but couldn't get enough air. Not with the gag in my mouth. Murphy had left some slack in it, though. Rubbing my cheek against my shoulder and shoving at the rag with my tongue, I quickly got my mouth clear and took deep, quick breaths.

As I calmed down, I started thinking.

First, I'd caught a mouthful of water in the bathtub.

Now this.

Both times, I'd fallen asleep dreaming of Judy, then gotten startled awake, only to find myself suffocating.

Maybe she's trying to tell me something.

What am I supposed to do, go back and cut her down before she has to gnaw her hand off?

Maybe she's already done it!

Hell, she couldn't chew her hand off even if she wanted to. It was too high above her head.

I realized that I wouldn't be able to chew mine off, either.

What if we're both stuck?

Don't worry about it, I told myself. For one thing, I can probably get free if I really have to. For another, I won't have to. Murphy should be getting back pretty soon.

How soon?

I had no idea how long he'd been gone. I'd fallen asleep almost right away, but how long had I been under? It didn't *seem* like very long. Ten or twenty minutes?

He'll be back any time now, I told myself.

How do you know?

583

Where's his bank?

He hadn't told me, but it had to be somewhere in town, probably no more than a ten-minute drive from here.

Ten minutes each way. That makes a total of twenty. And there might be a line inside the bank. So give him another ten minutes for the line.

That adds up to half an hour.

But maybe the line is really long.

Or they give him trouble about making such a large withdrawal.

Or he decides to take care of another errand or two before coming back.

Or his car breaks down.

Or he has an accident.

Or the bank gets robbed while he's there.

And the bank robbers take him hostage.

Or shoot him.

Or he drops dead of a heart attack.

Or an aneurism.

HE'S NOT DEAD, DAMN IT! HE CAN'T BE! HE LOVES ME!

Calm down, I told myself. For one thing, he's *not* dead. For another, he doesn't *love* me. That was Judy saying that. In a dream. Has nothing to do with reality.

Like I said before, dreams stink. They're no good for anything. They only exist to torture you any way they can.

He doesn't love me, I told myself.

But he *will* be back.

The bank *didn't* get robbed while he was there. That's nonsense. Paranoia.

He'll be back any minute.

Sure he will.

But maybe with cops in tow.

Maybe he's been lying to me from the start and right now he's telling the cops all about me.

No, he wouldn't dare.

No matter what story he might tell the cops, he'd be in a world of trouble the moment they found me tied to the bed. A naked woman, roped down, with numerous minor injuries and his semen inside.

Before you know it, they'll be thinking *he* killed Tony and abducted Judy and me.

For a while, I tried to come up with a good story to explain how it all worked. Maybe the four of us went to the park together on a double-date. I was Tony's date and Judy was Murphy's date. But then Murphy decided he wanted *both of us*, so he killed Tony, chopped him up and put him in the trunk . . .

How does Milo the Killer Slob fit in?

Maybe Judy escaped from Murphy, only to be grabbed by Milo – a thrill-killer lurking around in the woods in search of victims. He jumps her and takes her to his camp . . .

Awfully far-fetched.

Keep it nice and simple.

I could just say Judy ran off into the woods and I don't know what happened to her after that.

But what about Tony's car? I'd have to explain how it ended up back at Judy's apartment building – with his body in it.

That'd be a good trick.

It's probably not the only problem, either.

What about the tape from Tony's answering machine? If the cops showed up and cut me free, they would be sure to find it under the pillow.

Murphy put it there.

Simple.

But how could I possibly come up with a sensible story that explained everything?

Claim amnesia.

Good idea.

Tell the cops I don't know how *anything* happened. Last I

remember, I was walking back to my garage after watching the television in Serena and Charlie's den.

That should work.

At least until Judy spills the beans.

If she talks, I'm screwed.

I should've killed her when I had the chance.

Maybe it's not too late.

I suddenly had an urge to get free, run out to Judy's car and speed over to Miller's Woods, find the camp and finish her off.

Do it now. Get out of here before Murphy comes back.

But the ropes held me down.

I strained at them with my arms and legs. They were nothing but pieces of old clothesline, and seemed to stretch as I pulled. They also tightened around my wrists and ankles. I kept pulling, anyway. For all I knew, Murphy might've done a lousy job tying the other ends around the legs of the bed. Maybe something would give, down there. Or maybe I could break the ropes by sheer strength.

They held, but I didn't give up.

I pulled, jerked, kicked, squirmed and bucked. Soon, I was out of breath and pouring sweat.

I quit struggling, and rested.

The ropes had tightened so much that they'd cut off my circulation. My hands and feet were numb. The pillow case and sheet underneath me felt soaked.

Gasping for air, I blinked sweat out of my eyes.

And thought, Maybe I *can't* get loose.

I can! I will!

Just give me a minute to catch my breath.

While I was waiting to make my next try, someone rang the doorbell.

Chapter Thirty-six

Invader

At any time of the day or night, I hate the sound of a doorbell. It almost always means someone has shown up uninvited.

An intruder is barging into your life.

Invading.

No matter what, it's annoying and a little scary.

But just try having the doorbell ring when you're naked in the bedroom of a guy you hardly know, you're tied down, and your legs are spread apart about as far as they'll go.

When I heard that doorbell, I felt as if someone had shot a hose full of ice water up my bowels.

I froze.

The bell rang again.

Nobody's home! Go away!

What if it's the cops?

So what if it is? I told myself. Cops can't come into a place without being invited. Not unless they have a search warrant.

They can't possibly have a search warrant.

Can they?

The bell rang again.

Go AWAY!

Calm down, I told myself. Whoever it is, they can't get in. Sooner or later, they'll give up and go away.

Again, the bell rang.

Persistent . . .

What if it's burglars?

They do that. They pick a place that looks deserted. But before they break in, they ring the doorbell to make sure nobody

587

is home. If someone comes to the door, they have a little story to tell. 'Is Doug there? No? Oh, I must have the wrong address.' But if nobody answers the doorbell, they figure the place is empty and safe to rob.

In they come . . .

And find me like this.

Should I call out?

And say what? *I'm here, but I can't come to the door right now!* Like I'm on the john, or something. *Could you come back in a few minutes?*

No, I thought. Don't do it. Keep your mouth shut.

The little town of Chester has its share of crime. I mean, what place doesn't? But the odds had to be slim that the doorbell was being rung by a burglar. *Especially* when you consider that, since just after last midnight, I'd run into a weirdo flasher *and* a serial killer. On top of all that, a *burglar*? Not likely.

Not impossible, either. But . . .

Someone used a key on the front door. I heard its quiet ratchety sound as it slid into a lock, heard the latch click back, heard the knob rattle, heard a sigh of hinges as the door swung open.

Shit! Now what?

A man's voice called out, 'Murphy? Yo, Murph? You home? Helllllo? It's only me from across the sea!' He waited a few seconds, then said, 'Yo ho ho, guess you're not home.'

I heard the door shut, but I didn't know whether he was inside or out.

Until I heard his footsteps on the carpet.

Great! I'm gonna get found!

Some creep I don't even know is gonna see me like this.

He must be Murphy's best friend or brother or something. You don't give a spare key to just anyone.

This guy is about to have the surprise of his life.

I heard the television come on. It sounded like CNN's *Headline News*.

That's right, I thought. Sit down in the living room and watch some TV news. Just stay put. Don't move. Murphy'll be home pretty soon. He'll figure a way to steer you out of the place, and you'll never be the wiser.

From the TV came a nifty British voice talking about tribal massacres in some African country. Zaire or Rwanda or some damn place.

Suddenly, during a pause in the broadcast, I heard footsteps again. These were quiet, as if the intruder had taken off his shoes.

What's he doing?

Going into the kitchen for a beer?

The only route to the kitchen – or just about anywhere else in the apartment – would take him past the open bedroom door.

Maybe he won't look in.

Fat chance.

I shut my eyes and went limp.

The footsteps suddenly stopped. The intruder said, 'Whoa!'

I kept my eyes shut and tried to keep my breathing shallow and slow.

Let him think I'm out cold or dead or something. I sure didn't want to strike up a conversation with the guy.

'What the hell's going on here?' he muttered, and came walking slowly into the room. 'Lady?' he asked.

I didn't stir.

He said, 'My God, what's Murphy *done*?'

He sounded as if he were standing at the foot of the bed. I tried not to think about the view he had. But I could feel myself blushing.

I was blushing, sweating, and my heart was pounding fast. Couldn't he see any of that?

Not where he's probably looking.

'Wow,' he said. 'Oh, Murphy, Murphy. How'd you land a babe like this?'

Down between my legs, the mattress sank in.

The mattress shook, making me wobble.

What's he doing?

A hand patted me on the thigh. Very high up on my thigh.

'Hello?' he asked. 'Young lady? Can you hear me?'

I didn't respond.

'Must be out cold,' he muttered.

Moments later, a light fabric fell across my face.

Then two hands were gently caressing my thighs. 'What a piece,' he muttered. 'Man, oh man. Murph, you lucky dog. No wonder you tied her down. Couldn't let something like this get away from you.'

His tongue got me. I gasped and flinched with the sudden shock of it, and knew the game was up. With no more need to play possum, I writhed as his mouth stayed where it was and his hands roamed up my body and found my breasts. He caressed them, gently massaged them, squeezed my nipples and pulled while his tongue flicked and delved. Soon, I was panting, thrashing against the ropes.

His mouth lifted off me. 'Looks like I've awakened Sleeping Beauty. Does this mean I'm a prince?'

It was the same, fake voice.

But this time, I recognized the mind behind it.

'You bastard!' I gasped out.

Opening my eyes, I found a pale blue shirt on top of my face. Murphy swept it aside and smiled down at me. He was kneeling between my legs, totally naked and erect.

'What do you think you're doing?' I asked.

'What do you think?'

'You scared the hell out of me.'

'Good,' he said. Then he came down and planted his mouth on my mouth and pushed himself slowly into me until I had all of him. Then he pulled most of the way out, and thrust in so hard that the ropes bit into my ankles and I yelped into his mouth.

He murmured, 'Sorry.'

Then he clutched me by the shoulders to hold me still so the ropes wouldn't hurt me again.

And went at it.

He went crazy on me, plunging and ramming as if he needed to get someplace where nobody'd ever gone before.

By damn, I think he succeeded.

He blew the roof off the joint, so to speak.

I'd never gone through anything like it. My guess is, neither had he.

When he was done, he stayed inside and settled down heavily on top of me, gasping for air. When he could talk, he said, 'Are you okay?'

I answered by flexing some muscles down there.

He said, 'Ooooh.'

After a while, I said, 'That was a rotten trick, you know.'

'Huh?'

'Faking me out. Pretending you were somebody else.'

'Oh. That. Yeah. Figured I owed you one.'

'Very nice.'

'I enjoyed it,' he said.

'You've got a real mean streak,' I told him.

'That makes two of us.'

'So, did you get the money okay?'

'Yep. Everything went smooth as silk.'

I gave him a couple more flexes, and felt him starting to grow.

'How come no condom?' I asked.

'Didn't see much point. Not after the way you got me before.'

'For which you decided to pay me back by impersonating a stranger and scaring me shitless.'

'Not exactly.'

'No?'

'That's just . . . the way it turned out. What I'd planned to do was come straight in, strip naked and jump on you. No tricks. But when I showed up, there was a bunch of Jehovah's Witnesses at the front door.'

'You're kidding. That was a Jehovah's Witness ringing the doorbell?'

'Yep.'

'Never figured that.'

'I figured you were probably freaking.'

'I wasn't *freaking*.'

He laughed. It felt strange and great, the way he shook on top of me and deep inside me while he laughed.

'I might've been mildly concerned,' I admitted.

He laughed some more.

'What freaked me,' I explained, 'was when some sneaky, rotten son-of-a-bitch unlocked the door and came in.'

'That was me,' he said.

I said, 'Duh.'

He laughed again.

'Bastard.'

'You loved it.'

'Not the trick, I didn't. That really stank.'

'Who did you think I was?'

'One of your horny buddies. Or maybe a brother.'

'Whoever you thought I was, you must've liked him. I didn't hear any complaints.'

'That's only because I was trying to play possum.'

'If you *hadn't* been playing possum, you would've seen right away that it was only me. The moment I walked into the bedroom. I didn't throw the shirt over your face until pretty far along.'

'What if I *hadn't* figured it was you?' I asked. 'Were you just going to screw me and leave, so I'd go on thinking it was someone else?'

'I knew you'd recognize me. I'm surprised it took you as long as it did.'

'It was the prince crack,' I explained, and had to smile.

'Ah, well.'

'When I heard that, I knew it was you.'

'Not only beautiful, but smart.'

'That's me,' I said. Turning my head, I kissed the side of his face. Then I asked, 'You gonna let me up, now?'

'Maybe I will and maybe I won't.'

'My hands and feet are numb.'

'Oh. Uh-oh.' He pushed himself up and slid out of me. Frowning, he said, 'I should've untied you first thing. I didn't realize the ropes were that tight. I'm sorry.'

'Hey, it's fine.'

Kneeling over my chest, he leaned forward, reached out with both hands, and started trying to untie my left wrist.

It reminded me a lot of my Judy dream.

Except that Judy'd had breasts and a knife.

Soon, Murphy managed to pluck open the knot. He loosened the rope around my wrist, and I pulled my hand free. It really was numb. I shook it, trying to get some feeling back, while he worked on the knot at my other wrist.

'I shouldn't have made these so tight,' he muttered.

'Had to make it look good.'

'Not really,' he said. 'I came back without any cops.'

'See? It worked.'

He laughed, and kept on struggling with the knot.

With circulation coming back, my left hand began to feel hot and get pins and needles. I kept flapping it around and wiggling my fingers.

'This one's sure tight,' he said.

'Maybe you should get a knife.'

'Yeah. That might save a lot of trouble.'

He tried for another few seconds, then climbed off me and the bed.

'Back in a second,' he said.

I raised my head off the pillow and watched him stride toward the doorway. His tan stopped just above his rear end, and started again at the tops of his legs. His ass looked pale as cream, and smooth. The firm, round buttocks took turns flexing as he walked.

In the doorway, he turned around.

I liked the front view better.

Leaning sideways, he rested a shoulder against the door frame and smiled at me. 'Can I get you anything else while I'm in the kitchen? A glass of water for your Morning Dehydration Syndrome? A Pepsi? A beer?'

'Just hurry, okay? If I'm tied up much longer, something may have to get amputated.'

He raised his eyebrows. 'If anything has to come off, may I have it?'

Chapter Thirty-seven

Identity Crisis

Very funny,' I muttered.

'I'll take anything. I'm not picky.'

'Every piece of me is precious?'

'You got it.'

'Go!'

He laughed and hurried away.

With my free left hand, I reached under the pillow and grabbed the miniature cassette. I thought about hiding it on my person, so to speak. But what if Murphy decided to have another go at me while it was in there?

So I just slid it between my back and the mattress, where it would be easy to reach.

I no sooner had it out of sight than Murphy came hurrying in with a knife. He carried it in his right hand, down low by his side. Its blade, at least eight inches long, was straight out and pointing at me.

The blade wasn't all that was pointing at me.

They were level with each other, both tilting at the same slightly upward angle, and one about as long as the other. While the knife swung back and forth at the end of Murphy's arm, the thick shaft bounced and swayed with each step he took.

'You come well armed,' I said.

He smirked and shook his head, but didn't say anything.

Stopping beside my right hand, he bent over and eased the blade down onto the rope. He wouldn't be going for the knot, but for the clothesline itself where it was tight around my wrist. Only the thickness of the rope – less than half an inch – stood between the blade's edge and my skin. 'Don't move,' he muttered. 'I don't want to cut you.'

The way he was hunkered over with his head down, his hair fell across his brow and hid his eyes. He looked like a big kid with a messy mop of hair.

As he gently sawed the rope, his hair hardly moved at all, but the motions of his arm were enough to shake his rigid penis from side to side.

Finally, he cut me.

'Ow!'

'Sorry,' he said, quickly stepping back. 'Are you all right?'

'Yeah. Probably. What's one more cut?'

'I think that'll do it, though. Try giving a hard pull.'

I jerked my arm downward. The rope held it for a moment, then made a quiet *puh!* and let me go.

'I'll get your feet,' Murphy said and stepped toward the other end of the bed.

I brought my right hand down. It was surrounded by a deep red indentation from the rope. The knife had made a shallow, half-inch slice. Bright red blood was sliding out, streaking my wrist and forearm. I quickly licked the streaks away, then covered the wound with my mouth.

Murphy was watching. 'Maybe I'd better get you a bandage,' he said.

'It's no big deal. Why don't you go ahead and cut me loose? We can worry about a bandage later. Anyway, we may need several by the time you're done.'

'I'll be a lot more careful,' he said. 'And this time, I'll go for the knots.'

'Good idea.'

Bending over my left foot, he started to work the knife back and forth. Its edge made soft, rubbing sounds against the rope.

'I haven't really had much practice at this sort of thing,' he said. 'Not since I was a kid.' He lifted his head and smiled. 'In my neighborhood, we were *always* tying people up.'

'Sounds like you lived in an interesting neighborhood,' I told him.

'I never tied up anyone like you, that's for sure. But I *wished* I could. I've always wanted to. This was like . . .' He shook his head and sighed. 'Unbelievable,' he said.

'Any time,' I told him.

He grinned, then lowered his head and resumed cutting.

He managed to slice the ropes off both my ankles without drawing any more blood.

When he was done, he asked, 'How's that?'

'Great. Thanks. But I don't think I can move.'

He picked up my legs and eased them together. Then he sat

on the end of the bed, turned sideways, and raised my feet onto his lap. He massaged them with both hands. 'Let me know when they're better,' he said. 'I'll help you into the bathroom and we'll take care of your cut.'

'Okay. Thanks.'

'And I don't think we should make that drive to Culver City.'

'You don't?'

'Screw them,' he said. 'I'll FedEx the books. It won't kill them to wait a day longer.'

'I don't want to be responsible . . .'

'Oh, don't worry about it.'

'What if I hadn't been here?'

He shrugged. 'Who knows? But that's not how it went down.'

'So, if we're not going to Culver City, what'll we do?'

'Whatever we want.'

'I want my five grand,' I told him.

He grinned. 'I want to hear your story.'

I said, 'Okay.' Though I smiled, I suddenly had a bad feeling inside – which must've showed.

'Something wrong?' Murphy asked.

Something was wrong, all right.

So far, he and I . . . we'd been getting along awfully well. I liked him better than any guy I'd ever known. A lot better.

Maybe I was even falling in love with him.

And maybe he had similar feelings about me.

But if I told him my story – the truth – it would probably ruin everything.

I mean, the truth might make me look pretty bad in his eyes. Might even disgust him. Especially when he hears about the way I chopped Tony into pieces, and about some of the things I did to Judy.

I can't tell him!

We kept looking at each other.

Frowning, Murphy asked, 'Are you feeling okay?'

'It's just . . . I've got a little headache. Do you have any aspirin, or . . .?'

'Sure. I'll get it for you.' He slid a hand up the bottom of my leg, gave my calf a friendly pat, then lifted my feet off his lap, stood up and lowered them to the mattress. 'Would you rather have Excedrin, Tylenol or Bufferin?' he asked.

'You must get a lot of headaches.'

'I get my share. What'll it be?'

'How about Excedrin?'

Nodding, he took a few steps away from the bed, crouched and picked up his trunks.

'You're getting dressed?'

'You've got a headache.'

'What does one have to do with the other?'

'You mean it wasn't a hint?' he asked, looking flustered.

'I'm not much for hinting. But if you want to go ahead and get dressed . . .'

'Well . . .' He shrugged and smiled. 'Maybe we should give you some time to get over your headache before we, uh, do anything too strenuous.'

'Maybe so.'

He stepped into his trunks, pulled them up, then left the room without putting on a shirt.

I reached under my back and grabbed the cassette. Shoving it into my mouth, I climbed off the bed. Then I swooped down and snatched my skirt off the floor. On my way to the door, I swept the skirt around my waist and fastened its buttons. Then I took the cassette out of my mouth. Clutching it in my right hand, I stepped through the doorway.

No sign of Murphy.

From the television came the voice of a man praising the courage of Paula Jones.

From the bathroom came a sound of rushing water.

Walking fast, I crossed the living room. Went straight to

my purse near the end of the couch. Bent over it and spread it open.

All I meant to do was drop the cassette inside.

But I gaped at what was in there.

The usual stuff: lipstick, my compact, some tissues, a couple of tampons, my sunglasses, and so on.

Plus two sets of keys – mine and Judy's.

And the note pad with Tony's new telephone number.

And my wallet.

My wallet!

With my own driver's license inside.

With my photo on it.

And my true name.

And real address.

'Oh, my Christ,' I murmured.

My hand trembling, I shoved the cassette down deep into the purse.

I felt sick.

Had Murphy looked?

He could've. He'd been out here alone before going to the bank, and then again after returning.

But did he?

Maybe he'd turned on the television so the voices would cover any sounds he might make while searching my purse.

But he'd been busy taking off his clothes.

And probably excited by his plans for me.

His blue jeans were draped over the cushion at the other end of the couch. His socks and shoes were on the floor over there.

'Oh, you're out,' he said.

I turned around to face him. 'Dressed, too.'

'Well, sort of.' He glanced at my chest, then quickly raised his eyes to my face.

'I thought maybe I had some chewing gum in my purse, but I guess not.'

'I'm afraid I don't have any,' he said, 'or I'd get you some.' He came toward me holding a glass of water in one hand, a plastic container of Excedrin in the other. 'You don't seem like the chewing gum type,' he said.

'What type is that?'

'Airhead.'

'Keeps my breath minty fresh,' I chirped, and stepped around to the front of the coffee table.

'Nothing wrong with your breath.'

A couple of strides away from me, he stopped.

I reached out for the glass of water, but he pulled it back slightly. 'Now, be careful,' he said. 'Let's not spill, this time.'

'If I do, I won't be getting my blouse wet.'

'Guess not.' Blushing deep crimson, he gave the glass to me. While I held it, he opened the Excedrin. I put out my left hand. He shook a couple of tablets into my palm. I tossed them into my mouth and washed them down with the water.

He waited until I'd lowered the glass, then asked, 'How's the cut?'

I glanced at it. 'Not so bad. See? The bleeding's stopped.'

'Does it hurt?'

'Nah. It's just a nick. I'm fine.'

'We'd better put something on it, anyway.'

'How about your lips?'

He laughed and blushed. A real blusher, that Murphy.

'I was thinking of an antiseptic,' he said. He took the glass from me and set it on the table. He put down the Excedrin bottle, too. Then, holding my hand, he led me across the room. 'We'll touch up the rest of you, too, while we're at it.'

'I can use a little touching up.'

In the bathroom, he poured some hydrogen peroxide onto a cotton ball and patted the cut on my wrist. It felt cold. It fuzzed a little on the slit.

After bandaging my little cut, he took out a fresh ball of

cotton. He soaked it with hydrogen peroxide and started dabbing at my other injuries – the scratches and nicks and gouges from last night's accidents. The liquid touched me with coldness. Here and there, it dribbled down my skin.

When it stung the wound on my belly, I gasped and stiffened. 'Sorry,' he said.

'That's okay. A little pain is good for the soul.'

'I'm not so sure about that.'

'It feels so good when it stops.'

'Can't argue with that one,' he said.

'I like how this stuff feels, though. It's so nice and cool.'

He said, 'Hmm.' With a fresh, dripping ball, he gently swabbed my right nipple.

Unaware of any injury there, I looked down. My nipple appeared to be fine. The chilly fluid made it pucker and jut out. 'Now you're treating places that aren't hurt,' I pointed out.

'Yep,' he said, and moved the cotton ball to my other nipple. I shivered a little with the good feel of it.

Then I undid my buttons, and my skirt fell to the bathroom floor. 'Anywhere else need a touch-up?' I asked.

He squatted down in front of me. 'I should say so,' he said. 'You've gotten yourself banged up pretty good.'

'Do what you can. I'm in your hands.'

Each time he touched me with a wet ball of cotton, I flinched a bit. Not because it hurt, but because it felt so cold on my hot skin.

Down low in front of me, he found a scratch here, a scrape there. He dabbed them. And he dabbed places where I had no injuries at all.

I turned around. He touched chilly balls of cotton to the backs of my thighs and to my buttocks. Then I felt his lips, his tongue. He kissed and licked his way up my back until he was standing.

When he pressed himself against my body, I found out that

his trunks were gone. He was smooth and bare all the way down. And I could feel the hard length of him pressing against my lower back.

Nibbling the side of my neck, he reached around me with both hands and took gentle hold of my breasts.

The cotton balls and the bottle of hydrogen peroxide must've been down on the bathroom floor with his trunks.

He writhed against my back, sucked my neck and squeezed my breasts. Then one of his hands roamed down my front and slipped between my legs. Moaning, I squirmed against him.

After a while, I managed to turn around so we were facing each other. By then, I was in such a frantic delirium that I hardly knew what was happening.

He slammed me against the door frame.

As he pulled at my buttocks, I climbed his body and wrapped my legs around him.

He thrust into me.

I hugged him with my arms and legs.

He pounded me against the frame as he tried to ram up higher and deeper.

Then suddenly he was throbbing and pumping.

I clung to him, shuddering with my own release.

As our frenzy subsided, we remained clutching each other, my back against the door frame, my feet off the floor, my legs and arms around him. He stayed in me. We both panted for air.

I gasped, 'My God, Murphy.'

He gasped, 'My God, Alice.'

Chapter Thirty-eight

The Slip

Every time I remember it, I get the same awful, sick feeling in the pit of my guts.

Murphy saying my name.

My real name.

(Not Alice, by the way. But my real name was on my driver's license and on a dozen other items in my wallet, and that's the name that came out of Murphy's mouth as we clutched each other in the bathroom doorway.)

Alice, not Fran.

He *had* searched my purse.

He knew who I was and where I lived.

Letting go of his back, I clutched his hair with both hands and jerked his head back, tilting his face toward mine.

'What'd you say?' I asked.

'Huh? When?'

'Just now.'

'Huh?'

'You called me Alice.'

'Huh?'

'Why'd you call me Alice?'

'Did I?'

'You looked in my purse!' I blurted into his face. Then my right hand let go of his hair and I hit him with my fist. Punched him in the cheek so hard it jolted his head sideways.

And then he staggered backward.

Lurched backward, turning as if he wanted to set me down in

the middle of the bathroom floor. But he didn't really have his balance anymore.

He couldn't stop.

Couldn't set me down.

It might've turned out all right, but too many things went wrong.

For one, Murphy kicked over the bottle of hydrogen peroxide. I heard it go over and roll, and heard its liquid gurgling out, slicking the tiles.

For another, Murphy had me clinging to him. Had me spitted on his cock so I couldn't jump down, couldn't get free, couldn't do anything to stop his sudden backward voyage across the bathroom.

Perched high and able to see over the top of his head, I saw what was coming.

'*Watch out!*' I yelled.

But he couldn't.

A moment later, the bathtub kicked his legs out from under him.

I flew face-first toward the tile wall on the other side of the tub. Throwing out my hands, I slapped the wall. My arms folded. I turned my face and my cheek struck one of my forearms.

From lower down came an awful thud like a coconut dropped on a concrete sidewalk. I not only heard it, but I *felt* it. Felt Murphy jolt between my legs and in me.

Suddenly, I felt a quick, sucking pull inside, and heard a slurp, and he was out.

And I was falling.

I threw my legs apart so Murphy wouldn't land on them.

My bare feet slapped against the bottom of the tub. For a moment, I seemed to be standing, hunched low over Murphy as if looking for a good way to sit on him. It seemed like a *long* moment. I saw him down there, looking limp and odd. I sure didn't want to sit on him. But I probably would've done it, anyway, if I'd had a choice.

I didn't.

Because it *was* only a moment, and I might've *seemed* to be standing, but I wasn't.

I was just pausing in mid-fall.

Waving my arms, I tumbled backward. My butt slapped against the edge of the tub – between Murphy's knees. Then my legs flew up and I dropped to the floor.

My back *smacked* the tile floor.

Then my head thumped it.

And that, as they say, was 'all she wrote'.

At least for a pretty long while.

I don't know what I dreamed about. Probably something bad. Whatever it might've been, though, at least I didn't wake up choking.

Just with a horrid headache.

I was lying on my back with my legs up, calves resting on the edge of the tub. The way Murphy's feet were sticking out, I figured he was probably in the reverse of my position, and inside the tub.

'Murph?' I asked.

He didn't answer.

Then I remembered the sound and feel of his head striking the wall – and my glimpse of him as I fell.

'Murph?' I asked again. 'Are you okay?'

Nothing.

'Are you dead?'

Nothing.

'God,' I muttered.

Then I started to cry.

A word of advice: don't ever cry when you've got a splitting headache. The crying does something to the pressure inside your head. Pretty soon, I felt like I had a team of maniacs chewing and clawing through my brain.

It seemed to get worse and worse. I tore off my wig of red hair and flung it aside. I felt a little better without it, but not much.

The pain still raging, I clutched both sides of my head.

Finally, I figured my position on the floor wasn't helping matters. I needed to get up. So I drew in my legs. They were pretty numb from the calves down because of how they'd been resting on the tub's edge. But I brought them to my side of the tub, anyway, and shoved with my feet.

My back slid over the tile floor. As I scooted, the top of my head ran into Murphy's trunks and pushed them along in front of me. I ended up in the puddle of hydrogen peroxide with the plastic bottle against my shoulder.

For a while, I just lay there on my back, sobbing and holding my head, my legs straight out on the floor.

I knew I should be trying to get away.

But I couldn't.

And didn't really care.

I felt too miserable to care about anything.

I'd killed Murphy.

I'd damn near busted my own head open.

Maybe I did!

Raising my head slightly, I explored it with my fingers. My hair was wet – maybe with blood. But I found no gaping fissures, no spilling brains. Just a bump high on the back of my head, as if half a golf ball had been stuffed underneath my scalp.

I looked at my fingers. They were wet, but not bloody.

Pretty soon, I rolled over. I crawled out of the bathroom. Off the tiles and onto the carpet of the living room.

As I crawled toward the coffee table, CNN blared at me about some damn ferry boat sinking in some Godforsaken corner of the world.

Like I could give a shit. I had problems of my own.

The voices made my head throb.

So I took a detour to the television. Kneeling in front of it, I had to squint because of the picture's brightness. But I found the power button and hit it with a knuckle. The TV suddenly went dark and silent.

Much better.

Turning around, I crawled the rest of the way to the table. I grabbed its edge and pushed myself up. On my knees, I studied the clutter for a few seconds.

I was looking for the Excedrin and the water glass, but the first thing I saw was Murphy's book. The one that he'd autographed for me. *Deep Dead Eyes.*

It wasn't something I wanted to be seeing just then.

I looked away from it fast.

When I spotted the plastic bottle of Excedrin, I reached out and grabbed it. I pulled it over to me, then got hold of the glass.

It was half full of water.

I tossed four Excedrin tablets into my mouth. Then, with a shuddering hand, I picked up the glass. I gulped the water and swallowed the tablets.

They went down fine.

I was still awfully thirsty, though. Holding on to the glass, I struggled to my feet. I staggered into the kitchen, turned on the faucet, and filled the glass with cold water. I drank it all. Then I refilled the glass. This time, I sipped it slowly and looked around.

Murphy's kitchen seemed to double for an office. Its breakfast table held a computer, piles of paper and stacks of books. I could almost see him sitting at the table, rubbing his hair and frowning with thought.

No more books for him.

Starting to feel worse, I turned away and saw a clock above the kitchen's entryway.

1:25.

Early afternoon. A lot earlier than I would've thought.

What'll I do?

I wanted to lie down on a nice bed and sleep. Make my headache go away. Make *all this* go away. At least for a while.

Lie down in my own bed . . .

But I couldn't do that, couldn't leave, not without taking care of the evidence.

A major clean-up to get rid of every trace of me.

It seemed like a huge, impossible job.

The way I felt . . .

I filled the glass once more with water, then carried it out of the kitchen and into Murphy's bedroom.

As I made my way toward the bed, I saw three of the ropes he'd used on me. They lay on the carpet like pale, dead snakes. Each was still tied to a leg of the bed.

I'll have to take those . . .

I saw the condom, too. On the floor where I'd dropped it when I took Murphy into my mouth.

The pale white disk looked like a sea creature you might find washed up on a beach, dead.

I'll have to get rid of it.

But I could do nothing, now.

I set the glass of water on the nightstand, then crawled onto the bed, sprawled myself out on its rumpled sheet, and buried my face in the pillow.

Chapter Thirty-nine

So Long, My Sweet

Most of my headache was gone when I woke up. I was still facedown on Murphy's bed, as if I hadn't moved at all during my nap.

I'd drooled all over his pillow.

The sheet underneath me was sodden with my sweat.

I thought how nice it might be to take a shower, but then I remembered that Murphy was in the tub.

Dead.

I'd killed him.

I hadn't *meant* to, but that didn't count for much: he was just as dead, either way.

And here I was, sprawled on his bed like Goldilocks.

What if somebody shows up?

I've gotta get out of here.

So I rolled over, twisted sideways until my legs fell off the edge of the mattress, and sat up. I groaned. My body felt ruined. I was sore and stiff and achy almost everywhere. But at least my head no longer burned with pain.

I could think again.

I could function.

I *could*, but *didn't*.

Not for a while, anyway.

For a while, I just sat on the edge of the bed, my head hanging, my back bent, my elbows on my thighs, my feet on the floor.

Almost like that statue, *The Thinker*.

But if anyone did a statue of how I looked then, he'd have to name it *The Wasted*.

I knew that I needed to get off my butt and destroy every trace of my presence in Murphy's apartment and go home. But I couldn't bring myself to get started.

What's the point?

I felt as if nothing mattered anymore.

Why not just stay here?

Sooner or later, somebody would show up and find me, find Murphy, call the cops.

Who cares?

Why not go to the phone and call the cops, myself? Tell them everything. Put an end to all this.

But doing even that would've taken too much effort.

So I just kept sitting there.

Finally, I *had* to get up. It was either that, or flood the bedroom. Gritting my teeth, I made it to my feet. But I couldn't stand up straight. Hunched over slightly, I hurried to the bathroom. I slipped on the wet tile floor, but didn't fall. With my eyes fixed on the floor just in front of my feet, I found my way to the toilet and sat down without looking at Murphy.

I kept my head low while I went.

Stared at the floor.

But I could see him, anyway. That peripheral vision thing. The tub was a short distance over to my right. Even with my eyes down, I could see its long, white side. And Murphy's legs sticking out over the edge. And his face. He seemed to be peeking at me from around the side of his left knee.

Finally, I looked at him.

His eyes were open, but he wasn't seeing me.

He wasn't exactly Murphy, anymore. Whatever'd been Murphy was gone. The thing in the tub was just a fair likeness, that's all. Somebody might've dropped by while I was asleep, snatched his body and replaced it with a dummy from a wax museum.

A dummy that didn't quite get it right.

Which was a good thing, I guess. I couldn't have stood it if *my* Murphy'd been in the tub.

But he wasn't.

When I finished on the toilet, I flushed and stood up and walked across the wet tiles to the side of the tub.

I stared down at the body.

And wondered what to do with it.

Leave it just as it is.

Sure. Why not? I didn't have the strength or desire to take it anywhere.

Besides, what could be accomplished by moving it?

I might try, if I had a good reason.

In spite of the difficulties and risks, I could probably haul Murphy's body to the parking lot of Judy's apartment building, or into Tony's apartment, or even over to Miller's Woods. But why? How could his body fit into the rest of it in any logical way?

I didn't see how.

No matter where they find him, it'll just add to the confusion.

If they find him just as he is, I thought, it'll look like an accident. While getting ready to take a shower, he somehow slipped and fell backward and bashed his head on the wall beside the tub.

Which had the advantage of being almost true.

Unless I did some major clean-up, however, they would also figure out that he'd been having sex with a woman just before his accident. And they might suspect she'd had a hand in his death.

If they got that far, they would look for samples of her hair, fluids etc.

I'd *have* to make the clean-up effort.

I started with the bathroom. Taking care of the worst part first, I climbed into the tub, straddled Murphy's body and wiped the wall where I'd hit it with my hands. I didn't like standing there. Not one bit. I knew that *he* wasn't under me, but *something* was. Not a wax dummy, either – a naked stiff. It made me nervous. Like I half expected a spook of some sort to take over the body and make a grab for me. Or lurch up between my legs and give me a bite.

Me and my imagination.

I got a good case of goosebumps, but I was okay as soon as I'd climbed out of the tub.

Next, I put away the package of cotton balls and the hydrogen peroxide – which wasn't completely empty. (Naturally, I wiped the plastic bottle to take care of my prints.) Then I found all the used cotton balls on the floor and in the waste basket. I flushed them down the toilet.

Then I mopped the bathroom floor.

I wiped the toilet seat and the flush handle.

That was about it for the bathroom. For now. I'd be back again, but not until just before time to leave.

After putting away the mop and bucket, I went into the living room for my purse. As I headed for the couch, though, I saw a brown leather attaché case standing beside the front door. Though it must've been there before, this was the first time I'd noticed it.

Right away, I knew what must be inside.

I crouched beside it, set it down flat on the floor, snapped open its latches, and raised the lid.

The case was *loaded* with money.

Neat packets of one-dollar bills, fives, tens, and twenties.

He'd gotten it for me in small bills, just as I'd asked.

Murphy's idea of a joke, I guess.

I would've thought it was pretty funny if he'd been there to enjoy the gag with me.

But he wasn't.

I smiled for about a second, then fell apart.

This was the worst yet. You'd think I'd never seen anything

as heartbreaking as those five thousand dollars in small bills. I *bawled*. Tears poured down my face and spasms wracked my body. I ended up stretched out on the carpet by the door, crying onto my crossed arms.

When I finally ran out of tears, I felt empty and lazy. I was dangerously close to falling asleep, so I pushed myself up. Leaving the attaché case by the door, I hurried into the kitchen. I jerked a couple of paper towels off a roll by the sink, and used them to cover my hands while I pulled open a few cupboards.

I found Murphy's stash of grocery bags. The paper bags were folded neatly in a row inside a cupboard. I took out two, stuffed one inside another for double thickness, then returned to the living room.

Squatting over the attaché case, I double-bagged my cash.

Then I carried Murphy's empty case into the kitchen, set it down by the table where he used to work, and wiped it carefully with a paper towel.

I'd planned to do the bedroom next, but suddenly had an urge to take care of my kitchen chores. So I made a couple of trips into the living room to gather the beer mugs, bottles and water glass. I washed and put away the mugs and glass. I wiped the bottles and dropped them into Murphy's recycling bin.

Back in the living room, I saw the bag of pretzels on the coffee table. I had not only touched its cellophane bag, but I'd reached into it. My fingerprints might actually be *inside* the bag. So instead of trying to clean it, I decided to take it with me. It went into the grocery sack along with the money.

Well, I'm beginning to see that it might take me all day to describe every single step in detail. And who really wants to read about all that stuff, anyway? So I'll just summarize the rest of it, if that's okay with you.

Here's what I did – pretty much in order – before leaving Murphy's apartment:

1. Placed my autographed copy of *Deep Dead Eyes* in grocery bag.
2. Put bottle of Excedrin in my purse.
3. Untied ropes from all four bed legs and tossed them into grocery bag.
4. Found knife Murphy had used to cut the ropes (and me), washed it in the kitchen, and put it away.
5. Flushed condom and condom wrapper down toilet (and again wiped handle).
6. Removed pillow case and sheets from bed, stuffed them into grocery sack.
7. Put clean sheets on bed, fresh pillow case on pillow.
8. Artfully arranged Murphy's trunks and Bear Whizz Beer T-shirt on bed mattress as if flung there in haphazard manner.
9. Took five copies of *The Dark Pit* from box, wrapped them for mailing, and labeled package with address Murphy'd copied onto the back cover of *TV Guide* (and his return address).
10. In bathroom, turned on shower so it sprayed down on Murphy.
11. Left shower curtain open and shower running.
12. Gathered my clothes and shoes, got dressed.
13. Put wig on.
14. Rearranged contents of grocery bag so that package of books went in on top of money.
15. Set grocery bags and purse near front door.

That's pretty much all I did. It took a while – especially getting the books ready for mailing. I had to find tape and scissors, cut up a grocery bag, and be careful not to leave prints on any of the books or wrapping materials. A major chore.

I felt pretty good about doing it, though. I'd killed the poor guy, but at least he might get his chance at a movie deal.

Finally, all dressed and ready to go, I made the rounds one more time. I picked up a few odds and ends that shouldn't be left behind, and gave a quick wipe to whatever I might've touched but couldn't take with me.

I didn't go into the bathroom, though. The floor was too wet from the shower, and the air was so thick with steam that I couldn't even see Murphy in the tub.

Returning to the front door, I tossed a few things into the grocery bag with the money, books etc. I didn't think I'd be able to manage two bags, so I mashed down the one holding the dirty sheets and pillow case, and stuffed it into the other bag. Then I slipped my purse strap onto my shoulder. I put on my sunglasses and picked up the full bag.

It was pretty heavy. With my right arm, I hugged it against my chest. I used my left hand – wrapped in my skirt – to open the door.

For a few seconds, I stood there and looked out through the screen door. Nothing seemed to be going on outside.

From one of the nearby units came the noisy whine of a vacuum cleaner. I also heard television voices coming from somewhere.

But I saw nobody.

So I stepped out, pulled the main door shut, and walked briskly toward the sidewalk. I was several paces away from Murphy's unit by the time its screen door bammed shut.

Chapter Forty

Last Tasks

Eyes turned toward me as I entered the post office. Mostly belonging to guys, of course. Scoping out this flashy red-haired babe with the body to die for, the slit up her skirt and her blouse half open.

I recognized nobody.

I don't think anyone looked high enough to see my face.

But I had my sunglasses on, just in case.

Holding the wrapped books low in front of me to keep the view of my cleavage clear, I walked straight over to the waiting line. There were ten or twelve people ahead of me.

I planned to send the books First Class.

I'd considered Overnight Express Mail, but it was after four o'clock by the time I reached the post office. I thought that might be too late in the afternoon for guaranteed next-day delivery, so why go to the extra expense?

Besides, if I sent the books Overnight, I would have to stand around and fill out a special label. I didn't want to fool with that.

First Class would get the books to the producers soon enough.

If not tomorrow, the day after tomorrow.

While I stood in the line, I set the package down on the floor in front of my feet. Then I took a twenty-dollar bill out of my purse. I also took out a couple of tissues.

Squatting down, I casually used the tissues to wipe the outside of the parcel where I'd touched it. (Cops *can* lift fingerprints off paper, you know.) I didn't pay attention to who might be watching, and didn't really care. A person's got every right to clean off a package before mailing it, right? It's nobody's business why, and who would ever guess I was doing it to ruin possible fingerprint evidence? Nobody, that's who.

Keeping a tissue in one hand and my twenty in the other so that my fingertips didn't touch the package, I picked it up again.

Then I just waited in line for my turn at one of the windows.

I kept my head down. Nobody talked to me, and I spoke to no one. It was a pretty long wait, though.

People are amazing. They'll go to a place like the post office, and half of them don't seem to have a clue. They'll step up to the window with a box that's still open, for instance, and ask to borrow some tape. Or when it comes time to pay, they'll have to spend five minutes hunting for their checkbook. Amazing.

Not to mention, the postal workers were in no hurry to set any speed records.

Finally, my turn came anyway.

I set my package onto the counter, smiled, and said, 'Good afternoon,' to the clerk.

She gave me back a friendly smile, and said, 'What can I do for you, honey?'

'I'd like to mail these books,' I told her. My parcel was too large to fit through the slot under the panel of bullet-proof glass (or acrylic, or whatever), so she opened the panel like a door. I slid the package toward her, leaving the twenty on top, and said, 'I'd like it to go First Class, please.'

Nodding, she shut the panel. When she set the parcel on a scale, its weight and cost appeared on a computer screen. After slapping on some stickers, she pushed my change under the window and asked if I would like to have a receipt.

'No,' I said. 'I don't think I'll be needing one. Thanks.'

'You have a nice day,' she said.

'Thanks. You, too.'

I turned away from her window.

'Next in line,' she called.

The line had dwindled. Only three customers were waiting.

Two women – one in her twenties and the other at least seventy – and a young guy probably no older than eighteen. Guess which one was looking at me.

He gaped at me, his jaw drooping.

But I doubt that he saw my face at all.

I walked on past him and out the door.

Just so the flashy redhead who mailed Murphy Scott's books would not be connected directly to Judy's car (on the slim chance that an investigator might actually look into the situation), I had parked her car a block away from the post office and around a corner.

Nobody followed me around the corner.

I climbed in and drove away.

I had no more chores to run. Only one thing still needed to be done: ditch Judy's car.

Abandon it somewhere, and walk home.

Walk home carrying the grocery sack loaded with my pretzels, my personally inscribed and autographed copy of *Deep Dead Eyes*, my souvenir pieces of rope, a pair of used bedsheets and a pillow case, and my five thousand dollars in small bills.

It wasn't terribly heavy, now that I'd gotten rid of the five hardcover books.

But heavy enough. I didn't care to trudge five or ten miles with it.

There was, of course, a simple solution to the problem. Why not drive straight home, park in the garage and haul the sack up to my room, *then* take off again to find a distant dumping-spot for the car?

Simple, but not for me.

I just didn't have the guts to go driving Judy's car brazenly all over creation. Even the trip from Murphy's neighborhood to the post office had nearly undone me. Too much time had gone by since leaving Judy, Milo and Tony. Too much might've happened. What if Judy had already been reported missing?

What if somebody had stumbled upon Milo's camp? Suppose Judy had escaped from the woods and told the cops all about me? What if Tony's body had already been discovered in the parking lot of her apartment building?

If anything of the sort had happened, every cop in Chester might be on the lookout for her car.

I wanted to be far away from it.

The sooner, the better.

Even if it meant a tough hike home.

But I couldn't just leave it *anywhere*. For one thing, I didn't want people to notice me getting out. For another, it really should, if possible, be abandoned in a place where nobody would pay attention to it for a while.

I came up with one idea after another, but found flaws in all of them.

Until I thought of the perfect place.

The mall!

The vast, indoor shopping plaza over by the highway was surrounded by acres of parking lots with probably more than a dozen entances and exits.

There was no parking fee, which meant no gates or cashiers.

With a steady flow of cars coming and going, one more would hardly be noticed.

I would hardly be noticed, entering, parking, walking away with my bag.

To top it all off, the lots were never completely empty. Even after the mall's closing time, plenty of vehicles remained because of people parking there, then walking over to nearby establishments. Scattered all around were mini-marts, restaurants, bars, and fast-food joints. There was even a supermarket. Some stayed open late, while others (including the supermarket) stayed open *always*.

In short, the mall's parking lots offered *anonymity*.

I could anonymously drop off Judy's car and walk away.

Her car might anonymously sit there, day after day, night after night, lost among the others.

Delighted, I headed for the mall.

About halfway there, I swung onto a little sidestreet. I pulled over and stopped the car in front of a house that had a For Sale sign on the front lawn. The house looked empty. Across the street was a vacant lot. Looking all around, I saw nobody.

So I grabbed one of the legs that I'd cut off Tony's jeans last night and climbed out of the car. With the denim leg, I wiped the exterior door handles and everywhere else that I might've touched.

Then I climbed in and did the interior.

Then I double-checked the whole car, inside and out, to make sure I hadn't missed anything. Judy's purse was still on the floor, partly hidden under the driver's seat. Fine. It could stay there.

Satisfied that I'd removed every trace of myself (to the extent that it can be done in a few minutes with a rag), I tossed both the legs into my grocery bag, started up the car again, and drove the rest of the way to the mall.

Plenty of other cars were coming and going.

I entered a parking lot over on the Macy's side of the complex, found an empty space, pulled in and shut off the engine.

Just for the heck of it, I left Judy's key in the ignition.

I wiped off the keys and key case, the shift handle and the steering wheel.

My purse and grocery bag were on the front passenger seat. Leaning sideways, I grabbed them.

I climbed out of Judy's car. Purse hanging by my side, I set down the bag. Then I looked around. Several people were in sight, some heading toward mall entrances, others returning to their cars. None paid any attention to me.

With one of the denim legs, I cleaned the interior door handle.

Then I flopped the leg back into the sack, hoisted the sack off the pavement, stepped out of the way, and flung the door shut with my knee.

Even as the door thunked, I realized that I'd forgotten to lock it.

I'd *meant* to lock it.

But this is better.

Leave it unlocked, key in the ignition.

With any luck, some creep might come along and steal the thing.

Walking away from Judy's car, I couldn't help but smile.

Chapter Forty-one

Going Home

Freedom's just another word for nothing left to fear.

As soon as I walked away from Judy's car, I felt hugely, enormously, wonderfully free.

I was done!

I'd severed my last major connection with the series of accidents and/or crimes that had started last night when I killed Tony. Sure, I still had possession of a few items such as the money and autographed book, but nothing that could draw me in as a suspect.

I was, as they say, 'home free.'

But several miles from home.

I started to hike across the parking lot, the grocery sack clutched to my chest. It was heavy enough that I needed to hold it with both hands.

Gonna be a long hike.

I hadn't walked very far, though, before I noticed that many of the kids roaming across the lot were carrying book bags on their backs.

Just what I needed!

Instead of striking out for home, I made a detour into the mall.

It was good to be in such a familiar place. Rarely a week ever went by that I didn't visit the mall at least once. I would spend a couple of hours there, just wandering, browsing through the stores, having a nice lunch at the food court. It was a quiet, pleasant place – and just about the *only* place in town worth going to, except for the cineplex.

Wandering the mall, a person can pretty much stay anonymous.

Pretty much but not completely.

If you visit the same shops or food stands time after time, certain employees will start to recognize you. They have no way to learn your name unless you introduce yourself or pay with a credit card or check, but some are bound to know your face.

Some might even know it well enough to wonder how come, today, I was wearing a bright red wig.

So my first stop, after entering the mall, was the ladies' restroom.

As I understand it, California has a law against security cameras in toilet cubicles. You can't blow your nose in this state without breaking the criminal code, but this is one law I really go for. I mean, you don't want some horny degenerate of a security guard watching you on TV while you're doing your stuff, if you get my meaning.

They're allowed to spy on you with hidden cameras just about everywhere else, but not when you're in a stall.

So that's where I went.

First, I availed myself of the toilet since it happened to be there anyway and it didn't look hideous. Unbelievable as this may seem, the last person using this public toilet had actually flushed it. Not only that, but (hold on to your hat) she hadn't left a puddle – or worse – on the seat! I was impressed and grateful.

Shit, I wanted to *meet* her!

Never mind.

With my purse hanging from a hook on the door and my grocery sack down on the floor, I hoisted my skirt, pulled my panties down around my ankles, and hovered a couple of inches above the seat. (Even if the seat looks clean, you sure don't want to sit on it. You don't even want to *think* about what's been on it.)

The toilet paper dispenser, of course, turned out to be empty. Always prepared, I used some tissues from my purse.

Then I flushed the toilet.

I've possibly done some lousy things in my life, but I've always flushed after myself.

Anybody who doesn't is nothing short of a pig.

After flushing, I pulled up my panties, stood in front of the toilet, and let my skirt drift down around my legs. Then I took off my gaudy red wig and stuffed it into the grocery sack.

Anything else I should do while I've got some privacy?

Of course!

It wasn't easy to do in the confines of the toilet stall, but I bent over, reached down deep into my sack, and pulled out a few packets of cash. I transferred some denominations back and forth. Finally, I ended up with about three hundred dollars, mostly in twenties and tens. I put that money into my purse.

Then I crumpled down the top of my sack so nobody would be able to see inside. I picked it up, took my purse off the hook, unlatched the door, and stepped out of the stall.

I stopped in front of a mirror. The redhead was gone. I looked like myself again. Almost.

Nobody else was using the restroom, just then, so I set

down the bag, took a brush out of my purse, and spent a couple of minutes working my hair into shape. When I was done, it still wouldn't win any prizes. It no longer looked frightful, though.

Now that I was resuming my own identity, I fastened the upper buttons of my blouse. I also took off my big, hoop earrings and tucked them away in my purse.

All set, I picked up my grocery sack and walked out of the restroom. I strolled the length of the mall, entered J.C. Penney's, found myself a nice green book bag (or backpack, as the case may be), and bought it with cash.

Right in front of the clerk, I removed its tags and stickers, stuffed my grocery sack inside, then swung the pack onto my back and slipped my arms through its straps.

On my way out, I wondered if I needed anything else before leaving the mall.

How about supper?

Wong's Kitchen in the food court had great orange chicken, barbecued pork, fried wonton, etc. I was tempted. But on the other hand, remaining at the mall would increase my chances of running into someone who knew me.

Get out now.

Go home.

I went straight to the nearest exit and walked out into the heat and glare of late afternoon. My sunglasses helped against the glare. After putting them on, I paused long enough to stuff my purse into the backpack.

Then I was off.

I started with a brisk pace, but couldn't keep it up for long. Though a breeze sometimes stirred against me, the day was too hot for hurrying. And I was in lousy shape from too little sleep, too many injuries, too much prolonged stress, and the ungodly amount of stenuous physical activity I'd gone through since the start of my problems last night.

Soon, I was short of breath, my heart was racing, and sweat was pouring out of me.

I slowed down.

Slow and steady gets the job done.

Before long, I was feeling a lot better.

I knew from my many trips to the mall, however, that it was six miles from home. At my usual pace, I could walk more than four miles per hour. This was probably half that speed.

Six miles at two miles per hour.

I did some tricky math.

A three-hour hike?

Dismayed by the idea of not making it home until about eight o'clock, I decided to pick up my pace as much as possible.

I must've been an interesting sight for the motorists as I hurried down the sidewalk. Even without the wig, I was conspicuous in my bright yellow blouse and flowing green skirt. Not to mention, as we all know, I'm built like a brick shithouse. Plus, my bra hadn't exactly been designed for maximum support, so my quick and bouncy strides made for a lot of bust action – which was exaggerated still more by the backpack. The pack's weight thrust my chest forward, while its straps drew my shoulders back and pulled at the front of my blouse as if trying to rip it open. If that weren't enough, every stride sent my bare leg swinging out through the slit in my skirt.

Every now and then, guys in passing cars tooted at me, whistled at me, or called out. Because of traffic noise, I couldn't really hear what they were yelling. Probably a combination of compliments, critical remarks, suggestions and offers – all crude.

When guys shout at you from car windows, they never say anything that *isn't* crude.

Before too long, the inevitable happened.

A car passed me, then slowed down, pulled over to the side of the road and stopped.

I felt only a slight sinking sensation. This was no cause

for alarm – just a nuisance. Probably some jerk hoping to get lucky.

I kept walking, but picked up my speed as I neared the car.

When I came up alongside it, the passenger door swung open. Not even glancing in, I started to step around the door.

'Alice?'

A man, and he knew my name.

Instead of my name, it might've been the squeak and crackle of ice beginning to break under my feet – if I were standing on a frozen lake a mile from any shore.

This can't be good!

I lurched to a halt, ducked, and peered in through the open door. Nobody in the passenger seat.

The driver looked familiar, but . . . I suddenly recognized him, and the ice froze solid again.

I felt so relieved that I was almost *glad* to see him.

'Elroy?' I asked.

'That's my name, don't wear it out.'

The same old Elroy.

'I've got room for two in my buggy,' he said.

'Are you offering me a ride?'

'Hop right in.'

So I took off my pack. Holding it in front of me with both hands, I climbed into Elroy's car. Then I leaned out and pulled the door shut. 'This is really nice of you,' I said.

'Just call me Mr Nice Guy.'

In the past, I had generally called him Dork-head, but not to his face.

A couple of years earlier, he and I had worked in the same law office for about six months. We were both employed as secretaries. I couldn't stand him, but I'd always treated him okay, and he'd apparently liked me quite a lot.

'Buckle up for safety,' he said.

Realizing that he probably wouldn't start driving until I'd

complied with the rules, I brought the seatbelt down across my chest and latched it.

'I just couldn't believe my eyes when I saw it was you,' he said, and checked the side mirror. 'I said to myself, "Elroy, that woman bears a striking resemblance to our Alice. Is it possible?" Well, then I kept watching you and saw that it was not only possible, but factual.' He found an opening in the traffic and steered us onto the road. 'I'm *so* glad to see you again. You're looking utterly splendid.'

'Thanks,' I said. 'You're looking great, yourself.'

So I'm a liar.

The one way Elroy did not look, and never would, was 'great.' A skinny little guy with slicked-down black hair, big ears and a pointy nose, he looked mostly like a rat. A dapper rat, he nearly always wore a white shirt and blue bow-tie. He didn't seem to have changed much – including his outfit – since I'd last seen him.

'I must say,' he said, 'we've missed you at the office.'

'They can't be missing me much. Hell, they fired me.'

'*I* miss you.'

'Well, thanks.'

'You always . . . cheered the place up.'

'My manic charm.'

'The other girls . . . they're all such snotty bitches. You were always nice to me.'

'Well . . . thanks.'

'It's *so* good to see you again. I just can't believe we've run into each other this way. I thought you'd left town.'

'No such luck,' I said.

'I'm sure someone told me you'd moved to El Paso.'

'Someone's wishful thinking,' I said.

'Are you still living above that garage?'

'Still there. But you don't need to spread the word around at the office.'

Giving me a sly glance, he said, 'Mum's the word.'

'Thanks. Let them keep on thinking I'm in El Paso.'

'It'll be our little secret.'

'How *is* my old friend, Mr Heflin, by the way?'

'Oh, Mr Heflin. Polite. He is very polite to all the ladies. And he keeps his hands entirely to himself.'

'Glad to hear it. And how is he around stairways?'

'Careful. Very careful.'

'Has he made a complete recovery?'

'I shouldn't say "complete." No. Hardly complete. He limps. I suspect he'll *always* limp.'

'Sorry to hear that,' I said.

Which brought a squeaky laugh out of Elroy. He said, 'Oh, Alice, I love it. You haven't changed a *bit*. Not one *smidgen*. You're such a terror.'

'That's me.'

'So, where can I take you?'

'Where would you *like* to take me?' I asked.

Chapter Forty-two

The Invitation

'Oh, my,' Elroy said.

I gave him the eye and asked, 'You didn't go and get married, did you?'

Fat chance.

But you never know. It's amazing, some of the losers who end up getting married. All they need to do is find someone who's an *even bigger* loser.

'Nope,' Elroy said. 'No ball and chain for yours truly. I've gotta have my freedom.'

'Going with anyone?'

'Aren't *we* inquisitive?'

'I wouldn't want to get you into hot water with your sweetie.'

'Hot water? How?'

'By having you over for dinner tonight. I happen to be house-sitting for my friends, this week. I've got their whole house all to myself. We could have cocktails by the swimming pool, and I'll barbecue some steaks on the outdoor grill. How about it?'

I'd been watching his face go through changes. The way I read it, he was shocked and delighted by the invitation, but afraid I might be trying to embarrass him with a phony offer.

Casting me a smirk, he said, 'Surely you jest.'

I tried to look hurt. 'I thought you said you were glad to see me.'

'I *am*,' he insisted. 'It's just that . . . You aren't serious about . . . what you just said about dinner. Are you?'

'Of course I'm serious.'

'Well, it sounds lovely, but . . .'

'Turn right at the next light.'

'Why?'

'It's how we get there,' I explained, smiling.

'No, I mean . . . I'd be happy to just drop you off. You don't have to make dinner for me.'

'I don't have to, I want to.'

'That's the part I don't get.'

To be frank, I didn't quite get it, myself.

Until running into Elroy, I'd only wanted to get home as soon as possible and be alone. Have a drink, have a meal, take a nice long bath, and go to bed. And sleep and sleep and sleep.

However. Being given the car ride would save me at least two hours of hard walking. I owed Elroy for that. Besides, I could spend an hour or so treating him to dinner, and still be ahead of the game timewise.

Another thing. I needed a chance to figure out whether or not Elroy was a threat to me. If asked, he could testify as to the time and place he'd picked me up. But did it matter? If it *did* matter, I needed to figure out how to prevent him from talking.

And. This may seem odd, considering. For one thing, I'm pretty much of a loner. For another, I'd always figured Elroy for a dork. But I actually liked the idea of having him around when I got home.

Life is strange.

I don't know why anything happens. Why did I *really* ask Elroy to have dinner with me?

Maybe it was in my genes to invite him. Or in the cards. Or in the stars. Maybe I was programmed to do it by the Great Computer. Or moved by the Master of Games. Maybe God made me do it. Or the Devil.

If you want the truth, though, I guess the main reason must've had to do with Murphy.

It was Murphy, more than anything, that made me reluctant to be alone.

Too bad it couldn't be him instead of Elroy keeping me company.

But Elroy would be better than nobody.

I supposed.

'What are you scared of?' I asked him in a tesing way.

'Me?' Elroy asked. 'I'm not scared.'

'You seem awfully nervous.'

'Do I? I'm just . . . surprised, that's all. We haven't seen each other in *ages*, and all of a sudden you're inviting me over to your place for dinner.'

'My friend's place. Anyway, it seems like a fine idea to me. I always felt that we should've gotten to know each other better.'

'I asked you out, remember? You turned me down.'

I remembered, all right. He'd asked me out three different times, and I had always politely refused, claiming to have prior commitments.

'I had a rule against dating anyone at work,' I explained. 'But now that I don't work there anymore, I don't see any reason for us to stay away from each other. Do you?'

'Me? No. I never did.'

'Then you'll have dinner with me?'

'I'd be most honored.'

'Good deal.'

After that, I gave him directions now and then, while he filled me in on doings at the office, gave me a summary of his own recent activities (dull as mud), and asked about mine. I didn't want to admit much of the truth, so I told him that I was now a mystery writer.

'Oh, how exciting! Have you had anything published?'

'Just one book, so far.'

'But that's *spectacular*! I'm so excited for you.'

'Thanks.'

'The big bad girl makes good!'

I smiled at him. 'Watch it, buddy.'

'So, what's the title of your book?'

'*Depths of Darkness.*'

'Excellent! It's so . . . evocative! And is it published under your own name? I do hope so. You've such an absolutely *luscious* name for a mystery writer.'

'Think so?'

'Oh, indeed,' he said. 'But did you? Use your own name?'

'Absolutely.'

'Oh, good for you!' He spoke my name slowly and dramatically, so it almost sounded like poetry. (My *actual* name, not Alice.) 'It's so perfect, I just bet everyone must *think* it's a pen name.'

'Maybe so,' I said, starting to regret the fabrication.

' "*She writes with a poison pen.*" '

'Good one,' I said.

'I can't wait to read it. It isn't about intrigue in a law office, is it?'

'Not exactly.'

'Am *I* in it?'

Throwing him a mysterious smile, I said, 'You'll have to read it and find out.'

'Oooh. This is *so* exciting.'

'I'll give you a copy if I can ever manage to get my hands on some.'

'*You don't have any?*' He sounded shocked and appalled.

'Not at the moment. I only had twenty to start with. By the time I gave copies to my relatives and a few friends . . . and sent half a dozen to this film producer in Culver City . . . I'm trying to get more, but it isn't easy.'

'That's awful.'

'Well, it's ridiculous. Seems like everybody has the book but me.'

'You don't even have a copy for *yourself*?'

'Not at the moment. I loaned my last copy to a friend. But don't worry about it, I'll send you one the moment I get a new shipment.'

'I can hardly wait. Now, tell me about the movie version.'

This is the sort of crapola one gets into, on occasion, when one lies.

So I kept making up more lies, sometimes telling him to make turns, until finally we reached Serena and Charlie's house.

'And here we are! Just go ahead and pull into the driveway.'

He slowed his car, made the turn, and the house came into sight.

I nearly panicked.

What if I missed something?

I'd done my best to clean up the place and get rid of every

trace of Tony, but I suddenly wasn't at all sure that I hadn't overlooked something.

A gob of brain on the front stoop . . .

I should've kept my mouth shut, let Elroy drop me off at the curb, told him thanks and goodbye – *not invite him in!*

Better yet, I never should've gotten into his car in the first place.

Thanks for the offer, Elroy, but I'm not allowed to ride with strangers – and I don't know anyone stranger than you.

'This is an absolutely lovely house,' he said, and stopped his car. 'I can't *wait* to feast my eyes on the interior.'

'It's pretty nice,' I admitted.

Gosh, Elroy, you know what? I'm not feeling so well all of a sudden. It wouldn't be a lie.

Would you mind terribly if we didn't do this tonight? Why don't I give you a rain check? Better yet, why don't you give me your phone number, and I'll call you?

Very cute.

Only two problems with it. First, I would look like a creep. Second, I didn't really *want* to get rid of him.

I did a fine job of cleaning up. He won't find anything.

And if he does?

'Are you having second thoughts?' he asked.

'No. Are you kidding? This'll be great.' With that, I opened the car door.

'Wait,' Elroy said, opening his door. 'I'll come around to your side and give you a hand.'

'No, that's . . .'

He leaped out.

Clutching the backpack against my chest, I burst from the car. I made it to my feet about two seconds before Elroy arrived.

'Here,' he said. 'Allow me to take that.'

'I'm fine.'

He reached for my pack, anyway.

'No!' I snapped, and whirled around to put my back in the way. 'I'm perfectly capable of carrying it myself.'

'Whoa! Jeezle-peezle! Okay! Sorry.'

'That's all right,' I said, and turned around to face him.

'What do you have in there, the Crown Jewels?'

Terrific. Now I've made him curious.

Grinning, I said, 'Curiosity killed the Elroy.'

He laughed. 'You are such a stitch, Alice. You haven't changed a single whit.'

'I've changed my underwear once or twice.'

His face went crimson.

'Sorry,' I said. 'I didn't mean to embarrass you.'

'Of *course* you meant to embarrass me. It's part of your charm.'

'Really?'

'Such a naughty girl.'

'That's me,' I said, and stepped around him. 'Let's go this way.'

He stayed by my side as I walked down the driveway. When we came to the rear corner of the house, I quickly scanned the pool area, the back yard and the edge of the forest. I saw no one. Everything looked fine.

'Why don't you make yourself comfortable over by the pool?' I suggested. 'I need to trot upstairs and take care of a few things, then I'll be right down and make us some drinks.'

'Fine and dandy,' he said.

But as I headed for the garage, he kept walking beside me.

'Is this *your* garage?' he asked.

'It's where I live. I just rent the upstairs.'

'I'd be curious to see what it looks like.'

I was beginning to remember *why* I'd formed such a strong dislike for Elroy.

'Maybe some other time,' I told him.

'I'll stay out of your way.'

'Why don't you just wait over there by the pool?'

'Are you sure you wouldn't like me to carry your pack up the stairs for you? You could go up first and unlock the door.'

'No, that's fine. I can take care of it.'

'I'd be more than happy to help.'

'I'll be down in a few minutes,' I said, hurrying forward.

This time, he stayed put.

I started trotting up the wooden stairway.

With the pack clutched against my chest, I couldn't see the steps in front of my feet.

So, of course, I fell.

Chapter Forty-three

No Place Like Home

Rammed myself down on my pack.

It contained my purse and the grocery sack with an open bag of pretzels, four lengths of rope, two denim legs, two sheets and a pillow case, my autographed copy of *Deep Dead Eyes*, and most of my five thousand dollars in small bills. None of which did much to soften my impact with the stairs.

I slammed down hard on top of the pack, mashing my breasts, pounding my ribcage and belly, knocking my wind out.

From the sound of things, I instantly pulverized the pretzels.

From the feel of things, a corner of Murphy's novel tried to punch its way through the gouge in my stomach.

I let out a cry of pain.

A split second after impact, I began skidding down the stairs feet first, knees bumping, thighs scraping, arms being pummeled as they hugged the pack.

The first thing I heard from Elroy was a gasp of, 'Oh, dear me!' Then I heard him charging up the stairs below me.

Suddenly, he grabbed the backs of my legs, clamping down hard on them and stopping me.

'I've got you,' he gasped. 'Don't worry.'

'Thanks.'

'Are you all right?'

'Fine. I'm fine.'

'Just don't move.'

I had little intention of moving – at least until I could breathe again and the pain subsided. Even after that, I wouldn't be *able* to move until he let go of my legs. He had a firm grip. And his hands were way up there, almost high enough to touch my butt.

'Don't get fresh,' I told him.

'Ha ha, very funny.'

'I guess I should've . . . let you carry the pack.'

'I'm not one to rub it in.'

Oh, sure you are.

'But I did rather expect something of this sort,' he added.

I *should've* expected it. I'd had so many falls lately, I was starting to feel like a river.

With Elroy still holding me, I pulled my arms out from under the pack. They seemed to work okay. I placed both hands on a stair to brace myself, then said, 'Why don't you sort of ease off my legs, and I'll try to get up?'

'Be careful,' he warned.

'Get ready to grab me again, just in case.'

When he let go, I pushed at the stair, raising myself off the pack. But suddenly I started to slip.

I gasped.

Elroy grabbed me by the hips.

But I only slipped an inch or two before my knees settled onto a lower stair, stopping me.

'There,' I said.

'Okay?'

'I'll be fine now. But I can't get up till you're out of the way.'

'Okay.'

A true gentleman, he let go of my hips without giving me so much as a squeeze or a pat, and descended the stairs. I got to my feet. With a hand on the railing, I turned halfway around and smiled down at him. 'Thanks for catching me,' I said.

'Glad to be of service, ma'am.'

'See you in a while.'

'Are you sure you won't be needing me again?'

'I'll be all right. I'm not due for another fall until about six-thirty or seven.'

He laughed. 'You fall a lot, do you?'

'Lately. I need to start being more careful.' With that, I turned away, climbed up to my pack, bent over it, and lifted it by the straps. It came swinging back and bumped gently against my thighs.

I stayed on my feet.

At the top of the stairs, I set it down, opened its flap, and took out my purse.

Elroy stood at the foot of the stairs and watched me.

'Go on over to the pool,' I said. 'I'll be down in a couple of minutes.'

'Are you sure you wouldn't like to invite me up?'

'Don't make a pest of yourself, Elroy.'

'You can't blame a fellow for trying.'

'Don't count on it.'

With a smirk on his face, he winked an eye, pointed a finger at me, and said, 'Later.'

Which would've been truly cool coming from Paul Newman or John Travolta. Coming from Elroy, it was sort of sad and funny, but mostly annoying.

As he swiveled around and started swaggering toward the

pool, I took the keys out of my purse. I unlocked the door, opened it, then picked up my pack and went in.

I made sure the door was locked.

Then I hauled the pack over to my closet, pushed my way through some hanging clothes, and set it down on the floor. There, it was basically out of sight. You could only spot it by squatting down low and peering in under the clothes. You couldn't spot it that way, either, after I'd shut the closet door.

Good enough.

I wasn't trying to hide the stuff from Sherlock Holmes. My only concern, just then, was Elroy.

Not that I had any intention of allowing him into my room. You can't be too careful, though. Elroy might seem harmless and easy to control, but guys like that will sometimes go nuts on you. I wanted my pack to be out of sight – out of mind – in case he flipped out and came barging in.

Or in case *I* went nuts and brought him in, myself.

Fat chance.

With the pack nicely hidden, I spent a minute or two inspecting my latest injuries. I found minor scrapes on my arms, shins and knees, but no new damage anywhere else – not even where the corner of Murphy's book had jabbed me in the belly. Nothing needed treatment.

I decided against changing any of my clothes.

In the bathroom, I took a few minutes to 'freshen up.' Which means I washed, brushed my hair and dabbed on a bit of Tropical Nights perfume.

I wouldn't be needing my purse, so I stuck it away inside a dresser drawer.

With nothing except my key case, I stepped outside. Elroy waved at me from a lounger beside the pool. I waved back, then made sure the door was locked before I started down the stairs.

I reached the bottom, still standing.

Elroy got to his feet as I walked over to him.

'Ready for the Happy Hour?' I asked.

'The sun's well over the yardarm,' he said.

'Let's go in and concoct something. And I'll see what I can do about finding a couple of nice, thick steaks for dinner.'

The sliding glass doors were all locked from inside, so I led Elroy around to the front of the house. Along the way, I kept watch for any telltale signs of Tony.

Everything looked fine.

I unlocked the front door and entered the house. Elroy stepped in after me. I shut the door.

The house felt hot and stuffy.

It was very silent.

I'd left all the curtains shut, so the rooms were filled with murky, yellow light.

'Hang on a second,' I whispered. 'I'll turn on the air conditioning.'

As if nervous about being here, Elroy stayed in the foyer and looked around while I hurried down the hall to turn on the air.

I flicked the switch and heard the blower start.

The sound was good to hear. I hadn't liked that silence.

'Things'll cool off fast, now,' I said, returning to the foyer.

'Are you sure it's all right for us to be here?'

'Sure I'm sure. I have the keys, don't I? Come on,' I said, and headed for the kitchen. 'What do you like to drink?'

'Oh, I don't know.'

'How about margaritas?'

'Are we going to use *their* stuff?'

'Sure.'

'Is it all right to do that?' he asked.

'Would I be doing it if it weren't?'

'Maybe. I don't know, would you?'

'Nope. Not me. I ain't no thief.'

In the kitchen, I went straight for the cupboard where they kept the liquor. I opened it and took out a bottle of tequila.

639

'The deal is,' I explained, 'they like me to use their stuff when I'm staying here. They even stock up on my favorite foods and drinks and things. They want me to live it up. They're on vacation, and they want this to be like a vacation for me.'

'Really?'

'Don't you believe me?'

'I just don't want to get into any trouble,' he said.

'Relax. Everything's fine. What they don't know won't hurt them.'

Elroy's face contorted. He blurted, 'Oh, my God. I've gotta get out of here.'

I burst out laughing.

'It's not funny. I'm leaving.'

'I was *kidding*! It was a *joke*. The owners are my best friends. I've got the run of the place. You're not going to get into any trouble. If they walked in the door right now, they'd be delighted to find us here and they'd make the drinks *for* us.'

'Honest?' Elroy asked.

'So help me.'

After that, he seemed to be all right. He even helped me. Soon, we had a blender full of margarita. While Elroy salted the rims of our glasses, I studied the meat situation.

It came as no surprise.

Except for some hot dogs and salami in the refrigerator, everything else was frozen. The freezer compartment was full of goodies: steaks, pork chops, lamb chops, chicken breasts. But they were as solid as bricks.

'If you don't want grilled weenies,' I explained, 'we'll have to thaw out something.'

'I thought we were having steaks.'

'We still *can* have steaks.'

'But they're frozen?'

'I'll just nuke 'em till they thaw.'

'That'll be tasty.'

'Well, we could thaw them out *naturally*, but that might take a few hours.'

'I'm not in any hurry,' he said, smiling and wiggling his eyebrows.

'Well, let's see how it goes.' I opened the freezer compartment again. 'We can have anything in here. Would you rather have lamb, or . . .?'

'You promised me a steak.'

For a guest, Elroy seemed awfully damn insistent.

'Then a steak you shall have,' I told him, and took out a couple of T-bones.

What is it, anyway, with people and slabs of beef? Hey, I like the things, too. But I'm not wild for them. Steaks aren't the be-all and end-all. If you ask me, lamb and pork have more flavor. And chicken is usually more tender. Besides, steaks are tricky devils. If you don't cook them just right, they get all dry inside. And sometimes, for reasons I've never figured out, you cook up a perfectly good steak and it ends up tasting like liver. I just don't see what the infatuation is.

Anyway, I ripped the butcher paper off the T-bones. Serena was in the habit of freezing her meat in pairs, so the steaks were not only as solid as slabs of concrete, but also stuck together.

I didn't even try to part them.

Smiling at Elroy, I hammered the counter a couple of times and said, 'Dinner will be a while.'

'No problem,' he said.

'These can at least marinate . . .'

'*Marinate*?'

'You know, maybe some teryaki sauce.'

'No. Perish the thought. Do you want to ruin them?'

Figures!

'Let's not marinate them,' I suggested.

'Just a dab of salt and pepper before they go on the fire,' Elroy said.

'Excellent. I'll let you take care of it.'

Looking very pleased with himself, he said, 'Happy to oblige.' Then he turned away. He gave the blender a quick buzz that swirled the margarita concoction, whipped it to forth and sent it climbing the sides of the pitcher.

As he filled our glasses, he asked, 'Do we have anything to nibble on?'

I thought of Murphy's pretzels.

'What would you like?'

'Tortilla chips, if you have them.'

'I'll see if *Serena* has any,' I said, and headed for the cupboard where she kept various bags of chips.

'Who is this Serena?'

'She owns the joint. She and her husband.'

'Our out-of-town hosts?'

'Right.'

'Let's see what they've got,' he said, and joined me in front of the cupboard.

There were plenty of nibbles to choose from. Elroy decided on a bag of lightly salted, fat-free, taste-free corn tortilla chips.

'Shall we take it all outside and enjoy it by the pool?' I asked.

'Absolutely,' Elroy said.

Carrying the bag of chips, I left the kitchen. Elroy followed with the drinks.

Wanting to avoid the den – I'd never gotten around to cleaning its glass door – I started across the living room. My plan was to open the drapes and let us out through the sliding door.

But along the way, striding by the fireplace, I turned my head to take a look at the saber.

What if it's wet?

What if it's dripping blood?

What if Elroy gets curious and takes a close look . . .?

But I didn't need to worry about any of that.

The saber was gone.

Chapter Forty-four

Adamant Elroy

Yeah, I thought. Sure it's gone.

I looked away and kept moving.

Where'd I leave it? I wondered. In the den?

I opened the curtains, then stepped over to the sliding door. As I unlocked it, I recalled having the saber with me when I took my bath early that morning. Had I left it in the bathroom?

No.

I slid open the glass door.

Didn't leave it in the bathroom. Wanted everything back in place. Could've sworn I hung it back over the fireplace.

I DID.

I remembered, now. After breakfast, I'd put the saber on its hooks where it belonged.

So where is it now?

Very quickly, I stepped outside. In my mind, I imagined myself letting out a squeal, flinging my sack of tortilla chips at the sky, and running like hell.

But I simply walked over to the table. From the other side, I watched Elroy step out of the house, a margarita in each hand. He didn't have a hand to spare for closing the door, so I hurried over and rolled it shut.

Elroy placed the drinks on the table, then pulled out a chair for me. I thanked him and sat down, even though the chair put my back to the door.

He dragged one of the other chairs around the table, and sat down beside me. Then he handed me a margarita and took the other for himself. 'Shall I propose a toast?' he suggested.

'Toast away.'

'To you and me, and lucky encounters.'

'Lucky, huh?'

You'd change your tune if you knew what was going on.

'It most certainly *was* lucky,' he said.

'Maybe so,' I muttered.

We clicked our glasses together, then drank.

Lowering his glass, Elroy said, 'Imagine the odds against me just happening to drive by just the right place at just the right time . . . not to mention *recognizing* you. I call that lucky. I usually don't even pay attention to people on the sidewalks. For that matter, I wouldn't have *been* there if my wristwatch hadn't died on me this morning. It's not my usual route home. Our paths wouldn't have crossed at all except for the fact that I had to make a stop at the mall for a new watch battery.'

'I was at the mall, myself.'

'Ah! I should've known. We were only a few blocks away when I spotted you.' He drank some more of his margarita, then asked, 'Are you in the habit of walking to the mall and back? It's a good, long distance.'

Nodding, I said, 'About six miles each way. It's my chief form of exercise. I try to do it a couple of times a week.'

'You certainly dress well for your hikes.'

'Well, I like to look good at the mall.'

'Aren't you at all . . . nervous about it?'

'About what?'

'Walking that far by yourself. There are so many psychos in this world.'

'You're telling me.'

'Doesn't it make you the least bit nervous?' Elroy asked.

'A little. But I don't let it stop me. Besides, I've been known to be dangerous, myself.'

Elroy let out a laugh. 'You can say that again.' Then he tore open the bag of tortilla chips and turned it toward me.

I took a handful.

'It didn't occur to me until just this moment,' he said, 'but look at the irony we've just encountered. *You* fell down the stairs. You, who pushed Mr Heflin down the stairs. Isn't that just marvelously ironic?'

'Oh, yeah. Marvelously.' I popped a chip into my mouth and crunched down on it. It was thin and nearly tasteless.

Do you know what else would be marvelously ironic, Elroy? If our 'lucky encounter' ends with both of us getting murdered by a saber-wielding maniac.

I drank some more of my margarita.

And wondered if I should warn him.

I wouldn't need to tell him the whole story, just explain that somebody must've broken into the house sometime today and stolen the saber.

And might be anywhere.

He'll say we should call the cops.

Obviously, that was out of the question.

So what can we do?

Flee.

'This is a *lovely* place,' Elroy said. 'It must be fabulous to live here.'

'It's nice, all right.'

'I should imagine that some of our furry friends must wander out of the woods now and again.'

'Sure. We get all sorts of critters. Deer, raccoons, squirrels . . .'

Midnight swimmers.

'I'd love to see some deer come out,' Elroy said.

'Stick around, there's no telling what you might see.'

He leered at me. 'Is that so?' he asked.

'You never know.'

'Well, well.'

'But you know what?'

'What?'

'I think we oughta go *out* for dinner tonight.'

'Out? We are out.'

'I mean like to a real restaurant.'

'You're kidding.'

'No, I'm serious. If we have to wait for those steaks to thaw out, we won't be eating till eight or nine. I just don't think I can wait that long. I'm already starving.'

'Have some more nibbles.'

'It'll be my treat. And you can pick the restaurant. Anywhere you like.'

'I like it here. It's so peaceful and pleasant. Of course, I'm sure you're used to it. You live here. But I live in an apartment house. I don't have any lawn at all, much less a swimming pool and a beautiful *forest*. You want to take me away from all *this*? I can eat in a restaurant any old time.'

'I'm not trying to cheat you out of the barbecue. Why don't we just postpone it till tomorrow. That way, I'll have time to prepare for it. We won't have to worry about frozen steaks. You can even come over early, and we'll make a day of it. How does that sound?'

'Lousy.'

'Lousy?'

'You promised me cocktails and barbecued steaks by the swimming pool. Tonight, not tomorrow. If you'd said tomorrow in the first place, that'd be different. But you didn't, so you got me all set to *expect* it. We can go to a restaurant tomorrow, if you want. But tonight, I want my barbecued steak like you promised.'

'When I made the promise,' I said, 'I counted on being able to thaw the steaks in the microwave.'

'Well, you can't do that. They'd be ruined.'

'But it was my plan. You can't hold me to a promise if you won't let me follow my plan.'

'Why not?'

'It isn't fair.'

'It isn't fair of *you* to promise me a barbecued steak by your swimming pool, and get me out here, and then say, "Oh, dear, I don't want to do this, after all. Let's go to a *restaurant*." '

'I'm starting to think I don't want to eat with you at all.'

'Oh, isn't that just dandy?'

'I'm trying to be reasonable, Elroy, but . . .'

'It's either your way or the highway, is that it?'

'I just think you should cut me a little slack, that's all. This barbecue thing isn't working out, so let's do it another time. For tonight, why don't we just try to make the best of things and go to a restaurant?'

Elroy let out a deep sigh. Then he raised his glass and drained it. Staring into his empty glass, he muttered, 'You said it'd be okay to wait for them to thaw. Remember? In the kitchen? We talked about the fact that it'd take a few hours, and you said it wouldn't be a problem. Only now it *is* a problem. Why do you suppose that is?'

'I never said it wouldn't be a problem.'

'Maybe not in so many words. But you were all ready to go along with it. You even wanted to marinate them.'

'I can still *get* steak teriyaki if we go to a restaurant.'

He narrowed his eyes at me. 'Is that what this is all about? Because I wouldn't let you ruin the steaks with teriyaki sauce?'

'No, of course not.'

'Then what *is* it about? Why have you suddenly *turned* on me?'

I stared into his eyes.

'I haven't turned on you, Elroy. Though I do think you have a cruddy attitude about all this.'

'You promised me, and now you want to take it away.'

'There's something going on here that you don't know about.'

With a wary look in his eyes, he said, 'Such as?'

Don't tell him!

'Somebody was here,' I said.

'What do you mean?'

Leaning over close to him, I said quietly, 'I think someone might've broken into the house while I was gone. There's supposed to be a Civil War saber hanging above the fireplace. It was there when I left to go to the mall this afternoon. Now, it's gone.'

'You're kidding, right?'

'Take a look for yourself. You don't even have to get up.'

Twisting in his seat, he peered over his shoulder.

I took a sip of my margarita.

'And where is this saber supposed to be?' Elroy asked.

'You see the fireplace?'

'Yeah.'

'There's a framed citation above it?'

'I see that.'

'That's where the saber is supposed to be, but isn't. I think somebody must've broken into the house and taken it.'

'Hmm.'

'For all I know, he might still be in the house. Hiding somewhere. Maybe just waiting for a chance to jump us. That's why I think we oughta get out of here.'

Elroy turned toward me. 'Instead of running off to a restaurant, shouldn't we call the police?'

'No!'

He smirked slightly. 'And why not?'

'Because.'

'Excellent reason.'

'Because if he's already gone,' I said, 'the cops won't do any good, anyway. If he's *not* gone . . . well, all the phones are inside the house. I don't want to get chopped up trying to call the cops, do you?'

Elroy's smirk grew. 'Don't you have a telephone in your suite above the garage?'

Damn it!

I gave the matter some thought, then said, 'Yes, but I can't get to it without my keys. Which I left on the kitchen counter.'

'Ah, you have an answer for everything.'

'I'm telling you the truth about this, Elroy.'

'I'm sure you are.'

'You think I'm lying.'

'Far be it from me to call you a liar.'

'Well, thank you one hell of a lot for believing in me.'

'I tell you what,' he said. 'Just to prove how much I believe in you, I'll go inside, myself, and make the call to the police.'

With that, he scooted back his chair.

Grabbing his arm, I said, 'Don't you dare.'

'Ha! I knew it.'

'Okay,' I said. 'I admit it.'

'You admit what?'

He hadn't believed me, anyway. Some people just don't listen, even when you're trying to help them.

'There never was any saber,' I said. 'I made up the whole business about the break-in.'

'Surprise, surprise.'

'I just wanted to go to a restaurant, that's all.'

He gave my shoulder a squeeze and said, 'Maybe tomorrow night.' His hand tightened its grip. 'But from now on, no more stories. Save them for your books.'

'Okay. I'm sorry.'

'No harm, no foul,' he said, and released my shoulder. 'Looks like we can both use refills.' Rising to his feet, he said, 'Why don't I bring out the whole pitcher?'

'Good idea. And while you're in there, see if you can pry the steaks apart. They'll thaw out a lot faster that way.'

'Your wish is my command, my dear.'

'Oh, and would you mind bringing out my keys? They should be on the counter near the blender.'

649

'My pleasure.' Grinning, he said, 'Now, are you *sure* you wouldn't like me to go ahead and dial up the cops?'

'That won't be necessary.'

'Thought not,' he said, and stepped out of sight behind me.

I heard him slide open the door and enter the house. But I didn't hear the door shut, so I got out of my chair to do it, myself.

As I rolled it shut, I saw Elroy striding across the living room. He didn't so much as glance at the place above the fireplace where the saber should've been.

If he'd bothered to take a close look, he would've seen the hooks.

He could've at least looked, the bastard.

So damn sure of himself.

So damn sure that I'm a liar.

'The hell with him,' I muttered.

But I was afraid of what I might see if I kept peering in through the glass door, so I turned away from it.

I strolled over to the side of the pool.

The early evening sun made the surface of the water glare and flash. Even with my sunglasses on, I had to squint. A warm breeze was blowing. It stirred softly against my face and arms, and drifted my skirt against the fronts of my legs. I felt a bead of sweat dribble down my spine.

Elroy'll be fine, I told myself.

Chapter Forty-five

Where is Elroy?

Or maybe not.

As the minutes went by, I kept expecting to hear the door slide open. But no sounds came from the house.

What's he doing in there?

Playing games, probably.

Payback games. He's staying inside, wasting time, trying to scare me.

I turned my back to the pool and stared at the living-room door. From where I was standing, though, the glass reflected too much. I could barely make out any details of the dim room.

I should probably just go in and see what's keeping him.

Yeah, sure, I thought. That's what he *wants* me to do. So he can jump out and scare the . . .

What if he's dead?

He isn't dead, I told myself. Whoever took the saber is probably long gone. You don't rob a house, then stick around. You get out as fast as you can.

Unless maybe it's not just a robbery.

Maybe the whole idea is to use the sword on me.

Who would want to do that? I wondered.

Judy. She got away, somehow, and now she wants revenge.

But she couldn't possibly know where I live. She knew nothing about me, certainly not my address or my real name.

Maybe my midnight swimmer came back for another try at me.

Get real, I told myself. A guy like that isn't going to show up in daylight. Or any other time, probably, since he had to figure I'd called the cops on him.

Somebody took the sword.

Probably.

But maybe not. Even though I had a specific memory of hanging it back up – had I taken it down again for some reason?

Maybe I'd done it while concentrating on something else. That sort of thing happens to me, sometimes. I suppose it happens to everyone. Haven't you ever, say, started off on a trip but then wanted to turn back because you couldn't recall turning off the stove or locking the front door? Even though you figure you *must've* done it (and you're right), you just cannot remember the act, no matter how hard you try?

It might've been that way with the saber.

Instead of getting all bent out of shape when I saw that it was gone, I should've made a quick search of the house. Maybe I would've found it in the den or bedroom or kitchen – exactly where I'd left it – and saved myself all this worry.

Why not do that now?

Staring at the shut door, I shook my head. This was about as close to the house as I wanted to get.

If Elroy comes out, maybe I'll go in for a look around.

If?

He'll come out, I told myself. Just let him get tired of his little game. He'll quit as soon as he realizes I'm not going to fall for it.

Never should've let him go in there. If he's dead, it'll be my fault.

No, it won't. I told him the truth, and he laughed at me. It'll be his own damn fault.

Anyway, he's fine. Probably wondering, right now, why I haven't come in to look for him yet.

Get used to it, creepazoid. I'm not coming in. You can wait till hell freezes over and our steaks thaw out, I'm staying right here.

Even as I thought that, I realized that it might be a very long wait. Elroy had already shown himself to be childish, stubborn, and inconsiderate. A guy like that would be very slow to quit.

I didn't exactly want to go on waiting.

For one thing, his absence made me nervous; I just couldn't help fearing foul play, even though I knew the odds were against it.

For another, I wanted my margarita refill.

'I'll get you out of there,' I muttered.

Then I turned away and walked alongside the pool. I rounded the corner. Stopping near the diving board, I turned to face the house again. The entire rear of it seemed to be glass. I couldn't see in. But Elroy could see out, if he wanted to. At least from the living room, where the curtains weren't shut. Other places, too, if he peeked through gaps at the edges of the curtains.

'Elroy!' I called.

But only once. With the house shut up tightly and the air conditioner on, he probably couldn't hear anything from outside.

Speaking quietly, to myself really, I said, 'Come out, come out, wherever you are.'

Then I started to undo the buttons of my blouse. I began at the top and worked my way slowly downward. Even though I took my sweet time, I didn't ham it up with any of that stripper stuff you see in the movies. That would've been too silly and embarrassing. I don't mind taking off my clothes, but I'm not going to act like a dork about it.

I slipped my blouse off. I didn't swing it around overhead, though, and give it a fling. I just dropped it to the concrete at my feet, then unfastened the couple of buttons at my hip and let my skirt fall.

Without looking down, I knew that I was pretty scratched and bruised. But I also knew that there was a lot more to look at than my injuries. My eyepatch panties didn't leave much to the imagination, and neither did my translucent red bra.

Balancing on one foot, then the other, I pulled off my shoes and socks.

Over at the house, there was still no sign of Elroy. The door remained shut.

I took off my sunglasses, crouched, and set them on my skirt. Then I stepped onto the diving board. I walked out slowly over the water. The board bounced a little with each stride. When I reached the end, I stopped moving and the board settled down.

Still, I didn't like standing up there. It was like being perched on a ledge. The slightest loss of balance, and I'd fall.

With my record for falling . . .

This time, at least, I would have a swimming pool underneath me.

I was tempted to go ahead and dive in while I still had control. *Not yet. Just wait. He's gotta see me up here. That's the whole point.*

So I stayed put, and turned my head to look at the house. Which upset my balance. Not much, but enough to make me start to tilt. I faced forward quickly, bending my knees and spreading my arms. It was iffy for a second or two, but I managed to get steady again.

After that, I knew better than to turn my head.

I also knew it was only a matter of time before I fell off the diving board.

Are you watching, Elroy? Come on out!

Apparently, he hadn't seen me yet, or he would be hot-footing it out for a closer look.

Maybe he can't see me.

He's down on the floor, dead.

Or maybe he's watching me, all right, but afraid to come out.

Or maybe he's got his face pressed to the glass, somewhere, and he's gazing out at me, spellbound, frantic to watch and see what I do next.

I thought about taking off my bra. *That* would sure give him something to see. But I suddenly pictured Elroy naked and squirming against the glass door, just like the guy last night. Then he *became* the guy last night.

Enough of this nonsense.

I kept my bra on, raised my arms high overhead, bent my knees and sprang off the board.

I'm not much of a diver. I'm not much of an athlete of any kind, really. But I knew I had to be looking pretty good. Even with the worst diving form in the world – and mine wasn't that bad – Elroy had to be drooling and erect watching me. *If* he was watching.

You better be watching, damn it.

I hit the water and went in cleanly and deep. It felt frigid, but only for a couple of seconds. After the first shock had passed, it felt okay. And then it felt just fine, cool and smooth, as I glided along below the surface. When I started to lose power from the dive, I swam underwater until I came to the shallow end of the pool. Then I stood up and turned toward the house.

And found myself looking at the den door.

First, I noticed the pale streaks down the glass.

Then I noticed a gap about ten or twelve inches wide at the door's edge.

It's open!

I hadn't done *that!* I might've misplaced the saber – though I doubted it – but no way on earth had I left the den door unlocked and open.

I hadn't left the curtains open, either.

But they were open now. In spite of the reflections on the glass, I could make out a few vague images inside the den. Not much, but enough to tell me that someone had opened the curtains.

Elroy must've done it.

Maybe he'd decided to give the house an inspection – just to make sure there really wasn't an intruder. Along the way, he might've opened some curtains, opened the den door . . .

It hardly seemed likely, though.

He wouldn't go around looking for intruders or signs of a

break-in. Not Elroy. He hadn't even looked to see if there were any hooks above the fireplace.

I suddenly knew the answer.

He did it as part of his plan to freak me out.

The bastard sure holds a grudge.

Or maybe he's just doing it to amuse himself. Doesn't mean to really scare me. Sees it as nothing more than a fun diversion, like hide 'n seek. A game to help pass the time while the steaks are thawing.

I called out, 'Very funny, Elroy. I know what you're doing, and I'm not falling for it. Why don't you stop screwing around and come out?'

No answer came.

Frankly, I didn't expect one.

But I hoped.

'I know you're in the den, watching me.'

I knew no such thing.

I only hoped.

Please, let it be a dumb game he's playing.

It has to be.

'I tell you what, Elroy.' My voice was shaking. 'I'll count to three. If you come out before I reach three, I'll take my bra off for you. Hell, I'll throw it to you. But only if you come out by the time I count to three. One.'

Nothing.

I went ahead and reached behind my back, anyway, to show him I meant business.

'Two.'

Nothing.

'Time's running out. This'll be your only chance, Elroy. If you don't pop your head out of that doorway in one second . . .'

It didn't pop out.

It rolled.

Chapter Forty-six

Reunion

Unfortunately, the rest of Elroy wasn't attached.

His head tumbled out of the den like a lopsided, mutant bowling ball, did a little hop over the door's threshold, then dropped to the concrete outside. As it dropped, his tongue was sticking out. The concrete clipped him on the chin, and he bit his tongue nearly off. It hung by a string of flesh as his head rolled a crooked course toward the pool – toward me.

He seemed to glance at me each time his face came up.

The stump of his neck flung blood through the air.

His tongue came off.

He bounced and rolled all the way to the pool. By the time he reached its edge, his nose was flat and his front upper teeth were broken out. He gave me a quick, awful grin, then sailed off the edge and plopped into the water about a yard in front of me.

The water went pink around his sinking head.

I waded backward as fast as I could.

Elroy's head seemed to pursue me.

But I stopped paying attention to it when the den door rumbled open.

Out stepped my midnight swimmer.

He held the saber in his right hand.

He wore nothing but shorts. From face to feet, he was spattered with blood. Except for his left arm, which was *sleeved* with it.

Somewhere in Serena and Charlie's house, he must've made an *awful* mess.

657

If he kills me, I thought, at least I won't have to worry about cleaning it up.

(You think odd stuff at times like that.)

He walked straight to the edge of the pool, then stopped and rested the point of the sword on the concrete beside his bare foot.

'Hello again,' he said. He seemed serious, but calm.

I didn't say anything. I was having trouble breathing. Then I flinched as something brushed against the side of my right leg.

'You must've known I'd come back for you.'

I took a step backward to get away from Elroy's head.

'Don't. Don't try to get away from me. You *can't* get away from me. I'm way too fast for you. And today, I'm the one with the sword. I could kill you in the blink of an eye. Or slice off small parts of you here and there. You don't want me to do that, do you?'

I shook my head.

'You be my good girl, then.'

I nodded.

'Don't move,' he said, then raised the saber, stepped off the edge, and dropped into the pool. As water splashed up around him, I took a single step backward. He didn't seem to notice. But he waded closer to me, and I didn't dare move away from him again. 'You're very lucky to have a pool,' he said. 'I wish I had one.'

Lowering his sword, he crouched down until the water covered his shoulders. Then he swished his left arm around, apparently trying to wash the blood off, and the water around it went pink.

'Your name is Alice, right?' he asked.

(Of course, he didn't say Alice. He said my real name, which is my secret.)

'How do you know?' I asked.

'I've heard.' He dunked his head.

658

I thought about making a break.

Before I could decide, his head came up, hair matted flat, water running down his face. With his left hand, which wasn't bloody anymore, he rubbed his face.

'I'm Steve,' he said.

'I'm charmed,' I said.

He smiled. 'Glad to hear it.'

'That's sarcasm, Stevie.'

His left hand smacked me hard across the face, burning my cheek and knocking my head sideways. My eyes filled with tears.

'That wasn't very nice,' I said.

'Depends which side you're on.'

'From this side, it sucked.'

'If you didn't like it, you'd better learn how to behave.'

'Consider me taught,' I said.

He grabbed me through the front of my bra, squeezed my nipple and lifted. Both my hands were free. I didn't try to fight him, though. Wincing, I went up on tiptoes and kept my hands down by my sides. Instead of begging him to stop, I hissed through my teeth and glared at him.

'Here's what we're going to do,' he said, keeping his grip. 'We're going to climb out of the pool, then have ourselves a nice party. Margaritas and barbecued steaks. You have my permission to marinate them. Say thank you.'

'Thank you,' I gasped.

'This could be a very pleasant experience for both of us.'

'I bet.'

He pinched me.

I flinched and tears ran down my face.

'You made me do that, Alice. And I *enjoyed* doing it. Did you enjoy it?'

'No.'

'Then why did you make me do it?'

'I don't know.'

'Would you like me to do it again?'

'No.'

'I can even do worse. Much worse.'

'You don't have to. I'll be good. I promise.'

'You'll be my good girl?'

'Yes.'

'My sweetheart?'

'Yes.'

'Cross your heart and hope to die?'

'Yes.'

He pinched me again. I jerked rigid with the pain, and cried out. He squeezed even harder. Writhing, I arched my spine and threw back my head. Tears spilled down my face.

And I felt his tongue.

Even as he kept pinching me, he licked the tears off my cheeks.

Finally, he let go of my nipple. He put his arm around my back and I sagged against him, sobbing. His hand caressed my back gently.

I thought about taking a bite out of his neck.

I could probably kill him if I did it well.

But he had the sword underwater in his right hand. Even mortally wounded, he could kill me with it in an instant.

Just wait, I told myself. Do everything he says. Be his good girl, his sweetheart, his slave, his whore, his anything-he-wants-me-to-be.

Sooner or later, I'll get him.

I'll get him good.

He doesn't know who he's dealing with.

Hasn't got a clue.

But he'll find out the hard way.

His hand slid down below the waistband of my panties, and gave my bare buttock a squeeze. 'So,' he said, 'are we ready to enjoy our party?'

'I'm ready,' I said.

I must've said it okay, because he didn't hurt me.

'Let's climb out of the pool,' he said. 'You go first. I'll be right behind you. Do everything I tell you to – without hesitation or wisecracks – and we'll have ourselves a merry time. I might even allow you to live.'

He let go of me, then stepped out of my way and gestured for me to step past him.

As I waded, I looked for Elroy's head.

I spotted it a couple of yards to my left, hovering just above the tile bottom of the pool, staring straight up as if he were trying to figure the best way of reaching the surface.

Poor bastard.

He'd been a schmuck, but he didn't deserve this.

I glared at Steve, but kept my mouth shut and waded on past him. At the wall of the pool, I braced myself with both hands and boosted myself up.

Steve swatted me across the ass with the saber.

Crying out, I flung myself over the edge and scurried to my feet. I hobbled away from the pool, clutching my buttocks. They felt as if they'd been lashed, but not slashed. There was no cut. He must've used the flat side of the blade.

'Looks count, too,' he informed me.

When I turned around, he was just standing up.

I kept rubbing my butt.

'You didn't have to kill him,' I said.

'That's a good one, coming from you.'

I gaped at him. 'What're you talking about?'

'You can't play innocent with me, honey. I saw what you did last night.'

'What I did?'

'You're about as cold-blooded as they come.' He smirked. 'Maybe that's why I find myself so strangely attracted to you. Let's go inside, now. Take me to the kitchen.'

661

I turned around and saw the trail of blood leading to the den's open door. 'Okay if we go in the other way?' I asked.

'Suit yourself.'

'May I please get dressed?' I asked.

'You may not. I like you just the way you are. Let's go.'

I led the way alongside the house, stepped behind the table and chairs, and slid open the living-room door. Steve followed me into the house.

Glancing over my shoulder, I asked, 'What do you think you saw me do last night?'

'I saw what you *did* do. Involving the sword and a certain unlucky young man who came to your door.'

'I thought he was you.'

'Isn't *that* a fine how-do-you-do?'

'Well, you had me scared.'

Entering the kitchen, I expected to find Elroy's headless body on the floor. But it wasn't there. Nor did I see any blood or signs of a struggle.

'Go ahead and marinate the steaks,' Steve said. 'I know you prefer them that way.'

'You were spying on us?' I asked, heading for the cupboard where Serena kept her sauces.

'You might say that.'

'Where were you?'

'Trade secret.'

I took down the bottle of teryaki, found a platter, and stepped over to the counter where I'd left the steaks. I tried to pry them apart, but they were still frozen together. 'Can you get them apart?' I asked Steve.

'They'll come apart in the natural course of time.'

'Thanks.'

'That comes perilously close to a wisecrack.'

'I'm sorry. I didn't mean it to sound that way.'

'Better watch yourself.'

'I will,' I said. I placed the steaks on the platter, drenched them with teryaki sauce, picked them up rubbed them with both hands to make sure they were wet everywhere, then put them back into the platter.

My hands were dripping with the spicy brown liquid. As I turned toward the sink, Steve said, 'Wait. I'll lick them clean.'

So I held out both my hands, fingers open and spread. Steve licked and sucked them.

It seemed like a weird thing to do – like licking my tears off. But I've got to admit, it felt pretty good. Especially when he sucked each one of my fingers all the way into his mouth. In other circumstances, it might've been a real turn-on. For instance, if someone like Murphy had been doing it to me. With Steve, I was too scared to enjoy it very much.

I had a big worry, for one thing, that he might bite one of my fingers off.

For another, I figured he had terrible plans for me, for later on.

As the last finger slurped out of his mouth, he smiled and said, 'Yummy. You're delicious.'

I almost said, '*Eat me*,' but stopped myself in the nick of time. Instead, I said, 'Thanks.'

'Now you may go ahead and wash your hands, if you like.'

I turned to the sink. I used soap and hot water on them. While I was drying my hands on a dish towel, Steve buzzed the blender a few times.

Then he said, 'Get me out a clean glass. I wouldn't want to use Elroy's. Might catch something.'

'Like what?'

'I wouldn't know. But he must've been gravely ill. He's dead, isn't he?'

Hilarious, I thought.

Keeping my mouth shut, I took down a clean glass for Steve. He lifted the pitcher of frothy margarita off the blender.

'Do you want salt on your rim?' I asked.

'I take my rims without.'

'Healthier that way.'

He chuckled. 'Do you really suppose I'm worried about my *health*? With my lifestyle, I'm looking forward to a lethal injection – or perhaps a bullet – but certainly not hardening of the arteries.'

'And what lifestyle is that?'

'I like to think of myself as a "thrill-killer".'

'Charming,' I muttered.

'Now, march,' he said.

'Where?'

'Out to the table. It's time for the Happy Hour.'

I stepped past him and left the kitchen. On our way across the living room, I asked, 'Did you get a thrill out of killing Elroy?'

'Not particularly, though it was amusing. I killed him because he was an obstacle in the way of you.'

'Where is he?'

'Here and there.'

'I know where his head is,' I pointed out. 'Where's the rest of him?'

'Already worrying about clean-up?'

'I just want to know.'

'He's in the guest bathroom.'

'You killed him in the bathroom?'

'Standing at the toilet, as a matter of fact. Took him completely by surprise. I'm afraid his aim got thrown off when he lost his head. Pissed all over the place. But he finally fell into the tub. Would you like to see?'

'No thanks.'

Chapter Forty-seven

The Happy Hour

'Remarkable woman,' Steve said as he filled my glass from the pitcher.

'Who is?'

'You, of course.'

'What do you know about it?' I said.

He poured margarita into his own glass, then placed the pitcher on the table. 'More than you might think,' he said. Before sitting down, he moved his chair around to the other side of the table.

He lowered the saber and leaned it against the side of his left thigh. Probably so he could go for it quickly with his right hand by reaching across his lap. The sword version of a cross-draw.

'I've been watching you,' he said, and took a sip. 'Very good margarita.'

'Yeah.'

'You're a fine figure of a woman.'

'So I've heard.'

'And extremely dangerous.'

I smiled sweetly.

'I've never run into a woman like you before. And, I must say, neither had Milo.'

'*Milo?*'

'Alas, poor Milo. We were partners, you know. Well, not exactly partners. Let's say Milo was my mentor. Until you killed him.'

'Killed him? I don't know what you're talking about.'

'Oh, please,' he said. Fortunately, he seemed amused, not angry. 'Spare me the innocent routine. I saw you do it.'

'Where?' I asked.

'Where do you think? At our camp in the woods.'

'You were *there*?'

'Oh, yes.'

'You must really get around,' I said.

A smile spread over his face. 'I do, I do. It's my specialty. Getting around. Coming and going. In a most sneaky fashion.'

'You weren't very sneaky last night in the pool.'

'That doesn't count. I *wanted* you to see me.'

'Sure you did.'

'Watch out, you're treading close to sarcasm. I may have to hurt you.'

'You're going to kill me, anyway.'

'That remains to be seen.'

'Sure.'

He leaned forward slightly in his chair, and something gouged my leg.

'Ow!' I scooted back my chair and looked down. On the side of my left calf, I now had a small, crescent-shaped wound. Made, probably, by the nail of Steve's big toe.

'Real nice,' I said.

'Be my good girl and these things won't happen.'

'I'm trying.'

'Not hard enough. When I tell you something, accept it.'

'Okay. I'm sorry. I was *supposed* to see you last night.'

'That's right. You *only* see me when you're supposed to.'

'Okay.'

Grinning, he said, 'Do you know that I spied on you yesterday afternoon?'

'No. Did you?'

'Absolutely. For a couple of hours. And you were completely unaware of my presence.'

'But I'm sure you were there.'

His eyes narrowed.

'Sorry,' I said.

'You were sunning yourself by the pool,' he said. 'A vision. That's when I decided I must have you.' He frowned. 'Not me so much as Milo, actually.'

'You wanted me for *him*? That fat, disgusting slob?'

'He always got firsties. That was our arrangement. I would've gotten you after he was done.'

'That's disgusting.'

'Cheer up. He won't get firsties anymore, thanks to you.'

'Good.'

'I could almost feel sorry for him. He was very much looking forward to you.'

'Is that so? Was he here, too?'

'Oh, no. I discovered you all on my own.'

'Where was Milo?'

'Back at camp with Marilyn.'

Marilyn? Must've been the dead woman in Milo's tent. *The woman he'd been eating.*

Had Steve been at her, too? I didn't want to think about it. 'If Milo was at the camp,' I said, 'how could he be looking forward to me?'

'Oh, I went back and told him all about you. And, of course, I showed him the photos.'

'*What* photos?'

'I took Polaroids of you.'

'You're kidding.'

'Not in the least. I always take snapshots of our special gals.' Grinning, he said, 'Before *and* after.'

'After?'

'You know.'

'Jeez.'

'We have quite a striking collection, really. We? Hum.

It's just me, now. I'm going to miss that big galoot. There may be lonely times ahead.' He drank some more of his margarita.

'So you not only spied on me yesterday afternoon, you also took pictures of me?'

'Exactly. I got several excellent shots, too. Close-ups. For a few of them, I was *this* close to you.'

'How close?'

'As close as I am now.'

Three feet? 'No way,' I said.

'Oh, yes way. I'm very good at sneaking about.'

'Those cameras are noisy.'

'I didn't say you were awake at the time. Let me tell you, your snoring was considerably louder than the camera. You were asleep right *there*,' he said, and pointed at the nearby padded lounger where I'd napped, off and on, through much of yesterday afternoon. 'When you weren't asleep,' he said, 'you were drinking Bloody Marys, reading a John D. MacDonald book called *A Tan and Sandy Silence*, and . . .'

'Okay, I get the picture. You were here.'

'You interrupted me.'

'I'm sorry. Go ahead.'

'I was about done, anyway.'

'What else did you do while I was asleep?'

'Nothing.'

'You didn't . . . touch me at all?'

'I was tempted. You looked absolutely scrumptious. As you do now. But you might've woken up. Anyway, it was my job to reconnoiter, not enjoy. Scout, and return with my findings to Milo.'

'So after you took those Polaroids of me, you ran back to camp and showed them to Milo?'

'He was enthralled. We're rarely lucky enough to get our hands on anyone as . . . attractive as you.'

'So then what happened?' I asked. 'After you showed him the photos?'

'Plenty. But I'm sure you don't want to hear about that. You want to know about my return last night.'

'Tell me about it.'

'Well, we decided that Milo would stay in camp to keep the home fires burning, and I would pay you a visit shortly after midnight.'

'Which is when I saw you.'

'I *let* you see me.'

'Okay.'

'I knew you were watching. That's why I took off my shorts.'

'Uh-huh.'

'I was hoping to lure you out.'

'*What?*'

'Lure you out.'

'You're kidding. You thought I'd come out if you stripped for me?'

'Oh, it's a tried-and-true technique.' He grinned. 'In fact, you were pulling much the same stunt in order to lure Elroy out of the house just a few minutes ago.'

'That was different.'

'Oh, really?'

'For one thing, I wasn't some stranger. For another, guys are crazy about breasts. It doesn't work the other way around.'

'It doesn't? I must say, that comes as a surprise to me. In my own experience, the stripping routine rarely fails. Of course, I don't always get completely naked. That depends on the woman. But I often let myself be seenin various stages of undress. I'm just there, keeping my distance, pretty much minding my own business, as if I've shown up by accident. And I allow them to watch me, to spy on me. The longer they watch me, the more intrigued – and aroused – they become. It works most of the time.'

'You're kidding.'

'Not at all. It's so easy. I don't have to break in and catch my victims, they come to me. More often than not. But you have to realize, I've already checked them out. They're always women. Always alone. In some cases, it's obvious that they're . . . hungry for romance. You, for instance.'

Feeling myself blush, I said, 'You had that wrong.'

'Did I?'

'You'd better believe it.'

'I *don't* believe it. It would've been obvious to anyone who saw you by the pool yesterday. That bikini you had on, the way you rubbed the suntan oil on your body, the way you sprawled on the lounger . . . you wanted *hands* on you. You wanted a man all over you and *in* you.'

'Wrong,' I said, and squirmed a little.

'I told Milo, "This gal's as hot to trot as they come. I might not be able to keep her off me." So, I must say, it came as a shock to find you calling the cops.'

'Couldn't have been *much* of a shock, the way you started humping the door.'

He looked confused for a moment, then grinned. 'Oh, that,' he said. 'Afraid I couldn't help it. You looked so . . . ravishing. You were wearing that silk robe. And your breast was out, you know.'

'Not on purpose.'

'Perhaps not.'

'No perhaps about it. It was an accident.'

'Are there any such things as accidents? Freud, I believe, said no.'

'Fuck Freud,' I said.

Chuckling softly, Steve lowered his eyes from my face to my breasts.

'Let me see them now,' he said. 'Take off the bra.'

I gave some thought to refusing. But he would've hurt me.

Besides, my bra was wet from the pool and not exactly comfortable. Also, it was a warm night with a soft breeze.

On top of all that, he had the saber. If he wanted my bra off, it would come off whether I refused or not.

I went ahead and took it off and dropped it to the concrete beside my chair.

'How's that?' I asked.

'Spectacular.'

I picked up my glass, finished the remains of my margarita, and set it down on the table. Standing up, Steve gave me a refill from the pitcher.

When he was seated again, I said, 'I wasn't really calling the police, you know.'

'Is that so?'

'I just wanted you to think I was. It was a wrong number. Somebody called the house by mistake. But you had no way of knowing that. For all you could tell, it was me calling 911. I even turned on the light to make sure you would see me.'

'What a gal. Gorgeous, tough, *and* tricky.'

'Obviously, not tricky enough. Or as tricky as you. You didn't really go away, did you? You just wanted me to *think* I'd scared you off.'

'That's right. I ran off into the woods, but then I circled back.'

'Weren't you afraid the cops might show up?'

'Not in the least. If they'd come, I simply would've disappeared into the woods. I'm very good at disappearing.' He took a sip of his drink, then looked at me. First at my breasts, then at my face. Then he said, 'So who *did* show up?'

'You don't know?'

He raised his eyebrows.

'Not as smart as you think you are,' I said.

He lurched forward over the table and his hand flew out and slapped me across the face. Then, smiling mildly, he settled back in his chair and asked, 'So, who *did* show up?'

I rubbed my cheek and said, 'A guy named Tony. I didn't even know him. He was the one who'd called. I'd told him about you on the phone, and I guess he decided to come over and protect me. I *guess* that's what he had in mind. He never told me anything.'

'He came to save you from me, and you smote him with your sword.'

'I suppose you saw that.'

'Sure did. I saw everything, from the moment you opened the front door till you drove away with his pieces. It was a rather amazing spectacle.' Shaking his head, Steve said, 'I could hardly believe my eyes when you started to dismember him. It seemed – so over the top.'

'He was too heavy, that's all. It was the only way I could get him into the trunk.'

'I was awestruck. And rather smitten with you, I must admit. Not only was your behavior truly extraordinary, but you were stark naked much of the time. A sight to behold.' With a grin, he asked, 'Were you naked by accident?'

'I didn't want to get everything bloody, that's all.'

'Well, I thank you. It was magnificent to watch you at work, all bare and sweaty. God, how I *wanted* you!'

'So, how come you didn't jump me?'

'Oh, that would've interrupted your show. I wanted to see it through to the finish.' With a small laugh, he said, 'I *will* be lucky enough to catch the end, though. I'll be a *participant* in it. But I regret missing some of the middle parts. I wanted so badly to follow you when you drove away with poor Tony in pieces in your trunk.'

'What did you do, go running back to the woods to tell Milo all about it, show him some more photos?'

'I didn't have the camera. It's no good at night. The flash would give me away. No, I stayed at the house. I wanted to be there when you came back. So I waited and waited. I waited an awfully long time. It was just an agony, the waiting, because I longed for you so much. Finally, I decided to call it a night, and try again tomorrow. So I bid your house a fond farewell and hiked back through the woods to our campsite . . . and who should I find there but *you*? *YOU*, my splendid savage, in the very midst of a life and death struggle with my dear demented friend, Milo!'

'And you did nothing but hide and watch?'

'It was a splendid show. All of it.'

'You just . . . let me go ahead and kill him?'

'Certainly.'

'Why didn't you try to save him?'

'Oh, I don't know.' He shrugged. 'Why, oh why? Perhaps because you might've killed me? You had that pistol. I've never much fancied the notion of being shot. I certainly didn't want to risk a bullet for Milo's sake. I'd grown weary of him. He was so bossy. And he always had to have firsties. One gets tired of sloppy seconds.'

A thoughtful look on his face, Steve said, 'I suppose I was pulling for you to win. That would be a reason for not trying to save Milo, wouldn't it? Also, I was enjoying the show too much to join in. There's nothing like a good fight, especially when a woman is involved. Especially when the woman is you.

'And then, after slaying Milo, you enthralled me with your bizarre treatment of Judy.'

'You watched everything?'

'And *heard* most of everything. It was wonderful.'

'And then what happened? When I left. Did you follow me then?'

'Ah, no. I gave it some thought, but . . . I was exhausted by then. So I let you go away, figuring I would stay at camp and take care of loose ends and save you for another day.' With a languid smile, he added, 'A day like today.'

'What about Judy?' I asked.
'What about her?'
'What did you do to her?'
'Let me put it this way, darling. I cut her down.'

Chapter Forty-eight

Body Heat

Steve stuck a tortilla chip into his mouth and crunched it. 'Uck. These are terrible.'

'They're healthy chips,' I pointed out. 'Low fat, cholesterol free, salt free.'

'Taste like paper.' He took a long drink of margarita to wash the chip down. Then he said, 'Are you starving? I'm starving. Why don't we go ahead and barbecue those steaks?'

'They're probably still frozen.'

'Let's have a look.'

'Fine with me.'

Steve and I got up from the table. Holding the saber in his right hand, he followed me into the house. At the kitchen counter, I lifted the T-bones out of the teryaki sauce. They were wet and slippery, and still stuck together. With Steve beside me and leaning forward to watch, I dug my fingertips into the edges where the two steaks met, and pulled hard. Suddenly, they came apart with a sound like ripping cloth.

'Bravo!' Steve said.

I set them down on the platter. 'They're still awfully frozen, but . . .'

'I'll thaw them out,' Steve said. Taking me by the arm, he

turned me toward him. Then, using both hands, he lifted the dripping steaks off the platter and pushed them against my breasts.

I gasped and flinched with their frigid touch.

'This'll warm them up fast,' he said, grinning.

'Come on,' I said. 'Quit it.'

'Nothing like body heat for thawing out steaks.'

'Please.'

'Don't make me hurt you,' he warned.

I almost grabbed his wrists, but stopped myself in time.

I *did* back away from him. He came after me, though, grinning and rubbing me with the steaks. Before I got far, my retreat was stopped by a turn in the counter. Steve cornered me and slid the steaks all over my breasts. They felt like slabs of ice. They made my skin burn. My nipples were rigid and aching. My breasts dripped with teryaki sauce, and dribbles ran down my belly.

Finally, he tossed the steaks onto the counter. They thunked the tile surface and skidded a few inches.

Clutching my sides with his wet hands, he crouched in front of me and started to clean the sauce off me with his mouth. First, he licked the dribbles off my belly. Then he slid his tongue over my breasts. He licked and sucked.

After the frigid beef, the heat of his mouth felt good.

It all felt good, especially what he was doing to my nipples with his tongue and lips.

But I worried about his teeth.

What's to stop him from biting me?

What's to stop him from eating me?

His buddy, Milo, ate Marilyn.

Maybe they both did.

I clutched Steve's shoulders, ready to thrust him away in case of trouble.

And stared at the saber.

Needing both hands for his games with the steaks, he'd left the saber propped upright against the counter, five or six feet behind him.

But he was in the way, hunched down, working my breasts with his mouth.

One good shove . . .

He would land on his back within easy reach of the saber.

If he gets it before I do . . .

I couldn't think straight because of what he was doing to me, but I knew this wouldn't be a good time to risk an attack on him.

Wait till it's a sure thing.

What if it's never a sure thing?

Just not now.

He suddenly bit my right nipple. I cried out and rammed my knee up. As it caught him in the chest, his mouth sprang open, freeing my nipple, and I shoved him backward by the shoulders. His back slammed against the kitchen floor.

Just as I figured, he landed beside the saber.

Before he could make a reach for it, I lurched forward between his legs and tried to kick him in the groin. It was a powerful kick. It would've knocked his balls into next Tuesday. But his hand shot down and caught my ankle and stopped my kick cold.

He could stop my foot, but not me.

Even as he gripped my ankle, I dropped onto him, driving my knees down hard into his belly.

He had solid stomach muscles. But not solid enough.

The moment my knees hit him, he let go of my ankle. His lips formed an O. He said, '*Ooomph!*' His eyes bugged out, and his head and shoulders came up off the floor.

For me, it was like kneeling on a raft shooting the rapids. I didn't stand a chance of staying up. Thanks to the fact that Steve had been clutching my right foot, I'd gone down on him with my body slightly turned – facing the saber. So I fell toward it.

As Steve's face got jammed with the left side of my ribcage, I reached high with my right hand and got hold of the blade. Then I flung myself over, trying to roll off him. But he hugged me around the rump. I rolled off him, all right, but he stayed with me. I ended up on my back, Steve on top with his face between my breasts.

His breath was still knocked out, so he was wheezing and gagging and not very strong.

He was trying to pull his arms out from under me.

Clutching the saber where I'd first grabbed it – high on the blade – I pounded the top of Steve's head with the hilt. The blade hurt my hand. That close to the hilt, though, it wasn't very sharp. I didn't think it had cut me.

But the hilt *clobbered* Steve.

I got him with the metal part that curves over to protect your hand during a sword fight.

He grunted and flinched. Then he jerked his arms out from under my ass and I was afraid of what he might do, so instead of worrying about my hand, I hammered him with the hilt about five more times hard and fast. My hand hurt with each blow, but I bashed the crap out of Steve's head and knocked him out cold.

He lay on top of me as if he'd suddenly fallen asleep.

Blood poured out of his torn scalp, soaked his hair, spilled all over my chest.

Bucking and twisting, I threw him off me.

He landed on his back, and I got to my feet. My right hand hurt like mad. I switched the saber to my left, then checked the damage. Not much. The blade had pressed several deep dents across my hand and fingers, but there were no cuts.

I'd gotten off lucky.

In more ways than one.

In *plenty* of ways.

I stared down at Steve. He still seemed to be unconscious. His head was lying in a nice puddle of blood.

I was all bloody, myself. I looked as if a small animal had died a messy death between my breasts.

Steve could've had a jolly time licking me clean.

I thought about waking him up and *making* him do it.

But he might bite me again. Or worse.

Over at the counter, I tore some paper towels off a roll and wiped the worst of the blood off me. I would've liked to take a shower.

But – as usual – I had too many other things to do.

Steve wouldn't stay unconscious forever.

Probably.

Right now, I had a choice to make: either kill him, or not.

No, that's wrong. Letting him live wasn't a real option.

For one thing, he knew too much. He knew my name and where I lived. He'd seen me kill Tony and Milo. He'd seen me abuse Judy, and had probably made her talk before killing her. If the cops got him alive, he would likely 'turn over' on me to get a deal.

For another thing, the guy had murdered Elroy and Judy and maybe Marilyn (the dead woman in Milo's tent). God only knows how many other people he and Milo had murdered as a team. He'd called himself a 'thrill-killer' and he was probably a cannibal, to boot.

Besides, given the chance, he would try to murder me.

So the real choices were between killing Steve here and now, or killing him somewhere else, later.

I was very tempted to do it here and now. Immediately, he would stop being a threat. (Dead men not only tell no tales, they *get* no tails. They don't rape, torture, or murder anyone ever again.)

But I would be stuck with Steve's body on the kitchen floor. And Elroy's headless body in the guest bathroom. And Elroy's head in the swimming pool. And various other, more manageable messes.

Quite frankly, I'd had enough of that shit.

He made the messes, let him clean them up!

YEAH!

It would be risky. But I had the saber, now.

While I waited for him to regain consciousness, I wondered about tying him up. Some manner of restraint seemed necessary. But how could he pick up Elroy, and so on, if his hands were tied? How could he carry the body away from the house with his feet bound together?

Pretty soon, I came up with a good solution.

I hurried into the laundry room. Serena had a fifteen-foot electrical extension cord that she mostly used for her iron. I unplugged it, gathered it up, and hurried back into the kitchen with it. Steve looked as if he hadn't moved.

I set my saber on top of a counter, then took a small knife out of the butcher block knife holder. In Serena's 'junk drawer,' I found some heavy-duty strapping tape. The sort that has threads running through it, so it's almost unbreakable.

Kneeling by Steve's bare feet, I tied one end of the electrical cord around his left ankle. I knotted it as well as I could, but cords make lousy knots. You just can't pull them tight enough. So then I unspooled about a yard of tape and cut it off with the knife. I used the tape to wrap his ankle *and* the cord. Then used another length of tape, just to make sure.

When I was done, the cord seemed completely secure.

I had fashioned a 'foot-leash' for Steve.

I retrieved the saber. Then I put all the sharp kitchen knives into a drawer so they wouldn't be handy for Steve. When that was done, I picked up my end of the extension cord and gave it a couple of tugs.

'Hey, Steve!' I yelled. 'Wake up! We've got work to do!'

Chapter Forty-nine

Sleeping Beauty

Perhaps I'd bashed him *too* hard.

Though I yelled at him and gave him nudges with my foot, he refused to stir.

To make sure he wasn't faking, I gave the crotch of his shorts a couple of prods with the tip of my saber. He didn't react, so I was convinced.

Now what?

In his present condition, he was useless. Worse than useless. Not only could *he* not do any chores for me, but *I* couldn't leave his side.

Well, I could leave his side, but not the kitchen.

At any moment, he might come to. I needed to be nearby when that happened, not off somewhere bringing in the margarita pitcher or gathering up my clothes or cleaning Elroy's assorted fluids off the bathroom floor.

Standing over him, I tried to think . . . plan my moves.

Top priority was keeping control of Steve, so I crouched down and slid his right leg over against his left, then wrapped the cord around both his ankles. Just a simple precaution to keep him from making any quick attacks.

As an added precaution, I placed a kitchen chair on top of him. The chair didn't touch him. With its front legs under his armpits and its rear legs beside his thighs, its job was to keep him from getting up fast and silently.

Now that I seemed to be safe from a surprise attack, I went over to the counter and picked up the steaks. They were still frozen, but seemed to have a slight springiness. Maybe my body heat *had* quickened the thawing process.

I thought about giving Steve the treatment.

But that might wake him up. True, I wanted to get things over with as soon as possible. But if Steve would do me the favor of staying out cold for a while, I could take care of a few matters on my own.

I placed the steaks in the platter of teryaki sauce, turned them over, then washed my hands at the sink.

I wanted to wash my whole body. Even though I'd already done a quick job with some paper towels, I felt incredibly filthy – itchy and sticky from such items as sweat and teryaki sauce and Steve's spittle and blood.

A bath or shower would have to wait.

But now that I had some free time, I went to the kitchen sink, set the saber down on the counter within easy reach, and held a dish towel under the faucet. When the towel was heavy with cold water, I turned around to watch Steve, and mopped myself with the sopping cloth. The water just seemed to flood me. It felt heavenly. It ran all down my body and made a puddle around my feet.

With a fresh dish towel, I dried myself and wiped up the puddle.

I felt so much better!

I felt like celebrating with a drink. Of course, the pitcher of margarita was on the table out by the pool, and I didn't dare go after it. The makings were still on the kitchen counter, though. So I took down a clean glass, tossed in a couple of ice cubes, and poured myself some tequila.

I hopped up and sat on the counter. I was wearing nothing, of course, except my thong panties. The tiles were cool and smooth under my rump.

I took a sip of the gold tequila. It felt cool in my mouth, then seemed to scald my throat and stomach.

I said, 'Ahhh.'

It is astonishing – and maybe one of life's quiet miracles – how much better every situation becomes as soon as you find a chance to clean up, have a good drink and relax. You might still be in an awful pickle, but you *feel* so much better, regardless.

It also helps if you're alone. With Elroy dead and Steve unconscious, I was alone for all intents and purposes. There was nobody to contend with, nobody who needed to be lied to, tricked or fought. It was such a relief.

I just sat there on the counter with my feet dangling, kept a general eye on Steve, and enjoyed my drink. I'd already knocked down a couple of margaritas. They hadn't been nearly as soothing, though, as the tequila.

Soon, I was feeling fine and lazy.

I wished I could lie down for a nap, but that was out of the question.

I needed activity to keep from drowsing off, so I hopped down from the counter. I set aside my empty glass, picked up the saber and both the dish towels, and went over to Steve. Crouching by his head, I set down the saber. Then I used the wet towel to clean him up. As I wiped the blood off him, I kept a sharp watch for any sign that he might be coming awake.

There was none.

With the same wet towel, I mopped the blood off the floor. This required several trips to the sink and back, but didn't take terribly long. Anyway, it was something to do while I waited.

Next, I folded the other dish towel into a square pad, and placed it against the wounds on top of Steve's head. With long strips of strapping tape (which I cut with the saber), I fastened down its corners to his ears and the sides of his face. It made him look stupid. Which was fine with me.

Pigs deserve to look stupid.

With the mess cleaned up and Steve bandaged, I felt free to relax again. But I was hungrier than ever.

Over at the counter, I checked the steaks. Nearly thawed out, they felt springy and firm, but stiff in the center.

Why wait any longer? I thought. You can't barbecue them on the grill, anyway. Not unless Steve comes to about now.

Well, I could drag him outside.

Right. No way.

I tossed some more ice cubes into my glass, added more gold tequila, took a sip, and sighed.

Squatting and duck-walking, I searched one cupboard after another until I found Serena's work. I took it to the stove and set it on a burner. Then I hunted out her vegetable oil. I poured some into the work, turned the burner on, and spent the next couple of minutes cutting the two steaks into bite-sized chunks.

Naturally, I took time out, every half a minute or so, to make sure Steve hadn't moved.

I tossed the two bones into the waste basket beside the stove.

By the time I managed to find Serena's wooden stirring spoon, the oil in the work seemed good and hot.

I poured in the meat and teryaki sauce.

Hiss, sizzle, spit, spatter!

'Shit!' I yelped and leaped away, my belly and breasts stinging with a thousand pin-pricks of fire. My skin glittered with specks of oil.

Here's a cooking tip: never stir-fry topless.

Except for a few moments of amazing pain, no real damage was done.

The wok no longer seemed to be erupting, so after a glance at Steve, I picked up the wooden spoon and started to stir the mixture of oil, teryaki sauce, and chunks of steak.

If they cooked too long, they'd be tough. So I counted to sixty in my head a couple of times while I continued to stir. Then I shut off the burner, hurried over to a cupboard and snatched down a couple of dinner plates.

I piled about the same amount of steak teryaki onto each

plate. Which seemed pretty generous, considering Steve's treatment of me. Also considering it would probably be cold and ruined by the time he might get around to eating it.

I set aside Steve's dinner, then found myself a fork and hopped up onto the counter. The counter made a fine seat. Not only did it feel cool and smooth under me, but I liked having the elevation. Perched up there, I had an excellent view of Steve. And I could jump down and run over to him in about a second if I had to.

With the plate resting on my lap, I sipped my tequila and ate the tasty chunks of steak. There should've been a bed of those crispy, squiggly Chinese noodles underneath the meat and sauce. That would've been great, but I hadn't thought of it. At this point, I didn't want to bother hunting for the noodles.

I wished I hadn't thought of them, though. It's a lousy thing, when you're eating fabulous steak teriyaki, to ruin it by worrying about the noodles that might've been.

Forget about the noodles! Relish the meal you've got!

Words to live by.

Hey, have you ever noticed how much *better* food tastes when you're a little tipsy? For some reason, aromas and flavors seem so much more wonderful than when you're completely sober. If you're not a drinker, you're really missing a treat.

Of course, you're also missing the aftermath, where you feel crummy and may vomit.

I guess it's a toss-up.

Done with my meal, I hopped off the counter. I rinsed my plate and fork at the sink, and stowed them away in Serena's dishwasher. Then I had a little dab more tequila. When the glass was empty, I filled it with cold water and took a good, long drink.

Now what?

Steve was still out cold, and I'd run out of things to keep me busy.

Try to wake him up?

I refilled my glass with water, then added a few ice cubes. Taking the saber along, I walked over to the chair that I'd placed over Steve's torso. I sat down on it, my feet on the floor just above his shoulders, and rested the saber across my lap. Then I leaned forward and peered down between my knees.

He looked asleep.

'Steve?' I asked.

He didn't move.

I gave his shoulder a nudge with my foot. Still no response.

*If he's going to *stay* out cold . . .*

Instead of dumping the glassful of water onto his face, I drank it. When nothing was left except for a few ice cubes, I bent way down and set the empty glass on Steve's forehead.

Then I settled back, sliding my rump toward the front edge of the chair. I stretched out my legs, folded my hands down low on my belly, shut my eyes and let my head droop forward.

I know, I know, I know. I had to be crazy to try and take a nap under these circumstances.

But I was so damn worn out by then. I'd had too much excitement, too much stress, too much strenuous activity, too little sleep, and maybe a smidgen too much tequila.

And I figured that Steve was no great threat. Even if he should wake up before me, he was pinned under the chair with his legs bound together and a glass resting precariously on his forehead. He had a slim chance of taking me by surprise.

He *might* get the upper hand, but it didn't seem likely.

It wasn't likely enough to worry me.

Or keep me awake.

After positioning myself for the nap, I must've stayed awake, worrying, for about five seconds. If that.

This was a straight-backed, wooden chair without a seat pad, but I zonked right away. Which tells you how badly I needed some sleep.

I was dead to the world.

Until the noise of bursting glass shocked me awake in the near-dark room and the chair lurched, throwing me off.

Chapter Fifty

The Awakening

Earthquake!

That was my first thought. I'd been through some bad ones. They nearly always hit while you're asleep, roaring and shaking you furiously and scaring the crap out of you.

Falling sideways, I was halfway to the floor when I figured out this wasn't any quake.

This was Steve.

My right shoulder hit the floor, and I rolled. Rolled and tumbled as fast as I could, hanging on to the saber. The chair toppled over. Part of it pounded my back, but not very hard.

Clear of Steve and the chair, I scrambled to my feet.

He was already sitting up, but still trying to free his feet from the electrical cord.

'Stop!' I shouted.

He looked up and saw me coming at him.

Even though the kitchen was dim with the gloom of dusk, I must've been quite a sight charging across the kitchen in nothing but my panties, my breasts leaping, my saber high.

One glimpse of me, and Steve let out a yelp.

He quit fooling with the cord and stuck up his hands. 'I give!' he yelled. 'Don't do it! Please!'

I slid to a halt beside him. Still holding the saber overhead with both hands, I said, 'Lie down and don't move.'

He sank backward until he was stretched out flat.

Never turning away from him, I sidestepped to the nearest light switch. I flicked it up and brightness filled the kitchen.

As I approached Steve, he lifted his head off the floor. He winced and flinched, but didn't take his eyes off me. Fingering the dish towel that I'd taped to the top of his head, he asked, 'What's . . . going on?'

'I won, that's what.'

'I don't remember.'

'I don't doubt it.'

'What happened to my head?'

I shook the saber.

'You chopped my head open? Oh, my God!'

'Don't blow a gasket,' I said. 'I just gave you a few raps with the handle, that's all. If I'd used the blade, you wouldn't be asking me questions about it. Lie still, and I'll take care of your feet.'

'Okay,' he muttered.

'I'm not even gonna warn you about trying something.'

He eased his head down against the floor.

With the saber in my right hand ready to strike him, I squatted near his feet and used my left hand to unwind the cord. 'As long as you cooperate with me, you'll be fine.'

'I'll do whatever you want.'

'Good. I went ahead and ate, by the way. I couldn't wait for you.'

'That's okay.'

'But I saved you some.'

'Really?'

'Yeah.'

When his feet were no longer bound together, I stood up and backed away, the end of the cord in my left hand.

He pushed himself up to his elbows, looked, and saw how I'd fashioned a tether for his left ankle. 'Cute,' he said.

'It'll let you get around.'

'I guess so.' Meeting my eyes, he said, 'I can't say that I blame you for not trusting me.'

I laughed at him. Then I said, 'Get up and come over here.'

He made it to his feet, and I led him over to the counter where his plate was waiting. I was careful not to let him get close to me.

'Where do you want me to eat it?' he asked.

'Right there.'

'What about a fork?'

'So you can stab me with it? Use your fingers.'

He started to pick up the plate.

'Put it down,' I said. 'Leave it on the counter.'

He set it down. Then, bending over, he started picking up pieces of steak one at a time. He got a couple into his mouth before he really started chewing. 'Mmm,' he said. He shoved more in. 'Good.'

'I know it's not *human*, but it's the best I could do on short notice.'

'That was Milo's gig,' he said. The words came out mushy because of the meat in his mouth. 'Not mine.'

'You don't eat people?'

Grinning over his shoulder, he said, 'Not that way.'

'Very funny.'

'He was nuts. Milo.'

'He was your mentor.'

'Yeah, but he was a fuckin' cannibal. I'm no cannibal. Shit, he did all kinds of weird stuff. Not me.'

'Not you. Sure.'

'This is really good steak. Really delicious.'

'You should've had it when it was still hot.'

'Well. Can't have everything.' He shoved more into his mouth.

'I want to hear the rest of your story,' I told him.

'What do you want to know?'

'You said you watched me in your camp last night. When I took care of Milo and stuff. And then, after I left, you killed Judy. Then what?'

'Did I say that?' He gave me another grin. His lips were shiny with steak juice. 'I don't *believe* I said anything about killing Judy.'

'Yeah, you did.'

'If I said that, I must've been mistaken.'

I felt a strange, fluttery tightness inside. I don't know quite what it was. Hope? Fear? Excitement? In some ways, I wanted Judy to be dead. She was a loose end. She could get me in big trouble. But in other ways . . . Hell, I liked her.

'You *didn't* kill her?' I asked.

'No, no, absolutely not.'

'Bad choice of words, pal.'

'Huh?'

' "Absolutely not." Makes me think you're lying.'

'Oh. Jeez. I see what you mean. Protesting too much, huh?'

'What *did* happen after I left?'

He shoved a couple more chunks of steak into his mouth, chewed for a minute, and said, 'How about something to drink?'

'The sink's right there,' I said.

'A glass?'

'Use your hand.'

So he sidestepped to the sink, ran some water, cupped his hand under the faucet and took a few drinks.

'What about Judy?' I asked.

He slurped some more water out of his hand, and said, 'What about her?'

'If you didn't kill her, what happened to her after I left?'

Steve sighed, wiped his wet hand across his lips, then shut off the faucet and turned around and grinned at me. 'I cut her down.'

'You cut her down?'

'The ropes, the ropes. I freed her from the ropes from which she was so cruelly hanging, thanks to you.'

'I didn't do that to her.'

'But you didn't cut her down.'

I didn't need to be reminded of that.

'Are you done eating?' I asked.

'No!' Losing his grin, he turned away and hurried over to his plate and stuffed more steak into his mouth.

'Okay,' I said. 'So what happened after you ... took her down from the ropes?'

'Plenty.'

'Tell me.'

'Fucked the daylights out of her, for starters.'

I struck him hard across the ass with the flat of the saber blade. He shrieked and arched his back and clutched his buttocks. For a while, he stood there gasping for air. Then he bent forward a little and braced his hands on the counter top. I could see him shaking.

'You forgot who has the sword,' I told him.

'You asked ...'

'I didn't like your answer. I don't want to hear about that stuff. What *else* happened?'

'We ... we buried the bodies. Milo and Marilyn.'

'Where'd this Marilyn come from, anyway?'

'The tent. Milo had her in the tent.'

'Where'd she *come* from? Is she from around here? Did you catch her in Miller's Woods?'

'Huh? No. We grabbed her when we were on the road.'

'Tell me about it.'

'Well, we spotted her at a gas station. That was a few days ago, when we were up north. We'd stopped for a fill-up, and there she was, pumping gas into her Toyota. A real babe. She wore these short shorts . . .' He glanced back at me and at the saber. Then he went on. 'Anyway, we followed her when she left the station. We wanted her to rear-end us, so we got ahead of her, then slowed down. This Marilyn was impatient, so she tailgated us, trying to get us to speed up or pull over. A real bitch move. So then, when we came to a place where nobody was around, Milo suddenly stomped on the brakes. Wham! She rear-ended us. Well, we all got out to check the damage and exchange information. And that's when we snatched her. We threw her into the back of the van, I jumped in with her, and Milo drove off.'

'You have a van?' I asked.

'Sure. You've gotta have a van.'

'Where is it?'

'Oh, we've got it hidden in the woods. Not too far from a road, but far enough so it's out of sight.'

'So you brought Marilyn here to the woods?'

'Right. And put up our camp and had ourselves . . .' He gave the saber an uneasy glance. 'We kept her as our guest in the camp for a couple of days, and then she died.'

'Died, huh?'

'Well, Milo cut her throat.'

'Milo, huh?'

'Yeah.'

'How many other people have you two killed?'

'Between the two of us? Quite a few. I couldn't say for sure.'

'How long were you together?'

'Milo and me?'

'Yeah. Traveling around in your van, killing people.'

'A couple of years.'

'My God.'

He grinned at me. 'Just doing some population control. Environmentally speaking, over-population is a real . . .'

'Shut up.'

'Sorry.' He faced forward again.

'So what happened,' I asked, 'after you and Judy dug the graves last night?'

'Nothing. Well, we threw Milo and Marilyn in and covered them with dirt, of course. Then we went to sleep. That's all.' Reaching out, he picked up a single piece of steak. He looked at me, then stuck it into his mouth and started to chew.

'But you came back here today,' I told him. 'What'd you do with Judy when you left camp? Where is she?'

'Still there . . . in camp.'

'Alive?'

He nodded.

'Tied up?'

He grunted, then said, 'Tied and gagged. In the tent.'

'And in what condition?'

'Fine. She's fine.'

'She *can't* be fine.'

'*I* didn't hurt her.'

'Sure you didn't.'

'Not much.' He leered over his shoulder at me. 'I'd be glad to take you to her.'

'Not interested,' I said.

'Sure you are. You're *very* interested.'

'You know what I want?'

'Judy.'

'No. I want this house cleaned up. I want you to haul Elroy's body out – and get his head out of the pool. Then we'll take a little trip. You buried Milo and Marilyn somewhere near your camp?'

He nodded and stuffed more steak into his mouth.

'You have shovels?'

'Sure. Tools of the trade. Got a couple of them.'

'Okay. Then I guess we *will* go to camp. You can bury Elroy there with the others.'

'And you can have a nice reunion with Judy.'

Chapter Fifty-one

Teamwork

'Cut it out about Judy,' I said.

'Whatever you say. You're the boss.'

'Finish up with the food. We've gotta get on with this.'

He stuffed the last three or four pieces of steak into his mouth. Chewing, he sidestepped to the sink.

'You raped her, huh?' I asked.

He made a garbled sound.

'What?' I asked.

He shook his head and continued to chew. Then he ran the faucet, leaned forward and cupped water into his mouth like before. When the faucer was off, he stood up straight. He wiped his mouth. Then he turned around to face me. 'I thought you didn't want me to talk about Judy.'

'Yeah. You're right. I don't. Never mind.'

'Anyway, I *didn't* rape her.'

'But you said . . .'

'I said we fucked. I didn't say anything about rape. A rape requires force or coercion. She was quite willing. After all, I'd cut her down. *You* should've cut her down. Maybe you would've gotten lucky.'

'Okay, that's enough. Let's go find Elroy. You lead the way.'

Holding the end of the cord in one hand, the saber in the other, I followed Steve out of the kitchen. The rest of the house was pretty dark. As we walked through the foyer, I switched a light on.

'How long have you been here today?' I asked.

'Oh, I arrived around noon. Hoping to find you sunning yourself by the pool like yesterday. I was severely disappointed.'

'How did you get in?'

'Sliding doors are a cinch.'

He turned to the left and stepped into the guest bathroom. Now that he was no longer blocking my view, I saw a trail of blood drops on the hallway carpet. Steve must've made them carrying Elroy's head from the bathroom to the den. The trail was sure to continue on through the den.

Entering the bathroom, I said, 'Nice job on the carpet.' And then I saw the mess near the toilet. 'Oh, my God.'

Steve grinned and shrugged. 'What can I say? He made a nice splatter pattern. Could've been a lot worse, though. At least he fell into the tub.'

I walked closer to Steve, sidestepped to see past him, and spotted Elroy in the bathtub.

My memory flashed an image of Murphy, also dead in a tub. *Rub-a-dub dub, two men in a tub . . .*

Unlike Murphy, Elroy had his clothes on. And he wasn't sitting sideways in the tub, feet sticking out. He probably *had* been crooked, since he'd fallen from a standing position in front of the toilet. But now he was stretched out on his back, feet toward the drain. His penis was hanging out the open fly of his trousers. His blood-soaked shirt was still tucked in, and his bow-tie, no longer blue, was still in place at the throat of his shirt. Above the bow-tie, he had a ragged stump of neck.

'You want me to pick him up?' Steve asked.

'That's the idea.'

'And do what with him?'

'Get him out of the house, for starters.'

'He's bound to drip, you know.'

'Run the shower on him,' I said. 'That'll get the worst of the blood off.'

'Aye-aye, ma'am.' Steve stepped to the foot of the tub, started the shower spraying down onto Elroy, then slid the plastic curtain shut.

'We need something to put him in,' I said.

'A couple of plastic garbage bags should do the trick.'

'Those'd be out in the garage.'

'No problem.'

'Yeah, it's a problem,' I said. 'I'm not taking you all the way out there just to get some garbage bags.'

'Afraid I'll make a *break for it*?'

'Something like that.'

'Well, we could get a sandwich baggie from the kitchen and put it on his stump.'

'Very funny,' I said. But his suggestion made me realize that, if the shower did its job, we really didn't need to worry about blood from anywhere except Elroy's neck.

So we marched back to the kitchen. I instructed Steve where to look, and he found Serena's roll of cellophane wrap in the cupboard underneath the sink.

We returned to the bathroom.

While I held the saber and my end of the cord, Steve shut off the shower. He slid open the curtain, stepped into the tub, and got to work on Elroy.

First, he raised the body to a sitting position. Then he removed Elroy's bow-tie and opened the top two buttons of his shirt. After that, he tore off a foot-long section of plastic wrap and draped it over Elroy's neck stump. He squeezed it down firmly so it clung to the raw stuff inside. Finally, he tucked the edges of the cellophane underneath Elroy's shirt collar to hold the wrapping snug.

'That should do the trick,' he said.

'I think so,' I agreed.

The shower had done a fine job cleaning the blood off Elroy and his clothes. The white shirt was badly stained, but it wouldn't be dripping blood on the way out. With the neck stump secure, he was ready to move.

'Okay,' I said. 'Now pick him up and let's get him out of the house.'

Steve looked at me and raised his eyebrows. 'Are you going to lend a hand?'

'No.'

'But you're so *good* at body handling.'

'I've retired,' I said. 'You killed him, you carry him.'

'What a sweetheart.'

'That's me. Let's get going.'

Squatting behind Elroy's back, he reached beneath the arms, hugged him around the chest, and lifted.

As Steve hauled Elroy out of the tub, I backed away, giving him plenty of slack with the electric cord. Then I waited while he struggled to find the best way to carry the body. He ended up cradling Elroy in his arms the way you see guys carry their brides over the threshold in movies.

'Ready?' I asked.

'All set,' he said. 'You ready, Elroy?'

'Cut out the funny stuff,' I said. 'He was a nice guy.'

'Give me a break. He was a pain in the ass. You couldn't stand him.'

'Maybe so, but you shouldn't have killed him.'

Smirking, he said, 'You made me do it. I would chop the heads off an *army* to get my hands on you.'

'Go to hell,' I said.

Then I led us out of the bathroom. 'We'll take him out the front door,' I said, turning and moving backward for the foyer. As I walked, I watched Elroy. He dripped onto the carpet, but only water – so far as I could tell. The cellophane on his neck seemed to be working fine. 'We'll put him in his car and drive him to the woods.'

'Now, *that's* a good idea. I was afraid you might make me walk.'

'Can't leave his car here, anyway. We'll park it at the picnic area, and you can carry him the rest of the way to the camp.'

I opened the front door, glanced outside to make sure the coast was clear, then stepped out of the way. Turning sideways, Steve carried Elroy past me. I left the door open (since I had no keys on me) and followed them across the lawn to the driveway.

'You'd better put him in the trunk,' I said.

Nodding, Steve trudged to the rear of Elroy's car. 'How do we unlock it?' he asked.

'Use his keys,' I suggested. 'They're probably in a pocket of his pants.'

'How about coming over here and finding them for me?'

'Thanks, but no thanks. Do I look that stupid?'

'I won't try anything,' he said.

'I'm sure I believe you. Just put him down and get the keys yourself.'

He started to crouch, then apparently changed his mind. Instead of lowering Elroy onto the driveway, he eased the body down on the trunk of the car. Then he patted both front pockets of the trousers. I heard keys jingle.

The body started to slip, so Steve halted it with one hand. Holding it still, he shoved his other hand into the right front pocket. A moment later, he came out with a key case.

He tossed it to me and said, 'Catch.'

It sailed toward my left shoulder.

In my left hand, I held the end of the cord that led to his ankle.

I clutched the cord more tightly, and didn't go for the keys.

697

The leather case smacked me below my left shoulder, slid down my breast and fell to the grass.

'Nice catch,' he said.

'Nice try,' I told him.

He laughed softly. Then he said, 'I know it's asking a lot, but if I pick up your friend and move out of the way, would you be kind enough to unlock the trunk for us?'

'No.'

'Please? Pretty please with sugar?'

'Which hand do you want me to use for the keys?' I asked. 'The one with the saber in it, or the one with the cord in it?'

'Either would be fine,' he said.

'I'm sure.'

'You know what? I've got a terrific idea. Why don't we simply dispense with the cord altogether? In fact, why not forget this entire *captive* routine and work as a team?'

'You're dreaming.'

'Let's be partners from now on. How about it? It would make life so much easier for both of us if we start working together instead of fighting each other.'

'Only one problem with that,' I said. 'I'd turn up raped and dead.'

'No, no, no. Don't be ridiculous. I wouldn't hurt my partner.'

'Forget about it. Come over here and pick up the keys.' I gave the cord a couple of quick tugs.

'Okay, okay.' Leaving Elroy on the car's trunk, Steve came toward me. I backed away. 'I know you want me,' he said. 'You should've seen the look on your face last night when I was up against the door. *You* wanted to be the door. Not to *mention* in the kitchen tonight when I licked the teryaki off your incredible, luscious body . . .'

'Just shut up and grab the keys.'

He squatted, reached forward into the grass, and picked up

the key case. Staying low, he gazed at me and said, 'You want me, I want you. We'd be great together. We could go off tonight . . . Hell, we could leave Elroy here and drive away right now. I'll take you to my van, and we'll hit the roads. We'll leave *all this* behind. What do you say?'

'Eat shit and die.'

Laughing, he stood up. 'That's what I love about you. You're so tough. *And* you've got a sense of humor. Not to mention your killer figure.'

'He's slipping,' I said.

'Huh?'

'Elroy.'

Steve looked over his shoulder just in time to watch Elroy's body slide off the car's trunk and tumble onto the driveway. Facing me again, he shook his head, smiled, and said, 'All the guys fall for you.'

Chapter Fifty-two

Head Games

It worked out well. With Elroy sprawled on the drive-way, Steve was spared the extra chore of lifting him off the trunk.

I waited near the side of the car while Steve unlocked the trunk. As the lid swung up, he stuffed the keys into a front pocket of his shorts. Then he turned around, picked up Elroy, carried him over to the trunk and dropped him in. The car squeaked and rocked a little. Steve slammed the lid shut.

'Shall we be off?' he asked.

'Not quite yet,' I said. 'We're missing something.'

He grinned. 'I suppose we'd forget Elroy's head if it weren't attached.'

'Let's go get it.'

Worried that Steve might try to shut me out of the house, I stayed ahead of him, walking backward all the way to the front door.

I'd liked it better when he had his arms full.

In the foyer, I said, 'Let's make a stop in the kitchen, first.'

For that, I let him take the lead.

As we entered the kitchen, he warned, 'Careful of the broken glass.'

'Thanks,' I said.

'You're welcome. What are partners for?'

I stepped around the glass. 'We're not partners.'

'Maybe not yet. But soon.'

'Yeah, sure.' I spotted my own keys near the end of the counter, exactly where I'd left them after coming into the house with Elroy. 'Step over to the right,' I said.

Steve followed instructions. When he was out of my way, I walked toward the counter.

'Need your keys?' he asked.

I didn't bother to answer.

'Which hand will you pick them up with?' he asked. 'The one with the cord, or the one with the sword?'

'This may work,' I said. Then I tucked the plug under my right armpit. I clamped my upper arm tightly against my side to hold it there. 'Now if the cord gets away from me,' I said, 'I'll just have to chop your head off.'

'Hey, we're a team,' he said. 'Get your keys. I won't try anything.'

Watching him closely, I sidestepped to the counter and used my left hand to pick up the key case.

He watched *me* closely as I slipped the case down inside the front of my panties. The leather felt smooth and cool. 'Lucky keys,' he muttered.

'Shut up,' I said. 'Let's go get Elroy's head.'

Being careful again to avoid the broken glass on the floor, we left the kitchen. From there, we had several possible ways of getting to the pool. I decided on the den door, mostly because I wanted to inspect the carpet damage.

The trail of blood started at the doorway of the guest bathroom and dribbled along the hall toward the den. Not great quantities of blood, but enough. Too much.

'I don't know what the hell I'm going to do about these stains,' I said, walking a few paces behind Steve. 'They aren't going to clean up. Damn you, anyway. I've been cleaning up after myself ever since last night. I've covered up *everything*. I've worn myself out, cleaning up and covering up and . . . What am I gonna do about *this*? There's no way to make all these blood stains go away, you bastard.'

'Replace the carpet,' Steve suggested.

'Yeah, sure. You think my friends wouldn't notice a new carpet?'

He grinned over his shoulder. 'Come away with me, and it won't matter.'

'No way.'

He entered the den. I followed him, pausing long enough to hit a light switch with my elbow. A lamp came on, and I saw the dribble of blood leading to the den's sliding door. 'I guess I could tell them I got cut and it's *my* blood.'

'Excellent idea. You have such fine ideas. That's one of the things I love about you, darling. Along with your . . .'

'Shove it.'

'So sorry.'

'Why'd you have do that with his head, anyway?' I asked.

'Cut it off, you mean?'

'And carry it through the house and *roll* it at me.'

He chuckled. 'I was hoping to bowl you over.'

'You're a sick fuck,' I said.

'I'm a *splendid* fuck, as you'll soon learn.'

'Yeah? Has hell frozen over?'

As Steve neared the sliding door, I quickened my pace. I was about one stride behind him by the time he stepped outside.

I glimpsed the stains he'd put on the glass last night.

Then I stepped out, let him walk ahead, and gave the cord a sharp pull. Its other end jerked his left leg backward. Yelping with alarm, he fell headlong onto the concrete. He caught himself with his hands, but seemed to land fairly hard.

'Just another guy falling for me,' I remarked.

On his hands and knees, he looked back at me. I suspect he might've been scowling, but I couldn't see much of his expression because of the darkness.

'That's a lousy way to treat your partner,' he said, pushing himself up.

'Knock off the partner crap.'

'If you say so.'

'We aren't partners. We'll never *be* partners.'

'We're already accomplices,' he said. 'In the eyes of the law.'

'I don't plan for the eyes of the law to look in my direction. So just shut up about the eyes of the law and get in that pool and find Elroy's head.'

'All right. Partner.' Steve took a few steps and halted at the edge of the swimming pool. Then he stood there, slowly turning his head.

Pretty soon, he said, 'Oh, my.'

'What?'

'It's gotten dark.'

'I noticed.'

'I can't seem to locate the head.'

'It's down there someplace.'

'Does the pool have lights?'

'Give me a break,' I said. Stepping closer to the edge, myself, I looked down into the water. It might've been a pool of black ink.

'Do *you* see his head?' Steve asked.

'No.'

'I suggest we try the lights.'

We didn't seem to have much choice. 'Okay,' I said. 'They're over here. Come on.' I gave the cord a small tug.

'Don't do that.'

'I'll do whatever I want. Let's go.'

'Where?'

Using the saber, I pointed out the electrical panel on the wall behind the outdoor table. 'You first,' I said.

He started toward it, and I stayed a few strides behind him, giving the cord plenty of slack.

The bag of tortilla chips and the margarita pitcher were still on the table.

'Shall we take a break for cocktails?' Steve asked.

'Keep going. Don't touch that pitcher.'

'How about this?' he asked. Stepping around the table, he scooped up my bra with his bare right foot. It draped his foot like a huge red mask, flopping about but not falling off as he kept on walking. 'Of course,' he said, 'I prefer you without it.'

'Big surprise. You *made* me take it off.'

'But I'll let you have it, now.'

'Don't bother.'

He stopped at the electrical panel and flicked a couple of switches.

Lights suddenly flooded the patio. Glancing over my shoulder, I saw that the pool lights had come on, too. 'That'll do it,' I said.

'Excellent,' Steve said. Turning around, he swung up his foot and flipped the bra at me.

I snagged it out of the air with the saber. It slid down the blade until it met the crosspiece. 'Thanks,' I muttered.

'Aren't you going to put it on?'

'Maybe later.'

'It does look like your hands are full,' Steve said. 'Would you like *me* to lend you a hand?'

'Let's go get the head.'

I backed out of his way. He walked past me.

As I followed him, I lowered the saber. My bra slid down its blade and fell off. I stepped over it.

At the edge of the pool, I stood a couple of yards to Steve's left. The water was brightly lighted, and looked pale blue because of the pool's blue tiles. The hot night breeze ruffled its surface.

'Thar she blows!' he called out, and pointed.

Elroy's head had dropped into the pool at the shallow end. But it hadn't stayed there. It had wandered to the deep end, where it now rested under about twelve feet of water. It seemed to be face-down as if giving the drain a close inspection.

'Now we have a problem,' Steve said.

'Do we?'

'Who goes down for it?'

'You do.'

'Well, I don't believe the cord is long enough. Not if you're planning to stand here and hold it.'

'We'll see. Move over that way,' I told him, and gestured to the right with my saber. 'We'll get as close as we can.'

We both walked along the edge until Steve was adjacent to Elroy's head.

'We're still not close enough,' he said. 'The cord's too short.'

'Go anyway.'

'If you say so.' With that, he suddenly dived off the edge.

Before he even hit the water, I was leaping out. I held the

saber high in my right hand, the end of the cord low in my left. Feet first, I plunged deep.

Through a frothy curtain of bubbles, I saw Steve trying for the bottom. He was in front of me and lower in the water, nearly vertical, kicking and reaching. His shorts had almost come off in the dive. You could see a few inches of his butt crack. From neck to rump, his skin looked very pale and stark and wavery in the underwater lights.

Near his left ankle, his kicking flung the cord this way and that. But he still had slack.

And he still had slack when his right hand thrust down and clutched Elroy by the hair. Hanging on to the head, he curved away from the bottom and began to rise.

Which is when I tried to come up.

And couldn't.

For one thing, the saber weighed me down. For another, I held the cord in one hand and the saber in the other, leaving no hand free to paddle at the water. Though I struggled to kick my way to the surface, I didn't seem to be making any progress.

I didn't panic, though.

I was in no danger of drowning.

Before letting that happen, I would empty my hands and swim to safety.

But what kind of safety would it be if I left the saber at the bottom of the pool?

Just let go of the cord, I told myself.

But I kept my grip on it.

You've gotta let go!

Can't! He'll get away!

Suddenly the cord jerked and nearly flew out of my hand. I squeezed hard and kept hold of it by the plug.

The cord began to tow me through the water.

Chapter Fifty-three

The Getaway

Above me but still below the surface, Steve was swimming toward the shallow end of the pool. He must've known he was pulling me along behind him, but he didn't do anything about it.

He had no idea, I'm sure, that he was helping me.

If he'd known, he would've stayed in the deep water. That would've forced me to drop the cord or the saber or both.

But he towed me to safety.

Just when I was starting to ache for a breath of air, the bottom of the pool suddenly sloped up sharply under me. I tried to lower my legs and stand up. I couldn't manage it, though, with Steve still pulling me forward.

Then he stopped.

I planted my feet on the tile bottom and burst out of the water, gasping for breath and thrusting my saber high. I blinked my eyes clear.

I was standing in water high enough to touch the undersides of my breasts. Ahead of me, Steve turned around in water up to his waist.

The light shimmered on his slim body. He hadn't lost his shorts, but they were down below the pool's surface. So was Elroy's head. They wavered and undulated the way things do when they're under water.

'Have a nice ride?' he asked.

'Yeah, thanks.'

He lifted Elroy's head by its hair. It came up looking at me, water spilling down its face, its eyes and mouth wide open.

When the head was level with Steve's shoulders, he changed his hold on it. He put his left hand under the pulpy neck to act as a platform. Then his right hand let go of the hair and gripped the back of Elroy's head.

He turned the face toward himself. 'And how did *you* like the ride, Elroy?'

'*It was just super, Stevie boy,*' Steve responded on Elroy's behalf, speaking in an enthusiastic nasal voice and moving his lips like a lousy ventriloquist.

'Cut it out,' I said.

'*Stevie alweady cut if OFF, and boy did it hoit! Ouch!*'

'That's okay, Elroy,' I said, glaring at Steve. 'In about two seconds, I'll cut off *Steve's* head. You'll like that, won't you?'

'*Oh, dear me, yes! Give him a taste of steel, the bwute!*'

Ignoring Elroy, Steve said to me, 'You don't want to cut off my head. Not here in the pool. Think of the mess. Aside from the blood, you'd have two heads and a body to haul out.'

'Just turn around and get moving. I want to get done with all this.'

'Aye-aye.' He started backing away from me. I followed, taking a few strides into shallower water.

The level had slipped down to my waist when he suddenly stopped and frowned at Elroy's head. 'What's that? A secret?' He brought the head close to his ear and pretended to listen. He nodded. Then he said, 'No, I'm not going to ask her that. *You* ask her.'

He swiveled Elroy's head so it faced me again.

'Stop this,' I said, 'and get out of the pool right now.'

'But Elroy wants to ask you something.'

'I don't want to hear it. Get out.'

'*Pwease?*' Elroy begged.

'Steve!'

'*I wubb you, honey. I wub you so bad. Will you wet me kiss you?*'

707

'Shit. Knock it off, Steve. I'm warning you.' I raised the saber.

'*Juss one wittow kiss on the wips?*' Elroy asked.

And Steve hurled the head straight at my face.

I slashed at it, trying to knock it aside. But I swung too soon. The tip of my blade whipped across Elroy's gaping mouth, slicing through both cheeks. His mouth jumped wide open as if he suddenly wanted to take a really *big* bite out of me.

I flung up my left arm in front of my face and started to twist away.

The head crashed against my forearm.

The electrical cord jerked and flew out of my hand.

The head caromed off the bottom of my arm. I looked down just as Elroy's chin punched me in the solar plexus, snapping his mouth shut. I grunted with the sudden pain. He fell almost straight down, gazing up at me from between my breasts until he plopped into the water in front of my belly.

As he sank, I waded backward, doubling over and fighting for a breath.

I knew that I'd lost hold of the cord. But the place where Elroy had struck me is almost like your crazy bone, only worse. Blasted with pain, my main worry was staying on my feet.

Besides, I still had the saber.

And Steve wasn't attacking me, anyway.

While I stood there, hunched over and struggling for a breath, Steve waded for the end of the pool. The shallow end had underwater stairs at the corner nearer to the house, but he ignored them and charged straight forward. He came to the wall, slapped its top with both hands and lunged up. Water sluiced down his body. His shorts dropped, baring his ass and trapping his legs from the knees down. As he tried to spring to his feet, the shorts seemed to tackle him. He let out a yelp and fell sprawling onto the concrete.

By that time, I'd had a few moments to recover.

I still couldn't take a deep breath, but I no longer felt paralyzed by the blow.

Hunched over and gritting my teeth, I trudged toward the end of the pool.

Steve's feet were near the edge. The cord from his left ankle dangled down into the water, and I could see its length below the surface, curling toward me like a strange, skinny snake with a three-pronged head.

Grab it!

I tried to hurry, but the water pushed at me as if it had an urgent need to keep me away from the cord. I leaned forward and kneed my way through it.

Steve flipped over onto his back. He sat up. He saw me coming.

Looking somewhat alarmed, he leaned way forward over his outstretched legs, reached to his ankle and grabbed the cord and snatched it toward him.

Under the water, it darted away from me.

I dived for it, leaping as far as I could, slamming myself down through the water, stretching out my left arm.

And got it!

Tweezed the plug between two fingers.

But then it jumped free.

My hand struck the end of the pool. I reached up out of the water, pawing for the cord, but didn't touch it.

Fast as I could, I got my feet under me and stood up.

Blinking water from my eyes, I saw Steve staggering backward away from the pool. He held the cord in his teeth. It swayed in front of him, its other end still attached to his ankle. His hands were almost finished tugging up his shorts. His penis vanished under the waistband.

I could've been on him in a couple of seconds, except for the saber.

It's hard to climb out of a pool with a sword in your hand.

I wasn't about to let go of it, though.

I guess I could've gone for the stairs, but that probably would've taken even longer than climbing out the awkward way I did, boosting myself over the edge with the saber clutched in my right hand.

Steve never took his eyes off me. He backed farther and farther away while he watched my progress. He even took a few seconds, after his shorts were up, to tighten his belt.

As I got to my feet, he took the cord out of his teeth.

Holding it in his left hand, he whirled around and broke into a run.

'Stop!' I yelled.

Of course, he didn't stop. Why should he?

I went after him.

We sprinted over the warm dewy grass, Steve well ahead of me. I held the saber overhead, ready to strike him down.

If I could only get close enough.

Being built like 'a brick shithouse' is never a picnic. But it's a disaster when you're trying to chase someone. You want to be tall and slim and lithe. You want to be flat. And quick.

I didn't stand a chance of catching Steve.

The distance between us kept stretching.

I didn't give up, though. I stayed after him, running as hard as I could, saber waving high and breasts leaping, until he vanished into Miller's Woods.

Chapter Fifty-four

Wires

Lowering the saber until its tip met the ground, I slouched and huffed for air and didn't go any farther.

My lungs ached from the hard run.

My legs felt heavy, as if loaded with granite.

My heart raced like crazy.

I was drenched. A combination of sweat and pool water, probably. It spilled down my body, dribbles sliding down my skin, all over, tickling me. Drops fell from the tips of my nose and chin and breasts. I used a hand to wipe my face, but it wasn't much help.

I was worn out.

Vulnerable.

Saber or no saber, I would've been easy prey for Steve if he doubled back and jumped me. I was too exhausted. And much too close to the edge of the woods.

When I'd recovered a little, I trudged backward. I was too tired to move quickly, but I put more and more distance between myself and the woods.

I wanted to lie down on the grass.

The grass would make me itchy, though.

So I kept moving, and didn't stop until I reached the apron of the pool. There, I eased myself down and stretched out on the warm concrete. It felt awfully hard against the back of my head. It didn't feel that great under my heels, either. Otherwise, though, it felt okay. I liked that it was solid and dry.

I held on to the saber, my right arm on the concrete by my side, the blade resting across my thigh.

This isn't so bad, I thought. This is pretty nice.

But what do I do now?

Steve got away.

I got away.

We both escaped from each other.

After such a close call, Steve probably wouldn't be coming back. And he wasn't likely to tell any tales, since he's the one who'd murdered Elroy.

Just let him go. Call it even.

What about Judy? She'd promised to keep her mouth shut about me. I couldn't completely trust her about that, but she would probably never get a *chance* to do any damage. If she wasn't dead already (and I figured she might be, even though Steve claimed otherwise), Steve would almost certainly kill her sooner or later. She knew too much. He couldn't just let her walk away.

Maybe I can rescue her.

Yeah, right.

For one thing, you can't exactly rescue someone who's already dead. For another, supposing she isn't dead, why would I want to save her? Dead gals tell no tales.

Besides, I probably wouldn't be able to find the campsite, anyway.

And if I *did*, I'd end up facing Steve again.

I'd been damn lucky to survive this encounter with him. Next time, he might win.

Forget it.

Forget both of them. They're out of the picture.

And I'm almost home free. Just a few little matters to take care of . . .

Such as?

Elroy's head was still in the swimming pool, and the rest of him was locked inside the trunk of his car.

I needed to get rid of them.

Fish out the head, take it around to the car and throw it into the trunk and . . .

Steve's got the keys!

Out front by the car, I'd seen him drop them into a pocket of his shorts.

Without Elroy's keys, I wouldn't be able to open the trunk.

Or drive his car away.

When I realized that, I suddenly went all hot and squirmy inside. I sat up. And sat there, head down, groaning.

Doesn't it ever end?

My God, my God.

Killing Tony had been an accident!

All I ever wanted to do was get out from under it – make it go away so I could get on with my life.

It had seemed so simple, at first. Clean up the mess and drop off the body somewhere else. So simple.

But some things aren't simple, and some things can't be undone.

Maybe nothing can *ever* be undone.

That's probably more like the truth.

Once you've done it, it's been done forever and there's no making it go away.

Because too much is attached.

You might think you're dealing with just one matter – like Tony's body – but then it turns out that the body has a dozen wires attached to it. Or a hundred. And every wire leads off into the unknown. One's attached to Judy. Another to an answering machine. Another to poor Murphy. You go to cut those wires, but run into more. Elroy, for instance. And Milo and Steve. Always more wires leading off somewhere.

I guess this might sound like I'm talking about 'loose strings.'

I don't see them as strings, though. Strings are soft and you can usually break them with your bare hands. What I mean are thin, steel wires. If you try to break these with your hands, they'll cut into you.

They're everywhere, attached to every word out of your mouth, to your every action, to every person you encounter – and they all lead off somewhere else and drag new stuff into the picture – new stuff with wires leading off . . .

Sitting there by the side of the pool, I felt lost and desperate.

There has to be an end to it, somewhere!

Oh, yeah?

I'd gone through so much. I'd cut so many of those wires . . . A few more, and maybe I'd be free.

Fat chance.

There'll be more. Always more.

It's hopeless.

So what'll you do? I asked myself. Just call it quits, take a nice bath, go to bed, pretend everything is fine?

And go out for the newspaper tomorrow morning and find Elroy's car in the driveway?

I *had* to do something.

Start with Elroy's stupid head.

I sprang to my feet. Standing at the edge of the pool, I spotted his head deep in the water, migrating toward the drain again.

After scanning the grounds to make sure Steve wasn't sneaking toward me, I put down the saber and dived into the pool. The cold of the water shocked me. But then it felt good.

And I felt much better than before.

My despair had gone away.

Apparently, it had been *shoved* away by the mere act of making up my mind to get on with things.

Fuck the wires.

Take care of business.

You know the mistake I'd been making? Why I'd felt such despair a little earlier? Because I'd been looking at the Big Picture. It's the biggest mistake you can make.

Fuck the Big Picture.

Deal with one problem at a time, take care of it, move on to the next.

That's my advice. Take it from me, the deep thinker.

Speaking of deep, I went plunging down through about ten feet of water to reach Elroy's head. He happened to be face up, at the time. I would've preferred to grab him by the hair, but it wasn't convenient so I stuck my hand in his mouth and picked him up by the jaw.

Then I kicked for the surface. I rose at an angle, and came up close to the side of the pool. Holding the edge with one hand, I swung Elroy's head up with the other and set it on the concrete.

I'd left the saber on the other side, so I quickly swam the width of the pool, boosted myself up and climbed out.

As one who learns from her mistakes, I didn't attempt to swim back across. Not with the saber. Instead, I ran around to the side where I'd left Elroy's head. I snatched it up by the hair. With the head swinging by my left side, I jogged over to the garage.

At the side door, I set down the saber. I plucked the keys out of my panties, fumbled with them until I found the right key, then unlocked the door. Inside the garage, I slipped the keys back inside my panties and hurried past my car.

I knew right where to find everything. First, I put on a pair of gardening gloves. Then I went to the cupboard where Serena and Charlie kept their box of plastic garbage bags. I pulled one bag out of the box, shook it open, and dropped Elroy's head inside.

Unfortunately, I should've been holding the bag higher. Its bottom was resting against the concrete floor, so Elroy's head didn't have a nice, soft landing. It made such a nasty *THONK!* that I had to cringe.

Good thing he was already dead.

Anyway, I shut the top of the bag with its plastic drawstring, closed the cupboard, and hurried on out of the garage. I kept the gloves on.

After retrieving the saber, I ran to Elroy's car.

I had no idea whether I would find the doors locked.

But I set down the bag and tried the driver's door. It opened. The car's ceiling light came on. I flicked the lock switch to make sure all the doors were unlocked, then stepped to the back door and pulled it open. I picked up the bag and swung it in. After dropping it onto the floor, I stepped back and shut the back door.

Just for the hell of it, I put down the saber and climbed into the driver's seat to search for keys. You never know. Some people hide a spare set of keys in the glove compartment or under a floor mat or in a magnetic device underneath the dashboard.

Not Elroy, apparently.

And I had not the slightest idea about how to 'hot-wire' a car. It sure looks easy in the movies. I'd tried it a couple of times in the past, though, and knew I couldn't do it. So I didn't bother fooling with the wires under the dash.

Unable to find any hidden keys, I used my gloved hands to wipe any areas inside the car that I might've touched on the ride over. Then I climbed out. I left the door unlocked, and shut it.

After picking up my saber, I hurried to the other side of the car and wiped the handle of the passenger door.

Then I whirled away from Elroy's car and ran for the back of the house.

As fast as possible, I gathered up all my clothes. You don't want to be leaving home on an excursion in nothing but thong panties. I carried everything over to the table. I set the saber on top of the table, its handle in easy reach. Then, keeping an eye out for Steve, I got dressed.

Jeans and a dark top would've been more appropriate for the next stage of my plans, but they were upstairs in my room. I was in a hurry. So I wore what I had: my red bra, my bright yellow blouse and long green skirt with the slit up the side. Also, of course, my white sneakers.

All dressed, I picked up the pitcher and treated myself to a few gulps of margarita.

I took a couple of steps toward the switch panel, intending to kill the outdoor lights. But I changed my mind and decided to leave them on. They might help me find my way back, later.

Anything else?

A flashlight? Maybe an extra weapon of some kind?

I glanced into the house through the sliding glass door.

Don't waste any more time. Every minute counts. Get going!

Chapter Fifty-five

Into the Woods

Gasping for air after my sprint across the back yard, I stopped at the edge of the woods. Stopped and listened.

Steve was probably long gone.

But you never know.

He could be sneaky.

Last night, after pretending to run off, he'd circled around to the front of the house and spied on me. He'd actually bragged about it.

So I figured he might be just about anywhere.

After catching my breath and listening for a while, I entered the woods. I moved along as quickly as I dared.

No reason to sneak. If Steve was near enough to hear me tromping through the foliage, the noise wouldn't matter because he was probably already watching me.

I hadn't brought a flashlight, though. A little moonlight came down through the trees, speckling some areas and throwing patches of snowy brightness onto others. But mostly the forest was dark. All around me were dim shapes of gray and black.

Last time, I'd fallen plenty of times in the darkness and even crashed into that broken branch. I didn't want any more accidents like those, so I walked fairly fast but not *too* fast.

I soon managed to find a trail. It was a trail I'd probably used many times in daylight. In the darkness, though, it didn't seem familiar at all. I had only vague notions about where it might lead. All I knew for sure was that it was taking me deeper into Miller's Woods.

Good enough.

I didn't know how to find Steve's campsite, anyway.

And if I somehow found it, he might not even be there. I had no guarantee that he'd returned to his camp after getting away from me.

Maybe he'd gone there, packed up . . . finished off Judy . . . and hit the road in his van.

Taking Elroy's keys with him.

I'd be screwed.

What if I can't get my hands on the keys?

There must be another way to get rid of Elroy's car. That's all I really need to do – move it out of the driveway, leave it somewhere else. Just about anywhere, so long as it's a fair distance from Serena and Charlie's house.

I tried to think of a way.

It helped take my mind off other things.

How heavy the saber felt, for instance. It seemed to grow heavier every minute. Now and then, I had to switch it from one hand to the other.

How hot and sweaty I was, for another instance. I'd been better off without my clothes. They kept the air away from my skin. They clung to me, and seemed to hold the heat in. I didn't have socks on, so the shoes felt slimy under my feet.

I tried not to think about any of that, and concentrate instead on my *real* problem.

What'll I do with Elroy's car?

Can't get it started without the key. So how . . .?

There must be a way.

Call a tow truck? That'd open a whole new can of worms. I'd have to contend with the driver, his company records . . . who knows what else? Forget that.

How else can I move it?

I'm not exactly capable of pushing the car myself.

Hire some workers to push it away? But then I'd have them to worry about.

Kill them all. Ha ha.

I lifted my blouse and wiped sweat off my face.

So damn hot.

The heat was fine if you happened to be in an airconditioned house, or sitting around outside or enjoying cocktails or swimming in the pool. But when you're trudging through the woods with a saber in your hand . . .

I took off my blouse. That helped quite a lot. I didn't want to lose it, so I tucked it under the waistband at the back of my skirt and it hung behind me like a tail.

I kept my bra on. Even though it felt wet and uncomfortable, it stopped my breasts from bouncing and swinging all over the place. I kept the skirt on, too. It was wet and clingy against my rump, but otherwise okay. Besides, I figured it would be easier to wear than to carry. I also kept my shoes on. You don't want to go walking through dark woods barefoot.

With the blouse tucked behind me, I tried to focus my mind again on the problem of Elroy's car.

There must be a way to get rid of it!

How about pushing it with my car? That might work. Push

it backward out of the driveway. Once it's on the street, tow it away.

Yes!

Of course, I'd have to do it at night to lower the chances of being seen.

Out on the street in front of the house, I could fasten my rear bumper to Elroy's front bumper with some rope or electrical cord – or even pick up a chain at a store tomorrow, and save the job for tomorrow night. Tow Elroy's car into Miller's Woods. Leave it near the picnic area, maybe.

Fantastic!

It would mean a lot of work, and a whole new series of risks, but the plan should succeed fine if I didn't get caught in the act.

I was glad to have a back-up plan. But it sure made me want to find Steve and get my hands on Elroy's ignition key.

So where are you, Stevie boy?

I'd been walking for long enough to be fairly deep into the woods. I might even be somewhere near the camp.

Maybe fifty yards away from it.

Or half a mile.

Or a mile.

It might be dead ahead. Or somewhere to the left or the right.

For that matter, where was the creek? What about the picnic grounds? The parking area?

I'd be glad to find *any* familiar place. But even if I could get my bearings, I still might have trouble locating the campsite. I'd only stumbled onto it by accident, last night. With such a dim notion of where it might be, I probably had no chance at all of finding it again.

There's always *some* chance, I told myself.

Fat chance.

Maybe if Steve has an enormous bonfire . . .

Or if Judy screams . . .

Or I scream?

Shaking my head, I muttered, 'How nuts *am* I?'

Nuts enough, apparently.

I stopped walking, then took a deep breath and shouted, 'HELLO! IT'S ME! I CHANGED MY MIND! DON'T GO AWAY WITHOUT ME! I'M COMING! CAN YOU HEAR ME? I WANT TO GO WITH YOU!'

In the quiet of the woods, my voice must've carried awfully far.

I listened for an answer.

After a minute or two, I realized that Steve wouldn't call out, even if he'd heard me.

He might *come* for me, but he wouldn't call out.

'WAIT FOR ME!' I shouted.

As I walked on, I was still worn out and sweaty and breathing hard, but now I had fear mixed in.

By yelling, I'd probably improved my chances of meeting up with Steve – but I'd lost any chance of taking him by surprise. From now on, the element of surprise would be on *his* side.

'Idiot,' I muttered.

Just keep quiet and maybe he won't find me.

And I for damn sure won't find him, either. Or Elroy's key.

The key isn't worth dying for.

So why am I doing this?

I realized that I could turn around right now and hurry silently away, find my way back to the house and not have to deal with Steve tonight – or maybe ever again. I could take a bath and go to bed. Tomorrow, clean the house. If I couldn't get the blood off the carpet, I'd cut myself and make up a story for Serena and Charlie. They would probably believe whatever I decided to tell them. After dark, I'd tow away Elroy's car with his body in the trunk and his head in the back seat and be done with all this.

I could do that.

But even as it went through my mind, I kept on walking deeper into the woods.

I'm not sure why.

Maybe it was something inside me that didn't like to quit, that needed to see it through to the end, no matter what.

Something that needed to cut the last wires.

Nor only did I keep walking, but I started shouting again. This time, I used his name.

'STEVE! HEY, STEVE! WHERE ARE YOU? CAN YOU HEAR ME? I DON'T KNOW WHERE YOU ARE! COME AND GET ME!'

Even if Steve wanted to keep clear of me, I figured he might be tempted to come looking – to stop me from shouting his name through the woods.

No telling how far my voice might be carrying.

Or who might be listening.

More than likely, we weren't the only two people within the sound of my voice. There might be a couple of campers, or someone out for a jog or stroll, maybe some lovebirds or a dog walker or a wino, maybe even a criminal or two using the forest as a place to hide from the authorities or hunt for victims.

Or there might be only the two of us.

I didn't know, and neither did Steve.

'WHERE ARE YOU, STEVE?' I called out. 'COME AND FIND ME! DON'T YOU DARE LEAVE ME BEHIND! I'M NOT GONNA LET THEM NAIL ME FOR THIS. IF THE COPS GET ME, I'LL TELL EVERYTHING! I'M NOT GONNA TAKE THE FALL FOR YOU, STEVE! YOU'RE THE ONE WHO MURDERED HIM, NOT ME! I HAD NOTHING TO DO WITH IT. YOU DID IT ALL, AND I'LL TELL THE COPS THAT.'

I knocked off the yelling for a while, and just walked along and listened. I heard nothing except the usual sounds you hear on a hot summer night in a forest, such as birds and bugs and frogs and the breeze creeping through the trees and bushes.

'I SWEAR TO GOD, STEVE, YOU'D BETTER NOT LEAVE ME HERE! I'LL SPILL MY GUTS! I'LL TELL THEM ALL ABOUT HOW YOU CUT OFF ELROY'S HEAD! I'LL TELL THEM ABOUT YOU AND MILO, TOO! THE FBI WILL *LOVE* TO HEAR ABOUT YOU GUYS!'

I had a sudden inspiration.

Just in case a stranger *might* actually be listening to me and paying attention –

'I'LL TELL ABOUT HOW YOU CHOPPED UP TONY ROMANO, TOO! AND HOW YOU SNATCHED AND RAPED JUDY! AND MURDERED HER! I'LL TELL THEM EVERYTHING I KNOW IF YOU DON'T GET ME OUT OF HERE!'

I wondered if I should throw in Murphy for good measure.

No. Why drag poor Murphy into this? He was my own business, my own private loss.

Anyway, I was tired of yelling. I was out of breath and my throat hurt.

And I'd already shouted more than enough to draw Steve's attention – and wrath.

If he'd heard me, he would probably be on his way.

In a rage.

Chapter Fifty-six

I Fall for Steve

A few minutes later, as I went rushing down a dip in the trail, something tripped me. It caught me across the front of my right ankle, then my left. It felt like a taut rope or cord.

With both feet snagged, I plunged headlong.

I flung out my hands, hoping to break the fall. They probably helped a little. But the ground bashed them out of the way and I slammed down hard. By the time my body struck the trail, my feet were free from whatever had snagged them. I skidded down the sloping earth.

The moment I came to a stop, someone rushed out of the darkness beside the trail. A bare foot stomped down on my right wrist, pinning the saber to the ground. I figured it must be Steve's foot. Before I could do anything, he dropped a knee down, punching me between the shoulder blades. Then he clobbered me in the head. I felt an explosion of pain, glimpsed a bright flash, and then I was out.

But not for long.

At least, I don't think so.

While I was knocked out, Steve dismantled his booby-trap, brought it down to where I was sprawled on the trail, rolled me onto my back, removed my bra, and bound my hands together in front of me with the same length of electrical cord I'd used on him.

I woke up to find him standing in front of me. He held the saber in his right hand, an end of the cord in his left. Tugging the cord, he tried to pull me into a sitting position.

'Okay, okay,' I said.

'Ah, Sleeping Beauty wakes up.'

It sounded like something poor Murphy might've said. For a moment, I thought I was back in his bed . . . but then I remembered he'd fallen into the bathtub . . . with me on him. Fallen and broken his head open.

This wasn't Murphy, this was Steve.

I suddenly felt lost and sick.

'Go to hell,' I muttered.

'You don't sound very perky,' Steve said. 'Hope I didn't break you.'

'Fuck you,' I said.

Steve hauled away at the cord. It tightened around my wrists and stretched my arms. Leaning forward, I struggled to stand up. It wasn't easy. It wasn't successful, either. When I got to my knees, he jerked the cord and I flew forward and landed hard.

'You must try to be less clumsy,' he said.

I wanted to make another crack, but I couldn't because I'd started to cry and didn't want him to find out.

He gave the cord a couple of tugs. 'Up we go,' he said.

I shoved at the ground with my elbows and knees. I thought he'd probably try to pull me down again, but this time he let me stand up.

'Very good,' he said. 'Now, let's see. How'll we do this? I don't want to have you behind me, so . . . You take the lead.' He stepped to the left side of the trail and pointed the way with the saber. 'Ladies first,' he said.

As I walked by, he swatted me across the ass with the blade. I flinched and gasped. Then he came in behind me, holding the cord low. It dangled from my wrists and hung against the side of my left leg.

'We'll just stick to the trail for a while,' he said. 'I'll tell you where to go.'

Pretty soon, he asked, 'You weren't satisfied with getting out alive?'

'I . . . want to go away with you.'

'So I heard. So *everyone* must've heard in ten counties. But I figure you were lying about that. Just like you were lying when you said I killed Tony. I didn't rape or kill Judy, either. Bad enough you were yelling your head off like a lunatic and accusing me of all kinds of shit, but making *false* accusations . . . That really takes the cake. How could you do that to me?'

'I'm sorry,' I muttered. 'I just figured . . . I don't know . . . I thought if I said enough really awful things about you, you'd *have* to come and get me.'

'It worked,' he said, and laughed.

'I was telling the truth, though, about going away with you. I want to be your partner.'

'I don't think so.'

'You said you wanted me.'

'Still do, hon. And I aim to *have* you. But maybe not for my partner. I happen to think you're playing games about that. You'll be all nice and chummy till you get the upper hand, then you'll nail me.'

'No, I won't. We'll hit the road together. I'll help you . . .'

'No, you won't.'

'I will! I want to!'

'You're just saying this to save your sweet rear end. That's about all you're interested in. You don't want to be my partner. You hate me.'

'I do not.'

'I've got a nasty wound on my head that says otherwise.'

'I only did that because you were hurting me. You *bit* me!'

'Ah, yes. I was enjoying a taste of tit teryaki.'

Real cute.

'We could be great together,' I told him. 'You know damn well how tough I am.'

'Tough? Not at all. I've rarely put my lips around such nice, tender tits. Love 'em.'

'They go where I go,' I told him. 'Take me on as your partner, and we'll all be together.'

'Or I could take them *without* you.'

Don't let him get to you!

'I won't be much good to you dead.'

'Oh, I wouldn't say that.'

'I mean as a partner.'

'Oh, that. True.'

'You're going to need a partner.'

'Now that you've killed Milo?' he asked.

'Right. Exactly. And you owe me for that, don't you?'

'Owe you how?'

'No more sloppy seconds.'

'True, true,' he said. 'I thank you.'

'And now you need a *new* partner, and I'll be it. I can drive for you. I can do all sorts of stuff. Like help you get girls. I can even . . . you know . . . help *do* stuff to them.'

'*Do* stuff?' he asked.

'Like tie them up, help you kill them or whatever, help you dispose of their bodies. Whatever you want.' I looked over my shoulder at him. 'You *know* I can do that sort of stuff.'

'Yeah, you're a bad cat.'

'Bad enough.'

'Not *nearly* bad enough, honey.'

'I am, too.'

'You're a pussy.'

'Tough enough to kill Milo and Tony and knock *your* brains half out of your head.'

Again, I couldn't bring myself to mention Murphy. I didn't want him to be part of this.

'If you had what it takes,' Steve said, 'you would've taken care of Judy. You left a living *witness*.'

'She didn't know enough to get me in trouble.'

'Bullshit. She knew plenty. You didn't kill her, because you're not as tough as you think you are. You *liked* her, so you let her live.'

'No.'

'You had the hots for her.'

'Did not.'

'You fell for her, so you didn't have the heart to take her down.'

'You're nuts.'

'That so?'

'Yeah. So maybe I didn't kill her, I beat the crap out of her and left her for dead. I figured she'd never get out of the woods alive.'

'Who are you trying to kid?' Steve said.

'Nobody.'

'*She's* probably the real reason you came out here tonight. You never had any intention of hitting the road with me, you came out here to save that girl's ass.'

'You're nuts.'

'Or maybe *whip* it,' he added, and laughed softly.

'Judy had nothing to do with this,' I insisted. 'I came because I want to go away with you. That's the only reason. After you got away . . . never mind.'

'No, no. Please, don't stop now. I can't wait to hear it.'

'Why should I waste my breath? You won't believe me, anyway.'

'Oh, try me.'

Looking over my shoulder again, I said, 'I missed you.'

'How sweet.'

'I figured we'd probably never see each other again, and I suddenly realized how much I . . . I wanted to be with you. I know it sounds crazy. And you probably don't believe me, anyway. But there's something about you. I can't explain it. All I know is that I suddenly felt this horrible emptiness inside after you were gone. And I knew that the emptiness was because . . .

I was afraid I might not be able to find you, that I might have to go the rest of my life without you.'

'I'm deeply moved,' he said. 'You loved me so much that you came after me with a sword.'

'It wasn't meant for you.'

'But I've got it, and I thank you.'

'That isn't what I . . . I only brought the saber along for protection. I never intended to use it against *you*.'

'And you never will.'

'That's fine. I would've *handed* it to you, if you'd asked. You didn't have to ambush me for it.'

'You know something, Alice?'

'Plenty.'

'You *are* marvelous. I've mentioned that before. But the more we're together, the more I discover. Now I find that you're not only sexy and stacked and gutsy and witty and tough – but you're a quite a fine liar, too.'

'I don't lie.'

A laugh burst out of him. 'You could be President!'

'I just want to be your partner.'

'There you go again. But you know what? Considering your many wonderful attributes, I might just be willing to let you have a go at it.'

'At being your partner?'

'Exactly.'

This was pretty much what I'd been hoping to hear, but I sensed trouble. 'What's the catch?' I asked.

'No catch. There will be an audition, though.'

'What do you mean?'

'You don't know what an audition is?'

'Of course I do. But I don't see the point. I mean, you've already seen me in action.'

'My dear, I've *felt* you in action.'

'So why do I have to prove myself?'

'It's simple. You're not the only sweet young thing interested in the role.'

'You're kidding.'

'Judy.'

'*Judy?*'

He laughed. 'Of course! Who else *would* it be? Marilyn? Marilyn's a looker, but she's much too stiff for the part. Of course it's Judy.'

'She really is alive?'

Steve had claimed, before, that he hadn't killed her. But I'd figured he must be lying. *Now* I believed him. Now that I'd have to be going up against her for the 'role' of Steve's partner.

It made me feel strange, somehow, to find out she wasn't dead. Relieved, I guess. Nervous. Excited.

I felt dread, too.

Because I would probably *have* to kill her, this time.

'What makes you think Judy wants to be your partner?' I asked.

'Told me so, herself. Fact is, until *you* came along shouting all that shit for the whole world to hear, I'd say that Judy pretty much had it in the bag. I don't think she'll be very pleased to find out she has competition.'

'She'd make a lousy partner for you,' I said.

'Oh, I'm not so sure of that. I happen to think she'll make a spectacular partner. Better than you, in some ways. She's younger than you, certainly more beautiful. Though she's lacking your magnificent figure, she has a certain innocence that I find very appealing, tremendously sexy.'

'Yeah, well, that's her problem. She can't be partners with a *thrill-killer*. She's a fuckin' goody-two-shoes.'

'Which is why we need the audition,' Steve said. 'She'll have to prove that she has what it takes.'

Chapter Fifty-seven

Searching the Dark

'Let's head over in that direction,' Steve said. Stepping up close behind me, he pointed to the right with the saber. 'We don't have much farther to go.'

I could see nothing over there except more dark forest. I stepped off the trail, though, and started hiking through the undergrowth. The ground was rougher, littered with rocks and fallen limbs. There were also plenty of unexpected dips and rises. I walked very carefully. I'd already had too many falls, and sure didn't want to go down with my hands tied together.

As I made my way along, low bushes clawed at my skirt and pushed at my legs as if trying to keep me back. Higher limbs slid their moist leaves against my bare arms and breasts and face. Some limbs scraped across my skin like dull claws. Others poked and scratched me, drawing blood. I couldn't see the blood, but felt it dribbling down my skin, here and there.

Every so often, Steve gave me instructions about which way to turn. I tried to do what he said. Sometimes, though, I displeased him. Either I didn't move fast enough, or my turn wasn't exactly what he wanted. He'd jerk the cord, hurting my wrists and twisting me around. Or he'd smack me with the flat of the saber blade. Once, he even jabbed me in the right buttock hard enough to make me bleed. The seat of my skirt got so wet that it stuck to my rump, and I felt blood trickling down the back of my leg.

After he did that, I said, 'I'll make you a better partner if you don't wreck me.'

'But I enjoy wrecking you. Anyway, I need to soften you up a little for Judy.'

'What do you mean, soften me up?'

'You're bigger and stronger than she is.'

'So?'

'We need a level playing-field.'

'What for?'

'The audition, of course.'

'What're you gonna do, have us *fight*?'

'Among other things,' he said, sounding very chipper. 'Winner becomes my partner. Loser loses.'

'But I've got to be "softened up"?'

'Exactly.'

'That's not fair.'

'We've got to be fair to Judy, don't we? You have all the natural advantages. Besides, she's been through a lot.'

'*I've* been through a lot.'

'Not as much as Judy. She was rather roughly used by Milo, myself *and* you. In her present condition, she wouldn't stand much of a chance.'

'Then let's just skip this "audition" crap, and you can declare me winner by default.'

'Not a chance. I think you'd better hang a left about now.'

'If I'm so much better than she is . . .'

He jabbed my other buttock.

'OW!'

I turned left and kept on walking.

He kept giving directions.

After a while, he kicked one of my feet sideways, tripping me. As I stumbled forward out of control, he said, 'Oops!' Then I fell. With my hands bound together, I couldn't catch myself. I struck the ground hard.

'What a klutz!' he said, and laughed.

I pushed myself up, and we continued through the woods.

Finally, Steve took the lead. He stayed well ahead of me, pulling the cord so it stayed taut between us. This went on for a while.

'Are we lost?' I asked.

'We'll find it. I know we're close. I had no way to keep the fire going, though. I was gone most of the day, and Judy was certainly in no position to add any wood.'

'How'll we find it if there isn't a fire?'

'I know the area pretty well.'

'Not well enough, apparently.'

He gave the cord a rough tug. It jerked my wrists, stretched my arms, and made me lurch forward, staggering. This time, though, I didn't fall.

We kept walking.

After a while, I said, 'Do you mind if I make a suggestion?'

'Suggest away.'

'Not if you're gonna hurt me for it.'

'What have you got in mind?'

'Maybe you should try calling out to Judy.'

'I don't think she'll answer.'

'What kind of partner *is* she?'

'I left her with a gag on.'

'Maybe she got it off. Why don't you at least *try* calling her? These are big woods. We might *never* find your camp.'

Stopping, Steve turned around and faced me. 'You call her,' he said. 'She's more likely to answer if it's you.'

'After everything I did to her?'

'It's not half what I did. Tell her you ran into me and killed me and now you want to help her get free.'

'She won't believe that.'

'Make her believe it.'

I gazed through the darkness at Steve.

If I refused to call Judy, maybe we *wouldn't* be able to find her. It might save her life. Or mine.

'Do it,' he said.

'What if I don't?' I asked.

Steve walked slowly toward me. 'You want to find her as much as I do,' he said.

'So she and I can have some sort of *fight to the death*?'

'Against her, you stand a chance.' He raised the saber blade and moved it slowly torward my chest. Because of the way my wrists were tied, my breasts were pushed close together by my upper arms. They had a deep, narrow crevice between them. Steve slipped the blade in. Then he flicked it from right to left to right to left, paddling the sides of my breasts a few times. Not very hard. Gentle slaps that didn't hurt much, but made me flinch anyway. And worried me.

If he turns the blade . . .

'Think you stand a chance against *me*?' he asked.

'Not at the moment,' I said.

'Call out to Judy. Make her answer.'

He gave the saber a quick, hard flick. It slapped the side of my right breast.

'JUDY!' I shouted. 'IT'S ME! ALICE! WHERE ARE YOU?'

Steve and I stood in silence, listening.

Nothing.

'CAN YOU HEAR ME? STEVE'S DEAD. I TOOK HIM BY SURPRISE AND KILLED HIM! HE CAN'T HURT YOU ANYMORE! I WANT TO SET YOU FREE! ARE YOU AT THE CAMP? WHERE ARE YOU? MAKE SOME SOUNDS SO I CAN FIND YOU!'

No sounds came.

Just the breeze and the birds and the bugs.

'You'll have to do better than that,' Steve whispered. He slipped the blade deeper into the crevice until its point met my chest.

'COME ON, JUDY! I'M SORRY ABOUT EVERYTHING, OKAY? I KNOW I HURT YOU. I WENT TOO FAR, AND I'M SORRY. NOW LET ME HELP YOU.'

Nothing.

'Maybe she couldn't get the gag off,' I whispered to Steve.

'Or she might be afraid to speak up,' he said. 'I knew the gag might not be enough to keep her quiet, so I gave her a gentle warning. I said if I heard her yelling, I'd come back and do some very nasty things to her. You know. With my teeth. With burning sticks.' I couldn't see Steve's smile, but I knew it had to be there. 'In tender, intimate places.'

'You pig.'

He stuck me.

'*OW!*'

'Be nice to the man with the sword. Now, try again.'

I felt a thin stream of blood sliding down between my breasts. 'What do you want me to say?' I asked.

'Whatever works.'

'Maybe she can't hear me. Maybe she's already gotten away.'

'I don't think so. Try again.'

'JUDY!' I shouted. 'HE'S ALIVE. HE'S GOT ME. KEEP YOUR MOUTH SHUT, AND MAYBE HE WON'T FIND . . .'

'Fucking . . .!' he blurted, and jerked the blade up.

While I tried to back away, the point sliced a vertical slit up the middle of my chest, missed my throat, and nicked the front of my chin. Then I was falling backward.

I slammed the ground. It smashed my breath out, but at least I didn't land on anything terribly hard or sharp.

Steve lunged at me with the sword.

Its tip popped through the front of my skirt, pierced my panties and poked me.

'No!' I cried out.

And Judy, somewhere not very far away, shouted, 'STOP IT! I'M OVER HERE!'

Steve turned his head toward the sound of her voice.

'LEAVE HER ALONE, STEVE! DON'T HURT HER!

I'M RIGHT HERE IN CAMP WHERE YOU LEFT ME.'

'Okay,' he called. 'Stay put, and keep talking till we find you.'

He raised the saber and stepped away from me. When the slack was gone, the cord grew tight and pulled at my wrists. To save myself pain, I didn't resist. I sat up, then struggled to my feet.

'Speak to me, Judy,' Steve said.

'I'm over here.'

He towed me in that direction.

'Speak up.'

'Are you okay, Alice?' Judy asked.

'Sure. Dandy. How about you?'

'I've been better.'

'What'd Steve do to you?'

'He . . .'

'All right, all right, ladies. Knock it off. Just count, Judy.'

'Just die,' Judy said.

'Count. One, two, three, four . . .'

'Go to hell.'

When she said that, Steve jerked my cord. I stumbled forward. Arms stretched forward like a diver (thanks to the cord), I flew off my feet.

Not again!

I cried out, '*AHH!*' and crashed down to the ground in front of Steve's feet.

'What'd you do to her?' Judy called.

'*I* didn't do anything to her – *you* did.'

Instead of giving me time to stand up, he trudged backward, pulling the cord, dragging me.

'Alice?' Judy asked.

She sounded no more than a few yards away.

'RUN!' I shouted as Steve dragged me closer to her. 'GET AWAY!'

'I can't.'

Chapter Fifty-eight

The Audition

He made me lie flat on the ground, face down, my legs spread wide apart and my arms stretched overhead. 'Don't move,' he told me.

Crouching just beyond my bound hands, he worked on the fire. He got a small blaze going, then added sticks from a nearby pile. The flames grew. I could feel their warmth. The fire crackled and hissed and popped. He added larger chunks of wood. Soon, he had a roaring, hot campfire with flames leaping two and three feet into the air.

'Okay,' he said. 'Get up on your knees.'

I pushed myself up. Kneeling, I settled back on my haunches.

And scanned the campsite. It looked pretty much the same as last night, but Judy was no longer hanging by her wrists from the tree limb. I didn't see her anywhere.

Leaving my hands tied together, Steve shoved my wrists in against my belly, then wrapped the cord around me a couple of times like a belt. He drew it backward and looped what was left of it around my ankles.

'Now,' he said, 'stay put.'

He picked up the saber, then headed for the tent. Twisting sideways, I watched him. He flung one of the tent flaps aside, poked the saber into the ground nearby, then ducked into the dark opening.

A few moments later, he scuttled out backward. He was bent over, straddling Judy, dragging her by her upper arms. Her head was between his feet. She had it raised and turned sideways, trying to keep her face off the ground.

She was naked, of course.

And hogtied with rope – hands bound together behind her back, feet forced up and tied almost within reach of her hands.

As Steve dragged her toward me, she strained upward, arching her back. She managed to get her upper body off the ground so she was skidding along on just her thighs.

About six feet away from me, Steve hoisted her to her knees. Leaving her, he hurried over to the tent and retrieved the saber. With the weapon in his right hand, he took up a position midway between us but slightly off to the side where he wouldn't obstruct our views.

Judy and I stared at each other.

The old, red bandana hung around her neck.

She looked awful. And beautiful.

Her sweaty body was smudged with dirt, smeared and streaked with blood. She gleamed like gold in the firelight. She was a battered ruin of welts, bruises, scratches and cuts. I'd given many of them to her myself.

Including a bullet wound to the right side of her head. The gouge from that was out of sight, hidden under the curls of her wet, blonde hair. I knew she had it, though. And knew I'd done it.

Shot her. My God. Tried to kill her.

What's the matter with me?

'I'm so sorry,' I whispered.

'Shut up,' Steve said. 'You can look, but don't talk.'

So I kept on looking.

In spite of all the damage to her body, Judy didn't seem beaten. Hurt, badly hurt, but not beaten.

She knelt like a proud soldier at attention, her body straight and rigid, belly sucked in, chest out, shoulders back, chin up. She had a fierce look in her eyes. The only sign of weakness or vulnerability – her lower lip was clamped between her teeth.

My throat felt tight and thick, but I managed to say, 'I wish I'd never gotten you into . . .'

'Shut up,' Steve said.

'Go to hell,' I told him.

He smiled at me. 'Better be nice. Only one of you gets to be my loyal sidekick. The other stays here, toes up, ticket cancelled, farm bought, dead as dirt. And I'm the sole judge. In other words, you'd better start kissing up.'

'Kiss my ass,' I said.

'I'm sure I'll get to it sooner or later,' he said. 'Now, let's start the audition. Is everyone feeling well rested and fit as a fiddle?'

Judy and I looked at each other, but said nothing.

'Good!' Steve blurted. 'Let's begin. Who would like to go first?'

'Go first?' I said. 'I thought we were supposed to have a fight.'

'All in good time, my dear. This'll be a multi-part audition, with the fight as the finale.' Grinning, he added, 'We'll work our way up to it.'

'So what else do we have to do?' I asked.

'Anything I say. Now. Who would like to start? Do we have a volunteer?' He turned his grin from me to Judy. 'How about you, sweet thing?'

She glared up at him, but didn't answer.

'Remember, ladies, cooperation counts.'

'What do I have to do?' Judy asked.

'Competition number one?' Raising the saber high, he used his other hand to unfasten his belt. 'The Great Suck-off!' he announced. His cut-offs dropped around his ankles.

Even though I despised him and he disgusted me, I've got to admit he had a wonderful body. All slender and smooth, with sleek muscles and a small, tight rear end. His penis stuck out straight in front of him. It was only about half erect, but already seemed pretty huge.

Resting the saber on his shoulder, he stepped out of his shorts and walked over to Judy.

She stared straight forward, her lips pressed together in a tight line.

Steve stopped by her left side.

'Turn and face me,' he said.

She turned. It didn't look like an easy task, the way she was tied. But she managed.

'Excellent,' Steve said. He moved closer to her. When he stopped, he was almost touching her lips.

Judy's mouth was shut. Apparently breathing only through her nostrils, she sucked in air as if she'd just finished a sprint. The quick panting made her chest swell and contract, her breasts lift and fall. She looked as if she'd been dipped in melted butter.

'Open wide,' Steve said.

She didn't.

He prodded her lips, but she kept them shut.

'Do you want to lose by forfeit?' he asked.

'*I'll* do it,' I told him.

'I'm talking to Judy,' he snapped. All the tease was gone from his voice.

'Do me instead! She doesn't want you. I do. Come on over here and put it in. I'll suck your brains out.'

'Your turn'll come. Now butt out.' To Judy, he said, 'Open up, honey. Right now.'

She shook her head.

So then Steve grabbed her by the hair and jerked her head back. Her mouth stayed shut.

'Don't!' I cried out.

Ignoring me, he did a little prance. I couldn't tell exactly what was going on, but he must've knocked her in the belly with either a knee or a foot. She suddenly grunted and her mouth sprang open. With the hand clutching her hair, he jerked her head forward.

He shoved himself in.

'Yes!' he cried out. 'Now *suck*, honey, *suck!*'

He waved his saber high.

Judy wheezed and gagged as he thrust.

'Stop it!' I yelled. 'Leave her alone!'

'You're next!' he shouted.

'*Bite him, Judy! Bite his fucking cock off!*'

Maybe afraid she might follow my advice, Steve suddenly flung her away. She fell onto her back, her tied arms trapped beneath her and her knees in the air.

Steve tossed the saber aside. Hands free, he threw himself on top of Judy. His hips shoved her legs even farther apart. He clutched her shoulders to pin her down. Then his ass rammed forward and she gasped and I knew he was in her.

'*NO!*' I shrieked. '*STOP THAT!*'

He hadn't done much of a job securing me.

I had no trouble at all working my feet free. By the time I'd managed to stand up, the cord that Steve had wrapped around my waist was hanging in a couple of loose coils down my rump and legs.

But my hands were still lashed together.

I struggled to jerk them free. The cord had no give, and only dug into my wrists.

But I didn't intend to let it stop me.

Steve was still on top of Judy, grunting and thrusting.

I couldn't take the risk of going for the saber. It was in his line of sight – if he happened to look up from Judy. Besides, it'd be a tricky weapon for someone whose hands are bound together.

Whereas the carving knife was conveniently located high on the inner side of my right thigh – and just the perfect size for one-handed use.

It had come from Serena and Charlie's kitchen.

Before setting out to hunt for Steve, I'd decided against a flashlight but in favor of a knife.

Hurrying toward him now as he raped Judy, I used both hands to reach in through the slit of my skirt. With my left hand, I drew the knife downward, freeing it from the single strip of tape that held it to my thigh.

The way Steve was huffing and thrusting, he must've been just about ready to come.

I changed the knife to my right hand and twisted my wrist so the blade pointed forward.

Judy was writhing and sobbing under him.

Steve's firelit ass bobbed up and down, buttocks flexing.

I dropped toward him, my hands low, the blade straight out like a steel version of his penis and aiming for the shadowy crack between his cheeks.

The blade slid in easily and deep.

Suck this, asshole!

Steve squealed.

I gave the handle a hard twist, turning the blade, and his squeal jumped an octave higher. My ears hurt. He jerked and thrashed under me. Hot fluids flooded out over my hands. Mostly blood, I suppose.

He tried to throw me off, but he didn't stand a chance. Not the way he was caught between Judy and me. Not the way his nervous system had gotten trashed with the first thrust of my attack.

I'd nailed him but good.

As badly as I wanted to climb off and escape from Steve's gushing ass, I wanted even worse to keep at him until the job was done. So I stayed on him with the knife buried deep, and went on working its blade around, really ripping him up inside.

For quite a long time, he shuddered and twitched and screamed.

Finally he settled down.

Chapter Fifty-nine

And the Winner is . . .

Underneath me, underneath Steve, Judy wept.

'It's okay,' I told her. 'It's over.'

'Is . . . is he dead?'

'If he isn't, he wishes he was.'

'Could you . . . get him off me? He's . . .' She started crying too hard to go on.

I shoved myself off Steve's back. On my feet behind him, I bent over and grabbed him, clutching his right ankle with my right hand. As I dragged him off Judy, his face rubbed between her breasts and down her belly. About the time his mouth got to her navel, I gave his ankle a strong jerk and stumbled backward. His face sped the rest of the way. The slight rise of her pubic mound must've acted like a ramp. Going over, his head jumped up as if he needed to take a last peek at her. Then he dropped off and his face struck the ground.

I kept staggering backward as fast as I could, dragging him by the foot, until our momentum ran out. Then I let go and stood above him and tried to catch my breath.

Judy rolled onto her side. She lay there sobbing quietly.

Crouching, I pulled the knife out of Steve's butt.

Then I stood up straight. I raised my hands and studied them in the firelight. They were crossed at the wrists and tightly wrapped with the electrical extension cord.

Right away, it was obvious that I wouldn't be able to reach the cord with the knife's blade.

I could think of only one way, without help, to free my hands from the cord.

743

By loosening it *with my teeth*.

Both my hands were bathed with blood and filth from Steve. I brought my hands toward my mouth, anyway, but the stench made me gag.

Forget it.

Maybe there was a way to use the knife, after all.

Bending over, I spread my skirt open and clamped the knife's handle between my knees so that the blade pointed upward. Then I lowered my arms, easing my wrists down until the blade slipped between them.

I moved my hands up and down, rubbing the cord against the blade's edge.

The coating of the cord – rubber or plastic, I guess – was so hard that the blade didn't have much effect on it.

Maybe try it with the saber.

This'll work. Just gonna take a while.

I tried to apply more pressure, but my knee-grip wasn't secure enough so the knife slipped.

'What're you doing?' Judy asked, her voice quiet and shaky.

'Trying to cut this damn cord off me.'

'Can't you . . . just untie it?'

'Not with my hands tied.'

'I'll do it for you.'

'Thanks anyway,' I said, and kept rubbing. Pretty soon, my legs began to tremble from keeping such a tight hold on the knife. Also, my back started to ache.

'Are you afraid of me?' Judy asked.

'Give me a break.'

'Then why won't you let me help?'

'I'd have to cut you loose.'

'So . . . now I'm *your* prisoner? Again?'

'I don't know.'

'Just great,' she murmured. 'I thought . . . after all this . . . you've saved my *life*, Alice. Twice.'

'I know.'

'You just . . . killed Steve for me.'

'For both of us.'

'I'm the one he was raping.'

'Yeah.'

'You're the best friend I've ever had.'

'Sure.'

'And you're afraid I'll . . . *jump* you?'

'You might,' I said.

'I won't.'

'Sure.'

'So what are you going to do, kill me?'

When she said that, I pushed too hard or flinched or something. I'm not sure exactly what went wrong, but my knees let go of the knife and it fell to the ground. I blurted, 'Shit!' and almost felt like crying, myself.

'Just come here and I'll take care of you,' Judy said.

'Okay. Okay.' I squatted, picked up the knife, and walked over to her with the long end of the cord trailing behind me.

'Do you know what I think?' Judy asked.

'What?'

'I think we should go away together.'

'Huh?'

'Just disappear. You and I.'

'Yeah, right.' Crouching behind her, I slipped the knife blade under the taut line connecting her hands and feet. With one hard tug, I severed it.

Judy said, 'Ah.' She straightened her legs. 'Oh, God,' she said, and stretched. 'That feels so good. Thank you.'

Her feet were still tied together. I decided to leave them that way, and started to cut through the rope binding her wrists together.

'No funny stuff,' I said, 'or I *will* kill you.'

'I mean it about going away together,' she said.

I stopped cutting. 'The hell you do,' I told her.

'These guys have a van,' she said.

'I know.'

'Maybe we can find it. They sure as heck don't need it anymore. We can use it for our getaway.'

'You don't want to run away with me. Hey, I was pulling the same stunt with Steve. So were you, apparently. It's not a bad ploy if you can pull it off, but . . .'

'This is different.'

'Oh, yeah? How?'

'I hated him. I don't hate you.'

'You should. Everything I did to you.'

'You were just scared, that's all. Trying to protect yourself.'

'By killing you.'

'But you didn't kill me,' she said. 'And you saved me from Steve *and* Milo. I owe you.'

'No, you don't. You don't owe me for anything. After all the awful things I did to you . . .'

'Forget about that stuff, Alice.'

'Sure.'

'I think we'd be great together. We could take their van and hit the road.'

'Why?' I asked.

'You know why.'

'You tell me.'

'Because we're in this whole thing too deep,' Judy said.

'*You're* not. You're just a victim.'

'The cops won't know that. My ex-boyfriend's body is in the trunk of his car – in the parking lot of *my* apartment building. I'll be a suspect right from the start. And one look at me, they'll know I've been tangling with someone.'

'Right. Milo and Steve. And me.'

'That's the point, Alice. I can't tell the truth without telling on you. And I won't do that. So I'll be in deep trouble if I stick around.'

'I guess you're right about that,' I admitted.

She *was* right. We'd gone way past the point where all might be explained by a few simple lies.

The truth would get Judy off the hook – if the cops believed her – but it would destroy me.

'You'd really . . . give up everything and go away with me?' I asked.

'What's to give up? I've got no family, no boyfriend, a crummy job. We can drive off and start all over, just you and me. Change our names, maybe dye our hair . . . Wouldn't it be great?'

'Sounds pretty good to me,' I said.

If we went away together, I supposed I would miss my room above the garage, and Serena and Charlie and their kids. But my life hadn't really been all that spectacular so far, anyway. I wouldn't be giving up much, that's for sure.

And the idea of going off with Judy . . . I felt almost like a kid on the eve of a great adventure.

Not that it's going to happen.

'Do you really mean it?' I asked.

'Yeah. I mean it.'

I went ahead and finished cutting her hands loose. 'Oh, that feels so great,' she said. She rolled onto her back. Sighing, she rubbed her wrists. 'Thanks. Give me a second or two, okay?'

'Sure.'

While she stretched and rubbed her wrists and tried to recover, I crouched by her feet and sliced through the rope between them.

She said, 'Ah,' and, 'Thanks.' Then she sat up and rubbed her ankles. 'Feels so good.' Smiling up at me, she said, 'Now, let's take care of that cord.'

On our knees, we faced each other.

I still held the knife in my right hand.

'What're you gonna do with that?' she asked.

'It's just in case.'

Leaning forward, Judy put her hands gently on both sides of my face. She gazed into my eyes.

God, she was so beautiful.

'What kind of friends are we going to be?' she asked. 'If you feel you need a knife . . .?'

'You don't really want to go away with me,' I said.

'Yes, I do.'

I swallowed hard, and said, 'Bull.'

'Trust me, Alice.'

'I'd like to trust you,' I said. 'But I can't.'

'Yes, you can. You *can* trust me. You can *depend* on me. We'll be best friends, now and forever.'

'Yeah, sure,' I said. My eyes filled with tears.

Judy put her hands on my shoulders. 'You won't have to be lonely anymore. Neither will I. We've both been so lonely . . . and hurt. But no more. We have each other, now.' She leaned in closer and gently kissed each of my wet eyes and then the tip of my nose.

I let the knife fall from my hand.

Judy sighed as if very relieved. Then she whispered, 'Thanks,' and leaned back and picked up the knife. With a strange smile on her firelit face, she said, 'Now *I'm* the one with the weapon and *you're* the one tied up.'

'That's right,' I said.

I suddenly felt cold and sick inside.

'You believed me?' Judy asked. 'You really *believed* you could trust me?'

'I guess,' I said, my voice shaking. Her beautiful, golden face was blurry through my tears.

'You really thought I wanted to be your best friend? And *run away* with you?'

'Yeah. No. I guess not. But . . . but I *wanted* to believe you. I wanted it so badly.'

Then I was bawling like a kid with a crushed heart and I couldn't stop.

Not even when Judy tossed aside the knife and freed my hands from the electric cord.

Not even when she pulled me against her and hugged me tightly and stroked my hair.

Not even when she whispered, 'Believe,' in my ear.

Epilogue

How do you like that?

Judy had *meant* it.

When I was finally able to settle down and stop crying, I found myself to be about the happiest I'd ever been in my whole life. Filthy, worn out and hurting all over, but . . . *spectacular*!

So that's pretty much where the story ends.

I've got to stop it somewhere, right? This seems like a good place, since all the bad guys are dead, Judy and I are safe, and we've agreed to hit the road, together, for parts unknown.

There are still a few things that ought to be told, but I'll try to be brief.

For starters, there at the camp when I finally finished crying, I took off my skirt and we both used it to wipe most of the blood and assorted yuck off our bodies.

Then I searched the pockets of Steve's shorts and gathered all the keys.

We buried Steve. Now, that was a chore!

When he was underground, we took down the tent and made the whole campsite go away.

We searched out the van, tossed the tent and some other odds and ends inside (including an astonishing and horrible collection of Polaroid photos that we'd found in the tent), started up the van with Steve's keys, and drove back to Serena and Charlie's house.

There, we took a quick shower in the master bathroom. (How wonderful to be really clean again!) Then we helped patch each other with an assortment of bandages, pads and tape. You should've seen us. We ended up looking like a couple of mummies.

We got dressed, borrowing shorts and tops and footwear from Serena.

By that time, it was about one o'clock in the morning. We still had quite a lot of night left. So we shuttled Elroy's car (with him in it), back to Miller's Woods and left it in the parking area near the picnic grounds.

Then we drove the van over to Judy's apartment building. Scouting around, we found Tony's car in the parking structure. The neighborhood seemed quiet. Maybe the body *had* been discovered and the place was staked out by cops. But we doubted it.

If I'd had Tony's keys, I might've moved his car to a new location. But I'd long ago (the previous night), thrown them into the campfire. I could've dug them out while Judy and I were breaking camp, but it hadn't occurred to me. Anyway, I suppose it's just as well. Trying to move Tony's car might've set off a whole new series of problems. You know how it is: everything is connected. Wires, wires, everywhere. So his car stayed put.

Up in Judy's apartment, I helped her pack. We made several trips down to the van. Though we had to leave a lot of her stuff behind, we took everything that was truly important to her. Then we drove on back to Serena and Charlie's house.

We parked the van in the garage.

Judy hurried upstairs with me, and helped me pack. We made a few trips down to the van. When I was satisfied that I had everything truly important – including the tapes from the answering machines, the five thousand dollars in cash from poor Murphy, and the autographed copy of his book – I locked up my room for the last time. Downstairs, I removed the license plates from my car and put them on the van. I also spent a couple of minutes in my car, signing it over to Serena.

Then, with me carrying the saber, we went to the main house. The sun was rising. We desperately needed to sleep, but we couldn't risk it. Before too much longer, one of the bodies was sure to be discovered.

They were all over the town and woods, like bombs that might go off at any moment.

So we didn't even try to sleep. Instead, we went to work cleaning up the mess that Elroy had left behind, thanks to Steve. In the guest bathroom, we scrubbed the walls and toilet and tub and floor. Then we worked on the carpet stains.

Which were pretty much hopeless.

I'd known they would be.

There was just no easy way around those stains. Lies would probably work with Serena and Charlie, but if the police should get involved . . .

Anyway, I would be gone. They could make whatever they wanted of the bloodstains.

By the time Judy and I finished our attempts to clean things up, it was about eight o'clock in the morning. Together, we made coffee and breakfast for ourselves, for each other. We had a delicious, leisurely meal.

While Judy cleaned up the breakfast mess, I wrote a note. It went like this:

Dear Serena and Charlie,

Great news! An old friend dropped by – someone I hadn't seen in years. We really hit it off. The upshot is, I'm going away with him. Whatever I've left behind, including my car, is yours. I've signed the pink slip for you. It's in the glove compartment.

I'm not sure when I'll be back this way again. But thanks for everything. You've been great friends and landlords. I'll miss you and the kids.

Give my love to Debbie and Jeff.

When I get settled, I'll give you a call.

Love and kisses,
Alice

P.S. I'm so sorry about the blood stains on your carpet. I had a minor accident with a beer bottle. Jim and I did our best to clean the stains, but you may need to replace the carpet. Maybe you can pay for it by selling my car.

Bye,
Me

I propped up the note in the middle of the kitchen table.

Just before leaving, I cleaned the saber, dried it thoroughly, and hung it up on the wall above the fireplace where it belonged.

On our way out of town in the van, we stopped at our bank. We both had accounts at the same branch, which was not very strange when you consider the size of Chester. We went in separately, ten minutes apart, and withdrew our money. It didn't come to much. But added to the cash from Murphy, we had enough to get by on for a while.

Back in the van, we headed for the city limits.

During our travels, we followed the newspaper, TV and radio accounts of what came to be known as the Miller's Woods Massacre. It was a big story. A huge story. I mean, you're not supposed to have that sort of slaughter in quiet, small towns like Chester.

Here are the basics.

Elroy's body, found where we'd left it, triggered a major search of Miller's Woods. Which led to the discoveries of several shallow graves. They not only dug up Milo, Steve and Marilyn, but two more female corpses that *we* knew nothing about.

When they found Tony's dismembered body in the trunk of his car, they figured he'd been done in by the same culprit who cut off Elroy's head. This connected Tony to the Miller's Woods Massacre, even though his body was discovered several miles away, in a parking space at Judy's apartment building.

Which dragged Judy into the picture.

Judy, missing and presumed dead. The authorities seem to think that she's buried somewhere in Miller's Woods, but they eventually quit looking for her body.

Murphy Scott, the manager of Tony's apartment complex, may or may not have been murdered in connection with the Miller's Woods Massacre. His death might've been an unrelated murder, or an accident. They just don't know. Nicely ironic, if you ask me. The mystery writer's death, in the midst of so much mayhem, remains a mystery.

In the course of the entire investigation, so far as I know, my name has never come up.

As for all that has happened to Judy and I since leaving Chester, I could make another whole book out of it. But I won't. Not for now, anyway. Maybe never.

There are a couple of items I should mention, though.

For one thing, I was in the doctor's office last month and read in *Entertainment Weekly* that this really major actor has signed on to star in a film version of a movie called *The Dark Pit*, from the novel of that title by the late Murphy Scott.

Cool, huh?

He would've liked that.

It made me awfully sad, though.

The other thing is, Judy and I are going to be mothers. Both of us. We're due at about the same time, early in April. Sounds corny, I know. I mean, like a soap opera or something. But you might say it's sort of a mixed blessing.

The father of my baby has to be Murphy. Which is wonderful, I think. Wonderful and sad, like the fact that they're going to make a movie of his book, only better than that, and worse. Him being dead . . .

But Judy's child – well, we don't know who the father is.

Possibly Tony. But he's a long shot, considering the time element. The father is almost certainly Milo or Steve.

Not exactly the best news.

Genes count for plenty. Do we really want to bring a kid into the world if half his genes come from a vicious rapist, a sadist, a thrill-killer, a cannibal?

Judy and I talked about terminating the pregnancy.

But we decided against it.

For one thing, we wanted nothing more to do with killing.

For another, half the baby's genes will be from Judy, and that's got to count for plenty.

The Richard Laymon Collection Volume 2

Richard Laymon

THE WOODS ARE DARK

In the woods are six dead trees. The Killing Trees. That's where they take them. Innocent travellers on the road in California. Seized and bound, stripped of their valuables and shackled to the Trees. To wait. In the woods. In the dark . . .

OUT ARE THE LIGHTS

The Vampire movie came first, then the story of the Axeman. This was the horror movie series to end them all. Cinema buffs admired the grainy, amateur camera work – it suggested the action was the real thing. But it couldn't be – could it?

'If you've missed Laymon, you've missed a treat' Stephen King

'A brilliant writer' *Sunday Express*

'This author knows how to sock it to the reader' *The Times*

0 7553 3169 9

headline

The Richard Laymon Collection Volume 3

Richard Laymon

NIGHT SHOW

When he was in high school, Tony Johnson locked school beauty Linda Allison in a haunted house for the night. Now he has moved to Hollywood determined to break into horror movies and he's forgotten all about her. But Linda is a girl with vengeance in her heart – and she certainly hasn't forgotten him . . .

ALLHALLOW'S EVE

The Sherwood house has been deserted since the horrific killing of a local family in the sleepy town of Ashburg. When invitations to a mysterious party to be held there are sent out, nobody is particularly surprised – after all, *everyone* wants to party in a house of death on Allhallow's Eve.

'If you've missed Laymon, you've missed a treat' Stephen King

'A gut-crunching writer' *Time Out*

0 7553 3170 2

headline

The Richard Laymon Collection Volume 4

Richard Laymon

BEWARE!

Elsie doesn't normally shut shop early, but neither is it normal for meat cleavers to fly through the air by themselves, or for Elsie to wind up on the meat counter neatly wrapped and jointed. Something very strange is happening in the small town of Oasis and everyone had better . . . BEWARE!

DARK MOUNTAIN

It was supposed to be a peaceful escape for the two families camping high in the California mountains. But they made the mistake of camping at Mesquite Lake, home to two of the wilderness's most terrifying inhabitants: an aged hag with gruesome powers and her depraved son whose unnatural lusts even she cannot control . . .

'If you've missed Laymon, you've missed a treat' Stephen King

'In Laymon's books, blood doesn't so much as drip as explode, splatter and coagulate' *Independent*

0 7553 3171 0

headline